MARCEL PROUST was born in Auteuil in 1871. In his twenties, following a year in the army, he became a conspicuous society figure, frequenting the most fashionable Paris salons of the day. After 1899, however, his chronic asthma, the death of his parents, and his growing disillusionment with humanity caused him to lead an increasingly retired life. From 1907 on, he rarely emerged from a cork-lined room in his apartment on boulevard Haussmann. There he insulated himself against the distractions of city life and the effects of trees and flowers—though he loved them, they brought on his attacks of asthma. He slept by day and worked by night, writing letters and devoting himself to the completion of *In Search of Lost Time*. He died in 1922.

LYDIA DAVIS, a 2003 MacArthur Fellow, is the author of a novel, *The End of the Story*, and three volumes of short fiction, the latest of which is *Samuel Johnson Is Indignant*. She is also the translator of numerous works by Maurice Blanchot, Michel Leiris, Pierre Jean Jouve, and many others and was recently named a Chevalier of the Order of Arts and Letters by the French government. Her essay on close translation of Proust appeared in the April 2004 issue of the *Yale Review*.

Marcel Proust

Swann's Way

Translated with an Introduction
and Notes by Lydia Davis

GENERAL EDITOR:
CHRISTOPHER PRENDERGAST

PENGUIN BOOKS

PENGUIN BOOKS

Published by the Penguin Group
Penguin Group (USA) Inc., 375 Hudson Street, New York, New York 10014, U.S.A.
Penguin Group (Canada), 10 Alcorn Avenue, Toronto,
Ontario, Canada M4V 3B2 (a division of Pearson Penguin Canada Inc.)
Penguin Books Ltd, 80 Strand, London WC2R 0RL, England
Penguin Ireland, 25 St Stephen's Green, Dublin 2, Ireland (a division of Penguin Books Ltd)
Penguin Group (Australia), 250 Camberwell Road, Camberwell,
Victoria 3124, Australia (a division of Pearson Australia Group Pty Ltd)
Penguin Books India Pvt Ltd, 11 Community Centre,
Panchsheel Park, New Delhi - 110 017, India
Penguin Group (NZ), Cnr Airborne and Rosedale Roads, Albany,
Auckland, New Zealand (a division of Pearson New Zealand Ltd)
Penguin Books (South Africa) (Pty) Ltd, 24 Sturdee Avenue,
Rosebank, Johannesburg 2196, South Africa

Penguin Books Ltd, Registered Offices:
80 Strand, London WC2R 0RL, England

First published in the United States of America by Viking Penguin,
a member of Penguin Group (USA) Inc. 2003
Published in Penguin Books 2000, 2004

1   3   5   7   9   10   8   6   4   2

Translation, introduction, and notes copyright © Lydia Davis, 2002
All rights reserved

THE LIBRARY OF CONGRESS HAS CATALOGED THE HARDCOVER EDITION AS FOLLOWS:
Proust, Marcel, 1871–1922
[Du côté de chez Swann. English]
Swann's way / Marcel Proust ; translated with an introduction and
notes by Lydia Davis ; general editor, Christopher Prendergast.
p.   cm.
ISBN 0-670-03245-X (hc.)
ISBN 0 14 24.3796 4 (pbk.)
I. Davis, Lydia.   II. Prendergast, Christopher.   III. Title.
PQ2631.R63D813   2003
843'.912–dc21   2003049743

Printed in the United States of America
Set in Berthold Garamond
Designed by Francesca Belanger

Contents

Introduction

Many passages from Marcel Proust's *Swann's Way* are by now so well known that they have turned into clichés and reference points and occupy a permanent place in contemporary Western culture. Scenes and episodes are familiar even to many who have not actually read the book: say "Proust" and they will immediately think "madeleine" and "tea," if not "cork-lined room." Yet confronting the book itself is an entirely different, and individual, experience. One will have one's own way of visualizing the narrator's childhood bedtime scene with his mother, his visits to his hypochondriac aunt, his teasing of the servant Françoise, his embrace of the prickly hawthorns, his vision of the three steeples, and his first piece of serious writing. Swann's agonizing love affair with Odette and the narrator's youthful infatuation with Swann's daughter Gilberte will be colored by the personal associations of each reader, who will likewise have unexpected memories, recalled by unexpected stimuli, that will enable him or her to identify with the narrator in the most famous scene of all, in which the taste of a tea-soaked madeleine suddenly incites his full recollection of his childhood in the village of Combray and, from this, leads to the unfolding of all the subsequent action in the three-thousand-page novel.

One will find, too, that the better acquainted one becomes with this book, the more it yields. Given its richness and resilience, Proust's work may be, and has been, enjoyed on every level and in every form—as quotation, as excerpt, as compendium, even as movie and comic book—but in the end it is best experienced, for most, in the way it was meant to be, in the full, slow reading and rereading of every word, in complete submission to Proust's subtle psychological analyses, his precise portraits, his compassionate humor, his richly colored and lyrical landscapes, his extended digressions, his architectonic sentences, his symphonic structures, his perfect formal designs.

Swann's Way is divided into three parts: "Combray," "Swann in Love," and "Place-Names: The Name." "Combray," itself divided into two parts, opens with the bedtime of the narrator as a grown man: he describes how he used to spend the sleepless portions of his nights remembering events from earlier in his life and finally describes the episode of the madeleine. A second and much longer section of "Combray" follows, containing the memories of his childhood at Combray that were summoned by the taste of the "petite madeleine" and that came flooding back to him in unprecedentedly minute and sensuous detail. This first part of the book, having opened at bedtime, closes—itself like a long sleepless night—at dawn.

"Swann in Love," which jumps back in time to a period before the narrator was born, consists of the self-contained story of Swann's miserable, jealousy-racked love for the shallow and fickle Odette, who will one day be his wife; the narrator with whom we began the book scarcely appears at all.

The third and last part, "Place-Names: The Name," much shorter than the rest of the volume, includes the story of the narrator's infatuation, as a boy, with Swann's daughter Gilberte during the weeks they play together on the chilly lawns of the Champs-Élysées and ends with a sort of coda which jumps forward in time: on a late November day, at the time of the writing, the narrator, walking through the Bois de Boulogne, muses on the contrast between the beauties of the days of his childhood and the banality of the present, and on the nature of time.

The story is told in the first person. Proust scholars have identified a handful of slightly different *I*'s in the novel as a whole, but the two main *I*'s are those of the rather weary, middle-aged narrator as he tells the story and the narrator as a child and young man. The first person, however, is abandoned for shorter or longer intervals in favor of what is in effect an omniscient narrator, as when, in "Combray," we witness conversations between his aunt Léonie and the servant Françoise which the boy could not have heard; and most remarkably during nearly the whole of "Swann in Love."

The story is told in the first person, the protagonist is referred to several times in the course of *In Search of Lost Time*, though not in *Swann's Way*, as "Marcel," and the book is filled with events and characters closely resembling those of Proust's own life, yet this novel is not autobiography wearing a thin disguise of fiction but, rather, something more complex—fiction created out of real life, based on the experiences and beliefs of its author, and presented in the guise of autobiography. For although Proust's own life experience is the material from which he forms his novel, this material has been altered, recombined, shaped to create a coherent and meaningful fictional artifact, a crucial alchemy—art's transformation of life—which is itself one of Proust's preoccupations and a principal subject and theme of the book.

The episode of the madeleine, for instance, was based on an experience of Proust's own, but what Proust apparently dipped in his tea was a rusk of dry toast, and the memory that then returned to him was his morning visits to his grandfather. The scene of the goodnight kiss was set, not in a single actual home of Proust's childhood, but in a melding of two—one in Auteuil, the suburb of Paris where he was born, and the other in Illiers, a town outside Paris where he spent many summers. Similarly, the characters in the novel are composites, often more perfectly realized ideals or extremes, of characters in his own life: the annoying Mme. Verdurin is based closely on a certain Mme. X of Proust's acquaintance, but to avoid offending her by too blatantly describing her, Proust attributed her habit of incessantly painting pictures of roses to another character, Mme. de Villeparisis.

What is introduced in this inaugural volume of *In Search of Lost Time*? As Samuel Beckett remarks in his slim study *Proust*, "The whole of Proust's world comes out of a teacup, and not merely Combray and his childhood. For Combray brings us to the two 'ways' and to Swann, and to Swann may be related every element of the Proustian experience and consequently its climax in revelation. . . . Swann is the cornerstone of the entire structure, and the central figure of the narrator's childhood, a childhood that involuntary memory, stimulated or charmed by the long-forgotten taste of a madeleine steeped in an infusion of tea, conjures in all the relief and colour of its essential significance from the shallow well of a cup's inscrutable banality."

Through Charles Swann, the faithful friend and constant dinner guest of the narrator's family, we are led, either directly or indirectly, to all the most important characters of *In Search of Lost Time*. As Proust himself says, describing the book in a letter to a friend: "There are a great many characters; they are 'prepared' in this first volume, in such a way that in the second they will do exactly the opposite of what one would have expected from the first." Nearly all, in fact, are introduced in *Swann's Way:* the young protagonist, his parents and his grandmother; Swann, his daughter Gilberte, and Odette, whose is both the mysterious "lady in pink" early in the book and later the lovely Mme. Swann; Françoise, the family servant; the narrator's boyhood friend, the bookish Bloch; and the aristocrat Mme. de Villeparisis. Stories are told about them that will be echoed later by parallel stories, just as the story of the young protagonist's longing for his mother is echoed within this volume by the story of Swann's longing for Odette and the narrator's, when he was a boy, for Gilberte. Stories are begun that will be continued, hints are dropped that will be picked up, and questions are asked that will be answered in later volumes; places are described that will reappear in greater detail. "Combray," which contains some of the most beautiful writing in the novel, sets the stage for the rest, and in its first pages introduces the principal themes which will be elaborated in subsequent volumes: childhood, love, betrayal, memory, sleep, time, homosexuality, music, art, manners, taste, society, historic France. The later volumes, in turn, give "Combray" an ever richer meaning, and reveal more fully the logical interrelation of its parts. As Proust himself, again, in the same letter, says: "And from the point of view of composition, it is so complex that it only becomes clear much later when all the 'themes' have begun to coalesce."

In the narrator's recovery of his early memories through the tasting of the tea-soaked madeleine, for instance, we first learn of Proust's conception of the power of involuntary memory: the madeleine is only the first of a number of inanimate objects that will appear in the course of *In Search of Lost Time,* each of which provides a sensuous experience which will in turn provoke an involuntary memory (the uneven cobblestones in a courtyard, for instance, or the touch of a stiffly starched napkin on the lips). The incident of the madeleine will itself be taken up again and revealed in a new light in the final volume.

In the narrator's early passion for his mother and Swann's for Odette, we are introduced to the power of love for an elusive object, the obstinate perversity with which one's passion is intensified, if not in fact created, by the danger of losing one's beloved. The narrator's infatuation with Gilberte in the present volume will be echoed by his more fully developed passion, as an adult, for Albertine in a subsequent volume. In the very first pages of *Swann's Way,* the notion of escape from time is alluded to, and the description of the magic lantern which follows soon after hints at how time will be transcended through art. The wistful closing passage in the Bois de Boulogne introduces the theme of the receding, in time, and the disappearance, of beloved places and people, and their resurrection in our imagination, our memory, and finally our art. For only in recollection does an experience become fully significant, as we arrange it in a meaningful pattern, and thus the crucial role of our intellect, our imagination, in our perception of the world and our re-creation of it to suit our desires; thus the importance of the role of the artist in transforming reality according to a particular inner vision: the artist escapes the tyranny of time through art.

In one early scene, for example, the young protagonist sees the object of his devotion, the Duchesse de Guermantes, in the village church. He has never seen her before; what he has loved has been his own image of her, which he has created from her name and family history, her country estate, her position and reputation. In the flesh, she is disappointing: she has a rather ordinary face, and a pimple beside her nose. But immediately his imagination goes to work again, and soon he has managed to change what he sees before him into an object once again worthy of his love. Similarly, later in the novel Swann finds that his love of Odette is wonderfully strengthened, even transformed, the moment he realizes how closely she resembles a favorite painting of his:

he now sees the painting, as well, when he looks at her. The power of the intellect, and the imagination, have come to transform the inadequacy or tediousness of the real.

Proust began writing *Du côté de chez Swann* when he was in his late thirties, sometime between the summer of 1908 and the summer of 1909, as near as we can make out from references in his letters and conversations. His mother, with whom he had lived, had died in 1905, and following a stay of some months in a sanatorium, he had moved into an apartment at Versailles while friends searched for a suitable place for him to settle. This place turned out to be an apartment at 102, boulevard Haussmann, which was already familiar to him since the building had been in the possession of his family for some years; his uncle had died in the apartment and his mother had often visited it. The building is now owned by a bank, but one can still view Proust's high-ceilinged bedroom with its two tall windows and marble fireplace. In this room, of modest dimensions, Proust spent most of the rest of his life—slept, rested, ate, received visitors, read, and wrote. It was here that most of *À la recherche du temps perdu* came into being.

In a sense, the book had already been in preparation for several years before it began to take the form of a novel. It was never destined to be composed in a neatly chronological manner in any case, and elements of it had been emerging piecemeal in various guises: paragraphs, passages, scenes were written and even published in earlier versions, then later reworked and incorporated into the novel. The famous description in *Swann's Way* of the steeples of Martinville, for example, had an earlier incarnation as an article on road travel; and versions of many scenes had appeared in Proust's first, unfinished, and unpublished novel, *Jean Santeuil*, which juxtaposed the two childhood homes that Proust would later combine to form the setting of the drama of the goodnight kiss.

Proust had been projecting a number of shorter works, most of them essays. At a certain point he realized they could all be brought together in a single form, a novel. What became its start had, immediately before, begun as an essay contesting the ideas of the literary critic Charles-Augustin Sainte-Beuve, a work which he conceived as having a fictional opening: the mother of the main character would come to his bedside in the morning and the two of them would begin a conversation about Sainte-Beuve. The first drafts of this essay evolved into the novel, and at last, by midsummer of 1909, Proust was actually referring to his work-in-progress as a novel. Thereafter the work continued to develop somewhat chaotically, as Proust wrote many different parts of the book at the same time, cutting, expanding, and revising endlessly. Even as he wrote the opening, however, he foresaw the conclusion, and in fact the end of the book was completed before the middle began to grow.

A version of the present first volume, *Du côté de chez Swann,* was in existence by January 1912, and extracts including "A Ray of Sun on the Balcony" and "Village Church" were published that year in the newspaper *Le Figaro.*

Although the publisher Eugène Fasquelle had announced that in his opinion "nothing must interfere with the *action*" in a work of fiction, Proust nevertheless submitted to him a manuscript of the book in October 1912. At this point, admitting that his novel was very long but pointing out that it was "very concise," he proposed a book in two volumes, one called *Le Temps perdu* (Time Lost) and the other *Le Temps retrouvé* (Time Found Again), under the general title *Les Intermittences du coeur* (The Intermittences of the Heart). (He had not yet found the title *Du côté de chez Swann.*)

He received no answer from Fasquelle and, in November 1912, wrote to the Nouvelle Revue Française, a more literary publisher which had developed from a literary journal of the same name founded by André Gide and was later to take the name of its director, Gaston Gallimard. Now he was considering three volumes.

In December 1912, Gallimard and Fasquelle both returned their copies of the manuscript. Fasquelle did not want to risk publishing something "so different from what the public is used to reading." Gide later admitted to Proust: "The rejection of this book will remain the most serious mistake ever made by the NRF—and (since to my shame I was largely responsible for it) one of the sorrows, one of the most bitter regrets of my life."

At the end of December 1912, Proust approached another publisher, Ollendorff. He offered not only to pay the costs of publication but also to share with the publisher any profits that might derive from it. Ollendorff's rejection came in February and included the comment: "I don't see why a man should take thirty pages to describe how he turns over in bed before he goes to sleep." At last Proust submitted the manuscript to the energetic young publisher Bernard Grasset, offering to pay the expenses of publishing the book and publicizing it, and Grasset accepted.

By April 1913, Proust was beginning to work on proofs. He said in a letter to a friend: "My corrections so far (I hope this won't continue) are not corrections. There remains not a single line out of 20 of the original text. . . . It is crossed out, corrected in every blank part I can find, and I am pasting papers at the top, at the bottom, to the right, to the left, etc. . . ." He said that although the resulting text was actually a bit shorter, it was a "hopelessly tangled mess."

During this time, he made final decisions about titles. Ideally, he would have preferred simply the general title, *À la recherche du temps perdu*, followed by "Volume I" and "Volume II" with no individual titles for the two volumes. However, his publisher wanted individual titles for commercial reasons. Proust decided the first volume would be called *Du côté de chez Swann* and the second probably *Le Côté de Guermantes*. He explained several times what these titles meant, that in the country around Combray there were two directions in which to take a walk, that one asked, for example: "Shall we go in the direction of M. Rostand's house?" (His friend Maurice Rostand had in fact suggested the title of the first volume.) *Du côté de chez Swann* would, most literally translated, be the answer: "in the direction of Swann's place" or "toward Swann's."

But the title also had a metaphorical signification. *Chez Swann* means not only "Swann's home, Swann's place," but also "on the part of Swann, about Swann"; i.e., the title refers not just to where Swann lives but to the person Swann is, to Swann's mind, opinions, character, nature. And by extension the first volume concerns not just Swann's manner of living, thinking, but also Swann's world, the worldly and artistic domain, while *Le Côté de Guermantes* (now the third volume of the novel) concerns the ancient family of the Guermantes and their world, the domain of the aristocracy. And it is true that the character of Swann gives the volume its unity. (By the end of the novel, the two divergent walks are symbolically joined.)

Proust's friend Louis de Robert did not like the title, and Proust mentioned a few others—rather idly, as it turns out, since he was not really going to change his mind: "Charles Swann," "Gardens in a Cup of Tea," and "The Age of Names." He said he had also thought of "Springtime." But he argued: "I still don't understand why the name of that Combray path which was known as 'the way by Swann's' with its earthy reality, its local truthfulness, does not have just as much poetry in it as those abstract or flowery titles."

The work of the printer was finished by November 1913—an edition of 1,750 was printed—and the book was in the bookstores November 14. Reviews by Lucien Daudet and Jean Cocteau, among others, appeared. Not all the reviews were positive. The publisher submitted the book for the Prix Goncourt, but the prize was won, instead, by a book called *Le Peuple de la mer* (The People of the Sea), by Marc Elder.

A later edition was published in 1919 by Gallimard with some small changes. A corrected edition was published by Gallimard in its Bibliothèque de la Pléiade series in 1954 and another, with further corrections and additions, in 1987.

The first English translation of *Du côté de chez Swann*, C. K. Scott Moncrieff's *Swann's Way*, was done in Proust's lifetime and published in 1922. Sixty years later, a revision of Scott Moncrieff's translation by Terence Kilmartin, based on the corrected edition of the French, brought the translation closer to the original, cutting gratuitous additions and embellishments and correcting Scott Moncrieff's own misreadings, though it did not go as far as it could have in eliminating redundancy and also introduced the occasional grammatical mistake and mixed metaphor; in addition, Kilmartin's ear for the English language was not as sensitive as Scott Moncrieff's. In 1992, after Kilmartin's death and after the publication of the still-more-definitive 1987 Pléiade edition, the translation was further revised by D. J. Enright. The two revisions of Scott Moncrieff's *Swann's Way* retain so much of his original work that they cannot be called new translations. Thus, there existed, until the present volume, only one other translation of *Du côté de chez Swann,* and that was *Swann's Way* (Canberra, 1982) as translated by James Grieve, a writer and professor of French literature in Australia. Grieve's approach was not to follow the original French as closely as possible, as had been Scott Moncrieff's, but to study the text for its meaning and then re-create it in a style which might have been that of an author writing originally in English. He therefore brings to his version a greater degree of freedom in word choice, order, and syntax.

If Proust has been reputed by some to be difficult reading, this can be attributed perhaps to several factors. One is that the interest of this novel, unlike that of the more traditional novel, is not merely, or even most of all, in the story it tells. (In one letter, Proust himself describes the work as a novel, but then, having second thoughts, qualifies that description with typical subtlety and precision by adding that, at least, "the novel form" is the form from which "it departs least.") In fact it does not set out to tell a linear, logically sequential story, but rather to create a world unified by the narrator's governing sensibility, in which blocks of a fictional past life are retrieved and presented, in roughly chronological order, in all their nuances. A reader may feel overwhelmed by the detail of this nuance and wish to get on with the story, and yet the only way to read Proust is to yield, with a patience equal to his, to his own unhurried manner of telling the story.

Another factor in Proust's reputed difficulty for Anglophone readers in particular may be that in the Scott Moncrieff translation, which has been virtually the only one read hitherto by readers of Proust in English, Proust's own lengthy, yet concise, expatiations were themselves amplified by a certain consistent redundancy which makes the translation at all points longer than the original. Proust's single word "strange" is rendered in English by Scott Moncrieff, for the sake of euphony or rhythm, as "strange and haunting"; "uninteresting" becomes "quite without interest"; "he" becomes "he himself." At the same time Proust's prose was heightened by Scott Moncrieff, by the replacement throughout of a plain word such as "said" by a more colorful one such as "remarked," "murmured," "asserted," etc.; he was given, regularly, a more sentimental or melodramatic turn: the "entrance to the Underworld," in the original French, becomes "the Jaws of Hell." The effect of all these individual choices was to produce a text which, although it "flows" very well and follows the original remarkably closely in word order and construction, is wordier and "dressier" than the original. It remains a very powerful translation, but, as with many of the first translations of seminal literary works, somewhat misrepresents the style of the original, which was, in this case, essentially natural and direct, and far plainer than one might have guessed.

Yet another factor in Proust's "difficulty" may be his famously long sentences. Proust never felt that great length was desirable in itself. He categorically rejected sentences that were artificially amplified, or that were overly abstract, or that groped, arriving at a thought by a succession of approximations, just as he despised empty flourishes; when he describes Odette as having a *sourire sournois*, or "sly smile," the alliteration is there for a purpose, to further unite the two words in one's mind. As he proceeded from draft to draft, he not only added material but also condensed. "I prefer concentration," he said, "even in length." And in fact, according to a meticulous count of the sentences in *Swann's Way* and the second volume of the novel, reported by Jean Milly in his study of the Proustian sentence, *La Phrase de Proust,* nearly forty percent of the sentences in these two books are reasonably short—one to five lines—and less than one-quarter are very long—ten lines or more.

Proust felt, however, that a long sentence contained a whole, complex thought, a thought that should not be fragmented or broken. The shape of the sentence was the shape of the thought, and every word was necessary to the thought: "I really have to weave these long silks as I spin them," he said. "If I shortened my sentences, it would make little pieces of sentences, not sentences." He wished to "encircle the truth with a single—even if long and sinuous—stroke."

Many contemporaries of Proust's insisted that he wrote the way he spoke, although when *Du côté de chez Swann* appeared in print, they were startled by what they saw as the severity of the page. Where were the pauses, the inflections? There were not enough empty spaces, not enough punctuation marks. To them, the sentences seemed longer when read on the page than they did when they were spoken, in his extraordinary hoarse voice: his voice punctuated them.

One friend, though surely exaggerating, reported that Proust would arrive late in the evening, wake him up, begin talking, and deliver one long sentence that did not come to an end until the middle of the night. The sentence would be full of asides, parentheses, illuminations, reconsiderations, revisions, addenda, corrections, augmentations, digressions, qualifications, erasures, deletions, and marginal notes. It would, in other words, attempt to be exhaustive, to capture every nuance of a piece of reality, to reflect Proust's entire thought. To be exhaustive is, of course, an infinite task: more events can always be inserted, and more nuance in the narration, more commentary on the event, and more nuance within the commentary. Growing by association of ideas, developing internally by contiguity, the long sentences are built up into pyramids of subordinate clauses.

These sentences are constructed very tightly, with their many layers, the insertion of parenthetical remarks and digressions adding color and background to the main point, and delaying the outcome, the conclusion of the sentence, which is most often a particularly strong or climactic word or pair of words. They are knit together using a variety of conscious and unconscious stylistic techniques that become fascinating to observe and analyze: repetition, apposition, logical contrast, comparison; extended metaphors; nuanced qualifications within the metaphors themselves; varieties of parallel structures; balanced series of pairs of nouns, adjectives, or phrases; and lavish aural effects—as in the alliteration of this phrase: *faisait refluer ses reflets;* or the ABBA structure of vowel sounds in this one: *lâcheté qui nous détourne de toute tâche;* or the cooing of the dove at the end of this paragraph: *Et son faîte était toujours couronné du roucoulement d'une colombe.*

And yet Proust's economy prevails, and extends even to his punctuation, with in particular a marked underuse of the comma. The effect of this light punctuation is, again, that the whole thought is conveyed with as little fragmentation as possible, and that it travels more quickly from writer to reader, has a more noticeably powerful trajectory. The punctuation, of course, in part determines the pace and the breath span of the prose. If, as occasionally and conspicuously happens in *Swann's Way,* a sentence is chopped into a succession of short phrases separated by commas which halt its flow, the prose gasps for air; whereas the very long sentence, relatively unimpeded by stops, gives the impression of a headlong rush to deliver the thought in one exhalation. In this translation I have attempted to stay as close to Proust's own style as possible, in its every aspect, without straying into an English style that is too foreign or awkward; with particular attention to word order and word choice, his punctuation, too, can often be duplicated in English, and commas which might have seemed necessary can quite happily be eliminated or reduced.

One last comment concerning word choice: often the closest, most accurate, and even most euphonious equivalent may be a word more commonly used decades ago than it is now: for instance, the French *chercher* means both "to look for" and "to try," so its perfect equivalent in English is our "seek," still current today but rarer and more specialized than its equivalents. Or, to go further back in time, for the French *corsage,* the part of a woman's dress extending from the neck to the hips and also known as the "waist" or "body" of the dress, the perfect equivalent is "bodice," which in fact means the same thing. I have chosen to use both of these and many other close equivalents. Other perfectly identical English equivalents have simply receded too far into the past by now and will be too obscure to be understood: Proust's *solitude,* which in French can mean "a lonely spot," has that meaning in English, too, but will no longer be understood in that sense. A couple of centuries ago, we referred, in English, to a "piece of water" just as Proust does to *une pièce d'eau,* and meant,

like him, an ornamental pool or pond. And then there are some bor-
derline cases, some perfect equivalents which may not convey as
much to the contemporary reader as a close approximation, so that
what one gains in exactness one loses in expressive power; some of
these I have reluctantly bypassed (such as "parvis," identical to the
French, which means the area in front of a sacred building and is the
name neatly given by Proust to the part of the garden outside
Françoise's "temple" and for which I have substituted "temple yard");
but others I have used because they were too perfect to give up. One
of these was "aurora" for *aurore:* it is the rosy or yellow-gold light in
the sky just before the sun rises, and it follows *aube,* the first appearance of light in the sky.

A Note on the Translation

The present translation came into being in the following way. A project was conceived by the Penguin UK Modern Classics series in which the whole of *In Search of Lost Time* would be translated freshly on the basis of the latest and most authoritative French text, *À la recherche du temps perdu*, edited by Jean-Yves Tadié (Paris: Pléiade, Gallimard, 1987–89). The translation would be done by a group of translators, each of whom would take on one of the seven volumes. The project was directed first by Paul Keegan, then by Simon Winder, and was overseen by general editor Christopher Prendergast. I was contacted early in the selection process, in the fall of 1995, and I chose to translate the first volume, *Du côté de chez Swann*. The other translators are James Grieve, for *In the Shadow of Young Girls in Flower;* Mark Treharne, for *The Guermantes Way;* John Sturrock, for *Sodom and Gomorrah;* Carol Clark, for *The Prisoner;* Peter Collier, for *The Fugitive;* and Ian Patterson, for *Finding Time Again*.

Between 1996 and the delivery of our manuscripts, the tardiest in mid-2001, we worked at different rates in our different parts of the world—one in Australia, one in the United States, the rest in various parts of England. After a single face-to-face meeting in early 1998, which most of the translators attended, we communicated with one another and with Christopher Prendergast by letter and e-mail. We agreed, often after lively debate, on certain practices that needed to be consistent from one volume to the next, such as retaining French titles like Duchesse de Guermantes, and leaving the quotations that occur within the text—from Racine, most notably—in the original French, with translations in the notes.

At the initial meeting of the Penguin Classics project, those present had acknowledged that a degree of heterogeneity across the volumes was inevitable and perhaps even desirable, and that philosophical differences would exist among the translators. As they proceeded, therefore, the translators worked fairly independently, and decided for themselves how close their translations should be to the original—how many liberties, for instance, might be taken with the sanctity of Proust's long sentences. And Christopher Prendergast, as he reviewed all the translations, kept his editorial hand relatively light. The Penguin UK translation appeared in October 2002, in six hardcover volumes and as a boxed set.

Some changes may be noted in this American edition, besides the adoption of American spelling conventions. One is that the UK decision concerning quotes within the text has been reversed, and all the French has been translated into English, with the original quotations in the notes. We have also replaced the French punctuation of dialogue, which uses dashes and omits certain opening and closing quotation marks, with standard American dialogue punctuation, though we have respected Proust's paragraphing decisions—sometimes long exchanges take place within a single paragraph, while in other cases each speech begins a new paragraph. Last, I have gone through the text of the British edition and made whatever small changes seemed to me called for when I read it freshly in print.

Suggestions for Further Reading

Beckett, Samuel. *Proust*. New York: Grove Press, 1931.

Carter, William C. *Marcel Proust: A Life*. New Haven and London: Yale University Press, 2000.

Milly, Jean. *La Phrase de Proust*. Paris: Éditions Champion, 1983.

Painter, George D. *Proust: The Later Years*. Boston: Atlantic-Little, Brown, 1965.

Proust, Marcel. *Remembrance of Things Past*, Vol. I: *Swann's Way*, tr. C. K. Scott Moncrieff. New York: Random House, 1934.

——. *À la recherche du temps perdu: Combray*, ed. Germaine Brée and Carlos Lynes Jr. New York: Appleton-Century-Crofts, Inc., 1952.

——. *In Search of Lost Time*, Vol. I: *Swann's Way*, tr. C. K. Scott Moncrieff and Terence Kilmartin. London and New York: Chatto & Windus and Random House, 1981.

——. *A Search for Lost Time: Swann's Way*, tr. James Grieve. Canberra: Australian National University, 1982.

——. *À la recherche du temps perdu*, ed. Jean-Yves Tadié, Vol. I: *Du côté de chez Swann*. Paris: Pléiade, Gallimard, 1987. Introduction by Pierre-Louis Rey and Jo Yoshida.

——. *In Search of Lost Time*, Vol. I: *Swann's Way*, tr. C. K. Scott Moncrieff and Terence Kilmartin, rev. D. J. Enright. New York: Random House, 1992.

Shattuck, Roger. *Proust's Binoculars: A Study of Memory, Time and Recognition in* À la recherche du temps perdu. New York: Random House, 1963.

——. *Proust's Way: A Field Guide to* In Search of Lost Time. New York: W. W. Norton & Co., 2000

Tadié, Jean-Yves. *Marcel Proust: A Life*, tr. Euan Cameron. New York: Viking, 2000.

White, Edmund. *Marcel Proust*. New York: Viking, 1999.

PART I

Combray

I

OR A LONG TIME, I went to bed early. Sometimes, my candle scarcely out, my eyes would close so quickly that I did not have time to say to myself: "I'm falling asleep." And, half an hour later, the thought that it was time to try to sleep would wake me; I wanted to put down the book I thought I still had in my hands and blow out my light; I had not ceased while sleeping to form reflections on what I had just read, but these reflections had taken a rather peculiar turn; it seemed to me that I myself was what the book was talking about: a church, a quartet, the rivalry between François I and Charles V. This belief lived on for a few seconds after my waking; it did not shock my reason but lay heavy like scales on my eyes and kept them from realizing that the candlestick was no longer lit. Then it began to grow unintelligible to me, as after metempsychosis do the thoughts of an earlier existence; the subject of the book detached itself from me, I was free to apply myself to it or not; immediately I recovered my sight and I was amazed to find a darkness around me soft and restful for my eyes, but perhaps even more so for my mind, to which it appeared a thing without cause, incomprehensible, a thing truly dark. I would ask myself what time it might be; I could hear the whistling of the trains which, remote or nearby, like the singing of a bird in a forest, plotting the distances, described to me the extent of the deserted countryside where the traveler hastens toward the nearest station; and the little road he is following will be engraved on his memory by the excitement he owes to new places, to unaccustomed activities, to the recent conversation and the farewells under the unfamiliar lamp that follow him still through the silence of the night, to the imminent sweetness of his return.

I would rest my cheeks tenderly against the lovely cheeks of the pillow, which, full and fresh, are like the cheeks of our childhood. I would strike a match to look at my watch. Nearly midnight. This is the hour when the invalid who has been obliged to go off on a journey and has had to sleep in an unfamiliar hotel, wakened by an attack, is cheered to see a ray of light under the door. How fortunate, it's already morning! In a moment the servants will be up, he will be able to ring, someone will come help him. The hope of being relieved gives him the courage to suffer. In fact he thought he heard footsteps; the steps approach, then recede. And the ray of light that was under his door has disappeared. It is midnight; they have just turned off the gas; the last servant has gone and he will have to suffer the whole night through without remedy.

I would go back to sleep, and would sometimes afterward wake again for brief moments only, long enough to hear the organic creak of the woodwork, open my eyes and stare at the kaleidoscope of the darkness, savor in a momentary glimmer of consciousness the sleep into which were plunged the furniture, the room, that whole of which I was only a small part and whose insensibility I would soon return to share. Or else while sleeping I had effortlessly returned to a period of my early life that had ended forever, rediscovered one of my childish terrors such as my great-uncle pulling me by my curls, a terror dispelled on the day—the dawn for me of a new era—when they were cut off. I had forgotten that event during my sleep, I recovered its memory as soon as I managed to wake myself up to escape the hands of my great-uncle, but as a precautionary measure I would completely surround my head with my pillow before returning to the world of dreams.

Sometimes, as Eve was born from one of Adam's ribs, a woman was born during my sleep from a cramped position of my thigh. Formed from the pleasure I was on the point of enjoying, she, I imagined, was the one offering it to me. My body, which felt in hers my own warmth, would try to find itself inside her, I would wake up. The rest of humanity seemed very remote compared with this woman I had left scarcely a few moments before; my cheek was still warm from her kiss, my body aching from the weight of hers. If, as sometimes happened, she had the features of a woman I had known in life, I would devote myself entirely to this end: to finding her again, like those who go off on a journey to see a longed-for city with their own eyes and imagine that one can enjoy in reality the charm of a dream. Little by little the memory of her would fade, I had forgotten the girl of my dream.

A sleeping man holds in a circle around him the sequence of the hours, the order of the years and worlds. He consults them instinctively as he wakes and reads in a second the point on the earth he occupies, the time that has elapsed before his waking; but their ranks can be mixed up, broken. If toward morning, after a bout of insomnia, sleep overcomes him as he is reading, in a position quite different from the one in which he usually sleeps, his raised arm alone is enough to stop the sun and make it retreat, and, in the first minute of his waking, he will no longer know what time it is, he will think he has only just gone to bed. If he dozes off in a position still more displaced and divergent, after dinner sitting in an armchair for instance, then the confusion among the disordered worlds will be complete, the magic armchair will send him traveling at top speed through time and space, and, at the moment of opening his eyelids, he will believe he went to bed several months earlier in another country. But it was enough if, in my own bed, my sleep was deep and allowed my mind to relax entirely; then it would let go of the map of the place where I had fallen asleep and, when I woke in the middle of the night, since I did not know where I was, I did not even understand in the first moment who I was; I had only, in its original simplicity, the sense of existence as it may quiver in the depths of an animal; I was more destitute than a cave dweller; but then the memory—not yet of the place where I was, but of several of those where I had lived and where I might have been—would come to me like help from on high to pull me out of the void from which I could not have got out on my own; I

crossed centuries of civilization in one second, and the image confusedly glimpsed of oil lamps, then of wing-collar shirts, gradually re-
composed my self's original features.

Perhaps the immobility of the things around us is imposed on
them by our certainty that they are themselves and not anything else,
by the immobility of our mind confronting them. However that may
be, when I woke thus, my mind restlessly attempting, without success,
to discover where I was, everything revolved around me in the darkness, things, countries, years. My body, too benumbed to move,
would try to locate, according to the form of its fatigue, the position
of its limbs so as to deduce from this the direction of the wall, the
placement of the furniture, so as to reconstruct and name the
dwelling in which it found itself. Its memory, the memory of its ribs,
its knees, its shoulders, offered in succession several of the rooms
where it had slept, while around it the invisible walls, changing place
according to the shape of the imagined room, spun through the shadows. And even before my mind, hesitating on the thresholds of times
and shapes, had identified the house by reassembling the circumstances, it—my body—would recall the kind of bed in each one, the location of the doors, the angle at which the light came in through the
windows, the existence of a hallway, along with the thought I had had
as I fell asleep and that I had recovered upon waking. My stiffened
side, trying to guess its orientation, would imagine, for instance, that
it lay facing the wall in a big canopied bed and immediately I would
say to myself: "Why, I went to sleep in the end even though Mama
didn't come to say goodnight to me," I was in the country in the
home of my grandfather, dead for many years; and my body, the side
on which I was resting, faithful guardians of a past my mind ought
never to have forgotten, recalled to me the flame of the night-light of
Bohemian glass, in the shape of an urn, which hung from the ceiling
by little chains, the mantelpiece of Siena marble, in my bedroom at
Combray, at my grandparents' house, in faraway days which at this
moment I imagined were present without picturing them to myself
exactly and which I would see more clearly in a little while when I was
fully awake.

Then the memory of a new position would reappear; the wall would slip away in another direction: I was in my room at Mme. de Saint-Loup's, in the country; good Lord! It's ten o'clock or even later, they will have finished dinner! I must have overslept during the nap I take every evening when I come back from my walk with Mme. de Saint-Loup, before putting on my evening clothes. For many years have passed since Combray, where, however late we returned, it was the sunset's red reflections I saw in the panes of my window. It is another sort of life one leads at Tansonville, at Mme. de Saint-Loup's, another sort of pleasure I take in going out only at night, in following by moonlight those lanes where I used to play in the sun; and the room where I fell asleep instead of dressing for dinner—from far off I can see it, as we come back, pierced by the flares of the lamp, a lone beacon in the night.

These revolving, confused evocations never lasted for more than a few seconds; often, in my brief uncertainty about where I was, I did not distinguish the various suppositions of which it was composed any better than we isolate, when we see a horse run, the successive positions shown to us by a kinetoscope. But I had seen sometimes one, sometimes another, of the bedrooms I had inhabited in my life, and in the end I would recall them all in the long reveries that followed my waking: winter bedrooms in which, as soon as you are in bed, you bury your head in a nest braided of the most disparate things: a corner of the pillow, the top of the covers, a bit of shawl, the side of the bed and an issue of the *Débats roses*,[1] which you end by cementing together using the birds' technique of pressing down on it indefinitely; where in icy weather the pleasure you enjoy is the feeling that you are separated from the outdoors (like the sea swallow which makes its nest deep in an underground passage in the warmth of the earth) and where, since the fire is kept burning all night in the fireplace, you sleep in a great cloak of warm, smoky air, shot with the glimmers from the logs breaking into flame again, a sort of immaterial alcove, a warm cave dug out of the heart of the room itself, a zone of heat with shifting thermal contours, aerated by drafts which cool your face and come from the corners, from the parts close to the window or far from the hearth, and which have grown cold again: summer bed-rooms where you delight in becoming one with the soft night, where the moonlight leaning against the half-open shutters casts its en-chanted ladder to the foot of the bed, where you sleep almost in the open air, like a titmouse rocked by the breeze on the tip of a ray of light; sometimes the Louis XVI bedroom, so cheerful that even on the first night I had not been too unhappy there and where the slender columns that lightly supported the ceiling stood aside with such grace to show and reserve the place where the bed was; at other times, the small bedroom with the very high ceiling, hollowed out in the form of a pyramid two stories high and partly paneled in mahogany, where from the first second I had been mentally poisoned by the unfamiliar odor of the vetiver, convinced of the hostility of the violet curtains and the insolent indifference of the clock chattering loudly as though I were not there; where a strange and pitiless quadrangular cheval glass, barring obliquely one of the corners of the room, carved from deep inside the soft fullness of my usual field of vision a site for itself which I had not expected; where my mind, struggling for hours to dis-lodge itself, to stretch upward so as to assume the exact shape of the room and succeed in filling its gigantic funnel to the very top, had suffered many hard nights, while I lay stretched out in my bed, my eyes lifted, my ear anxious, my nostril restive, my heart pounding, until habit had changed the color of the curtains, silenced the clock, taught pity to the cruel oblique mirror, concealed, if not driven out completely, the smell of the vetiver and appreciably diminished the apparent height of the ceiling. Habit! That skillful but very slow housekeeper who begins by letting our mind suffer for weeks in a temporary arrangement; but whom we are nevertheless truly happy to discover, for without habit our mind, reduced to no more than its own resources, would be powerless to make a lodging habitable.

Certainly I was now wide-awake, my body had veered around one last time and the good angel of certainty had brought everything around me to a standstill, laid me down under my covers, in my bed-room, and put approximately where they belonged in the darkness my chest of drawers, my desk, my fireplace, the window onto the street and the two doors. But even though I knew I was not in any of the houses of which my ignorance upon waking had instantly, if not presented me with the distinct picture, at least made me believe the presence possible, my memory had been stirred; generally I would not try to go back to sleep right away; I would spend the greater part of the night remembering our life in the old days, in Combray at my great-aunt's house, in Balbec, in Paris, in Doncières, in Venice, elsewhere still, remembering the places, the people I had known there, what I had seen of them, what I had been told about them.

At Combray, every day, in the late afternoon, long before the moment when I would have to go to bed and stay there, without sleeping, far away from my mother and grandmother, my bedroom again became the fixed and painful focus of my preoccupations. They had indeed hit upon the idea, to distract me on the evenings when they found me looking too unhappy, of giving me a magic lantern, which, while awaiting the dinner hour, they would set on top of my lamp; and, after the fashion of the first architects and master glaziers of the Gothic age, it replaced the opacity of the walls with impalpable iridescences, supernatural multicolored apparitions, where legends were depicted as in a wavering, momentary stained-glass window. But my sadness was only increased by this since the mere change in lighting destroyed the familiarity which my bedroom had acquired for me and which, except for the torment of going to bed, had made it tolerable to me. Now I no longer recognized it and I was uneasy there, as in a room in some hotel or "chalet" to which I had come for the first time straight from the railway train.

Moving at the jerky pace of his horse, and filled with a hideous design, Golo would come out of the small triangular forest that velveted the hillside with dark green and advance jolting toward the castle of poor Geneviève de Brabant. This castle was cut off along a curved line that was actually the edge of one of the glass ovals arranged in the frame which you slipped between the grooves of the lantern. It was only a section of castle and it had a moor in front of it where

Geneviève stood dreaming, wearing a blue belt. The castle and the moor were yellow, and I had not had to wait to see them to find out their color since, before the glasses of the frame did so, the bronze sonority of the name Brabant had shown it to me clearly. Golo would stop for a moment to listen sadly to the patter read out loud by my great-aunt, which he seemed to understand perfectly, modifying his posture, with a meekness that did not exclude a certain majesty, to conform to the directions of the text; then he moved off at the same jerky pace. And nothing could stop his slow ride. If the lantern was moved, I could make out Golo's horse continuing to advance over the window curtains, swelling out with their folds, descending into their fissures. The body of Golo himself, in its essence as supernatural as that of his steed, accommodated every material obstacle, every hindersome object that he encountered by taking it as his skeleton and absorbing it into himself, even the doorknob he immediately adapted to and floated invincibly over with his red robe or his pale face as noble and as melancholy as ever, but revealing no disturbance at this transvertebration.

Certainly I found some charm in these brilliant projections, which seemed to emanate from a Merovingian past and send out around me such ancient reflections of history. But I cannot express the uneasiness caused in me by this intrusion of mystery and beauty into a room I had at last filled with myself to the point of paying no more attention to the room than to that self. The anesthetizing influence of habit having ceased, I would begin to have thoughts, and feelings, and they are such sad things. That doorknob of my room, which differed for me from all other doorknobs in the world in that it seemed to open of its own accord, without my having to turn it, so unconscious had its handling become for me, was now serving as an astral body for Golo. And as soon as they rang for dinner, I hastened to run to the dining room where the big hanging lamp, ignorant of Golo and Bluebeard, and well acquainted with my family and beef casserole, shed the same light as on every other evening; and to fall into the arms of Mama, whom Geneviève de Brabant's misfortunes made all the dearer to me, while Golo's crimes drove me to examine my own conscience more scrupulously.

After dinner, alas, I soon had to leave Mama, who stayed there talking with the others, in the garden if the weather was fine, in the little drawing room to which everyone withdrew if the weather was bad. Everyone, except my grandmother, who felt that "it's a pity to shut oneself indoors in the country" and who had endless arguments with my father on days when it rained too heavily, because he sent me to read in my room instead of having me stay outdoors. "That's no way to make him strong and active," she would say sadly, "especially that boy, who so needs to build up his endurance and willpower." My father would shrug his shoulders and study the barometer, for he liked meteorology, while my mother, making no noise so as not to disturb him, watched him with a tender respect, but not so intently as to try to penetrate the mystery of his superior qualities. But as for my grandmother, in all weathers, even in a downpour when Françoise had rushed the precious wicker armchairs indoors so that they would not get wet, we would see her in the empty, rain-lashed garden, pushing back her disordered gray locks so that her forehead could more freely drink in the salubriousness of the wind and rain. She would say: "At last, one can breathe!" and would roam the soaked paths—too symmetrically aligned for her liking by the new gardener, who lacked all feeling for nature and whom my father had been asking since morning if the weather would clear—with her jerky, enthusiastic little step, regulated by the various emotions excited in her soul by the intoxication of the storm, the power of good health, the stupidity of my upbringing, and the symmetry of the gardens, rather than by the desire, quite unknown to her, to spare her plum-colored skirt the spots of mud under which it would disappear up to a height that was always, for her maid, a source of despair and a problem.

When these garden walks of my grandmother's took place after dinner, one thing had the power to make her come inside again: this was—at one of the periodic intervals when her circular itinerary brought her back, like an insect, in front of the lights of the little drawing room where the liqueurs were set out on the card table—if my great-aunt called out to her: "Bathilde! Come and stop your husband from drinking cognac!" To tease her, in fact (she had brought into my father's family so different a mentality that everyone poked fun at her and tormented her), since liqueurs were forbidden to my grandfather, my great-aunt would make him drink a few drops. My poor grandmother would come in, fervently beg her husband not to taste the cognac; he would become angry, drink his mouthful despite her, and my grandmother would go off again, sad, discouraged, yet smiling, for she was so humble at heart and so gentle that her tenderness for others, and the lack of fuss she made over her own person and her sufferings, came together in her gaze in a smile in which, unlike what one sees in the faces of so many people, there was irony only for herself, and for all of us a sort of kiss from her eyes, which could not see those she cherished without caressing them passionately with her gaze. This torture which my great-aunt inflicted on her, the spectacle of my grandmother's vain entreaties and of her weakness, defeated in advance, trying uselessly to take the liqueur glass away from my grandfather, were the kinds of things which you later become so accustomed to seeing that you smile as you contemplate them and take the part of the persecutor resolutely and gaily enough to persuade yourself privately that no persecution is involved; at that time they filled me with such horror that I would have liked to hit my great-aunt. But as soon as I heard: "Bathilde, come and stop your husband from drinking cognac!," already a man in my cowardice, I did what we all do, once we are grown up, when confronted with sufferings and injustices: I did not want to see them; I went up to sob at the very top of the house next to the schoolroom,[2] under the roofs, in a little room that smelled of orris root and was also perfumed by a wild black-currant bush which had sprouted outside between the stones of the wall and extended a branch of flowers through the half-open window. Intended for a more specialized and more vulgar use, this room, from which during the day you could see all the way to the keep of Roussainville-le-Pin, for a long time served me as a refuge, no doubt because it was the only one I was permitted to lock, for all those occupations of mine that demanded an inviolable solitude: reading, reverie, tears, and sensuous pleasure. Alas! I did not know that, much more than her husband's little deviations from his regimen, it was my weak will, my delicate health, the uncertainty they cast on my future that so sadly preoccupied my grandmother in the course of those incessant perambulations, afternoon and evening, when we would see, as it passed and then passed again, lifted slantwise toward the sky, her beautiful face with its brown furrowed cheeks, which with age had become almost mauve like the plowed fields in autumn, crossed, if she was going out, by a veil half raised, while upon them, brought there by the cold or some sad thought, an involuntary tear was always drying.

My sole consolation, when I went upstairs for the night, was that Mama would come kiss me once I was in bed. But this goodnight lasted so short a time, she went down again so soon, that the moment when I heard her coming up, then the soft sound of her garden dress of blue muslin, hung with little cords of plaited straw, passing along the hallway with its double doors, was for me a painful moment. It ushered in the moment that would follow, in which she would have left me, in which she would have gone back down. So that I came to wish that this goodnight I loved so much would take place as late as possible, so as to prolong the time of respite in which Mama had not yet come. Sometimes when, after kissing me, she opened the door to go, I wanted to call her back, to say "kiss me one more time," but I knew that immediately her face would look vexed, because the concession she was making to my sadness and agitation by coming up to kiss me, by bringing me this kiss of peace, irritated my father, who found these rituals absurd, and she would have liked to try to induce me to lose the need for it, the habit of it, far indeed from allowing me to acquire that of asking her, when she was already on the doorstep, for one kiss more. And to see her vexed destroyed all the calm she had brought me a moment before, when she had bent her loving face down over my bed and held it out to me like a host for a communion of peace from which my lips would draw her real presence and the power to fall asleep. But those evenings, when Mama stayed so short a time in my room, were still sweet compared to the ones when there was company for dinner and when, because of that, she did not come up to say goodnight to me. That company was usually limited to M. Swann, who, apart from a few acquaintances passing through, was almost the only person who came to our house at Combray, sometimes for a neighborly dinner (more rarely after that unfortunate marriage of his, because my parents did not want to receive his wife), sometimes after dinner, unexpectedly. On those evenings when, as we sat in front of the house under the large chestnut tree, around the iron table, we heard at the far end of the garden, not the copious high-pitched bell that drenched, that deafened in passing with its ferruginous, icy, inexhaustible noise any person in the household who set it off by coming in "without ringing," but the shy, oval, golden double tinkling of the little visitors' bell, everyone would immediately wonder: "A visitor—now who can that be?" but we knew very well it could only be M. Swann; my great-aunt speaking loudly, to set an example, in a tone of voice that she strained to make natural, said not to whisper that way; that nothing is more disagreeable for a visitor just coming in who is led to think that people are saying things he should not hear; and they would send as a scout my grandmother, who was always glad to have a pretext for taking one more walk around the garden and who would profit from it by surreptitiously pulling up a few rose stakes on the way so as to make the roses look a little more natural, like a mother who runs her hand through her son's hair to fluff it up after the barber has flattened it too much.

We would all remain hanging on the news my grandmother was going to bring us of the enemy, as though there had been a great number of possible assailants to choose among, and soon afterward my grandfather would say: "I recognize Swann's voice." In fact one could recognize him only by his voice, it was difficult to make out his face, his aquiline nose, his green eyes under a high forehead framed by blond, almost red hair, cut Bressant-style,³ because we kept as little light as possible in the garden so as not to attract mosquitoes, and I would go off, as though not going for that reason, to say that the syrups should be brought out; my grandmother placed a great deal of importance, considering it more amiable, on the idea that they should not seem anything exceptional, and for visitors only. M. Swann, though much younger, was very attached to my grandfather, who had been one of the closest friends of his father, an excellent man but peculiar, in whom, apparently, a trifle was sometimes enough to interrupt the ardor of his feelings, to change the course of his thinking. Several times a year I would hear my grandfather at the table telling anecdotes, always the same ones, about the behavior of old M. Swann upon the death of his wife, over whom he had watched day and night. My grandfather, who had not seen him for a long time, had rushed to his side at the estate the Swanns owned in the vicinity of Combray and, so that he would not be present at the coffining, managed to entice him for a while, all in tears, out of the death chamber. They walked a short way in the park, where there was a little sunshine. Suddenly M. Swann, taking my grandfather by the arm, cried out: "Oh, my old friend, what a joy it is to be walking here together in such fine weather! Don't you think it's pretty, all these trees, these hawthorns! And my pond—which you've never congratulated me on! You look as sad as an old nightcap. Feel that little breeze? Oh, say what you like, life has something to offer despite everything, my dear Amédée!" Suddenly the memory of his dead wife came back to him and, no doubt feeling it would be too complicated to try to understand how he could have yielded to an impulse of happiness at such a time, he confined himself, in a habitual gesture of his whenever a difficult question came into his mind, to passing his hand over his forehead, wiping his eyes and the lenses of his lorgnon. Yet he could not be consoled for the death of his wife, but, during the two years he survived her, would say to my grandfather: "It's odd, I think of my poor wife often, but I can't think of her for long at a time." "Often, but only a little at a time, like poor old Swann," had become one of my grandfather's favorite phrases, which he uttered apropos of the most different sorts of things. I would have thought Swann's father was a monster, if my grandfather, whom I considered a better judge and whose pronouncement, forming a legal precedent for me, often allowed me later to dismiss offenses I might have been inclined to condemn, had not exclaimed: "What! He had a heart of gold!"

For many years, even though, especially before his marriage, the younger M. Swann often came to see them at Combray, my great-aunt and my grandparents did not suspect that he had entirely ceased to live in the kind of society his family had frequented and that, under the sort of incognito which this name Swann gave him among us, they were harboring—with the perfect innocence of honest inn-keepers who have under their roof, without knowing it, some cele-brated highwayman—one of the most elegant members of the Jockey Club,[4] a favorite friend of the Comte de Paris[5] and the Prince of Wales,[6] one of the men most sought after by the high society of the Faubourg Saint-Germain.

Our ignorance of this brilliant social life that Swann led was obvi-ously due in part to the reserve and discretion of his character, but also to the fact that bourgeois people in those days formed for them-selves a rather Hindu notion of society and considered it to be made up of closed castes, in which each person, from birth, found himself placed in the station which his family occupied and from which noth-ing, except the accidents of an exceptional career or an unhoped-for marriage, could withdraw him in order to move him into a higher caste. M. Swann, the father, was a stockbroker; "Swann the son" would find he belonged for his entire life to a caste in which fortunes varied, as in a tax bracket, between such and such fixed incomes. One knew which had been his father's associations, one therefore knew which were his own, with which people he was "in a position" to con-sort. If he knew others, these were bachelor acquaintances on whom old friends of the family, such as my relatives, would close their eyes all the more benignly because he continued, after losing his parents, to come faithfully to see us; but we would have been ready to wager that these people he saw, who were unknown to us, were the sort he would not have dared greet had he encountered them when he was with us. If you were determined to assign Swann a social coefficient that was his alone, among the other sons of stockbrokers in a position equal to that of his parents, this coefficient would have been a little lower for him because, very simple in his manner and with a long-standing "craze" for antiques and painting, he now lived and amassed his collections in an old town house which my grandmother dreamed of visiting, but which was situated on the quai d'Orléans, a part of town where my great-aunt felt it was ignominious to live. "But are you a connoisseur? I ask for your own sake, because you're likely to let the dealers unload some awful daubs on you," my great-aunt would say to him; in fact she did not assume he had any competence and even from an intellectual point of view had no great opinion of a man who in conversation avoided serious subjects and showed a most prosaic preciseness not only when he gave us cooking recipes, entering into the smallest details, but even when my grandmother's sisters talked about artistic subjects. Challenged by them to give his opinion, to express his admiration for a painting, he would maintain an almost ungracious silence and then, on the other hand, redeem himself if he could provide, about the museum in which it was to be found, about the date at which it had been painted, a pertinent piece of information. But usually he would content himself with trying to entertain us by telling a new story each time about something that had just happened to him involving people selected from among those we knew, the Combray pharmacist, our cook, our coachman. Certainly these tales made my great-aunt laugh, but she could not distinguish clearly if this was because of the absurd role Swann always assigned himself or because of the wit he showed in telling them: "You are quite a character, Monsieur Swann!" Being the only rather vulgar person in our family, she took care to point out to strangers, when they were talking about Swann, that, had he wanted to, he could have lived on the boulevard Haussmann or the avenue de l'Opéra, that he was the son of M. Swann, who must have left four or five million, but that this was his whim. One that she felt moreover must be so amusing to others that in Paris, when M. Swann came on New Year's Day to bring her her bag of marrons glacés,[7] she never failed, if there was company, to say to him: "Well, Monsieur Swann! Do you still live next door to the wine warehouse, so as to be sure of not missing the train when you go to Lyon?"[8] And she would look out of the corner of her eye, over her lorgnon, at the other visitors.

But if anyone had told my great-aunt that this same Swann, who, as the son of old M. Swann, was perfectly "qualified" to be received by all the "best of the bourgeoisie," by the most respected notaries or lawyers of Paris (a hereditary privilege he seemed to make little use of), had, as though in secret, quite a different life; that on leaving our house, in Paris, after telling us he was going home to bed, he retraced his steps as soon as he had turned the corner and went to a certain drawing room that no eye of any broker or broker's associate would ever contemplate, this would have seemed to my aunt as extraordinary as might to a better-educated lady the thought of being personally on close terms with Aristaeus and learning that, after having a chat with her, he would go deep into the heart of the realms of Thetis, into an empire hidden from mortal eyes, where Virgil shows him being received with open arms; or—to be content with an image that had more chance of occurring to her, for she had seen it painted on our petits-fours plates at Combray—of having had as a dinner guest Ali Baba, who, as soon as he knows he is alone, will enter the cave dazzling with unsuspected treasure.

One day when he had come to see us in Paris after dinner apologizing for being in evening clothes, Françoise having said, after he left, that she had learned from the coachman that he had dined "at the home of a princess," "Yes, a princess of the demimonde!" my aunt had responded, shrugging her shoulders without raising her eyes from her knitting, with serene irony.

Thus, my great-aunt was cavalier in her treatment of him. Since she believed he must be flattered by our invitations, she found it quite natural that he never came to see us in the summertime without having in his hand a basket of peaches or raspberries from his garden and that from each of his trips to Italy he would bring me back photographs of masterpieces.

They did not hesitate to send him off in search of it when they needed a recipe for gribiche sauce or pineapple salad for large dinners to which they had not invited him, believing he did not have sufficient prestige for one to be able to serve him up to acquaintances who were coming for the first time. If the conversation turned to the princes of the House of France: "people you and I will never know, will we, and we can manage quite well without that, can't we," my great-aunt would say to Swann, who had, perhaps, a letter from Twickenham[9] in his pocket; she had him push the piano around and turn the pages on the evenings when my grandmother's sister sang, handling this creature, who was elsewhere so sought after, with the naive roughness of a child who plays with a collector's curio no more carefully than with some object of little value. No doubt the Swann who was known at the same time to so many clubmen was quite different from the one created by my great-aunt, when in the evening, in the little garden at Combray, after the two hesitant rings of the bell had sounded, she injected and invigorated with all that she knew about the Swann family the dark and uncertain figure who emerged, followed by my grandmother, from a background of shadows, and whom we recognized by his voice. But even with respect to the most insignificant things in life, none of us constitutes a material whole, identical for everyone, which a person has only to go look up as though we were a book of specifications or a last testament; our social personality is a creation of the minds of others. Even the very simple act that we call "seeing a person we know" is in part an intellectual one. We fill the physical appearance of the individual we see with all the notions we have about him, and of the total picture that we form for ourselves, these notions certainly occupy the greater part. In the end they swell his cheeks so perfectly, follow the line of his nose in an adherence so exact, they do so well at nuancing the sonority of his voice as though the latter were only a transparent envelope that each time we see this face and hear this voice, it is these notions that we encounter again, that we hear. No doubt, in the Swann they had formed for themselves, my family had failed out of ignorance to include a host of details from his life in the fashionable world that caused other people, when they were in his presence, to see refinements rule his face and stop at his aquiline nose as though at their natural frontier; but they had also been able to garner in this face disaffected of its prestige, vacant and spacious, in the depths of these depreciated eyes, the vague, sweet residue—half memory, half forgetfulness—of the idle hours spent together after our weekly dinners, around the card table or in the garden, during our life of good country neighborliness. The corporeal envelope of our friend had been so well stuffed with all this, as well as with a few memories relating to his parents, that this particular Swann had become a complete and living being, and I have the impression of leaving one person to go to another distinct from him, when, in my memory, I pass from the Swann I knew later with accuracy to that first Swann—to that first Swann in whom I rediscover the charming mistakes of my youth and who in fact resembles less the other Swann than he resembles the other people I knew at the time, as though one's life were like a museum in which all the portraits from one period have a family look about them, a single tonality—to that first Swann abounding in leisure, fragrant with the smell of the tall chestnut tree, the baskets of raspberries, and a sprig of tarragon.

Yet one day when my grandmother had gone to ask a favor from a lady she had known at the Sacré-Coeur[10] (and with whom, because of our notion of the castes, she had not wished to remain in close contact despite a reciprocal congeniality), this lady, the Marquise de Villeparisis of the famous de Bouillon[11] family, had said to her: "I believe you know M. Swann very well; he is a great friend of my nephew and niece, the des Laumes." My grandmother had returned from her visit full of enthusiasm for the house, which overlooked some gardens and in which Mme. de Villeparisis had advised her to rent a flat, and also for a waistcoat maker and his daughter, who kept a shop in the courtyard where she had gone to ask them to put a stitch in her skirt, which she had torn in the stairwell. My grandmother had found these people wonderful, she declared that the girl was a gem and the waistcoat maker was most distinguished, the finest man she had ever seen. Because for her, distinction was something absolutely independent of social position. She went into ecstasies over an answer the waistcoat maker had given her, saying to Mama: "Sévigné[12] couldn't have said it any better!" and, in contrast, of a nephew of Mme. de Villeparisis whom she had met at the house: "Oh, my dear daughter, how common he is!"

Now the remark about Swann had had the effect, not of raising him in my great-aunt's estimation, but of lowering Mme. de Villeparisis.

It seemed that the respect which, on my grandmother's faith, we accorded Mme. de Villeparisis created a duty on her part to do nothing that would make her less worthy, a duty in which she had failed by learning of Swann's existence, by permitting relatives of hers to associate with him. "What! She knows Swann? A person you claim is a relation of the Maréchal de MacMahon?"[13] My family's opinion regarding Swann's associations seemed confirmed later by his marriage to a woman of the worst social station, practically a cocotte, whom, what was more, he never attempted to introduce, continuing to come to our house alone, though less and less, but from whom they believed they could judge—assuming it was there that he had found her—the social circle, unknown to them, that he habitually frequented.

But one time, my grandfather read in a newspaper that M. Swann was one of the most faithful guests at the Sunday lunches given by the Duc de X . . . , whose father and uncle had been the most prominent statesmen in the reign of Louis-Philippe.[14] Now, my grandfather was interested in all the little facts that could help him enter imaginatively into the private lives of men like Molé, the Duc Pasquier, the Duc de Broglie.[15] He was delighted to learn that Swann associated with people who had known them. My great-aunt, however, interpreted this news in a sense unfavorable to Swann: anyone who chose his associations outside the caste into which he had been born, outside his social "class," suffered in her eyes a regrettable lowering of his social position. It seemed to her that he gave up forthwith the fruit of all the good relations with well-placed people so honorably preserved and stored away for their children by foresightful families (my great-aunt had even stopped seeing the son of a lawyer we knew because he had married royalty and was therefore in her opinion demoted from the respected rank of lawyer's son to that of one of those adventurers, former valets or stableboys, on whom they say that queens sometimes bestowed their favors). She disapproved of my grandfather's plan to question Swann, the next evening he was to come to dinner, about these friends of his we had discovered. At the same time my grandmother's two sisters, old maids who shared her nobility of character, but not her sort of mind, declared that they could not understand what pleasure their brother-in-law could find in talking about such foolishness. They were women of lofty aspirations, who for that very reason were incapable of taking an interest in what is known as tittle-tattle, even if it had some historic interest, and more generally in anything that was not directly connected to an aesthetic or moral subject. The disinterestedness of their minds was such, with respect to all that, closely or distantly, seemed connected with worldly matters, that their sense of hearing—having finally understood its temporary uselessness when the conversation at dinner assumed a tone that was frivolous or merely pedestrian without these two old spinsters being able to lead it back to the subjects dear to them—would suspend the functioning of its receptive organs and allow them to begin to atrophy. If my grandfather needed to attract the two sisters' attention at such times, he had to resort to those bodily signals used by alienists with certain lunatics suffering from distraction: striking a glass repeatedly with the blade of a knife while speaking to them sharply and looking them suddenly in the eye, violent methods which these psychiatrists often bring with them into their ordinary relations with healthy people, either from professional habit or because they believe everyone is a little crazy.

They were more interested when, the day before Swann was to come to dinner, and had personally sent them a case of Asti wine, my aunt, holding a copy of the *Figaro* in which next to the title of a painting in an exhibition of Corot,[16] these words appeared: "From the collection of M. Charles Swann," said: "Did you see this? Swann is 'front page news' in the *Figaro*." "But I've always told you he had a great deal of taste," said my grandmother. "Of course you would! Anything so long as your opinion is not the same as *ours*," answered my great-aunt, who, knowing that my grandmother was never of the same opinion as she, and not being quite sure that she herself was the one we always declared was right, wanted to extract from us a general condemnation of my grandmother's convictions against which she was trying to force us into solidarity with her own. But we remained silent. When my grandmother's sisters expressed their intention of speaking to Swann about this mention in the *Figaro*, my great-aunt advised them against it. Whenever she saw in others an advantage, however small, that she did not have, she persuaded herself that it was not an advantage but a detriment and she pitied them so as not to have to envy them. "I believe you would not be pleasing him at all; I am quite sure I would find it very unpleasant to see my name printed boldly like that in the newspaper, and I would not be at all gratified if someone spoke to me about it." But she did not persist in trying to convince my grandmother's sisters; for they in their horror of vulgarity had made such a fine art of concealing a personal allusion beneath ingenious circumlocutions that it often went unnoticed even by the person to whom it was addressed. As for my mother, she thought only of trying to persuade my father to agree to talk to Swann not about his wife but about his daughter, whom he adored and because of whom it was said he had finally entered into this marriage. "You might just say a word to him; just ask how she is: It must be so hard for him." But my father would become annoyed: "No, no; you have the most absurd ideas. It would be ridiculous."

But the only one of us for whom Swann's arrival became the object of a painful preoccupation was I. This was because on the evenings when strangers, or merely M. Swann, were present, Mama did not come up to my room. I had dinner before everyone else and afterward I came and sat at the table, until eight o'clock when it was understood that I had to go upstairs; the precious and fragile kiss that Mama usually entrusted to me in my bed when I was going to sleep I would have to convey from the dining room to my bedroom and protect during the whole time I undressed, so that its sweetness would not shatter, so that its volatile essence would not disperse and evaporate, and on precisely those evenings when I needed to receive it with more care, I had to take it, I had to snatch it brusquely, publicly, without even having the time and the freedom of mind necessary to bring to what I was doing the attention of those individuals controlled by some mania, who do their utmost not to think of anything else while they are shutting a door, so as to be able, when the morbid uncertainty returns to them, to confront it victoriously with the memory of the moment when they did shut the door. We were all in the garden when the two hesitant rings of the little bell sounded. We knew it was Swann; even so we all looked at one another question-ingly and my grandmother was sent on reconnaissance. "Remember to thank him intelligibly for the wine, you know how delicious it is and the case is enormous," my grandfather exhorted his two sisters-in-law. "Don't start whispering," said my great-aunt. "How comfortable would you feel arriving at a house where everyone is speaking so qui-etly!" "Ah! Here's M. Swann. Let's ask him if he thinks the weather will be good tomorrow," said my father. My mother thought that one word from her would wipe out all the pain that we in our family might have caused Swann since his marriage. She found an opportu-nity to take him aside. But I followed her; I could not bring myself to part from her by even one step while thinking that very soon I would have to leave her in the dining room and that I would have to go up to my room without having the consolation I had on the other eve-nings, that she would come kiss me. "Now, M. Swann," she said to him, "do tell me about your daughter; I'm sure she already has a taste for beautiful things like her papa." "Here, come and sit with the rest of us on the veranda," said my grandfather, coming up to them. My mother was obliged to stop, but she derived from this very constraint one more delicate thought, like good poets forced by the tyranny of rhyme to find their most beautiful lines: "We can talk about her again when we're by ourselves," she said softly to Swann. "Only a mother is capable of understanding you. I'm sure her own mother would agree with me." We all sat down around the iron table. I would have pre-ferred not to think about the hours of anguish I was going to endure that evening alone in my room without being able to go to sleep; I tried to persuade myself they were not at all important, since I would have forgotten them by tomorrow morning, and to fix my mind on ideas of the future that should have led me as though across a bridge beyond the imminent abyss that frightened me so. But my mind, strained by my preoccupation, convex like the glance which I shot at my mother, would not allow itself to be penetrated by any foreign im-pressions. Thoughts certainly entered it, but only on condition that they left outside every element of beauty or simply of playfulness that could have moved or distracted me. Just as a patient, by means of an anesthetic, can watch with complete lucidity the operation being performed on him, but without feeling anything, I could recite to myself some lines that I loved or observe the efforts my grandfather made to talk to Swann about the Duc d'Audiffret-Pasquier, without the former making me feel any emotion, the latter any hilarity. Those efforts were fruitless. Scarcely had my grandfather asked Swann a question relating to that orator than one of my grandmother's sisters, in whose ears the question was resonating like a profound but untimely silence that should be broken for the sake of politeness, would address the other: "Just imagine, Céline, I've met a young Swedish governess who has been telling me about cooperatives in the Scandinavian countries; the details are most interesting. We really must have her here for dinner one evening." "Certainly!" answered her sister Flora,[17] "but I haven't been wasting my time either. At M. Vinteuil's I met a learned old man who knows Maubant[18] very well, and Maubant has explained to him in the greatest detail how he creates his parts. It's most interesting. He's a neighbor of M. Vinteuil's, I had no idea; and he's very nice." "M. Vinteuil isn't the only one who has nice neighbors," exclaimed my aunt Céline in a voice amplified by her shyness and given an artificial tone by her premeditation, while casting at Swann what she called a meaningful look. At the same time my aunt Flora, who had understood that this phrase was Céline's way of thanking Swann for the Asti, was also looking at Swann with an expression that combined congratulation and irony, either simply to emphasize her sister's witticism, or because she envied Swann for having inspired it, or because she could not help making fun of him since she thought he was being put on the spot. "I think we can manage to persuade the old gentleman to come for dinner," continued Flora; "when you get him started on Maubant or Mme. Materna,[19] he talks for hours without stopping." "That must be delightful," sighed my grandfather, in whose mind, unfortunately, nature had as completely failed to include the possibility of taking a passionate interest in Swedish cooperatives or the creation of Maubant's parts as it had forgotten to furnish those of my grandmother's sisters with the little grain of salt one must add oneself, in order to find some savor in it, to a story about the private life of Molé or the Comte de Paris. "Now, then," said Swann to my grandfather, "what I'm going to say has more to do than it might appear with what you were asking me, because in certain respects things haven't changed enormously. This morning I was rereading something in Saint-Simon[20] that would have amused you. It's in the volume about his mission to Spain;[21] it's not one of the best, hardly more than a journal, but at least it's a marvelously well written one, which already makes it rather fundamentally different from the deadly boring journals we think we have to read every morning and evening." "I don't agree, there are days when reading the papers seems to me very pleasant indeed . . ." my aunt Flora interrupted, to show that she had read the sentence about Swann's Corot in *Le Figaro*. "When they talk about things or people that interest us!" said my aunt Céline, going one better. "I don't deny it," answered Swann with surprise. "What I fault the newspapers for is that day after day they draw our attention to insignificant things whereas only three or four times in our lives do we read a book in which there is something really essential. Since we tear the band off the newspaper so feverishly every morning, they ought to change things and put into the newspaper, oh, I don't know, perhaps . . . Pascal's *Pensées*!" (He isolated this word with an ironic emphasis so as not to seem pedantic.) "And then, in the gilt-edged volume that we open only once in ten years," he added, showing the disdain for worldly matters affected by certain worldly men, "we would read that the Queen of Greece has gone to Cannes or that the Princesse de Léon has given a costume ball. This way, the proper proportions would be reestablished." But, feeling sorry he had gone so far as to speak even lightly of serious things: "What a lofty conversation we're having," he said ironically; "I don't know why we're climbing to such 'heights'"—and turning to my grandfather: "Well, Saint-Simon describes how Maulévrier[22] had the audacity to offer to shake hands with Saint-Simon's sons. You know, this is the same Maulévrier of whom he says: 'Never did I see in that thick bottle anything but ill-humor, vulgarity, and foolishness.'" "Thick or not, I know some bottles in which there is something quite different," said Flora vivaciously, determined that she too should thank Swann, because the gift of Asti was addressed to both of them. Céline laughed. Swann, disconcerted, went on: " 'I cannot say whether it was ignorance or a trap,' wrote Saint-Simon. 'He tried to shake hands with my children. I noticed it in time to prevent him.' " My grandfather was already in ecstasies over "ignorance or a trap," but Mlle. Céline, in whom the name of Saint-Simon—a literary man—had prevented the complete anesthesia of her auditory faculties, was already growing indignant: "What? You admire that? Well, that's a fine thing! But what can it mean; isn't one man as good as the next? What difference does it make whether he's a duke or a coachman, if he's intelligent and good-hearted? Your Saint-Simon had a fine way of raising his children, if he didn't teach them to offer their hands to all decent people. Why, it's quite abominable. And you dare to quote that?" And my grandfather, terribly upset and sensing how impossible it would be, in the face of this obstruction, to try to get Swann to tell the stories that would have amused him, said quietly to Mama: "Now remind me of the line you taught me that comforts me so much at times like this. Oh, yes! 'What virtues, Lord, Thou makest us abhor!'²³ Oh, how good that is!"

I did not take my eyes off my mother, I knew that when we were at the table, they would not let me stay during the entire dinner and that, in order not to annoy my father, Mama would not let me kiss her several times in front of the guests as though we were in my room. And so I promised myself that in the dining room, as they were beginning dinner and I felt the hour approaching, I would do everything I could do alone in advance of this kiss which would be so brief and furtive, choose with my eyes the place on her cheek that I would kiss, prepare my thoughts so as to be able, by means of this mental beginning of the kiss, to devote the whole of the minute Mama would grant me to feeling her cheek against my lips, as a painter who can obtain only short sittings prepares his palette and, guided by his notes, does in advance from memory everything for which he could if necessary manage without the presence of the model. But now before the dinner bell rang my grandfather had the unwitting brutality to say: "The boy looks tired, he ought to go up to bed. We're dining late tonight anyway." And my father, who was not as scrupulous as my grandmother and my mother about honoring treaties, said: "Yes, go on now, up to bed with you." I tried to kiss Mama, at that moment we heard the dinner bell. "No, really, leave your mother alone, you've already said goodnight to each other as it is, these demonstrations are ridiculous. Go on now, upstairs!" And I had to leave without my viaticum; I had to climb each step of the staircase, as the popular expression has it, "against my heart,"[24] climbing against my heart which wanted to go back to my mother because she had not, by kissing me, given it license to go with me. That detested staircase which I always entered with such gloom exhaled an odor of varnish that had in some sense absorbed, fixated, the particular sort of sorrow I felt every evening and made it perhaps even crueler to my sensibility because, when it took that olfactory form, my intelligence could no longer share in it. When we are asleep and a raging toothache is as yet perceived by us only in the form of a girl whom we attempt two hundred times to pull out of the water or a line by Molière that we repeat to ourselves incessantly, it is a great relief to wake up so that our intelligence can divest the idea of raging toothache of its disguise of heroism or cadence. It was the opposite of this relief that I experienced when my sorrow at going up to my room entered me in a manner infinitely swifter, almost instantaneous, at once insidious and abrupt, through the inhalation—far more toxic than the intellectual penetration—of the smell of varnish peculiar to that staircase. Once in my room, I had to stop up all the exits, close the shutters, dig my own grave by undoing my covers, put on the shroud of my nightshirt. But before burying myself in the iron bed which they had added to the room because I was too hot in the summer under the rep curtains of the big bed, I had a fit of rebelliousness, I wanted to attempt the ruse of a condemned man. I wrote to my mother begging her to come upstairs for something serious that I could not tell her in my letter. My fear was that Françoise, my aunt's cook who was charged with looking after me when I was at Combray, would refuse to convey my note. I suspected that, for her, delivering a message to my mother when there was company would seem as impossible as for a porter to hand a letter to an actor while he was onstage. With respect to things that could or could not be done she possessed a code at once imperious, extensive, subtle, and intransigent about distinctions that were impalpable or otiose (which made it resemble those ancient laws which, alongside such fierce prescriptions as the massacre of children at the breast, forbid one with an exaggerated delicacy to boil a kid in its mother's milk, or to eat the sinew from an animal's thigh). This code, to judge from her sudden obstinacy when she did not wish to do certain errands that we gave her, seemed to have anticipated social complexities and worldly refinements that nothing in Françoise's associations or her life as a village domestic could have suggested to her; and we had to say to ourselves that in her there was a very old French past, noble and ill understood, as in those manufacturing towns where elegant old houses testify that there was once a court life, and where the employees of a factory for chemical products work surrounded by delicate sculptures representing the miracle of Saint Théophile or the four sons of Aymon.[25] In this particular case, the article of the code which made it unlikely that except in case of fire Françoise would go bother Mama in the presence of M. Swann for so small a personage as myself simply betokened the respect she professed not only for the family—as for the dead, for priests, and for kings—but also for the visitor to whom one was offering one's hospitality, a respect that would perhaps have touched me in a book but that always irritated me on her lips, because of the solemn and tender tones she adopted in speaking of it, and especially so this evening, when the sacred character she conferred on the dinner might have the effect of making her refuse to disturb its ceremonial. But to give myself a better chance, I did not hesitate to lie and tell her that it was not in the least I who had wanted to write to Mama, but that it was Mama who, as she said goodnight to me, had exhorted me not to forget to send her an answer concerning something she had asked me to look for; and she would certainly be very annoyed if this note was not delivered to her. I think Françoise did not believe me, for, like those primitive men whose senses were so much more powerful than ours, she could immediately discern, from signs imperceptible to us, any truth that we wanted to hide from her; she looked at the envelope for five minutes as if the examination of the paper and the appearance of the writing would inform her about the nature of the contents or tell her which article of her code she ought to apply. Then she went out with an air of resignation that seemed to signify: "If it isn't a misfortune for parents to have a child like that!" She came back after a moment to tell me that they were still only at the ice stage, that it was impossible for the butler to deliver the letter right away in front of everyone, but that, when the mouth-rinsing bowls[26] were put round, they would find a way to hand it to Mama. Instantly my anxiety subsided; it was now no longer, as it had been only a moment ago, until tomorrow that I had left my mother, since my little note, no doubt annoying her (and doubly because this stratagem would make me ridiculous in Swann's eyes), would at least allow me, invisible and enraptured, to enter the same room as she, would whisper about me in her ear; since that forbidden, hostile dining room, where, just a moment before, the ice itself—the "*granité*"[27]—and the rinsing bowls seemed to me to contain pleasures noxious and mortally sad because Mama was enjoying them far away from me, was opening itself to me and, like a fruit that has turned sweet and bursts its skin, was about to propel, to project, all the way to my intoxicated heart, Mama's attention as she read my lines. Now I was no longer separated from her; the barriers were down, an exquisite thread joined us. And that was not all: Mama would probably come!

I thought Swann would surely have laughed at the anguish I had just suffered if he had read my letter and guessed its purpose; yet, on the contrary, as I learned later, a similar anguish was the torment of long years of his life and no one, perhaps, could have understood me as well as he; in his case, the anguish that comes from feeling that the person you love is in a place of amusement where you are not, where you cannot join her, came to him through love, to which it is in some sense predestined, by which it will be hoarded, appropriated; but when, as in my case, this anguish enters us before love has made its appearance in our life, it drifts as it waits for it, vague and free, without a particular assignment, at the service of one feeling one day, of another the next, sometimes of filial tenderness or affection for a friend. And the joy with which I served my first apprenticeship when Françoise came back to tell me my letter would be delivered Swann too had known well, that deceptive joy given to us by some friend, some relative of the woman we love when, arriving at the house or theater where she is, for some dance, gala evening, or premiere at which he is going to see her, this friend notices us wandering outside, desperately awaiting some opportunity to communicate with her. He recognizes us, speaks to us familiarly, asks us what we are doing there. And when we invent the story that we have something urgent to say to his relative or friend, he assures us that nothing could be simpler, leads us into the hall, and promises to send her to us in five minutes. How we love him, as at that moment I loved Françoise—the well-intentioned intermediary who with a single word has just made tolerable, human, and almost propitious the unimaginable, infernal festivity into the thick of which we had been imagining that hostile, perverse, and exquisite vortices of pleasure were carrying away from us and inspiring with derisive laughter the woman we love! If we are to judge by him, the relative who has come up to us and is himself also one of the initiates in the cruel mysteries, the other guests at the party cannot have anything very demoniacal about them. Those inaccessible and excruciating hours during which she was about to enjoy unknown pleasures—now, through an unexpected breach, we are entering them; now, one of the moments which, in succession, would have composed those hours, a moment as real as the others, perhaps even more important to us, because our mistress is more involved in it, we can picture to ourselves, we possess it, we are taking part in it, we have created it, almost: the moment in which he will tell her we are here, downstairs. And no doubt the other moments of the party would not have been essentially very different from this one, would not have had anything more delectable about them that should make us suffer so, since the kind friend has said to us: "Why, she'll be delighted to come down! It'll be much nicer for her to chat with you than to be bored up there." Alas! Swann had learned by experience that the good intentions of a third person have no power over a woman who is annoyed to find herself pursued even into a party by someone she does not love. Often, the friend comes back down alone.

My mother did not come, and with no consideration for my pride (which was invested in her not denying the story that she was supposed to have asked me to let her know the results of some search) asked Françoise to say these words to me: "There is no answer," words I have so often since then heard the doormen in grand hotels or the footmen in bawdy houses bring back to some poor girl who exclaims in surprise: "What, he said nothing? Why, that's impossible! Did you really give him my note? All right, I'll go on waiting." And—just as she invariably assures him she does not need the extra gas jet which the doorman wants to light for her, and remains there, hearing nothing further but the few remarks about the weather exchanged by the doorman and a lackey whom he sends off suddenly, when he notices the time, to put a customer's drink on ice—having declined Françoise's offer to make me some tea or to stay with me, I let her return to the servants' hall, I went to bed and closed my eyes, trying not to hear the voices of my family, who were having their coffee in the garden. But after a few seconds, I became aware that, by writing that note to Mama, by approaching, at the risk of angering her, so close to her that I thought I could touch the moment when I would see her again, I had shut off from myself the possibility of falling asleep without seeing her again, and the beating of my heart grew more painful each minute because I was increasing my agitation by telling myself to be calm, to accept my misfortune. Suddenly my anxiety subsided, a happiness invaded me as when a powerful medicine begins to take effect and our pain vanishes: I had just formed the resolution not to continue trying to fall asleep without seeing Mama again, to kiss her at all costs even though it was with the certainty of being on bad terms with her for a long time after, when she came up to bed. The calm that came with the end of my distress filled me with an extraordinary joy, quite as much as did my expectation, my thirst for and my fear of danger. I opened the window noiselessly and sat down on the foot of my bed; I hardly moved so that I would not be heard from below. Outdoors, too, things seemed frozen in silent attention so as not to disturb the moonlight which, duplicating and distancing each thing by extending its shadow before it, denser and more concrete than itself, had at once thinned and enlarged the landscape like a map that had been folded and was now opened out. What needed to move, a few leaves of the chestnut tree, moved. But their minute quivering, complete, executed even in its slightest nuances and ultimate refinements, did not spill over onto the rest, did not merge with it, remained circumscribed. Exposed against this silence, which absorbed nothing of them, the most distant noises, those that must have come from gardens that lay at the other end of town, could be perceived detailed with such "finish" that they seemed to owe this effect of remoteness only to their pianissimo, like those muted motifs so well executed by the orchestra of the Conservatoire that, although you do not lose a single note, you nonetheless think you are hearing them far away from the concert hall and all the old subscribers—my grandmother's sisters too, when Swann had given them his seats—strained their ears as if they were listening to the distant advances of an army on the march that had not yet turned the corner of the rue de Trévise.

I knew that the situation I was now placing myself in was the one that could provoke the gravest consequences of all for me, coming from my parents, much graver in truth than a stranger would have supposed, the sort he would have believed could be produced only by truly shameful misdeeds. But in my upbringing, the order of misdeeds was not the same as in that of other children, and I had become accustomed to placing before all the rest (because there were probably no others from which I needed to be more carefully protected) those whose common characteristic I now understand was that you lapse into them by yielding to a nervous impulse. But at the time no one uttered these words, no one revealed this cause, which might have made me believe I was excusable for succumbing to them or even perhaps incapable of resisting them. But I recognized them clearly from the anguish that preceded them as well as from the rigor of the punishment that followed them; and I knew that the one I had just committed was in the same family as others for which I had been severely punished, though infinitely graver. When I went and placed myself in my mother's path at the moment she was going up to bed, and when she saw that I had stayed up to say goodnight to her again in the hallway, they would not let me continue to live at home, they would send me away to school the next day, that much was certain. Well! Even if I had had to throw myself out of the window five minutes later, I still preferred this. What I wanted now was Mama, to say goodnight to her, I had gone too far along the road that led to the fulfillment of that desire to be able to turn back now.

I heard my parents' footsteps as they saw Swann out; and when the bell on the gate let me know he had gone, I went to the window. Mama was asking my father if he had thought the lobster was good and if M. Swann had had more coffee-and-pistachio ice. "I found it quite ordinary," said my mother; "I think next time we'll have to try another flavor." "I can't tell you how changed I find Swann," said my great-aunt, "he has aged so!" My great-aunt was so used to seeing Swann always as the same adolescent that she was surprised to find him suddenly not as young as the age she continued to attribute to him. And my family was also beginning to feel that in him this aging was abnormal, excessive, shameful, and more deserved by the unmarried, by all those for whom it seems that the great day that has no tomorrow is longer than for others, because for them it is empty and the moments in it add up from morning on without then being divided among children. "I think he has no end of worries with that wretched wife of his who is living with a certain Monsieur de Charlus, as all of Combray knows. It's the talk of the town." My mother pointed out that in spite of this he had been looking much less sad for some time now. "He also doesn't make that gesture of his as often, so like his father, of wiping his eyes and running his hand across his forehead. I myself think that in his heart of hearts he no longer loves that woman." "Why, naturally he doesn't love her anymore," answered my grandfather. "I received a letter from him about it a long time ago, by now, a letter with which I hastened not to comply and which leaves no doubt about his feelings, at least his feelings of love, for his wife. Well now! You see, you didn't thank him for the Asti," added my grandfather, turning to his two sisters-in-law. "What? We didn't thank him? I think, just between you and me, that I put it quite delicately," answered my aunt Flora. "Yes, you managed it very well: quite admirable," said my aunt Céline. "But you were very good too." "Yes, I was rather proud of my remark about kind neighbors." "What? Is that what you call thanking him?" exclaimed my grandfather. "I certainly heard that, but devil take me if I thought it was directed at Swann. You can be sure he never noticed." "But see here, Swann isn't stupid, I'm sure he appreciated it. After all, I couldn't tell him how many bottles there were and what the wine cost!" My father and mother were left alone there, and sat down for a moment; then my father said: "Well, shall we go up to bed?" "If you like, my dear, even though I'm not the least bit sleepy; yet it couldn't be that perfectly harmless coffee ice that's keeping me so wide-awake; but I can see a light in the servants' hall, and since poor Françoise has waited up for me, I'll go and ask her to unhook my bodice while you're getting undressed." And my mother opened the latticed door that led from the vestibule to the staircase. Soon, I heard her coming upstairs to close her window. I went without a sound into the hallway; my heart was beating so hard I had trouble walking, but at least it was no longer pounding from anxiety, but from terror and joy. I saw the light cast in the stairwell by Mama's candle. Then I saw Mama herself; I threw myself forward. In the first second, she looked at me with astonishment, not understanding what could have happened. Then an expression of anger came over her face, she did not say a single word to me, and indeed for much less than this they would go several days without speaking to me. If Mama had said one word to me, it would have been an admission that they could talk to me again and in any case it would perhaps have seemed to me even more terrible, as a sign that, given the gravity of the punishment that was going to be prepared for me, silence, and estrangement, would have been childish. A word would have been like the calm with which you answer a servant when you have just decided to dismiss him; the kiss you give a son you are sending off to enlist, whereas you would have refused it if you were simply going to be annoyed with him for a few days. But she heard my father coming up from the dressing room where he had gone to undress and, to avoid the scene he would make over me, she said to me in a voice choked with anger: "Run, run, so at least your father won't see you waiting like this as if you were out of your mind!" But I repeated to her: "Come say goodnight to me," terrified as I saw the gleam from my father's candle already rising up the wall, but also using his approach as a means of blackmail and hoping that Mama, to avoid my father's finding me there still if she continued to refuse, would say: "Go back to your room, I'll come." It was too late, my father was there in front of us. Involuntarily, though no one heard, I murmured these words: "I'm done for!"

It was not so. My father was constantly refusing me permission for things that had been authorized in the more generous covenants granted by my mother and grandmother because he did not bother about "principles" and for him there was no "rule of law." For a completely contingent reason, or even for no reason at all, he would at the last minute deny me a certain walk that was so customary, so consecrated that to deprive me of it was a violation, or, as he had done once again this evening, long before the ritual hour he would say to me: "Go on now, up to bed, no arguments!" But also, because he had no principles (in my grandmother's sense), he was not strictly speaking intransigent. He looked at me for a moment with an expression of surprise and annoyance, then as soon as Mama had explained to him with a few embarrassed words what had happened, he said to her: "Go along with him, then. You were just saying you didn't feel very sleepy, stay in his room for a little while, I don't need anything." "But my dear," answered my mother timidly, "whether I'm sleepy or not doesn't change anything, we can't let the child get into the habit . . ." "But it isn't a question of habit," said my father, shrugging his shoulders, "you can see the boy is upset, he seems very sad; look, we're not executioners! You'll end by making him ill, and that won't do us much good! There are two beds in his room; go tell Françoise to prepare the big one for you and sleep there with him tonight. Now then, goodnight, I'm not as high-strung as the two of you, I'm going to bed."

It was impossible to thank my father; he would have been irritated by what he called mawkishness. I stood there not daring to move; he was still there in front of us, tall in his white nightshirt, under the pink and violet Indian cashmere shawl that he tied around his head now that he had attacks of neuralgia, with the gesture of Abraham in the engraving after Benozzo Gozzoli[28] that M. Swann had given me, as he told Sarah she must leave Issac's side. This was many years ago. The staircase wall on which I saw the rising glimmer of his candle has long since ceased to exist. In me, too, many things have been destroyed that I thought were bound to last forever and new ones have formed that have given birth to new sorrows and joys which I could not have foreseen then, just as the old ones have become difficult for me to understand. It was a very long time ago, too, that my father ceased to be able to say to Mama: "Go with the boy." The possibility of such hours will never be reborn for me. But for a little while now, I have begun to hear again very clearly, if I take care to listen, the sobs that I was strong enough to contain in front of my father and that broke out only when I found myself alone again with Mama. They have never really stopped; and it is only because life is now becoming quieter around me that I can hear them again, like those convent bells covered so well by the clamor of the town during the day that one would think they had ceased altogether but which begin sounding again in the silence of the evening.

Mama spent that night in my room; when I had just committed such a misdeed that I expected to have to leave the house, my parents granted me more than I could ever have won from them as a reward for any good deed. Even at the moment when it manifested itself through this pardon, my father's conduct toward me retained that arbitrary and undeserved quality that characterized it and was due to the fact that it generally resulted from fortuitous convenience rather than a premeditated plan. It may even be that what I called his severity, when he sent me to bed, deserved that name less than my mother's or my grandmother's, for his nature, in certain respects more different from mine than theirs was, had probably kept him from discovering until now how very unhappy I was every evening, something my mother and my grandmother knew well; but they loved me enough not to consent to spare me my suffering, they wanted to teach me to master it in order to reduce my nervous sensitivity and strengthen my will. As for my father, whose affection for me was of another sort, I do not know if he would have been courageous enough for that: the one time he realized that I was upset, he had said to my mother: "Go and comfort him." Mama stayed in my room that night and, as though not to allow any remorse to spoil those hours which were so different from what I had had any right to expect, when Françoise, realizing that something extraordinary was happening when she saw Mama sitting next to me, holding my hand and letting me cry without scolding me, asked her: "Why, madame, now what's wrong with Monsieur that he's crying so?" Mama answered her: "Why, even he doesn't know, Françoise, he's in a state; prepare the big bed for me quickly and then go on up to bed yourself." And so, for the first time, my sadness was regarded no longer as a punishable offense but as an involuntary ailment that had just been officially recognized, a nervous condition for which I was not responsible; I had the relief of no longer having to mingle qualms of conscience with the bitterness of my tears, I could cry without sin. I was also not a little proud, with respect to Françoise, of this turnabout in human affairs which, an hour after Mama had refused to come up to my room and had sent the disdainful answer that I should go to sleep, raised me to the dignity of a grown-up and brought me suddenly to a sort of puberty of grief, of emancipation from tears. I ought to have been happy: I was not. It seemed to me that my mother had just made me a first concession which must have been painful to her, that this was a first abdication on her part from the ideal she had conceived for me, and that for the first time she, who was so courageous, had to confess herself beaten. It seemed to me that, if I had just gained a victory, it was over her, that I had succeeded, as illness, affliction, or age might have done, in relaxing her will, in weakening her judgment, and that this evening was the beginning of a new era, would remain as a sad date. If I had dared, now, I would have said to Mama: "No, I don't want you to do this, don't sleep here." But I was aware of the practical wisdom, the realism as it would be called now, which in her tempered my grandmother's ardently idealistic nature, and I knew that, now that the harm was done, she would prefer to let me at least enjoy the soothing pleasure of it and not disturb my father. To be sure, my mother's lovely face still shone with youth that evening when she so gently held my hands and tried to stop my tears; but it seemed to me that this was precisely what should not have been, her anger would have saddened me less than this new gentleness which my childhood had not known before; it seemed to me that with an impious and secret hand I had just traced in her soul a first wrinkle and caused a first white hair to appear. At the thought of this my sobs redoubled, and then I saw that Mama, who never let herself give way to any emotion with me, was suddenly overcome by my own and was trying to suppress a desire to cry. When she saw that I had noticed, she said to me with a smile: "There now, my little chick, my little canary, he's going to make his mama as silly as himself if this continues. Look, since you're not sleepy and your mama isn't either, let's not go on upsetting each other, let's do something, let's get one of your books." But I had none there. "Would you enjoy it less if I took out the books your grandmother will be giving you on your saint's day? Think about it carefully: you mustn't be disappointed not to have anything the day after tomorrow." On the contrary, I was delighted, and Mama went to get a packet of books, of which I could not distinguish, through the paper in which they were wrapped, more than their shape, short and thick, but which, in this first guise, though summary and veiled, already eclipsed the box of colors from New Year's Day and the silkworms from last year. They were *La Mare au Diable, François le Champi, La Petite Fadette,* and *Les Maîtres Sonneurs.* My grandmother, as I learned afterward, had first chosen the poems of Musset, a volume of Rousseau, and *Indiana;*[29] for though she judged frivolous reading to be as unhealthy as sweets and pastries, it did not occur to her that a great breath of genius might have a more dangerous and less invigorating influence on the mind even of a child than would the open air and the sea breeze on his body. But as my father had nearly called her mad when he learned which books she wanted to give me, she had returned to the bookstore in Jouy-le-Vicomte herself, so that I would not risk not having my present (it was a burning-hot day and she had come home so indisposed that the doctor had warned my mother not to let her tire herself out that way again) and she had resorted to the four pastoral novels of George Sand. "My dear daughter," she said to Mama, "I could not bring myself to give the boy something badly written."

In fact, she could never resign herself to buying anything from which one could not derive an intellectual profit, and especially that which beautiful things afford us by teaching us to seek our pleasure elsewhere than in the satisfactions of material comfort and vanity. Even when she had to make someone a present of the kind called "useful," when she had to give an armchair, silverware, a walking stick, she looked for "old" ones, as though, now that long desuetude had effaced their character of usefulness, they would appear more disposed to tell us about the life of people of other times than to serve the needs of our own life. She would have liked me to have in my room photographs of the most beautiful monuments or landscapes. But at the moment of buying them, and even though the thing represented had an aesthetic value, she would find that vulgarity and utility too quickly resumed their places in that mechanical mode of representation, the photograph. She would try to use cunning and, if not to eliminate commercial banality entirely, at least to reduce it, to substitute for the greater part of it more art, to introduce into it in a sense several "layers" of art: instead of photographs of Chartres Cathedral, the Fountains of Saint-Cloud, or Mount Vesuvius, she would make inquiries of Swann as to whether some great painter had not depicted them, and preferred to give me photographs of Chartres Cathedral by Corot, of the Fountains of Saint-Cloud by Hubert Robert,[30] of Mount Vesuvius by Turner,[31] which made one further degree of art. But if the photographer had been removed from the representation of the masterpiece or of nature and replaced by a great artist, he still reclaimed his rights to reproduce that very interpretation. Having deferred vulgarity as far as possible, my grandmother would try to move it back still further. She would ask Swann if the work had not been engraved, preferring, whenever possible, old engravings that also had an interest beyond themselves, such as those that represent a masterpiece in a state in which we can no longer see it today (like the engraving by Morghen[32] of Leonardo's *Last Supper* before its deterioration). It must be said that the results of this interpretation of the art of gift giving were not always brilliant. The idea I formed of Venice from a drawing by Titian that is supposed to have the lagoon in the background was certainly far less accurate than the one I would have derived from simple photographs. We could no longer keep count, at home, when my great-aunt wanted to draw up an indictment against my grandmother, of the armchairs she had presented to young couples engaged to be married or old married couples which, at the first attempt to make use of them, had immediately collapsed under the weight of one of the recipients. But my grandmother would have believed it petty to be overly concerned about the solidity of a piece of wood in which one could still distinguish a small flower, a smile, sometimes a lovely invention from the past. Even what might, in these pieces of furniture, answer a need, since it did so in a manner to which we are no longer accustomed, charmed her like the old ways of speaking in which we see a metaphor that is obliterated, in our modern language, by the abrasion of habit. Now, in fact, the pastoral novels of George Sand that she was giving me for my saint's day were, like an old piece of furniture, full of expressions that had fallen into disuse and turned figurative again, the sort you no longer find anywhere but in the country. And my grandmother had bought them in preference to others just as she would sooner have rented an estate on which there was a Gothic dovecote or another of those old things that exercise such a happy influence on the mind by filling it with longing for impossible voyages through time.

Mama sat down by my bed; she had picked up *François le Champi*, whose reddish cover and incomprehensible title gave it, in my eyes, a distinct personality and a mysterious attraction. I had not yet read a real novel. I had heard people say that George Sand was an exemplary novelist. This already predisposed me to imagine something indefinable and delicious in *François le Champi*. Narrative devices intended to arouse curiosity or emotion, certain modes of expression that make one uneasy or melancholy, and that a reader with some education will recognize as common to many novels, appeared to me—who considered a new book not as a thing having many counterparts, but as a unique person, having no reason for existing but in itself—simply as a disturbing emanation of *François le Champi*'s peculiar essence. Behind those events so ordinary, those things so common, those words so current, I sensed a strange sort of intonation, accentuation. The action began; it seemed to me all the more obscure because in those days, when I read, I often daydreamed, for entire pages, of something quite different. And in addition to the lacunae that this distraction left in the story, there was the fact, when Mama was the one reading aloud to me, that she skipped all the love scenes. Thus, all the bizarre changes that take place in the respective attitudes of the miller's wife and the child and that can be explained only by the progress of a nascent love seemed to me marked by a profound mystery whose source I readily imagined must be in that strange and sweet name "Champi," which gave the child, who bore it without my knowing why, its vivid, charming purplish color. If my mother was an unfaithful reader she was also, in the case of books in which she found the inflection of true feeling, a wonderful reader for the respect and simplicity of her interpretation, the beauty and gentleness of the sound of her voice. Even in real life, when it was people and not works of art which moved her to compassion or admiration, it was touching to see with what deference she removed from her voice, from her motions, from her words, any spark of gaiety that might hurt some mother who had once lost a child, any recollection of a saint's day or birthday that might remind some old man of his advanced age, any remark about housekeeping that might seem tedious to some young scholar. In the same way, when she was reading George Sand's prose, which always breathes that goodness, that moral distinction which Mama had learned from my grandmother to consider superior to all else in life, and which I was to teach her only much later not to consider superior to all else in books too, taking care to banish from her voice any pettiness, any affectation which might have prevented it from receiving that powerful torrent, she imparted all the natural tenderness, all the ample sweetness they demanded to those sentences which seemed written for her voice and which remained, so to speak, entirely within the register of her sensibility. She found, to attack them in the necessary tone, the warm inflection that preexists them and that dictated them, but that the words do not indicate; with this inflection she softened as she went along any crudeness in the tenses of the verbs, gave the imperfect and the past historic the sweetness that lies in goodness, the melancholy that lies in tenderness, directed the sentence that was ending toward the one that was about to begin, sometimes hurrying, sometimes slowing down the pace of the syllables so as to bring them, though their quantities were different, into one uniform rhythm, she breathed into this very common prose a sort of continuous emotional life.

My remorse was quieted, I gave in to the sweetness of that night in which I had my mother close to me. I knew that such a night could not be repeated; that the greatest desire I had in the world, to keep my mother in my room during those sad hours of darkness, was too contrary to the necessities of life and the wishes of others for its fulfillment, granted this night, to be anything other than artificial and exceptional. Tomorrow my anxieties would reawaken and Mama would not stay here. But when my anxieties were soothed, I no longer understood them; and then tomorrow night was still far away; I told myself I would have time to think of what to do, even though that time could not bring me any access of power, since these things did not depend on my will and seemed more avoidable to me only because of the interval that still separated them from me.

So it was that, for a long time, when, awakened at night, I remembered Combray again, I saw nothing of it but this sort of luminous panel, cut out among indistinct shadows, like those panels which the glow of a Bengal light or some electric projection will cut out and illuminate in a building whose other parts remain plunged in darkness: at the rather broad base, the small parlor, the dining room, the opening of the dark path by which M. Swann, the unconscious author of my sufferings, would arrive, the front hall where I would head toward the first step of the staircase, so painful to climb, that formed, by itself, the very narrow trunk of this irregular pyramid; and, at the top, my bedroom with the little hallway and its glass-paned door for Mama's entrance; in a word, always seen at the same hour, isolated from everything that might surround it, standing out alone against the darkness, the bare minimum of scenery (such as one sees prescribed at the beginnings of the old plays for performances in the provinces) needed for the drama of my undressing; as though Combray had consisted only of two floors connected by a slender staircase and as though it had always been seven o'clock in the evening there. The fact is, I could have answered anyone who asked me that Combray also included other things and existed at other times of day. But since what I recalled would have been supplied to me only by my voluntary memory, the memory of the intelligence, and since the information it gives about the past preserves nothing of the past itself, I would never have had any desire to think about the rest of Combray. It was all really quite dead for me.

Dead forever? Possibly.

There is a great deal of chance in all this, and a second sort of chance event, that of our own death, often does not allow us to wait long for the favors of the first.

I find the Celtic belief very reasonable, that the souls of those we have lost are held captive in some inferior creature, in an animal, in a plant, in some inanimate object, effectively lost to us until the day, which for many never comes, when we happen to pass close to the tree, come into possession of the object that is their prison. Then they quiver, they call out to us, and as soon as we have recognized them, the spell is broken. Delivered by us, they have overcome death and they return to live with us.

It is the same with our past. It is a waste of effort for us to try to summon it, all the exertions of our intelligence are useless. The past is hidden outside the realm of our intelligence and beyond its reach, in some material object (in the sensation that this material object would give us) which we do not suspect. It depends on chance whether we encounter this object before we die, or do not encounter it.

For many years, already, everything about Combray that was not the theater and drama of my bedtime had ceased to exist for me, when one day in winter, as I returned home, my mother, seeing that I was cold, suggested that, contrary to my habit, I have a little tea. I refused at first and then, I do not know why, changed my mind. She sent for one of those squat, plump cakes called *petites madeleines* that look as though they have been molded in the grooved valve of a scallop shell. And soon, mechanically, oppressed by the gloomy day and the prospect of another sad day to follow, I carried to my lips a spoonful of the tea in which I had let soften a bit of madeleine. But at the very instant when the mouthful of tea mixed with cake crumbs touched my palate, I quivered, attentive to the extraordinary thing that was happening inside me. A delicious pleasure had invaded me, isolated me, without my having any notion as to its cause. It had immediately rendered the vicissitudes of life unimportant to me, its disasters innocuous, its brevity illusory, acting in the same way that love acts, by filling me with a precious essence: or rather this essence was not merely inside me, it was me. I had ceased to feel mediocre, contingent, mortal. Where could it have come to me from—this powerful joy? I sensed that it was connected to the taste of the tea and the cake, but that it went infinitely far beyond it, could not be of the same nature. Where did it come from? What did it mean? How could I grasp it? I drink a second mouthful, in which I find nothing more than in the first, a third that gives me a little less than the second. It is time for me to stop, the virtue of the drink seems to be diminishing. Clearly, the truth I am seeking is not in the drink, but in me. The drink has awoken it in me, but does not know this truth, and can do no more than repeat indefinitely, with less and less force, this same testimony which I do not know how to interpret and which I want at least to be able to ask of it again and find again, intact, available to me, soon, for a decisive clarification. I put down the cup and turn to my mind. It is up to my mind to find the truth. But how? Such grave uncertainty, whenever the mind feels overtaken by itself; when it, the seeker, is also the obscure country where it must seek and where all its baggage will be nothing to it. Seek? Not only that: create. It is face-to-face with something that does not yet exist and that only it can accomplish, then bring into its light.

And I begin asking myself again what it could be, this unknown state which brought with it no logical proof, but only the evidence of its felicity, its reality, and in whose presence the other states of consciousness faded away. I want to try to make it reappear. I return in my thoughts to the moment when I took the first spoonful of tea. I find the same state again, without any new clarity. I ask my mind to make another effort, to bring back once more the sensation that is slipping away. And, so that nothing may interrupt the thrust with which it will try to grasp it again, I clear away every obstacle, every foreign idea, I protect my ears and my attention from the noises in the next room. But feeling my mind grow tired without succeeding, I now compel it to accept the very distraction I was denying it, to think of something else, to recover its strength before a supreme attempt. Then for a second time I create an empty space before it, I confront it again with the still recent taste of that first mouthful, and I feel something quiver in me, shift, try to rise, something that seems to have been unanchored at a great depth; I do not know what it is, but it comes up slowly; I feel the resistance and I hear the murmur of the distances traversed.

Undoubtedly what is palpitating thus, deep inside me, must be the image, the visual memory which is attached to this taste and is trying to follow it to me. But it is struggling too far away, too confusedly; I can just barely perceive the neutral glimmer in which the elusive eddying of stirred-up colors is blended; but I cannot distinguish the form, cannot ask it, as the one possible interpreter, to translate for me the evidence of its contemporary, its inseparable companion, the taste, ask it to tell me what particular circumstance is involved, what period of the past.

Will it reach the clear surface of my consciousness—this memory, this old moment which the attraction of an identical moment has come from so far to invite, to move, to raise up from the deepest part of me? I don't know. Now I no longer feel anything, it has stopped, gone back down perhaps; who knows if it will ever rise up from its darkness again? Ten times I must begin again, lean down toward it. And each time, the laziness that deters us from every difficult task, every work of importance, has counseled me to leave it, to drink my tea and think only about my worries of today, my desires for tomorrow, upon which I may ruminate effortlessly.

And suddenly the memory appeared. That taste was the taste of the little piece of madeleine which on Sunday mornings at Combray (because that day I did not go out before it was time for Mass), when I went to say good morning to her in her bedroom, my aunt Léonie would give me after dipping it in her infusion of tea or lime blossom. The sight of the little madeleine had not reminded me of anything before I tasted it; perhaps because I had often seen them since, without eating them, on the shelves of the pastry shops, and their image had therefore left those days of Combray and attached itself to others more recent; perhaps because of these recollections abandoned so long outside my memory, nothing survived, everything had come apart; the forms and the form, too, of the little shell made of cake, so fatly sensual within its severe and pious pleating—had been destroyed, or, still half asleep, had lost the force of expansion that would have allowed them to rejoin my consciousness. But, when nothing subsists of an old past, after the death of people, after the destruction of things, alone, frailer but more enduring, more immaterial, more persistent, more faithful, smell and taste still remain for a long time, like souls, remembering, waiting, hoping, upon the ruins of all the rest, bearing without giving way, on their almost impalpable droplet, the immense edifice of memory.

And as soon as I had recognized the taste of the piece of madeleine dipped in lime-blossom tea that my aunt used to give me (though I did not yet know and had to put off to much later discovering why this memory made me so happy), immediately the old gray house on the street, where her bedroom was, came like a stage set to attach itself to the little wing opening onto the garden that had been built for my parents behind it (that truncated section which was all I had seen before then); and with the house the town, from morning to night and in all weathers, the Square, where they sent me before lunch, the streets where I went on errands, the paths we took if the weather was fine. And as in that game enjoyed by the Japanese in which they fill a porcelain bowl with water and steep in it little pieces of paper until then indistinct which, the moment they are immersed, stretch and twist, assume colors and distinctive shapes, become flowers, houses, human figures, firm and recognizable, so now all the flowers in our garden and in M. Swann's park, and the water lilies of the Vivonne, and the good people of the village and their little dwellings and the church and all of Combray and its surroundings, all of this which is acquiring form and solidity, emerged, town and gardens alike, from my cup of tea.

2

COMBRAY, FROM A DISTANCE, for ten leagues¹ around, seen from the railway when we arrived there the last week before Easter, was no more than a church summing up the town, representing it, speaking of it and for it into the distance, and, when one approached, holding close around its high dark cloak, in the middle of a field, against the wind, like a shepherdess her sheep, the woolly gray backs of the gathered houses, which a vestige of medieval ramparts girdled here and there with a line as perfectly circular as a small town in a primitive painting. To live in, Combray was a little dreary, like its streets, whose houses, built of the blackish stones of the countryside, fronted by outside steps, capped with gables that cast shadows down before them, were so dark that once the daylight began to fade one had to draw back the curtains in the "formal rooms"; streets with the solemn names of saints (of whom many were connected to the history of the earliest seigneurs of Combray): the rue Saint-Hilaire, the rue Saint-Jacques, in which my aunt's house stood, the rue Sainte-Hildegarde, along which her railings ran, and the rue du Saint-Esprit, onto which opened the little side gate of her garden; and these streets of Combray exist in a part of my memory so withdrawn, painted in colors so different from those that now coat the world for me, that in truth all of them, and also the church that rose above them on the square, appear to me even more unreal than the projections of the magic lantern; and that at certain moments, it seems to me that to be able to cross the rue Saint-Hilaire again, to be able to take a room in the rue de l'Oiseau—at the old Hôtellerie de l'Oiseau Flesché, from whose basement windows rose a smell of cooking that now and then still rises in me as intermittently and as warmly—would be to enter into contact with the Beyond in a manner more marvelously supernatural than making the acquaintance of Golo or chatting with Geneviève de Brabant.

My grandfather's cousin—my great-aunt—in whose house we lived, was the mother of that Aunt Léonie who, after the death of her husband, my uncle Octave, no longer wished to leave, first Combray, then within Combray her house, then her bedroom, then her bed and no longer "came down," always lying in an uncertain state of grief, physical debility, illness, obsession, and piety. Her own rooms looked out on the rue Saint-Jacques, which ended much farther away in the Grand-Pré (as opposed to the Petit-Pré, a green in the middle of the town where three streets met), and which, smooth and gray, with the three high steps of sandstone before almost every door, seemed like a narrow passage hewn by a cutter of Gothic images from the same stone out of which he would have sculpted a crèche or a calvary. My aunt effectively confined her life to two adjoining rooms, staying in one of them in the afternoon while the other was aired. These were the sorts of provincial rooms which—just as in certain countries entire tracts of air or ocean are illuminated or perfumed by myriad protozoa that we cannot see—enchant us with the thousand smells given off by the virtues, by wisdom, by habits, a whole secret life, invisible, superabundant, and moral, which the atmosphere holds in suspension; smells still natural, certainly, and colored by the weather like those of the neighboring countryside, but already homey, human and enclosed, an exquisite, ingenious, and limpid jelly of all the fruits of the year that have left the orchard for the cupboard; seasonal, but movable and domestic, correcting the piquancy of the hoarfrost with the sweetness of warm bread, as lazy and punctual as a village clock, roving and orderly, heedless and foresightful, linen smells, morning smells, pious smells, happy with a peace that brings only an increase of anxiety and with a prosiness that serves as a great reservoir of poetry for one who passes through it without having lived in it. The air was saturated with the finest flower of a silence so nourishing, so succulent, that I could move through it only with a sort of greed, especially on those first still cold mornings of Easter week when I tasted it more keenly because I had only just arrived in Combray: before I went in to say good morning to my aunt, they made me wait for a moment, in the first room where the sun, still wintry, had come to warm itself before the fire, already lit between the two bricks and coating the whole room with an odor of soot, having the same effect as one of those great rustic open hearths, or one of those mantels in country houses, beneath which one sits hoping that outdoors there will be an onset of rain, snow, even some diluvian catastrophe so as to add to the comfort of reclusion the poetry of hibernation; I would take a few steps from the prayer stool to the armchairs of stamped velvet always covered with a crocheted antimacassar; and as the fire baked like a dough the appetizing smells with which the air of the room was all curdled and which had already been kneaded and made to "rise" by the damp and sunny coolness of the morning, it flaked them, gilded them, puckered them, puffed them, transforming them into an invisible, palpable country pastry, an immense "turnover" in which, having barely tasted the crisper, more delicate, more highly regarded but also drier aromas of the cupboard, the chest of drawers, the floral wallpaper, I would always come back with an unavowed covetousness to ensnare myself in the central, sticky, stale, indigestible, and fruity smell of the flowered coverlet.

In the next room, I would hear my aunt talking all alone in an undertone. She always talked rather softly because she thought there was something broken and floating in her head that she would have displaced by speaking too loudly, but she never remained for long, even alone, without saying something, because she believed it was beneficial to her throat and that if she prevented the blood from stopping there, she would reduce the frequency of the fits of breathlessness and the spasms from which she suffered; besides, in the absolute inertia in which she lived, she attributed to the least of her sensations an extraordinary importance; she endowed them with a mobility that made it difficult for her to keep them to herself, and lacking a confidant to whom she could communicate them, she announced them to herself, in a perpetual monologue that was her only form of activity. Unfortunately, having acquired the habit of thinking out loud, she did not always take care to see that there was no one in the next room, and I often heard her saying to herself: "I must be sure to remember that I did not sleep" (for never sleeping was her great claim, and the language we all used deferred to it and was marked by it: in the morning Françoise did not come to "wake" her, but "entered" her room; when my aunt wanted to take a nap during the day, we said she wanted to "reflect" or "rest"; and when she happened to forget herself, while chatting, so far as to say: "what woke me up" or "I dreamed that," she would blush and correct herself instantly).

After a moment I would go in and kiss her; Françoise would be steeping her tea; or, if my aunt was feeling agitated, she would ask instead for her infusion and I would be the one entrusted with pouring from the pharmacy bag onto a plate the quantity of lime blossom which then had to be put into the boiling water. The drying of the stems had curved them into a whimsical trelliswork in whose interlacings the pale flowers opened, as if a painter had arranged them, posing them in the most ornamental way. The leaves, having lost or changed their aspect, looked like the most disparate things, a fly's transparent wing, the white back of a label, a rose petal, but these things had been heaped up, crushed, or woven as in the construction of a nest. A thousand small useless details—the charming prodigality of the pharmacist—that would have been eliminated in an artificial preparation gave me, like a book in which one is amazed to encounter the name of a person one knows, the pleasure of realizing that these were actually stems of real lime blossoms, like those I saw in the avenue de la Gare, altered precisely because they were not duplicates but themselves, and because they had aged. And since here, each new characteristic was only the metamorphosis of an old characteristic, in some little gray balls I recognized the green buds that had not come to their term; but especially the pink luster, lunar and soft, that made the flowers stand out amid the fragile forest of stems where they were suspended like little gold roses—a sign, like the glow on a wall that still reveals the location of a fresco that has worn away, of the difference between the parts of the tree that had been "in color" and those that had not—showed me that these petals were in fact the same ones that, before filling the pharmacy bag with flowers, had embalmed the spring evenings. That candle-pink flame was their color still, but half doused and drowsing in the diminished life that was theirs now, and that is a sort of twilight of flowers. Soon my aunt would be able to dip into the boiling infusion, of which she savored the taste of dead leaf or faded flower, a small madeleine, a piece of which she would hold out to me when it had sufficiently softened.

On one side of her bed was a large yellow chest of drawers of lemon wood and a table that was akin to both a dispensary and a high altar, on which, below a small statue of the Virgin and a bottle of Vichy-Célestins, could be found her missals and her medical prescriptions, everything needed for following from her bed both the services and her regimen, for not missing the hour either of her pepsin or of Vespers. On the other side, her bed lay by the window, she had the street there before her eyes and on it from morning to night, to divert her melancholy, like the Persian princes, would read the daily but immemorial chronicle of Combray, which she would afterward comment upon with Françoise.

I would not have been with my aunt five minutes before she would send me away for fear that I would tire her. She would hold out to my lips her sad, pale, dull forehead, on which, at this morning hour, she had not yet arranged her false hair, and where the bones showed through like the points of a crown of thorns or the beads of a rosary, and she would say to me: "Now, my poor child, off you go, get ready for Mass; and if you see Françoise downstairs, tell her not to stay too long amusing herself with all of you, she should come up soon to see if I need anything."

Françoise, who had been in her service for years and did not suspect at that time that one day she would enter exclusively into ours, did in fact neglect my aunt a little during the months when we were there. There had been a time, in my childhood, before we went to

Combray, when my aunt Léonie still spent the winters in Paris with her mother, when Françoise was such a stranger to me that on the first of January, before entering my great-aunt's, my mother would put a five-franc coin in my hand and say to me: "Take great care not to give it to the wrong person. Wait until you hear me say, 'Good morning, Françoise'; at the same time, I'll touch you lightly on the arm." Hardly had we arrived in my aunt's dim hall than we would see in the shadows, under the flutes of a dazzling bonnet as stiff and fragile as if it were made of spun sugar, the concentric ripples of an anticipatory smile of gratitude. It was Françoise, standing motionless in the frame of the little door of the corridor like the statue of a saint in its niche. When we were a little used to this chapel darkness, we could distinguish on her face the disinterested love of humanity, the fond respect for the upper classes excited in the best regions of her heart by the hope of a New Year's gift. Mama would pinch my arm violently and say in a loud voice: "Good morning, Françoise." At this signal, my fingers would open and I would release the coin, which found a bashful but outstretched hand to receive it. But ever since we had begun going to Combray I knew no one better than Françoise, we were her favorites, she had for us, at least during the first years, not only as much regard as for my aunt, but also a keener liking, because we added, to the prestige of being part of the family (she had, for the invisible bonds formed between the members of a family by the circulation of the same blood, as much respect as a Greek tragedian), the charm of not being her usual masters. And so with what joy would she welcome us, commiserate with us that we did not yet have finer weather, the day of our arrival, just before Easter, when there was often an icy wind, while Mama would ask her for news of her daughter and her nephews, whether her grandson was a pretty child, what they were planning to make of him, whether he was going to be like his grandmother.

And when there was no one else there, Mama, knowing that Françoise still mourned her parents, who had died years ago, would talk to her about them gently, ask her for a thousand details about what sort of life they had led.

She had guessed that Françoise did not like her son-in-law and that he spoiled the pleasure she took in being with her daughter, with whom she could not chat as freely when he was there. And so, when Françoise went to see them, a few leagues from Combray, Mama would say to her, smiling: "Isn't it so, Françoise, if Julien is obliged to be away and you have Marguerite all to yourself all day long, you'll be sorry, but you'll make the best of it?" And Françoise would say, laughing: "Madame knows everything; Madame is worse than those X rays" (she said X with an affected difficulty and a smile to poke fun at herself, an ignorant woman, for using that erudite term) "that they brought in for Mme. Octave and that see what you have in your heart," and disappeared, embarrassed that someone was paying attention to her, perhaps so that we would not see her cry; Mama was the first person who gave her that sweet sensation, the feeling that her life as a countrywoman, her joys, her sorrows could be of some interest, could be a reason for pleasure or sadness in someone other than herself. My aunt was resigned to managing with less help from her during our stay, knowing how much my mother appreciated the service of this maid who was so intelligent and active, who was as handsome at five o'clock in the morning in her kitchen, under a bonnet whose dazzling rigid flutes appeared to be made of porcelain, as she was when going to High Mass; who did everything well, working like a horse, whether she was in good health or not, but without a fuss, as though it were nothing, the only one of my aunt's maids who, when Mama asked for hot water or black coffee, brought them really boiling; she was one of those servants who, in a household, are at the same time those most immediately displeasing to a stranger, perhaps because they do not bother to win him over and are not attentive to him, knowing very well they have no need of him, that one would stop seeing him rather than dismiss them; and who are, on the other hand, those most valued by masters who have tested their real capacities, and do not care about the superficial charm, the servile chatter that makes a favorable impression on a visitor, but that often cloaks an ineducable incompetence.

When Françoise, having seen that my parents had everything they needed, went back for the first time to give my aunt her pepsin and ask what she would like to have for lunch, it was quite rare that she was not already required to offer an opinion or provide explanations about some event of importance:

"Françoise, imagine, Mme. Goupil went past more than a quarter of an hour late going to fetch her sister; if she lingers along the way it wouldn't surprise me at all if she were to arrive after the Elevation."

"Well, there wouldn't be anything astonishing in that," answered Françoise.

"Françoise, if you had come five minutes earlier you would have seen Mme. Imbert go past carrying some asparagus twice as fat as Mère Callot's; now try to find out from her maid where she got them. You have been serving us asparagus in every sauce this year; you of all people might have found some like those for our travelers."

"It wouldn't be surprising if they came from M. le Curé's," said Françoise.

"Ah! Do you expect me to believe that, my poor Françoise?" answered my aunt, shrugging her shoulders. "From M. le Curé's! You know very well he grows only wretched, spindly little asparagus. I tell you these were as fat as a woman's arm. Not your arm, of course, but one like mine, poor thing, which has got so much thinner again this year."

"Françoise, didn't you hear those chimes that nearly split my head open?"

"No, Madame Octave."

"Ah, my poor girl, you must have a hard head, you can thank the Good Lord for that. It was Maguelone coming to get Dr. Piperaud. He came back out with her right away and they turned down the rue de l'Oiseau. Some child must be ill."

"Oh my, dear God," sighed Françoise, who could not hear of a misfortune occurring to a stranger, even in a distant part of the world, without beginning to lament.

"Françoise, now who were they ringing the passing bell for? Oh, dear God, it must have been for Mme. Rousseau. I'm blessed if I hadn't forgotten that she passed away the other night. Oh, it's time for the Good Lord to call me home, I don't know what I've done with my head since my poor Octave died. But I'm wasting your time, my girl."

"Not at all, Madame Octave, my time is not so precious; He who made it did not sell it to us. I'm only just going to see that my fire isn't out."

In this way Françoise and my aunt together appraised, during that morning session, the first events of the day. But sometimes those events assumed a character so mysterious and so grave that my aunt felt she could not wait for the moment when Françoise would come up, and four astounding peals of the bell would echo through the house.

"But Madame Octave, it isn't time for your pepsin yet," Françoise would say. "Were you feeling faint?"

"Not at all, Françoise," my aunt would say; "what I mean is yes, you know very well there is seldom a time, now, when I don't feel faint; one day I'll pass away like Mme. Rousseau without even time to collect myself; but that's not why I rang. Would you believe that I just saw Mme. Goupil as clearly as I see you now with a little girl whom I don't know at all? Now go fetch two sous' worth of salt at Camus's. It's not often that Théodore can't tell you who someone is."

"But that'll be M. Pupin's daughter," Françoise would say, preferring to be satisfied with an immediate explanation since she had already been to Camus's twice that morning.

"M. Pupin's daughter! Oh, do you expect me to believe that, my poor Françoise? And you think I wouldn't have recognized her?"

"But I don't mean the big one, Madame Octave, I mean the little one that's away at school in Jouy. I think I saw her once already this morning."

"Ah! That must be it," said my aunt. "She must have come for the holidays. That's it! There's no need to ask, she will have come for the holidays. But then anytime now we might very likely see Mme. Sazerat come and ring at her sister's for lunch. That's what it is! I saw Galopin's boy going past with a tart! You'll see, the tart was on its way to Mme. Goupil's."

"Once Mme. Goupil has a visitor, Madame Octave, it won't be long before you'll see all her folk coming back for lunch, because it's not so early as it was," said Françoise, who, in a hurry to go back down and see to lunch, was not sorry to leave my aunt the prospect of this distraction.

"Oh, not before noon!" answered my aunt in a tone of resignation, casting an uneasy glance at the clock, yet furtively so as not to let it be seen that she, who had renounced everything, nevertheless took such a lively pleasure in learning whom Mme. Goupil was having to lunch, a pleasure that would unfortunately have to wait a little more than an hour longer. "And on top of that, it will happen during my lunch!" she added half aloud to herself. Her lunch was enough of a distraction for her so that she did not wish for another one at the same time. "Now you won't forget to give me my eggs with cream in a flat plate?" These were the only plates with pictures on them, and my aunt amused herself at each meal by reading the inscription on the one she was served that day. She would put on her glasses and spell out: Ali Baba and the Forty Thieves, Aladdin or the Magic Lamp, and smile, saying: "Very good, very good."

"I would certainly have gone to Camus's . . ." Françoise would say, seeing that now my aunt would not send her there.

"No, no, it's not worth the trouble anymore, it's certainly Mlle. Pupin. My poor Françoise, I'm sorry to have made you come up for nothing."

But my aunt knew perfectly well it was not for nothing that she had rung for Françoise, since, in Combray, a person "whom one did not know at all" was a creature as scarcely believable as a mythological god, and in fact one could not remember when, anytime one of these stupefying apparitions had occurred, in the rue du Saint-Esprit or on the square, well-conducted research had not ended by reducing the fabulous character to the proportions of a "person one knew," either personally or abstractly, in his or her civil status, as having such and such a degree of kinship with some people of Combray. It was Mme. Sauton's son returning from military service, Abbé Perdreau's niece leaving the convent, the curé's brother, a tax collector at Châteaudun, who had just retired or had come to spend the holidays. One had had, upon seeing them, the shock of believing that there were in Combray people whom one did not know at all, simply because one had not recognized them right away. And yet, long in advance, Mme. Sauton and the curé had let everyone know they were awaiting their "travelers." When in the evening I went upstairs, after returning home, to describe our walk to my aunt, if I was so imprudent as to tell her that we had met, near Pont-Vieux, a man my grandfather did not know, "A man Grandfather did not know at all!" she would cry. "Ah! I don't believe it!" Nonetheless somewhat disturbed by this news, she would want to clear the matter up, my grandfather would be summoned. "Now who did you meet near Pont-Vieux, Uncle? A man you didn't know?" "But I did know him," my grandfather would answer, "it was Prosper, the brother of Mme. Bouilleboeuf's gardener." "Ah! All right," my aunt would say, calmed and a little flushed; shrugging her shoulders with an ironic smile, she would add: "Now, he told me you had met a man you didn't know!" And they would advise me to be more circumspect the next time and not to go on agitating my aunt with thoughtless remarks. One knew everybody so well, in Combray, both animals and people, that if my aunt had chanced to see a dog pass by "whom she did not know at all," she would not stop thinking about it and devoting to this incomprehensible fact all her talents for induction and her hours of leisure.

"That must be Mme. Sazerat's dog," Françoise would say, without great conviction but in order to pacify my aunt, and so that she would not "split her head."

"As if I didn't know Mme. Sazerat's dog!" my aunt would answer, her critical mind not accepting a fact so easily.

"Ah! Then it will be the new dog M. Galopin brought back from Lisieux."

"Ah! That must be it."

"It seems it's quite an affable creature," added Françoise, who had got the information from Théodore, "as clever as a person, always in a good humor, always friendly, always as agreeable as you might wish. It's uncommon for an animal of that age to be so well behaved already. Madame Octave, I will have to leave you, I haven't time to enjoy myself, here it's almost ten o'clock, and my stove not lit yet, even, and I still have my asparagus to scrape."

"What, Françoise, more asparagus! Why, you've got a regular mania for asparagus this year. You'll make our Parisians grow tired of it!"

"Why, no, Madame Octave, they're very fond of it. You'll see, they'll come home from church with a good appetite and they won't push it about with the backs of their spoons."

"Church! Why, they must be there already. You'd do well not to waste any time. Go and look after your lunch."

While my aunt was conferring thus with Françoise, I was going to Mass with my parents. How I loved it, how clearly I can see it again; our church! The old porch by which we entered, black, pocked like a skimming ladle, was uneven and deeply hollowed at the edges (like the font to which it led us), as if the gentle brushing of the country-women's cloaks as they entered the church and of their timid fingers taking holy water could, repeated over centuries, acquire a destructive force, bend the stone and carve it with furrows like those traced by the wheel of a cart in a boundary stone which it knocks against every day. Its tombstones, under which the noble dust of the abbots of Combray, who were buried there, formed for the choir a sort of spiritual pavement, were themselves no longer inert and hard matter, for time had softened them and made them flow like honey beyond the bounds of their own square shapes, which, in one place, they had overrun in a flaxen billow, carrying off on their drift a flowery Gothic capital letter, drowning the white violets of the marble; and into which, elsewhere, they had reabsorbed themselves, further contracting the elliptical Latin inscription, introducing a further caprice in the arrangement of those abridged characters, bringing close together two letters of a word of which the others had been disproportionately distended. Its windows never sparkled as much as on the days when the sun hardly appeared, so that, if it was gray outside, we were sure it

would be beautiful inside the church; one was filled to its very top by
a single figure like a king in a game of cards, who lived up there,
under an architectural canopy, between heaven and earth (and in
whose slanting blue light, on weekdays sometimes, at noon, when
there is no service—at one of those rare times when the church, airy,
vacant, more human, luxurious, with some sun on its rich furniture,
looked almost habitable, like the hall of a medieval-style mansion, of
sculpted stone and stained glass—one would see Mme. Sazerat kneel
for a moment, setting down on the next prayer stool a packet of petits
fours tied with string that she had just picked up from the pastry shop
across the street and was going to take back home for lunch); in another, a mountain of pink snow, at whose foot a battle was being
fought, seemed to have frosted onto the glass itself, blistering it with
its cloudy sleet like a windowpane on which a few snowflakes remained, but snowflakes lit by some aurora (the same, no doubt, that
flushed the reredos of the altar with tints so fresh they seemed set
there for a moment by a gleam from outside about to vanish, rather
than by colors attached forever to the stone); and all were so old that
here and there one saw their silvery age sparkle with the dust of the
centuries and show, shimmering and worn down to the thread, the
weft of their soft tapestry of glass. One of them, a tall compartment,
was divided into a hundred or so small rectangular panes in which
blue predominated, like a great deck of cards resembling those meant
to entertain King Charles VI;[2] but either because a beam of sunlight
was shining, or because my gaze, as it moved, carried across the glass,
snuffed and lit again by turns, a precious moving conflagration, the
next moment it had assumed the changing luster of a peacock's train,
then trembled and undulated in a flaming chimerical rain that
dripped from the top of the dark rocky vault, along the damp walls, as
if this were the nave of some grotto iridescent with sinuous stalactites
into which I was following my parents, who were carrying their prayer
books; a moment later the little lozenge-shaped panes had assumed
the deep transparency, the infrangible hardness of sapphires which
had been juxtaposed on some immense breastplate, but behind which
one felt, more beloved than all these riches, a momentary smile of

sunlight; it was as recognizable in the soft blue billow with which it bathed the precious stones as on the pavement of the square or the straw of the marketplace; and even on our first Sundays when we had arrived before Easter, it consoled me for the earth being still bare and black, by bringing into bloom, as in a historical springtime dating from the age of Saint Louis's successors, this dazzling gilded carpet of glass forget-me-nots.

Two high-warp tapestries represented the coronation of Esther (tradition had it that Ahasuerus had been given the features of a king of France and Esther those of a lady of Guermantes with whom he was in love), to which their colors, by melting, had added expression, relief, light: a little pink floated over Esther's lips outside the tracing of their outline; the yellow of her dress spread so unctuously, so thickly, that it acquired a kind of solidity and stood out boldly from the receding atmosphere; and the green of the trees, remaining vivid in the lower parts of the panel of silk and wool, but "gone" at the top, brought out in a paler tone, above the dark trunks, the lofty yellowing branches, gilded and half obliterated by the abrupt, slanting illumination of an invisible sun. All this, and still more the precious objects that had come into the church from figures who were for me almost legendary (the gold cross worked, they said, by Saint Eloi[3] and given by Dagobert, the tomb of the sons of Louis the Germanic,[4] of porphyry and enameled copper), because of which I moved through the church, when we went to our seats, as though through a valley visited by the fairies, in which a country person is amazed to see in a rock, a tree, a pool, the palpable trace of their supernatural passage, all this made it, for me, something entirely different from the rest of the town: an edifice occupying a space with, so to speak, four dimensions—the fourth being Time—extending over the centuries its nave which, from bay to bay, from chapel to chapel, seemed to vanquish and penetrate not only a few yards but epoch after epoch from which it emerged victorious; hiding the rough, savage eleventh century in the thickness of the walls, from which it appeared with its heavy arches plugged and blinded by crude blocks of ashlar only in the deep gash incised near the porch by the tower staircase, and even there concealed by the graceful Gothic arcades that crowded coquettishly in front of it like older sisters who, to hide him from strangers, place themselves smiling in front of a younger brother who is boorish, sulky, and badly dressed; lifting into the heavens above the square its tower which had contemplated Saint Louis and seemed to see him still; and plunging down with its crypt into a Merovingian night, in which, groping their way as they guided us under the dark vault as powerfully ribbed as the wing of an immense stone bat, Théodore and his sister would light for us with a candle the tomb of Sigebert's[5] little daughter, on which a deep scallop—like the mark of a fossil—had been dug, it was said, "by a crystal lamp which, on the night the Frankish princess was murdered, had separated of its own accord from the golden chains by which it hung on the site of the present apse and without the crystal breaking, without the flame going out, had sunk deep into the stone which gave way softly under it."

The apse of the Combray church; what can one say about it? It was so crude, so lacking in artistic beauty and even religious spirit. From outside, because the crossroads which it commanded was on a lower level, its crude wall rose up from a subbasement of quite unpolished ashlar, bristling with flints, and having nothing particularly ecclesiastical about it, the windows seemed to have been pierced at an excessive height, and the whole looked more like the wall of a prison than the wall of a church. And certainly, later, when I recalled all the glorious apses I had seen, it would never have occurred to me to compare them with the apse of Combray. But, one day, at the bend of a little street in a country town, I noticed, opposite the crossing of three lanes, a rough and unusually high wall with windows pierced far above and the same asymmetrical appearance as the apse of Combray. Then I did not ask myself as at Chartres or Rheims how powerfully it expressed religious feeling, but involuntarily exclaimed: "The church!"

The church! Familiar; flanked, in the rue Saint-Hilaire, where its north door was situated, by its two neighbors, M. Rapin's pharmacy and Mme. Loiseau's house, which it touched without any separation; a simple citizen of Combray that could have had its number in the street if the streets of Combray had had numbers, and where it seems that the postman should have had to stop in the morning when he was making his rounds, before going into Mme. Loiseau's and upon coming out of M. Rapin's, there existed, however, between it and everything that was not it a demarcation that my mind was never able to cross. Even though Mme. Loiseau might have at her window fuchsias which developed the bad habit of forever allowing their branches to run all over with heads lowered, and whose flowers had no business more pressing, when they were large enough, than to go and cool their flushed, violet cheeks against the dark front of the church, for me the fuchsias did not for this reason become holy; between the flowers and the blackened stone against which they leaned, if my eyes perceived no interval, my mind reserved an abyss.

One could recognize the steeple of Saint-Hilaire from quite far off inscribing its unforgettable form on the horizon where Combray had not yet appeared; when from the train which, in Easter week, was bringing us from Paris, my father caught sight of it slipping by turns over all the furrows of the sky and sending its little iron weathercock running in all directions, he would say to us: "Come, gather up the rugs, we're here." And on one of the longest walks we took from Combray, there was a spot where the narrow road emerged suddenly on an immense plateau closed at the horizon by jagged forests above which rose only the delicate tip of the steeple of Saint-Hilaire, but so thin, so pink, that it seemed merely scratched on the sky by a fingernail which wanted to give this landscape, this exclusively natural picture, that little mark of art, that indication of human presence. When one drew near and could see the remains of the half-destroyed square tower which, not as high, still stood next to it, one was struck most of all by the dark, reddish shade of the stones; and on a misty morning in autumn one might have thought it, rising above the stormy violet of the vineyards, a ruin of purple nearly the color of a wild vine.

Often in the square, when we were coming home, my grandmother would make me stop to look at it. From the windows of its tower, placed two by two one above the other, with the exact and original proportion in their spacing that gives beauty and dignity not just to human faces, it loosed, dropped at regular intervals, volleys of crows which, for a moment, circled about shrieking, as if the old stones that allowed them to hop and flutter about without appearing to see them had suddenly become uninhabitable and emitted some principle of infinite agitation, struck them and driven them out. Then, after striping in every direction the violet velvet of the evening air, they would return suddenly calm to be reabsorbed into the tower, which was no longer baneful but once again benign, a few of them sitting here and there, apparently motionless, but perhaps snapping up some insect, on the tip of a turret, like a seagull as still as a fisherman on the crest of a wave. Without really knowing why, my grandmother found in the steeple of Saint-Hilaire that absence of vulgarity, of pretension, of meanness, which made her love and believe rich in beneficent influence not only nature, when the hand of man had not, as had my great-aunt's gardener, shrunk and reduced it, but also works of genius. And certainly, every part of the church that one could see distinguished it from all other buildings by a sort of thoughtfulness that was infused into it, but it was in the steeple that it seemed to become aware of itself, affirm an individual and responsible existence. It was the steeple that spoke for it. I believe above all that, confusedly, my grandmother found in the steeple of Combray what for her had the highest value in the world, an air of naturalness and an air of distinction. Knowing nothing about architecture, she would say: "My children, make fun of me if you like, perhaps it isn't beautiful according to the rules, but I like its strange old face. I'm sure that if it could play the piano it would not play *dryly*." And looking at it, following with her eyes the gentle tension, the fervent inclination of its slopes of stone, which approached each other as they rose like hands meeting in prayer, she would join so fully in the effusion of the spire that her gaze seemed to soar with it; and at the same time she would smile in a friendly way at the worn old stones, of which the setting sun now illuminated only the topmost part and which, the moment they entered that sunny region, softened by the light, appeared suddenly to have risen much higher, to be quite far away, like a song taken up again in "a head voice" an octave above.

It was the steeple of Saint-Hilaire that gave all the occupations, all the hours, all the viewpoints of the town their shape, their crown, their consecration. From my bedroom, I could see only its base, which had been covered with slates; but when, on Sunday, I saw them, on a warm summer morning, blazing like a black sun, I would say to myself: "Good Heavens! Nine o'clock! I'd better get ready for Mass if I want to have time to go and give Aunt Léonie a kiss first," and I knew exactly the color of the sun on the square, the heat and dust of the market, the shadow made by the awning of the store which Mama would perhaps enter before Mass in an odor of un-bleached linen, to buy some handkerchief which would be displayed to her under the direction of the shopkeeper, his chest outthrust, who, as he prepared to close, had just gone into the back of the shop to put on his Sunday jacket and soap his hands, which it was his habit, every five minutes, even in the most melancholy of circumstances, to rub together with an air of enterprise, celebration, and success.

When after Mass we went in to ask Théodore to bring us a brioche larger than usual because our cousins had taken advantage of the fine weather to come from Thiberzy to have lunch with us, we would have the steeple there in front of us, itself golden and baked like a greater blessed brioche, with flakes and gummy drippings of sun, pricking its sharp point into the blue sky. And in the evening, when I was coming home from a walk and thinking about the moment when I would soon have to say goodnight to my mother and not see her anymore, it was on the contrary so soft, at the close of day, that it looked as if it had been set down and crushed like a cushion of brown velvet against the pale sky which had yielded under its pressure, hollowing slightly to give it room and flowing back over its edges; and the cries of the birds that wheeled around it seemed to increase its silence, lift its spire to a greater height, and endow it with something ineffable.

Even on the errands we had to do behind the church, where we could not see it, everything seemed to be arranged in relation to the steeple, which would rise up here or there between the houses, per-haps even more affecting when it appeared that way, without the church. And certainly, there are many others that are more beautiful when seen this way, and I have in my memory vignettes of steeples rising above roofs which have a different artistic character from those composed by the sad streets of Combray. I will never forget, in a curious town in Normandy near Balbec, two charming eighteenth-century houses that are in many respects dear to me and venerable and between which, when you look at it from the lovely garden that descends from the front steps to the river, the Gothic spire of a church hidden behind them soars up, appearing to complete, to surmount their facades, but in a material so different, so precious, so annulated, so pink, so polished, that you see clearly it no more belongs to them than does the crimson crenellated spire of some seashell, tapering to a turret and glazed with enamel, to the two handsome, smooth pebbles between which it is caught on the beach. Even in Paris, in one of the ugliest parts of the city, I know a window from which you can see, beyond a foreground, middle ground, and even third ground composed of the piled-up roofs of several streets, a violet bell, sometimes ruddy, sometimes also, in the noblest "proofs" of it printed by the atmosphere, a decanted cindery black, which is in fact the dome of Saint-Augustin and which gives this view of Paris the character of certain views of Rome by Piranesi. But since into none of these little engravings, with whatever taste my memory may have executed them, was it able to put what I had lost a long time ago, the feeling that makes us not consider a thing a spectacle, but believe in it as in a creature without equivalent, none of them holds in subjection an entire profound part of my life, as does the memory of those views of the Combray steeple from the streets behind the church. Whether we saw it at five o'clock, when we went to get the letters at the post office, a few houses away from us to the left, abruptly lifting with an isolated peak the ridgeline of the roofs; or whether, on the other hand, if we wanted to go in to ask for news of Mme. Sazerat, our eyes followed that line, low again after the descent of its other slope, knowing we would have to turn at the second street after the steeple; or whether, again, going on farther, if we went to the station, we saw it obliquely, showing in profile new edges and surfaces like a solid caught at an unfamiliar moment of its revolution; or whether, from the banks of the Vivonne, the apse, muscularly gathered and raised to a greater height by the perspective, seemed to spring with the effort the steeple was making to hurl its spire into the heart of the sky: it was always to the steeple that we had to return, always the steeple that dominated everything, summing up the houses with an unexpected pinnacle, raised before me like the finger of God, whose body might be hidden in the crowd of humans, though I would not confuse it with them because of that. And even today, if in a large provincial town or a part of Paris I do not know well, a passing stranger who has "put me on the right path" shows me in the distance, as a reference point, some hospital belfry, some convent steeple lifting the peak of its ecclesiastical cap at the corner of a street I am supposed to take, if only my memory can obscurely find in it some small feature resembling the dear departed form, the stranger, if he turns around to make sure I am not going astray, may, to his astonishment, see me, forgetting the walk I had begun or the necessary errand, remain there in front of the steeple for hours, motionless, trying to remember, feeling deep in myself lands recovered from oblivion draining and rebuilding themselves; and then no doubt, and more anxiously than a short time before when I asked him to direct me, I am still seeking my path, I am turning a corner . . . but . . . I am doing so in my heart . . .

As we returned home from Mass, we would often meet M. Legrandin, who was detained in Paris by his profession of engineer and, except during the summer vacation, could come to his property in Combray only from Saturday evening until Monday morning. He was one of those men who, quite apart from a career in science in which they have in fact been brilliantly successful, possess an entirely different culture, one that is literary, artistic, which their professional specialization does not make use of and which enriches their conversation. Better read than many men of letters (we did not know at that time that M. Legrandin had a certain reputation as a writer and we were very surprised to see that a famous musician had composed a melody to some verses of his), gifted with more "facility" than many painters, they imagine that the life they are leading is not the one that really suits them and they bring to their actual occupations either an indifference mingled with whimsy, or an application that is sustained and haughty, scornful, bitter, and conscientious. Tall, with a handsome figure, a fine, thoughtful face with a long, blond mustache and disenchanted blue eyes, exquisitely courteous, a conversationalist such as we had never heard before, he was in the eyes of my family, who always cited him as an example, the epitome of the superior man, approaching life in the noblest and most delicate way. My grandmother reproached him only for speaking a little too well, a little too much like a book, for not having the same naturalness in his language as in his loosely knotted lavaliere bow ties, in his short, straight, almost schoolboyish coat. She was also surprised by the fiery tirades he often launched against the aristocracy, against fashionable life, against snobbery, "certainly the sin which Saint Paul has in mind when he speaks of the sin for which there is no forgiveness."

Worldly ambition was a sentiment that my grandmother was so incapable of feeling or even, almost, of understanding, that it seemed to her quite pointless to bring so much ardor to stigmatizing it. What was more, she did not think it in very good taste that M. Legrandin, whose sister near Balbec was married to a titled gentleman of Lower Normandy, should indulge himself in such violent attacks against the nobility, going so far as to reproach the Revolution for not having had them all guillotined.

"Greetings, my friends!" he would say, coming up to us. "How fortunate you are to live here for such extended periods of time; tomorrow I must return to Paris, to my little nook.

"Oh!" he would add, with his own particular smile, gently ironical, disappointed and slightly distracted, "of course my house contains every useless thing in the world. It lacks only the one essential, a large piece of sky like this one. Always try to keep a piece of sky over your life, little boy," he would add, turning to me. "You have a lovely soul, of a rare quality, an artist's nature, don't ever let it go without what it needs."

When we returned home and my aunt sent to ask us if Mme. Goupil had been late coming to Mass, we could not give her any information. Instead, we increased her disturbance by telling her there was a painter at work in the church copying the window of Gilbert the Bad. Françoise, sent immediately to the grocery, came back empty-handed owing to the absence of Théodore, whose two professions, that of chorister with a part in the maintenance of the church and of grocer's boy, gave him connections in all worlds and therefore knowledge that was universal.

"Ah!" sighed my aunt, "I wish it were time for Eulalie. She's really the only one who will be able to tell me."

Eulalie was an active old maid, lame and hard-of-hearing, who had "retired" after the death of Mme. de la Bretonnerie, with whom she had been in service since her childhood, and had then taken a room next to the church, descending from it constantly either for the services or, when there was no service, to say a little prayer or give Théodore a hand; the rest of the time she visited invalids like my aunt Léonie, to whom she would describe what had happened at Mass or at Vespers. She was not above adding some revenue to the small pension paid her by the family of her former employers by going from time to time to look after the curé's linen or that of some other prominent personality in Combray's clerical world. Above a cloak of black cloth she wore a small white hood almost like a nun's, and a skin disease gave parts of her cheeks and her hooked nose the bright pink tones of an impatiens. Her visits were the great diversion of my aunt Léonie, who hardly received anyone else now, apart from M. le Curé. My aunt had gradually eliminated all the other visitors because all of them made the mistake, in her eyes, of belonging to one of two categories of people whom she detested. One group, the worst, whom she had got rid of first, were the ones who advised her not to "listen to herself" so, and subscribed, if only negatively, manifesting it only by certain disapproving silences or by certain dubious smiles, to the subversive doctrine that a little walk in the sun and a good rare beefsteak (even though two wretched sips of Vichy water would lie on her stomach for fourteen hours!) would do her more good than her bed and her medicines. The other category was made up of the people who seemed to believe she was more seriously ill than she thought, that she was as seriously ill as she said she was. And so, those she had allowed to come up after some hesitation and upon Françoise's kindly meant entreaties and who, in the course of their visit, had shown how very unworthy they were of the favor being done them by timidly risking a "Don't you think that if you were to move about a little when the weather's fine," or who, on the contrary, when she said to them: "I'm very low, very low, this is the end, my poor friends," answered her: "Ah! when our health fails us! Still, you may last awhile longer yet as you are"—these, the former as well as the latter, were certain never to be received again. And if Françoise was amused by my aunt's horrified look when from her bed she saw one of these people in the rue du Saint-Esprit apparently coming toward her house or when she heard the doorbell ring, she would laugh more heartily still, and as though at a good trick, at my aunt's ever-victorious ruses for managing to have them turned away, and at their discomfited expressions as they went off without having seen her, and at heart admired her mistress, whom she felt to be superior to all these people since she did not want to receive them. In short, my aunt required that her visitors at the same time commend her on her regimen, commiserate with her for her sufferings, and encourage her as to her future.

This was where Eulalie excelled. My aunt might say to her twenty times in a minute: "This is the end, my poor Eulalie," twenty times Eulalie would answer: "Knowing your illness as you know it, Madame Octave, you will live to be a hundred, as Mme. Sazerin was saying to me just yesterday." (One of Eulalie's firmest beliefs, which the impressive number of denials contributed by experience had not been enough to shake, was that Mme. Sazerat's name was Mme. Sazerin.)

"I am not asking to live to a hundred," answered my aunt, who preferred not to see her days assigned a precise term.

And since along with this Eulalie knew better than anyone else how to distract my aunt without tiring her, her visits, which took place regularly every Sunday, barring an unforeseen obstacle, were for my aunt a pleasure, the prospect of which kept her on those days in a state that was at first pleasant, but quite soon painful like an excessive hunger, if Eulalie was even a little late. Overly prolonged, this ecstasy of waiting for Eulalie became a torment, my aunt looked constantly at the time, yawned, felt faint. The sound of Eulalie's chime, if it came at the very end of the day, when she was no longer expecting it, would almost make her ill. The fact was that on Sunday, she thought only of this visit, and as soon as lunch was finished, Françoise would be in a hurry for us to leave the dining room so that she could go up and "occupy" my aunt. But (especially once the fine weather settled in at Combray) a good long time would go by after the haughty hour of noon, descending from the Saint-Hilaire steeple, which it had emblazoned with the twelve momentary rosettes of its sonorous crown, had echoed around our table close to the consecrated bread which had also come in, familiarly, after church, while we remained sitting in front of the *Thousand and One Nights* plates, oppressed by the heat and especially by the meal. For, upon a permanent foundation of eggs, cutlets, potatoes, jams, biscuits which she no longer even announced to us, Françoise would add—depending on the labors in the fields and orchards, the fruit of the tide, the luck of the marketplace, the kindness of neighbors, and her own genius, and with the result that our menu, like the quatrefoils carved on the portals of cathedrals in the thirteenth century, reflected somewhat the rhythm of the seasons and the incidents of daily life—a brill because the monger had guaranteed her that it was fresh, a turkey hen because she had seen a large one at the Roussainville-le-Pin market, cardoons with marrow because she had not made them for us that way before, a roast leg of mutton because fresh air whets the appetite and it would have plenty of time to "descend" in the next seven hours, spinach for a change, apricots because they were still uncommon, gooseberries because in two weeks there would not be any more, raspberries that M. Swann had brought especially, cherries, the first that had come from the cherry tree in the garden after two years in which it had not given any, cream cheese, which I liked very much at one time, an almond cake because she had ordered it the day before, a brioche because it was our turn to present it. When all of that was finished, there came a work of art composed expressly for us, but more particularly dedicated to my father who was so fond of it, a chocolate custard, the product of Françoise's personal inspiration and attention, ephemeral and light as an occasional piece into which she had put all her talent. If anyone had refused to taste it, saying: "I'm finished, I'm not hungry anymore," that person would immediately have been relegated to the rank of those barbarians who, even in a gift an artist makes them of one of his works, scrutinize its weight and its material when the only things of value in it are its intention and its signature. To leave even a single drop of it on the plate would have been to display the same impoliteness as to stand up before the end of a piece under the very nose of the composer.

At last my mother would say to me: "Now, don't stay here all day, go up to your room if you're too hot outdoors, but get a little fresh air first so that you don't start reading right after leaving the table." I would go and sit down beside the pump and its trough, often ornamented, like a Gothic font, with a salamander which sculpted on the rough stone the mobile relief of its allegorical tapering body, on the backless bench shaded by a lilac, in the little corner of the garden that opened through a service gate onto the rue du Saint-Esprit and from whose untended earth the scullery rose by two steps, projecting from the house like an independent structure. One could see its red paving stones gleaming like porphyry. It looked not so much like Françoise's lair as a little temple of Venus. It overflowed with the offerings of the dairyman, the fruit man, the vegetable monger, who had come sometimes from quite remote hamlets to dedicate to it the first fruits of their fields. And its roof was forever crowned with the cooing of a dove.

In earlier years I did not linger in the sacred grove surrounding it, since, before going upstairs to read, I would enter the little sitting room that my uncle Adolphe, a brother of my grandfather and a veteran who had retired with the rank of major, occupied on the ground floor, and which, even when its open windows let in the heat, if not the rays of the sun, which seldom reached that far, gave off inexhaustibly that dark cool smell of both forest and ancien régime, that makes your nostrils linger in a daydream when you venture into certain abandoned hunting lodges. But for a number of years now I had not gone into my uncle Adolphe's room, since he no longer came to Combray because of a quarrel that had occurred between him and my family, through my fault, in the following circumstances.

Once or twice a month, in Paris, I used to be sent to pay him a visit as he was finishing lunch wearing a plain loose-fitting jacket and waited on by his servant who was dressed in a work jacket of striped duck, violet and white. He would grumble complaining that I had not come for a long time, grumble that we were abandoning him; he would offer me a marzipan cake or a tangerine, we would pass through a drawing room in which no one ever stopped, where no one ever made a fire, whose walls were ornamented with gilded moldings, its ceilings painted with a blue that was meant to imitate the sky and its furniture upholstered in satin as at my grandparents', but yellow; then we would go on into what he called his "study," whose walls were hung with some of those engravings depicting, against a dark background, a fleshy pink goddess driving a chariot, standing on a globe, or wearing a star on her forehead, which were admired during the Second Empire[6] because they were felt to have a Pompeiian look about them, were then hated, and are beginning to be admired again for one reason and one reason only, despite the others that are given, and that is that they have such a Second Empire look about them. And I would stay with my uncle until his valet came to him from the coachman to ask what time the latter should harness up. My uncle would then sink into a deep meditation while his admiring valet, afraid of disturbing him by the slightest movement, waited curiously for the result, which was always identical. At last, after the greatest hesitation, my uncle would unfailingly utter these words: "At quarter past two," which the valet would repeat with surprise, but without disputing them: "At quarter past two? Very good . . . I'll go and tell him . . ."

In those days I loved the theater, with a platonic passion since my parents had not yet allowed me to enter a theater, and I pictured to myself so inaccurately the pleasures one might experience there that I almost believed that each spectator looked as though into a stereoscope at a scene that was for him alone, though similar to the thousand others being looked at, each one for himself, by the rest of the audience.

Every morning I would run to the Morris column[7] to see what shows were being announced. Nothing was more disinterested or happier than the daydreams inspired in my imagination by each play that was announced, daydreams conditioned both by the images inseparable from the words that made up its title and also by the color of the posters, still damp and blistered with paste, against which that title stood out. Except for those strange works like *Le Testament de César Girodot* or *Oedipe-Roi*, which were inscribed, not on the green poster of the Opéra-Comique, but on the wine-red poster of the Comédie-Française, nothing seemed to me more different from the sparkling white plume of *Les Diamants de la Couronne* than the smooth, mysterious satin of *Le Domino Noir*,[8] and, since my parents had told me that when I went to the theater for the first time I would have to choose between these two plays, as I tried to study exhaustively and in turn the title of one and then the title of the other, since this was all I knew of them, so as to attempt to discern the pleasure each one promised me and compare it to the pleasure that lay concealed within the other, I managed to picture to myself so forcefully, on the one hand a play that was dazzling and proud, on the other a play that was soft and velvety, that I was as incapable of deciding which I would prefer as if, for dessert, I had been given the choice between rice *à l'Impératrice* and chocolate custard.

All my conversations with my friends concerned these actors whose art, though unknown to me, was the first form, of all those it assumes, in which Art allowed me a presentiment of what it was. Between the manner in which one actor and another delivered, nuanced a declamatory speech, the tiniest differences seemed to me to have an incalculable importance. And I would rank them in order of talent, according to what I had been told about them, in lists that I recited to

myself all day long, and that in the end hardened in my brain and obstructed it with their immovability.

Later, when I was in school, each time I wrote to a new friend during class as soon as the teacher's head was turned, my first question
was always whether he had been to the theater yet and whether he
thought the greatest actor really was Got, the second best Delaunay,
etc. And if, in his opinion, Febvre came only after Thiron, or Delaunay only after Coquelin, the sudden mobility that Coquelin, losing
his stony rigidity, would develop in my mind in order to pass to second place, and the miraculous agility, the fecund animation with
which Delaunay would be endowed in order to withdraw to fourth,
would restore the sensation of flowering and life to my newly supple
and fertilized brain.

But if the actors preoccupied me so, if the sight of Maubaut coming out of the Théâtre-Français one afternoon had filled me with the
ecstasy and suffering of love, how much more did the name of a star,
blazing on the door of a theater, how much more did the sight, at the
window of a brougham passing in the street, its horses blossoming
with roses in their headbands, of a woman I thought might be an actress, leave me in a state of prolonged disturbance, as I tried impo-
tently and painfully to imagine her life! I would rank the most
illustrious in order of talent, Sarah Bernhardt, La Berma, Bartet,
Madeleine Brohan, Jeanne Samary, but all of them interested me.
Now my uncle knew many of them and also some courtesans whom I
did not distinguish clearly from the actresses. He would entertain
them at home. And if we went to see him only on certain days, this
was because on the other days women came whom his family could
not have met, or so at least they thought, since my uncle himself, on
the contrary, was only too ready to pay pretty widows who had perhaps never been married, and countesses with high-sounding names
which were doubtless only noms de guerre, the courtesy of introducing them to my grandmother or even of presenting them with some
of the family jewels, tendencies which had already embroiled him
more than once with my grandfather. Often, when an actress's name
came into the conversation, I would hear my father say to my mother,

smiling: "A friend of your uncle's"; and I would think that the novi-
tiate pointlessly endured for perhaps years on end by eminent men at
the door of some woman who would not answer their letters and
would ask her doorman to turn them away could have been spared a
boy like me by my uncle, who could introduce him in his own home
to the actress who, unapproachable by so many others, was for him
an intimate friend.

And so—using the excuse that a lesson which had been moved now
came at such an awkward hour that it had prevented me several times
and would continue to prevent me from seeing my uncle—one day,
different from the day set apart for the visits we made to him, taking
advantage of the fact that my parents had had lunch early, I went out
and, instead of going to look at the column of posters, for which I
was allowed to go out alone, I ran to him. I noticed in front of his
door a carriage with two horses, each of which had a red carnation at
its blinkers, as did the coachman in his buttonhole. From the staircase
I heard a laugh and a woman's voice, and, as soon as I rang, a silence,
then the sound of doors being shut. The valet came to open the door,
and when he saw me seemed embarrassed, told me my uncle was very
busy, probably would not be able to see me, and when he went to let
him know anyway, the same voice I had heard before said: "Oh, yes!
do let him come in; just for a minute, I would enjoy it so much. In
the photograph you have on your desk, he looks so much like his
mother, your niece; that's her photograph next to his, isn't it? I would
so like to see the boy, just for a moment."

I heard my uncle grumble, become cross, finally the valet showed
me in.

On the table, there was the same plate of marzipan as always; my
uncle had on his usual jacket, but across from him, in a pink silk dress
with a long string of pearls around her neck, sat a young woman who
was eating the last of a tangerine. My uncertainty as to whether I
should call her Madame or Mademoiselle made me blush and, not
daring to turn my eyes too much in her direction for fear of having to
talk to her, I went to kiss my uncle. She looked at me, smiling, my
uncle said to her, "My nephew," without telling her my name, or

telling me hers, probably because, ever since the difficulties he had had with my grandfather, he had been trying as far as possible to avoid any association of his family with this sort of acquaintance.

"How much like his mother he is," she said.

"But you've never seen my niece except in a photograph," said my uncle brusquely.

"I beg your pardon, my dear friend, I passed her on the stairs last year when you were so ill. It's true that I saw her for only a split second and your stairs are quite dark, but that was enough for me to admire her. This young man has her beautiful eyes and also *that*," she said, drawing a line with her finger along the lower part of her forehead. "Does Madame, your niece, have the same name as you, my dear?" she asked my uncle.

"He looks like his father more than anyone," muttered my uncle, who was no more anxious to introduce them at a distance by saying Mama's name than to do so at close quarters. "He is exactly like his father and also my poor mother."

"I don't know his father," said the lady in pink with a slight inclination of her head, "and I never knew your poor mother, my dear. You remember, it was shortly after your bereavement that we met."

I was feeling a little disappointed, because this young lady was no different from the other pretty women I had sometimes seen in my family, in particular the daughter of a cousin of ours to whose house I went every year on the first of January. Better dressed, only, my uncle's friend had the same quick and kind glance, she seemed as open and affectionate. In her I found no trace of the theatrical appearance that I admired in photographs of actresses, nor of the diabolical expression that would have suited the life she must lead. I had trouble believing she was a courtesan and I especially would not have believed she was a stylish courtesan, if I had not seen the carriage and pair, the pink dress, the pearl necklace, if I had not known that my uncle was acquainted only with those of the highest sort. But I wondered how the millionaire who had given her her carriage and her house and her jewels could enjoy squandering his fortune on a person whose appearance was so simple and proper. And yet, as I thought about what her life must be like, the immorality of it disturbed me perhaps more than if it had taken concrete form before my eyes in some special guise—it was so invisible, like the secret of some romantic story, of some scandal which had driven out of the home of her bourgeois parents and consigned to the public, which had brought to a bloom of beauty and raised to the demimonde and to notoriety, this woman, the play of whose features, the intonations of whose voice, the same as so many others I knew already, made me consider her despite myself to be a young woman from a good family, though she was no longer from any family.

We had gone into the "study," and my uncle, appearing somewhat ill at ease because of my presence, offered her a cigarette.

"No," she said, "my dear, you know I've become used to the ones the grand duke sends me. I told him you were jealous." And from a case she drew cigarettes covered with gilded foreign writing. "Why yes," she added abruptly, "I must have met this young man's father at your house. Isn't he your nephew? How could I have forgotten? He was so good, so exquisite to me," she said modestly and sensitively. But as I thought about what might have been my father's brusque greeting which she had found so exquisite, I, who knew his reserve and his coldness, was embarrassed, as by an indelicacy he had committed, by this disparity between the excessive gratitude that was bestowed on it and his insufficient cordiality. It seemed to me later that it was one of the touching aspects of the role of these idle and studious women that they devote their generosity, their talent, a free-floating dream of beauty in love—for, like artists, they do not carry it to fruition, do not bring it into the framework of a shared existence—and a gold that costs them little, to enrich with a precious and refined setting the rough and ill-polished lives of men. Just as this one, in the smoking room where my uncle was wearing his plain jacket to receive her, generously diffused her soft and sweet body, her dress of pink silk, her pearls, the elegance that emanates from the friendship of a grand duke, so in the same way she had taken some insignificant remark of my father's, had worked it delicately, turned it, given it a precious appellation, and enchasing it with one of her glances of the finest water, tinged with humility and gratitude, had given it back changed into an artistic jewel, into something "completely exquisite."

"Come now, it's time for you to go," my uncle said to me.

I stood up, I had an irresistible desire to kiss the hand of the lady in pink, but it seemed to me this would have been something as bold as an abduction. My heart pounded as I said to myself: "Should I do it, should I not do it," then I stopped asking myself what I should do so as to be able to do something. And with a blind and senseless gesture divested of all the reasons I had found in its favor a moment ago, I carried to my lips the hand she was holding out to me.

"How nice he is! How gallant! Why, the boy's a bit of a ladies' man already: he takes after his uncle. He'll be a perfect *gentleman*,"[9] she added, clenching her teeth to give the phrase a slightly British accent. "Couldn't he come have *a cup of tea* with me sometime, as our neighbors the English say? He need only send me a 'blue'[10] in the morning."

I did not know what a "blue" was. I did not understand half the words the lady said, but my fear that there was some question concealed in them which it would have been impolite of me not to answer made me keep on listening to them with close attention, and this made me very tired.

"Oh no, that's not possible," said my uncle, shrugging his shoulders, "he's very busy, he works hard. He wins all the prizes at school," he added in a low voice so that I would not hear this lie and contradict it. "Who knows? Perhaps the boy will be a little Victor Hugo, another Vaulabelle,[11] you know."

"I adore artists," answered the lady in pink, "they're the only ones who understand women . . . besides a few superior creatures like you. Excuse my ignorance, my dear, but who is Vaulabelle? Is it those giltedged volumes in the little glass bookcase in your sitting room? You know you promised to lend them to me, I'll take great care of them."

My uncle, who hated lending his books, said nothing in answer and took me to the front hall. Crazed with love for the lady in pink, I covered my old uncle's tobacco-filled cheeks with mad kisses, and, while with some embarrassment he let me know without venturing to tell me openly that he would just as soon I not talk about this visit to my parents, I said to him, tears in my eyes, that the memory of his goodness was so powerful within me that one day I would certainly find the means to show him my gratitude. It was so powerful, in fact, that two hours later, after a few mysterious phrases that did not seem to me to give my parents a distinct enough idea of the new importance with which I was endowed, I found it more explicit to describe to them every last detail of the visit I had just paid. I did not think that in doing this I was causing problems for my uncle. How could I have thought that, since I did not wish it? And I could not imagine that my parents would see any harm in a visit in which I saw none. Doesn't it happen every day that a friend asks us to be sure to apologize for him to a woman to whom he has been prevented from writing, and that we neglect to do it, feeling that this person cannot attach any importance to a silence that has none for us? I imagined, like everyone else, that the brain of another person was an inert and docile receptacle, without the power to react specifically to what one introduced into it; and I did not doubt that in depositing in my parents' brains the news of the acquaintance I had made through my uncle, I was transmitting to them at the same time, as I wished to, the kindly opinion that I had of this introduction. My parents unfortunately deferred to principles entirely different from those I was suggesting they adopt, when they wished to appraise my uncle's action. My father and grandfather had some violent arguments with him; of this, I was indirectly informed. A few days later, encountering my uncle outdoors as he was passing in an open carriage, I was filled with all the pain, the gratitude, the remorse that I would have liked to express to him. Compared to their immensity, I felt that raising my hat would be shabby and might make my uncle think I did not believe I owed him more than an ordinary sort of courtesy. I decided to refrain from that inadequate gesture and I turned my head away. My uncle thought that in doing this I was following my parents' orders, he did not forgive them, and he died many years later without any of us ever seeing him again.

And so I no longer went into my uncle Adolphe's sitting room, now closed, and would linger in the vicinity of the scullery until Françoise appeared in her temple yard and said to me: "I'm going to let my kitchen maid serve the coffee and take up the hot water, I must fly to Mme. Octave," when I would decide to go back in and would go straight upstairs to read in my room. The kitchen maid was an abstract entity, a permanent institution whose invariable set of attributes assured her a sort of continuity and identity, through the succession of temporary forms in which she was incarnated, for we never had the same one two years running. The year we ate so much asparagus, the kitchen maid usually given the job of "scraping" them was a poor, sickly creature, in a state of pregnancy already rather advanced when we arrived at Easter, and we were in fact surprised that Françoise allowed her to do so many errands and so much heavy work, for she was beginning to have difficulty carrying before her the mysterious basket, rounder every day, whose magnificent form one could divine under her ample smocks. These smocks reminded me of the cloaks worn by certain of Giotto's symbolic figures, photographs of whom I had been given by M. Swann. He himself was the one who had pointed this out to us and when he asked for news of the kitchen maid he would say: "How is Giotto's Charity?" What was more, she herself, poor girl, fattened by her pregnancy even in her face, even in her cheeks, which descended straight and square, rather resembled, in fact, those strong, mannish virgins, matrons really, in whom the virtues are personified in the Arena. And I realize now that those Virtues and Vices of Padua[12] resembled her in still another way. Just as the image of this girl was increased by the added symbol she carried before her belly without appearing to understand its meaning, without expressing in her face anything of its beauty and spirit, as a mere heavy burden, in the same way the powerful housewife who is represented at the Arena below the name "Caritas," and a reproduction of whom hung on the wall of my schoolroom at Combray, embodies this virtue without seeming to suspect it, without any thought of charity seeming ever to have been capable of being expressed by her vulgar, energetic face. Through a lovely invention of the painter, she is trampling upon the treasures of the earth, but absolutely as if she were treading grapes to extract their juice or rather as she would have climbed on some sacks to raise herself up; and she holds her flaming heart out to God, or, to put it more exactly, "hands" it to him, as a cook hands a corkscrew through the vent of her cellar to someone who is asking her for it at the ground-floor window. Envy, too, might have had more of a particular expression of envy. But in this fresco too, the symbol occupies such a large place and is represented as so real, the serpent hissing at the lips of Envy is so fat, it fills her wide-open mouth so completely, that the muscles of her face are distended to contain it, like those of a child swelling a balloon with its breath, and that Envy's attention—and ours along with it—entirely concentrated as it is on the action of her lips, has scarcely any time for envious thoughts.

Despite all the admiration M. Swann professed for these figures of Giotto, for a long time I took no pleasure in contemplating, in our schoolroom, where the copies he had brought back to me had been hung, this Charity without charity, this Envy which looked like nothing more than a plate in a medical book illustrating the compression of the glottis or uvula by a tumor of the tongue or by the introduction of the operating surgeon's instrument, a Justice whose grayish and meanly regular face was the very same which, in Combray, characterized certain pretty, pious, and unfeeling bourgeois ladies I saw at Mass, some of whom had long since been enrolled in the reserve militia of Injustice. But later I understood that the startling strangeness, the special beauty of these frescoes was due to the large place which the symbol occupied in them, and the fact that it was represented, not as a symbol, since the thought symbolized was not expressed, but as real, as actually experienced or physically handled, gave something more literal and more precise to the meaning of the work, something more concrete and more striking to the lesson it taught. In the case of the poor kitchen maid, too, wasn't one's attention constantly brought back to her belly by the weight that pulled on it; and in the same way, also, the thoughts of the dying are quite often turned toward the aspect of death that is real, painful, dark, visceral, toward the underside of death, which is in fact the side it presents to them and so harshly makes them feel, and which more closely resembles a crushing burden, a difficulty breathing, a need to drink, than what we call the idea of death.

There must have been a good deal of reality in those Virtues and Vices of Padua, since they seemed to me as alive as the pregnant servant, and since she herself did not appear to me much less allegorical. And perhaps this (at least apparent) nonparticipation of a person's soul in the virtue that is acting through her has also, beyond its aesthetic value, a reality that is, if not psychological, at least, as they say, physiognomical. When, later, I had occasion to meet, in the course of my life, in convents for instance, truly saintly embodiments of practical charity, they generally had the cheerful, positive, indifferent, and brusque air of a busy surgeon, the sort of face in which one can read no commiseration, no pity in the presence of human suffering, no fear of offending it, the sort which is the ungentle face, the antipathetic and sublime face of true goodness.

While the kitchen maid—involuntarily causing Françoise's superiority to shine forth, just as Error, by contrast, renders more dazzling the triumph of Truth—served coffee which according to Mama was merely hot water, and then took up to our rooms hot water which was barely lukewarm, I had lain down on my bed, a book in my hand, in my room which tremulously protected its frail transparent coolness from the afternoon sun behind its nearly closed shutters, through which a gleam of daylight had nonetheless contrived to pass its yellow wings, remaining motionless between the wood and the windowpane, in a corner, like a poised butterfly. It was barely light enough to read, and the sensation of the splendid brightness of the day came to me only from the blows struck in the rue de la Cure by Camus (told by Françoise that my aunt was "not resting" and that one could make noise) against some dusty crates, which, however, reverberating in the sonorous atmosphere peculiar to hot weather, seemed to send scarlet

stars flying into the distance; and also by the houseflies that performed for me, in a little concert, a sort of chamber music of summer: this music does not evoke summer in the same way as a melody
of human music, which, when you happen to hear it during the warm
season, afterward reminds you of it; it is connected to the summer by
a more necessary bond: born of the fine days, born again only with
them, containing a little of their essence, it not only awakens their
image in our memory, it guarantees their return, their presence, actual, ambient, immediately accessible.

This dim coolness of my room was to the full sun of the street
what a shadow is to a ray of light, that is to say, it was just as luminous
and offered my imagination the full spectacle of summer, which my
senses, had I been out walking, could have enjoyed only piecemeal;
and so it was quite in harmony with my repose, which (because of the
stirring adventures narrated in my books) sustained, like the repose of
an unmoving hand in the midst of a stream of water, the shock and
animation of a torrent of activity.

But my grandmother, even if the hot weather had turned bad, if a
storm or merely a squall had arisen, would come and beg me to go
out. And not wanting to stop my reading, I would go and continue it
in the garden, at least, under the chestnut tree, in a little hooded chair
of wicker and canvas, in the depths of which I would sit and think I
was hidden from the eyes of the people who might come and pay a
visit to my parents.

And wasn't my mind also like another crib in the depths of which
I felt I remained ensconced, even in order to watch what was happening outside? When I saw an external object, my awareness that I was
seeing it would remain between me and it, lining it with a thin spiritual border that prevented me from ever directly touching its substance; it would volatize in some way before I could make contact
with it, just as an incandescent body brought near a wet object never
touches its moisture because it is always preceded by a zone of evapo-
ration. In the sort of screen dappled with different states of mind
which my consciousness would simultaneously unfold while I read,
and which ranged from the aspirations hidden deepest within me to

the completely exterior vision of the horizon which I had, at the bottom of the garden, before my eyes, what was first in me, innermost, the constantly moving handle that controlled the rest, was my belief in the philosophical richness and the beauty of the book I was reading, and my desire to appropriate them for myself, whatever that book might be. For, even if I had bought it in Combray, having seen it in front of Borange's grocery, which was too far away from the house for Françoise to be able to do her shopping there as she did at Camus's, but which was better stocked as stationer and bookshop, held in place by some strings in the mosaic of pamphlets and monthly serials that covered the two panels of its door, which was itself more mysterious, more sown with ideas than the door of a cathedral, the fact was that I had recognized it as having been mentioned to me as a remarkable work by the teacher or friend who appeared to me at that period to hold the secret of the truth and beauty half sensed, half incomprehensible, the knowledge of which was the goal, vague but permanent, of my thoughts.

After this central belief, which moved incessantly during my reading from inside to outside, toward the discovery of the truth, came the emotions aroused in me by the action in which I was taking part, for those afternoons contained more dramatic events than does, often, an entire lifetime. These were the events taking place in the book I was reading; it is true that the people affected by them were not "real," as Françoise said. But all the feelings we are made to experience by the joy or the misfortune of a real person are produced in us only through the intermediary of an image of that joy or that misfortune; the ingeniousness of the first novelist consisted in understanding that in the apparatus of our emotions, the image being the only essential element, the simplification that would consist in purely and simply abolishing real people would be a decisive improvement. A real human being, however profoundly we sympathize with him, is in large part perceived by our senses, that is to say, remains opaque to us, presents a dead weight which our sensibility cannot lift. If a calamity should strike him, it is only in a small part of the total notion we have of him that we will be able to be moved by this; even more, it is only in a part of the total notion he has of himself that he will be able to be moved himself. The novelist's happy discovery was to have the idea of replacing these parts, impenetrable to the soul, by an equal quantity of immaterial parts, that is to say, parts which our soul can assimilate. What does it matter thenceforth if the actions, and the emotions, of this new order of creatures seem to us true, since we have made them ours, since it is within us that they occur, that they hold within their control, as we feverishly turn the pages of the book, the rapidity of our breathing and the intensity of our gaze. And once the novelist has put us in that state, in which, as in all purely internal states, every emotion is multiplied tenfold, in which his book will disturb us as might a dream but a dream more lucid than those we have while sleeping and whose memory will last longer, then see how he provokes in us within one hour all possible happinesses and all possible unhappinesses just a few of which we would spend years of our lives coming to know and the most intense of which would never be revealed to us because the slowness with which they occur prevents us from perceiving them (thus our heart changes, in life, and it is the worst pain; but we know it only through reading, through our imagination: in reality it changes, as certain natural phenomena occur, slowly enough so that, if we are able to observe successively each of its different states, in return we are spared the actual sensation of change).

Already less interior to my body than these lives of the characters, next came, half projected in front of me, the landscape in which the action unfolded and which exerted on my thoughts a much greater influence than the other, the one I had before my eyes when I lifted them from the book. It was thus that during two summers, in the heat of the garden at Combray, I felt, because of the book I was reading then, homesick for a mountainous and fluvial country, where I would see many sawmills and where, in the depths of the clear water, pieces of wood rotted under tufts of watercress: not far off, climbing along low walls, were clusters of violet and reddish flowers. And since the dream of a woman who would love me was always present in my mind, during those summers that dream was impregnated with the coolness of the running waters; and whichever woman I conjured up, clusters of violet and reddish flowers would rise immediately on either side of her like complementary colors.

This was not only because an image of which we dream remains forever stamped, is adorned and enriched, by the glimmer of the colors not its own that may happen to surround it in our daydream; for the landscapes in the books I read were for me not merely landscapes more vividly portrayed in my imagination than those which Combray set before my eyes but otherwise analogous. Because the author had chosen them, because of the faith with which my mind went to meet his word as though it were a revelation, they seemed to be—an impression hardly ever given me by the countryside in which I happened to be, and especially by our garden, the unmagical product of the perfectly correct conception of the gardener so despised by my grandmother—an actual part of Nature itself, worthy to be studied and explored.

If my parents had allowed me, when I was reading a book, to go visit the region it described, I would have believed I was taking an invaluable step forward in the conquest of truth. For even if we have the sensation of being always surrounded by our own soul, it is not as though by a motionless prison: rather, we are in some sense borne along with it in a perpetual leap to go beyond it, to reach the outside, with a sort of discouragement as we hear around us always that same resonance, which is not an echo from outside but the resounding of an internal vibration. We try to rediscover in things, now precious because of it, the glimmer that our soul projected on them; we are disappointed to find that they seem to lack in nature the charm they derived in our thoughts from the proximity of certain ideas; at times we convert all the forces of that soul into cunning, into magnificence, in order to have an effect on people who are outside us, as we are well aware, and whom we will never reach. Thus, if I always imagined the woman I loved surrounded by the places I longed for most at that time, if I would have liked her to be the one who took me to visit them, who opened the way for me into an unknown world, it was not because of a simple chance association of thoughts; no, it was because my dreams of travel and of love were only moments—which I am separating artificially today as if I were cutting sections at different heights of an apparently motionless iridescent jet of water—in a single inflexible upsurge of all the forces of my life.

Lastly, continuing to trace from the inside to the outside these states simultaneously juxtaposed in my consciousness, and before reaching the real horizon that enveloped them, I find pleasures of another kind, the pleasure of being comfortably seated, of smelling the good scent of the air, of not being disturbed by a visit; and, when an hour rang in the bell tower of Saint-Hilaire, of seeing fall piece by piece what was already consumed of the afternoon, until I heard the last stroke, which allowed me to add up the total and after which the long silence that followed it seemed to commence in the blue sky that whole part that was still granted me for reading until the good dinner which Françoise was preparing and which would restore me from the hardships I had incurred, during the reading of the book, in pursuit of its hero. And at each hour it would seem to me only a few moments since the preceding hour had rung; the most recent would come and inscribe itself close to the other in the sky, and I would not be able to believe that sixty minutes were held in that little blue arc comprised between their two marks of gold. Sometimes, even, this premature hour would ring two strokes more than the last; there was therefore one that I had not heard, something that had taken place had not taken place for me; the interest of the reading, as magical as a deep sleep, had deceived my hallucinated ears and erased the golden bell from the azure surface of the silence. Lovely Sunday afternoons under the chestnut tree in the garden at Combray, carefully emptied by me of the ordinary incidents of my own existence, which I had replaced by a life of foreign adventures and foreign aspirations in the heart of a country washed by running waters, you still evoke that life for me when I think of you and you contain it in fact from having gradually encircled and enclosed it—while I went on with my reading in the falling heat of the day—in the crystalline succession, slowly changing and spanned by leafy branches, of your silent, sonorous, redolent, and limpid hours.

Sometimes I would be drawn from my reading, in the middle of the afternoon, by the gardener's daughter, who would run like a lunatic, overturning an orange tree in its tub as she went by, cutting a finger, breaking a tooth, and shouting, "They're coming, they're coming!" so that Françoise and I should run out too and not miss any of the show. This was on the days when the regiment passed through Combray on its way to garrison maneuvers, generally going down the rue Sainte-Hildegarde. While our servants, sitting in a row on chairs outside the railings, gazed at the people of Combray taking their Sunday walk and allowed themselves to be gazed at in return, the gardener's daughter through a slit left between two distant houses in the avenue de la Gare had caught sight of the glitter of helmets. The servants had rushed to bring in their chairs, for when the cuirassiers paraded down the rue Sainte-Hildegarde, they filled its entire breadth, and the cantering horses grazed the houses, covering pavements submerged like banks that offer too narrow a bed for a torrent unleashed.

"Poor children," said Françoise, having barely reached the railings and already in tears; "poor boys, to be mown down like grass in a meadow; the very thought of it gives me a shock," she added, putting her hand on her heart, where she had received that *shock.*

"A fine sight, isn't it, Madame Françoise, all these youngsters with no care for their lives?" said the gardener to get a "rise" out of her.

He had not spoken in vain:

"No care for their lives? Well, now, what should we care for if we don't care for our lives, the only gift the dear Lord never gives us twice over? Alas, dear God! It's quite true, though, they don't care! I saw them in '70; in those wretched wars they've no fear of death left in them; they're nothing more nor less than madmen; and then they're not worth the rope to hang them with; they're not men anymore, they're lions." (For Françoise, the comparison of a man to a lion, which she pronounced lie-on, was not at all complimentary.)

The rue Sainte-Hildegarde turned too sharply for us to be able to see anything coming from far off, and it was through that slit between the two houses in the avenue de la Gare that we saw more and more new helmets flowing and shining in the sun. The gardener wanted to know if there were many more still to come, and he was thirsty, because the sun was beating down. So, all of a sudden, his daughter, leaping out as though from a place besieged, would sally forth, gain the corner of the street, and after braving death a hundred times, come back to us bringing, along with a carafe of licorice water, the news that there were at least a thousand of them coming without a break from the direction of Thiberzy and Méséglise. Françoise and the gardener, reconciled, would discuss what action should be taken in case of war.

"You see, Françoise," said the gardener, "revolution would be better, because when they declare a revolution, it's only them that wants to that goes."

"Well now, at least I can understand that, it's more honest."

The gardener believed that when war was declared they would stop all the railway trains.

"Of course! So we doesn't run off," said Françoise.

And the gardener: "Oh, they're clever ones!" because he would not admit that war was not a kind of bad trick that the State tried to play on the people, and that if only they had the means to do it, there was not a single person who would not have run away from it.

But Françoise would hurry back to my aunt, I would return to my book, the servants would settle in front of the gate again to watch as the dust subsided along with the emotion roused by the soldiers. Long after calm had descended, an unaccustomed flow of people out walking would continue to darken the streets of Combray. And in front of each house, even those where it was not the custom, the servants or even the masters, sitting and watching, would festoon the sill with a border as dark and irregular as the border of seaweed and shells whose crepe and embroidery are left on the shore by a strong tide after it recedes.

Except on those days, however, I could usually read in peace. But the interruption and the commentary that a visit of Swann's once produced as I was in the midst of reading a book by an author quite new to me, Bergotte, had the consequence that for a long time afterward it was not against a wall adorned with spikes of violet flowers, but against a quite different background, before the portal of a Gothic cathedral, that the image now appeared of one of the women I dreamed of.

I had heard Bergotte mentioned for the first time by a friend of mine older than I whom I greatly admired, Bloch. When he heard me admit how much I admired "La Nuit d'Octobre,"[13] he had exploded in laughter as noisy as a trumpet and said to me: "Beware this rather low fondness of yours for the Honorable de Musset. He's an extremely pernicious individual and a rather sinister brute. I must admit, however, that he and even our man Racine did, each of them, in the course of their lives, make one fairly rhythmical line of verse that also has in its favor what I believe to be the supreme merit of meaning absolutely nothing. They are: 'The white Oloossone and the white Camyre' and 'The daughter of Minos and Pasiphaë.'[14] They were pointed out to me in defense of those two rogues in an article by my very dear master, old Leconte, acceptable to the Immortal Gods. Speaking of which, here's a book I don't have time to read right now which is recommended, it seems, by that colossal fellow. I've been told he considers the author, the Honorable Bergotte, to be a most subtle individual; and even though he may evince, at times, a goodness of heart rather hard to explain, for me his word is a Delphic Oracle. Do read these lyrical pieces of prose, therefore, and if the titanic rhymester who composed 'Bhagavat' and 'Le Lévrier de Magnus'[15] has spoken the truth, by Apollo, you will taste, dear master, the nectarine joys of Olympos." It was in a sarcastic tone that he had asked me to call him "dear master" and that he called me the same. But in reality we took a certain pleasure in this game, since we were still close to the age when one believes one creates what one names.

Unfortunately, I was unable to talk to Bloch and ask him for an explanation in order to quiet the disturbance he had caused in me when he told me that fine lines of poetry (from which I expected nothing less than a revelation of the truth) were all the finer if they meant nothing at all. For Bloch was not invited to the house again. At first he had been made quite welcome. It was true that my grandfather claimed that each time I formed a closer attachment to one of my friends than the others and brought him home, he was always a Jew, which would not have displeased him in principle—even his friend Swann was of Jewish extraction—had he not felt that it was not from among the best that I had chosen him. And so when I brought home a new friend, he very seldom failed to hum "Oh God of our Fathers" from *La Juive*[16] or "Israel, break thy bond,"[17] singing only the tune, naturally (Ti la lam talam, talim), but I was afraid my friend would know it and restore the words.

Before he saw them, simply from hearing the name, which quite often had nothing particularly Jewish about it, he would guess not only the Jewish background of those of my friends who were in fact Jewish, but even whatever might be distressing about their family.

"And what is the name of this friend of yours who's coming this evening?"

"Dumont, Grandfather."

"Dumont! Oh, now I'm suspicious!"

And he would sing:

> Archers, be on your guard!
> Watch without rest, without sound.[18]

And after adroitly asking us a few more specific questions, he would cry out: "On guard! On guard!" or, if it was the victim himself, already there, whom he had forced, by a subtle interrogation, unwittingly to confess his origins, then, to show us he no longer had any doubts, he would simply gaze at us while barely perceptibly humming:

> Let you now guide
> The steps of this timid Israelite![19]

or:

> Fields of our fathers, sweet valley of Hebron.[20]

or else:

Yes, I am of the chosen race.[21]

These little idiosyncrasies of my grandfather's did not imply any feeling of ill will toward my friends. But Bloch had displeased my family for other reasons. He had begun by irritating my father, who, noticing that he was wet, had said to him with lively interest:

"Why, Monsieur Bloch, what's the weather like? Has it been raining? I don't understand this at all, the barometer couldn't have been better."

The only answer he had drawn from him had been this:

"Monsieur, I absolutely cannot tell you if it has been raining. I live so resolutely beyond physical contingencies that my senses do not bother to notify me of them."

"Why, my poor son, that friend of yours is an idiot," my father had said to me when Bloch had gone. "My goodness! He can't even tell me what the weather's like! Why, nothing is more interesting! He's an imbecile."

Then Bloch had displeased my grandmother because after lunch, when she said she was feeling a little indisposed, he had stifled a sob and wiped away a few tears.

"How can you tell me he's sincere?" she said to me. "He doesn't know me; unless he's out of his mind, of course."

And finally he had annoyed everyone because, having come for lunch an hour and a half late covered with mud, instead of apologizing, he had said:

"I never allow myself to be influenced either by atmospheric perturbations or by the conventional divisions of time. I would happily instate the use of the opium pipe and the Malay kris,[22] but I know nothing about the use of those infinitely more pernicious and also insipidly bourgeois implements, the watch and the umbrella."

He would have returned to Combray despite all this. He was not, of course, the friend my parents would have wanted for me; in the end they had believed that the tears he shed over my grandmother's indisposition were not feigned; but they knew, either instinctively or from experience, that our impulsive emotions have little influence over the course of our actions or the conduct of our lives, and that regard for moral obligations, loyalty to friends, the completion of a piece of work, obedience to a rule of life, have a surer foundation in blind habits than in those momentary transports, ardent and sterile. They would have preferred for me, over Bloch, companions who would have given me no more than is suitable to give one's friends, according to the laws of bourgeois morality; who would not unexpectedly send me a basket of fruits because they had been thinking of me with affection that day, but who, being incapable of tipping in my favor the correct balance of the obligations and claims of friendship by a simple impulse of their imagination and sensibility, would also not tamper with it to my detriment. Even our offenses will not easily divert from their duty toward us those natures of which the model was my great-aunt, who, estranged for years from a niece to whom she never spoke, did not for this reason change the will in which she left that niece her entire fortune, because she was her closest relative and it "was proper."

But I liked Bloch, my parents wanted to make me happy, the insoluble problems I posed for myself concerning the meaningless beauty of the daughter of Minos and Pasiphaë tired me more and made me more ill than further conversations with him would have done, even though my mother felt they were harmful. And he would still have been received at Combray, if, after that dinner, having just informed me—news that later had a great deal of influence on my life and made it first happier, then less happy—that no woman ever thought about anything but love and that there was not one whose resistance could not be overcome, he had not assured me that he had heard most positively that my great-aunt had had a wild youth and had been known to be a kept woman. I could not stop myself from repeating these remarks to my parents, he was shown the door when he returned, and when I approached him afterward in the street, he was extremely cold to me.

But on the subject of Bergotte what he had said was true.

In the first few days, like a melody with which one will become infatuated but which one cannot yet make out, what I was to love so much in his style was not apparent to me. I could not put down the novel of his that I was reading, but thought I was interested only in the subject, as during that first period of love when you go to meet a woman every day at some gathering, some entertainment, thinking you are drawn to it by its pleasures. Then I noticed the rare, almost archaic expressions he liked to use at certain moments, when a hidden wave of harmony, an inner prelude, would heighten his style; and it was also at these moments that he would speak of the "vain dream of life," the "inexhaustible torrent of beautiful appearance," the "sterile and delicious torment of understanding and loving," the "moving effigies that forever ennoble the venerable and charming facades of our cathedrals," that he expressed an entire philosophy, new to me, through marvelous images which seemed themselves to have awakened this harp song which then arose and to whose accompaniment they gave a sublime quality. One of these passages by Bergotte, the third or fourth that I had isolated from the rest, filled me with a joy that could not be compared to the joy I had discovered in the first one, a joy I felt I was experiencing in a deeper, vaster, more unified region of myself, from which all obstacles and partitions seemed to have been removed. What had happened was that, recognizing the same preference for rare expressions, the same musical effusion, the same idealist philosophy that had already, the other times, without my realizing it, been the source of my pleasure, I no longer had the impression I was in the presence of a particular passage from a certain book by Bergotte, tracing on the surface of my mind a purely linear figure, but rather of the "ideal passage" by Bergotte, common to all his books, to which all the analogous passages that merged with it had added a sort of thickness, a sort of volume, by which my mind seemed enlarged.

I was not quite Bergotte's only admirer; he was also the favorite writer of a friend of my mother's, a very well read woman, while Dr. du Boulbon would keep his patients waiting as he read Bergotte's most recent book; and it was from his consulting room, and from a park near Combray, that some of the first seeds of that predilection for Bergotte took flight, a rare species then, now universally wide-spread, so that all through Europe, all through America, even in the smallest village, one can find its ideal and common flower. What my mother's friend and, it seems, Dr. du Boulbon liked above all in Bergotte's books, as I did, was that same melodic flow, those old-fashioned expressions, a few others which were very simple and famil-iar, but which enjoyed, to judge from the places in which he focused attention on them, a particular preference on his part; lastly, in the sad passages, a certain brusqueness, a tone that was almost harsh. And no doubt he himself must have felt that these were his greatest charms. For in the books that followed, if he had found out some great truth, or the name of a famous cathedral, he would interrupt his narrative and, in an invocation, an apostrophe, a long prayer, he would give vent to those exhalations which in his early works re-mained interior to his prose, revealed only by the undulations of its surface, even sweeter, perhaps, more harmonious, when they were thus veiled and one could not have pointed out precisely where their murmur rose, where it died. These passages in which he took such pleasure were our favorite passages. I myself knew them by heart. I was disappointed when he resumed the thread of his narrative. Each time he talked about something whose beauty had until then been hidden from me, about pine forests, about hail, about Notre-Dame Cathedral, about *Athalie* or *Phèdre*,[23] with one image he would make that beauty explode into me. And so, realizing how many parts of the universe there were that my feeble perception would not be able to distinguish if he did not convey them to me, I wanted to possess an opinion of his, a metaphor of his, for everything in the world, espe-cially those things that I would have an opportunity to see myself, and, of the latter, particularly some of the historic buildings of France and certain seascapes, because the insistence with which he men-tioned them in his books proved that he considered them rich in meaning and beauty. Unfortunately, concerning almost everything in the world I did not know what his opinion was. I did not doubt that it was entirely different from my own, since it came down from an un-known world toward which I was trying to rise: persuaded that my thoughts would have looked like pure ineptitude to that perfect mind, I had made such a clean sweep of them all that, when by chance I happened to encounter in one of his books a thought that I had already had myself, my heart would swell as though a god in his goodness had given it back to me, had declared it legitimate and beautiful. It happened now and then that a page of his would say the same things that I often wrote to my grandmother and my mother at night when I could not sleep, so that this page by Bergotte seemed like a collection of epigraphs to be placed at the beginnings of my letters. Later still, when I began writing a book, and the quality of certain sentences was not high enough to persuade me to continue it, I would find their equivalent in Bergotte. But it was only then, when I read them in his book, that I could enjoy them; when I was the one composing them, anxious that they should reflect exactly what I perceived in my thoughts, afraid I would not "make a good likeness," I hardly had time to ask myself whether what I was writing was agreeable! But in fact there was no other sort of sentence, no other sort of idea, that I really loved. My uneasy and dissatisfied efforts were themselves a sign of love, a love without pleasure but profound. And so, when I suddenly found sentences like these in a book by another person, that is, without having to suffer my usual qualms, my usual severity, without having to torment myself, I would at last abandon myself with delight to my partiality for them, like a cook who, when for once he does not have to prepare the meal, at last finds the time to gormandize. One day, when I encountered in a book by Bergotte a joke about an old servant woman which the writer's magnificent and solemn language made even more ironical, but which was the same joke I had often made to my grandmother when talking about Françoise, another time when I saw that he did not think it unworthy to portray in one of those mirrors of truth which were his books a remark similar to one I had had occasion to make about our friend M. Legrandin (remarks about Françoise and M. Legrandin that were certainly among those I would most resolutely have sacrificed to Bergotte, persuaded that he would find them uninteresting), it seemed to me suddenly that my humble life and the realms of the truth were not as widely separated as I had thought, that they even coincided at certain points, and from confidence and joy I wept over the writer's pages as though in the arms of a father I had found again.

From his books, I imagined Bergotte to be a frail, disappointed old man who had lost several of his children and never recovered. And so I would read, I would sing his prose to myself, more *dolce*, more *lento*²⁴ perhaps than it was written, and the simplest sentence spoke to me with a more tender intonation. Above all else I loved his philosophy, I had pledged myself to it for life. It made me impatient to reach the age when I would enter secondary school and enroll in the class called Philosophy. But I did not want to do anything else there but live according to Bergotte's ideas exclusively, and, had I been told that the metaphysicians to whom I would be devoting myself by then would not resemble him at all, I would have felt the despair of a lover who wants his love to be lifelong and to whom one talks about the other mistresses he will have later.

One Sunday, as I was reading in the garden, I was disturbed by Swann, who had come to see my parents.

"What are you reading? May I look? Well, well! Bergotte! Now, who told you about his books?" I said it was Bloch.

"Ah, yes! The boy I saw here once, who looks so much like the portrait of Mohammed II by Bellini.²⁵ Oh, it's quite striking! He has the same circumflex eyebrows, the same curved nose, the same jutting cheekbones. When he has a goatee, he'll be the same person. Well, he has good taste, in any case, because Bergotte is quite enchanting." And seeing how much I appeared to admire Bergotte, Swann, who never talked about the people he knew, out of kindness made an exception and said to me:

"I know him very well. If you would like him to write a few words in the front of your book, I could ask him."

I did not dare accept his offer, but asked Swann some questions about Bergotte. "Could you tell me which is his favorite actor?"

"Actor? I don't know. But I do know that he doesn't consider any man on the stage equal to La Berma; he puts her above everyone else. Have you seen her?"

"No, monsieur, my parents don't allow me to go to the theatre."

"That's unfortunate. You ought to ask them. La Berma in *Phèdre,* in *Le Cid,*[26] is only an actress, you might say, but you know, I'm not much of a believer in the *'hierarchy!'* of the arts" (and I noticed, as had often struck me in his conversations with my grandmother's sisters, that when he talked about serious things, when he used an expression that seemed to imply an opinion about an important subject, he took care to isolate it in a tone of voice that was particularly mechanical and ironic, as though he had put it between quotation marks, seeming not to want to take responsibility for it, as though saying *"hierarchy,* you know, as it is called by silly people?" But then if it was so silly, why did he say hierarchy?). A moment later, he added: "It will give you as noble a vision as any masterpiece, I don't know, really . . . as"– and he began to laugh–"the Queens of Chartres!"[27] Until then his horror of ever expressing a serious opinion had seemed to me a thing that must be elegant and Parisian and that was the opposite of the provincial dogmatism of my grandmother's sisters; and I also suspected that it was a form of wit in the social circles in which Swann moved, where, reacting against the lyricism of earlier generations, they went to an extreme in rehabilitating those small, precise facts formerly reputed to be vulgar, and proscribed "fine phrases." But now I found something shocking in this attitude of Swann's toward things. It appeared that he dared not have an opinion and was at his ease only when he could with meticulous accuracy offer some precise piece of information. But if that was the case, he did not realize that to postulate that the accuracy of these details was important was to profess an opinion. I thought again of that dinner at which I was so sad because Mama would not be coming up to my room and at which he had said that the balls given by the Princesse de Léon were of no importance whatsoever. But it was to just that sort of pleasure that he devoted his life. I found all this contradictory. For what other lifetime was he reserving the moment when he would at last say seriously what he thought of things, formulate opinions that he did not have to put between quotation marks, and no longer indulge with punctilious politeness in occupations which he declared at the same time to be ridiculous? I also noticed in the way Swann talked to me about Bergotte something that was, on the other hand, not peculiar to him, but shared at the time by all the writer's admirers, by my mother's friend, by Dr. du Boulbon. Like Swann, they said about Bergotte: "He's quite enchanting, so individual, he has his own way of saying things which is a little overly elaborate, but so pleasing. You don't need to see the signature, you know right away that it's by him." But none of them would have gone so far as to say: "He's a great writer, he has a great talent." They did not even say he had talent. They did not say it because they did not know it. We are very slow to recognize in the particular features of a new writer the model that is labeled "great talent" in our museum of general ideas. Precisely because these features are new, we do not think they fully resemble what we call talent. Instead, we talk about originality, charm, delicacy, strength; and then one day we realize that all of this is, in fact, talent.

"Are there any books by Bergotte in which he talks about La Berma?" I asked M. Swann.

"I think so, in his slim little volume on Racine, but it must be out of print. There may have been a reissue, though. I'll find out. I can also ask Bergotte anything you like; there isn't a week in the whole year when he doesn't come to dinner at our house. He's my daughter's greatest friend. They go off together visiting old towns, cathedrals, castles."

Since I had no notion of social hierarchy, for a long time the fact that my father found it impossible for us to associate with Mme. and Mlle. Swann had had the effect above all, by making me imagine a great distance between them and us, of giving them prestige in my eyes. I was sorry my mother did not dye her hair and redden her lips as I had heard our neighbor Mme. Sazerat say that Mme. Swann did in order to please, not her husband, but M. de Charlus, and I thought we must be an object of scorn to her, which distressed me most of all because of Mlle. Swann, who, from what I had been told, was such a pretty little girl and about whom I often dreamed, giving her each time the same arbitrary and charming face. But when I learned that day that Mlle. Swann was a creature of so rare a condition, bathing as though in her natural element in the midst of such privileges, that when she asked her parents if anyone was coming to dinner, she would be answered by those syllables filled with light, by the name of that golden dinner guest who was for her only an old friend of the family: Bergotte; that for her the intimate talk at the table, the equivalent for me of my great-aunt's conversation, would be Bergotte's words on all the subjects he had not been able to broach in his books, and on which I would have liked to hear him pronounce his oracles; and that, lastly, when she went to visit other towns, he would walk along next to her, unknown and glorious, like the Gods who descended among mortals; then I was conscious both of the worth of a creature like Mlle. Swann and also of how crude and ignorant I would appear to her, and I felt so keenly the sweetness and the impossibility of my being her friend that I was filled with both desire and despair. Most often, now, when I thought of her, I would see her in front of a cathedral porch, explaining to me what the statues signified and, with a smile that said good things about me, introducing me as her friend to Bergotte. And always the charm of all those ideas awakened in me by the cathedrals, the charm of the hills of Île-de-France and the plains of Normandy, cast its glimmers over the picture I was forming of Mlle. Swann: this was what it meant to be on the point of falling in love with her. Our belief that a person takes part in an unknown life which his or her love would allow us to enter is, of all that love demands in order to come into being, what it prizes the most, and what makes it care little for the rest. Even women who claim to judge a man by his appearance alone see that appearance as the emanation of a special life. This is why they love soldiers, firemen; the uniform makes them less particular about the face; they think that under the breastplate they are kissing a different heart, adventurous and sweet; and a young sovereign, a crown prince, may make the most flattering conquests in the foreign countries he visits without needing the regular profile that would perhaps be indispensable to a stockbroker.

While I read in the garden, something my great-aunt would not have understood my doing except on a Sunday, a day when it is forbidden to occupy oneself with anything serious and when she did not sew (on a weekday, she would have said to me, "What? Still *amusing* yourself with a book? This isn't Sunday, you know," endowing the word *amusement* with the meaning of childishness and waste of time), my aunt Léonie would gossip with Françoise, waiting until it was time for Eulalie. She would announce that she had just seen Mme. Goupil go by "without an umbrella, in that silk dress she had made for her at Châteaudun. If she has far to go before Vespers, she could very well get it properly drenched."

"Maybe, maybe" (meaning maybe not), said Françoise so as not to rule out absolutely the possibility of a more favorable alternative.

"Oh dear," said my aunt, striking her forehead, "that reminds me I never found out if she arrived at church after the Elevation. I will have to remember to ask Eulalie . . . Françoise, just look at that black cloud behind the steeple, and that pitiful sunlight on the slates. It's sure to rain before the day is done. It couldn't possibly stay like this, it was too hot. And the sooner the better, because until the storm breaks, my Vichy water won't go down," added my aunt, in whose mind her desire to hasten the descent of her Vichy water was infinitely more important than her fear of seeing Mme. Goupil ruin her dress.

"Maybe, maybe."

"And the fact is, when it rains on the square there isn't much shelter. What, three o'clock?" my aunt cried out suddenly, turning pale. "Why, my goodness, Vespers has begun and I've forgotten my pepsin! Now I know why my Vichy water was lying on my stomach."

And swooping down on a missal bound in violet velvet, with gilt clasps, from which, in her haste, she let escape a few of those pictures edged with a band of yellowing paper lace that mark the pages of the feast days, my aunt, while swallowing her drops, began reading the sacred texts as fast as she could, her comprehension of them slightly obscured by her uncertainty as to whether the pepsin, taken so long after the Vichy water, would still be able to catch up with it and make it go down. "Three o'clock! It's unbelievable how the time passes!"

A little tap against the windowpane, as though something had struck it, followed by a copious light spill, as of grains of sand dropping from a window above, then the spill extending, becoming regular, finding a rhythm, turning fluid, resonant, musical, immeasurable, universal: it was the rain.

"Well, now, Françoise! What did I tell you? How it's coming down! But I think I heard the bell at the garden gate: go and see who could be outside in such weather."

Françoise returned:

"It was Mme. Amédée" (my grandmother). "She said she was going for a little walk. And yet it's raining hard."

"That doesn't surprise me at all," said my aunt, lifting her eyes to the heavens. "I've always said that her way of thinking is different from everyone else's. I'd rather it be her than me outdoors just now."

"Mme. Amédée is always as different as she can be from everyone else," said Françoise gently, refraining until she should be alone with the other servants from saying that she believed my grandmother was a little "touched."

"Now, *see?* The Benediction is over! Eulalie won't be coming," sighed my aunt; "the weather must have frightened her away."

"But it's not five o'clock, Madame Octave, it's only half-past four."

"Only half-past four? And I had to raise the little curtains to get a wretched glimmer of daylight. At half-past four! One week before the Rogations! Oh, my poor Françoise, the Good Lord must be sorely vexed with us. The world is going too far these days! As my poor Octave used to say, we have forgotten the Good Lord too often and he's taking his revenge."

A bright flush enlivened my aunt's cheeks; it was Eulalie. Unfortunately, scarcely had she been shown in before Françoise returned and, with a smile that was meant to indicate her participation in the joy she was sure her words would give my aunt, articulating the syllables to show that, despite her use of the indirect style, she was reporting, good servant that she was, the very words the visitor had condescended to use:

"M. le Curé would be delighted, enchanted, if Mme. Octave is not resting and could see him. M. le Curé does not wish to disturb. M. le Curé is downstairs; I told him to go into the parlor."

In fact, the curé's visits did not give my aunt as much pleasure as Françoise supposed, and the air of jubilation with which Françoise thought she must illuminate her face each time she had to announce him did not entirely correspond to the invalid's feelings. The curé (an excellent man with whom I am sorry I did not have more conversations, for if he understood nothing about the arts, he did know many etymologies), being in the habit of enlightening distinguished visitors with information about the church (he even intended to write a book about the parish of Combray), fatigued her with endless explanations that were in fact always the same. But when his visit came at the very same time as Eulalie's, it became frankly unpleasant for my aunt. She would have preferred to make the most of Eulalie and not have all her company at once. But she did not dare decline to see the curé and only made a sign to Eulalie not to leave at the same time, so that she could keep her there by herself for a little while after he was gone.

"Monsieur le Curé, what's this they've been telling me, that a painter has set up his easel in your church and is copying a window? I must say, old as I am, I've never in my life heard of such a thing! What is the world coming to? And the ugliest part of the church, too!"

"I will not go so far as to say it is the ugliest, for if there are some parts of Saint-Hilaire that are well worth a visit, there are others that are very old now, in my poor basilica, the only one in all the diocese that has never even been restored! My Lord, the porch is dirty and ancient, but still it is really majestic in character; the same is true of the tapestries of Esther, for which personally I would not give two sous but which the experts rank immediately below those at Sens. I can quite see, too, that apart from certain rather realistic details, they offer other details that show a genuine power of observation. But don't talk to me about the windows! Is it really sensible to leave us with windows that give no light and even deceive our eyes with patches of color I would never be able to identify, in a church where no two paving stones are on the same level and they refuse to replace them for me, giving the excuse that these are the tombstones of the Abbés de Combray and the Seigneurs de Guermantes, the old Comtes de Brabant? The direct ancestors of the present Duc de Guermantes and of the Duchesse too since she's a Demoiselle de Guermantes who married her cousin." (My grandmother, who, because she took no great interest in "persons," ended by confusing all names, would claim, each time anyone mentioned the Duchesse de Guermantes, that she must be a relative of Mme. de Villeparisis. Everyone would burst out laughing; she would try to defend herself by citing as proof a certain letter containing an announcement: "It seems to me I recall there was something about Guermantes in it." And for once I would side with the others against her, unable to admit that there was any connection between her friend from boarding school and the descendant of Geneviève de Brabant.) "Look at Roussainville, today it is no more than a parish of farmers, though in ancient times the locality experienced a great boom in the commerce of felt hats and clocks. (I'm not sure of the etymology of Roussainville. I'm inclined to think the original name was Rouville [*Radulfi villa*], analogous to Châteauroux [*Castrum radulfi*], but we can talk about that some other time.) Well! The church has superb windows, almost all modern, including that impressive *Entry of Louis-Philippe into Combray,* which would be more suited to Combray itself and is just as good, they say, as the famous windows at Chartres. Only yesterday I saw Dr. Percepied's brother, who goes in for these things and who regards it as a very fine piece of work. But, as I in fact said to this artist, who seems very courteous, by the way, and who is apparently a veritable virtuoso with the paintbrush, I said, now what do you find so extraordinary about this window, which is if anything a little darker than the others?"

"I'm sure that if you asked the bishop," my aunt said feebly, beginning to think she was going to be tired, "he would not refuse you a new window."

"You may depend upon it, Madame Octave," answered the curé. "But it was His Lordship himself who started all the fuss about this wretched window by proving that it represented Gilbert the Bad, Sire de Guermantes, a direct descendant of Geneviève de Brabant, who was a Demoiselle de Guermantes, receiving absolution from Saint Hilaire."

"But I can't see where Saint Hilaire would be."

"Why, in the corner of the window—you never noticed a lady in a yellow dress? Well, now, that's Saint Hilaire, who in certain provinces is also called, you know, Saint Illiers, Saint Hélier, and even, in the Jura, Saint Ylie. And these various corruptions of *sanctus Hilarius* are not the most curious that have occurred in the names of the blessed. For instance, your own patron, my good Eulalie, *sancta Eulalia*—do you know what she is in Burgundy? *Saint Éloi,* quite simply: she has become a male saint. You see Eulalie?—after you die they will turn you into a man."

"Monsieur le Curé always has a joke for us."

"Gilbert's brother, Charles the Stammerer, was a pious prince, but having early in life lost his father, Pépin the Mad, who died as a result of his mental infirmity, he wielded the supreme power with all the arrogance of a man who has had no discipline in his youth, and if in a certain town he saw a man whose face he didn't like, he would massacre every last inhabitant. Gilbert, wishing to take revenge on Charles, caused the church of Combray to be burned down, the original church at the time, which Théodebert, when he and his court left the country house he had near here, at Thiberzy (which would be *Theodeberciacus*), to go fight the Burgundians, had promised to build over the tomb of Saint Hilaire if the Blessed One would grant him the victory. Nothing remains of it now but the crypt which Théodore must have taken you down into, for Gilbert burned the rest. Finally, he defeated the unfortunate Charles with the help of William the Conqueror" (the curé pronounced it Will'am), "which is why so many English visitors come to see it. But he apparently was unable to win the affection of the people of Combray, for they rushed upon him as he was coming out of Mass and cut off his head. Théodore has a little book he lends out to people that explains it all.

"But what is unquestionably the most extraordinary thing about our church is the view from the belfry, which is magnificent. Certainly in your case, since you're not strong, I would never advise you

to climb our ninety-seven steps, exactly half the number of the celebrated dome in Milan. It's quite tiring enough for someone in good
health, especially as you must go up bent double if you don't want to
crack your head, and you collect all the cobwebs off the stairwell on
your clothes. In any case you would have to wrap yourself up quite
snugly," he added (without noticing my aunt's indignation at the idea
that she was capable of climbing into the belfry), "because there's
quite a breeze once you get to the top! Some people declare they have
felt the chill of death up there. Nonetheless, on Sundays there are always groups coming even from a long way off to admire the beauty
of the panorama, and they go away enchanted. Now next Sunday, if
the weather holds, you'll be sure to find some people there, since it's
Rogation Day. It really must be admitted, though, that from that spot
the scene is magical, with what you might call vistas over the plain
that have quite a special charm of their own. On a clear day, you can
see all the way to Verneuil. But the marvelous thing is that you can
see, all in one glance, things you can't usually see except one at a time
separately, like the course of the Vivonne and the ditches at Saint-
Assise-lès-Combray, which are separated by a screen of tall trees, or
the different canals at Jouy-le-Vicomte (*Gaudiacus vice comitis,* as you
know). Each time I've gone to Jouy-le-Vicomte, of course, I've seen a
bit of the canal, and then I've turned a corner and seen another bit,
but by then I could no longer see the preceding bit. I could put them
together in my mind, but that didn't have much of an effect for me.
But from the Saint-Hilaire belfry it's different, the whole area seems
to have been caught in one great net. But you can't see any water;
it's as though there were deep clefts dividing the town into different neighborhoods so neatly it looks like a brioche still holding
together after it has been sliced. To do it right, you'd have to be in
both places at the same time, in the steeple of Saint-Hilaire and at
Jouy-le-Vicomte."

The curé had so exhausted my aunt that he was scarcely gone before she had to send Eulalie away too.

"Here, my poor Eulalie," she said weakly, drawing a coin from a little purse that she had within reach of her hand, "this is so that you won't forget me in your prayers."

"Oh, Madame Octave! I don't know if I should; you know I don't come here for that!" Eulalie would say with the same hesitation and the same awkwardness, each time, as if it were the first, and with an appearance of dissatisfaction that diverted my aunt but did not displease her, because if one day Eulalie looked a little less vexed than usual as she took the coin, my aunt would say:

"I don't know what was bothering Eulalie; I gave her the same as usual, and yet she didn't look happy."

"I think she has nothing to complain about, all the same," Françoise would sigh, inclined to consider as small change anything my aunt gave her for herself or her children and as treasure madly squandered on an ingrate the little coins placed in Eulalie's hand each Sunday, but so discreetly that Françoise never managed to see them. It was not that Françoise would have wanted for herself the money my aunt gave Eulalie. She took sufficient pleasure in what my aunt possessed, knowing that the mistress's wealth both elevated and embellished her servant in everyone's eyes; and that she, Françoise, was distinguished and renowned in Combray, Jouy-le-Vicomte, and other places, on account of my aunt's many farms, the curé's frequent and extended visits, the singular number of bottles of Vichy water consumed. She was greedy only for my aunt; if it had been up to her to manage my aunt's fortune, which would have been her dream, she would have preserved it from the encroachments of others with a maternal ferocity. She would not, however, have seen any great harm in what my aunt, whom she knew to be incurably generous, allowed herself to give away, as long as it went to rich people. Perhaps she thought that they, having no need of gifts from my aunt, could not be suspected of showing fondness for her because of them. Besides, gifts made to people of eminence and wealth, like Mme. Sazerat, M. Swann, M. Legrandin, Mme. Goupil, to persons "of the same rank" as my aunt who "were well suited," appeared to her to belong to the customs of the strange and brilliant life of the wealthy who hunt, give balls, visit back and forth, people whom she admired and smiled upon. But it was not the same if the beneficiaries of my aunt's generosity were what Françoise called "people like me, people who are no better than me," the ones of whom she was most scornful unless they called her "Madame Françoise" and considered themselves to be "less than her." And when she saw that despite her advice my aunt did just as she pleased and threw her money away—as Françoise saw it, at least—on the unworthy, she began to think the gifts my aunt made to her were quite small compared to the imaginary sums lavished on Eulalie. There was not a single farm in the vicinity of Combray so substantial that Françoise did not suppose Eulalie could easily have bought it with all she earned from her visits. It is true that Eulalie formed the same estimate of the immense and hidden riches of Françoise. It was Françoise's habit, when Eulalie had gone, to make unkind predictions about her. She detested her, but she was also afraid of her and believed that when Eulalie was there she had to present a "good face." She made up for it after Eulalie's departure, without ever naming her, in fact, but proffering sibylline oracles or pronouncements of a general character like those in Ecclesiastes, whose application could not escape my aunt. After watching through a corner of the curtain to see if Eulalie had closed the gate behind her, she would say: "Flatterers know how to make themselves welcome and collect a little pocket money; but have patience, the Good Lord will punish them all one fine day," with the sidelong glance and the insinuation of Joas thinking only of Athalie when he says:

The happiness of the wicked rushes down like a mountain stream.[28]

But when the curé had come as well and his interminable visit had exhausted my aunt's strength, Françoise would leave the bedroom behind Eulalie and say:

"Madame Octave, I will let you rest, you look very tired."

And my aunt would not even answer, breathing a sigh that must, it seemed, be the last, her eyes closed, as though dead. But scarcely had Françoise gone down than four peals dealt with the greatest violence would echo through the house, and my aunt, upright on her bed, would cry out:

"Has Eulalie gone yet? Can you believe it—I forgot to ask her if Mme. Goupil arrived at Mass before the Elevation! Quick, run after her!"

But Françoise would return without having been able to catch up with Eulalie.

"It's vexing," my aunt would say, shaking her head. "The only important thing I had to ask her!"

In this way life went on for my aunt Léonie, always the same, in the sweet uniformity of what she called, with affected disdain and deep tenderness, her "little routine." Preserved by everyone, not only in the house, where we had all experienced the futility of advising her to adopt a better health regimen and so had gradually resigned ourselves to respecting the routine, but even in the village where, three streets away from us, the goods packer, before nailing his crates, would send word to ask Françoise if my aunt was "resting"—this routine was, however, disturbed once during that year. Like a hidden fruit that had ripened without anyone's noticing and had dropped spontaneously, one night the kitchen maid gave birth. But her pains were intolerable, and since there was no midwife in Combray, Françoise had to go off before daybreak to find one in Thiberzy. My aunt could not rest because of the kitchen maid's cries, and since Françoise, despite the short distance, did not come back until very late, my aunt missed her very much. And so my mother said to me in the course of the morning: "Go up, why don't you, and see if your aunt needs anything." I went into the first room, and through the open door saw my aunt lying on her side sleeping; I heard her snoring lightly. I was going to go away quietly, but the noise I had made had probably interfered with her sleep and made it "shift gears," as they say about cars, because the music of her snoring broke off for a second and resumed on a lower note, then she woke up and half turned her face, which I could now see; it expressed a sort of terror; she had obviously just had a horrible dream; she could not see me the way she was positioned, and I stayed there not knowing if I should go in to her or leave; but already she seemed to have returned to a sense of reality and had recognized the falsity of the visions that had frightened her; a smile of joy, of pious gratitude to God who permits waking life to be less cruel than dreams, weakly illuminated her face, and in the habit she had formed of talking to herself half aloud when she thought she was alone, she murmured: "God be praised! Our only worry is the kitchen maid, who is having a baby. And here I've gone and dreamed that my poor Octave had come back to life and was trying to make me go for a walk every day!" Her hand went out toward her rosary, which lay on the little table, but sleep was overcoming her again and did not leave her the strength to reach it: she fell asleep, soothed, and I crept out of the room without her or anyone else ever finding out what I had heard.

When I say that except for very rare events, like that confinement, my aunt's routine never suffered any variation, I am not speaking of those variations which, always the same and repeated at regular intervals, introduced into the heart of that uniformity only a sort of secondary uniformity. And so, for instance, every Saturday, because Françoise went to the Roussainville-le-Pin market in the afternoon, lunch was, for everyone, an hour earlier. And my aunt had so thoroughly acquired the habit of this weekly violation of her habits that she clung to it as much as to the others. She was so well "routined" to it, as Françoise said, that if she had had to wait, some Saturday, to have lunch at the regular hour, this would have "disturbed" her as much as if on another day she had had to move her lunch forward to the Saturday hour. What was more, this early lunch gave Saturday, for all of us, a special face, indulgent and almost kindly. At the time of day when one usually has another hour to live through before the relaxation of the meal, we knew that in a few seconds we would see the arrival of some precocious endives, a gratuitous omelette, an undeserved beefsteak. The return of this asymmetrical Saturday was one of those little events, internal, local, almost civic, which, in peaceful lives and closed societies, create a sort of national bond and become the favorite theme of conversations, jokes, stories wantonly exagger-

ated: it would have been the ready-made nucleus for a cycle of legends, if one of us had had an epic turn of mind. First thing in the
morning, before we were dressed, for no particular reason, for the
pleasure of feeling the strength of our comradeship, we would say to
one another with good humor, warmth, patriotism: "There's no time
to lose; don't forget—it's Saturday!" while my aunt, conferring with
Françoise and remembering that the day would be longer than usual,
would say: "You might make them a nice bit of veal, since it's Saturday." If at ten-thirty one of us absentmindedly drew out his watch and
said: "Let's see, still an hour and a half before lunch," everyone was
delighted to have to say to him: "Come now, what are you thinking
of, you're forgetting it's Saturday!"; we would still be laughing over it
a quarter of an hour after and we would promise ourselves to go up
and report this lapse to my aunt to amuse her. Even the face of the sky
seemed changed. After lunch, the sun, aware that it was Saturday,
would linger an hour longer at the top of the sky, and when someone,
thinking we were late for our walk, said, "What, only two o'clock?,"
watching, as they passed, the two strokes from the Saint-Hilaire
steeple (which do not usually encounter anyone yet on paths which
are deserted because of the midday meal or the afternoon nap, alongside the lively white stream which even the fisherman has abandoned,
and go on alone into the empty sky where only a few lazy clouds remain), we would all answer him in chorus: "But you're wrong, we had
lunch an hour early; you know very well it's Saturday!" The surprise
of a barbarian (this was what we called anyone who did not know
what was special about Saturday) who, arriving at eleven o'clock to
talk to my father, found us at the table, was one of the things in her
life which most amused Françoise. But if she found it funny that the
dumbfounded visitor did not know we had lunch earlier on Saturday,
she found it even more comical (while at the same time sympathizing
from the bottom of her heart with this narrow chauvinism) that my
father himself had not realized that the barbarian might not know this
and had responded with no further explanation to his astonishment
at seeing us already in the dining room: "Well what do you expect, it's
Saturday!" Having reached this point in her story, she would wipe

away a few tears of hilarity and, to increase her own pleasure, would prolong the dialogue, invent what had been said in answer by the visitor, to whom this "Saturday" did not explain anything. And quite far from complaining about her embellishments, we would feel they were not enough for us and we would say: "But I think he also said something else. It was longer the first time you told it." Even my great-aunt would put down her needlework, lift her head, and look over her glasses.

What was also special about Saturday was that on this day, during the month of May, we would go out after dinner to attend the "Month of Mary."

Since there we would sometimes meet M. Vinteuil, who was very severe about "the deplorable fashion of slovenliness in young people, which seems to be encouraged these days," my mother would take care that nothing was wrong with my appearance, then we would leave for church. It was in the Month of Mary that I remember beginning to be fond of hawthorns. Not only were they in the church, which was so holy but which we had the right to enter, they were put up on the altar itself, inseparable from the mysteries in whose celebration they took part, their branches running out among the candles and holy vessels, attached horizontally to one another in a festive preparation and made even lovelier by the festoons of their foliage, on which were scattered in profusion, as on a bridal train, little bunches of buds of a dazzling whiteness. But, though I dared not do more than steal a glance at them, I felt that the ceremonious preparations were alive and that it was nature herself who, by carving those indentations in the leaves, by adding the supreme ornament of those white buds, had made the decorations worthy of what was at once a popular festivity and a mystical celebration. Higher up, their corollas opened here and there with a careless grace, still holding so casually, like a last and vaporous adornment, the bouquets of stamens, delicate as gossamer, which clouded them entirely, that in following, in trying to mime deep inside myself the motion of their flowering, I imagined it as the quick and thoughtless movement of the head, with coquettish glance and contracted eyes, of a young girl in white, dreamy and alive. M. Vinteuil had come in with his daughter and sat down beside us. He was from a good family and had been my grandmother's sisters' piano teacher, and when, after his wife died and he came into an inheritance, he retired near Combray, we often entertained him at the house. But he was extremely prudish, and stopped coming so as not to meet Swann, who had made what he called "an unsuitable marriage, as is the fashion these days." My mother, after learning that he composed, had said to him in a friendly way that when she went to see him, he would have to let her hear something of his. M. Vinteuil would have taken great joy in this, but he was so scrupulous in his politeness and kindness that, always putting himself in the place of others, he was afraid he would bore them and appear egotistical if he pursued or even allowed them to infer his own desires. The day my parents had gone to visit him at his home, I had gone with them, but they had allowed me to stay outside and, since M. Vinteuil's house, Montjouvain, stood at the foot of a brush-covered hillock where I had hidden, I had found I was on a level with the second-floor drawing room, a foot or two from the window. When the servant had come to announce my parents, I had seen M. Vinteuil hurry to place a piece of music in a conspicuous position on the piano. But once my parents had entered, he had taken it away and put it in a corner. No doubt he had been afraid of letting them think he was happy to see them only so that he could play them some of his compositions. And each time my mother had made a fresh attempt in the course of the visit, he had repeated several times: "I don't know who put that on the piano, it doesn't belong there," and had diverted the conversation to other subjects, precisely because they interested him less. His only passion was for his daughter, and she, with her boyish appearance, seemed so robust that one could not help smiling at the sight of the precautions her father took for her sake, always having extra shawls to throw over her shoulders. My grandmother pointed out what a gentle, delicate, almost shy expression often came into the eyes of that rough-mannered child, whose face was covered with freckles. After she made a remark, she would hear it with the minds of the people to whom she had made it, would grow alarmed at possible misunderstandings, and one would see, illuminated, showing through as though by transparency, under the mannish face of the "good fellow" that she was, the more refined features of a young girl in tears.

When, before leaving the church, I kneeled in front of the altar, I suddenly smelled, as I stood up, a bittersweet scent of almonds escaping from the hawthorns, and then I noticed, on the flowers, little yellower places under which I imagined that scent must be hidden, as the taste of a frangipani must be hidden under the burned parts, or that of Mlle. Vinteuil's cheeks under their freckles. Despite the silence and stillness of the hawthorns, this intermittent scent was like the murmuring of an intense life with which the altar quivered like a country hedge visited by living antennae, of which I was reminded by the sight of certain stamens, almost russet red, that seemed to have preserved the springtime virulence, the irritant power, of insects now metamorphosed into flowers.

We would talk with M. Vinteuil for a moment in front of the porch on our way out of the church. He would intervene among the children squabbling in the square, take up the defense of the little ones, deliver a lecture to the older ones. If his daughter said to us in her loud voice how happy she was to see us, it would immediately seem as if a more sensitive sister within her were blushing at this thoughtless, tomboyish remark, which might have made us think she was asking to be invited to our house. Her father would throw a cloak over her shoulders, they would get up into a little cabriolet, which she would drive herself, and the two of them would return to Montjouvain. As for us, since it was Sunday the next day and we would not get up until it was time for High Mass, if there was moonlight and the air was warm, instead of having us go home directly, my father, out of a love of personal glory, would take us by way of the Calvary on a long walk which my mother's little capacity for orienting herself, or knowing what road she was on, made her consider the feat of a strategic genius. Sometimes we would go as far as the viaduct, whose giant strides of stone began at the railway station and represented to me the exile and distress that lay outside the civilized world, because each year as we came from Paris we were warned to pay careful attention, when Combray came, not to let the station go by, to be ready ahead of time because the train would leave again after two minutes and would set off across the viaduct beyond the Christian countries of which Combray marked for me the farthest limit. We would return by way of the station boulevard, which was lined by the most pleasant houses in the parish. In each garden the moonlight, like Hubert Robert, scattered its broken staircases of white marble, its fountains, its half-open gates. Its light had destroyed the Telegraph Office. All that remained was one column, half shattered but still retaining the beauty of an immortal ruin. I would be dragging my feet, I would be ready to drop with sleep, the fragrance of the lindens that perfumed the air would seem to me a reward that one could win only at the cost of the greatest fatigue and that was not worth the trouble. From gates far apart, dogs awakened by our solitary steps would send forth alternating volleys of barks such as I still hear at times in the evening and among which the station boulevard (when the public garden of Combray was created on its site) must have come to take refuge, for, wherever I find myself, as soon as they begin resounding and replying, I see it again, with its lindens and its pavement lit by the moon.

Suddenly my father would stop us and ask my mother: "Where are we?" Exhausted from walking but proud of him, she would admit tenderly that she had absolutely no idea. He would shrug his shoulders and laugh. Then, as if he had taken it out of his jacket pocket along with his key, he would show us the little back gate of our own garden, which stood there before us, having come, along with the corner of the rue du Saint-Esprit, to wait for us at the end of these unfamiliar streets. My mother would say to him admiringly: "You are astonishing!" And from that moment on, I would not have to take another step, the ground would walk for me through that garden where for so long now my actions had ceased to be accompanied by any deliberate attention: Habit had taken me in its arms, and it carried me all the way to my bed like a little child.

* * *

If Saturday, which began an hour earlier and deprived her of Françoise, passed more slowly than other days for my aunt, she nonetheless awaited its return with impatience from the beginning of the week, because it contained all the novelty and distraction that her weakened and finical body was still able to endure. And yet this was not to say that she did not now and then aspire to some greater change, that she did not experience those exceptional moments when we thirst for something other than what we have, and when people who from a lack of energy or imagination cannot find a source of renewal in themselves ask the next minute that comes, the postman as he rings, to bring them something new, even if it is something worse, some emotion, some sorrow; when our sensibility, which happiness has silenced like an idle harp, wants to resonate under some hand, even a rough one, and even if it might be broken by it; when the will, which has with such difficulty won the right to surrender unimpeded to its own desires, to its own afflictions, would like to throw the reins into the hands of imperious events, even if they may be cruel. Doubtless, since my aunt's strength, drained by the least fatigue, returned to her only drop by drop deep within her repose, the reservoir was very slow to fill up, and months would go by before she had that slight overflow which others divert into activity and which she was incapable of knowing, and deciding, how to use. I have no doubt that then—just as the desire to replace them by potatoes with béchamel sauce ended after a certain time by being born from the very pleasure she felt at the daily return of the mashed potatoes of which she never "got tired"— she would derive from the accumulation of those monotonous days which she valued so the expectation of some domestic cataclysm lasting only a moment but forcing her to effect once and for all one of those changes which she recognized would be beneficial to her and to which she could not of her own accord make up her mind. She truly loved us, she would have taken pleasure in mourning us; had it come at a moment when she felt well and was not in a sweat, the news that the house was being consumed by a fire in which all of us had perished already and which would soon leave not a single stone of the walls standing, but from which she would have ample time to escape without hurrying, so long as she got out of bed right away, must often have lingered among her hopes, since it combined, with the secondary advantages of allowing her to savor all her tenderness for us in an extended grief and to be the cause of stupefaction in the village as she led the funeral procession, courageous and stricken, dying on her feet, that other much more precious advantage of forcing her at the right moment, with no time to lose, no possibility of an enervating hesitation, to go and spend the summer on her pretty farm, Mirougrain, where there was a waterfall. As no event of that sort had ever occurred, the outcome of which she would certainly contemplate when she was alone, absorbed in her innumerable games of patience (and which would have reduced her to despair at the first moment of its realization, at the first of those little unforeseen developments, the first word announcing the bad news, whose accent can never be forgotten afterward, all those things that bear the imprint of real death, so different from its logical, abstract possibility), she would from time to time resort to introducing into her life, to make it more interesting, imaginary incidents which she would follow with passion. She enjoyed suddenly pretending that Françoise was stealing from her, that she herself had been cunning enough to make sure of it, that she had caught her in the act; being in the habit, when she played cards alone, of playing both her own hand and that of her opponent, she would utter out loud to herself Françoise's embarrassed excuses and would answer them with so much fire and indignation that if one of us entered at that moment, we would find her bathed in perspiration, her eyes sparkling, her false hair dislodged and revealing her bald forehead. Françoise would perhaps sometimes hear from the next room mordant pieces of sarcasm addressed to her the invention of which would not have relieved my aunt sufficiently if they had remained in a purely immaterial state and if by murmuring them half aloud she had not given them more reality. Sometimes, even this "theater in bed"[29] was not enough for my aunt, she wanted to have her plays performed. And so, on a Sunday, all doors mysteriously closed, she would confide to Eulalie her doubts about Françoise's honesty, her intention of getting rid of her, and another time, to Françoise, her suspicions about the faithlessness of Eulalie, to whom the door would very soon be closed; a few days later, she would be disgusted with her confidante of the day before and once again consort with the traitor, though for the next performance the two of them would exchange roles yet again. But the suspicions that Eulalie was at times able to inspire in her amounted only to a straw fire and died down quickly, for lack of fuel, since Eulalie did not live in the house. It was not the same for those that concerned Françoise, of whose presence under the same roof my aunt was perpetually conscious, though for fear of catching cold if she left her bed, she did not dare go down to the kitchen to verify whether they were well founded. Gradually her mind would come to be occupied entirely by attempting to guess what, at each moment, Françoise could be doing and trying to hide from her. She would notice the most furtive movements of Françoise's features, a contradiction in something she said, a desire that she seemed to be concealing. And she would show Françoise that she had unmasked her, with a single word that would make Françoise turn pale and that my aunt seemed to find a cruel amusement in driving deep into the heart of the unfortunate woman. And the following Sunday, a revelation of Eulalie's—like those discoveries that suddenly open an unsuspected field to a young science that has got into something of a rut—would prove to my aunt that her own suppositions were far short of the truth. "But Françoise ought to know that, now that you've given her a carriage." "Given her a carriage!" my aunt would cry. "Oh, well, I don't know really. I thought, well, I saw her passing just a short time ago in a calash, proud as Artaban,[30] going to the market at Roussainville. I thought it was Mme. Octave who gave it to her." And so by degrees Françoise and my aunt, like quarry and hunter, would reach the point of constantly trying to anticipate each other's ruses. My mother was afraid Françoise would develop a real hatred for my aunt, who insulted her as brutally as she could. Certainly Françoise came more and more to pay an extraordinary attention to the least of my aunt's remarks, to the least of her gestures. When she had to ask her something, she would hesitate for a long time over how she should go about it. And when she had tendered her request, she would observe my aunt covertly, trying to guess from the look on her face what she thought and what she would decide. And so—while some artist who reads the memoirs of the seventeenth century and wants to be like the great King, and thinks he will be making progress in that direction if he fabricates a genealogy for himself that traces his own descent from a historic family or if he carries on a correspondence with one of the current sovereigns of Europe, is actually turning his back on what he mistakenly sought in forms that were identical and consequently dead—an old lady from the provinces who was simply yielding to irresistible manias and to a malice born of idleness, saw, without ever thinking of Louis XIV, the most insignificant occupations of her day, those concerned with her rising, her lunch, her afternoon rest, acquire, because of their despotic singularity, some of the interest of what Saint-Simon called the "mechanics" of life at Versailles,³¹ and could also believe that her silences, a nuance of good humor or disdain in her features, were for Françoise the object of a commentary as passionate, as fearful as were the silence, the good humor, the disdain of the King when a courtier, or even his greatest lords, handed him a petition at the bend of an avenue at Versailles.

One Sunday when my aunt had had a visit from the curé and Eulalie at the same time and had afterward rested, we all went up to say good evening to her, and Mama offered her her condolences on the bad luck that always brought her visitors at the same hour:

"I know that things turned out poorly again this afternoon, Léonie," she said to her gently, "you had all your company here at the same time."

Which my great-aunt interrupted with: "Too much of a good thing can do no harm . . ." because, ever since her daughter had become ill, she had believed it was her duty to cheer her up by consistently showing her the bright side of everything. But now my father spoke:

"I would like to take advantage," he said, "of the fact that the whole family is together to tell you all about something without having to begin all over again with each of you separately. I'm afraid we've had a falling-out with Legrandin: he barely said hello to me this morning."

I did not stay to hear my father's story, because I had actually been with him after Mass when we met M. Legrandin, and I went down to the kitchen to ask about the menu for our dinner, which diverted me every day like the news in the paper and excited me like the program for some festivity. When M. Legrandin had passed near us as he was coming out of the church, walking by the side of a lady from a neighboring château whom we knew only by sight, my father had greeted him in a way that was at once friendly and reserved, though we had not stopped; M. Legrandin had barely responded, with a surprised look, as if he did not recognize us, and with that perspective in his gaze peculiar to people who do not want to be friendly and who, from the suddenly extended depths of their eyes, seem to perceive you at the end of an interminable road and at so great a distance that they confine themselves to addressing to you a minuscule nod in order to give it the proportions of your puppetlike dimensions.

Now the lady Legrandin was accompanying was a virtuous and esteemed person; it was quite out of the question that he was having an affair and embarrassed at being found out, and my father wondered how he might have annoyed Legrandin. "I would be especially sorry to know he is vexed," said my father, "because of the fact that among all those people dressed up in their Sunday best there is something about him, with his little straight jacket, his loose tie, that is so uncontrived, so truly simple, an air of ingenuousness, almost, that is extremely likable." But the family council was unanimously of the opinion that my father was imagining things, or that Legrandin, at that particular moment, was absorbed in some other thought. And in fact my father's apprehension was dispelled the very next evening. As we were returning from a long walk, near the Pont-Vieux we saw Legrandin, who because of the holidays was staying in Combray for a few days. He came up to us with his hand outstretched: "My young bookworm," he asked me, "do you know this line by Paul Desjardins:

The woods are dark, the sky still blue.[32]

Isn't that a fine rendering of this hour of the day? Perhaps you've never read Paul Desjardins. Read him, my child; today he is transforming himself, they tell me, into a sermonizing friar, but for a long time he was a limpid watercolorist . . .

The woods are dark, the sky still blue.

May the sky remain forever blue for you, my young friend; and even at the hour which is now approaching for me, when the woods are dark already, when night is falling fast, you will console yourself as I do by looking up at the sky." He took a cigarette out of his pocket, remained for a long time with his eyes on the horizon. "Good-bye, friends," he said suddenly, and he left us.

At the hour when I usually went downstairs to find out what the menu was, dinner would already have been started, and Françoise, commanding the forces of nature, which were now her assistants, as in fairy plays where giants hire themselves out as cooks, would strike the coal, entrust the steam with some potatoes to cook, and make the fire finish to perfection the culinary masterpieces first prepared in potters' vessels that ranged from great vats, casseroles, cauldrons, and fishkettles to terrines for game, molds for pastry, and little jugs for cream, and included a complete collection of pans of every shape and size. I would stop by the table, where the kitchen maid had just shelled them, to see the peas lined up and tallied like green marbles in a game; but what delighted me were the asparagus, steeped in ultramarine and pink, whose tips, delicately painted with little strokes of mauve and azure, shade off imperceptibly down to their feet—still soiled though they are from the dirt of their garden bed—with an iridescence that is not of this earth. It seemed to me that these celestial hues revealed the delicious creatures who had merrily metamorphosed themselves into vegetables and who, through the disguise of their firm, edible flesh, disclosed in these early tints of dawn, in these beginnings of rainbows, in this extinction of blue evenings, the precious essence that I recognized again when, all night long following a dinner at which I had eaten them, they played, in farces as crude and poetic as a fairy play by Shakespeare, at changing my chamber pot into a jar of perfume.

Poor Giotto's Charity, as Swann called her, instructed by Françoise to "scrape" them, would have them beside her in a basket, her expression as mournful as though she were suffering all the misfortunes of the earth; and the light crowns of azure that girded the asparagus stalks above their tunics of pink were delicately drawn, star by star, as, in the fresco, are the flowers bound around the forehead or tucked into the basket of Virtue at Padua. And meanwhile, Françoise would be turning on the spit one of those chickens, such as she alone knew how to roast, which had carried the fragrance of her merits through the far reaches of Combray and which, while she was serving them to us at the table, would cause the quality of gentleness to predominate in my particular conception of her character, the aroma of that flesh which she knew how to render so unctuous and so tender being for me only the specific perfume of one of her virtues.

But the day on which, while my father consulted the family council about the encounter with Legrandin, I went down to the kitchen, was one of those on which Giotto's Charity, very ill from her recent confinement, could not get out of bed; Françoise, having no help now, was late. When I arrived downstairs she was busy in the scullery that opened onto the poultry yard, killing a chicken which, by its desperate and quite natural resistance, but accompanied by Françoise, beside herself as she tried to split its neck under the ear, with cries of "Vile creature! Vile creature!," put the saintly gentleness and unction of our servant a little less in evidence than it would, at dinner the next day, by its skin embroidered with gold like a chasuble and its precious juice drained from a ciborium. When it was dead, Françoise collected the blood, which flowed without drowning her resentment, had another fit of anger, and looking at her enemy's cadaver, said one last time: "Vile creature!" I went back upstairs trembling all over; I wanted them to dismiss Françoise immediately. But who would have prepared me such cozy hot-water bottles, such fragrant coffee, and even . . . those chick-

ens? . . . And in fact, everyone had had to make this cowardly calculation, just as I had. For my aunt Léonie knew—as I did not yet know—
that Françoise, who would for her daughter, for her nephews, have
given her life without a murmur, was singularly hard-hearted toward
other people. Despite this my aunt had kept her, for if she was aware
of her cruelty, she valued her service. I gradually came to see that the
gentleness, the compunction, the virtues of Françoise concealed scullery tragedies, just as history reveals that the reigns of the kings and
queens who are portrayed with their hands joined in church windows
were marked by bloody incidents. I realized that, apart from her own
relatives, human beings inspired her with more pity for their afflictions
the farther away from her they lived. The torrents of tears she shed
while reading in the newspaper about the misfortunes of strangers
would dry up quickly if she could picture to herself at all precisely the
person concerned. On one of the nights following her confinement,
the kitchen maid was seized by appalling cramps: Mama heard her
moaning, got up, and woke Françoise, who, quite indifferent, declared
that all this wailing was a sham, that the girl wanted "to be the center
of attention." The doctor, who had been afraid of this sort of attack,
had put a marker in a medical book we had, at the page on which the
symptoms are described, and told us to consult it in order to find out
what kind of first aid to give. My mother sent Françoise to get the
book, warning her not to let the bookmark fall out. After an hour,
Françoise had not returned; my mother, indignant, thought she had
gone back to bed and told me to go to the library myself and see. There
I found Françoise, who, having wanted to look at what the marker
showed, was reading the clinical description of the attack and sobbing,
now that the patient was a hypothetical one whom she did not know.
At each painful symptom mentioned by the author of the article, she
would exclaim: "Oh dear, Holy Virgin, is it possible that the good Lord
would want a wretched human creature to suffer so? Oh, the poor girl!"

But as soon as I called her and she came back to the bedside of
Giotto's Charity, her tears immediately stopped flowing; she could
recognize neither the pleasant sensation of pity and tenderness which

she knew so well and which reading the newspapers had so often given her, nor any kindred pleasure, in the bother and irritation of having gotten up in the middle of the night for the kitchen-maid, and at the sight of the same sufferings whose description had made her cry, she now produced nothing more than bad-tempered mutterings, even nasty pieces of sarcasm, saying, when she thought we had gone and could no longer hear her: "She had only to stop herself doing what you do to get this way! Sure she enjoyed it well enough! So she needn't make a fuss now! Anyways, a boy must be quite forsaken by the good Lord to want to keep company with *that*. Ah, 'tis just as they used to say in my poor mother's own tongue:

> Love a dog's arse, and to thy nose
> 'Twill smell like a rose."[33]

Although when her grandson had a little cold in the head she would set off at night even if she was ill, instead of going to bed, to see if he needed anything, covering four leagues on foot before day-break in order to be back in time to do her work, this same love of her own people and her desire to ensure the future greatness of her house was expressed, in her policy toward the other servants, by a consistent principle, which was never to let a single one of them become attached to my aunt, whom she took, moreover, a sort of pride in not allowing to be approached by anyone, preferring, when she herself was ill, to get up out of bed in order to give her mistress her Vichy water rather than permit the kitchen maid access to the bedroom. And like the hymenopteran observed by Fabre,[34] the burrowing wasp who, so that its young may have fresh meat to eat after its death, summons anatomy in aid of its cruelty and, after capturing a few weevils and spiders, proceeds with a marvelous knowledge and skill to pierce them in the nerve center that governs the movement of their legs but not their other life functions, in such a way that the paralyzed insect near which it deposits its eggs provides the larvae, when they hatch, with prey that is docile, harmless, incapable of flight or resistance, but not in the least tainted, Françoise found, to serve her abiding desire to make the house intolerable to any other servant, ruses so clever and so

merciless that many years later we learned that if we had eaten asparagus almost every day that summer, it was because their smell provoked in the poor kitchen girl who was given the job of scraping them
attacks of asthma so violent that she was obliged in the end to leave.

Alas, we had to change our minds definitively about Legrandin. On
one of the Sundays following the meeting on the Pont-Vieux after
which my father had had to confess himself mistaken, as mass was ending and as something so far from holy was entering the Church, with
the sunlight and the noise from outdoors, that Mme. Goupil, Mme.
Percepied (all those people who not long before, when I arrived a little
late, had remained with their eyes absorbed in their prayers and who I
might even have believed had not seen me come in if, at the same
time, their feet had not gently pushed back the little kneeling bench
that was blocking my path to my seat) began to converse with us
loudly about quite temporal subjects as if we were already in the
square, we saw on the blazing threshold of the porch, looking out over
the motley tumult of the market, Legrandin being introduced by the
husband of that lady with whom we had just recently encountered him
to the wife of another large landowner of the area. Legrandin's face expressed an animation, and a zeal, that were quite extraordinary; he
made a deep bow with a secondary recoil that brought his back sharply
up past its starting position and that must have been taught him by the
husband of his sister, Mme. de Cambremer. This rapid straightening
caused Legrandin's bottom, which I had not supposed was so fleshy, to
flow back in a sort of ardent muscular wave; and I do not know why
that undulation of pure matter, that quite fleshly billow, with no expression of spirituality and whipped into a storm by a fully contemptible alacrity, suddenly awakened in my mind the possibility of a
Legrandin quite different from the one we knew. This lady asked him
to say something to her coachman, and as he went over to the carriage,
the imprint of timid and devoted joy which the introduction had set
upon his face persisted there still. He was smiling, enraptured in a sort
of dream, then he hurried back to the lady, and since he was walking
more quickly than was his habit, his two shoulders oscillated ridicu-
lously to the right and left, and so entirely did he abandon himself to

this, without concern for anything else, that he looked like the inert and mechanical plaything of happiness itself. Meanwhile, we were leaving the porch, we were going to pass right by him, he was too well mannered to turn his head away, but he fastened his gaze, suddenly burdened by a profound reverie, on so distant a point of the horizon that he could not see us and did not have to greet us. His face remained ingenuous above his straight and supple jacket that looked as though it had been led astray against its will into detestably splendid surroundings. And a polka-dotted lavaliere bow tie tossed by the wind in the square continued to float in front of Legrandin like the flag of his proud isolation and noble independence. Just as we reached the house, Mama realized that the Saint Honoré cake had been forgotten and asked my father to go back the way we had come, taking me with him, and tell them to bring it immediately. Near the church we met Legrandin, who was coming in the opposite direction escorting the same lady to her carriage. He passed close to us, did not break off his conversation with his neighbor, and from the corner of his blue eye gave us a little sign that was in some way interior to his eyelid and which, not involving the muscles of his face, could go perfectly unnoticed by the lady he was talking to; but seeking to compensate by intensity of feeling for the somewhat narrow field in which he had circumscribed its expression, in the azure corner assigned to us he set sparkling all the liveliness of a grace that exceeded playfulness, bordered on mischievousness; he overrefined the subtleties of amiability into winks of connivance, insinuations, innuendos, the mysteries of complicity; and finally exalted his assurances of friendship into protestations of affection, into a declaration of love, illuminating for us alone, at that moment, with a secret languor invisible to the lady, a love-smitten eye in a face of ice.

He had in fact asked my parents the day before to send me to dine with him that evening: "Come and keep your old friend company," he had said to me. "Like a bouquet sent to us by a traveler from a country to which we will never return, allow me to breathe from the distance of your adolescence those flowers that belong to the springtimes which I too traversed many years ago. Come with the primrose, the monk's beard, the buttercup, come with the sedum that makes the bouquet of love in Balzac's flora,[35] come with the flower of Resurrection Day, the Easter daisy, and the garden snowdrop, which is beginning to perfume your great-aunt's paths even though the last snows dropped by the Easter showers have not yet melted. Come with the glorious silk raiment of the lily worthy of Solomon himself, and with the polychrome enamel of the pansies, but above all come with the breeze still cool from the last frosts, that will open the petals, for the two butterflies that have waited at its door since morning, of the first Jerusalem rose."

At home they wondered if they still ought to send me to have dinner with M. Legrandin even so. But my grandmother refused to believe he had been impolite. "Even you admit that he goes about dressed in very simple clothes, hardly those of a man of high society." She declared that in any case, and at the very worst, if he had been, it was better to appear not to have noticed. In fact, my father himself, though he was the one most irritated by Legrandin's attitude, may still have harbored a last doubt as to what it meant. It was like any attitude or action that reveals a person's deep and hidden character: it has no connection with anything he has said before, we cannot seek confirmation from the culprit's testimony for he will not confess; we are reduced to the testimony of our own senses concerning which we wonder, confronting this isolated and incoherent memory, if they were not the victims of an illusion; so that these attitudes, the only ones of any importance, often leave us with some doubts.

I had dinner with Legrandin on his terrace; the moon was shining: "This silence has a nice quality, does it not?" he said to me; "for wounded hearts such as mine, a novelist whom you will read later asserts that the only fit companions are shadow and silence.[36] And you know, my child, in life there comes a time, still quite remote for you, when our weary eyes can tolerate only one light, that which a lovely night like this prepares and distills from the darkness, when our ears cannot listen to any other music but that which is played by the moonlight on the flute of silence." I was listening to M. Legrandin's words, which always seemed to me so pleasant; but disturbed by the memory of a woman I had seen recently for the first time, and thinking, now that I knew Legrandin was friends with several of the prominent local aristocracy, that perhaps he knew this one, plucking up my courage I said to him: "Monsieur, do you know the lady . . . the ladies of Guermantes?," happy too that in pronouncing this name I was assuming a sort of power over it, by the mere fact of bringing it out of my daydreams and giving it an objective existence in the world of sound.

But at the name of Guermantes, I saw a little brown notch appear in the center of each of our friend's blue eyes as if they had been stabbed by invisible pinpoints, while the rest of the pupil reacted by secreting floods of azure. The arc of his eyelids darkened and drooped. And his mouth, marked by a bitter fold, but recovering more quickly, smiled while his eyes remained sorrowful, like the eyes of a handsome martyr whose body bristles with arrows: "No, I don't know them," he said, but instead of giving so simple a piece of information, so unsurprising an answer in the natural, everyday tone that would have been appropriate, he declaimed it stressing each word, leaning forward, nodding his head, with the insistence one imparts, so as to be believed, to an improbable statement—as though the fact that he did not know the Guermantes could be due only to a curious accident of fate—and also with the expressive force of a person who, unable to keep silent about a situation that is painful to him, prefers to proclaim it so as to give others the idea that the confession he is making is one that causes him no embarrassment, is easy, pleasant, spontaneous, that the situation itself—the absence of relations with the Guermantes—could well have been, not suffered, but desired by him, could result from some family tradition, moral principle, or mystical vow specifically forbidding him any association with the Guermantes. "No," he went on, explaining his own intonation by what he said, "no, I don't know them, I've never wanted to, I've always made a point of safeguarding my complete independence; deep down I'm a Jacobin[37] in my thinking, you know. Many people have tried to save me, they told me I was wrong not to go to Guermantes, that I was making myself look like a savage, an old bear. But that's not the sort of reputation that dismays me, it's so very true! Deep down, I care for nothing in the world now but a few churches, two or three books, scarcely more paintings, and the light of the moon when the breeze of your youth brings me the fragrance of the flower beds that my old eyes can no longer distinguish." I did not understand very clearly why, in order not to go to the houses of people whom one did not know, it was necessary to cling to one's independence, or how this might make one look like a savage or a bear. But what I did understand was that Legrandin was not being completely truthful when he said he cared only for churches, moonlight, and youth; he cared very much for the people from the châteaux and in their presence was overcome by so great a fear of displeasing them that he did not dare let them see that some of his friends were bourgeois people, sons of notaries or stockbrokers, preferring, if the truth was to be revealed, that it be revealed in his absence, far away from him and "by default"; he was a snob. Certainly he never said any of this in the language my family and I loved so much. And if I asked: "Do you know the Guermantes?," Legrandin the talker would answer: "No, I have never wanted to know them." Unfortunately, he was not the first Legrandin to answer, but the second, because another Legrandin whom he kept carefully concealed deep inside himself, whom he did not exhibit because that Legrandin knew some compromising stories about our own, about his snobbishness, had already answered by the wound in his eyes, by the rictus of his mouth, by the excessive gravity in the tone of his answer, by the thousand arrows with which our own Legrandin had been instantly larded, languishing like a Saint Sebastian of snobbishness: "Alas! How you hurt me! No, I don't know the Guermantes, do not reawaken the great sorrow of my life." And since this troublemaker Legrandin, this blackmailer Legrandin, though he did not have the other's pretty language, had the infinitely quicker speech consisting of what are called "reflexes," when Legrandin the talker wished to impose silence on him, the other had already spoken, and though our friend might grieve over the poor impression that his *alter ego*'s revelations must have produced, he could only attempt to mitigate it.

And this certainly does not mean that M. Legrandin was not sincere when he ranted against snobs. He could not be aware, at least from his own knowledge, that he was one, since we are familiar only with the passions of others, and what we come to know about our own, we have been able to learn only from them. Upon ourselves they act only secondarily, by way of our imagination, which substitutes for our primary motives alternative motives that are more seemly. It was never Legrandin's snobbishness that advised him to pay frequent visits to a duchess. It would instruct Legrandin's imagination to make that duchess appear to him as being endowed with all the graces. Legrandin would become acquainted with the duchess, filled with esteem for himself because he was yielding to attractions of wit and virtue unknown to vile snobs. Only other people were aware that he was one himself; for, because they were incapable of understanding the intermediary work of his imagination, they saw, coupled together, Legrandin's social activity and its primary cause.

Now we at home no longer had any illusions about M. Legrandin, and our contacts with him became less frequent. Mama was infinitely amused each time she caught Legrandin in flagrante delicto in the sin that he would not confess, that he continued to call the sin without forgiveness, snobbishness. My father, on the other hand, had trouble accepting Legrandin's manifestations of disdain with such detachment and good humor; and when, one year, they thought of sending me to spend my summer vacation at Balbec with my grandmother, he said: "I absolutely must let Legrandin know that you'll be going to Balbec, to see if he offers to put you in touch with his sister. He probably doesn't remember telling us she lives only a mile from there." My grandmother, who believed that when staying at a seaside resort one should be on the beach from morning to evening inhaling the salt and that one ought not to know anyone thereabouts because visits and excursions were only so much time taken from the sea air, asked on the contrary that we not speak about our plans to Legrandin, as she could already see his sister, Mme. de Cambremer, arriving at the hotel just when we were about to go fishing and forcing us to remain confined indoors entertaining her. But Mama laughed at her fears, thinking privately that the danger was not so great, that Legrandin would not be in such a hurry to put us in touch with his sister. Yet no one had to mention Balbec to him, it was Legrandin himself who, never suspecting that we had any intention of going to those parts, walked into the trap of his own accord one evening when we met him on the banks of the Vivonne.

"There are very lovely violets and blues in the clouds this evening, are there not, my friend," he said to my father, "a blue, especially, more flowery than airy, the blue of a cineraria, which is surprising in the sky. And that little pink cloud, too, has it not the tint of some flower, a sweet william or hydrangea? Nowhere, perhaps, but on the Channel, between Normandy and Britanny, have I made richer observations of this sort of plant kingdom of the atmosphere. There, near Balbec, near those wild areas, there is a little bay, charmingly gentle, where the sunsets of the Auge country, the red and gold sunsets which I do not in the least disdain, let it be said, are characterless, insignificant; but in that damp and mild atmosphere, in the evening, you will see blooming in the space of a few instants celestial bouquets of blue and pink which are incomparable and often last for hours before they fade. There are others that lose their blossoms immediately, and then it is even lovelier to see the entire sky strewn with the scattering of their countless petals, sulfur or pink. In this bay, which they call Opal Bay, the golden beaches seem gentler still because they are chained like blond Andromedas[38] to those terrible rocks of the nearby coast, to that gloomy shore, famed for the number of its wrecks, where every winter many a vessel is lost to the perils of the sea. Balbec! The most ancient geological skeleton of our soil, truly Ar-mor, the Sea,[39] the land's end, the accursed region which Anatole France[40]—an enchanter whom our little friend here ought to read—has painted so well, under its eternal fogs, like the veritable country of the Cimmerians in the *Odyssey*.[41] From Balbec especially, where they are already building hotels, superimposing them upon the ancient and charming soil which they cannot change, what a delight it is to go for excursions just a step or two away through regions so primitive and so lovely!"

"Oh, do you know someone in Balbec?" asked my father. "As it happens, this boy of ours will be spending two months there with his grandmother, and my wife, too, perhaps."

Legrandin, caught unprepared by this question at a moment when he was looking directly at my father, could not turn his eyes away, but fastening them more intensely second by second—and at the same time smiling sadly—to the eyes of his questioner, with an expression of friendliness and frankness and of not being afraid to look him full in the face, he seemed to have gone right through that face as though it had become transparent, and to be seeing at that moment, far beyond and behind it, a bright and colorful cloud that created a mental alibi for him and would allow him to prove that at the moment when he had been asked if he knew someone at Balbec, he was thinking of something else and had not heard the question. Usually, such an expression makes the other person say: "What are you thinking about?" But my father, curious, irritated, and cruel, said again:

"You know Balbec so well—do you have friends in the area?"

In a last desperate effort, Legrandin's smiling gaze reached its highest degree of tenderness, vagueness, sincerity, and distraction, but, no doubt thinking there was nothing else he could do but answer, he said to us:

"I have friends wherever there are companies of trees, wounded but not vanquished, which huddle together with touching obstinacy to implore an inclement and pitiless sky."

"That was not what I meant," interrupted my father, as obstinate as the trees and as pitiless as the sky. "In case something should happen to my mother-in-law and she needed to feel she was not all alone in an out-of-the-way place, I was asking if you knew anyone there?"

"There as everywhere, I know everyone and I know no one," answered Legrandin, who was not going to give in so quickly; "I know a great deal about things and very little about people. But in that place the very things themselves seem to be people, rare people, delicate in their very essence, disappointed by life. Sometimes it is a manor house that you encounter on a cliff, by the side of a road, where it has stopped to point its sorrow toward the still pink evening where the golden moon rises while the returning boats, fluting the dappled water, hoist the flame of evening on their masts and carry its colors; sometimes it is a simple solitary house, rather ugly, its expression shy but romantic, which conceals from all eyes some imperishable secret of happiness and disenchantment. That land which is so lacking in truth," he added with a Machiavellian delicacy, "that land of pure fiction makes poor reading for a child, and is certainly not what I would choose and recommend for my little friend, already so inclined to sadness, for his heart, already so predisposed. Climates of amorous confessions and vain regrets may suit a disillusioned old man like me, but they are unhealthy for one whose temperament is not yet formed. Please believe me," he went on insistently, "the waters of that bay, already half Breton, may act as a sedative, though a questionable one, on a heart like mine that is no longer undamaged, on a heart for whose wounds there is no longer any compensation. They are contraindicated at your age, my boy. Good night, neighbors," he added, leaving us with that evasive abruptness which was his habit and, turning back toward us with a doctor's raised finger, he summed up his advice: "No Balbec before the age of fifty, and even then it must depend on the state of the heart," he called to us.

Although my father talked to him about this again in our subsequent encounters, torturing him with questions, it was a useless effort: like that erudite crook[42] who used to employ, in fabricating false palimpsests, a labor and a scholarship a hundredth part of which would have been enough to guarantee him a more lucrative, but honorable position, M. Legrandin, had we insisted further, would have ended by constructing a whole system of landscape ethics and a celestial geography of Lower Normandy, sooner than admit to us that his own sister lived a mile from Balbec and be obliged to offer us a letter of introduction which would not have been such an object of terror for him had he been absolutely certain—as in fact he should have been given his experience of my grandmother's character—that we would not have taken advantage of it.

We always returned in good time from our walks so that we could pay a visit to my aunt Léonie before dinner. At the beginning of the season, when the days ended early, when we reached the rue du Saint-Esprit there was still a reflection of the sunset on the windowpanes of the house and a band of crimson deep in the timbers of the Calvary, which was reflected farther off in the pool, a red which, often accompanied by a rather brisk chill, was associated in my mind with the red of the fire over which was roasting the chicken that would allow the poetic pleasure given me by the walk to be succeeded by the pleasure of gluttony, warmth and rest. But in the summer, when we returned, the sun was not yet setting; and during the visit we made to my aunt Léonie, its light, lowering and touching the window, had stopped between the great curtains and the curtain loops, divided, ramified, filtered, and, encrusting the lemon wood of the chest of drawers with little pieces of gold, illuminated the room obliquely with the delicacy it acquires in the forest undergrowth. But on certain very rare days, when we returned, the chest had lost its momentary encrustations long before, when we reached the rue du Saint-Esprit there was no reflection of the sunset spread over the windowpanes, and the pool at the foot of the Calvary had lost its red, sometimes it was already the color of opal and a long ray of moonlight that grew broader and broader and broke over all the wrinkles of the water traversed it entirely. Then, as we came near the house, we would see a figure on the doorstep and Mama would say to me:

"Dear me! There's Françoise, watching for us. Your aunt must be worried; that means we're late."

And, without taking the time to remove our things, we would quickly go up to my aunt Léonie's room to reassure her and show her that, contrary to what she was already imagining, nothing had happened to us, but that we had gone the "Guermantes way" and, bless us, when one took that walk, my aunt knew very well one could never be sure what time one would be back.

"There, Françoise," said my aunt, "what did I tell you? Didn't I say they must have gone the Guermantes way? Heavens! How hungry they must be! And your leg of lamb all dried up after waiting so long. What a time to be getting back! Well, imagine that, you went the Guermantes way!"

"But I thought you knew, Léonie," said Mama. "I thought Françoise saw us go out the little gate from the kitchen garden."

For in the environs of Combray there were two "ways" which one could go for a walk, in such opposite directions that in fact we left our house by different doors when we wanted to go one way or the other: the Méséglise-la-Vineuse way, which we also called the way by Swann's because we passed in front of M. Swann's estate when we went in that direction, and the Guermantes way. About Méséglise-la-Vineuse, to tell the truth, I never knew anything but the "way" and some strangers who used to come and stroll around Combray on a Sunday, people whom, this time, even my aunt, along with all the rest of us, "did not know at all" and whom because of this we assumed to be "people who must have come from Méséglise." As for Guermantes, I was to know more about it one day, but only much later; and during the whole of my adolescence, if for me Méséglise was something as inaccessible as the horizon, concealed from view, however far we went, by the folds of a landscape that already no longer resembled the landscape of Combray, Guermantes, on the other hand, appeared to me only as the terminus, more ideal than real, of its own "way," a sort of abstract geographical expression like the line of the equator, like the pole, like the Orient. So, "to set off toward Guermantes" in order to go to Méséglise, or the opposite, would have seemed to me an expression as devoid of meaning as to set off toward the east in order to go west. Since my father always talked about the Méséglise way as the most beautiful view of the plain that he knew and about the Guermantes way as a typical river landscape, I gave them, conceiving of them thus as two entities, the cohesion, the unity that belong only to the creations of our mind; the smallest part of either of them seemed to me precious and to manifest their particular excellence, while compared to them, before one reached the sacred ground of one or the other, the purely material paths in the midst of which they were set down as the ideal view of the plain and the ideal river landscape were no more worth the trouble of looking at than, for the spectator infatuated with the art of drama, the little streets next to a theater. But most importantly I set between them, much more than their distances in miles, the distance that lay between the two parts of my brain where I thought about them, one of those distances of the mind which not only moves things away from each other, but separates them and puts them on different planes. And that demarcation was made even more absolute because our habit of never going both ways on the same day, in a single walk, but one time the Méséglise way, one time the Guermantes way, shut them off, so to speak, far apart from each other, unknowable by each other, in the sealed and uncommunicating vessels of different afternoons.

When we wanted to go in the direction of Méséglise, we would go out (not too early, and even if the sky was overcast, because the walk was not very long and did not take us too far away) as though we were going anywhere at all, through the front door of my aunt's house on the rue du Saint-Esprit. We would be greeted by the gunsmith, we would drop our letters in the box, we would tell Théodore, from Françoise, as we passed, that she had no more oil or coffee, and we would leave town by the lane that ran along the white gate of M. Swann's park. Before reaching it, we would meet the smell of his lilacs, coming out to greet the strangers. From among the fresh green little hearts of their leaves, the flowers would curiously lift above the gate of the park their tufts of mauve or white feathers, glazed, even in the shade, by the sun in which they had bathed. A few, half hidden by the little tiled lodge called the Archers' House, where the caretaker lived, overtopped its Gothic gable with their pink minarets. The Nymphs of Spring would have seemed vulgar compared to these young houris, which preserved within this French garden the pure and vivid tones of Persian miniatures. Despite my desire to entwine their supple waists and draw down to me the starry curls of their fragrant heads, we would pass by without stopping because my parents had ceased to visit Tansonville since Swann's marriage, and, so as not to appear to be looking into the park, instead of taking the lane that goes along its fence and climbs directly up to the fields, we would take another that leads to the same place, but obliquely, and that brought us out too far away. One day, my grandfather said to my father:

"Don't you remember Swann's telling us yesterday that his wife and daughter were going off to Rheims and that he would take the opportunity to spend a day in Paris? We could go along by the park, since the ladies aren't there; it would make the walk that much shorter for us."

We stopped for a moment in front of the gate. Lilac time was nearly over; a few, still, poured forth in tall mauve chandeliers the delicate bubbles of their flowers, but in many places among the leaves where only a week before they had still been breaking in waves of fragrant foam, a hollow scum now withered, shrunken and dark, dry and odorless. My grandfather pointed out to my father how the look of the place had remained the same, and how it had changed, since the walk he had taken with M. Swann the day of his wife's death, and he used the occasion to tell the story of that walk one more time.

In front of us, an avenue bordered by nasturtiums climbed in full sun toward the house. To the right, the park extended over level ground. Darkened by the shade of the tall trees that surrounded it, an ornamental pond had been dug by Swann's parents; but even in his most artificial creations, man is still working upon nature; certain places will always impose their own particular empire on their surroundings, hoist their immemorial insignia in the middle of a park just as they would have done far from any human intervention, in a solitude which returns to surround them wherever they are, arising from the exigencies of the position they occupy and superimposed on the work of human hands. So it was that, at the foot of the path that overlooked the artificial pond, there might be seen in its two rows woven of forget-me-nots and periwinkles, a natural crown, delicate and blue, encircling the chiaroscuro brow of water, and so it was that the sword lily, bending its blades with a regal abandon, extended over the eupatorium and wet-footed frogbit the ragged fleurs-de-lis, violet and yellow, of its lacustrine scepter.

Mlle. Swann's departure, which—by taking from me the terrible chance that I might see her appear on a path, that I might be recognized and scorned by the privileged little girl who had Bergotte for a friend and went to visit cathedrals with him—made the contemplation of Tansonville a matter of indifference to me the first time it was allowed me, seemed on the contrary to add to that estate, in the eyes of my grandfather and my father, certain accommodations, a transitory charm, and, as does for an excursion into mountain country the absence of any cloud, to make that day exceptionally favorable for a walk in that direction; I would have liked their calculations to be foiled, a miracle to make Mlle. Swann appear with her father, so close to us that we would not have time to avoid her and would be obliged to make her acquaintance. And so, when suddenly I saw on the grass, like a sign of her possible presence, a creel sitting forgotten next to a line whose bob was floating on the water, I hastened to turn my father's and grandfather's eyes away in another direction. In any case, since Swann had told us it was bad of him to go off because he had family at the house just now, the line could belong to one of his guests. We heard no sound of steps on the avenues. Dividing the height of an unknown tree, an invisible bird, contriving to make the day seem short, explored the surrounding solitude with one prolonged note, but received from it a retort so unanimous, a repercussion so redoubled by silence and immobility, that one felt it had arrested forever that moment which it had been trying to make pass more quickly. The light fell so implacably from the still sky that one would have wanted to elude its attention, and the dormant water itself, whose sleep was perpetually irritated by insects, dreaming no doubt of some imaginary maelstrom, increased the disturbance into which I had been plunged by the sight of the cork float, by appearing to draw it at full speed over the silent reaches of the reflected sky; almost vertical, it seemed about to dive and I was already wondering if, quite beyond my desire to know her and my fear of knowing her, I did not have a duty to warn Mlle. Swann that the fish was biting—when I had to run to rejoin my father and grandfather, who were calling me, surprised that I had not followed them along the little lane they had already entered which leads up to the fields. I found it all humming with the smell of the hawthorns. The hedge formed a series of chapels that disappeared under the litter of their flowers, heaped

into wayside altars; below them, the sun was laying down a grid of
brightness on the ground as if it had just passed through a stained-
glass window; their perfume spread as unctuous, as delimited in its
form as if I were standing before the altar of the Virgin, and the flowers, themselves adorned also, each held out with a distracted air its
sparkling bunch of stamens, delicate radiating ribs in the flamboyant
style like those which, in the church, perforated the balustrade of the
rood screen or the mullions of the window and blossomed out into
the white flesh of a strawberry flower. How naive and folksy by comparison would seem the sweetbriers which, in a few weeks, would
climb in full sun the same country lane, in the smooth silk of their
blushing bodices undone by a breath.

But though I remained there in front of the hawthorns, breathing
in, bringing into the presence of my thoughts, which did not know
what to do with it, then losing and finding again their invisible and
unchanging smell, absorbing myself in the rhythm that tossed their
flowers here and there with youthful high spirits and at unexpected
intervals like certain intervals in music, they offered me the same
charm endlessly and with an inexhaustible profusion, but without letting me study it more deeply, like the melodies you replay a hundred
times in succession without descending further into their secrets. I
turned away from them for a moment, to accost them again with renewed strength. I pursued, all the way onto the embankment behind
the hedge that rose steeply toward the fields, some lost poppy, a few
cornflowers which had lazily stayed behind, which decorated it here
and there with their flower heads like the border of a tapestry on
which there appears, thinly scattered, the rustic motif that will domi-
nate the panel; infrequent still, spaced apart like the isolated houses
that announce the approach of a village, they announced to me the
immense expanse where the wheat breaks in waves, where the clouds
fleece, and the sight of a single poppy hoisting its red flame to the top
of its ropes and whipping it in the wind above its greasy black buoy
made my heart pound like the heart of a traveler who spies on a low-
land a first beached boat being repaired by a caulker and, before
catching sight of it, cries out: "The Sea!"

Then I came back to stand in front of the hawthorns as you do in front of those masterpieces which, you think, you will be able to see more clearly when you have stopped looking at them for a moment, but although I formed a screen for myself with my hands so that I would have only them before my eyes, the feeling they awakened in me remained obscure and vague, seeking in vain to detach itself, to come and adhere to their flowers. They did not help me to clarify it, and I could not ask other flowers to satisfy it. Then, filling me with the joy we feel when we see a work by our favorite painter that is different from the ones we knew, or if someone takes us up to a painting of which we had until then seen only a pencil sketch, if a piece heard only on the piano appears to us later clothed in the colors of the orchestra, my grandfather, calling me and pointing to the Tansonville hedge, said to me: "You love hawthorns—just look at this pink one. Isn't it lovely!" Indeed it was a hawthorn, but a pink hawthorn, even more beautiful than the white ones. It, too, wore finery for a holiday—for the only true holidays, which are the religious holidays, since they are not assigned by some fortuitous whim, as are the secular holidays, to an ordinary day that is not especially intended for them, that has nothing essentially festal about it—but their finery was even more opulent, for the flowers, attached to the branch one above another, in such a way as to leave no spot that was not decorated, like pom-poms garlanding a rococo shepherd's crook, were "in color," and consequently of a superior quality according to the aesthetics of Combray, if one judged it by the scale of prices in "the store" in the square, or at Camus's, where the more expensive sponge cakes were the pink ones. Even I preferred cream cheese when it was pink, when I had been allowed to crush strawberries in it. And these flowers had chosen precisely the color of an edible thing, or of a delicate embellishment to an outfit for an important holiday, one of those colors which, because they offer children the reason for their superiority, seem most obviously beautiful to the eyes of children, and for that reason will always seem more vivid and more natural to them than the other tints, even after the children have learned that they did not promise anything for the appetite and had not been chosen by the dressmaker. And certainly, I had felt at once, as I had felt in front of the white hawthorns but with more wonder, that it was in no artificial manner, by no device of human fabrication that the festive intention of the flowers was expressed, but that nature had spontaneously expressed it with the naïveté of a village shopkeeper laboring over her wayside altar, by overloading the shrub with these rosettes which were too delicate in their color and provincially pompadour in their style. At the tops of the branches, like those little rosebushes, their pots hidden in lace paper, whose thin spindles radiated from the altar on the major feast days, teemed a thousand little buds of a paler tint which revealed, when they began to open, as though at the bottom of a cup of pink marble, reds of a bloody tinge, and expressed even more than the flowers the particular, irresistible essence of the hawthorn which, wherever it budded, wherever it was about to flower, could do so only in pink. Inserted into the hedge, but as different from it as a young girl in a party dress among people in everyday clothes who are staying at home, the shrub was all ready for Mary's month, and seemed to form a part of it already, shining there, smiling in its fresh pink outfit, catholic and delicious.

Through the hedge we could see within the park an avenue edged with jasmines, pansies, and verbenas between which stocks opened their fresh purses, of a pink as fragrant and faded as an old piece of cordovan leather, while a long green-painted watering hose, uncoiling its loops over the gravel, sent up at each of the points where it was punctured, over the flowers whose fragrances it imbibed, the prismatic vertical fan of its multicolored droplets. Suddenly I stopped, I could not move, as happens when something we see does not merely address our eyes, but requires a deeper kind of perception and possesses our entire being. A little girl with reddish-blond hair, who appeared to be coming back from a walk and held a gardening spade in her hand, was looking at us, lifting toward us a face scattered with pink freckles. Her dark eyes shone, and since I did not know then, nor have I learned since, how to reduce a strong impression to its objective elements, since I did not have enough "power of observation," as they say, to isolate the notion of their color, for a long time afterward, whenever I thought of her again, the memory of their brilliance would immediately present itself to me as that of a vivid azure, since she was blonde: so that, perhaps if she had not had such dark eyes– which struck one so the first time one saw her–I would not have been, as I was, in love most particularly with her blue eyes.

I looked at her, at first with the sort of gaze that is not merely the messenger of the eyes, but a window at which all the senses lean out, anxious and petrified, a gaze that would like to touch the body it is looking at, capture it, take it away and the soul along with it; then, so afraid was I that at any second my grandfather and my father, noticing the girl, would send me off, telling me to run on a little ahead of them, with a second sort of gaze, one that was unconsciously suppli-cating, that tried to force her to pay attention to me, to know me! She cast her eyes forward and sideways in order to take stock of my grand-father and father, and no doubt the impression she formed of them was that we were absurd, for she turned away, and, with an indifferent and disdainful look, placed herself at an angle to spare her face from being in their field of vision; and while they, continuing to walk on without noticing her, passed beyond me, she allowed her glances to stream out at full length in my direction, without any particular ex-pression, without appearing to see me, but with a concentration and a secret smile that I could only interpret, according to the notions of good breeding instilled in me, as a sign of insulting contempt; and at the same time her hand sketched an indecent gesture for which, when it was directed in public at a person one did not know, the little dic-tionary of manners I carried inside me supplied only one meaning, that of intentional insolence.

"Gilberte, come here! What are you doing?" came the piercing, au-thoritarian cry of a lady in white whom I had not seen, while, at some distance from her, a gentleman dressed in twill whom I did not know stared at me with eyes that started from his head; the girl abruptly stopped smiling, took her spade, and went away without turning back toward me, with an air that was submissive, inscrutable, and sly.

So it was that this name, Gilberte, passed by close to me, given like a talisman that might one day enable me to find this girl again whom it had just turned into a person and who, a moment before, had been merely an uncertain image. Thus it passed, spoken over the jasmines and the stocks, as sour and as cool as the drops from the green watering hose; impregnating, coloring the portion of pure air that it had crossed—and that it isolated—with the mystery of the life of the girl it designated for the happy creatures who lived, who traveled in her company; deploying under the pink thicket, at the height of my shoulder, the quintessence of their familiarity, for me so painful, with her and with the unknown territory of her life which I would never be able to enter.

For a moment (as we moved away, my grandfather murmuring: "Poor Swann, what a role they make him play: they make him leave so that she can stay there alone with her Charlus—because it was him, I recognized him! And the little girl, mixed up in that disgraceful business!") the impression left in me by the despotic tone with which Gilberte's mother had spoken to her without her answering back, by presenting her to me as someone obliged to obey another person, as not being superior to everything in the world, calmed my suffering a little, restored some of my hope, and diminished my love. But very soon that love welled up in me again like a reaction by which my humiliated heart was trying to put itself on the same level as Gilberte or bring her down to its own. I loved her, I was sorry I had not had the time or the inspiration to insult her, hurt her, and force her to remember me. I thought her so beautiful that I wished I could retrace my steps and shout at her with a shrug of my shoulders: "I think you're ugly, I think you're grotesque, I loathe you!" But I went away, carrying with me forever, as the first example of a type of happiness inaccessible to children of my kind because of certain laws of nature impossible to transgress, the image of a little girl with red hair, her skin scattered with pink freckles, holding a spade and smiling as she cast at me long, cunning, and inexpressive glances. And already the charm with which the incense of her name had imbued that place under the pink hawthorns where it had been heard by her and by me together was beginning to reach, to overlay, to perfume everything that came near it, her grandparents, whom my own had had the ineffable happiness of knowing, the sublime profession of stockbroker, the harrowing neighborhood of the Champs-Élysées where she lived in Paris.

"Léonie," said my grandfather when we returned, "I wish we had had you with us this afternoon. You would not recognize Tansonville. If I had dared, I would have cut you a branch of those pink hawthorns you used to love so much." And so my grandfather told Aunt Léonie the story of our walk, either to entertain her or because they had not lost all hope of inducing her to go outdoors. For at one time she had liked that estate very much, and, too, Swann's visits had been the last she had received, when she had already closed her door to everyone else. And just as, when he now called to inquire after her (she was the only person in our house he still asked to see), she would tell them to answer him that she was tired, but that she would let him come in the next time, so she said, that evening: "Yes, someday when it's nice out, I'll take the carriage and go as far as the gate of the park." She said it sincerely. She would have liked to see Swann and Tansonville again; but this desire was enough for what strength remained to her; its fulfillment would have exceeded her strength. Sometimes the good weather restored a little of her energy, she would get up, get dressed; the fatigue would set in before she had gone into the other room and she would ask to go back to bed. What had begun for her—earlier, merely, than it usually happens—was the great renunciation which comes with old age as it prepares for death, wraps itself in its chrysalis, and which may be observed at the ends of lives that are at all extended, even in old lovers who have loved each other the most, even between friends bound by the closest ties of mutual sympathy, who, after a certain year, stop making the necessary journey or outing to see each other, stop writing to each other and know they will not communicate again in this world. My aunt must have known perfectly well that she would not see Swann again, that she would never again leave the house, but this final seclusion must have been made fairly comfortable to her for the very reason that, in our eyes, ought to have made it more painful for her: it was that this seclusion was required of her by the diminution in her strength which she could observe each day and which, making each action, each movement, a cause of fatigue, if not pain, in her eyes gave inaction, isolation, silence, the restorative and blessed sweetness of repose.

My aunt did not go to see the hedge of pink hawthorns, but again and again I asked my parents if she would not go, if at one time she had often gone to Tansonville, trying to make them talk about Mlle. Swann's parents and grandparents, who seemed to me as great as gods. When I was talking with my parents, I pined from the need to hear them say that name, Swann, which had become almost mythological for me, I did not dare pronounce it myself, but I drew them onto subjects that were close to Gilberte and her family, that concerned them, in which I did not feel I was exiled too far from them; and I would suddenly compel my father, by pretending to believe, for instance, that my grandfather's official appointment had been in our family before his time, or that the hedge of pink hawthorns which my aunt Léonie wanted to see was on communal land, to correct what I had said, to say to me, as though in opposition to me, as though of his own accord: "No, that appointment belonged to *Swann's* father, that hedge is part of *Swann's* park." Then I had to catch my breath, so effectively did that name, coming to rest as it did on the spot where it was always written inside me, oppress me to the point of suffocation, that name which, at the moment I heard it, seemed to me more massive than any other name because it was heavy with all the times I had uttered it beforehand in my mind. It gave me a pleasure that I was embarrassed at having dared to demand from my parents, because that pleasure was so great that it must have required considerable effort on their part to procure it for me, and without compensation, since it was not a pleasure for them. And so I would turn the conversation in another direction out of discretion. Out of compunction, too. All the odd allurements that I invested in this name Swann I would hear in it again when they pronounced it. Then it would suddenly seem to me that my parents could not fail to experience these allurements, that they must share my point of view, that they in their turn perceived, forgave, embraced my dreams, and I was unhappy, as if I had defeated them and corrupted them.

That year, when my parents had decided which day we would be returning to Paris, a little earlier than usual, on the morning of our departure, after they had had my hair curled for a photograph, and carefully placed on my head a hat I had never worn before and dressed me in a quilted velvet coat, after looking for me everywhere, my mother found me in tears on the steep little path beside Tansonville, saying good-bye to the hawthorns, putting my arms around the prickly branches, and, like the princess in the tragedy burdened by vain ornaments, ungrateful to the importunate hand that with such care had gathered up my hair in curls across my brow,[43] trampling underfoot my torn-out curl papers and my new hat. My mother was not moved by my tears, but she could not suppress a cry at the sight of my crushed hat and ruined coat. I did not hear it: "Oh, my poor little hawthorns," I said, weeping, "you're not the ones trying to make me unhappy, you aren't forcing me to leave. You've never hurt me! So I will always love you." And drying my tears, I promised them that when I was grown up I would not let my life be like the senseless lives of other men and that even in Paris, on spring days, instead of paying calls and listening to silly talk, I would go out into the countryside to see the first hawthorns.

Once in the fields, we did not leave them again during the rest of our walk toward Méséglise. They were perpetually crossed, as though by an invisible vagabond, by the wind that was for me the presiding spirit of Combray. Each year, the day we arrived, in order to feel that I was really in Combray, I would go up to find it again where it ran along the furrows and made me run after it. We always had the wind beside us when we went the Méséglise way, over that cambered plain where for leagues it encounters no rise or fall in the land. I knew that Mlle. Swann often went to Laon to spend a few days, and even though it was several miles away, since the distance was compensated for by the absence of any obstacle, when, on hot afternoons, I saw a single gust of wind, coming from the farthest horizon, first bend the most distant wheat, then roll like a wave through all that vast expanse and come to lie down murmuring and warm among the sainfoin and clover at my feet, this plain which was shared by us both seemed to bring us together, join us, and I would imagine that this breath of wind had passed close beside her, that what it whispered to me was some message from her though I could not understand it, and I would kiss it as it went by. On the left was a village called Champieu (*Campus pagani,* according to the curé). To the right, you could see beyond the wheat the two chiseled rustic spires of Saint-André-des-Champs, themselves as tapering, scaly, imbricated, checkered, yellowing, and granulose as two spikes of wheat.

At symmetrical intervals, in the midst of the inimitable ornamentation of their leaves, which cannot be confused with the leaves of any other fruit tree, the apple trees opened their broad petals of white satin or dangled the timid bouquets of their reddening buds. It was on the Méséglise way that I first noticed the round shadow that apple trees make on the sunny earth and those silks of impalpable gold which the sunset weaves obliquely under the leaves, and which I saw my father interrupt with his stick without ever deflecting them.

Sometimes in the afternoon sky the moon would pass white as a cloud, furtive, lusterless, like an actress who does not have to perform yet and who, from the audience, in street clothes, watches the other actors for a moment, making herself inconspicuous, not wanting anyone to pay attention to her. I liked finding its image again in paintings and books, but these works of art were quite different—at least during the early years, before Bloch accustomed my eyes and my mind to subtler harmonies—from those in which the moon would seem beautiful to me today and in which I would not have recognized it then. It might be, for example, some novel by Saintine,[44] some landscape by Gleyre[45] in which it stands out distinctly against the sky in the form of a silver sickle, one of those works which were naively incomplete, like my own impressions, and which it angered my grandmother's sisters to see me enjoy. They thought that one ought to present to children, and that children showed good taste in enjoying right from the start, those works of art which, once one has reached maturity, one will admire forever after. The fact is that they probably regarded aesthetic merits as material objects which an open eye could not help perceiving, without one's needing to ripen equivalents of them slowly in one's own heart.

It was along the Méséglise way, at Montjouvain, a house situated at the edge of a large pond and backed up against a brush-covered hillock, that M. Vinteuil lived. And so we often met his daughter on the road driving a cabriolet at top speed. One year, she was not alone when we met her, and from then on she was always accompanied by an older friend, a woman who had a bad reputation in the area and who one day moved permanently into Montjouvain. People said: "Poor M. Vinteuil must be blind with love not to realize what kind of rumors are going around—a man who is shocked by a single remark *out of place* letting his daughter bring a woman like that to live under his roof. He says she's a most superior woman, with a good heart, and that she would have had an extraordinary aptitude for music if she had cultivated it. He can be sure she's not dabbling in music when she's with his daughter." M. Vinteuil did say this; and in fact it is remarkable how a person always inspires admiration for her moral qualities in the family of the person with whom she is having carnal relations. Physical love, so unfairly disparaged, compels people to manifest the very smallest particles they possess of goodness, of self-abnegation, so much so that these particles glow even in the eyes of those immediately surrounding them. Dr. Percepied, whose loud voice and thick eyebrows permitted him to play to his heart's content the role of the villain to which his general appearance was not suited, without in the least compromising his unshakable and undeserved reputation as a kindly old curmudgeon, was capable of making the curé and everyone else laugh until they cried by saying gruffly: "Well, now! It seems young Mlle. Vinteuil is making music with her friend. You seem surprised. Now I don't know. It was old Vinteuil who told me just yesterday. After all, the girl certainly has a right to enjoy her music. It's not for me to go against a child's artistic vocation. Nor Vinteuil either, it seems. And then he himself plays music with his daughter's friend, as well. Heaven help us! There's certainly a good deal of music-making going on in that establishment. Well, why are you laughing? They play too much music, those people. The other day I met old Vinteuil near the cemetery. He was ready to drop."

For those like us who saw M. Vinteuil at that time avoiding people he knew, turning away when he saw them, aging in a few months, immersing himself in his sorrow, becoming incapable of any effort whose direct goal was not his daughter's happiness, spending whole days before the grave of his wife—it would have been difficult not to realize that he was dying of sorrow, or to imagine that he was not aware of the talk that was going around. He knew about it, maybe he even believed it. Perhaps there exists no one, however virtuous he may be, who may not be led one day by the complexity of his circumstances to live on familiar terms with the vice he condemns most expressly—without his fully recognizing it, moreover, in the disguise of particular details that it assumes in order to come into contact with him in that way and make him suffer: strange remarks, an inexplicable attitude, one evening, on the part of someone whom he has otherwise so many reasons for liking. But a man like M. Vinteuil must have suffered much more than most in resigning himself to one of those situations which are wrongly believed to be the exclusive prerogative of the bohemian life: they occur whenever a vice which nature itself plants in a child, like the color of its eyes, sometimes merely by mingling the virtues of its father and mother, needs to reserve for itself the space and the security it requires. But the fact that M. Vinteuil perhaps knew about his daughter's behavior does not imply that his worship of her would thereby be diminished. Facts do not find their way into the world in which our beliefs reside; they did not produce our beliefs, they do not destroy them; they may inflict on them the most constant refutations without weakening them, and an avalanche of afflictions or ailments succeeding one another without interruption in a family will not make it doubt the goodness of its God or the talent of its doctor. But when M. Vinteuil thought about his daughter and himself from the point of view of society, from the point of view of their reputation, when he attempted to place himself with her in the rank which they occupied in the general esteem, then he made this social judgment exactly as it would have been made by the most hostile inhabitant of Combray, he saw himself and his daughter in the lowest depths, and because of this his manner had recently acquired that humility, that respect for those who were above him and whom he saw from below (even if they had been well below him until then), that tendency to seek to climb back up to them, which is an almost automatic result of any downfall. One day as we were walking with Swann down a street in Combray, M. Vinteuil, who was emerging from another, found himself face-to-face with us too suddenly to have time to avoid us; and Swann, with the proud charity of a man of the world who, amid the dissolution of all his own moral prejudices, finds in another man's disgrace merely a reason for showing him a kindliness whose manifestations are all the more gratifying to the self-regard of the one offering them because he feels they are so precious to the one receiving them, had conversed with M. Vinteuil for a long time, although he had never spoken to him before then, and before leaving us had asked him if he would not send his daughter to play at Tansonville someday. This was an invitation which two years before would have incensed M. Vinteuil, but which now filled him with such feelings of gratitude that he believed he was obliged by them not to have the indiscretion of accepting it. Swann's friendliness toward his daughter seemed to him in itself so honorable and so delightful a support that he thought it would perhaps be better not to make use of it, so as to have the wholly platonic pleasure of preserving it.

"What a charming man," he said, when Swann had left us, with the same enthusiastic veneration that causes bright and pretty middleclass women to be awed and entranced by a duchess, even if she is ugly and foolish. "What a charming man! How unfortunate that he should have made such an entirely inappropriate marriage!"

And then, since even the most sincere people have a streak of hypocrisy in them which makes them put to one side their opinion of a person while they are talking to him, and express it as soon as he is no longer present, my parents deplored Swann's marriage along with M. Vinteuil in the name of principles and conventions which (by the very fact that they joined him in invoking them, as decent people of the same stamp) they seemed to be implying he had not violated at Montjouvain. M. Vinteuil did not send his daughter to Swann's house. And Swann was the first to regret it. For each time he left M. Vinteuil, he remembered that for some time now he had had a question to ask him about a person who bore the same name, a relative of his, he believed. And this time he had truly promised himself not to forget what he wanted to tell him when M. Vinteuil sent his daughter to Tansonville.

Since the walk along the Méséglise way was the shorter of the two that we took out of Combray and since, because of that, we saved it for uncertain weather, the climate along the Méséglise way was quite rainy and we would never lose sight of the edge of the Roussainville woods, in the thickness of which we could take cover.

Often the sun would hide behind a storm cloud, distorting its oval, yellowing the edges of the cloud. The brilliance, though not the brightness, would be withdrawn from the countryside, where all life seemed suspended, while the little village of Roussainville sculpted its white rooflines in relief upon the sky with an unbearable precision and finish. Nudged by a gust of wind, a crow flew up and dropped down again in the distance, and, against the whitening sky, the distant parts of the woods appeared bluer, as though painted in one of those monochromes that decorate the pier glasses of old houses.

But at other times the rain with which we had been threatened by the little hooded monk in the optician's window[46] would begin to fall; the drops of water, like migrating birds which take flight all at the same time, would descend in close ranks from the sky. They do not separate at all, they do not wander away during their rapid course, but each one keeps to its place, drawing along the one that comes after it, and the sky is more darkened by them than when the swallows leave. We would take refuge in the woods. When their flight seemed to be over, a few of them, feebler, slower, would still be arriving. But we would come back out of our shelter, because raindrops delight in leafy branches, and, when the earth was already nearly dry again, more than one would still linger to play on the ribs of a leaf and, hanging from the tip, tranquil and sparkling in the sun, would suddenly let go, slip off, and drop from the entire height of the branch onto one's nose.

Often, too, we would go and take shelter all crowded in together with the stone saints and patriarchs in the porch of Saint-André-des-Champs. How French that church was! Above the door, the saints, the knight-kings with fleurs-de-lis in their hands, wedding and funeral scenes, were depicted as they might have been in Françoise's soul. The sculptor had also narrated certain anecdotes involving Aristotle and Virgil just as Françoise in her kitchen was apt to talk about Saint Louis as if she had known him personally, usually in order to put my grandparents to shame by comparison since they were less "fair-minded." One felt that the notions which the medieval artist and the medieval countrywoman (living on into the nineteenth century) had acquired of ancient or Christian history, and which were distinguished by containing as much inaccuracy as simple good-heartedness, were derived not from books, but from a tradition that was at once very old and very direct, uninterrupted, oral, deformed, hardly recognizable, and alive. Another Combray character whom I also recognized, potential and prophesied, in the Gothic sculpture of Saint-André-des-Champs, was young Théodore, the delivery boy from Camus's grocery. Françoise, in fact, felt so clearly that he was a fellow countryman and a contemporary that when my aunt Léonie was too sick for Françoise by herself to turn her over in bed, or carry her to the armchair, instead of letting the kitchen maid come up and get into my aunt's "good books" she would send for Théodore. Now this boy, who was taken, and rightly, for such a ne'er-do-well, was so filled with the same spirit that had decorated Saint-André-des-Champs and especially with the feelings of respect that Françoise believed were owed to "poor sick folk," to "her poor mistress," that as he raised my aunt's head on her pillow he had the same naive and zealous expression as the little angels in the bas-reliefs, crowding around the fainting Virgin with tapers in their hands, as if the faces of sculpted stone, bare and gray as the woods in winter, were only a deep sleep, a reserve, about to blossom into life again in numberless common faces, reverent and crafty like Théodore's, illuminated with the redness of a ripe apple. No longer affixed to the stone like those little angels, but detached from the porch, of larger than human size, standing on a pedestal as though on a stool that spared her putting her feet on the damp ground, one saint had the full cheeks, the firm breast swelling the folds of the cloth like a cluster of ripe grapes in a horsehair sack, the narrow forehead, the short and saucy nose, the deep-set eyes, the able-bodied, impassive, and courageous demeanor of the countrywomen of the region. This resemblance, which insinuated into the statue a sweetness I had not looked for in it, was often authenticated by some girl from the fields, who, like us, had come to take cover, and whose presence, like the presence of the leaves of a climbing plant that has grown up next to some sculpted leaves, seemed intended to allow us, by confronting it with nature, to judge the truthfulness of the work of art. Before us in the distance, a promised land or an accursed one, Roussainville, was now, when the rain had already stopped for us, either continuing to be chastised like the village in the Bible by all the slanting spears of the storm, which scourged the dwellings of its inhabitants, or else had already been pardoned by God the Father, who caused to descend upon it, unequal in length, like the rays of an altar monstrance, the frayed golden shafts of his reappearing sun.

Sometimes the weather was completely spoiled, we had to go back home and stay shut up in the house. Here and there, far off in the countryside, which because of the dark and the wet resembled the sea, a few isolated houses, clinging to the side of a hill plunged in watery night, shone forth like little boats that have folded their sails and stand motionless out at sea all night long. But what did the rain matter, what did the storm matter! In summer, bad weather is only a passing, superficial mood on the part of the steady, underlying good weather, which is very different from the fluid and unstable good weather of winter, and having settled on the earth, where it has taken solid form in dense branches of leaves on which the rain may drip without compromising the resistance of their permanent joy, has hoisted for the whole season, even in the streets of the village, on the walls of the houses and gardens, its flags of white or violet silk. Sitting in the little drawing room, where I waited for the dinner hour while I read, I would hear the water dripping from our chestnut trees, but I knew that the downpour was only varnishing their leaves and that they would promise to stay there, like pledges of summer, all the rainy night, ensuring that the good weather would continue; that rain as it might, tomorrow little heart-shaped leaves would undulate just as numerous above the white gate of Tansonville; and it was without sadness that I saw the poplar in the rue des Perchamps meet the storm praying and bowing in despair; it was without sadness that I heard at the back of the garden the last rolls of thunder warbling among the lilacs.

If the weather was bad in the morning, my parents would give up the walk and I would not go out. But I later acquired the habit of going out to walk alone on those days along the Méséglise-la-Vineuse way, during the autumn in which we had to come to Combray to settle my aunt Léonie's estate, because she had at last died, proving correct both those who had claimed that her enfeebling regimen would end by killing her, and those who had always maintained that she suffered from an illness that was not imaginary but organic, to the evidence of which the skeptics would certainly be obliged to yield when she succumbed to it; and causing no great suffering by her death except to a single person, but to that one, a grief that was savage. During the two weeks of my aunt's final illness, Françoise did not leave her for an instant, did not undress, did not allow anyone else to care for her in any way, and did not leave her body until it was buried. Then we realized that the kind of dread in which Françoise had lived, of my aunt's ill-natured remarks, suspicions, angry moods, had developed a feeling in her that we had taken for hatred and that was actually veneration and love. Her true mistress, whose decisions were impossible to foresee, whose ruses were difficult to foil, whose good heart was easy to touch, her sovereign, her mysterious and all-powerful monarch, was no more. Next to her we counted for very little. The time was by now far in the past when, as we began coming to spend our holidays at Combray, we possessed as much prestige as my aunt in Françoise's eyes. That autumn, completely occupied as they were with the formalities that had to be observed, the interviews with notaries and tenants, my parents, having scarcely any time to go on excursions, which the weather frustrated in any case, fell into the habit of letting me go for walks without them along the Méséglise way, wrapped in a great plaid that protected me from the rain and that I threw over my shoulders all the more readily because I sensed that its Scottish patterning scandalized Françoise, into whose mind one could not have introduced the idea that the color of one's clothes had nothing to do with mourning and to whom, in any case, the sorrow that we felt over the death of my aunt was not very satisfactory, because we had not offered a large funeral dinner, because we did not adopt a special tone of voice in speaking of her, because I even hummed to myself now and then. I am sure that in a book—and in this I was actually quite like Françoise—such a conception of mourning, in the manner of the *Chanson de Roland*[47] and the portal of Saint-André-des-Champs, would have appealed to me. But as soon as Françoise came near me, some demon would goad me to try to make her angry, I would seize the slightest pretext to tell her that I missed my aunt because she was a good woman despite her ridiculous ways, but not in the least because she was my aunt, that she might have been my aunt and still seemed odious to me, and then her death would not have caused me any pain, remarks that would have seemed to me absurd in a book.

If Françoise then, filled like a poet with a flood of confused thoughts about bereavement, about family memories, excused herself for not knowing how to answer my theories and said: "I don't know how to *espress* myself," I would gloat over that admission with a harsh and ironic common sense worthy of Dr. Percepied; and if she added: "All the same, she was your own kith and kindred,[48] and there's a proper respect we owe to our kith and kindred, you know,' I would shrug my shoulders and say to myself: "Look at me, arguing with an illiterate woman who makes such blunders," adopting, in judging Françoise, the mean-spirited attitude of men whose behavior those people who despise them the most when contemplating them impartially are quite capable of adopting, when actually playing one of life's vulgar scenes.

My walks that autumn were all the more pleasant because I took them after long hours spent over a book. When I was tired from reading all morning in the parlor, throwing my plaid over my shoulders I would go out: my body, which had had to keep still for so long, but which had accumulated, as it sat, a reserve of animation and speed, now needed, like a top that has been released, to expend them in all directions. The walls of the houses, the Tansonville hedge, the trees of the Roussainville woods, the thickets at the back of Montjouvain, submitted to the blows of my umbrella or walking stick, heard my shouts of joy, these being both merely confused ideas that exhilarated me and found no repose in the light of understanding, because they had preferred, instead of a slow and difficult clarification, the pleasure of an easier diversion toward an immediate outcome. Most of the supposed expressions of our feelings merely relieve us of them in this way by drawing them out of us in an indistinct form that does not teach us to know them. When I try to count up what I owe to the Méséglise way, the humble discoveries for which it was the fortuitous setting or the necessary inspiration, I recall that it was that autumn, on one of those walks, near the bushy hillock that protects Montjouvain, that I was struck for the first time by this discord between our impressions and their habitual expression. After an hour of rain and wind which I had fought cheerfully, as I came to the edge of the Montjouvain pond, beside a little hut covered in tiles where M. Vinteuil's gardener stowed his gardening tools, the sun had just reappeared, and its gildings, washed by the downpour, glistened freshly in the sky, on the trees, on the wall of the hut, on its still-wet tile roof along the crest of which a hen was walking. The wind that was blowing tugged at the wild grass growing in the side of the wall and the downy plumage of the hen, the one and the other streaming out at full length horizontally before its breath, with the abandon of things that are weightless and inert. In the pond, reflective again under the sun, the tile roof made a pink marbling to which I had never before given any attention. And seeing on the water and on the face of the wall a pale smile answering the smile of the sky, I cried out to myself in my enthusiasm, brandishing my furled umbrella: "Damn, damn, damn, damn." But at the same time I felt I was in duty bound not to stop at these opaque words, but to try to see more clearly into my rapture.

And it was at that moment, too—because of a countryman who was passing by, who seemed rather cross already and was more so when my umbrella nearly went in his face, and who responded without warmth to my "fine weather, isn't it, perfect for a walk"—that I learned that the same emotions do not arise simultaneously, in a preestablished order, in all men. Later, each time a rather prolonged session of reading had put me in a mood to chat, the friend I was so eager to talk to would himself have just been indulging in the pleasure of conversation and now wanted to be left to read in peace. If I had just been thinking tenderly about my parents and making the wisest decisions, those most likely to please them, they would have been employing the same time in discovering some peccadillo I had forgotten, and they would reproach me severely for it just at the moment I bounded toward them to give them a hug.

Sometimes the exhilaration I felt at being alone was joined by another kind that I was not able to separate distinctly from it, and that came from my desire to see a peasant girl appear in front of me whom I could clasp in my arms. Born suddenly, and without my having had time to identify exactly what had caused it, from among very different thoughts, the pleasure which accompanied it seemed to me only one degree higher than that which those other thoughts had given me. Everything that was in my mind at that moment acquired an even greater value, the pink reflection of the tile roof, the wild grass, the village of Roussainville to which I had been wanting to go for so long now, the trees of its woods, the steeple of its church, as a result of this new emotion which made them appear more desirable only because I thought it was they that had provoked it, and which seemed only to wish to carry me toward them more rapidly when it filled my sail with a powerful, mysterious, and propitious wind. But if, for me, this desire that a woman should appear added something more exhilarating to the charms of nature, the charms of nature, in return, broadened what would have been too narrow in the woman's charm. It seemed to me that the beauty of the trees was also hers and that the soul of those horizons, of the village of Roussainville, of the books I was reading that year, would be given to me by her kiss; and as my imagination drew strength from contact with my sensuality, as my sensuality spread through all the domains of my imagination, my desire grew boundless. And, too—just as during those moments of reverie in the midst of na-ture when, the effect of habit being suspended, and our abstract no-tions of things set aside, we believe with a profound faith in the originality, in the individual life of the place in which we happen to be—the passing woman summoned by my desire seemed to be, not an ordinary exemplar of that general type—woman—but a necessary and natural product of this particular soil. For at that time everything which was not I, the earth and other people, appeared to me more pre-cious, more important, endowed with a more real existence than they appear to grown men. And I did not separate the earth and the people. I desired a peasant girl from Méséglise or Roussainville, a fisherwoman from Balbec, just as I desired Méséglise and Balbec. The pleasure they might give me would have appeared less real to me, I would no longer have believed in it, if I had modified its conditions as I pleased. To meet a fisherwoman from Balbec or a countrywoman from Méséglise in Paris would have been like receiving a seashell I could not have seen on the beach, a fern I could not have found in the woods, it would have subtracted from the pleasure which the woman would give me all those pleasures in which my imagination had enveloped her. But to wander through the woods of Roussainville without a peasant girl to hold in my arms was to see these woods and yet know nothing of their hidden treasure, their profound beauty. For me that girl, whom I could only envisage dappled with leaves, was herself like a local plant, merely of a higher species than the rest and whose structure enabled one to approach more closely than one could in the others the essential fla-vor of the country. I could believe this all the more readily (and also that the caresses by which she would allow me to reach that flavor would themselves be of a special kind, whose pleasure I would not have been able to experience through anyone else but her) because I was, and would be for a long time to come, at an age when one has not yet abstracted this pleasure from the possession of the different women with whom one has tasted it, when one has not reduced it to a general notion that makes one regard them from then on as the interchangeable instruments of a pleasure that is always the same. This pleasure does not even exist, isolated, distinct and formulated in the mind, as the aim we are pursuing when we approach a woman, as the cause of the previous disturbance that we feel. We scarcely even contemplate it as a pleasure which we will enjoy; rather, we call it her charm; for we do not think of ourselves, we think only of leaving ourselves. Obscurely awaited, immanent and hidden, it merely rouses to such a paroxysm, at the moment of its realization, the other pleasures we find in the soft gazes, the kisses of the woman close to us, that it seems to us, more than anything else, a sort of transport of our gratitude for our companion's goodness of heart and for her touching predilection for us, which we measure by the blessings, by the beatitude she showers upon us.

Alas, it was in vain that I implored the castle keep of Roussainville, that I asked it to have some child from its village come to me, appealing to it as to the only confidant I had had of my earliest desires, when at the top of our house in Combray in the little room smelling of orris root, I could see nothing but its tower in the middle of the pane of the half-open window, while with the heroic hesitations of a traveler embarking on an exploration or of a desperate man killing himself, with a feeling of faintness, I would clear an unknown and I thought fatal path within myself, until the moment when a natural trail like that left by a snail added itself to the leaves of the wild black currant that leaned in toward me. In vain did I appeal to it now. In vain did I hold the whole expanse of the country before me within the field of my vision, draining it with my eyes which tried to extract a woman from it. I would go as far as the porch of Saint-André-des-Champs; there I would never find the countrywoman I would inevitably have met had I been with my grandfather and therefore prevented from striking up a conversation with her. I would stare endlessly at the trunk of a distant tree from behind which she was going to appear and come to me; the scanned horizon would remain uninhabited, night would fall, hopelessly my attention would attach itself, as though to aspirate the creatures they might harbor, to that sterile ground, to that exhausted earth; and it was no longer with a light heart, but with rage, that I struck the trees of the Roussainville woods, from among which no more living creatures emerged than if they had been trees painted on the canvas background of a panorama, when, unable to resign myself to going back to the house without having held in my arms the woman I had so desired, I was nevertheless obliged to continue along the road to Combray admitting to myself that there was less and less chance that she had been placed in my path. And if she had been there, would I have dared talk to her? It seemed to me she would have thought I was mad; I no longer believed that the desires which I formed during my walks, and which were not fulfilled, were shared by other people, that they had any reality outside of me. They now seemed to me no more than the purely subjective, impotent, illusory creations of my temperament. They no longer had any attachment to nature, to reality, which from then on lost all its charm and significance and was no more than a conventional framework for my life, as is, for the fiction of a novel, the railway carriage on the seat of which a traveler reads it in order to kill time.

It was perhaps from an impression received also near Montjouvain, a few years later, an impression that remained obscure to me at the time, that there emerged, well after, the idea which I formed of sadism. As will be seen later, for quite other reasons the the memory of this impression was to play an important part in my life. It was during a spell of very hot weather; my parents, who had had to leave for the whole day, had told me to return home as late as I pleased; and having gone as far as the Montjouvain pond, where I liked to look at the reflections of the tile roof again, I had lain down in the shade and fallen asleep among the bushes of the hillock that overlooks the house, in the same spot where I had once waited for my father on a day when he had gone to see M. Vinteuil. It was almost night when I awoke, I wanted to stand up, but I saw Mlle. Vinteuil (insofar as I actually recognized her, because I had not seen her very often in Combray, and only when she was still a child, whereas now she was growing into a young woman), who had probably just come home, opposite me, a few inches from me, in the room in which her father had entertained my father and which she had made into her own little drawing room. The window was half open, the lamp was lit, I could see her every movement without her seeing me, but if I had gone away I would have made rustling sounds among the bushes, she would have heard me, and she might have thought I had hidden there to spy on her.

She was in deep mourning, because her father had died a short time before. We had not gone to see her, my mother had not wanted to because of a virtue of hers which alone limited the effects of her goodness: her sense of decency; but she pitied her deeply. My mother recalled the sad end of M. Vinteuil's life, completely absorbed as it was first in giving his daughter the care of a mother or a nursemaid, then in the suffering his daughter had caused him; she could still see the tormented expression on the old man's face during that last period; she knew he had entirely given up completing the task of transcribing in clean copies all his work of the last few years, insignificant pieces by an old piano teacher, by a former village organist, which we could well imagine had scarcely any value in themselves, but which we did not disdain because they had so much value for him, having been his reason for living before he sacrificed them for his daughter, and which, for the most part not even written down, preserved only in his memory, a few jotted on scattered sheets of paper, unreadable, would remain unknown; my mother thought of that other, even crueler renunciation which had been forced upon M. Vinteuil, the renunciation of a future of decent and respectable happiness for his daughter; when she remembered all this extreme distress on the part of my aunts' old piano teacher, she was moved by real sorrow and thought with horror of the far more bitter sorrow that Mlle. Vinteuil must be feeling, mingled as it was with remorse at having more or less killed her father. "Poor M. Vinteuil," my mother would say, "he lived and died for his daughter, without getting any reward for it. Will he get it after his death, and in what form? It could only come to him from her."

At the back of Mlle. Vinteuil's drawing room, on the mantelpiece, stood a small portrait of her father which she quickly went to get at the moment when the rattle of a carriage could be heard from the road outside, then she threw herself down on a couch, drew a little table close to her, and set the portrait on it, just as M. Vinteuil had once placed beside him the piece that he wanted to play for my parents. Soon her friend came in. Mlle. Vinteuil greeted her without standing up, both hands behind her head, and withdrew to the other end of the sofa as though to make room for her. But immediately she felt that by doing this she seemed to be forcing her friend into a position that might be annoying to her. She thought her friend might prefer to be some distance away from her on a chair, she thought she had been indiscreet, her tactful heart grew alarmed; moving so that she now occupied all the space on the sofa again, she closed her eyes and began yawning to imply that she had only stretched out like that because she was sleepy. Despite the crude and overweening familiarity with which she treated her friend, I recognized her father's obsequious and reticent gestures, his sudden qualms. Soon she stood up and pretended to be trying to close the shutters without success.

"No, leave them open, I'm hot," said her friend.

"But it's a nuisance, someone will see us," answered Mlle. Vinteuil.

But she must have guessed that her friend would think she had said these words only to goad her into answering with certain others that she in fact wanted to hear, but that out of discretion she wanted to leave her friend the initiative of uttering. And so her face, which I could not see, must have assumed the expression that my grandmother liked so much, as she quickly added:

"When I say see us, I mean see us reading; it's such a nuisance to think that whatever insignificant thing you may be doing, other eyes are watching you."

Out of an instinctive generosity and an involuntary courtesy she did not speak the premeditated words that she had felt were indispensable to the full realization of her desire. And time and again, deep inside her, a timid and supplicant virgin entreated and forced back a rough and swaggering brawler.

"Yes, I'm sure people are watching us at this hour, in this densely populated countryside," her friend said ironically. "And what if they are?" she added (thinking she had to give a mischievous, tender wink as she uttered these words, which she recited good-naturedly like a text she knew Mlle. Vinteuil liked, in a tone that she tried to make cynical). "If someone saw us, so much the better."

Mlle. Vinteuil shuddered and stood up. Her scrupulous and sensitive heart did not know what words ought to come to her spontaneously to suit the scene that her senses demanded. She searched as far away from her true moral nature as she could to find a language that would fit the depraved girl she wanted to be, but the words she thought that girl would have uttered sincerely seemed false on her own lips. And the little she allowed herself to say was said in a stiff tone of voice in which her habitual shyness paralyzed her inclinations toward boldness, and was interlarded with: "You're not too cold, are you, you're not too warm, would you rather be alone and read?"

"Mademoiselle seems to be having rather libidinous thoughts this evening," she said at last, probably repeating a phrase she had heard before on her friend's lips.

Mlle. Vinteuil felt her friend plant a kiss in the opening of her crepe blouse, she gave a little cry, broke free, and they began chasing each other, leaping, fluttering their wide sleeves like wings, and clucking and cheeping like two amorous birds. At last Mlle. Vinteuil collapsed on the couch, with her friend's body covering her. But the friend had her back turned to the little table on which the old piano teacher's picture was placed. Mlle. Vinteuil realized that her friend would not see it if her attention was not drawn to it, and she said to her, as if she had only just noticed it:

"Oh! That picture of my father is looking at us. I don't know who could have put it there. I've told them a dozen times that it doesn't belong there."

I remembered that these were the same words M. Vinteuil had spoken to my father in connection with the piece of music. They were probably in the habit of using the portrait for ritual profanations, because her friend answered her in words which must have been part of her liturgical response:

"Oh, leave him where he is. He's not here to bother us anymore. Just think how he would start whining and try to make you put your coat on if he could see you there with the window open, the ugly old monkey."

Mlle. Vinteuil answered with words of gentle reproach—"Come, come"—which proved the goodness of her nature, not because they were dictated by the indignation she might have felt at this way of referring to her father (evidently this was a feeling that she had grown used to silencing in herself at these times, with the help of who knows what sophistical reasonings), but because they were a sort of curb that she herself, so as not to seem selfish, was applying to the pleasure that her friend was trying to give her. And, too, such smiling forbearance in response to these blasphemies, such a tender, hypocritical reproach, may have appeared to her frank and generous good nature a particularly unspeakable form, a saccharine form of the wickedness she was trying to emulate. But she could not resist the attraction of the pleasure she would feel at being treated with such tenderness by a woman so implacable toward a defenseless dead man; she jumped on her friend's knees, and chastely presented her forehead for a kiss, as a daughter might have done, with the delightful sensation that the two of them were achieving an extreme of cruelty by robbing M. Vinteuil, even in his grave, of his fatherhood. Her friend took her head in her hands and set a kiss on her forehead with a docility that came easily to her because of her great affection for Mlle. Vinteuil and her desire to bring some amusement into the orphan's life, now so sad.

"Do you know what I would like to do to him—that old horror?" she said, picking up the portrait.

And she murmured in Mlle. Vinteuil's ear something I could not hear.

"Oh, you wouldn't dare!"

"I wouldn't dare spit on him? On *that old thing*?" said her friend with deliberate savagery.

I did not hear any more, because Mlle. Vinteuil, with a manner that was weary, awkward, fussy, honest, and sad, came and closed the shutters and the window, but now I knew that for all the suffering which M. Vinteuil had endured on his daughter's account during his lifetime, this was what he had received from her as his reward after his death.

And yet I have thought, since then, that if M. Vinteuil had been able to witness this scene, he still might not have lost his faith in his daughter's good heart, and perhaps he would not even have been entirely wrong in that. It was true that in Mlle. Vinteuil's habits, the appearance of evil was so complete that it would have been hard to find it so perfectly represented in anyone other than a sadist; it is behind the footlights of a popular theater rather than in the lamplight of an actual country house that one expects to see a girl encouraging her friend to spit on the portrait of a father who lived only for her; and almost nothing else but sadism provides a basis in real life for the aesthetics of melodrama. In reality, even when she is not a sadist, a girl might perhaps have failings as cruel as those of Mlle. Vinteuil with regard to the memory and wishes of her dead father, but she would not deliberately express them in an act of such rudimentary and naive symbolism; what was criminal about her behavior would be more veiled from the eyes of others and even from her own, and she would do evil without admitting it to herself. But, beyond appearances, even in Mlle. Vinteuil's heart, the evil, in the beginning at least, was probably not unmixed. A sadist of her sort is an artist of evil, something that an entirely bad creature could not be, for then evil would not be exterior to her, it would seem to her quite natural, would not even be distinguishable from her; and as for virtue, memory of the dead, and filial tenderness, since she would not be devoutly attached to them she would take no sacrilegious pleasure in profaning them. Sadists of Mlle. Vinteuil's kind are creatures so purely sentimental, so naturally virtuous that even sensual pleasure seems to them something bad, the privilege of the wicked. And when they allow themselves to yield to it for a moment, they are trying to step into the skin of the wicked and to make their partner do so as well, so as to have the illusion, for a moment, of escaping from their scrupulous and tender soul into the inhuman world of pleasure. And I understood how much she longed for it when I saw how impossible it was for her to succeed in it. At the very moment when she wanted to be so different from her father, what she at once suggested to me were the old piano teacher's ways of thinking, of speaking. Far more than his photograph, what she really desecrated, what she was really using for her pleasures, though it remained between them and her and kept her from enjoying them directly, was the resemblance between her face and his, his own mother's blue eyes which he had handed down to her like a family jewel, those kind gestures which interposed between Mlle. Vinteuil's vice and herself a style of talking, a mentality that was not made for it and that prevented her from recognizing it as something very different from the numberless obligatory courtesies to which she usually devoted herself. It was not evil which gave her the idea of pleasure, which seemed agreeable to her; it was pleasure that seemed to her malign. And since each time she indulged in it, it was accompanied by these bad thoughts which were absent the rest of the time from her virtuous soul, she came to see pleasure as something diabolical, to identify it with Evil. Perhaps Mlle. Vinteuil felt that her friend was not fundamentally bad and was not really sincere when she talked to her in this blasphemous way. At least she had the pleasure of kissing her friend's face with its smiles and glances that might have been feigned but were similar in their depraved and base expression to the smiles and glances of, not a kind, suffering person, but one given to cruelty and pleasure. She could imagine for a moment that she was really playing the games that would have been played, with so unnatural a confederate, by a girl who actually had these barbaric feelings toward her father's memory. Perhaps she would not have thought that evil was a state so rare, so extraordinary, so disorienting, and to which it was so restful to emigrate, if she had been able to discern in herself, as in everyone else, that indifference to the sufferings one causes which, whatever other names one gives it, is the terrible and lasting form assumed by cruelty.

If it was fairly simple to go the Méséglise way, it was another matter to go the Guermantes way, because the walk was long and we wanted to be sure what sort of weather we would be having. When we seemed to be entering a succession of fine days; when Françoise, desperate because not a single drop of water had fallen on the "poor crops," and seeing only rare white clouds swimming on the calm blue surface of the sky, exclaimed with a moan: "Why, they look just like a lot of dog-fishes playing about up yonder showing us their muzzles! Ah, they never think to make it rain a little for the poor farmers! And then as soon as the wheat is well up, that's when the rain will begin to fall pit-a-pat pit-a-pat without a break, and think no more of where it's falling than if 'twas falling on the sea"; when my father had been given the same unvarying favorable responses by both the gardener and the barometer, then we would say over dinner: "Tomorrow, if the weather's the same, we'll go the Guermantes way." We would leave right after lunch by the little garden gate and we would tumble out into the rue des Perchamps, narrow and bent at a sharp angle and filled with different varieties of grasses among which two or three wasps would spend the day botanizing, a street as odd as its name, which it seemed to me was the source of its curious peculiarities and its cantankerous personality, a street one would seek in vain in Combray now, for on its old path the school now stands. But in my daydreams (like those architects, pupils of Viollet-le-Duc,[49] who, thinking they will find under a Renaissance rood screen or a seventeenth-century altar the traces of a Romanesque choir, restore the whole edifice to the state in which it must have been in the twelfth century) I do not leave one stone of the new structure standing, I pierce through it and "reinstate" the rue des Perchamps. And for these reconstructions I also have more precise data than restorers generally have: a few pictures preserved by my memory, perhaps the last still in existence now, and destined soon to be obliterated, of what Combray was during the time of my childhood; and, because Combray itself drew them in me before disappearing, they are as moving—if one may compare an obscure portrait to those glorious representations of which my grandmother liked to give me reproductions—as those old engravings of the Last Supper or that painting by Gentile Bellini, in which one sees, in a state in which they no longer exist, da Vinci's masterpiece and the portal of Saint Mark's.[50]

In the rue de l'Oiseau we would pass in front of the old Hôtellerie de Oiseau Flesché, which in the seventeenth century had sometimes seen in its great courtyard the coaches of the Duchesses de Montpensier, de Guermantes, and de Montmorency when they had to come to Combray for some dispute with their tenants or to accept their homage. We would reach the mall, among whose trees the Saint-Hilaire steeple would appear. And I would have liked to be able to sit down and stay there the whole day reading while I listened to the bells; because it was so lovely and tranquil that, when the hour rang, you would have said not that it broke the calm of the day, but that it relieved the day of what it contained and that the steeple, with the indolent, painstaking precision of a person who has nothing else to do, had merely—in order to squeeze out and let fall the few golden drops which had slowly and naturally collected there in the heat—pressed at the proper moment the fullness of the silence.

The greatest charm of the Guermantes way was that we had next to us, almost the whole time, the course of the Vivonne. We crossed it first, ten minutes after leaving the house, on a footbridge called the Pont-Vieux. The day after we arrived, following the sermon on Easter Sunday, if the weather was fine, I would run there to see, amid all the disorder that prevails on the morning of a great festival, when the sumptuous preparations make the household utensils that are still lying about appear more sordid than usual, the river already promenading along dressed in sky blue between lands still black and bare, accompanied only by a flock of cuckooflowers that had arrived early and primroses ahead of their time, while here and there a violet with a blue beak bowed its stem under the weight of the drop of fragrance it held in its throat. The Pont-Vieux led to a towpath which at this spot would be draped in summer with the blue foliage of a hazel under which a fisherman in a straw hat had taken root. In Combray, where I knew which particular farrier or grocer's boy was concealed within the verger's uniform or choirboy's surplice, this fisherman is the only person whose identity I never discovered. He must have known my parents, because he would raise his hat when we passed; I would then try to ask his name, but they would signal me to keep quiet so as not to frighten the fish. We would enter the towpath, which ran along an embankment a few feet above the stream; on the other side the bank was low, extending in vast meadows to the village and to the train station far away. They were strewn with the remains, half buried in the grass, of the château of the old counts of Combray, who during the Middle Ages had had the stream of the Vivonne as defense on this side against the attacks of the lords of Guermantes and the abbots of Martinville. These remains were now no more than a few fragments of towers embossing the grassland, barely apparent, a few battlements from which in the old days the crossbowman would hurl stones, from which the watchman would keep an eye on Novepont, Clairefontaine, Martinville-le-Sec, Bailleau-l'Exempt, all of them vassal lands of Guermantes among which Combray was enclosed, today level with the grass, gazed down upon by the children of the friars' school, who came here to learn their lessons or play at recreation time—a past that had almost descended into the earth, lying by the edge of the water like some hiker enjoying the cool air, but giving me a great deal to think about, making me add to the little town of today, under the name of Combray, a very different town, captivating my thoughts with its incomprehensible face of long ago, which it half concealed under the buttercups. There were a great many of them in this spot, which they had chosen for their games on the grass, solitary, in couples, in groups, yellow as the yellow of an egg, shining all the more, it seemed to me, because, since I could not channel the pleasure which the sight of them gave me into any impulse to taste them, I would let it accumulate in their golden surface, until it became potent enough to produce some useless beauty; and I did this starting from my earliest childhood, when I would stretch my arms out toward them from the towpath though I could not yet correctly spell their pretty name,⁵¹ the name of some prince from a French fairy tale, whereas perhaps they had come from Asia many centuries ago, but were now naturalized for good in the village, content with the modest horizon, liking the sun and the water's edge, faithful to the little view of the station, but still retaining, like some of our old paintings in their folksy simplicity, a poetic luster of the Orient.

I liked to look at the carafes which the boys put in the Vivonne to catch little fish, and which were filled by the river that in turn enclosed them, so that they became at once a "container" with transparent sides like hardened water and a "content" immersed in a larger container of coursing liquid crystal, and evoked the image of coolness more deliciously and vexingly than they would have done on a table laid for dinner, by showing it only in that perpetual alliterative flight between the water without consistency in which my hands could not capture it and the glass without fluidity in which my palate could not enjoy it. I promised myself I would return there later with some fishing lines; I persuaded them to take out a bit of bread from the provisions for our snack; I threw it into the Vivonne in pellets that seemed sufficient to provoke a phenomenon of supersaturation, for the water immediately solidified around them in ovoid clusters of starving tadpoles which until then it had no doubt been holding in solution, invisible, on the point of beginning to crystallize.

Soon the course of the Vivonne is obstructed by water plants. First they appear singly, like this water lily, for instance, which was allowed so little rest by the current in the midst of which it was unfortunately placed that, like a mechanically activated ferry boat, it would approach one bank only to return to the one from which it had come, eternally crossing back and forth again. Pushed toward the bank, its peduncle would unfold, lengthen, flow out, reach the extreme limit of its tension at the edge where the current would pick it up again, then the green cord would fold up on itself and bring the poor plant back to what may all the more properly be called its point of departure because it did not stay there a second without starting off from it again in a repetition of the same maneuver. I would find it again, walk after walk, always in the same situation, reminding me of certain neurasthenics among whose number my grandfather would count my aunt Léonie, who present year after year the unchanging spectacle of the bizarre habits they believe, each time, they are about to shake off and which they retain forever; caught in the machinery of their maladies and their manias, the efforts with which they struggle uselessly to abandon them only guarantee the functioning and activate the triggers of their strange, unavoidable, and morose regimes. This water lily was the same, and it was also like one of those miserable creatures whose singular torment, repeated indefinitely throughout eternity, aroused the curiosity of Dante, who would have asked the tormented creature himself to recount its cause and its particularities at greater length had Virgil, striding on ahead, not forced him to hurry after immediately, as my parents did me.

But farther on the current slows down, it crosses an estate to which access was opened to the public by the man who owned it, who had delighted in creating works of aquatic horticulture, turning the little pools formed by the Vivonne into true flowering gardens of white water lilies. Because the banks were heavily wooded here, the trees' great shadows gave the water a depth that was usually dark green although sometimes, when we came home on an evening that was calm again after a stormy afternoon, I saw that it was a light, raw blue verging on violet, cloisonné in appearance and Japanese in style. Here and there on the surface, the flower of a water lily blushed like a strawberry, with a scarlet heart, white on its edges. Farther off, the more numerous flowers were paler, less smooth, coarser-grained, creased, and grouped by chance in coils so graceful that one thought one saw, floating adrift as after the melancholy dismantling of some gay party, loosened garlands of moss roses. In another place one corner seemed reserved for the various common species, of a tidy white or pink like dame's rocket, washed clean like porcelain with housewifely care, while a little farther off, others, pressed against one another in a true floating flower border, suggested garden pansies that had come like butterflies to rest their glossy blue-tinged wings on the transparent obliquity of that watery bed; of that celestial bed as well: for it gave the flowers a soil of a color more precious, more affecting than the color of the flowers themselves; and, whether it sparkled beneath the water lilies in the afternoon in a kaleidoscope of silent, watchful, and mobile contentment, or whether toward evening it filled, like some distant port, with the rose and reverie of the sunset, ceaselessly changing so as to remain in harmony, around the more fixed colors of the corollas themselves, with all that is most profound, most fleeting, most mysterious—all that is infinite—in the hour, it seemed to have caused them to flower in the middle of the sky itself.

As it left this park, the Vivonne flowed freely again. How often did I see, and want to imitate, as soon as I should be at liberty to live as I chose, a rower who, having let go of his oars, had lain flat on his back, his head down, in the bottom of his boat, and allowing it to drift, seeing only the sky gliding slowly above him, bore on his face a foretaste of happiness and peace!

We would sit down among the irises at the edge of the water. One idle cloud would linger in the holiday sky. Now and then, oppressed by boredom, a carp would stand up from the water with an anxious gasp. It was time for our snack. Before starting off again we would stay there on the grass for a long time eating fruit, bread, and chocolate, and we would hear, coming all the way to us, horizontal, weakened, but still dense and metallic, the peals of the Saint Hilaire bell which had not melted into the air they had been traversing for so long and which, ribbed by the successive palpitation of all their waves of sound, vibrated as they brushed over the flowers, at our feet.

Sometimes, at the edge of the water and surrounded by woods, we would come upon what is called a "vacation house,"[52] isolated and secluded, seeing nothing of the world but the river that bathed its feet. A young woman whose pensive face and elegant veils did not belong to this region and who had probably come to "bury herself" here, as the expression has it, to taste the bitter sweetness of feeling that her name, and more importantly the name of the one whose heart she had not been able to hold fast, were unknown here, stood framed in a window that did not allow her to look farther than the boat moored near the door. She would absently lift her eyes as she heard, behind the trees along the riverbank, the voices of people passing of whom, even before she glimpsed their faces, she could be certain that they had never known the faithless one nor ever would know him, that nothing in their past bore his imprint, that nothing in their future would have occasion to receive it. One sensed that, in her renunciation, she had deliberately withdrawn from places where she might at least have glimpsed the man she loved, in favor of these places which had never seen him. And I watched her, as she came back from some walk on a path along which she knew he would not pass, drawing from her resigned hands long gloves of a useless grace.

Never in our walk along the Guermantes way could we go as far as the sources of the Vivonne, of which I had often thought and which had in my mind an existence so abstract, so ideal, that I had been as surprised when I was told they could be found within the *département*, at a certain distance in miles from Combray, as I was the day I learned there was another precise spot on the earth where the opening lay, in ancient times, of the entrance to the Underworld. Never, either, could we go all the way to the end point that I would so much have liked to reach, all the way to Guermantes. I knew this was where the castellans, the Duc and Duchesse de Guermantes, lived, I knew they were real and presently existing figures, but when I thought about them, I pictured them to myself sometimes made of tapestry, like the Comtesse de Guermantes in our church's *Coronation of Esther*, sometimes in changing colors, like Gilbert the Bad in the stained-glass window where he turned from cabbage green to plum blue, depending on whether I was still in front of the holy water or was reaching our seats, sometimes completely impalpable like the image of Geneviève de Brabant, ancestor of the Guermantes family, which our magic lantern sent wandering over the curtains of my room or up to the ceiling—but always wrapped in the mystery of Merovingian times and bathing as though in a sunset in the orange light emanating from that syllable *antes*. But if despite this they were, as duke and duchess, real human beings for me, even if strange ones, on the other hand their ducal person was inordinately distended, became immaterial, in order to contain within itself this Guermantes of which they were duke and duchess, all this sunlit "Guermantes way," the course of the Vivonne, its water lilies and its tall trees, and so many lovely afternoons. And I knew that they did not merely bear the title of Duc and Duchesse de Guermantes, but that since the fourteenth century when, after uselessly trying to defeat its former lords, they had formed an alliance with them through marriages, they were also Comtes de Combray, and thus the foremost citizens of Combray, and yet the only ones who did not live there. Comtes de Combray, possessing Combray in the midst of their name, of their person, and no doubt actually having within them that strange and pious sadness that was special to Combray; proprietors in the town, but not of a private house, probably dwelling outdoors, in the street, between sky and earth, like Gilbert de Guermantes, of whom I could see, in the windows of the apse of Saint-Hilaire, only the reverse side, of black lake, if I raised my head as I went to get salt at Camus's.

And along the Guermantes way I would sometimes pass damp little enclosures over which climbed clusters of dark flowers. I would stop, thinking I was about to acquire some precious idea, because it seemed to me that there before my eyes I possessed a fragment of that fluvial region I had so much wanted to know ever since I had seen it described by one of my favorite writers. And it was with this, with its imaginary ground traversed by currents of seething water, that Guermantes, changing its appearance in my mind, was identified when I heard Dr. Percepied talk to us about the flowers and beautiful spring waters that could be seen in the park of their country house. I dreamed that Mme. de Guermantes had summoned me there, smitten with a sudden fancy for me; all day long she would fish for trout with me. And in the evening, holding me by the hand as we walked past the little gardens of her vassals, she would show me the flowers that leaned their violet and red stems along the low walls, and would teach me their names. She would make me tell her the subjects of the poems that I intended to compose. And these dreams warned me that since I wanted to be a writer someday, it was time to find out what I meant to write. But as soon as I asked myself this, trying to find a subject in which I could anchor some infinite philosophical meaning, my mind would stop functioning, I could no longer see anything but empty space before my attentive eyes, I felt that I had no talent or perhaps a disease of the brain kept it from being born. Sometimes I counted on my father to make it all come out right. He was so powerful, in such favor with people in office, that he had succeeded in having us transgress the laws that Françoise had taught me to consider more ineluctable than the laws of life and death, to procure for our house alone, in the whole neighborhood, a year's postponement of the work of "replastering," to obtain permission from the minister for Mme. Sazerat's son, who wanted to go take the waters, to pass his *baccalauréat* two months ahead of time, in the series of candidates whose names began with *A,* instead of waiting for the turn of the *S*s. If I had fallen seriously ill, if I had been captured by bandits, convinced that my father was in too close communication with the supreme powers, had letters of recommendation to the Good Lord too irresistible for my illness or captivity to be anything but empty simulacra that posed no danger to me, I would have waited calmly for the inevitable hour of my return to the correct reality, the hour of my rescue or recovery; perhaps my lack of talent, the black hole that opened in my mind when I looked for the subject of my future writings, was also merely an illusion without substance, and this illusion would cease through the intervention of my father, who must have agreed with the government and Providence that I would be the foremost writer of the day. But at other times, as my parents grew impatient at the sight of me lingering behind and not following them, my present life, instead of seeming to me an artificial creation of my father's that he could modify as he liked, appeared to me on the contrary to be included in a reality that had not been made for me, against which there was no recourse, within which I had no ally, which concealed nothing beyond itself. At those times it seemed to me that I existed the same way other men did, that I would grow old, that I would die like them, and that among them I was simply one of those who have no aptitude for writing. And so, discouraged, I would give up literature forever, despite the encouragement I had been given by Bloch. This intimate, immediate awareness I had of the worthlessness of my ideas prevailed against all the praise that might be heaped on me, as do, in a wicked man whose good deeds are universally commended, the qualms of his conscience.

One day my mother said to me: "You're always talking about Mme. de Guermantes. Well, because Dr. Percepied took such good care of her four years ago she's coming to Combray to attend his daughter's wedding. You'll be able to see her at the ceremony." It was from Dr. Percepied, in fact, that I had heard the most talk about Mme. de Guermantes, and he had even shown us an issue of an illustrated magazine in which she was depicted in the costume she wore to a fancy-dress ball at the home of the Princesse de Léon.

Suddenly during the wedding service, a movement made by the verger as he shifted his position allowed me to see, sitting in a chapel, a blond lady with a large nose, piercing blue eyes, a full tie of smooth, shiny, new mauve silk, and a little pimple at the corner of her nose. And because on the surface of her face, which was red, as though she were very warm, I could distinguish bits of resemblance, diluted and barely perceptible, to the picture I had been shown, especially because the particular features that I observed in her, if I tried to enunciate them, were formulated in exactly the same words—a large nose, blue eyes—which Dr. Percepied had used when he described the Duchesse de Guermantes in my presence, I said to myself: "That lady looks like Mme. de Guermantes"; now the chapel where she was attending Mass was that of Gilbert the Bad, under the flat tombstones of which, golden and distended like cells of honey, rested the former counts of Brabant, and which, I recalled, was reserved, according to what I had been told, for the Guermantes family when any one of its members came to Combray for a ceremony; there probably could not be more than one woman who resembled Mme. de Guermantes's picture, who on that day, the very day when she was in fact supposed to come, was in that chapel: it was she! I was very disappointed. My disappointment came from the fact that I had never noticed, when I thought of Mme. de Guermantes, that I was picturing her to myself in the colors of a tapestry or a stained-glass window, in another century, of a material different from that of other living people. I had never realized that she might have a red face, a mauve tie like Mme. Sazerat, and the oval of her cheeks reminded me so much of people I had seen at our house that the suspicion touched me, dissipating immediately, however, that this lady, in her generative principle, in all her molecules, was perhaps not essentially the Duchesse de Guermantes, that instead, her body, unaware of the name applied to it, belonged to a certain female type that also included the wives of doctors and shopkeepers. "So that's Mme. de Guermantes—that's what she is, that's all she is!" said the attentive and astonished expression with which I contemplated an image of course quite unrelated to those which under the same name of Mme. de Guermantes had appeared so many times in my daydreams, since this one, this particular one, had not like the others been arbitrarily created by me, but had leaped to my eyes for the first time just a moment before, in the church; an image which was not of the same kind, was not colorable at will like those which had so readily absorbed the orange tint of a syllable, but was so real that everything, even the little pimple flaring up at the corner of her nose, attested to its subjection to the laws of life, just as, in a transformation scene in a theater, a fold of the fairy's dress, a trembling of her little finger, betray the physical presence of a living actress, whereas we had not been sure if we were not looking at a simple projection of light.

But at the same time, I was trying to apply to this image, which the prominent nose, the piercing eyes pinned into my vision (perhaps because it was they that had first reached it, that had made the first notch in it, at a moment when I had not yet had time to imagine that the woman who appeared before me could be Mme. de Guermantes), to this entirely recent, unchangeable image, the idea: "It's Mme. de Guermantes," without managing to do more than maneuver it in front of the image, like two disks separated by a gap. But this Mme. de Guermantes of whom I had so often dreamed, now that I could see that she actually existed outside of me, acquired from this an even greater power over my imagination, which, paralyzed for a moment by this contact with a reality so different from what it had expected, began to react and say to me: "Glorious since before Charlemagne, the Guermantes had the right of life and death over their vassals; the Duchesse de Guermantes is a descendant of Geneviève de Brabant. She does not know, nor would she consent to know, any of the people here."

And—oh, the marvelous independence of the human gaze, tied to the face by a cord so lax, so long, so extensible that it can travel out alone far away from it—while Mme. de Guermantes sat in the chapel above the tombs of her dead, her gaze strolled here and there, climbed up the pillars, paused even on me like a ray of sunlight wandering through the nave, but a ray of sunlight which, at the moment I received its caress, seemed to me conscious. As for Mme. de Guermantes herself, since she remained motionless, sitting there like a mother who does not appear to see the bold pranks and indiscreet enterprises of her children, who play and call out to people she does not know, it was impossible for me to tell if she approved or disapproved, in the idleness of her soul, of the vagabondage of her gaze.

I felt it was important that she not leave before I had looked at her enough, because I remembered that for years now I had considered the sight of her eminently desirable, and I did not detach my eyes from her, as if each gaze could physically carry away, and put in reserve inside me, the memory of that prominent nose, those red cheeks, all the particular details that seemed to me so many precious, authentic, and singular pieces of information about her face. Now that I was impelled to consider it beautiful by all the thoughts I had brought to bear on it—and perhaps most of all by what is a kind of instinct to preserve the best parts of ourselves, by the desire we always have not to be disappointed—placing her once again (since she and that Duchesse de Guermantes whom I had evoked until then were one and the same) above the rest of humanity among whom the pure and simple sight of her body had for a moment made me confound her, I was irritated to hear people around me say: "She's better looking than Mme. Sazerat, she's better looking than Mlle. Vinteuil," as if she were comparable to them. And as my gaze stopped at her blond hair, her blue eyes, the fastening of her collar, and omitted the features that might have reminded me of other faces, I exclaimed in front of this sketch, deliberately incomplete: "How beautiful she is! How noble! What I see before me is indeed a proud Guermantes and a descendant of Geneviève de Brabant!" And the attention with which I illuminated her face isolated her to such an extent that today, if I think back to that ceremony, it is impossible for me to see a single one of the people who were present except for her and the verger who responded affirmatively when I asked him if that lady was really Mme. de Guermantes. But I can still see her, especially at the moment when the procession entered the sacristy, which was lit by the hot and intermittent sun of a day of wind and storm, and in which Mme. de Guermantes found herself surrounded by all those people of Combray whose names she did not even know, but whose inferiority too loudly proclaimed her supremacy for her not to feel a sincere benevolence toward them, and whom, besides, she hoped to impress even more by her good grace and simplicity. Thus, not being able to bestow those deliberate gazes charged with specific meaning which we address to someone we know, but only to allow her distracted thoughts to break free incessantly before her in a wave of blue light which she could not contain, she did not want that wave to disturb or appear to disdain those common people whom it encountered in passing, whom it touched again and again. I can still see, above her silky, swelling mauve tie, the gentle surprise in her eyes, to which she had added, without daring to intend it for anyone but so that all might take their share of it, the slightly shy smile of a sovereign who looks as though she is apologizing to her vassals and loves them. That smile fell on me, who had not taken my eyes off her. Recalling, then, the gaze she had rested on me during the Mass, as blue as a ray of sunlight passing through Gilbert the Bad's window, I said to myself: "Why, she's actually paying attention to me." I believed that she liked me, that she would still be thinking of me after she had left the church, that because of me perhaps she would be sad that evening at Guermantes. And immediately I loved her, because if it may sometimes be enough for us to fall in love with a woman if she looks at us with contempt, as

I had thought Mlle. Swann had done, and if we think she will never belong to us, sometimes, too, it may be enough if she looks at us with kindness, as Mme. de Guermantes was doing, and if we think she may someday belong to us. Her eyes turned as blue as a periwinkle which was impossible to pick, yet which she had dedicated to me; and the sun, threatened by a cloud but still beating down with all its strength on the square and in the sacristy, gave a geranium flesh tint to the red carpets that had been laid on the ground for the solemnities and over which Mme. de Guermantes advanced smiling, and added to their woolly weave a rosy velvet, an epidermis of light, the sort of tenderness, the sort of grave sweetness amid pomp and joy that characterize certain pages of *Lohengrin*,[53] certain paintings by Carpaccio,[54] and that explain why Baudelaire[55] was able to apply to the sound of the trumpet the epithet *delicious.*

How much more distressing still, after that day, during my walks along the Guermantes way, did it seem to me than it had seemed before to have no aptitude for literature, and to have to give up all hope of ever being a famous writer! The sorrow I felt over this, as I daydreamed alone, a little apart from the others, made me suffer so much that in order not to feel it anymore, my mind of its own accord, by a sort of inhibition in the face of pain, would stop thinking altogether about poems, novels, a poetic future on which my lack of talent forbade me to depend. Then, quite apart from all these literary preoccupations and not connected to them in any way, suddenly a roof, a glimmer of sun on a stone, the smell of the road would stop me because of a particular pleasure they gave me, and also because they seemed to be concealing, beyond what I could see, something which they were inviting me to come take and which despite my efforts I could not manage to discover. Since I felt that it could be found within them, I would stay there, motionless, looking, breathing, trying to go with my thoughts beyond the image or the smell. And if I had to catch up with my grandfather, continue on my way, I would try to find them again by closing my eyes; I would concentrate on recalling precisely the line of the roof, the shade of the stone which, without my being able to understand why, had seemed to me so full, so ready to open, to yield me the thing for which they themselves were merely a cover. Of course it was not impressions of this kind that could give me back the hope I had lost, of succeeding in becoming a writer and a poet someday, because they were always tied to a particular object with no intellectual value and no reference to any abstract truth. But at least they gave me an unreasoning pleasure, the illusion of a sort of fecundity, and so distracted me from the tedium, from the sense of my own impotence which I had felt each time I looked for a philosophical subject for a great literary work. But so arduous was the task imposed on my consciousness by the impressions I received from form, fragrance or color—to try to perceive what was concealed behind them—that I would soon look for excuses that would allow me to save myself from this effort and spare myself this fatigue. Fortunately, my parents would call me, I would feel I did not have the tranquillity I needed at the moment for pursuing my search in a useful way, and that it would be better not to think about it anymore until I was back at home, and not to fatigue myself beforehand to no purpose. And so I would stop concerning myself with this unknown thing that was enveloped in a form or a fragrance, feeling quite easy in my mind since I was bringing it back to the house protected by the covering of images under which I would find it alive, like the fish that, on days when I had been allowed to go fishing, I would carry home in my creel covered by a layer of grass that kept them fresh. Once I was back at the house I would think about other things, and so there would accumulate in my mind (as in my room the flowers I had gathered on my walks or objects I had been given) a stone on which a glimmer of light played, a roof, the sound of a bell, a smell of leaves, many different images beneath which the reality I sensed but did not have enough determination to discover had died long before. Once, however—when our walk had extended far beyond its usual duration and we were very happy to encounter halfway home, as the afternoon was ending, Dr. Percepied, who, going past at full speed in his carriage, recognized us and invited us to climb in with him—I had an impression of this kind and did not abandon it without studying it a little. They had had me climb up next to the coachman, we were going like the wind because, before returning to Combray, the doctor still had to stop at Martinville-le-Sec to see a patient at whose door it had been agreed that we would wait for him. At the bend of a road I suddenly experienced that special pleasure which was unlike any other, when I saw the two steeples of Martinville, shining in the setting sun and appearing to change position with the motion of our carriage and the windings of the road, and then the steeple of Vieuxvicq, which, though separated from them by a hill and a valley and situated on a higher plateau in the distance, seemed to be right next to them.

As I observed, as I noted the shape of their spires, the shifting of their lines, the sunlight on their surfaces, I felt that I was not reaching the full depth of my impression, that something was behind that motion, that brightness, something which they seemed at once to contain and conceal.

The steeples appeared so distant, and we seemed to approach them so slowly, that I was surprised when we stopped a few moments later in front of the Martinville church. I did not know why I had taken such pleasure in the sight of them on the horizon and the obligation to try to discover the reason seemed to me quite painful; I wanted to hold in reserve in my head those lines moving in the sun, and not think about them anymore now. And it is quite likely that had I done so, the two steeples would have gone forever to join the many trees, rooftops, fragrances, sounds, that I had distinguished from others because of the obscure pleasure they gave me which I never thoroughly studied. I got down to talk to my parents while we waited for the doctor. Then we set off again, I was back in my place on the seat, I turned my head to see the steeples again, a little later glimpsing them one last time at a bend in the road. Since the coachman, who did not seem inclined to talk, had hardly answered anything I said, I was obliged, for lack of other company, to fall back on my own and try to recall my steeples. Soon their lines and their sunlit surfaces split apart, as if they were a sort of bark, a little of what was hidden from me inside them appeared to me, I had a thought which had not existed a moment before, which took shape in words in my head, and the pleasure I had just recently experienced at the sight of them was so increased by this that, seized by a sort of drunkenness, I could no longer think of anything else. At that moment, as we were already far away from Martinville, turning my head I caught sight of them again, quite black this time, for the sun had already set. At moments the bends of the road would hide them from me, then they showed themselves one last time, and finally I did not see them again.

Without saying to myself that what was hidden behind the steeples of Martinville had to be something analogous to a pretty sentence, since it had appeared to me in the form of words that gave me pleasure, I asked the doctor for a pencil and some paper and I composed, despite the jolts of the carriage, and in order to ease my conscience and yield to my enthusiasm, the following little piece that I have since found again and that I have not had to submit to more than a few changes:

"Alone, rising from the level of the plain, and appearing lost in the open country, the two steeples of Martinville ascended toward the sky. Soon we saw three: wheeling around boldly to position itself opposite them, the laggard steeple of Vieuxvicq had come along to join them. The minutes were passing, we were going fast, and yet the three steeples were still far away ahead of us, like three birds poised on the plain, motionless, distinguishable in the sunlight. Then the steeple of Vieuxvicq moved away, receded into the distance, and the steeples of Martinville remained alone, illuminated by the light of the setting sun, which even at that distance I saw playing and smiling on their sloping sides. We had taken so long approaching them that I was thinking about the time we would still need in order to reach them, when suddenly the carriage turned and set us down at their feet; and they had flung themselves so roughly in front of it that we had only just time to stop in order not to run into the porch. We continued on our way; we had already left Martinville a little while before, and the village, after accompanying us for a few seconds, had disappeared, when, lingering alone on the horizon to watch us flee, its steeples and that of Vieuxvicq still waved good-bye with their sunlit tops. At times one of them would draw aside so that the other two could glimpse us again for an instant; but the road changed direction, they swung around in the light like three golden pivots and disappeared from my gaze. But a little later, when we were already close to Combray, and the sun had set, I caught sight of them one last time from very far away, seeming now no more than three flowers painted on the sky above the low line of the fields. They reminded me, too, of the three young girls in a legend, abandoned in a solitary place where darkness was already falling; and while we moved off at a gallop, I saw them timidly seek their way and, after some awkward stumbling of their noble silhouettes, press against one another, slip behind one another, now forming, against the still pink sky, no more than a single black shape, charming and resigned, and fade away into the night." I never thought of this page again, but at that moment, when in the corner of the seat where the doctor's coachman usually placed in a basket the poultry he had bought at the market in Martinville, I had finished writing it, I was so happy, I felt it had so perfectly relieved me of those steeples and what they had been hiding behind them, that, as if I myself were a hen and had just laid an egg, I began to sing at the top of my voice.

All day long, during those walks, I had been able to dream about what a pleasure it would be to be a friend of the Duchesse de Guermantes, to fish for trout, to go out in a boat on the Vivonne, and, greedy for happiness, ask no more from life in those moments than for it always to be made up of a succession of happy afternoons. But when on the way back I saw on the left a farm which was fairly distant from two others very close to each other, and from which, in order to enter Combray, one had only to go down an avenue of oaks bordered on one side by meadows, each of which was part of a little enclosure and was planted at equal intervals with apple trees that wore, when they were lit by the setting sun, the Japanese design of their shadows, my heart would abruptly begin to beat faster, I would know that within half an hour we would be home and that, as was the rule on the days when we had gone the Guermantes way and dinner was served later, they would send me to bed as soon as I had had my soup, so that my mother, kept at the table as though there were company for dinner, would not come up to say goodnight to me in my bed.

The region of sadness I had just entered was as distinct from the region into which I had hurled myself with such joy only a moment before, as in certain skies a band of pink is separated as though by a line from a band of green or black. One sees a bird fly into the pink, it is about to reach the end of it, it is nearly touching the black, then it has entered it. The desires that had surrounded me a short time ago, to go to Guermantes, to travel, to be happy, were so far behind me now that their fulfillment would not have brought me any pleasure. How I would have given all that up in order to be able to cry all night in Mama's arms! I was trembling, I did not take my anguished eyes off my mother's face, which would not be appearing that evening in the room where I could already see myself in my thoughts, I wanted to die. And that state of mind would continue until the following day, when the morning rays, like the gardener, would lean their bars against the wall clothed in nasturtiums that climbed up to my window, and I would jump out of bed to hurry down into the garden, without remembering, now, that evening would ever bring back with it the hour for leaving my mother. And so it was from the Guermantes way that I learned to distinguish those states of mind that follow one another in me, during certain periods, and that even go so far as to share out each day among them, one returning to drive out the other, with the punctuality of a fever; contiguous, but so exterior to one another, so lacking in means of communication among them, that I can no longer comprehend, no longer even picture to myself in one, what I desired, or dreaded, or accomplished in the other.

And so the Méséglise way and the Guermantes way remain for me linked to many of the little events of that life which, of all the various lives we lead concurrently, is the most abundant in vicissitudes, the richest in episodes, I mean our intellectual life. No doubt it progresses within us imperceptibly, and the truths that have changed its meaning and its appearance for us, that have opened new paths to us, we had been preparing to discover for a long time; but we did so without knowing it; and for us they date only from the day, from the minute in which they became visible. The flowers that played on the grass then, the water that flowed past in the sunlight, the whole landscape that surrounded their appearance continues to accompany the memory of them with its unconscious or abstracted face; and certainly when they were slowly studied by that humble passerby, that child dreaming—as a king is studied by a memorialist lost in the crowd—that corner of nature, that bit of garden could not have believed it would be thanks to him that they would be elected to survive in all their most ephemeral details; and yet the fragrance of hawthorn that forages along the hedge where the sweetbriers will soon replace it, a sound of echoless steps on the gravel of a path, a bubble formed against a water plant by the current of the stream and bursting immediately—my exaltation has borne them along with it and managed to carry them across so many years in succession, while the paths round about have disappeared and those who walked on them have died, and the memory of those who walked on them. At times the piece of landscape thus transported into the present detaches itself in such isolation from everything else that it floats uncertain in my mind like a flowery Delos,[56] while I cannot say from which country, which time—perhaps quite simply which dream—it comes. But it is most especially as deep layers of my mental soil, as the firm ground on which I still stand, that I must think of the Méséglise way and the Guermantes way. It is because I believed in things and in people while I walked along them, that the things and people they revealed to me are the only ones that I still take seriously today and that still bring me joy. Whether it is that the faith which creates has dried up in me, or that reality takes shape in memory alone, the flowers I am shown today for the first time do not seem to me to be real flowers. The Méséglise way with its lilacs, its hawthorns, its cornflowers, its poppies, its apple trees, the Guermantes way with its river full of tadpoles, its water lilies and buttercups, formed for me for all time the contours of the countrysides where I would like to live, where I demand above all else that I may go fishing, drift about in a boat, see ruins of Gothic fortifications, and find among the wheat fields a church, like Saint-André-des-Champs, monumental, rustic, and golden as a haystack; and the cornflowers, the hawthorns, the apple trees that I still happen, when traveling, to come upon in the fields, because they are situated at the same depth, on the level of my past, communicate immediately with my heart. And yet, because places have something individual about them, when I am seized by the desire to see the Guermantes way again, you would not satisfy it by taking me to the bank of a river where the water lilies were just as beautiful, more beautiful than in the Vivonne, any more than on my return home in the evening—at the hour when there awakened in me that anguish which later emigrates into love, and may become forever inseparable from it—I would have wished that the mother who came to say goodnight to me would be one more beautiful and more intelligent than my own. No; just as what I needed so that I could go to sleep happy, with that untroubled peace which no mistress has been able to give me since that time because one doubts them even at the moment one believes in them, and can never possess their hearts as I received in a kiss my mother's heart, complete, without the reservation of an afterthought, without the residue of an intention that was not for me—was that it should be her, that she should incline over me that face marked below the eye by something which was, it seems, a blemish, and which I loved as much as the rest, so what I want to see again is the Guermantes way that I knew, with the farm that is not very far from the two that come after pressed so close together, at the entrance to the avenue of oaks; those meadows on which, when the sun turns them reflective as a pond, the leaves of the apple trees are sketched, that landscape whose individuality sometimes, at night in my dreams, clasps me with an almost uncanny power and which I can no longer recover when I wake up. No doubt, by virtue of having forever indissolubly united in me different impressions merely because they had made me experience them at the same time, the Méséglise way and the Guermantes way exposed me, for the future, to many disappointments and even to many mistakes. For often I have wanted to see a person again without discerning that it was simply because she reminded me of a hedge of hawthorns, and I have been led to believe, to make someone else believe, in a revival of affection, by what was simply a desire to travel. But because of that very fact, too, and by persisting in those of my impressions of today to which they may be connected, they give them foundations, depth, a dimension lacking from the others. They add to them, too, a charm, a meaning that is for me alone. When on summer evenings the melodious sky growls like a wild animal and everyone grumbles at the storm, it is because of the Méséglise way that I am the only one in ecstasy inhaling, through the noise of the falling rain, the smell of invisible, enduring lilacs.

Thus I would often lie until morning thinking back to the time at Combray, to my sad sleepless evenings, to the many days, too, whose image had been restored to me more recently by the taste—what they would have called at Combray the "fragrance"—of a cup of tea, and, by an association of memories, to what, many years after leaving that little town, I had learned, about a love affair Swann had had before I was born, with that precision of detail which is sometimes easier to obtain for the lives of people who died centuries ago than for the lives of our best friends, and which seems as impossible as it once seemed impossible to speak from one town to another—as long as we do not know about the expedient by which that impossibility was circumvented. All these memories added to one another now formed a single mass, but one could still distinguish between them—between the oldest, and those that were more recent, born of a fragrance, and then those that were only memories belonging to another person from whom I had learned them—if not fissures, if not true faults, at least that veining, that variegation of coloring, which in certain rocks, in certain marbles, reveal differences in origin, in age, in "formation."

Of course by the time morning approached, the brief uncertainty of my waking would long since have dissipated. I knew which room I was actually in, I had reconstructed it around me in the darkness and—either by orienting myself with memory alone, or by making use, as a clue, of a faint glimmer that I perceived, under which I placed the casement curtains—I had reconstructed it entirely and furnished it like an architect and a decorator who retain the original openings of the windows and doors, I had put back the mirrors and restored the chest of drawers to its usual place. But scarcely had the daylight—and no longer the reflection of a last ember on the brass curtain rod which I had mistaken for it—traced on the darkness, as though in chalk, its first white, correcting ray, than the window along with its curtains would leave the doorframe in which I had mistakenly placed it, while, to make room for it, the desk which my memory had clumsily moved there would fly off at top speed, pushing the fireplace before it and thrusting aside the wall of the passageway; a small courtyard would extend in the spot where only a moment before the dressing room had been, and the dwelling I had rebuilt in the darkness would have gone off to join the dwellings glimpsed in the maelstrom of my awakening, put to flight by the pale sign traced above the curtains by the raised finger of the dawn.

PART II

Swann in Love

To BELONG TO the "little set," the "little circle," the "little clan" attached to the Verdurins, one condition was sufficient but necessary: You had to abide tacitly by a Credo one of whose articles was that the young pianist patronized by Mme. Verdurin that year, of whom she would say: "It ought to be against the law to be able to play Wagner like that!," "was miles above" both Planté[1] and Rubinstein[2] and that Dr. Cottard was a better diagnostician than Potain.[3] Any "new recruit" who could not be persuaded by the Verdurins that the soirées given by people who did not come to the Verdurins' house were as tiresome as rain was immediately excluded. Because the women were more rebellious in this respect than the men when it came to setting aside their curiosity about society, their desire to find out for themselves how amusing the other salons might be, and because the Verdurins felt that this spirit of investigation and this demon of frivolity could in fact be fatally contagious to the orthodoxy of the little church, they had been led to expel one after another all the "faithful" of the female sex.

Apart from the doctor's young wife, they were reduced almost exclusively that year (even though Mme. Verdurin herself was virtuous and from a respectable bourgeois family, an extremely rich and entirely obscure one with which she had by degrees and of her own accord ceased to have any contact) to a person almost of the demimonde, Mme. de Crécy, whom Mme. Verdurin called by her first name, Odette, and declared to be "a love," and to the pianist's aunt, who must once have been employed as a caretaker; both of them being women ignorant of the world whom, in their naïveté, it had been so easy to delude into believing that the Princesse de Sagan and the Duchesse de Guermantes were obliged to pay certain poor wretches in order to have any guest at their dinners, that if you had offered to get them invitations to the homes of these two great ladies, the former concierge and the cocotte would disdainfully have refused.

The Verdurins did not invite you to dinner: you had, at their house, a "place set for you." For the soirée there was no program. The young pianist would play, but only if "he fancied," because they did not force anyone and, as M. Verdurin said: "Anything for our friends. Here's to friendship!" If the pianist wanted to play the ride from *The Valkyrie* or the prelude from *Tristan*,[4] Mme. Verdurin would protest, not because she did not like that music, but on the contrary because it made too strong an impression on her. "Then you want me to have one of my migraines? You know perfectly well the same thing happens every time he plays that. I can count on it! Tomorrow when I try to get up—that's it, not possible!" If he did not play, people would chat and one of the friends, most often their favorite painter at the time, would "spin," as M. Verdurin said, "a damn funny tale that would make 'em all shriek with laughter," especially Mme. Verdurin, for such was her habit of taking literally the figurative expressions for the emotions she was feeling that Dr. Cottard (a young novice at the time) would one day have to set her jaw after she dislocated it from laughing too much.

Evening clothes were forbidden because one was "among friends" and also so as not to look like the "bores" whom they avoided like the plague and invited only to the larger soirées, given as rarely as possible and only if it might amuse the painter or help to promote the musician. The rest of the time, they were content to play charades, have supper in fancy dress, but only among themselves, not mixing any strangers in with the little "clan."

But as the "pals" had assumed more of a place in Mme. Verdurin's life, the "bores," the "pariahs" were anything that kept the friends away from her, anything that now and then kept them from being free, whether it was the mother of one, the profession of another, the country house or the bad health of a third. If Dr. Cottard thought he ought to leave just after he got up from the table in order to return to a patient who was dangerously ill, "Who knows," Mme. Verdurin would say to him, "he might be better off if you don't go disturbing him again this evening; without you, he'll have a good night; tomorrow morning early you'll go there and find him quite recovered." At the beginning of December, she would be sick at the thought that the faithful would "let them down" on Christmas Day and the first of January. The pianist's aunt insisted that he come to dinner with the family that day at her mother's home:

"You seem to think your mother might die," Mme. Verdurin exclaimed harshly, "if you don't have dinner with her on New Year's Day the way they do in the *provinces!*"

Her worries revived during Holy Week:

"Doctor, since you're such a scholar and freethinker, may I assume you will be coming on Good Friday just as you would on any other day?" she said confidently to Cottard the first year, as if she were sure what the answer would be. But she trembled as she waited for him to utter it, because if he did not come, she might find herself alone.

"I will come on Good Friday . . . to say good-bye to you, because we're going to be spending the Easter holiday in Auvergne."

"In Auvergne? You'll be eaten alive by fleas and vermin! Much good may it do you!"

And after a silence:

"If only you had told us, we would have tried to organize something; we could have made the trip together in comfort."

Likewise, if one of the "faithful" had a friend or if one of the ladies had a beau who might make them "desert" occasionally, the Verdurins, who were not afraid of a woman having a lover provided she had him at their house, loved him in their midst, and did not prefer his company to theirs, would say: "Well, bring your friend along!" And they would engage him on trial, to see if he was capable of having no secrets from Mme. Verdurin, if he was worthy of being enrolled in the "little clan." If he was not, the "regular" who had introduced him would be taken aside and helped to break with his friend or his mistress. In the opposite case, the "newcomer" would in his turn become one of the faithful. And so when, that year, the demimondaine told M. Verdurin she had made the acquaintance of a charming man, M. Swann, and insinuated that he would be very pleased to be received at their home, M. Verdurin transmitted the request to his wife then and there. (He never formed an opinion until she had formed hers, his particular role being to carry out her wishes, along with those of the faithful, with great and resourceful ingenuity.)

"My dear, Mme. de Crécy has something to ask you. She would like to introduce one of her friends to you, a M. Swann. What do you think?"

"Well, now, who could refuse anything to a little angel like that? Quiet, no one asked your opinion. I tell you you're an angel."

"Well, if you say so," answered Odette in a mincing tone, and she added: "You know I'm not *fishing for compliments.*"⁵

"All right! Bring your friend, if he's nice."

Of course the "little clan" had no connection to the society in which Swann moved, and true men of fashion would have felt there was little point in enjoying, as he did, an exceptional position only to end up with an introduction to the Verdurins. But Swann was so fond of women that once he had come to know more or less all the women in aristocratic circles and they had nothing more to teach him, he had ceased to regard those naturalization papers, almost a patent of nobility, which the Faubourg Saint-Germain had bestowed upon him, except as a sort of negotiable bond, a letter of credit with no value in itself but which allowed him to improvise a status for himself in some little provincial hole or obscure circle of Paris where the daughter of a squire or clerk had struck him as pretty. For at such times desire or love would revive in him a feeling of vanity from which he was now quite free in his everyday life (although it was doubtless this feeling that had originally pointed him toward the career as man of fashion in which he had wasted his intellectual gifts in frivolous pleasures and allowed his erudition in matters of art to be used to advise society ladies what pictures to buy and how to decorate their houses), and which made him want to shine, in the eyes of any unknown woman with whom he was infatuated, with an elegance which the name Swann in itself did not imply. He wanted this most especially if the unknown woman was in humble circumstances. Just as it is not by another man of intelligence that an intelligent man will be afraid of being thought stupid, so it is not by a great lord but by a country bumpkin that a man of fashion will be afraid of seeing his elegance go unappreciated. Three-quarters of the expenditure of wit and the lies told out of vanity that have been squandered since the world began by people who in doing so merely diminish themselves have been squandered on inferiors. And though Swann was unaffected and casual with a duchess, he trembled at being scorned by a chambermaid, and posed in front of her.

He was not like so many people who from laziness or a resigned sense of the obligation created by social grandeur to remain moored to a certain shore, abstain from the pleasures real life offers them outside the high-society position in which they live billeted and encamped until their death, contenting themselves in the end with describing as pleasures, for lack of any better, once they have managed to become used to them, the mediocre amusements or bearable tedium it contains. Swann did not try to convince himself that the women with whom he spent his time were pretty, but to spend his time with women he already knew were pretty. And these were often women of a rather vulgar beauty, for the physical qualities that he looked for without realizing it were the direct opposite of those he admired in the women sculpted or painted by his favorite masters. Depth of expression, melancholy, would freeze his senses, which were, however, immediately aroused by flesh that was healthy, plump, and pink.

If when travelling he met a family whom it would have been more stylish not to seek to cultivate, but in which one woman presented herself to his eyes adorned with a charm he had never experienced before, to "stand on his dignity" and cheat the desire she had awoken in him, to substitute a different pleasure for the pleasure he might have experienced with her, by writing to a former mistress to come and join him, would have seemed to him as cowardly an abdication before life, as stupid a renunciation of a new happiness as if instead of touring the countryside, he had shut himself up in his room and looked at pictures of Paris. He did not enclose himself in the edifice of his relationships, but had transformed that edifice, in order to be able to raise it again effortlessly on site wherever he found a woman who pleased him, into one of those collapsible tents of the kind explorers carry with them. As for what was not transportable or exchangeable for a new pleasure, he would have given it away for nothing, however enviable it might appear to others. How often had his credit with a duchess, built up from the desire she had been accumulating over the years to do something kind for him without having found the occasion, been spent all at once by his sending her an indiscreet message asking for a recommendation by telegraph that would put him in touch, immediately, with one of her stewards whose daughter he had noticed in the country, just as a starving man would barter a diamond for a piece of bread! He had even, after the fact, been amused by it, for there existed in him, compensated for by uncommon refinements, a certain boorishness. Then, too, he belonged to that category of intelligent men who have lived idle lives and who seek a consolation and perhaps an excuse in the idea that this idleness offers their intelligence objects just as worthy of interest as art or scholarship could offer, that "Life" contains situations more interesting, more novelistic than any novel. So he declared, at least, and easily convinced even the sharpest of his society friends, in particular the Baron de Charlus, whom he liked to entertain with tales of the racy adventures he had had, such as when he had met a woman on the railway train and afterward taken her back home with him, and then discovered that she was the sister of a monarch who at that time held in his hands all the mingled threads of European politics, thus finding he was kept abreast of them in a most agreeable way, or when, through a complex play of circumstances, the choice about to be made by the conclave[6] was going to determine whether or not he succeeded in sleeping with somebody's cook.

And it was not only the brilliant phalanx of virtuous dowagers, generals, and academicians with whom he was particularly close, whom Swann compelled with such cynicism to serve him as go-betweens. All his friends were used to receiving periodic letters from him in which a word of recommendation or introduction was asked of them with a diplomatic skill that, persisting as it did through his successive love affairs and different pretexts, revealed, more than moments of awkwardness would have done, a permanent trait in his character and an unvarying quest. I often asked to hear, many years later when I began to take an interest in his character because of the resemblances it offered to my own in completely different respects, how when he wrote to my grandfather (who was not my grandfather yet, for it was about the time of my birth that Swann's great love affair began, and it interrupted these habits for a long time), the latter, recognizing his friend's handwriting on the envelope, would exclaim: "It's Swann, about to ask for something: on guard!" And either from mistrust, or from the unconsciously diabolical spirit that incites us to offer a thing only to the people who do not want it, my grandparents would issue a blunt refusal to the most easily satisfied requests he addressed to them, as for instance to introduce him to a girl who dined at the house every Sunday, and whom they were obliged, each time Swann mentioned it to them again, to pretend they were no longer seeing, whereas all week long they would wonder who in the world they could invite with her, often finding no one in the end, because they would not ask the one who would have been so happy to come.

Sometimes a certain couple, friends of my grandparents who until then had complained of never seeing Swann, would announce to them with satisfaction and perhaps a little desire to arouse their envy that he had become as charming as could be, that he was never out of their house. My grandfather did not want to cloud their pleasure but would look at my grandmother and hum:

> What is then this mystery?
> I cannot understand.[7]

or:

> Fleeting vision . . .[8]

or:

In these affairs
'Tis better to be blind.⁹

A few months later, if my grandfather asked Swann's new friend: "And Swann—do you still see as much of him as ever?" the face of the man he was talking to would grow long: "Never mention his name to me again!" "But I thought you were so close . . ." For several months he had, for instance, been intimate friends with cousins of my grandmother, dining almost every day at their house. Suddenly, and without letting them know, he stopped coming. They thought he was ill, and my grandmother's cousin was about to send word asking for news of him, when in the pantry she found a letter from him left inadvertently in the cook's account book. In it he told the woman he was leaving Paris, that he would not be able to continue seeing her. She was his mistress, and when he broke it off with her, she was the only one he thought he needed to tell.

But when his mistress of the moment was a woman of rank or at least one whose background was not too humble or her situation too irregular for him to arrange for her to be received in society, then for her he would return to it, but only to the particular orbit in which she moved or into which he had drawn her. "No use depending on Swann for this evening," they would say. "Don't you remember? It's his American's night at the Opera." He would see to it that she was invited to the particularly exclusive salons where he was a constant guest, where he had his weekly dinners, his poker; every evening, after a slight crimp was added to the brush cut of his red hair, tempering with some gentleness the vivacity of his green eyes, he would choose a flower for his buttonhole and go off to join his mistress at dinner at the home of one or another of the women of his circle; and then, thinking of the admiration and affection which the fashionable people for whom he was the be-all and end-all and whom he was going to see there would lavish on him in the presence of the woman he loved, he would once again find some charm in this worldly life to which he had become indifferent but whose substance, penetrated and warmly colored by a flame that had been insinuated into it and flickered there, seemed to him precious and beautiful as soon as he had incorporated into it a new love.

But, while each of these love affairs, or each of these flirtations, had been the more or less complete fulfillment of a dream inspired by the sight of a face or body that Swann had spontaneously, without making any effort to do so, found charming, on the contrary when he was introduced to Odette de Crécy one day at the theater by an old friend of his, who had spoken of her as an entrancing woman with whom he might perhaps have some success, but making her out to be more difficult than she really was in order to appear to have done him a bigger favor by introducing her to him, she had seemed to Swann not without beauty, certainly, but of a type of beauty that left him indifferent, that aroused no desire in him, even caused him a sort of physical repulsion, one of those women such as everyone has his own, different for each, who are the opposite of the kind our senses crave. Her profile was too pronounced for his taste, her skin too delicate, her cheekbones too prominent, her features too pinched. Her eyes were lovely, but so large they bent under their own mass, exhausted the rest of her face, and always gave her a look of being in ill health or ill humor. Sometime after this introduction at the theater she had written to ask if she could see his collections, which interested her so, "she, an ignoramus with a taste for pretty things," saying that it seemed to her she would understand him better when she had seen him in "his home,"[10] where she imagined him to be "so comfortable with his tea and his books," though she had not hidden her surprise that he should live in that part of town, which must be so dreary and "which was so un-*smart* for a man who was so very smart himself." And after he had allowed her to come, as she left she had told him how sorry she was to have spent such a short time in a house that she had been so glad to enter, speaking of him as though he meant something more to her than the other people she knew, and seeming to establish between their two persons a sort of romantic bond that had made him smile. But at the age, already a little disillusioned, which Swann was approaching, at which one knows how to content oneself with being in love for the pleasure of it without requiring too much reciprocity, this closeness of two hearts, if it is no longer, as it was in one's earliest youth, the goal toward which love necessarily tends, still remains linked to it by an association of ideas so strong that it may become the cause of love, if it occurs first. At an earlier time one dreamed of possessing the heart of the woman with whom one was in love; later, to feel that one possesses a woman's heart may be enough to make one fall in love with her. And so, at an age when it would seem, since what one seeks most of all in love is subjective pleasure, that the enjoyment of a woman's beauty should play the largest part in it, love may come into being—love of the most physical kind—without there having been, underlying it, any previous desire. At this time of life, one has already been wounded many times by love; it no longer evolves solely in accordance with its own unknown and inevitable laws, before our astonished and passive heart. We come to its aid, we distort it with memory, with suggestion. Recognizing one of its symptoms, we recall and revive the others. Since we know its song, engraved in us in its entirety, we do not need a woman to repeat the beginning of it—filled with the admiration that beauty inspires—in order to find out what comes after. And if she begins in the middle—where the two hearts come together, where it sings of living only for each other—we are accustomed enough to this music to join our partner right away in the passage where she is waiting for us.

Odette de Crécy came to see Swann again, then visited him more and more often; and certainly each visit renewed the disappointment he felt at finding himself once again in the presence of that face whose details he had somewhat forgotten in the meantime and which he had not recalled as being either so expressive or, despite her youth, so faded; he felt sorry, as she talked to him, that her considerable beauty was not the type he would spontaneously have preferred. Odette's face seemed thinner and sharper, in fact, because her forehead and the upper part of her cheeks, those smoother and flatter surfaces, were covered by the masses of hair which women wore at that time drawn forward in fringes, lifted in "switches," spread in stray locks down along the ears; and as for her body, which was admirably formed, it was difficult to discern its continuity (because of the fashions of the period, and even though she was one of the best-dressed women in Paris), because her blouse, jutting out as though over an imaginary paunch and ending abruptly in a point, below which the balloon of the double skirts swelled out, made a woman look as though she were composed of different parts poorly fitted inside one another; because the flounces, the flutes, the vest followed so independently, according to the whimsy of their design or the consistency of their material, the line that led to the knots, the puffs of lace, the perpendicular fringes of jet, or that directed them along the corset, but were in no way attached to the living person, who, depending on whether the architecture of these frills and furbelows approached too closely or moved too far away from her own, was either encased or lost in them.

But when Odette had left, Swann would smile, thinking of how she had told him the time would drag until he allowed her to come again; he would recall the worried, shy air with which she had begged him once that it should not be too long, and the expression in her eyes at that moment, fastened on him in anxious entreaty, which made her look so touching under the bouquet of artificial pansies fastened to the front of her round white straw hat with its black velvet ribbons. "And you," she had said, "wouldn't you come to my house just once for tea?" He had pleaded unfinished work, a study—in reality abandoned years before—of Vermeer of Delft.[11] "I realize I can't do anything, pitiful little me, compared with all you great scholars," she had answered. "I would be like the frog in front of the Areopagus.[12] And yet I would so love to educate myself, to be informed, to know things. How amusing it must be to bury your nose in old papers!" she had added with the self-satisfaction a stylish woman adopts to assert that she is happiest abandoning herself with no fear of getting dirty to some messy job, like doing a little cooking "with her own hands in the dough." "You're going to make fun of me, but that painter who keeps you from seeing me—" (she meant Vermeer) "I've never heard of him; is he still alive? Can I see any of his things in Paris, so that I could imagine what it is you like, so that I could have some idea what's behind that great forehead that works so hard, inside that mind that I always sense is so busy with its thoughts, so that I could say to myself: There, this is what he's thinking about. What a joy it would be, to share in your work!" He apologized for his fear of new friendships, for what he had called, out of politeness, his fear of being unhappy. "You're afraid of affection? How odd; that's all I ever look for, I would give my life to find it," she had said in a voice so natural, so convinced, that he had been moved. "Some woman must have hurt you. And you think all other women are like her. She must not have understood you; you're such an unusual person. That's what I liked about you right away, I really felt you weren't like anyone else." "And you too," he had said to her, "I know very well what women are like, you must be busy with a great many things, you must not have much time." "Me! I never have anything to do! I'm always free, I will always be free for you. At any hour of the day or night that might be convenient for you to see me, send for me and I'll be only too happy to come immediately. Will you do it? Do you know what would be nice—if you could obtain an introduction to Mme. Verdurin; I go to her house every evening. Just imagine if we met there and I thought it was partly because of me that you were there!"

And as he recalled their conversations this way, as he thought of her this way when he was alone, he was no doubt merely turning over her image among those of many other women in his romantic daydreams; but if, due to some circumstance (or even perhaps not due to it, since a circumstance that presents itself at the moment when a state of mind, latent until then, comes out into the open may possibly not have influenced it in any way) the image of Odette de Crécy came to absorb all these daydreams, if these daydreams were no longer separable from the memory of her, then the imperfection of her body would no longer have any importance, nor would the fact that it might be, more or less than some other body, to Swann's taste, since, now that it had become the body of the woman he loved, it would be the only one capable of filling him with joy and torment.

As it happened, my grandfather had known—which was more than could be said of any of their current friends—the family of these Verdurins. But he had lost all contact with "young Verdurin," as he called him, whom he regarded, somewhat approximately, as having fallen—even while holding on to his many millions—among bohemians and riffraff. One day, he received a letter from Swann asking him if he could put him in touch with the Verdurins: "On guard! On guard!" my grandfather had exclaimed. "This doesn't surprise me at all; it's just where Swann was bound to end up. A nice group they are! In the first place, I can't do what he asks, because I don't know the gentleman in question anymore. And secondly, there must be a woman in it somewhere, and I never get mixed up in such affairs. Well, well! We shall have a rather amusing time of it if Swann falls in with the young Verdurins."

And after my grandfather returned a negative answer, it was Odette herself who had taken Swann to the Verdurins'.

The Verdurins had had to dinner, on the day Swann made his first appearance there, Dr. and Mme. Cottard, the young pianist and his aunt, and the painter who was in their favor at the time, and these were joined during the evening by several other faithful regulars.

Dr. Cottard was never quite certain of the tone in which he ought to answer someone, whether the person addressing him wanted to make a joke or was serious. And just in case, he would add to each of his facial expressions the offer of a conditional and tentative smile whose expectant shrewdness would exculpate him from the reproach of naïveté, if the remark that had been made to him was found to have been facetious. But since, so as to respond to the opposite hypothesis, he did not dare allow that smile to declare itself distinctly on his face, one saw an uncertainty perpetually floating upon it in which could be read the question he did not dare ask: "Are you saying this in earnest?" He was no more sure how he ought to behave in the street, and even in life generally, than in a drawing room, and he could be seen greeting passersby, carriages, and any minor event that occurred with the same ironic smile that removed all impropriety from his attitude in advance, since he was proving that if the attitude was not a fashionable one he was well aware of it and that if he had adopted it, it was as a joke.

On all points, however, where a direct question seemed to him permissible, the doctor did not fail to endeavor to reduce the field of his doubts and complete his education.

And so, acting on the advice given him by a foresightful mother when he left her province, he never let pass either an expression or a proper name that was unknown to him, without trying to acquire documentation about it.

In the case of expressions, he was insatiable for enlightenment, because, sometimes assuming they had a more precise meaning than they had, he wanted to know exactly what was meant by those he heard used most often: the bloom of youth, blue blood, a fast life, the hour of reckoning, to be a prince of refinement, to give carte blanche, to be nonplussed, etc., and in which specific cases he in his turn could introduce them into his conversation. If there were none, he would substitute puns he had learned. As for new names of people mentioned in his presence, he contented himself merely with repeating them in a questioning tone that he thought sufficient to procure him explanations without his appearing to ask for them.

Since he completely lacked the critical faculty which he thought he exercised on everything, that refinement of politeness which consists in declaring to a person to whom you are doing a favor, without however expecting to be believed, that you are in fact indebted to him, was a waste of effort with the doctor, who took everything literally. Whatever Mme. Verdurin's blindness with respect to him, she had in the end, while continuing to find him very subtle, been annoyed to see that, when she invited him to share a box near the stage for a performance by Sarah Bernhardt, saying to him, to be especially gracious: "It was too kind of you to come, Doctor, especially since I'm sure you've already heard Sarah Bernhardt many times, and we may also be too close to the stage," Dr. Cottard, who had entered the box with a smile that was waiting to become more pronounced or to disappear as soon as some authoritative person informed him as to the quality of the entertainment, answered her: "It's true that we're much too close and one begins to tire of Sarah Bernhardt. But you expressed a desire that I should come. And your desire is my command. I am only too happy to do you this small service. Is there anything one would not do in order to please you, you're so good!" And he added: "Sarah Bernhardt—she is in fact the Golden Voice, isn't she? And they often write that she sets the stage on fire. That's an odd expression, isn't it?" in hope of commentaries which were not forthcoming.

"You know," Mme. Verdurin had said to her husband, "I believe we're steering the wrong course when we belittle our gifts to the doctor out of modesty. He's a man of science, out of touch with the practical side of life, he has no idea of the value of things and relies on what we tell him." "I hadn't dared say anything to you, but I had noticed," answered M. Verdurin. And the following New Year's Day, instead of sending Dr. Cottard a three-thousand-franc ruby, remarking that it was only a trifle, M. Verdurin paid three hundred francs for an artificial stone, implying that it would be hard to find one as beautiful.

When Mme. Verdurin had announced that they would be having M. Swann at the soirée, "Swann?" the doctor had exclaimed in a tone of voice made rough by surprise, for the slightest piece of news always caught him more off guard than anyone else, though this was a man who believed he was perpetually prepared for anything. And seeing that no one answered him, "Swann? Who's this Swann?" he roared, filled with an anxiety that suddenly abated when Mme. Verdurin said: "Why, the friend Odette told us about." "Ah, good, good! That's all right then," answered the doctor, pacified. As for the painter, he was delighted by the introduction of Swann to Mme. Verdurin's, because he assumed Swann was in love with Odette and he liked to encourage love affairs. "There's nothing I enjoy more than arranging a marriage," he confided in Dr. Cottard's ear. "I've already managed a good many, even between women!"

By telling the Verdurins that Swann was very "*smart,*" Odette had awoken in them the fear that he would be a "bore." However, he made an excellent impression, of which, without their knowing it, his association with fashionable society was one of the indirect causes.

He had, in fact, over men who have never mixed in high society, even intelligent men, one of the superior qualities of those who have had some experience of it, which is that they no longer transfigure it out of the desire or the horror it inspires in their imagination, considering it unimportant. Their friendliness, disassociated from all snobbishness and from a fear of seeming too friendly, thus quite independent, has that ease, that grace characteristic of the motions of people whose supple limbs perform exactly what they want, without any indiscreet or awkward participation of the rest of the body. The simple elementary gymnastics of a man of the world extending his hand with good grace to the unknown young man who is being introduced to him, and bowing with reserve to the ambassador to whom he is being introduced, had in the end passed, without his being aware of it, into Swann's whole social attitude, so that toward people of a social circle inferior to his, like the Verdurins and their friends, he instinctively displayed a marked attention, permitted himself to make advances, from which, according to them, a bore would have refrained. He had a moment of coldness only with Cottard: seeing the doctor wink at him and smile ambiguously before they had spoken to each other (a dumb show that Cottard called "wait-and-see"), Swann thought the doctor probably recognized him from a previous encounter in some house of pleasure, even though he himself went to such places very seldom, having never inhabited the world of dissipation. Finding the allusion in bad taste, especially in the presence of Odette, who might receive a poor impression of him from it, he assumed an icy manner. But when he learned that the lady standing near him was Mme. Cottard, he thought that such a young husband would not have tried to allude to amusements of that sort in front of his wife; and he ceased to give the doctor's knowing look the meaning he had feared. The painter immediately invited Swann to come to his studio with Odette; Swann thought he was nice. "Perhaps he'll favor you more than he has me," said Mme. Verdurin in a tone of mock resentment, "perhaps he'll show you Cottard's portrait" (she had commissioned it from the painter). "Make sure, 'Monsieur' Biche," she reminded the painter, whom it was a sacred joke to address as Monsieur, "to capture that nice look in his eye, that subtle, amusing little way he has of glancing at you. As you know, what I want most of all is his smile; what I asked you for was a portrait of his smile." And since the phrase seemed to her noteworthy, she repeated it very loudly to make sure a number of guests heard it, and even, using some vague pretext, summoned a few of them over to her first. Swann asked to be introduced to everyone, even to an old friend of the Verdurins, Saniette, whose shyness, simplicity, and good nature had lost him all the esteem he had won by his skill as an archivist, his substantial fortune, and the distinguished family he came from. When he talked, there was a sort of mushy sound to his pronunciation that was charming because one sensed that it betrayed not so much an impediment in his speech as a quality of his soul, a sort of vestige of early childhood innocence that he had never lost. Each consonant he could not pronounce appeared to be another instance of a hardness of which he was incapable. In asking to be introduced to M. Saniette, Swann appeared to Mme. Verdurin to be reversing roles (to the degree that in response, she said, insisting on the difference: "Monsieur Swann, would you have the goodness to allow me to introduce to you our friend Saniette"), but aroused in Saniette a warm feeling of congeniality which the Verdurins, however, never revealed to Swann, for Saniette irritated them a little, and they were not anxious to make friends for him. But, on the other hand, Swann touched them infinitely by believing he ought to ask immediately to be introduced to the pianist's aunt. She was in a black dress, as always, because she thought one always looked nice in black and that it was most distinguished, and her face was extremely red, as it always was after she had just eaten. She bowed to Swann with respect, but straightened with majesty. Because she had no education and was afraid of making mistakes in grammar, she deliberately pronounced things in a garbled way, thinking that if she made a blunder it would be fogged over by such indefiniteness that no one would be able to make it out with any certainty, so that her conversation was reduced to an indistinct hawking, from which emerged now and then the few vocables of which she felt confident. Swann thought he could poke a little fun at her when he was talking to M. Verdurin, but the latter was offended.

"She's such an excellent woman," he answered. "I grant you she's not brilliant; but I assure you she can be most agreeable when you talk to her on your own." "I don't doubt it," Swann hastened to concede. "I meant to say she did not seem to me 'eminent,'" he added, isolating the adjective, "and really that's rather a compliment!" "Well, now," said M. Verdurin, "this will surprise you: she writes charmingly. You've never heard her nephew? He's wonderful, isn't he, Doctor? Would you like me to ask him to play something, Monsieur Swann?" "Why, it would be a joy . . ." Swann was beginning to answer, when the doctor interrupted him with a mocking look. In fact, having acquired the notion that in conversation, to be emphatic, to employ formal expressions was old-fashioned, as soon as he heard a solemn word used seriously, as the word *joy* had just been used, he thought the person who haduttered it had just been guilty of pomposity. And if, in addition, the word happened to occur in what he called an old cliché, however current it might be in other respects, the doctor would assume that the sentence that had been begun was ridiculous and would finish it ironically using the platitude he seemed to be accusing the speaker of having wanted to deploy, although the latter had never thought of it.

"A joy forever!" he cried mischievously, raising his arms for emphasis.

M. Verdurin could not help laughing.

"What are those good people laughing about! You don't seem to be having such a bad time over there in your corner," cried Mme. Verdurin. "I hope you don't think I'm enjoying myself here in disgrace all alone," she added in a tone of childish chagrin.

Mme. Verdurin was sitting on a high Swedish chair of waxed pine, which she had been given by a violinist from that country and which she had kept, though it looked rather like a stool and was at odds with the beautiful old furniture that she had, but she insisted on keeping in evidence the gifts which the faithful regulars were in the habit of giving her from time to time, so that the givers would have the pleasure of spotting them when they came. And so she tried to persuade them to give her nothing but flowers and sweets, which are at least perishable; but she was not successful, and her home contained a collection of foot warmers, cushions, clocks, screens, barometers, and urns, in an accumulation of useless, repetitive, and incongruous offerings.

From this elevated spot she took energetic part in the conversation of the faithful and revelled in their practical jokes, but after the accident involving her jaw, she no longer took pains to explode in true laughter and performed instead a conventionalized pantomime that signified, without fatigue or risk for her, that she was laughing to the point of tears. At the mildest remark fired off by a regular against a bore or against a former regular who had been flung back into the camp of the bores—and to the greatest despair of M. Verdurin, who for a long time had had pretensions of being as affable as his wife, but who, when laughing in earnest, would soon get out of breath and so had been outdistanced and defeated by this ruse of incessant and fictive hilarity—she would utter a little cry, entirely close her birdlike eyes, which were slightly dimmed by leucoma, and abruptly, as if she had only just had time to avoid some indecent spectacle or avert a fatal blow, plunging her face in her hands, which covered it and allowed nothing of it to be seen, would appear to be doing her best to suppress, to annihilate a fit of laughter which, had she given way to it, would have caused her to faint. So, dazed by the gaiety of the faithful, drunk with good-fellowship, scandal-mongering, and approbation, Mme. Verdurin, poised on her perch, like a bird whose seedcake has been soaked in warm wine, sobbed with affability.

Meanwhile, M. Verdurin, after asking Swann's permission to light his pipe ("we don't stand on ceremony here, we're among friends"), begged the young musician to sit down at the piano.

"Now don't bother him, he didn't come here to be tormented," exclaimed Mme. Verdurin, "I won't have him tormented!"

"But why on earth should it bother him?" said M. Verdurin. "Perhaps M. Swann doesn't know the Sonata in F-sharp which we've discovered. He'll play the piano arrangement for us."

"Oh, no, no, not my sonata!" cried Mme. Verdurin. "I don't want to be made to weep till I get a cold in my head and neuralgia in my face, like the last time. Thanks for your offer, but I don't intend to repeat that performance. You're so kind, all of you; it's easy to see you're not the ones who'll be spending the next week in bed!"

This little scene, which was reenacted each time the pianist prepared to play, enchanted her friends as much as if it had been brand-new, because it was proof of the *"Patronne's"*[13] charming originality and sensitivity to music. Those who were near her signaled to those farther away who were smoking or playing cards to come closer, that something was happening, saying to them, as they do in the Reichstag[14] at interesting moments: "Listen, listen." And the next day they would tell those who had not been able to be there how sorry they were, reporting that the scene had been even more entertaining than usual.

"Well, all right then," said M. Verdurin. "He'll just play the andante."

"Just the andante! What are you saying!" exclaimed Mme. Verdurin. "It's precisely the andante that completely paralyzes me. Listen to the *Patron*! He's really marvelous! It's as if he said: In the Ninth we'll just hear the finale, or in *The Meistersingers*[15] we'll just hear the overture."

The doctor, however, urged Mme. Verdurin to let the pianist play, not because he thought the troubling effects the music had on her were feigned—he recognized certain neurasthenic symptoms in them—but from a habit which many doctors have, of immediately relaxing the severity of their prescriptions when something is involved that seems much more important to them, like some social gathering at which they are present and in which the person they are advising for once to forget his dyspepsia or his grippe is an essential factor.

"You won't become ill this time, you'll see," he told her, trying to hypnotize her with his eyes. "And if you do, we'll look after you."

"Really and truly?" answered Mme. Verdurin, as if the hope of such a favor left her no alternative but to capitulate. Perhaps also, because she said she would be ill, there were times when she did not recall that it was a lie and took on the character of an ill person. For invalids, tired of always having to make the rarity of their attacks dependent on their prudence, like to indulge in the belief that they can with impunity do all of the things that give them pleasure and usually hurt them, as long as they put themselves in the hands of a powerful person who, without their having to take any pains, with a word or a pill will put them back on their feet.

Odette had gone to sit on a tapestry-covered couch near the piano: "You know I have my own little spot," she said to Mme. Verdurin.

The latter, seeing Swann on a chair, made him get up:

"You're not very comfortable there: now go and sit next to Odette. You'll make room for M. Swann there, won't you, Odette?"

"What a pretty Beauvais," said Swann before he sat down, trying to be pleasant.

"Oh, I'm glad you appreciate my couch," answered Mme. Verdurin. "And let me tell you, if you think you're ever going to see another one as beautiful, you may abandon the idea at once. They never did anything else like it. The little chairs are marvels too. You can look at them in a moment. Each bronze is an emblem that corresponds to the little subject on the chair; you know, you'll have a great deal to entertain you if you want to look at them. I can promise you a good time. Even the little friezes around the edges—look at that, look at the little vine against the red background in the Bear and the Grapes. Isn't it well drawn? What do you say? I think they really knew how to draw! Doesn't that vine make your mouth water? My husband claims I don't like the fruit you get from it, because I don't eat as many as he does. The fact is, actually, I'm more of a glutton than any of you, but I don't need to put them in my mouth because I enjoy them with my eyes. What are you all laughing about, now? Ask the doctor, he'll tell you—for me those grapes are a regular purgative. Other people take the cure at Fontainebleau, I take my little Beauvais cure. But, Monsieur Swann, you won't go away without feeling the little bronzes on the backs! Isn't the patina soft? No, no—with your whole hand: feel them properly."

"Ah, if Madame Verdurin begins fondling the bronzes, we won't hear any music tonight," said the painter.

"You be quiet. You're a rascal. In fact," she said, turning to Swann, "we women are forbidden to do things far less voluptuous than this. But no flesh can compare to it! When M. Verdurin did me the honor of being jealous of me—come now, be polite at least, don't say you never were . . ."

"But I said absolutely nothing. Doctor, be my witness: did I say anything?"

Swann was feeling the bronzes to be polite and did not dare stop right away.

"Come, you can caress them later; now you're the one who's going to be caressed. Your ears are going to be caressed; you'll like that, I think; here's the dear young man who'll be doing it."

Now after the pianist had played, Swann was even friendlier to him than to the others who were present. This is why:

The year before, at a soiree, he had heard a piece of music performed on the piano and violin. At first, he had experienced only the physical quality of the sounds secreted by the instruments. And it had been a keen pleasure when, below the little line of the violin, slender, unyielding, compact, and commanding, he had seen the mass of the piano part all at once struggling to rise in a liquid swell, multiform, undivided, smooth, and colliding like the purple tumult of the waves when the moonlight charms them and lowers their pitch by half a tone. But at a certain moment, without being able to distinguish an outline clearly, or give a name to what was pleasing him, suddenly charmed, he had tried to gather up and hold on to the phrase or harmony—he himself did not know which—that was passing by him and that had opened his soul so much wider, the way the smells of certain roses circulating in the damp evening air have the property of dilating our nostrils. Maybe it was because of his ignorance of music that he had been capable of receiving so confused an impression, the kind of impression that is, however, perhaps the only one which is purely musical, immaterial, entirely original, irreducible to any other order of impression. An impression of this kind is, for an instant, so to speak, *sine materia*. No doubt the notes we hear then tend already, depending on their loudness and their quantity, to spread out before our eyes over surfaces of varying dimensions, to trace arabesques, to give us sensations of breadth, tenuousness, stability, whimsy. But the notes vanish before these sensations are sufficiently formed in us not to be submerged by those already excited by the succeeding or even simultaneous notes. And this impression would continue to envelop with its liquidity and its "mellowness" the motifs that at times emerge from it, barely discernible, immediately to dive under and disappear, known only by the particular pleasure they give, impossible to describe, to recall, to name, ineffable—if memory, like a laborer working to put down lasting foundations in the midst of the waves, by fabricating for us facsimiles of these fleeting phrases, did not allow us to compare them to those that follow them and to differentiate them. And so, scarcely had the delicious sensation which Swann had felt died away than his memory at once furnished him with a transcription that was summary and temporary but at which he could glance while the piece continued, so that already, when the same impression suddenly returned, it was no longer impossible to grasp. He could picture to himself its extent, its symmetrical groupings, its notation, its expressive value; he had before him this thing which is no longer pure music, which is drawing, architecture, thought, and which allows us to recall the music. This time he had clearly distinguished one phrase rising for a few moments above the waves of sound. It had immediately proposed to him particular sensual pleasures which he had never imagined before hearing it, which he felt could be introduced to him by nothing else, and he had experienced for it something like an unfamiliar love.

With a slow rhythm it led him first here, then there, then elsewhere, toward a happiness that was noble, unintelligible, and precise. And then suddenly, having reached a point from which he was preparing to follow it, after an instant's pause, abruptly it changed direction, and with a new movement, quicker, slighter, more melancholy, incessant, and sweet, it carried him off with it toward unfamiliar vistas. Then it disappeared. He wished passionately to see it a third time.

And it did indeed reappear but without speaking to him more clearly, bringing him, indeed, a sensual pleasure that was less profound. But once he was back at home he needed it, he was like a man into whose life a woman he has glimpsed for only a moment as she passed by has introduced the image of a new sort of a beauty that increases the value of his own sensibility, without his even knowing if he will ever see this woman again whom he loves already and of whom he knows nothing, not even her name.

It even seemed, for a moment, that this love for a phrase of music would have to open in Swann the possibility of a sort of rejuvenation. He had for so long given up directing his life toward an ideal goal and limited it to the pursuit of everyday satisfactions that he believed, without ever saying so formally to himself, that this would not change as long as he lived; much worse, since his mind no longer entertained any lofty ideas, he had ceased to believe in their reality, though without being able to deny it altogether. Thus he had acquired the habit of taking refuge in unimportant thoughts that allowed him to ignore the fundamental essence of things. Just as he did not ask himself if it would have been better for him not to go into society, but on the other hand knew quite certainly that if he had accepted an invitation he ought to go and that if he did not pay a call afterward he must at least leave cards, so in his conversation he endeavored never to express with any warmth a personal opinion about things, but to furnish material details that had some sort of value in themselves and allowed him not to show his real capacities. He was extremely precise when it came to the recipe for a dish, the date of a painter's birth or death, the nomenclature of his works. Now and then, despite everything, he went so far as to utter a judgment on a work, on someone's interpretation of life, but he would then give his remarks an ironic tone, as if he did not entirely subscribe to what he was saying. Now, like certain confirmed invalids in whom, suddenly, a country they have arrived in, a different diet, sometimes a spontaneous and mysterious organic development seem to bring on such a regression of their ailment that they begin to envisage the unhoped-for possibility of belatedly starting a completely different life, Swann found within himself, in the recollection of the phrase he had heard, in certain sonatas he asked people to play for him, to see if he would not discover it in them, the presence of one of those invisible realities in which he had ceased to believe and to which, as if the music had had a sort of sympathetic influence on the moral dryness from which he suffered, he felt in himself once again the desire and almost the strength to devote his life. But, since he had not succeeded in finding out who had composed the work he had heard, he had not been able to acquire it for himself and had ended by forgetting it. True, during the week he had encountered several people who had been with him at that party and he had asked them about it; but many had arrived after the music or left before; some were indeed there while it was performed but had gone into the other drawing room to talk, and others, who had stayed to listen, had heard no more of it than had the first group. As for the master and mistress of the house, they knew it was a recent work which the musicians whom they had hired had asked to play; since the latter had gone off on a tour, Swann could not find out anything more. He had many friends who were musicians, but though he recalled the special and inexpressible pleasure the phrase had given him, and saw before his eyes the shapes it outlined, he was not able to sing it for them. Then he stopped thinking about it.

Now, scarcely a few minutes after the young pianist had begun playing at Mme. Verdurin's, suddenly, after a high note held for a long time through two measures, he saw it approaching, escaping from under that prolonged sonority stretched like a curtain of sound hiding the mystery of its incubation, he recognized it, secret, murmuring, and, divided, the airy and redolent phrase that he loved. And it was so particular, it had a charm so individual, which no other charm could have replaced, that Swann felt as though he had encountered in a friend's drawing room a person whom he had admired in the street and despaired of ever finding again. In the end, diligent, purposeful, it receded through the ramifications of its perfume, leaving on Swann's face the reflection of its smile. But now he could ask the name of his stranger (they told him it was the andante from the Sonata for Piano and Violin by Vinteuil), he possessed it, he could have it in his house as often as he liked, try to learn its language and its secret.

And so when the pianist had finished, Swann went up to him to express a gratitude whose warmth was very pleasing to Mme. Verdurin.

"He's a charmer, isn't he?" she said to Swann. "You might say he knows a thing or two about that sonata, the little devil. You didn't know the piano could achieve such things. It's everything–except a piano! My word! I'm startled by it every time; I think I'm hearing an orchestra. Though it's even more beautiful than an orchestra, more complete."

The young pianist bowed, and with a smile, stressing the words as if he were making a witty remark:

"You're very generous to me," he said.

And while Mme. Verdurin was saying to her husband: "Come, give him some orangeade, he certainly deserves it," Swann was describing to Odette how he had been in love with that little phrase. When Mme. Verdurin, nearby, said: "Well now, it seems to me someone is saying sweet things to you, Odette," she answered: "Yes, very sweet," and Swann found her simplicity delightful. Meanwhile, he was asking for information about Vinteuil, about his work, about the period of his life in which he had composed this sonata, about what the little phrase could have meant to him, this was what he would have liked most of all to know.

But all these people who professed to admire that musician (when Swann had said that his sonata was truly beautiful, Mme. Verdurin had exclaimed: "I should say it's beautiful! But one simply doesn't admit that one does not know Vinteuil's sonata, one is not allowed not to know it," and the painter had added: "Ah, yes! It's a work of genius, isn't it? It may not be what you would call 'obvious' or 'popular,' is it? But it makes a very great impression on us artists"), these people seemed never to have asked themselves these questions, for they were incapable of answering them.

Even in answer to one or two particular remarks that Swann made about his favorite phrase, Mme. Verdurin said:

"Well now, that's funny, I never paid any attention. I'll tell you, I don't very much enjoy nitpicking or discussing fine points; we don't waste our time splitting hairs here, it's not that kind of a house," while Dr. Cottard watched her with blissful admiration and scholarly zeal as she frolicked in this billow of stock expressions. He and Mme. Cottard, however, with a kind of good sense which is also possessed by certain people from humble backgrounds, carefully refrained from offering an opinion or feigning admiration for a sort of music which they confessed to each other, once they were back home, they did not understand any more than the painting of "Monsieur Biche." Since, of the charm, the grace, the forms of nature, the public knows only what it has absorbed from the clichés of an art slowly assimilated, and since an original artist begins by rejecting these clichés, M. and Mme. Cottard, being in this sense typical of the public, found neither in Vinteuil's sonata, nor in the painter's portraits, what for them created the harmony of music and the beauty of painting. It seemed to them when the pianist played the sonata that he was randomly attaching to the piano notes that were not in fact connected to the forms they were used to, and that the painter was randomly hurling colors onto his canvases. When they were able to recognize a form in these canvases, they found it heavy and vulgarized (that is, lacking the elegance of the school of painting through which they viewed all living creatures, even in the street), and lacking truth, as if Monsieur Biche did not know how a shoulder was constructed or that women do not have lavender hair.

However, when the regulars had dispersed, the doctor felt this was a favorable opportunity, and while Mme. Verdurin was saying a last word about Vinteuil's sonata, like a beginning swimmer who throws himself into the water in order to learn, but chooses a moment when there are not too many people to see him, he exclaimed with sudden determination:

"Now, this is what one calls a musician *di primo cartello!*"[16]

Swann learned only that the recent appearance of Vinteuil's sonata had caused quite a stir among the most advanced school of musicians, but was entirely unknown to the larger public.

"I know someone quite well named Vinteuil," said Swann, think-ing of the piano teacher who had taught my grandmother's sisters.

"Perhaps it's him," exclaimed Mme. Verdurin.

"Oh, no!" Swann answered, laughing. "If you had ever spent just a minute or two with him, you wouldn't ask."

"Then, to ask the question is to answer it?" said the doctor.

"But he could be a relative," Swann went on. "That would be rather sad, but the fact is, a man of genius can be cousin to an old fool. If this is so, I confess I would submit to any kind of torture to get the old fool to introduce me to the composer of that sonata: start-ing with the torture of associating with the old fool, which would be frightful."

The painter knew that Vinteuil was very ill at the moment and that Dr. Potain was afraid he would not be able to save him.

"What!" cried Mme. Verdurin. "Are there people who still go to Potain?"

"Ah, Madame Verdurin!" said Cottard, in a tone of witty repartee. "You forget that you're talking about one of my colleagues, I should say one of my teachers."

The painter had heard that Vinteuil was threatened with mental ill-ness. And he declared that one could perceive it in certain passages of his sonata. Swann did not find this comment absurd, but it bothered him; for since a pure work of music contains none of the logical rela-tionships whose alteration in language reveals madness, madness rec-ognized in a sonata seemed to him something as mysterious as the madness of a bitch, the madness of a horse, though these can indeed be observed.

"Don't upset me with talk about your 'teachers.' You know ten times as much as he does," Mme. Verdurin answered Dr. Cottard, in the tone of a person who has the courage of her convictions and stoutly holds her own against those who are not of the same opinion. "At least you don't kill your patients!"

"But Madame, he belongs to the Academy,"[17] replied the doctor ironically. "If a patient would rather die by the hand of one of the princes of science ... It's much more stylish to be able to say: 'I'm being treated by Potain.'"

"Ah! It's more stylish?" said Mme. Verdurin. "So there's such a thing as style in illness now? I wasn't aware of that ... How funny you are!" she exclaimed suddenly, dropping her face in her hands. "And I was such a silly fool, talking about it seriously without seeing that you were pulling my leg."

As for M. Verdurin, finding it rather a strain to force a laugh over such a trifle, he contented himself with drawing on his pipe, musing sadly that he would never be able to rival his wife in a contest of amiability.

"You know, we like your friend very much," said Mme. Verdurin to Odette when the latter was wishing her a good night. "He's so unaffected, he's so charming; if all the friends you think of introducing to us are like him, you may certainly bring them."

M. Verdurin pointed out that Swann had not, however, appreciated the pianist's aunt.

"The man felt a little out of his element," answered Mme. Verdurin. "Now you wouldn't expect him to have caught the tone of the house already, the very first time, like Cottard, who has been one of our little clan for years. The first time doesn't count; it was useful for breaking the ice. Odette, it's agreed that he'll meet us tomorrow at the Châtelet. Will you pick him up?"

"No, he doesn't want me to."

"Ah! Whatever you like, then. As long as he doesn't go and abandon us at the last minute!"

To Mme. Verdurin's great surprise, he never abandoned them. He went to meet them wherever they were, sometimes in restaurants in the outlying districts where no one went much yet, because it was not the season, more often to the theater, which Mme. Verdurin liked very much; and because one day, at her house, she said in his presence that on evenings when there were premieres, or galas, a pass would have been very useful to them, that it had inconvenienced them very much not to have one the day of Gambetta's funeral,[18]

Swann, who never talked about his distinguished connections, but only about those which were not very highly esteemed, which he thought it indelicate to conceal, and among which he had, in the Faubourg Saint-Germain, fallen into the habit of including his relations with the official world, answered:

"I promise to take care of it, you'll have it in time for the revival of *Les Danicheff*.[19] As it happens, I'm having lunch with the prefect of police tomorrow at the Élysée Palace."

"What? At the Élysée Palace?" shouted Dr. Cottard in a thunderous voice.

"Yes, at M. Grévy's,"[20] answered Swann, a little embarrassed by the effect his remark had produced.

And the painter said to the doctor as a joke:

"Do you have these attacks very often?"

Generally, once an explanation had been given, Cottard would say: "Oh, I see, that's all right then," and not show a trace more of emotion. But this time, Swann's last words, instead of procuring him the usual peace of mind, raised to a fever pitch his astonishment that a man with whom he had dined, who had no official position, no celebrity of any sort, would hobnob with the Head of State.

"What do you mean, M. Grévy? You know M. Grévy?" he said to Swann with the stupid and incredulous look of a policeman on guard at the palace who is asked by a stranger to see the President of the Republic, and who, realizing from these words "what sort of person he is dealing with," as the newspapers say, assures the poor lunatic that he will be received immediately and leads him to the special infirmary of the central police station.

"I know him slightly, we have friends in common." (He did not dare say that one of them was the Prince of Wales.) "Actually, he entertains a good deal, and I assure you these lunches aren't in the least amusing, they're also very simple, there are never more than eight at table," answered Swann, trying to expunge what had seemed to be too dazzling, in the doctor's eyes, about his relations with the President of the Republic.

Immediately Cottard, trusting in the truth of what Swann had said, adopted the opinion, concerning the value of an invitation to M. Grévy's, that it was not a very desirable thing and could be picked up anywhere. From then on, he was no longer surprised that Swann, or anyone else, should visit the Élysée Palace, and he was even a little sorry for him because he had to go to lunches which Swann himself admitted were boring.

"Oh, I see, that's quite all right then," he said in the tone of a customs inspector who, though suspicious a moment before, after hearing your explanations stamps your passport and lets you go through without opening your bags.

"Oh, I believe you, I'm sure those lunches must not be very amusing, and it's good of you to go to them," said Mme. Verdurin, who saw the President of the Republic as a bore to be especially dreaded because he had at his disposal various means of seduction and compulsion which, if employed upon the faithful, would be quite capable of making them desert her. "Apparently he's as deaf as a doorpost and eats with his fingers."

"In that case, certainly it must not be much fun to go there," said the doctor with a touch of commiseration; and, recalling that eight was the number of guests at table: "Are these intimate lunches?" he asked sharply with a linguist's zeal more than a snoop's curiosity.

But the prestige of the President of the Republic in the eyes of the doctor ended by prevailing over both Swann's modesty and Mme. Verdurin's animosity, and at each dinner Cottard would ask with interest: "Will we be seeing M. Swann this evening? He's on personal terms with M. Grévy. Is he in fact what one would call a *gentleman*?"[21] He even went so far as to present him with an invitation card for the dentistry exhibition.

"This will admit you, along with anyone you might like to bring with you, but they won't let dogs in. You understand, I tell you this because some friends of mine didn't know and kicked themselves for it afterward."

As for M. Verdurin, he noticed the bad effect produced on his wife by the discovery that Swann had influential friends whom he had never mentioned.

If they had not arranged a party somewhere, it was at the Verdurins' that Swann would join the little clan, but he came only in the evening, and almost never agreed to have dinner there despite Odette's earnest requests.

"I could even have dinner alone with you, if you would like that better," she would tell him.

"And what about Mme. Verdurin?"

"Oh, that would be easy enough. I would simply tell her my dress wasn't ready, or my cab came late. There's always a way to manage it."

"You're very sweet."

But Swann said to himself that if he showed Odette (by agreeing only to meet her after dinner) that there were other pleasures he preferred to the pleasure of being with her, a long time would pass before her appetite for him was surfeited. And, too, since he infinitely preferred to Odette's kind of beauty the beauty of a little working girl as fresh and plump as a rose with whom he was smitten, he chose to spend the beginning of the evening with her, being sure of seeing Odette afterward. It was for the same reasons that he never agreed to have Odette pick him up on her way to the Verdurins'. The little working girl would wait for him near his house at a corner known to his coachman Rémi, she would get in beside Swann and stay there in his arms until the moment the carriage drew up in front of the Verdurins'. When he came in, as Mme. Verdurin, pointing to some roses he had sent that morning, said to him: "You deserve a scolding" and showed him a spot next to Odette, the pianist would play for the two of them the little phrase by Vinteuil that was like the anthem of their love. He would begin with the sustained violin tremolos that are heard alone for a few measures, occupying the entire foreground, then all of a sudden they seemed to move away and, as in those paintings by Pieter de Hooch,[22] which assume greater depth because of the narrow frame of a half-open door, away in the distance, in a different color, in the velvet of an interposed light, the little phrase would appear, dancing, pastoral, interpolated, episodic, belonging to another world. It rippled past, simple and immortal, distributing here and there the gifts of its grace, with the same ineffable smile; but Swann thought he could now distinguish within it some disenchantment. It seemed to realize how futile this happiness was to which it showed the way. In its light grace, there was something finished about it, like the detachment that follows regret. But this hardly mattered to him; he considered the phrase less in itself—in what it could express to a musician who was unaware of his existence or of Odette's when he composed it, and to all those who would hear it in the centuries to come—than as a token, a memory of his love which, even for the Verdurins, even for the young pianist, would remind them of Odette and him at the same time, would join them together; so much so that when Odette, capriciously, had begged him to, he had given up the idea of having some pianist play him the entire sonata, of which he knew as yet only this passage. "Why would you need the rest?" she said to him. "This is *our* piece." And in fact, pained by the thought that, at the moment when it passed so close and yet infinitely far away, though it was addressed to them it did not know them, he was almost sorry it had any meaning, any intrinsic and unalterable beauty, alien to them, just as in the jewels given to us, or even the letters written to us by a woman we love, we resent the water of the gem and the words of the language, because they are not created exclusively from the essence of a passing love affair and a particular person.

It often happened that he had lingered so late with the young working girl before going to the Verdurins' that after the little phrase had been played by the pianist, Swann would notice that it would soon be time for Odette to go home. He would drive her back as far as the door of her little house in the rue La Pérouse behind the Arc de Triomphe. And it was perhaps because of this, in order not to demand all her favors, that he sacrificed the less necessary pleasure of seeing her earlier, of arriving at the Verdurins' with her, to the exercise of this right to leave together which she recognized as his and to which he attached a greater value, since, because of it, he had the impression that no one else saw her, no one else came between them, stopped her from being with him still, after he left her.

And so she would go back in Swann's carriage; one night, when she had just stepped down from it and he was saying he would see her tomorrow, she rushed to pick a last chrysanthemum from the little garden in front of the house and gave it to him before he went off. He held it pressed against his lips on the way home, and when after a few days the flower withered, he locked it with great care in his secretary desk.

But he never went into her house. Only twice, he had gone there in the afternoon to participate in that operation which was of such capital importance for her: "having tea." The isolation and emptiness of the short streets (almost all of them lined with small contiguous private houses, whose monotony would suddenly be interrupted by some sinister street stall, the historic sign and sordid vestige of a time when these districts were still in bad repute), the snow lingering in the garden and on the trees, the slovenliness of the season, the proximity of nature, lent something more mysterious to the warmth, the flowers that he had found when he went in.

Leaving to the left, on the raised ground floor, Odette's bedroom, which looked out on a little parallel street in the back, a straight staircase between walls painted a dark color and hung with Oriental cloths, strings of Turkish beads, and a large Japanese lantern suspended from a slender silk cord (but which, so as not to deprive visitors of the latest comforts of Western civilization, was lit with gas) led up to the drawing room and the morning room. These were preceded by a narrow vestibule whose wall, checkered by a garden trellis, but a gilded one, was lined down its entire length by a rectangular box in which bloomed, as in a greenhouse, a row of those fat chrysanthemums which were still rare at that time, yet nothing like the ones that horticulturalists later succeeded in obtaining. Swann was irritated by the fashion that had favored them since the previous year, but he had taken pleasure, this time, in seeing the half-light of the room striped with pink, orange, and white by the fragrant rays of those ephemeral stars which light up on gray days. Odette had received him in a morning gown of pink silk, her neck and arms bare. She had had him sit next to her in one of the many mysterious alcoves that were contrived in the bays of the drawing room, protected by immense palm trees contained in china cachepots, or by screens festooned with photographs, bows of ribbon, and fans. She had said to him: "You aren't comfortable like that, wait, I'll fix you up," and with the conceited little laugh she would have given at some invention of her own, had settled behind Swann's head, and under his feet, cushions of Japanese silk which she kneaded as if she were lavish with these riches and careless of their value. But when the valet came bringing one after another the many lamps which, nearly all enclosed in large Chinese vases, burned singly or in pairs, all on different pieces of furniture as though on altars, and which had summoned back to the already almost nocturnal twilight of that late afternoon in winter a more lasting sunset, rosier and more human—perhaps making some lover stop and daydream in the street before the mystery of the presence that was at once disclosed and concealed by the glowing panes—she had watched the servant severely from the corner of her eye to see whether he was setting them down properly in their consecrated places. She thought that if even one were put where it should not be, the overall effect of her drawing room would be ruined, and her portrait, placed on a sloping stand draped in plush, would be poorly lit. And so she fervently followed the movements of the ungainly man and reprimanded him sharply when he went too close to two flower stands which she took care to clean herself for fear they would be damaged and which she now went over to examine to see if he had chipped them. She thought all her Chinese knickknacks had "amusing" shapes, as did the orchids, the cattleyas[23] especially, which were, along with the chrysanthemums, her favorite flowers, because they had the great merit of not resembling flowers, but of being made of silk, or satin. "This one looks as though it were cut from the lining of my coat," she said to Swann, showing him an orchid, with a suggestion of respect for this very "chic" flower, for this elegant and unexpected sister which nature had given her, so far removed from her on the scale of living creatures and yet so refined, more deserving than many women of being given a place in her drawing room. As she showed him, first, chimeras with tongues of fire decorating a vase or embroidered on a screen, then the corollas of a bouquet of orchids, then a dromedary of silver inlaid with niello with eyes encrusted with rubies that stood on the mantelpiece next to a jade toad, she affected, first, fear of the wickedness, or laughter at the oddity, of the monsters, then blushes at the indecency of the flowers and then an irresistible desire to go and kiss the dromedary and the toad, which she called "dears." And these affectations contrasted with the sincerity of certain of her devotions, notably to Our Lady of Laghet,[24] who had once, when she lived in Nice, cured her of a fatal illness, and whose gold medal she always wore, attributing to it unlimited powers. Odette made Swann "her" tea, asking him: "Lemon or cream?" and when he answered "Cream," said to him laughing: "A cloud!" And when he found it good: "You see I know what you like." This tea, in fact, seemed as precious a thing to Swann as it did to her, and love has such need to find for itself a justification, a guarantee that it will last, in pleasures which in fact would not be pleasures without it and which end when it ends, that when he left her at seven o'clock to go home and dress, during the whole trip that he made in his coupé, unable to contain the joy which the afternoon had given him, he kept repeating to himself: "How nice it would be to have a little woman like that in whose home one could always find that rare thing, a good cup of tea." An hour later, he received a note from Odette and immediately recognized the large handwriting, in which an affectation of British stiffness imposed an appearance of discipline on ill-formed letters that would perhaps have signified, to less prejudiced eyes, an untidiness of mind, an insufficient education, a lack of frankness and resolution. Swann had forgotten his cigarette case at Odette's. "If you had forgotten your heart here too, I would not have let you have it back."

A second visit he made to her was perhaps more important. Going to her house that day, as always when he was to see her, he pictured her to himself beforehand; and his need, if he was to find her face pretty, to limit what he imagined of her cheeks only to her fresh, pink cheekbones since the rest was so often yellow, languid, sometimes marked with little red specks, distressed him, as it seemed to prove that the ideal is inaccessible and happiness mediocre. He had brought her an engraving that she wanted to see. She was a little unwell; she received him in a mauve crepe de chine dressing gown, pulling the richly embroidered material over her chest like a cloak. Standing next to him, allowing her hair, which she had undone, to flow down her cheeks, bending one leg somewhat in the position of a dancer so that without getting tired she could lean over the engraving, which she looked at, inclining her head, with those large eyes of hers, so tired and sullen when she was not animated, she struck Swann by her resemblance to the figure of Zipporah, Jethro's daughter, in a fresco in the Sistine Chapel.[25] Swann had always had this peculiar penchant for amusing himself by rediscovering in the paintings of the masters not only the general characteristics of the real world that surrounds us, but what seems on the contrary the least susceptible to generalization, the individual features of the faces we know: for instance, in the material of a bust of the Doge Loredano by Antonio Rizzo,[26] the jut of the cheekbones, the slant of the eyebrows, altogether the very evident resemblance to his coachman Rémi; under the colors of a Ghirlandaio,[27] M. de Palancy's nose; in a portrait by Tintoretto,[28] the invasion of the cheek's fat by the first implanted hairs of the side-whiskers, the break in the nose, the penetration of the gaze, the congestion of the eyelids of Dr. du Boulbon. Perhaps because he had always continued to feel a touch of remorse that he had limited his life to worldly relationships, to conversation, he believed he could find a sort of indulgent pardon granted him by the great artists, in the fact that they too had contemplated with pleasure, introduced into their work, faces like these which give it a singular certificate of reality and of truth to life, a modern flavor; perhaps, also, he had allowed himself to be so caught up in the frivolity of the society people that he felt the need to look into an old work of art for these anticipated and rejuvenating allusions to current proper names. Perhaps, on the other hand, he still had enough of an artist's nature so that these individual characteristics gave him pleasure by assuming a more general meaning as soon as he saw them extirpated, emancipated, in the resemblance between an older portrait and an original which it did not represent. Whatever the case, and perhaps because the abundance of impressions that he had been receiving for some time, and even though this abundance had come to him more with his love of music, had enriched even his delight in painting, he now found a deeper pleasure–and this was to exert a permanent influence on Swann–in Odette's resemblance to Zipporah as painted by Sandro di Mariano, whom people call more often by his popular nickname of Botticelli, since that name evokes, not the painter's true work, but the idea of it that is vulgarized, banal, and false. He no longer appraised Odette's face according to the finer or poorer quality of her cheeks and the purely flesh-colored softness he supposed he must find when he touched them with his lips if he ever dared to kiss her, but as a skein of subtle and beautiful lines that his eyes reeled off, following their winding curve, joining the cadence of her nape to the effusion of her hair and the flexion of her eyelids, as in a portrait of her in which her type became intelligible and clear.

He looked at her; a fragment of the fresco appeared in her face and in her body, and from then on he would always try to find it in her again, whether he was with Odette or was only thinking of her, and even though he probably valued the Florentine masterpiece only because he found it again in her, nevertheless that resemblance conferred a certain beauty on her too, made her more precious. Swann reproached himself for having misunderstood the value of a creature who would have appeared captivating to the great Sandro, and he felt happy that his pleasure in seeing Odette could be justified by his own aesthetic culture. He told himself that, in associating the thought of Odette with his dreams of happiness, he had not been resigning himself to a second best as imperfect as he had believed until now, since she satisfied his most refined artistic tastes. He forgot that this did not make Odette any more the sort of woman he desired, since in fact his desire had always been oriented in a direction opposite to his aesthetic tastes. The words "Florentine painting" did Swann a great service. They allowed him, like a title, to bring the image of Odette into a world of dreams to which it had not had access until now and where it was steeped in nobility. And, while the simple view he had had of this woman in the flesh, by perpetually renewing his doubts about the quality of her face, her body, her whole beauty, had weakened his love, these doubts were vanquished, that love confirmed when he had instead, for a foundation, the principles of an unquestionable aesthetic; while the kiss and the possession that would seem natural and ordinary if they had been granted him by damaged flesh, coming as they did to crown the adoration of a museum piece appeared to him necessarily supernatural and delicious.

And when he was tempted to regret the fact that for months now he had done nothing but see Odette, he said to himself that it was reasonable to give a good deal of his time to an inestimable masterpiece, cast just this once in a different and particularly savory material, in a most rare exemplar that he contemplated sometimes with the humility, spirituality, and disinterestedness of an artist, and sometimes with the pride, egotism, and sensuality of a collector.

He placed on his worktable, as if it were a photograph of Odette, a reproduction of Jethro's daughter. He admired the large eyes, the delicate face, which allowed one to imagine the imperfect skin, the marvelous curls of the hair along the tired cheeks, and adapting what he had found aesthetically beautiful up to then to the idea of a living woman, he translated it into physical attractions which he rejoiced to find united in a creature whom he could possess. The vague feeling of sympathy that draws us toward a masterpiece as we look at it became, now that he knew the fleshly original of Jethro's daughter, a desire that henceforth compensated for the desire that Odette's body had not at first inspired in him. When he had looked at that Botticelli for a long time, he would think of his own Botticelli, whom he found even more beautiful, and, bringing the photograph of Zipporah close to him, he would believe he was clasping Odette against his heart.

And yet he strained his ingenuity not only to prevent Odette from becoming tired of him, but also, sometimes, to prevent himself from becoming tired of her; feeling that, ever since Odette had had every opportunity to see him, she did not seem to have much to say to him, he was afraid that the rather banal, monotonous, and more or less permanently predetermined manner she now had when they were together would end by killing the romantic hope he had that one day she would declare her passion, a hope which alone had made him fall in love and stay in love. And in order to work a little transformation in Odette's quite invariable attitude of mind, which he was afraid would make him grow tired of her, he would suddenly write her a letter full of feigned disappointment and simulated anger that he would send round to her before dinner. He knew that she would be dismayed, and would answer him, and he hoped that in the contraction of her soul caused by her fear of losing him, words would spring forth that she had never yet said to him—and in fact it was by doing this that he had obtained the most tender letters she had yet written to him, including one, which she had sent round to him at noon from La Maison Dorée[29] (it was the day of the Paris-Murcia fete, held for the flood victims of Murcia)[30] that began with these words: "My dearest, my hand is trembling so badly I can hardly write," and that he had kept in the same drawer as the dry chrysanthemum flower. Or, if she had not had time to write to him, when he arrived at the Verdurins' she would come up to him quickly, saying, "I have to talk to you," and he would gaze curiously at what he saw in her face and her words that she had until then kept hidden from him, of all that was in her heart.

Even as he approached the Verdurins', when he saw the large lamplit windows whose shutters were never closed, he was moved as he thought of the charming creature he was going to see in full bloom in their golden light. Now and then the figures of the guests stood out in silhouette, slender and black, screening the lamps, like those little pictures intercalated at intervals around a translucent lampshade whose other panels are plain light. He would try to distinguish Odette's silhouette. Then, as soon as he arrived, without his realizing it, his eyes would shine with such joy that M. Verdurin would say to the painter: "I think it's getting warm." And for Swann, Odette's presence did indeed add something to this house which none of the others in which he was entertained possessed: a sort of sensory apparatus, a nervous system ramifying through all the rooms and causing constant excitations in his heart.

And so the simple functioning of that social organism, the little "clan," automatically arranged daily meetings with Odette for Swann and allowed him to feign an indifference to seeing her, or even a desire not to see her, which did not make him run any great risks, since, whatever he wrote to her during the day, he would necessarily see her that evening and take her home.

But once when, having glumly contemplated that inevitable ride home together, he had taken his young working girl all the way to the Bois in order to delay the moment of going to the Verdurins', he arrived at their house so late that Odette, thinking he would not be coming, had already left. When he saw that she was no longer in the drawing room, Swann felt a pain in his heart; he trembled at being deprived of a pleasure that he was now measuring for the first time, having had until then that certainty of finding it when he wanted it which in the case of all pleasures diminishes for us, or even prevents us from perceiving at all, their greatness.

"Did you notice the look on his face when he saw she wasn't here?" said M. Verdurin to his wife. "I think one may say he's smitten!"

"The look on his face?" asked Dr. Cottard violently, since, having gone out briefly to see a patient and returned to pick up his wife, he did not know whom they were discussing.

"What, you didn't meet the most handsome of all Swanns at the front door . . ."

"No. M. Swann was here?"

"Oh, just for a moment. We had a very agitated, a very nervous Swann. You see, Odette had already left."

"You mean she and he are thick as thieves? She has given him the key to her city?" asked the doctor, cautiously testing the meaning of the expressions.

"No, no, there's absolutely nothing going on, and just between us, I think she's making a great mistake and behaving like a real idiot, which she is, in fact."

"Tut, tut, tut," said M. Verdurin. "What do you know about it, how do you know there's nothing going on? We haven't gone there to see for ourselves, have we?"

"She would have told me," retorted Mme. Verdurin proudly. "I tell you she lets me know about all her little affairs! As she hasn't anyone just now, I told her she ought to sleep with him. She claims she can't, she says she was certainly rather infatuated with him at first, but that he's shy with her, which makes her shy with him, and then anyway she doesn't love him that way, he's some sort of ideal for her, she's afraid of taking the bloom off the feeling she has for him, what do I know? Yet it would be just what she needs."

"Allow me to disagree with you," said M. Verdurin. "I'm not overly fond of the gentleman's manner; I think he's affected."

Mme. Verdurin froze, assumed an inert expression as if she had turned into a statue, a fiction that allowed it to be assumed that she had not heard that intolerable word *affected*, which seemed to imply that one could "be affected" with them, therefore that one was "better than them."

"Anyway, if there's nothing going on, I don't think it's because the gentleman thinks she's *virtuous*," M. Verdurin said ironically. "And after all, one can't say anything, since he seems to think she's intelligent. I don't know if you heard what he was declaiming to her the other evening about Vinteuil's sonata; I love Odette with all my heart, but to construct aesthetic theories for her benefit, you'd really have to be quite an imbecile!"

"Now, don't say bad things about Odette," said Mme. Verdurin, playing the child. "She's so charming."

"But she can still be charming. We aren't saying bad things about her, we're saying she's not a saint, she's not a genius. In fact," he said to the painter, "are you really so anxious for her to be virtuous? Who knows—perhaps she would be far less charming."

On the landing Swann had been approached by the butler, who was not there when he arrived and had been instructed by Odette—but this was already an hour before—to tell him, in case he should still come, that she would probably go and have some chocolate at Prévost's[31] before returning home. Swann left for Prévost's, but at every step of the way his carriage was stopped by other carriages or by people crossing the street, loathsome obstacles that he would gladly have knocked down if the policeman and his report would not have delayed him even more than the passage of a pedestrian. He counted the time he was taking, and added a few seconds to all the minutes to be sure of not having made them too short, which would have allowed him to think the chance was greater than it really was that he would arrive early enough and still find Odette. And at one point, like a man in a fever who has just been sleeping and who becomes aware of the absurdity of the dreams he has been contemplating without clearly distinguishing himself from them, Swann suddenly perceived how alien to himself were the thoughts he had been revolving since the moment he had been told at the Verdurins' that Odette had already left, how new the pain he was suffering in his heart, but noted it only as though he had just woken up. What? All this agitation because he would not see Odette till tomorrow, exactly what he had wanted, an hour ago, when he arrived at Mme. Verdurin's! He was obliged to acknowledge that in this same carriage which was taking him to Prévost's he himself was no longer the same, and that he was no longer alone, that a new person was there with him, attached to him, amalgamated to him, one from whom he might not be able to free himself, whom he was going to have to treat with circumspection, like a master or an illness. And yet for a moment now, since he had felt a new person had been added to him in this way, his life had seemed to him more interesting. He hardly said to himself that this possible meeting at Prévost's, however (the expectation of which so disordered, so denuded the moments preceding it that he could no longer find a single idea, a single memory within which he could rest his mind), would probably, if it took place, be like the others, not much of anything. As on every other evening, once he was with Odette, casting on her changing face a furtive glance which he would immediately turn away for fear that she would see in it his mounting desire and no longer believe in his disinterest, he would cease to be able to think about her, too occupied with finding pretexts that would permit him not to leave her right away and to make certain, without seeming to care about it, that he would see her again the next day at the Verdurins': that is, to prolong for the moment and to renew for yet one more day the disappointment and torment that came to him from the pointless presence of this woman whom he saw so regularly without daring to take her in his arms.

She was not at Prévost's; he wanted to look in every restaurant along the boulevards. In order to gain time, while he visited some he sent into the others his coachman Rémi (the Doge Loredano by Rizzo), for whom he then waited—having found nothing himself—at a place he had specified to him. The carriage did not return and Swann pictured to himself the approaching moment, as both the moment in which Rémi would say to him: "The lady is here," and the moment in which Rémi would say to him: "The lady was not in any of the cafés." And so he saw the end of the evening before him, one single outcome and yet an alternative as well, preceded either by a meeting with Odette which would put an end to his agony, or by a forced renunciation of finding her this evening, an acceptance of returning home without having seen her.

The coachman came back, but at the moment he stopped in front of Swann, Swann did not say to him: "Did you find the lady?" but: "Remind me, tomorrow, to order more wood; I think our supply must be almost exhausted." Perhaps he had told himself that if Rémi had found Odette in some café where she was waiting for him, the end of the ill-fated evening would already be canceled out by the fulfillment, which was just beginning, of the blissful end of the evening and that he did not need to rush to seize a happiness that was already captured and held in a safe place, that would not be able to break free. But it was also from the force of inertia; there was in his soul that lack of suppleness which can be seen in the bodies of certain people who, at the moment when they need to avoid a collision, to snatch a flame away from their clothing, to perform some other urgent motion, instead take their time, begin by remaining for a second in their original position, as though to find in it their springboard, their source of momentum. And no doubt, if the coachman had interrupted him by saying: "The lady is there," he would have answered: "Oh yes, of course, the errand I sent you on! Well, well! Is that so?" and would have gone on talking to him about supplies of wood in order to hide the emotion he felt and allow himself time to separate from his uneasiness and give himself up to his happiness.

But the coachman came back to tell him he had not found her anywhere, and added his opinion, old servant that he was:

"I think that all Monsieur can do now is go home."

But the indifference that Swann had no trouble feigning as long as Rémi could do nothing further to change the answer he had brought back fell from him, when he saw Rémi attempt to make him give up hope and abandon his search:

"No, not at all," he cried, "we must find the lady; it's terribly important. She would be extremely annoyed—it's a business matter—she would be extremely offended if she didn't see me."

"I don't see how the lady could be offended," answered Rémi, "since she's the one who left without waiting for Monsieur, and since she said she would go to Prévost's and then she wasn't there."

Lights were beginning to go out all around him. Under the trees on the boulevards, in a mysterious darkness, fewer people wandered past, barely recognizable. Now and then the shadow of a woman coming up to him, murmuring a word in his ear, asking him to take her home, would make Swann start. He brushed anxiously against all those dim bodies as if, among the phantoms of the dead, in the kingdom of darkness, he were searching for Eurydice.

Of all the modes by which love is brought into being, of all the agents which disseminate the holy evil, surely one of the most efficacious is this great gust of agitation which now and then sweeps over us. Then our fate is sealed, and the person whose company we enjoy at the time is the one we will love. It is not even necessary for us to have liked him better than anyone else up to then, or even as much. What is necessary is that our predilection for him should become exclusive. And that condition is fulfilled when—at a moment like this, when we do not have him with us—the quest for the pleasures that his charm gave us is suddenly replaced in us by an anxious need whose object is this person himself, an absurd need which the laws of this world make it impossible to satisfy and difficult to cure—the senseless and painful need to possess him.

Swann asked to be driven to the last remaining restaurants; it was only the hypothesis of happiness he had been able to envisage calmly; now he no longer hid his agitation, the value he placed on this meeting; and he promised a reward to his coachman if they were successful, as though, by inspiring him with a desire to succeed that would be added to his own, he could make Odette appear, even if she had already gone home to bed, in a restaurant on the boulevard. He pushed on as far as La Maison Dorée, went into Tortoni's[32] twice and, still without having seen her, had just come out of the Café Anglais[33] again, walking fast with a wild look on his face back to his carriage, which was waiting for him at the corner of the boulevard des Italiens, when he bumped into a woman coming in the opposite direction: it was Odette; later, she explained that she had not found a seat at Prévost's and so had gone to have supper at La Maison Dorée in an alcove where he had not noticed her, and she was on her way back to her carriage.

She had so little expected to see him that she recoiled in fear. And he himself had run all over Paris not because he thought it was possible to find her, but because it was too hard for him to give up the search. But the joy which his reason had continued to believe was beyond realization that night only seemed even more real now; for since he had not collaborated with it by foreseeing its probabilities, it remained external to him; he did not need to reach into his mind to furnish it with truth, the truth emanated from it, was projected by it toward him, that truth whose radiance dispelled like a dream the isolation he had so dreaded, that truth on which he now based, on which he now rested, without thinking, his happy reverie. In the same way, a traveler arriving at the Mediterranean shore on a day of fine weather, no longer certain that the lands he has just left behind really exist, allows his vision to be dazzled, rather than looking at them himself, by the rays of light emitted in his direction by the luminous, resistant azure of the waters.

He stepped up with her into the carriage that she had waiting there, and told his own to follow.

She was holding a bunch of cattleyas in her hand and Swann saw, under her lace scarf, that she had flowers of the same orchid in her hair, fastened to a plume of swan feathers. She was dressed, under her mantilla, in a flood of black velvet caught up on one side to reveal in a wide triangle the hem of a skirt of white faille and showing a yoke, also of white faille, at the opening of a low-necked bodice tucked with more cattleyas. She had barely recovered from the fright Swann had given her when some obstacle made the horse shy. They were roughly jolted, she cried out and began trembling all over, breathless.

"It's all right," he said, "don't be afraid."

And he put his arm around her shoulder, supporting her against himself; then he said:

"Now don't talk to me, just answer with a sign so you don't get even more out of breath. It won't bother you, will it, if I straighten the flowers in your bodice? They were knocked out of place when the carriage lurched. I'm afraid you may lose them, I'll push them in a little."

She was not used to seeing a man make such a fuss over her, and said, smiling:

"No, not at all. I don't mind in the least."

But he, intimidated by her answer, and perhaps also so as to appear to have been sincere when he had used that excuse, or even beginning to believe that he had been, exclaimed:

"No, no! Don't talk, you'll get out of breath again, you can answer me perfectly well with a gesture, I'll understand. Tell me sincerely, this doesn't bother you? You see, there's a little . . . I think there's some pollen sprinkled on you; will you let me wipe it off with my hand? I'm not doing it too quickly, I'm not being too rough? Am I tickling you a little, maybe? I don't want to touch the velvet of your dress, I'm afraid I might crush it. But look, it really was necessary to fasten them, they would have fallen; and this way, by pushing them in a little myself . . . Seriously; I'm not annoying you? And what if I just take a little sniff to see if they really have no fragrance? I've never smelled them. May I? Tell the truth."

Smiling, she shrugged her shoulders a little, as though to say "You're quite mad; you can see very well that I like it."

He ran his other hand up along Odette's cheek; she gazed at him steadily, with the grave and languid look of the women by the Florentine master whom he had discovered she resembled; protruding to the edges of her lids, her shining eyes, wide and thin, like theirs, seemed about to well out like two tears. She bent her neck as you see them all do, in the pagan scenes as well as in the religious pictures. And in a position which was no doubt habitual for her, which she knew was appropriate to moments like this and which she took care not to forget to adopt, she seemed to require all her strength to hold her face back, as though an invisible force were drawing it toward Swann. And it was Swann who, before she let her face fall, as though despite herself, onto his lips, held it back for an instant, at a certain distance, between his two hands. He had wanted to give his mind time to catch up, to recognize the dream it had caressed for so long and to be present at its realization, like a relative summoned to witness the success of a child she has loved very much. Perhaps Swann was also fastening upon this face of an Odette he had not yet possessed, an Odette he had not yet even kissed, this face he was seeing for the last time, the gaze with which, on the day of our departure, we hope to carry away with us a landscape we are about to leave forever.

But he was so timid with her that, having ended by possessing her that night, after beginning by arranging her cattleyas, either from dread of offending her, or from fear of appearing in retrospect to have lied, or from a lack of audacity in formulating a greater demand than this one (which he could renew since it had not angered Odette the first time), in the days following he made use of the same pretext. If she had cattleyas tucked in her blouse, he would say: "It's a pity, this evening the cattleyas don't need to be straightened, they haven't been jostled the way they were the other evening; it seems to me, though, that this one isn't quite straight. May I see if these have more fragrance than the others?" Or, if she had none: "Oh! No cattleyas tonight, no way for me to indulge in a little rearranging." So that, for some time, the order he had followed the first night, when he began by touching Odette's throat with his fingers and lips, was not changed, and his caresses still began this way each time; and much later, when the rearrangement (or the ritual simulacrum of rearrangements) of the cattleyas had long since been abandoned, the metaphor "make cattleya," having become a simple phrase they used without thinking about it when they wanted to signify the act of physical possession—in which, in fact, one possesses nothing—lived on in their language, commemorating it, after that forgotten custom. And perhaps this individual way of saying "make love" did not mean exactly the same thing as its synonyms. Even if one is tired of women, even if one believes that the possession of the most various women is always the same and familiar beforehand, this possession becomes a new pleasure if it involves women difficult enough—or believed to be so by us—so that we have to make it happen as a result of some episode in our relationship that is unforeseen, as had been for Swann, the first time, the rearranging of the cattleyas. He tremulously hoped, that night (but Odette, he told himself, if she was fooled by his ruse, would not be able to guess as much), that the possession of this woman was what would emerge from among their broad mauve petals; and the pleasure he felt already and that Odette was perhaps tolerating, he thought, only because she had not recognized it, seemed to him, because of that—as it might seem to the first man who tasted it among the flowers of earthly paradise—a pleasure that had not existed until then, that he was seeking to create, a pleasure—signaled by the special name he gave it—entirely individual and new.

Now, every evening, when he took her home, he had to go in, and often she came back out in a dressing gown and led him to his carriage, kissed him within view of the coachman, saying: "What difference does it make to me, what other people think of me?" On evenings when he did not go to the Verdurins' (which happened sometimes now that he had another way of seeing her), on the increasingly rare evenings when he went into society, she would ask him to come to see her on his way home, whatever the hour. It was spring, a clear and icy spring. Coming out of a party, he would get into his victoria, spread a rug over his legs, tell the friends who were going off at the same time and who had asked him to join them that he could not, that he was not going in the same direction, and the coachman would leave at a fast trot knowing where to go. They would be amazed, and, in fact, Swann was no longer the same. No one ever received a letter from him now asking for an introduction to some woman. He no longer paid any attention to women, avoided going to places where one might meet them. In a restaurant, in the country, his attitude was the opposite of the one by which, just recently, he could be recognized and which had seemed to have been his always. To such an extent does a passion manifest itself in us as a temporary and distinct character that replaces our other character and eliminates the signs, invariable until then, by which it was expressed! Now, however, what was invariable was that, wherever Swann might be, he did not fail to go to meet Odette. The path that separated him from her was the one he inevitably traveled as though it were the slope itself, rapid and irresistible, of his life. In truth, when he had stayed out late, he would often have preferred to go directly home without making that long trip, and not see her until the next day; but the very fact of taking the trouble to go to her house at an unusual hour, of guessing that the friends who were leaving him were saying to themselves: "He is tied hand and foot, some woman must be insisting that he go to her whatever the hour," made him feel he was leading the life of men known to be having a love affair and in whom the sacrifice they are making of their sleep and their other interests to a dream of sensuous pleasure produces an inner charm. Then again, without his realizing it, the certainty that she was waiting for him, that she was not somewhere else with other people, that he would not return without seeing her, neutralized the anguish, forgotten but always ready to be reawakened, which he had felt the night when Odette was not at the Verdurins', and of which the present assuagement was so sweet that it could be named happiness. Perhaps it was to this anguish that he owed the importance which Odette had now assumed for him. Other people usually leave us so indifferent that when we have invested in one of them such possibilities of causing us pain and joy, that person seems to belong to another universe, is surrounded with poetry, turns our life into a sort of expanse of emotion in which that person will be more or less close to us. Swann could not ask himself without anxiety what Odette would mean to him in the years to come. Now and then, as he saw, from his victoria, on those lovely cold nights, the shining moon spreading its brightness between his eyes and the deserted streets, he would think of that other face, bright and tinged with pink like the moon's, which, one day, had appeared in the forefront of his mind and, since then, had cast on the world the mysterious light in which he saw it. If he arrived after the hour when Odette sent her servants to bed, before ringing at the gate of the little garden he would first go into the street onto which looked out, on the ground floor, between the windows, all alike but dark, of the contiguous houses, the only one illuminated, the window of her room. He would rap at the pane, and she, alerted, would answer and go and wait for him on the other side, at the front door. He would find several of her favorite pieces open on the piano: the "Valse des Roses" or "Pauvre Fou" by Tagliafico[34] (which should, according to her wishes, which she had put into writing, be performed at her funeral); he would ask her to play instead the little phrase from Vinteuil's sonata, even though Odette played very badly, but the loveliest vision of a work of art that remains with us is often the one that transcended the wrong notes coaxed by unskillful fingers from an out-of-tune piano. For Swann the little phrase continued to be associated with the love he felt for Odette. He was aware that this love was something that did not correspond to anything external, anything verifiable by others besides him; he realized that Odette's qualities did not justify his attaching so much value to the time he spent with her. And often, when Swann's positive intelligence alone prevailed, he wanted to stop sacrificing so many intellectual and social interests to this imaginary pleasure. But as soon as he heard it, the little phrase had the power to open up within him the space it needed, the proportions of Swann's soul were changed by it; a margin was reserved in him for a bliss that also did not correspond to any external object, and yet, instead of being purely individual, like the enjoyment of that love, assumed for Swann a reality superior to that of concrete things. The little phrase incited in him this thirst for an unfamiliar delight, but it did not give him anything precise to assuage it. So that those parts of Swann's soul from which the little phrase had erased any concern for material interests, any considerations that were human and valid for all people, it left vacant and blank, and in them he was free to write Odette's name. Moreover, where Odette's affection might seem somewhat limited and disappointing, the little phrase came along to add to it, to amalgamate with it its mysterious essence. From the sight of Swann's face as he listened to the phrase, one would have said he was absorbing an anesthetic that allowed him to breathe more deeply. And the pleasure which the music gave him, and which was soon to create in him a true need, did indeed resemble, at those moments, the pleasure he would have found in testing fragrances, in entering into contact with a world for which we are not made, which seems formless to us because our eyes do not perceive it, meaningless because it evades our understanding, which we can attain only through a single sense. What great repose, what mysterious renewal for Swann—for him whose eyes, though refined lovers of painting, whose mind, though a shrewd observer of manners, bore forever the indelible trace of the aridity of his life—to feel himself transformed into a creature strange to humanity, blind, without logical faculties, almost a fantastic unicorn, a chimerical creature perceiving the world only through his hearing. And since he still searched the little phrase for a meaning to which his intellect could not descend, what strange drunkenness he felt, as he divested his innermost soul of all the help of reason and forced it to pass alone through the sieve, through the dark filter of sound! He began to become aware of all that was painful, perhaps even secretly unappeased in the depths of the sweetness of that phrase, but it could not hurt him. What did it matter if it told him love was fragile, his own love was so strong! He toyed with the sadness it diffused, he felt it pass over him, but in a caress that only deepened and sweetened his sense of his own happiness. He made Odette play it ten times, twenty times, demanding that while she did so she should not stop kissing him. Each kiss summons another. Ah, in those first days of our love, kisses come so naturally! So closely, in their profusion, do they crowd together; and it would be as hard for us to count the kisses we give each other in an hour as the flowers of a field in the month of May. Then she would make as if to stop, saying: "How can you expect me to play if you hold on to me? I can't do everything at once. Now decide what you want—should I play the piano or play with you?," he would become annoyed, she would burst out laughing, and her laughter would change and descend on him in a rain of kisses. Or she would look at him with a sullen expression, once again he would see before him a face worthy of figuring in Botticelli's *Life of Moses*, he would place her in it, he would give her neck the necessary inclination; and when he had well and truly painted her in distemper, in the fifteenth century, on the wall of the Sistine Chapel, the idea that she had nevertheless remained here, by the piano, in the present moment, ready to be kissed and possessed, the idea of her materiality and her life would intoxicate him with such force that, his eyes distracted, his jaw tensed as though to devour her, he would swoop down upon that Botticelli virgin and begin pinching her cheeks. Then, once he had left her, not without going back in to kiss her again because he had forgotten to carry away in his memory some detail of her fragrance or her features, while he was returning home in his victoria, he would bless Odette for allowing him these daily visits, which he felt could not give her very great joy, but which, by saving him from becoming jealous—by relieving him of the occasion for suffering again from the disease that had broken out in him on the evening when he had not found her at the Verdurins'—would help him to arrive, without having any more of those crises of which the first had been so painful and must remain the only one, at the end of this singular period of his life, these hours that were almost enchanted, like those in which he crossed Paris in the light of the moon. And noticing, during his return, that the star had now moved in relation to him and was almost at the edge of the horizon, feeling that his love, too, was obeying immutable and natural laws, he asked himself whether this period he had entered would last much longer, whether, soon, his thoughts would no longer see the dear face except as occupying a distant and diminished place, and nearly ceasing to radiate any charm. For Swann did find charm in things, now that he was in love, just as during the period when, as an adolescent, he had thought he was an artist; but this was no longer the same charm; Odette alone conferred it on them. He felt the inspirations of his youth, which had been dissipated by a frivolous life, reawakening in him, but they all bore the reflection, the mark of a particular being; and, in the long hours which he now found a delicate pleasure in spending at home, alone with his convalescing soul, little by little he became himself again, but possessed by another.

He went to her house only in the evening, and he knew nothing about how she spent her time during the day, any more than about her past, so much so that he lacked even that initial bit of information which, by allowing us to imagine for ourselves what we do not know, makes us want to know it. Thus, he did not ask himself what she might be doing, nor what sort of life she had had. He merely smiled sometimes at the thought that a few years before, when he did not know her, someone had spoken to him of a woman who, if he remembered rightly, must certainly have been she, as being a courtesan, a kept woman, one of those women to whom he still attributed, since he had spent very little time in their company, the willful, fundamentally perverse character with which they were for so long endowed by the imaginations of certain novelists. He would tell himself that often if one simply believes the opposite of the reputation the world has formed one will judge a person accurately, when he contrasted the character of such a woman with that of Odette, good, naive, enamored of idealism, so nearly incapable of not telling the truth that, after he begged her one day, so that he could have dinner alone with her, to write to the Verdurins telling them that she was unwell, the next day he had seen her, face-to-face with Mme. Verdurin, who was asking her if she felt better, blush, stammer, and reveal on her face despite herself what an affliction, what a torment it was for her to lie, and, while in her answer she multiplied the invented details of her alleged indisposition the day before, appear to be asking forgiveness, by her supplicating looks and her sorrowful voice, for the falseness of her words.

On certain days, however, though they were rare, she came to his home in the afternoon, interrupting his daydreams or the study of Vermeer he had resumed lately. His servant would come to tell him that Mme. de Crécy was in his morning room. He would go off to find her there, and when he opened the door, as soon as she saw

Swann, a smile would come and settle in Odette's rosy face, changing the shape of her mouth, the look in her eyes, the modeling of her cheeks. Once he was alone, he would see that smile again, he would see the one she had given him the day before, another with which she had greeted him on a different occasion, the smile which had been her answer, in the carriage, when he had asked if it annoyed her that he was straightening her cattleyas; and Odette's life during the rest of the time, since he knew nothing about it, appeared to him, with its neutral and colorless background, similar to those sheets of studies by Watteau[35] in which one sees here and there, in every space, from every angle, drawn in three colors on buff paper, innumerable smiles. But sometimes, in a corner of that life which Swann saw as completely empty, even if his mind told him it was not, because he could not imagine it, some friend, who, suspecting they loved each other, had not dared to tell him anything about her except what was insignificant, would describe to him Odette's form, which he had seen, that very morning, going up the rue Abbatucci[36] on foot in a "visiting cloak" trimmed with skunk, under a "Rembrandt-style" hat, and with a bouquet of violets in her bodice. This simple sketch was greatly disturbing to Swann because it suddenly made him see that Odette had a life which did not belong entirely to him; he wanted to know whom she had been trying to please with that outfit, which he did not know she possessed; he would promise himself to ask her where she had been going, at that moment, as if in the whole of his mistress's colorless life—almost inexistent, because it was invisible to him—there had been only one thing apart from all those smiles directed at him: her walking under a Rembrandt-style hat, with a bunch of violets in her bodice.

Except when he asked her for the little phrase by Vinteuil instead of "The Waltz of the Roses," Swann did not try to make her play things he liked or, any more in music than in literature, to correct her bad taste. He fully realized that she was not intelligent. When she told him she would like it so much if he would tell her about the great poets, she had imagined that she would immediately become familiar with heroic and romantic couplets like those by the Vicomte de

Borelli,[37] but even more moving. As for Vermeer of Delft, she asked if he had ever suffered because of a woman, if it was a woman who had inspired him, and when Swann admitted to her that no one knew anything about that, she lost interest in the painter. She often said: "I do believe, of course, that poetry—well, that there would be nothing more beautiful if it was true, if poets really believed everything they said. But quite often, those people are the most calculating of all. I know something about it, because a friend of mine was in love with a poet of sorts. In his poetry all he talked about was love, the sky, the stars. Oh, she was fooled all right! He did her out of more than three hundred thousand francs." If Swann then tried to teach her what artistic beauty was, how one should admire poetry or painting, after a moment she would stop listening, saying: "Yes . . . I didn't imagine it was like that." And he would sense that she was feeling such disappointment that he would prefer to lie, telling her that what he had said was nothing, that it was the least important part, that he did not have the time to go into things more deeply, that there was something else. But she would say to him sharply: "Something else? What? . . . Say it, then," but he would not say it, knowing it would seem feeble to her and different from what she was hoping for, less sensational and less touching, and fearing that, disillusioned by art, she would at the same time be disillusioned by love.

And in fact she found Swann intellectually inferior to what she would have imagined. "You're always so reserved. I can't make you out." She would marvel more at his indifference to money, his kindness to everyone, his refinement. And it often happens, in fact, to greater men than Swann, to a scientist or an artist, when he is not misunderstood by those around him, that the feeling on their part which proves that the superiority of his intelligence has compelled their recognition is not their admiration for his ideas, since these are beyond them, but their respect for his goodness. There was also the respect with which Odette was inspired by Swann's position in society, but she did not want him to try to secure invitations for her. Perhaps she felt that he might not be successful, or was even afraid that merely by talking about her he would prompt revelations that she dreaded. In any case, she had made him promise never to utter her name. The reason she did not want to go into society, she had told him, was a quarrel she had once had with a friend who, to avenge herself, had then said bad things about her. Swann objected: "But not everyone knew your friend." "Well, yes, but these things get around. The world is cruel." Swann did not understand this story, but on the other hand he knew that such precepts—"The world is cruel," "A slanderous remark spreads like a drop of oil"—were generally held to be true; there must be cases to which they applied. Was Odette's one of them? He wondered about this, but not for long, because he, too, was subject to the mental torpor that had burdened his father whenever he posed himself a difficult problem. Besides, this world which so frightened Odette did not, perhaps, inspire any great desire in her, because it was too far removed from the one she knew for her to picture it quite clearly. However, while she had remained in certain respects truly simple (for example she had kept as her friend a solitary little seamstress, whose steep, dark, and foul-smelling stair she climbed almost every day), she thirsted after fashion, but did not conceive of it as the fashionable people did. For them, fashion is a thing that emanates from a small number of individuals who project it to a considerable distance—more and more faintly the farther one is from the center of their closest associations—through the circle of their friends or the friends of their friends, whose names form a sort of register. Society people hold this register in their memory, they have an erudition about such matters, from which they have derived a sort of taste, a sort of discernment, so that if Swann, for example, read in a newspaper the names of the people who were at a dinner, he could immediately, without having to call upon his knowledge of the world, tell the exact degree of stylishness of that dinner, the way a literary person, simply by reading a sentence, can judge exactly the quality of its author. But Odette was one of those people (extremely numerous, whatever the fashionable world may think, and the likes of which exist in every class of society) who do not share these notions, who imagine a stylishness that is quite different, that assumes different guises according to the circle to which they belong, but has the particular characteristic—whether it be the sort of stylishness

Odette dreamed of, or the sort Mme. Cottard worshiped—of being directly accessible to everyone. The other, the stylishness of the society people, is accessible too, in truth, but only after a certain delay. Odette would say of someone:

"He only goes to the really smart places."

And if Swann asked her what she meant by that, she would answer him a little scornfully:

"Why, smart places! My goodness! If at your age you need to be taught what the smart places are, I don't know what to tell you. For example, the avenue de l'Impératrice[38] on Sunday mornings, the Tour du Lac[39] at five o'clock, the Éden Théâtre[40] on Thursdays, the Hippodrome[41] on Friday, the balls . . ."

"Now, what balls?"

"Why, the balls people give in Paris, the smart people, I mean. Well, Herbinger, you know, the one that has a job with a broker? But you must know him, he's one of the most successful men in Paris, that tall blond young man who's such a snob, who always has a flower in his buttonhole, a part at the back, light-colored overcoats; he goes about with that old thing who wears so much paint on her face, he takes her out to all the premieres. Well, he gave a ball the other night, and the smartest people in Paris were there. How I would have loved to go! But you had to show your invitation card at the door and I couldn't get one. Really, I'm just as glad I didn't go, I would have got killed in the crush, and I wouldn't have seen a thing. It's really just to be able to say you were at Herbinger's. And you know how I like to boast! Anyway, you can bet that out of a hundred girls who tell you they were there, half of them are lying . . . But actually, you're such a swell, I'm amazed you weren't there."

But Swann in no way tried to make her change this conception of fashionable life; thinking that his own was no more real, was also foolish, unimportant, he saw no point in instructing her about it, so that after some months she had no interest in the people whose homes he went to except as a means of obtaining enclosure passes for the horse races or tickets to the premieres. She wanted him to cultivate useful relationships of that kind, but in other respects she was persuaded they were not very smart, after she saw the Marquise de Villeparisis go past her in the street wearing a black woolen dress and a bonnet with strings.

"Why, she looks like a working-class woman, darling,[42] like an old concierge! That was a marquise! I'm no marquise, but you'd have to pay me handsomely to make me go about rigged out like that!"

She could not understand why Swann lived in the house on the quai d'Orléans which, though she did not dare admit it to him, she found unworthy of him.

Of course she claimed she loved "antiques" and assumed a rapturous and discriminating air when she said she adored spending a whole day "collecting curios," looking for "bric-a-brac," things "from the past." Although she persisted in a sort of point of honor (and as though she were obeying some family precept) in never answering questions or "accounting" for how she spent her days, she talked to Swann once about a friend who had invited her to her house, where everything was "period." But Swann could not manage to make her say what that period was. After some reflection, however, she answered that it was "medieval." By this she meant that there was wood paneling. Sometime later, she talked to him about her friend again and added, in the hesitant tone and with the knowing look with which you mention someone you have had dinner with the night before and whose name you never heard before, but whom your hosts seemed to consider someone so celebrated that you hope the person you are talking to will know who you are talking about: "Her dining room . . . is . . . eighteenth century!" She had thought the room was hideous, bare, as if the house were not finished, the women looked hideous in it too, and the fashion would never catch on. Finally, a third time, she talked about it again and showed Swann the address of the man who had made that dining room and whom she wanted to send for, when she had the money, to see if he could make one for her, not the same one, of course, but another which she was contemplating and which unfortunately the dimensions of her little house would not allow, one with tall sideboards, Renaissance furniture, and fireplaces like the ones in the Château de Blois.[43] That day, she let slip in Swann's presence what she thought of his home on the quai d'Orléans; because he had criticized the fact that Odette's friend preferred, not Louis XVI, for, he said, even though that was not done, it could be charming, but the fake antique: "You wouldn't want her to live the way you do, with your broken furniture and your threadbare carpets," she said to him, her bourgeois deference to public opinion prevailing, again, over her cocotte dilettantism.

People who liked collecting curios, were fond of poetry, despised crass calculations, dreamed of honor and love, she saw as an elite superior to the rest of humanity. One did not really have to have these predilections, provided one proclaimed them; of a man who had confessed to her at dinner that he loved to wander about the city, to get his hands dirty in the old shops, that he would never be appreciated by this commercial century, because he did not look after his own interests, and that because of this he belonged to another age, she returned home saying: "Why, he's a lovely person, so sensitive, I never would have guessed!" and she felt a sudden warm friendship for him. But men who, like Swann, had these tastes, yet did not talk about them, left her cold. No doubt she had to admit that Swann did not value money, but she would add sulkily: "But with him, it's not the same thing"; and in fact, what spoke to her imagination was not the practice of disinterestedness, but its vocabulary.

Feeling that he often failed to satisfy her dreams, he at least tried to see that she enjoyed being with him, not to oppose the vulgar ideas, the bad taste, which she displayed in all things, and which he loved, moreover, like everything else that emanated from her, which even enchanted him, for they were so many particular traits by which the woman's essence appeared to him, became visible. And so, when she looked happy because she was going to *La Reine Topaz*,[44] or when her gaze became serious, worried, and petulant, because she was afraid of missing the flower show or merely of not being in time for tea, with *muffins* and *toasts*,[45] at the "Thé de la rue Royale,"[46] regular attendance at which she believed was indispensable in establishing a woman's reputation for elegance, Swann, enchanted as one is by the naturalness of a child or the truthfulness of a portrait that seems about to speak, sensed so clearly his mistress's soul rising to the surface of her face that he could not resist going over to touch it with his lips. "Ah! She wants to be taken to the flower show, little Odette, she wants to be admired, well then, we'll take her, we must obey." Since Swann's vision was rather poor, he had resigned himself to wearing glasses for working at home, and to adopting, for going out in the world, a monocle, which was less disfiguring. The first time she saw him with one in his eye, she could not contain her joy: "I really do think for a man it's very smart! How it suits you! You look like a real gentleman. All you're missing is a title!" she added, with a touch of regret. He was happy that Odette was like this, just as, if he had been in love with a Breton woman, he would have enjoyed seeing her in a coif and hearing her tell him she believed in ghosts. Until then, as is true of many men whose taste for the arts develops independently from their sensuality, a bizarre disparity had existed between the satisfactions he conceded to one and those he conceded to the other, as he enjoyed, in the company of increasingly crude women, the seductions of increasingly refined works of art, taking a little housemaid to a closed orchestra box for the performance of a decadent play that he wanted to see or to an exhibition of Impressionist painting, and sure, in any case, that a cultivated woman of the world would not have understood any more about it, but would not have been able to keep quiet so nicely. But now that he loved Odette, to feel what she felt, to try to share but a single soul between the two of them, was so sweet to him that he sought to enjoy the things she liked, and his pleasure, not only in imitating her habits, but in adopting her opinions, was all the more profound because, since they had no roots in his own intelligence, they reminded him only of his love, because of which he preferred them. If he went to more than one performance of *Serge Panine*,[47] if he sought out opportunities to go to see Olivier Métra[48] conduct, it was for the sweetness of being initiated into all of Odette's ideas, of feeling he was sharing equally in all her tastes. This charm of bringing him close to her, which was possessed by the works or places that she liked, seemed to him more mysterious than the charm intrinsic to those that were lovelier but did not remind him of her. What was more, because he had allowed the intellectual beliefs of his youth to weaken, and because his skepticism as a man of the world had, unbeknownst to him, penetrated to them, he thought (or at least he had thought this for so long that he still said it) that the objects of one's preferences do not have an absolute value in themselves, but that they all depend on one's period, one's social class, they are all merely fashions, the most vulgar of which are equal to those that pass for the most distinguished. And just as he believed that the importance Odette attached to having tickets for the opening was not in itself a more ridiculous thing than the pleasure he used to take in lunching at the home of the Prince of Wales, likewise he did not think that the admiration she professed for Monte Carlo or for the Righi[49] was more unreasonable than the fondness he himself felt for Holland, which she imagined to be ugly, or for Versailles, which she found dreary. And so he denied himself those places, taking pleasure in telling himself that it was for her sake, that he chose not to feel things, love things, except with her.

Like everything else that was part of Odette's environment and no more, in some sense, than a means by which he could see her, talk to her, he enjoyed the company of the Verdurins. There, because at the center of all the amusements, meals, music, games, costumed suppers, excursions into the country, theater parties, even the rare "grand soirees" given for the "bores," was the presence of Odette, the sight of Odette, conversation with Odette, of which the Verdurins gave to Swann, by inviting him, the inestimable gift, he was happier among the "little clan" than anywhere else, and sought to attribute real merits to it, for by so doing he could imagine that, out of preference, he would associate with it all his life. For, since he did not dare to say to himself, afraid that he would not believe it, that he would always love Odette, at least by supposing that he would always associate with the Verdurins (a proposition that, a priori, raised fewer objections of principle on the part of his intelligence), he could see himself in the future continuing to meet Odette every evening; this did not perhaps quite amount to the same thing as always loving her, but for the moment, while he loved her, to believe that he would not stop seeing her one day was all that he asked. "What a charming place," he would say to himself. "How fundamentally real their life is! How much more intelligent, more artistic, they are there than high-society people! How sincere, despite some rather absurd little exaggerations, is Mme. Verdurin's love of painting, music—what a passion she has for works of art, and how she longs to please artists! The notion she has formed of society people is not accurate; but then again, society's notion of artistic circles is even more false! Perhaps I have no very great intellectual needs to satisfy in conversation, but I'm perfectly happy with Cottard though he does make inept puns. And as for the painter, his pretentiousness may be unpleasant when he's trying to surprise people, but on the other hand he has one of the finest minds I've ever known. And also, most of all, you feel free there, you do what you like without feeling constrained, without standing on ceremony. What a quantity of good humor is expended every day in that drawing room! Decidedly, apart from a few rare exceptions, I will never go anywhere else. More and more, that is where I will find my companionship and live my life."

And since the qualities that he believed to be intrinsic to the Verdurins were merely the reflection of the pleasures he enjoyed in their house because of his love for Odette, those qualities became more serious, more profound, more vital, along with those pleasures. Because Mme. Verdurin sometimes gave Swann the only thing that could constitute happiness for him; because, on a certain evening when he felt anxious because Odette had been talking to one guest more than another, and when, irritated at her, he did not want to take the initiative of asking her if she would return home with him, Mme. Verdurin brought him peace and joy by saying spontaneously: "Odette, you will take M. Swann home, won't you?"; because, when summer was approaching, and he had at first wondered uneasily if Odette would be going away without him, if he could continue to see her every day, Mme. Verdurin invited them both to spend it at her home in the country—Swann, unconsciously allowing gratitude and self-interest to infiltrate into his intelligence and influence his ideas, went so far as to proclaim that Mme. Verdurin was the soul of high-mindedness. Apropos of a few delightful or eminent people whom one of his old class-mates from the École du Louvre might mention to him, he would re-spond: "I prefer the Verdurins a hundred times over." And, with a solemnity that was new to him: "They are magnanimous people, and magnanimity is, fundamentally, the only thing that matters and that gives us distinction here on earth. You know, there are only two classes of people: the magnanimous ones and all the rest; and when you reach my age you have to choose, you have to decide once and for all whom you intend to like and, whom you intend to despise, stick with the ones you like, and, so as to make up for the time you've wasted with the others, not leave them again until you die. Well!" he added with that slight emotion you feel when, even without fully real-izing it, you say something not because it is true, but because you enjoy saying it and you listen to it in your own voice as if it came from somewhere other than from yourself, "my fate is settled, I have chosen to like only magnanimous hearts and to live from now on only in magnanimity. You ask me if Mme. Verdurin is truly intelli-gent. I assure you that she has given me proof of a nobility of heart, of a loftiness of soul which, you know, can't be attained without an equal loftiness of mind. Certainly she has a profound intelligence where the arts are concerned. But perhaps this is not her most ad-mirable quality; and every small, ingeniously, exquisitely good action that she has performed for me, every genial attention, every gesture of sublime familiarity, reveals a more profound understanding of life than any philosophical treatise."

Yet he could have said to himself that there were old friends of his parents just as simple as the Verdurins, friends of his youth as smitten with art, that he knew other greathearted people, and that neverthe-less, now that he had opted for simplicity, the arts, and magnanimity, he never saw them anymore. But these people did not know Odette, and, if they had known her, would never have thought of bringing the two of them together.

And so there was probably not, in the whole Verdurin circle, a sin-gle faithful partisan who liked them or thought he liked them as much as did Swann. And yet, when M. Verdurin had said he did not much care for Swann, he was not only expressing his own thoughts, but also guessing his wife's. Doubtless Swann's affection for Odette was too private and he had neglected to make Mme. Verdurin his daily confidante concerning it; doubtless the very discretion with which he had made use of the Verdurins' hospitality, often refraining from coming to dinner for a reason that they did not suspect and in place of which they saw a desire not to turn down an invitation to the home of some "bores"; doubtless, too, and despite all the precautions he had taken to hide it from them, their gradual discovery of his brilliant position in society, all fed their irritation with him. But the deeper reason for it was different. It was that they had very quickly sensed in him a reserved, impenetrable space where he continued to profess silently to himself that the Princesse de Sagan was not grotesque and that Cottard's jokes were not funny, in the end, and, even though he never deviated from his affability and never rebelled against their dogmas, they sensed, too, an impossibility of imposing them on him, of wholly converting him to them, the likes of which they had never encountered before in anyone. They would have forgiven him for associating with bores (to whom, for that matter, in his heart of hearts, he preferred the Verdurins and the whole of the little clan a thousand times over), if he had consented, as a good example, to renounce them in the presence of the faithful. But this was an abjuration they understood could not be wrung from him.

How different from a "newcomer" whom Odette had asked them to invite, though she had not met him more than a few times, and in whom they invested many hopes: the Comte de Forcheville! (It turned out that in fact he was Saniette's brother-in-law, which filled the faithful with surprise: the old archivist's manners were so humble that they had always thought he was from a social rank inferior to theirs and did not expect to learn that he belonged to a world that was rich and relatively aristocratic.) True, Forcheville was grossly snobbish, whereas Swann was not; true, he did not even dream of placing the circle of the Verdurins above all others, as Swann did. But he did not have the natural delicacy that stopped Swann from joining in with the too manifestly false criticisms that Mme. Verdurin leveled against people he knew. As for the vulgar and pretentious tirades the painter launched into on certain days, and as for the traveling-salesman jokes that Cottard ventured, for which Swann, who liked both men, could easily find excuses without having the heart or the hypocrisy to applaud them, Forcheville by contrast was of an intellectual caliber that allowed him to be dumbfounded, awestruck by the first, though he did not understand them, and to delight in the second. And in fact the first dinner at the Verdurins' at which Forcheville was present exposed all these differences, brought out his qualities, and precipitated Swann's fall from grace.

At this dinner there was, besides the regulars, a professor from the Sorbonne, Brichot, who had met M. and Mme. Verdurin at the spa and, if his duties at the university and his scholarly work had not given him very few hours of freedom, would willingly have come to their house often. For he had that curiosity, that excessive interest in life which, when combined with a degree of skepticism concerning the object of their studies, gives certain intelligent men in any profession, doctors who do not believe in medicine, schoolteachers who do not believe in Latin compositions, a reputation for having minds that are broad, brilliant, and even superior. At Mme. Verdurin's, he made a point of seeking his illustrations in whatever was most up-to-date when he spoke of philosophy and history, principally because he thought such subjects were only a preparation for real life and he imagined he would find the little clan putting into practice what he had known before now only from books, and then perhaps also because, having had instilled in him in the past, and having preserved without knowing it, a respect for certain subjects, he believed he was casting off his academic tendencies by taking liberties with them which, on the contrary, appeared such to him only because he had remained an academic.

At the very beginning of the meal, when M. de Forcheville, placed to the right of Mme. Verdurin, who had gone to great trouble over her appearance so as to please the "newcomer," said to her: "Quite original, that white dress," the doctor, who had been steadily observing him, so curious was he to find out what sort of man a "de," as he termed it, would be, and who was looking for a chance of attracting his attention and entering into closer contact with him, seized on the word *"blanche"* and, without lifting his nose from his plate, said: *"Blanche? Blanche de Castille?,"*⁵⁰ then, without moving his head, cast his eyes furtively to the right and left with an uncertain, smiling look. Whereas Swann, with his painful and useless attempt at a smile, revealed how stupid he thought the pun was, Forcheville had shown both that he relished its subtlety and that he had good manners, by containing within judicious limits a gaiety whose frankness had charmed Mme. Verdurin.

"What do you make of our man of science?" she had asked Forcheville. "It's impossible to have even two minutes of serious conversation with him. Is that the sort of thing you say to them at your hospital?" she had added, turning to the doctor. "It must be rather lively there, if that's the case. I see I'll have to get them to admit me as a patient."

"I think I heard the doctor talking about that old termagant, Blanche de Castille, if I dare express myself that way. Am I correct, madame?" Brichot asked Mme. Verdurin, who, swooning with laughter, her eyes shut, plunged her face into her hands, from which stifled cries escaped. "My God, madame, I wouldn't want to alarm whatever respectful souls there may be at this table, *sub rosa* . . . And I realize that our ineffable republic, Athenian as it is—how very much so!— might pay homage to that obscurantist Capetian lady as the very first truly authoritarian police prefect. Yes indeed, my dear host, yes indeed, yes indeed," he went on in his sonorous voice, detaching each syllable, in response to an objection of M. Verdurin's. "The *Chronique de Saint-Denis,* whose facts are incontestably reliable, leaves no doubt about this. No better choice of patron could have been made by a secularized proletariat than that mother of a saint to whom, incidentally, she gave a pretty rough time, as we are told by Suger and other Saint Bernards;⁵¹ for with her everyone got hauled over the coals."

"Who is this gentleman?" Forcheville asked Mme. Verdurin. "He seems first-rate."

"What? You haven't heard of the famous Brichot? Why, he's celebrated all over Europe."

"Oh! So that's Bréchot!" cried Forcheville, who had not heard the name clearly. "You must tell me all about him," he added, staring wide-eyed at the famous man. "It's always interesting to have dinner with a prominent person. But I must say, you certainly give your guests some choice dinner mates. No one's likely to get bored in your house."

"Oh you know, the most important thing," Mme. Verdurin said modestly, "is that they know they can trust us. They can talk about whatever they like, and the conversation is off and running. For instance, now, take Brichot. This is nothing: I've seen him, you know, when he's been absolutely dazzling here in my house, you feel you ought to go down on your knees before him. Well, now, at other people's houses, he's not the same man, he hasn't a scrap of wit, you have to force the words out of him, he's actually boring."

"How odd!" said Forcheville, surprised.

A wit like Brichot's would have been considered pure stupidity by the people among whom Swann had spent his youth, even though it might be compatible with real intelligence. And the professor's intelligence, vigorous and well nourished, probably would have been envied by many of the society people whom Swann considered witty. But those people had inculcated him so thoroughly with their own likes and dislikes, at least concerning anything to do with society life, including even that annexed part of it which should, instead, belong to the domain of intelligence–namely, conversation–that Swann could only find Brichot's jokes pedantic, vulgar, and sickeningly coarse. Then, too, being so accustomed to good manners, he was shocked by the rough military tone affected, each time he addressed anyone, by the jingoistic academic. Finally, perhaps he had lost some of his indulgence that evening in particular, seeing the friendliness Mme. Verdurin was displaying toward this man Forcheville whom Odette had had the singular idea of bringing. A little ill at ease with Swann, she had asked him when she arrived:

"What do you think of my guest?"

And he, realizing for the first time that Forcheville, whom he had known for a long time, might be attractive to a woman and was a rather handsome man, had answered: "Disgusting!" Of course, it did not occur to him to be jealous over Odette, but he did not feel as happy as usual, and when Brichot, having begun to tell the story of Blanche de Castille's mother, who "had been with Henry Plantagenet[52] for years before she married him," tried to prompt Swann to ask him what happened next by saying to him: "Isn't that so, Monsieur Swann?" in the martial tone one adopts to make oneself understood by a peasant or instill courage in a soldier, Swann spoiled Brichot's effect, to the fury of their hostess, by answering that they must please excuse him for being so uninterested in Blanche de Castille, but he had something to ask the painter. That afternoon, in fact, the painter had gone to see the show of a friend of Mme. Verdurin's, an artist who had died recently, and Swann wanted to find out from him (for he respected his taste) if there really was even more in these last works than the virtuosity that was already so astounding in the earlier ones.

"In that respect it was extraordinary, but it didn't seem to me to be an art that was, as they say, all 'elevated,'" said Swann, smiling.

"Elevated . . . to the height of an institution," interrupted Cottard, lifting his arms with mock gravity.

The whole table burst out laughing.

"Didn't I tell you? He won't allow anyone to be serious," said Mme. Verdurin to Forcheville. "Just when you least expect it, he comes out with a pun."

But she noticed that Swann alone had not brightened up. What was more, he was not very pleased that Cottard had made fun of him in front of Forcheville. But the painter, instead of answering Swann in an interesting way, which he probably would have done if he had been alone with him, preferred to win the admiration of the guests by contributing a little set piece on the skill of the deceased master.

"I went up to one of them," he said, "just to see how it was done. I stuck my nose into it. Well! Absolute truth! Impossible to say whether it was done with glue, or rubies, or soap, or sunshine, or leaven, or bronze, or caca!"

"And one makes twelve," cried the doctor, too late, so that no one understood his interruption.

"The thing looked as though it were made with nothing at all," the painter went on; "absolutely no way of discovering the trick, any more than in *The Night Watch* or *The Regents,* and the brushwork is even stronger than Rembrandt or Hals.⁵³ It's got everything in it—no, I swear."

And just as singers who have reached the highest note they can sing continue in falsetto, softly, he confined himself to murmuring, and smiling, as if in fact the painting had been absurdly beautiful:

"It smells good, it goes to your head, it takes your breath away, it tickles you, and you haven't a hope of knowing what it's made with, it's some kind of sorcery, it's a trick, it's a miracle" (bursting fully into laughter): "it's dishonest!" And stopping, gravely lifting his head, adopting a deep bass note which he tried to make harmonious, he added: "and it's so sincere!"

Except at the moment when he had said "stronger than *The Night Watch,*" a blasphemy that had provoked a protest from Mme. Verdurin, who considered *The Night Watch* the greatest masterpiece in the world along with the Ninth and the *Winged Victory,*⁵⁴ and at "made with caca," which had caused Forcheville to cast a circular glance at the table to see if the word was acceptable and had then brought to his mouth a prudish and conciliatory smile, all the guests except for Swann had fastened their eyes on the painter with gazes hypnotized by admiration.

"How he amuses me when he gets carried away like that," cried Mme. Verdurin when he was finished, delighted that the table was so interesting on the very day when M. de Forcheville had come for the first time. "And what about you, what's the matter with you, letting your mouth hang open that way like some great dog?" she said to her husband. "You know very well how he can talk; it's as if my husband had never heard you before. If only you could have seen the way he looked while you were talking, he was lapping you up. And tomorrow he'll repeat everything you said without losing a word."

"But it's no joke," said the painter, enchanted with his success, "you seem to think I'm giving you a sales talk, you think it's all a sham; I'll take you there to see for yourself, then you'll decide whether I'm exaggerating. I'll bet your boots you'll come back even more enthusiastic than I was!"

"But we don't think you're exaggerating, we just want you to eat your dinner, and we want my husband to eat too; give Monsieur some more sole normande, you can see that his is cold. We're not in such a hurry as all that, you're serving as if the house were on fire, now wait a little before you bring in the salad."

Mme. Cottard, who was modest and did not talk much, did not lack self-assurance when a happy inspiration caused her to hit upon a suitable remark. She felt that it would have some success, this gave her confidence, and what she did with it was not so much in order to shine as to be useful to her husband's career. And so she did not allow the word *salad* to escape after it was spoken by Mme. Verdurin.

"That wouldn't be Japanese salad, would it?" she said softly, turning to Odette.

And delighted and abashed by the appropriateness and boldness of making this allusion, so discreet, yet so clear, to the new and astonishing play by Dumas,[55] she burst into charming, ingenuous laughter, not very noisy, but so irresistible that for a few moments she could not control it. "Who is that lady? She's a lively one," said Forcheville.

"No, it's not, but we'll have some for you if you'll all come to dine with us on Friday."

"I'm going to seem very provincial to you, monsieur," said Mme. Cottard to Swann, "but I haven't yet seen the famous *Francillon* everyone's talking about. The doctor has already gone (I even recall that he told me he had the very great pleasure of spending the evening with you) and I confess that I didn't find it reasonable that he should pay for seats to go again with me. Obviously, at the Théâtre-Français, one never regrets one's evening, it's always well acted, but as we have very nice friends" (Mme. Cottard rarely uttered a proper name and simply referred to "some friends of ours" or "one of my friends," because it was more "distinguished," speaking in an artificial tone and with the air of importance of a person who names only those she chooses to) "who often have a box and are kind enough to take us to all the new productions that are worth going to, I'm certain to see *Francillon* sooner or later, and then I can form an opinion for myself. Yet I must confess I find I'm a bit embarrassed, for in every drawing room I visit, naturally the only thing they're talking about is that wretched Japanese salad. One even begins to be a little tired of it," she added, seeing that Swann did not seem as interested as she would have thought in so burning a topic. "I must admit, though, that it sometimes provides an excuse for some rather amusing notions. For instance, I have a friend who's most original, though she's a very pretty woman, very popular, very sought after, who claims she got her cook to make that Japanese salad at her house, putting in everything that Alexandre Dumas *fils* mentions in the play. She invited some friends to come and eat it. Unfortunately I wasn't one of the elect. But she told us about it at her next 'at-home'; apparently it was quite horrible, she made us laugh till we cried. But you know, it's all in the way you tell it," she said, seeing that Swann still looked grave.

And imagining that it was perhaps because he did not like *Francillon:*

"Anyway, I think I'll be disappointed. I don't think it's as good as *Serge Panine*, which Mme. de Crécy worships so. In that one, at least, there are deep things that make you think; but to give a recipe for salad on the stage of the Théâtre-Français! Whereas *Serge Panine*! But then, it's like everything that comes from Georges Ohnet's pen, it's always so well written. I don't know if you know *Le Maître de Forges*, which I like even better than *Serge Panine*."

"Forgive me," Swann said to her with irony, "but I confess that my lack of admiration is almost equally divided between the two masterpieces."

"Really, what have you got against them? Are you sure you aren't prejudiced? Do you think perhaps they're a little dreary? Anyway, as I always say, one should never argue about novels or plays. Everyone has his own way of looking at things and what you find detestable may be the very thing I like best."

She was interrupted by Forcheville addressing Swann. In fact, while Mme. Cottard was talking about *Francillon*, Forcheville had told Mme. Verdurin how much he admired what he called the painter's little "*speech.*"⁵⁶

"The gentleman has a facility for speaking, a memory," he had said to Mme. Verdurin when the painter was finished, "such as I have rarely encountered! By my bootlaces! I'd love to have such a gift. He would make an excellent preacher. One may say that with him and M. Bréchot, you have two real characters, one as good as the other, though for gift of the gab I'm not even sure this one would not in fact ace the professor. It comes out more naturally, it's less studied. Although now and then he does use words that are a bit on the vulgar side, but that's the thing to do nowadays. It's not often that I've seen anyone hold the floor so cleverly–'hold the spittoon,' as we used to say in the regiment, and come to think of it, it was in the regiment that I had a friend the gentleman rather reminded me of. Apropos of anything, I don't know what, this glass, for instance, he could rattle on for hours; no, not about this glass, that's a silly thing to say; but about the Battle of Waterloo, anything you like, and he would throw in things you never would have thought of. Why, Swann was in the same regiment; he must have known him."

"Do you see M. Swann often?" asked Mme. Verdurin.

"Oh no," answered M. de Forcheville, and since in order to approach Odette more easily he wanted to be pleasant to Swann, he attempted to seize this opportunity of flattering him by talking about his distinguished friends, but talking about them as a man of the world, in the tone of an affectionate critic and not as though he were congratulating him as on an unhoped-for success: "Isn't it so, Swann? I never see you. Anyway, how could I ever see him? The man is always hanging about with the La Trémoïlles,⁵⁷ with the Laumes, people like that! . . ." An imputation especially false, since, for a year now, Swann had hardly gone anywhere but to the Verdurins'. But the mere name of a person they did not know was greeted by a reproving silence on their part. M. Verdurin, afraid of the painful impression that these names of "bores," especially when tactlessly hurled thus in the faces of all the faithful, must have produced on his wife, secretly cast at her a glance full of worried solicitude. He saw then that in her resolution not to take action, not to have been affected by the news that had just been announced to her, not merely to remain dumb but to have been deaf as well, the way we pretend to be deaf when a friend who has offended us tries to slip into the conversation an excuse which we would seem to accept if we listened to it without protesting, or when someone utters in our presence the forbidden name of an ingrate, Mme. Verdurin, so that her silence would not seem to be a form of consent, but rather the ignorant silence of an inanimate object, had suddenly divested her face of all life, all mobility; her prominent forehead was now merely a lovely study in the round, which the name of those La Trémoïlles at whose house Swann was always hanging about had not been able to penetrate; her slightly wrinkled nose revealed an indentation that seemed copied from life. Her half-open mouth seemed about to speak. She was now merely a lost wax,[58] a plaster mask, a model for a monument, a bust for the Palais de l'Industrie[59] in front of which the public would certainly stop to admire how the sculptor, by expressing the indefeasible dignity of the Verdurins as opposed to that of the La Trémoïlles and the Laumes, whose equals they naturally were, as they were the equals of all the bores on earth, had managed to give an almost papal majesty to the whiteness and rigidity of the stone. But at last the marble came to life and insinuated that one could not be squeamish if one wanted to go to the homes of these people, because the wife was always drunk and the husband so ignorant that he said "collidor" instead of "corridor."

"You'd have to pay me handsomely before I'd let that sort enter my house," concluded Mme. Verdurin, looking at Swann with an imperious air.

She probably did not hope that he would be submissive enough to imitate the saintly simplicity of the pianist's aunt, who had just exclaimed: "You see that? What astonishes me is that there's still people who'll speak to them! I think I would be too afraid: once struck, out of luck! How can there still be folks low enough to go running after them?" But he might at least have answered like Forcheville: "Lord, she's a duchess; some people are still impressed by that," which had at least allowed Mme. Verdurin to reply: "Much good may it do them!" Instead of that, Swann merely laughed with an air that signified that he could not even take such extravagant nonsense seriously. M. Verdurin, continuing to cast furtive glances at his wife, saw with sadness and understood all too well that she was feeling the rage of a grand inquisitor who cannot manage to extirpate the heresy, and in order to try to lead Swann to a recantation, since the courage of one's convictions always seem to be a calculation and an act of cowardice in the eyes of those who do not share them, M. Verdurin challenged him:

"Now tell us frankly what you think of them, we won't repeat it to them."

To which Swann answered:

"Why, it's not in the least out of fear of the duchess (if you're talking about the La Trémoïlles). I assure you everyone likes to visit her. I'm not saying she's 'profound'" (he pronounced *profound* as if it were a ridiculous word, because his language still bore the trace of habits of mind which his recent rejuvenation, marked by a love of music, had temporarily made him lose, so that at times he now expressed his opinions warmly) "but I'm quite sincere when I say that she's intelligent and her husband is truly well read. They're charming people."

Whereupon Mme. Verdurin, feeling that because of this one infidel she would be prevented from creating a complete moral unanimity among the little clan, was unable to stop herself, in her rage against this stubborn man who did not see how much his words pained her, from crying out to him from the bottom of her heart:

"Believe it if you like, but at least don't say it to us."

"It all depends on what you call intelligence," said Forcheville, who felt it was his turn to shine. "Now, Swann, what do you mean by intelligence?"

"There you are!" exclaimed Odette. "That's the sort of big subject I'm always asking him to talk to me about, but he never will."

"But I do . . ." protested Swann.

"What tripe!" said Odette.

"Tripe with onions?" asked the doctor.

"As you see it," Forcheville went on, "does intelligence mean a gift of the gab, does it have to do with how people manage to worm their way in?"

"Finish up so they can take your plate," said Mme. Verdurin sourly, turning to Saniette, who, absorbed in thought, had stopped eating. And perhaps a little ashamed of the tone she had taken: "Never mind, take your time, I only said it for the sake of the others, because it holds up the next course."

"There is," said Brichot, rapping out the syllables, "a very curious definition of intelligence in that gentle anarchist, Fénelon . . ."⁶⁰

"Listen!" said Mme. Verdurin to Forcheville and the doctor. "He's going to give us Fénelon's definition of intelligence. Now that's interesting. It's not often you have a chance of hearing that."

But Brichot was waiting for Swann to give his own definition. Swann did not answer, and by evading them spoiled the brilliant contest that Mme. Verdurin was so delighted to be able to offer Forcheville.

"Of course. He's just like that with me all the time," said Odette sulkily. "I'm glad to see I'm not the only one he doesn't think is up to his level."

"Those de la Trémouailles,⁶¹ who are so little to be recommended, as Mme. Verdurin has shown us," asked Brichot with powerfully clear articulation, "are they descended from the folk whom Mme. de Sévigné, that good snob, admitted she was pleased to know because it was good for her peasants? Of course, the Marquise had another reason, and one that had to be more important to her, for as a woman of letters through and through, she put copy before all else. Now in the journal she used to send regularly to her daughter, it was Mme. de la Trémouaille, kept well informed by her great connections, who supplied the foreign politics."

"Why, no, I don't think it's the same family," ventured Mme. Verdurin.

Saniette, who, after hurriedly giving the butler his plate, which was still full, had plunged back into a meditative silence, emerged from it at last to tell them with a smile the story of a dinner he had attended with the Duc de La Trémoïlle at which it turned out that the Duc did not know George Sand was the pseudonym of a woman. Swann, who was fond of Saniette, thought he ought to supply him with a few particulars about the Duc's culture proving that such ignorance on the latter's part was materially impossible; but suddenly he stopped, realizing that Saniette did not need these proofs and knew the story was untrue for the simple reason that he had just invented it a moment ago. That excellent man suffered from being thought such a bore by the Verdurins; and, aware that he had been even duller than usual at this dinner, he had not wanted to let it end before he succeeded in amusing them. He capitulated so quickly, looked so unhappy at seeing that the effect on which he had counted had failed, and answered Swann in such a pitiful tone so that Swann would not persist in a refutation that was henceforth pointless, "All right, all right; and if I'm mistaken it's not a crime, I hope," that Swann would have liked to be able to say the story was true and delightful. The doctor, who had been listening to them, thought this was the moment to say: *Se non è vero,*[62] but he was not quite sure of the words and was afraid of getting muddled.

After dinner, Forcheville went up to the doctor.

"She must not have been too bad at one time, Mme. Verdurin, and she's a woman you can talk to; for me that's everything. Of course she's beginning to get a bit long in the tooth. But Mme. de Crécy—now there's a little woman who seems intelligent—oh yes, by God; you can see at a glance that she keeps her eyes peeled! We're talking about Mme. de Crécy," he said to M. Verdurin, who was approaching, his pipe in his mouth. "I would imagine that as a specimen of the female figure . . ."

"I'd rather have it in my bed than a slap with a wet fish," Cottard rushed to say, having waited in vain for some moments for Forcheville to pause for breath so that he could insert that old joke, which he feared would not be appropriate again if the conversation changed course, and which he delivered with that excess of spontaneity and assurance which attempts to mask the coldness and anxiety inseparable from a recitation. Forcheville was familiar with the joke, he understood it and was amused by it. As for M. Verdurin, he was unsparing with his mirth, because he had recently discovered a signal for expressing it different from the one used by his wife but equally simple and clear. Scarcely had he begun moving his head and shoulders in the manner of a person shaking with laughter than he would immediately begin coughing as if, in laughing too hard, he had swallowed smoke from his pipe. And still keeping the pipe in one corner of his mouth, he would prolong indefinitely this pantomime of suffocation and hilarity. Thus he and Mme. Verdurin, who, across the room from him, listening to the painter tell her a story, was closing her eyes before dropping her face into her hands, looked like two theater masks each representing merriment in its own way.

M. Verdurin had in fact been wise not to withdraw his pipe from his mouth, for Cottard, who needed to leave the room for a moment, made a joke under his breath that he had learned recently and that he repeated each time he had to go to the same place: "I must absent myself for a moment in aid of the Duc d'Aumale,"⁶³ so that M. Verdurin's fit began again.

"Take your pipe out of your mouth. Can't you see you're going to choke to death trying not to laugh?" Mme. Verdurin said to him as she came around offering the liqueurs.

"How charming your husband is, he has wit enough for four," declared Forcheville to Mme. Cottard. "Thank you, madame. An old soldier like me never refuses a drop."

"M. de Forcheville thinks Odette is charming," said M. Verdurin to his wife.

"Why, actually she would like to come to lunch with you some time. We're going to contrive to make it happen, but Swann mustn't hear of it. You know, he puts rather a damper on things. That doesn't mean you shouldn't join us for dinner, of course, we hope to have you often. With summer coming, we'll be dining outdoors quite frequently. That won't bore you, will it—little dinners in the Bois? Good, good, it'll be very nice. You! Aren't you going to go do your job now?" she cried out to the little pianist, in order to display, in front of a newcomer as important as Forcheville, both her wit and her tyrannical power over the faithful.

"M. de Forcheville was saying bad things to me about you," said Mme. Cottard to her husband when he returned to the drawing room.

And he, pursuing the idea of Forcheville's noble lineage, which had preoccupied him from the beginning of dinner, said to him:

"I'm treating a baroness just now, Baronne Putbus;[64] the Putbuses took part in the Crusades, didn't they? They have a lake in Pomerania that's so big it must be ten times the size of the place de la Concorde. I'm treating her for rheumatoid arthritis; she's a charming woman. In fact she knows Mme. Verdurin, I believe."

Which allowed Forcheville, finding himself, a moment later, alone with Mme. Cottard, to complete the favorable judgment that he had passed on her husband:

"And he's so interesting, you can tell he's acquainted with more than a few people. Lord, they know such a lot, these doctors!"

"I'm going to play the phrase from the sonata for M. Swann," said the pianist.

"My God! I trust we don't have the 'sonata-snake'[65] in our midst?" asked M. de Forcheville to create an effect.

But Dr. Cottard, who had never heard that pun, did not understand it and thought M. de Forcheville was making a mistake. He went up to them briskly to correct it:

"No, no, one doesn't say *serpent à sonates,* it's *serpent à sonnettes,* 'rattlesnake,'" he said in a tone that was zealous, impatient, and triumphant.

Forcheville explained the pun to him. The doctor blushed.

"Admit that it's funny, Doctor!"

"Oh, I've known it for too long," answered Cottard.

But they fell silent; under the agitation of the violin tremolos which protected it with their quivering extended two octaves above— and as in a mountainous countryside, behind the apparent and vertiginous immobility of a waterfall one sees, two hundred feet down, the minuscule form of a woman walking—the little phrase had just appeared, distant, graceful, protected by the long unfurling of its transparent, ceaseless curtain of sound. And Swann, in his heart, appealed to it as to a confidant of his love, as to a friend of Odette's who certainly should tell her to pay no attention to that Forcheville.

"Ah, you're late!" said Mme. Verdurin to a regular whom she had invited only "for coffee." "Brichot was incomparable—so eloquent! But he's gone. Isn't that right, Monsieur Swann? I believe it was the first time you and he had met," she said in order to point out to him that she was the one to whom he owed the introduction. "Wasn't our Brichot delicious?"

Swann bowed politely.

"No? He didn't interest you?" Mme. Verdurin asked him curtly.

"Why, of course, madame, very much, I was delighted. He is perhaps a little peremptory and a little jovial for my taste. I would like to see some hesitation, some gentleness now and then, but one senses that he knows so many things and he seems like an all-around decent man."

Everyone went home very late. Cottard's first words to his wife were:

"I've rarely seen Mme. Verdurin as spirited as she was this evening."

"What exactly is this Mme. Verdurin of yours, rather a mixed bag of goods?" said Forcheville to the painter, whom he had invited to ride with him.

Odette watched with regret as he went off; she did not dare decline to ride with Swann, but was in a bad mood in the carriage, and when he asked her if he ought to come in, she said, "Of course," shrugging her shoulders impatiently. When all the guests had gone, Mme. Verdurin said to her husband:

"Did you notice how Swann laughed foolishly when we were talking about Mme. La Trémoïlle?"

She had noticed that several times, when saying this name, Swann and Forcheville had omitted the particle. Having no doubt that they did this to show they were not intimidated by titles, she wanted to imitate their pride, but had not fully understood by which grammatical form it was expressed. And so her incorrect way of speaking won out over her republican intransigence, and she still said "the de la Trémoïlles" or rather, using an abbreviation current in the words of the café songs and caricature captions, which swallowed the *de*, "the d'La Trémoïlles," but she made up for it by saying: "Madame La Trémoïlle," "The *Duchesse*, as Swann calls her," she added ironically with a smile which proved she was only quoting and did not accept responsibility for so naive and ridiculous a denomination.

"I must tell you I found him extremely stupid."

And M. Verdurin answered her:

"He's not direct, he's cunning, always betwixt and between. He's a fellow who's always wanting to run with the hare and hunt with the hounds. How different from Forcheville! There's a man who at least tells you fair and square what he's thinking. You either agree with him or you don't. He's not like the other, neither fish nor fowl. Anyway, Odette really seems to prefer Forcheville, and I think she's right. And then, also, since Swann wants to play the society man with us, defender of duchesses, at least the other has his own title; he's still the Comte de Forcheville," he added delicately, as if, well informed about the history of that dignity, he was scrupulously weighing its particular value.

"I must tell you," said Mme. Verdurin, "that he felt called upon to direct some venomous and quite ridiculous insinuations against Brichot. Naturally, since he saw that Brichot was well liked in this house, it was a way of attacking us, of disparaging our dinner party. What I suspect is he's the sort of good friend who says nasty things about you on his way out."

"But that's what I told you," answered M. Verdurin. "He's a typical failure, the little fellow envious of anything that's at all big."

In reality there was not one of the faithful who was not more malicious than Swann; but they all took care to season their slander with familiar jokes, with little hints of anxiety and cordiality; whereas the slightest reserve that Swann allowed himself, omitting such conventional formulas as, "Now I don't mean to say anything bad," to which he did not deign to stoop, seemed perfidious. There are authors of true originality in whom the least boldness offends because they have not first flattered the tastes of the public and have not served it the commonplaces which it is used to; it was in the same way that Swann roused M. Verdurin's indignation. In Swann's case as in theirs, it was the novelty of his language that convinced one of the darkness of his intentions.

Swann was still unaware of the disgrace that threatened him at the Verdurins' and continued to regard all their absurdities in a favorable light, with the eyes of his love.

Most of the time, at least, he met Odette only in the evening; but during the day, though he was afraid of causing her to become tired of him by going to her house, he wanted at least not to cease to occupy her thoughts and was always looking for an opportunity of involving himself in them, but in a way that would be pleasant for her. If, in the window of a florist or a jeweler, the sight of a shrub or a jewel charmed him, instantly he would think of sending it to Odette, imagining that the pleasure it had given him would be felt by her too, increasing her affection for him, and he would immediately have it delivered to the rue La Pérouse so as not to delay the moment when, because she was receiving something from him, he would feel he was in some way close to her. He especially wanted her to receive it before she went out so that the gratitude she felt would win him a more tender welcome when she saw him at the Verdurins', or even—who knows?—if the shopkeeper was prompt enough, perhaps a letter which she would send him before dinner, or her arrival in person at his house, in a supplementary visit to thank him. Just as he had once tested Odette's nature for reactions of resentment, so now he sought by reactions of gratitude to extract from her intimate particles of feeling that she had not yet revealed to him.

Often, she had money troubles and, hard-pressed by a debt, would ask him for help. He was happy about that, as about everything that could give Odette a strong impression of the love he had for her, or simply a strong impression of his influence, of how useful he could be to her. No doubt if someone had said to him in the beginning: "It's your position that attracts her," and now: "It's because of your wealth that she loves you," he would not have believed it, and would also not have minded very much that people imagined she was attached to him—that people felt they were joined together—by something as powerful as snobbishness or money. But, even if he had thought it was true, perhaps he would not have been hurt by discovering within Odette's love for him that mainstay more durable than his charm or the good qualities she might find in him: namely, self-interest, a self-interest that would prevent the day ever coming when she would be tempted to stop seeing him. For the moment, by overwhelming her with presents, by doing her favors, he could rely upon advantages extrinsic to his person, his intelligence, to take over from him the exhausting responsibility of pleasing her by himself. And as for the pleasure of being in love, of living by love alone, the reality of which he doubted at times, it was increased in value for him, as dilettante of immaterial sensations, by the price he was paying her for it—as we observe that people who are uncertain whether the sight of the sea and the sound of its waves are delightful convince themselves of it and also of the exceptional quality and disinterest of their own taste, by paying a hundred francs a day for a hotel room that allows them to experience that sight and that sound.

One day when reflections of this kind were leading him back once again to the memory of the time when people had described Odette to him as a kept woman, and when he was amusing himself yet again by contrasting that strange personification, the kept woman—an iridescent amalgam of unfamiliar and diabolical elements, set, like some apparition by Gustave Moreau,[66] among venomous flowers interwoven with precious jewels—with the Odette on whose face he had seen the same feelings of pity for a sufferer, revolt against an injustice, gratitude for a favor, that he had seen in earlier days on his own mother's face and on the faces of his friends, the Odette whose conversation had so often turned on the things he knew best himself, on his collections, his room, his old servant, the banker who looked after his securities, it happened that this last image of the banker reminded him that he would have to call on him soon to draw some money. In fact, if this month he was less liberal when helping Odette out of her material difficulties than he had been the month before when he had given her five thousand francs, and if he did not present her with a diamond rivière that she wanted, he would not reawaken her admiration for his generosity, her gratitude, which made him so happy, and he would even risk making her think that his love for her, as she saw its manifestations become less abundant, had diminished. Then, suddenly, he wondered if this was not precisely what was meant by "keeping" her (as if, in fact, this notion of keeping could be derived from elements not at all mysterious or perverse but belonging to the intimate substance of his daily life, like that thousand-franc bill, domestic and familiar, torn and reglued, which his valet, after having paid the month's accounts and the quarter's rent for him, had locked in the drawer of the old desk from which Swann had taken it out again to send it with four others to Odette) and if one could not apply to Odette, starting from when he had come to know her (because he did not for a moment suspect that she could ever have received money from anyone before him), those words which he had believed so irreconcilable with her—"kept woman." He could not study this idea in greater depth, because an attack of that mental laziness which in him was congenital, intermittent, and providential, happened at that moment to extinguish all light in his intelligence, as abruptly as, later, when electric lighting had been installed everywhere, one could cut off the electricity in a house. His mind groped for a moment in the darkness, he took off his glasses, wiped the lenses, passed his hand over his eyes, and saw the light again only when he found himself in the presence of an entirely different idea, namely that he ought to try to send six or seven thousand francs to Odette next month instead of five, because of the surprise and pleasure it would give her.

In the evening, when he did not stay at home waiting for the hour when he would meet Odette at the Verdurins' or rather in one of the summer restaurants they favored in the Bois and especially at Saint-

Cloud, he would go and dine in one of those elegant houses where he had once been a habitual guest at table. He did not want to lose touch with people who—one never could tell—might perhaps be useful to Odette one day and through whom, in the meantime, he often succeeded in pleasing her. Also, his long habit of society, of luxury, had given him, at the same time as a disdain for them, a need for them, so that by the time he had come to regard the most modest houses as exactly on a par with the most princely, his senses were so accustomed to the latter that he experienced some indisposition at finding himself in the former. He had the same esteem—identical to a degree they could not have believed—for a petit bourgeois family which asked him up to a dance on the fifth floor, Stairway D, left at the landing, as for the Princess of Parma, who gave the finest parties in Paris; but he did not have the feeling of being actually at a ball while standing with the fathers in the bedroom of the mistress of the house and the sight of the washstands covered with towels, of the beds, transformed into cloakrooms, their coverlets piled with overcoats and hats, gave him the same stifling sensation that people today who are used to twenty years of electricity may experience at the smell of a lamp blackening or a night-light smoking. On the days when he dined in town, he would have the horses harnessed for seven-thirty; he would dress while thinking about Odette and so would not be alone, because the constant thought of Odette would give to the moments in which he was away from her the same particular charm as to those in which she was there. He would get into his carriage, but he would feel that this thought had leaped into it at the same time and settled on his knees like a beloved pet which one takes everywhere and which he would keep with him at the table, unbeknownst to the other guests. He would stroke it, warm himself at it, and, experiencing a sort of languor, yield to a light quivering that tensed his neck and his nose, and was new to him, all the while fastening the bunch of columbines in his buttonhole. Having felt unwell and sad for some time, especially from the time that Odette had introduced Forcheville to the Verdurins, Swann would have liked to go and rest a little in the country. But he would not have had the courage to leave Paris for a single day while Odette was there. The air was warm; these were the finest days of spring. And though he might cross a city of stone to immure himself in some town house, what was constantly before his eyes was a park that he owned near Combray, where, from four o'clock on, before reaching the asparagus patch, because of the wind that comes from the fields of Méséglise, one could savor as much coolness under an arbor as at the edge of the pond encircled by forget-me-nots and gladioli, and where, when he dined, it was at a table around which ran red currants and roses intertwined by his gardener.

After dinner, if the appointed meeting time at the Bois or Saint-Cloud was early, he would leave so soon after getting up from the table—especially if rain was threatening to fall and make the "faithful" go home earlier—that once the Princesse des Laumes (at whose home they had dined late and whom Swann had left before coffee was served in order to join the Verdurins on the island in the Bois) had said:

"Really, if Swann were thirty years older and had bladder trouble, one would excuse him for running off like that. But the fact is he doesn't care what people think."

He told himself that the charm of springtime which he could not go down to enjoy at Combray he could at least find on the Île des Cygnes[67] or at Saint-Cloud. But since he could think only about Odette, he did not even know if he had detected the smell of the leaves, if there had been any light from the moon. He was greeted by the little phrase from the sonata played in the garden on the restaurant piano. If there was no piano there, the Verdurins would take great pains to have one brought down from a bedroom or dining room: it was not that Swann had come back into favor with them, on the contrary. But the idea of organizing an ingenious pleasure for someone, even for someone they did not like, fostered in them, during the time required for these preparations, exceptional and ephemeral feelings of warmth and cordiality. Now and then he would say to himself that another spring evening was passing, he would force himself to pay attention to the trees, the sky. But the agitation with which Odette's presence filled him, and also a slight feverish indisposition that had hardly left him for some time now, denied him that sense of calm and well-being which is the indispensable background to the impressions we derive from nature.

One evening when Swann had agreed to dine with the Verdurins, and had just mentioned during dinner that the next day he was going to attend a banquet for old comrades, Odette answered him across the table, in front of Forcheville, who was now one of the faithful, in front of the painter, in front of Cottard:

"Yes, I know you have your banquet, so I won't see you till I get home, but don't be too late."

Even though Swann had never become very seriously offended by Odette's friendliness toward one or another of the faithful, he felt an exquisite pleasure on hearing her thus confess in front of everyone, with such a calm lack of modesty, to their regular meetings every night, his privileged position in her house, and the preference for him which it implied. Of course Swann had often reflected that Odette was in no way a remarkable woman, and the ascendancy he exerted over a creature so inferior to him was not something that ought to appear to him so flattering to see proclaimed to all the "faithful," but from the time he had first noticed that many men found Odette an enchanting and desirable woman, the attraction her body had for them had awoken in him a painful need to master her entirely even in the smallest parts of her heart. And he had begun to set an inestimable price on those times spent in her house at night, when he would sit her on his knees, make her say what she thought of one thing, of another, when he would count up the only goods whose possession he now valued on earth. And so, after this dinner, taking her aside, he did not fail to thank her effusively, endeavoring to teach her according to the degrees of gratitude he displayed to her, the scale of pleasures that she could give him, the highest of which was to guarantee him, during the time that his love should last and make him vulnerable to them, protection from the assaults of jealousy.

When he came away from the banquet the next day, it was pouring rain, all he had was his victoria; a friend offered to drive him home in his coupé, and because Odette, since she had asked him to

come, had given him the assurance that she was not waiting for anyone else, it was with a tranquil mind and a happy heart that, rather
than set off in the rain like this, he would have gone back home to
bed. But perhaps, if she saw that he did not seem anxious to spend the
last part of every evening without exception in her company, she
might neglect to reserve it for him, precisely the one time when he
particularly desired it.

He reached her house after eleven o'clock, and, as he was apologizing for not being able to come earlier, she complained that it was
indeed very late, the storm had made her unwell, she had a headache
and warned him that she would not keep him more than half an hour,
that at midnight she would send him away; and, soon afterward, she
felt tired and wanted to go to sleep.

"So, no cattleyas tonight," he said to her, "after I was so hoping
for a nice little cattleya."

And, a little sulky and irritable, she answered:

"No, no, darling, no cattleyas tonight, you can see I'm unwell!"

"It might have done you good, but I won't insist."

She asked him to put out the light before he went, he himself
closed the curtains of the bed and left. But when he was back at home,
the idea came to him abruptly that perhaps Odette had been waiting
for someone else that night, had only pretended to be tired, and had
asked him to put out the light only so that he would believe she was
going to go to sleep, that as soon as he left, she had put the light on
again, and let in the man who was going to spend the night with her.
He looked at the time. It was about an hour and a half since he had left
her, he went back out, took a hackney carriage, and stopped it very
close to where she lived, in a little street at right angles to the one
which lay behind her house and into which he sometimes went to
knock at her bedroom window so that she would come and open the
door for him; he got out of the carriage, the neighborhood was dark
and deserted, he had only to walk a few steps, and he came out almost
opposite her house. Amid the blackness of all the windows in the street
in which the lights had long since been put out, he saw just one from

which there spilled out—between shutters which pressed its mysterious golden pulp—the light which filled the bedroom and which, on so many other evenings, as soon as he saw it when he came into the street, lifted his spirits and announced to him: "She's there waiting for you" and which now tortured him by saying: "She's there with the man she was waiting for." He wanted to know who it was; he slipped along the wall as far as the window, but between the oblique slats of the shutters he could see nothing; all he heard in the silence of the night was the murmur of conversation. Certainly it hurt him to see that light and know that in its golden atmosphere, behind the sash, the unseen and detested pair were moving about, to hear the murmur revealing the presence of the man who had come after he left, Odette's duplicity, the happiness she was enjoying with him.

And yet he was glad he had come: the torment that had forced him to leave his house had become less acute as it became less vague, now that Odette's other life, of which he had had, back then, a sudden helpless suspicion, was now in his grasp, fully illuminated by the lamp, an unwitting prisoner in that room into which, when he chose, he could go to surprise it and capture it; or rather he would knock on the shutters as he often did when he came very late; this way at least, Odette would learn that he knew, that he had seen the light and heard the talking, and that, after having just a moment ago pictured her laughing with the other man at his illusions, he would now be the one to see them, confident in their error, actually outwitted by him whom they believed to be so very far away and who, in fact, already knew he was going to knock at the shutters. And perhaps, what he was feeling at this moment, which was almost pleasant, was also something different from the assuaging of a doubt and a distress: it was a pleasure in knowledge. If, ever since he had fallen in love, things had regained for him a little of the delightful interest they had once had for him, but only insofar as they were illuminated by the memory of Odette, now it was another of the faculties of his studious youth that his jealousy revived, a passion for truth, but for a truth that was likewise interposed between him and his mistress, taking its light only from her, a completely individual truth whose sole object, of an infinite value and almost disinterested in its beauty, was Odette's actions, her relationships, her plans, her past. At all other periods of his life, the little everyday words and deeds of a person had always seemed worthless to Swann if someone conveyed them to him as the subject of a bit of gossip, he found such gossip meaningless, and, while he listened to it, only the most vulgar part of his attention was interested; these were the times when he felt himself to be most mediocre. But in this strange phase of love, an individual person assumes something so profound that the curiosity he now felt awakening in him concerning the smallest occupations of this woman, was the same curiosity he had once had about History. And all these things that would have shamed him up to now, such as spying, tonight, outside a window, tomorrow perhaps, for all he knew, cleverly inducing neutral people to speak, bribing servants, listening at doors, now seemed to him to be, fully as much as were the deciphering of texts, the weighing of evidence, and the interpretation of old monuments, merely methods of scientific investigation with a real intellectual value and appropriate to a search for the truth.

On the point of knocking on the shutters, he felt a pang of shame thinking that Odette was going to know he had been suspicious, that he had come back, that he had posted himself in the street. She had often told him what a horror she had of jealous men, of lovers who spied. What he was about to do was very uncouth, and from now on she would detest him, whereas now, for the moment, so long as he had not knocked, perhaps, even while deceiving him, she loved him. How often we sacrifice the fulfillment of a possible happiness to our impatience for an immediate pleasure! But the desire to know the truth was stronger and seemed to him nobler. He knew that the reality of certain circumstances which he would have given his life to reconstruct accurately could be read behind that window striated with light, as under the gold-illuminated cover of one of those precious manuscripts to whose artistic richness itself the scholar who consults them cannot remain indifferent. He felt a delicious pleasure in learning the truth that so impassioned him from this unique, ephemeral, and precious transcript, made of a translucid substance so warm and so beautiful. Then, too, the advantage he felt he had—that he so needed to feel he had—over them lay perhaps less in knowing than in being able to show them he knew. He raised himself on his tiptoes. He knocked. They had not heard, he knocked again more loudly, the conversation stopped. A man's voice which he tried to distinguish from among the voices of those of Odette's friends whom he knew asked:

"Who's there?"

He was not sure he recognized it. He knocked again. The window was opened, then the shutters. Now there was no way to retreat, and since she was going to know everything, so as not to seem too wretched, too jealous and curious, he merely called out carelessly and gaily:

"Please don't go to any trouble. I was just passing by and I saw the light. I wanted to know if you were feeling better."

He looked. Before him, two old gentlemen were standing at the window, one holding a lamp, and then he saw the bedroom, a bedroom unknown to him. Because he was in the habit, when he came to Odette's house very late, of recognizing her window by the fact that it was the only one lit among windows that were all alike, he had made a mistake and knocked at the window after hers, which belonged to the adjoining house. He went away apologizing and returned home, happy that the satisfaction of his curiosity had left their love intact and that after having simulated a sort of indifference toward Odette for so long, he had not given her, by his jealousy, that proof of loving her too much which, between two lovers, exempts forever after, from loving enough, the one who receives it. He did not talk to her about this misadventure, he himself did not think about it further. But now and then his thoughts as they moved about would come upon the memory of it which they had not noticed, bump up against it, drive it further in, and Swann would feel a sudden, deep pain. As if it were a physical pain, Swann's mind could not lessen it; but at least with physical pain, because it is independent of thought, thought can dwell on it, note that it has diminished, that it has momentarily ceased. But with this pain the mind, merely by recalling it, re-created

it. To wish not to think about it was still to think about it, still to suffer from it. And when, chatting with friends, he forgot his hurt, all of
a sudden a word someone said to him would make him change expression, like a man with an injury whom some clumsy person has
just carelessly touched on his sore arm or leg. When he left Odette, he
was happy, he felt calm, he recalled her smiles, derisive when speaking
of this or that other person, and affectionate toward him, the heavi-
ness of her head which she had shifted from its axis to incline it, let it
fall, almost despite herself, onto his lips, as she had done the first time
in the carriage, the languishing looks she had cast at him while she
was in his arms, as with a shiver she pulled her inclined head in
against her shoulder.

But instantly his jealousy, as if it were the shadow of his love,
would furnish itself with a duplicate of the new smile she had given
him that very evening—and which, inverse now, mocked Swann and
was filled with love for another man; with that inclination of her head
but reversed toward other lips; with all the marks of affection, now
given to another man, that she had given him. And all the sensuous
memories he carried away from her house were like so many sketches,
"plans" like those a decorator submits to you, that allowed Swann to
form an idea of the ardent or swooning attitudes she might adopt
with other men. So that he came to regret every pleasure he enjoyed
with her, every invented caress whose sweetness he had been so imprudent as to point out to her, every grace he discovered in her, for he
knew that a moment later, they would supply new instruments for
torturing him.

This torture became still crueler when Swann remembered a brief
expression he had surprised, a few days before, and for the first time,
in Odette's eyes. It was after dinner, at the Verdurins'. Either because
Forcheville, feeling that Saniette, his brother-in-law, was not in favor
in their house, wanted to use him as a whipping boy and shine in
front of them at his expense, or because he had been irritated by a
clumsy remark which Saniette had just made to him and which, in
fact, had gone unnoticed by those present, who were not aware of the

unpleasant allusion it might contain quite contrary to the intentions of the one who had uttered it without any malice, or finally because for some time now he had been looking for an opportunity to induce them to banish from the house someone who was too well acquainted with him and whom he knew to be so refined that he felt embarrassed at certain moments merely by his presence, Forcheville answered this clumsy remark of Saniette's with such coarseness, hurling insults at him, and emboldened, as he shouted, by Saniette's pain, his dismay, his entreaties, that the wretched man, after asking Mme. Verdurin if he ought to stay, and receiving no answer, had left the house stammering, tears in his eyes. Odette had watched this scene impassively, but when the door closed on Saniette, lowering as it were by several notches her face's habitual expression, so as to be able to find herself, in her baseness, on an equal footing with Forcheville, she had put a sparkle in her eyes with a sly smile of congratulations for the audacity he had shown, of mockery for the man who had been its victim; she had cast him a glance of complicity in evil which was so clearly intended to say: "That finished him off, or I'm very much mistaken. Did you see how pathetic he looked? He was actually crying," that Forcheville, when his eyes met that glance, sobering in a moment from the anger or simulation of anger which still warmed him, smiled and answered:

"He needed only to be friendly, and he would still be here. A good rebuke does a man no harm at any age."

One day when Swann had gone out in the middle of the afternoon to pay a call, not having found the person he wanted to see, it occurred to him to go to Odette's house at an hour when he never went there, but when he knew she was always at home having her nap or writing letters before teatime, and when he would enjoy seeing her for a little while without bothering her. The concierge told him he thought she was there; he rang, thought he heard a noise, heard footsteps, but no one opened the door. Anxious, irritated, he went into the little street on which the other side of the house looked out, stood in front of the window of Odette's bedroom; the curtains prevented him from seeing anything, he knocked hard on the windowpanes, called out; no one opened the window. He saw that some neighbors were watching him. He went away, thinking that after all, perhaps he had been mistaken in believing he heard footsteps; but he remained so preoccupied by it that he could not think about anything else. An hour later, he came back. He found her there; she told him she had been at home earlier when he rang, but was sleeping; the bell had woken her, she had guessed it was Swann, she had run after him, but he had already left. She had certainly heard the sound of knocking at the windowpanes. Swann immediately recognized this statement as one of those fragments of true fact with which liars, when caught unprepared, console themselves by introducing into the composition of the falsehood they are inventing, believing they can accommodate it there and steal its resemblance to the Truth. Of course when Odette had just done something she did not want to reveal, she would hide it deep inside herself. But as soon as she found herself face-to-face with the man to whom she wanted to lie, she was overcome with uneasiness, all her ideas collapsed, her faculties of invention and reasoning were paralyzed, she found nothing in her head but emptiness, yet it was necessary to say something, and all she would find within reach was the very thing she had wanted to conceal and which, being true, was all that had remained there. She would detach a little piece from it, unimportant in itself, telling herself that after all this was better since the detail was authentic and did not present the same dangers as a false detail. "At least this is true," she would say to herself, "so much is gained, anyway. He may make inquiries and he'll see that it's true, so at least it won't be this that gives me away." She was wrong, it was this that gave her away, she did not realize that the true detail had angles that could fit only into the contiguous details of the true fact from which she had arbitrarily detached it, angles which, whatever the invented details among which she might place it, would always reveal, by the excess material and unfilled empty areas, that it was not from among these that it had come. "She admits that she heard me ring, then knock, and that she thought it was me, that she wanted to see me," Swann said to himself. "But this does not conform with the fact that no one opened the door."

But he did not point out this contradiction to her, because he thought that, left to herself, Odette would perhaps produce some lie that would be a faint indication of the truth; she would talk; he would not interrupt her, he would collect with an avid and painful piety the words she said to him, feeling (precisely because she was hiding it behind them as she talked to him) that, like the sacred veil, they retained the vague imprint, sketched the uncertain features, of that reality so infinitely precious and, alas! undiscoverable—what she had been doing that afternoon at three o'clock, when he came—of which he would never possess more than these lies, illegible and divine vestiges, and which now existed only in the memory of this woman, who would conceal it like stolen goods and contemplate it without being able to appreciate it, but would not hand it over to him. Of course, he fully suspected at times that in themselves Odette's daily actions were not passionately interesting, and that the relationships she might have with other men did not naturally, universally, and for every intelligent creature exhale a morbid sadness capable of infecting one with a feverish desire to commit suicide. He would then realize that this interest, this sadness existed only in him like a disease, and that, once this disease was cured, Odette's actions, the kisses she might have given would become once again as harmless as those of so many other women. But the fact that the painful curiosity which Swann brought to them now had its origin only in himself was not enough to make him think it was unreasonable to consider this curiosity important and to use every possible means to satisfy it. For Swann was reaching an age the philosophy of which—encouraged, in his case, by the current philosophy of the day, and also by that of the circle in which he had spent so much of his life, that of the social set attached to the Princess des Laumes, where one's intelligence was understood to be in direct ratio to one's skepticism and nothing was real and incontestable except the individual tastes of each person—is no longer that of youth, but the positive, almost medical philosophy of men who, instead of externalizing the objects of their aspirations, try to derive from the years they have already lived a stable residue of habits and passions which they can regard as characteristic and permanent and to which, deliberately, they will take care before anything else that the kind of life they adopt may provide satisfaction. Swann thought it prudent to make allowance in his life for the pain he felt at not knowing what Odette had been doing, just as he made allowance for the fresh outbreak which a damp climate might cause in his eczema; to provide in his budget for a sizable sum of available funds for obtaining information about how Odette spent her days, without which he would feel unhappy, just as he reserved the same for other partialities from which he knew he could expect to derive pleasure, at least before he had fallen in love, like his partiality for collections and for good food.

When he tried to say good-bye to Odette in order to leave for home, she asked him to stay longer and even held him back suddenly, by taking his arm, when he was about to open the door to go out. But he took no notice of this, because among the multitude of gestures, remarks, minor incidents that fill a conversation, it is inevitable that we should come close, without detecting anything in them to attract our attention, to those that hide a truth our suspicions are blindly seeking, and that we should stop, on the other hand, at those behind which there is nothing. She kept saying to him: "How unfortunate— you never come in the afternoon, and the one time you do come, I don't see you." He knew very well that she was not sufficiently in love with him to be so keenly distressed at having missed his visit, but, because she was good, desirous of pleasing him, and often sad when she had vexed him, he found it quite natural that she should be sad this time at having deprived him of the pleasure of spending an hour together, a very great pleasure, not for her, but for him. Yet it was a thing unimportant enough so that the pained air she continued to have ended by surprising him. She reminded him even more than usual, when she looked this way, of the faces of the women portrayed by the painter of the Primavera.[68] She had at this moment their down-cast and heartbroken expression which seems to be succumbing beneath the weight of a grief too heavy for them, when they are merely letting the child Jesus play with a pomegranate or watching Moses pour water into a trough.[69] He had once before seen the same sadness on her face, but he no longer knew when. And suddenly he remembered: it was when Odette had lied in talking to Mme. Verdurin the day after that dinner to which she had not come on the pretext that she was ill and in reality so that she could stay with Swann. Of course, even if she had been the most scrupulous of women, she might not have felt remorse over a lie as innocent. But the lies Odette generally told were less innocent and served to prevent discoveries that might have created for her, with one person or another, terrible difficulties. And so when she lied, struck by fear, aware that she was feebly armed to defend herself, uncertain of success, she wanted to cry, from exhaustion, like certain children who have not slept. And she also knew that her lie was usually doing serious harm to the man to whom she was telling it, and into whose power she was perhaps going to fall if she lied badly. And so she felt at once humble and guilty in his presence. And when she had to tell an insignificant social lie, the association of sensations and memories would leave her with the faintness that follows overexertion and the regret that follows an act of malevolence.

What depressing lie was she telling Swann that gave her this pained look, this plaintive voice which seemed to falter under the effort she demanded of herself and to ask for forgiveness? He had an idea that it was not merely the truth about the incident in the afternoon that she was endeavoring to hide from him, but something more immediate, that had perhaps not yet transpired and was quite imminent, something that might enlighten him about this truth. At that moment, he heard the bell ring. Odette did not stop talking, but her words were now no more than a long lament: her regret at not having seen Swann in the afternoon, at not having opened the door to him, had turned into true despair.

He could hear the front door closing again and the sound of a carriage, as if someone was going away again—probably the one Swann was not supposed to meet—after being told that Odette was out. Then, when he reflected that merely by coming at an hour when he was not in the habit of coming he had managed to disturb so many arrangements she did not want him to discover, he was overcome with a feeling of discouragement, almost despondency. But because he loved Odette, because he was in the habit of turning all his thoughts toward her, the pity he might have inspired in himself he felt for her instead, and he murmured: "Poor darling!" As he was leaving her, she picked up several letters that she had on her table and asked him if he would put them in the post. He took them away with him and, once he was home, saw that he had kept the letters on him. He returned as far as the post office, drew them from his pocket, and before tossing them into the box looked at the addresses. They were all for tradesmen except one which was for Forcheville. He held it in his hand. He said to himself: "If I saw what was inside it, I would know what she calls him, how she talks to him, if there's anything between them. It may even be that by not looking, I'm behaving with a lack of delicacy toward Odette, because this is the only way to free myself of a suspicion which is perhaps calumnious for her, which is in any case bound to hurt her, and which nothing would be able to destroy, once the letter was gone."

He returned home after leaving the post office, but he had kept that last letter with him. He lit a candle and held up close to it the envelope he had not dared to open. At first he could not read anything, but the envelope was thin and, by making it adhere to the stiff card that was enclosed in it, he could read, through its transparency, the last words. It was a very cold, formal ending. If he had not been the one looking at a letter addressed to Forcheville, but instead Forcheville reading a letter addressed to Swann, Forcheville would have seen words that were far more affectionate! He took firm hold of the card that danced in the envelope, which was larger than it was, then, sliding it with his thumb, brought its different lines one after another under the part of the envelope where the paper was not doubled, the only part through which one could read.

Despite this he could not distinguish anything very well. But it did not matter, because he had seen enough to realize that its subject was a minor, unimportant event that had nothing to do with a love affair; it was something relating to an uncle of Odette's. Swann had read clearly at the beginning of the line: "I was right," but had not understood what Odette had been right in doing, when suddenly, a word he had not at first been able to decipher appeared and illuminated the meaning of the entire sentence: "I was right to open the door, it was my uncle." Open the door! So Forcheville had been there that afternoon when Swann rang the bell, and she had made him leave, which was the source of the noise Swann had heard.

Then he read the whole letter; at the end she apologized for having acted so unceremoniously toward him and said he had forgotten his cigarettes at her house, the same sentence she had written to Swann one of the first times he had come. But in Swann's case she had added: "If you had left your heart here, I would not have let you take it away again." For Forcheville nothing like that: no allusion that might suggest that they were having an affair. And in fact, Forcheville was more deceived in all this than he, since Odette was writing to him to assure him that the visitor had been her uncle. In the end he, Swann, was the one she considered important, the one for whom she had dismissed the other. And yet, if there was nothing between Odette and Forcheville, why had she not opened the door right away, why had she said, "I did the right thing to open the door, it was my uncle"? if she was doing nothing wrong at that moment, how would Forcheville even be able to explain to himself the fact that she had not opened the door? Swann remained there, disconsolate, embarrassed and yet happy, with this envelope which Odette had handed over to him quite fearlessly, so absolute was her confidence in his discretion, but through the transparent glazing of which was revealed to him, along with the secret of an incident which he would never have believed it possible to discover, a little of Odette's life, as in a narrow illuminated section cut directly out of the unknown. Then his jealousy rejoiced over it, as if that jealousy had an independent, selfish vitality, voracious for anything that would feed it, even at Swann's own expense. Now it had something to feed on and Swann was going to be able to begin worrying each day over the visitors Odette might have received at about five o'clock, and begin trying to learn where Forcheville had been at that hour. For Swann's affection continued to preserve the same character imprinted on it from the very beginning by his ignorance as to how Odette spent her days and by the mental laziness that stopped him from compensating for his ignorance with his imagination. He had not been jealous at first of Odette's whole life, but only of the times when some circumstances, perhaps wrongly interpreted, led him to suppose that Odette might have deceived him. His jealousy, like an octopus that casts a first, then a second, then a third mooring, attached itself solidly first to that time, five o'clock in the afternoon, then to another, then to yet another. But Swann was not capable of inventing his sufferings. They were merely the memory, the perpetuation of a suffering that had come to him from outside himself.

From outside, however, everything brought him more suffering. He wanted to separate Odette from Forcheville, take her away to spend a few days in the south. But he believed all the men who happened to be in the hotel desired her and that she desired them. And so he who in former days, when traveling, had sought out new people, large groups, now appeared unsociable, appeared to be fleeing the company of men as if it had cruelly wounded him. And how could he not be misanthropic, when he saw every man as a possible lover of Odette's? And so his jealousy, even more than the sensuous and lighthearted feeling he had at first had for Odette, altered Swann's character and changed entirely, in the eyes of other people, the very appearance of the external signs by which that character was manifested.

A month after the day on which he had read the letter addressed by Odette to Forcheville, Swann went to a dinner which the Verdurins were giving in the Bois. As they were preparing to leave, he noticed some confabulations between Mme. Verdurin and several of the guests and thought he heard them reminding the pianist to come to a party at Chatou[70] the next day; yet, he, Swann, had not been invited.

The Verdurins had spoken in low voices and in vague terms, but the painter, probably inattentive, exclaimed:

"There must be no lights on and he must play the 'Moonlight Sonata' in the dark so we can watch how things become illuminated."

Mme. Verdurin, seeing that Swann was two steps away, now wore that expression in which the desire to make the person who is talking be quiet and the desire to maintain a look of innocence in the eyes of the person who is hearing neutralize each other in an intense nullity of gaze, in which the motionless sign of intelligence and complicity is concealed beneath an innocent smile, and which in the end, being common to all those who find themselves making a social blunder, reveals it instantly, if not to those making it, at least to the one who is its victim. Odette suddenly had the desperate look of one who has given up fighting the crushing difficulties of life, and Swann anxiously counted the minutes that separated him from the time when, after leaving the restaurant, during the drive home with her, he would be able to ask her for an explanation, persuade her not to go to Chatou the next day or to see that he was invited, and to soothe in her arms the anguish he was feeling. At last the carriages were sent for. Mme. Verdurin said to Swann:

"Well now, good-bye, we'll see you soon, I trust?" attempting by the amiableness of her gaze and the constraint of her smile to keep him from realizing that she was not saying to him, as she had always done until now: "Tomorrow, then, at Chatou, the day after at my house."

M. and Mme. Verdurin made Forcheville get in with them, Swann's carriage had pulled up behind theirs, and he was waiting for theirs to leave so that he could help Odette into his.

"Odette, we're taking you home," said Mme. Verdurin, "we have a little spot for you here next to M. de Forcheville."

"Yes, madame," answered Odette.

"What? I thought I was driving you home," cried Swann, saying what had to be said without dissembling, because the carriage door was open, the seconds were numbered, and he could not go home without her in his present state.

"But Mme. Verdurin asked me . . ."

"Now, you can certainly go home alone, we've let you have her to yourself often enough," said Mme. Verdurin.

"But I had something important to say to Madame."

"Well, you can write it to her in a letter . . ."

"Good-bye," Odette said, holding out her hand.

He tried to smile but looked utterly crushed.

"Did you see the way Swann permits himself to behave with us now?" said Mme. Verdurin to her husband when they were back at home. "I thought he was going to eat me alive because we were taking Odette with us. It's quite unseemly, really! Let him just say right out that we're running a house of assignation! I don't understand how Odette can tolerate such behavior. He absolutely seems to be saying: You belong to me. I'm going to tell Odette what I think, I hope she'll understand."

And she also added, a moment later, angrily:

"No, really, the vile creature!" using, without realizing it, and perhaps responding to the same obscure need to justify herself—like Françoise at Combray when the chicken did not want to die—the same words which the last twitches of an inoffensive animal in its death throes wring from the countryman who is killing it.

And when Mme. Verdurin's carriage had left and Swann's came forward, his coachman looked at him and asked if he was not ill or if there had not been an accident.

Swann sent him away, he wanted to walk, and he returned home on foot through the Bois. He talked to himself out loud, in the same slightly artificial tone he had always used when he enumerated the charms of the little clan and extolled the magnanimity of the Verdurins. But just as Odette's conversation, smiles, kisses became as odious to him as he had once found them sweet, if they were addressed to another man, in the same way the Verdurins' salon, which only recently had still seemed to him amusing, inspired with a real enthusiasm for art and even a sort of moral nobility, now that a man other than himself was the one Odette was going there to meet, to love without restraint, exhibited to him its absurdities, its foolishness, its ignominy.

He pictured to himself with disgust the next day's soiree at Chatou. "The idea of going to Chatou anyway! Like drapers after shutting up shop! These people really are sublimely bourgeois, they can't really exist, they must have come out of a Labiche comedy!"[71]

The Cottards would be there, maybe Brichot. "It's quite grotesque, the lives of these nonentities, always in each other's pockets like this. They would feel utterly lost, I swear, if they didn't all meet up again tomorrow *at Chatou!*" Alas! the painter would be there too, the painter who enjoyed "matchmaking," who would invite Forcheville to come to his studio with Odette. He could see Odette in clothes far too formal for this country outing, "because she's so vulgar and worst of all, poor little thing, such a fool!!!"

He could hear the jokes that Mme. Verdurin would make after dinner, jokes which, whoever the bore might be at whom they were aimed, had always amused him because he saw Odette laughing, laughing with him, almost inside him. Now he felt that perhaps they would be making Odette laugh at him. "What fetid humor!" he said, twisting his mouth into an expression of disgust so powerful that he felt the muscular sensation of his grimace even in his neck, flung back against the collar of his shirt. "And how can a creature whose face is made in the image of God find anything to laugh about in those nauseating jokes? Any nose of any delicacy at all would turn away with horror so as not to allow itself to be offended by such musty odors. It's really incredible to think that a human being could fail to understand that, by permitting herself to smile at the expense of a fellow human being who has loyally reached out his hand to her, she is sinking down into a mire from which it will be impossible, even with the best will in the world, to rescue her. I live too many miles above the swamp in which these vermin are gabbling and wallowing to be splattered by the jokes of a Verdurin," he cried, lifting his head, proudly throwing back his shoulders. "As God is my witness, I have honestly tried to pull Odette up out of there, and lift her into a nobler and purer atmosphere. But no human being has more than just so much patience, and mine is exhausted," he said to himself, as if this mission to tear Odette away from an atmosphere of sarcasm dated from further back than the last few minutes and as if he had not taken it upon himself only when he thought perhaps these sarcasms were aimed at him and were attempting to separate Odette from him.

He could see the pianist preparing to play the "Moonlight Sonata" and the faces Mme. Verdurin would make as she grew dismayed at the harm that Beethoven's music was going to do to her nerves: "Idiot, liar!" he exclaimed. "And the woman pretends to love *Art*!" She would tell Odette, after having adroitly insinuated a few words of praise for Forcheville, as she had so often done for him: "Make a little room next to you for M. de Forcheville." "In the dark! The pimp, the procuress!" *Procuress* was also the name he applied to the music that would invite them to be quiet, to dream together, to look at each other, to take each other by the hand. He found there was some good to be said for the severity toward the arts displayed by Plato, by Bossuet,[72] and by the old school of French education.

In fact, the life one led at the Verdurins' and which he had so often called "real life" seemed to him the worst of all, and their little clan the lowest of social circles. "It really is," he said, "the lowest thing on the social ladder, Dante's last circle.[73] No doubt about it, the venerable text refers to the Verdurins! Really, the fashionable folk, whom one may vilify, but who all the same are different from these gangs of riffraff, show a most profound sagacity in refusing to know them, or even to dirty the tips of their fingers with them! What sound intuition there is in the Faubourg Saint-Germain's *Noli me tangere!*"[74] He had long since left the avenues of the Bois, he had nearly reached his house, and still, not yet sobered from his pain and from the insincere exuberance with which the deceitful intonations, the artificial sonority of his own voice, pouring into him more abundantly every minute, had intoxicated him, he continued to perorate out loud in the silence of the night: "Society people have their faults, as no one knows better than I do, but all the same really these are people for whom certain things are out of the question. For instance, one fashionable woman I knew was far from perfect, but all the same really she had a basic decency, a sense of honor in her dealings that would have made her incapable, whatever the circumstances, of any sort of treachery and which is quite sufficient to put a vast gulf between her and a vixen like Verdurin. Verdurin! What a name! Oh, one may truly say they are the ultimate, perfect specimens of their kind! Thank God—it was high time I stopped condescending to mix in utter promiscuousness with such infamy, such excrement."

But, just as the virtues he had attributed that same afternoon to the Verdurins would not have been enough, had they even really possessed them but had not encouraged and protected his love, to provoke in Swann that intoxication in which he was moved by their magnanimity and which, even if it was propagated through other people, could only come to him from Odette—in the same way, the immorality that he now saw in the Verdurins, had it been real, would have been powerless, had they not invited Odette with Forcheville and without him, to unleash his indignation and cause him to vilify "their infamy." And no doubt Swann's voice was more perceptive than he was himself, when it refused to pronounce these words filled with disgust for the Verdurin social circle and joy at being done with it, otherwise than in an artificial tone and as if they were chosen to appease his anger rather than to express his thoughts. The latter, in fact, while he was indulging in these invectives, were probably, without his noticing it, occupied with a completely different object, for, once he reached home, scarcely had he closed the carriage gate behind him than suddenly he struck himself on the forehead, and, opening the gate again, went out exclaiming in a natural voice this time: "I think I know a way of getting invited to the dinner at Chatou tomorrow!" But the way must have been a poor one, for Swann was not invited: Dr. Cottard, who, summoned to the country on a serious case, had not seen the Verdurins for several days and had not been able to go to Chatou, said, the day after that dinner, as he sat down at the table at their house:

"Why, won't we be seeing M. Swann this evening? He is certainly what you would call a personal friend of . . ."

"Why, I should hope not!" cried Mme. Verdurin. "May the Lord preserve us from him, he is deadly dull, stupid, and ill-mannered."

At these words Cottard showed surprise and submission at the same time, as though confronted with a truth contrary to everything he had believed up to then, but irresistibly obvious; and, lowering his nose nervously and timidly into his plate, confined himself to answering: "Ah! Ah! Ah! Ah! Ah!," traversing along a descending scale, in his forced but orderly retreat into the depths of himself, the entire register of his voice. And at the Verdurins', Swann was never mentioned again.

So the salon which had brought Swann and Odette together became an obstacle to their meetings. She no longer said to him as she had in the early days of their love: "We'll see each other tomorrow night anyway, there's a supper at the Verdurins'," but: "We won't be able to see each other tomorrow night, there's a supper at the Verdurins'." Or else the Verdurins were to take her to the Opéra-Comique to see *Une Nuit de Cléopatre*[75] and Swann would read in Odette's eyes a fear that he would ask her not to go, which once upon a time he would not have been able to keep himself from kissing as it passed over his mistress's face, and which now exasperated him. "It's not anger, however," he said to himself, "that I feel when I see that she wants to go and scratch about in that excremental music. It's sorrow, not for myself certainly, but for her; sorrow at seeing that after more than six months of living in daily contact with me, she has not managed to change enough to eliminate Victor Massé spontaneously! Especially for not having come to understand that there are evenings when a person of any subtlety must know how to give up a pleasure, when one asks it of her. She ought to know how to say 'I won't go,' if only by using her intelligence, since it is on the basis of her answer that one will rate once and for all the quality of her soul." And having persuaded himself that it really was only in order to be able to pass a more favorable judgment on Odette's spiritual value that he wanted her to stay with him that evening instead of going to the Opéra-Comique, he presented her with the same reasoning, with the same degree of insincerity as he had presented it to himself, and even with one degree more, for now he was also responding to a desire to capture her through her self-love.

"I swear," he said to her a few moments before she left for the theater, "that in asking you not to go out, my every wish, if I were selfish, would be for you to refuse me, because I have a thousand things to do this evening and I will find myself trapped and thus quite annoyed if against all expectations you answer me that you won't go. But my own occupations, my own pleasures, aren't everything, I have to think of you. There may come a day when, seeing me gone from you forever, you will be justified in reproaching me for not having warned you in the crucial moments when I sensed that I was going to bring down upon you one of those severe judgments against which love cannot resist for long. You see, *Une Nuit de Cléopatre* (what a title!) doesn't really matter. What we must find out is whether you are really that creature which ranks lowest in mentality, and even in charm, the contemptible creature who is incapable of giving up a pleasant thing. Now, if this is what you are, how could anyone love you, for you're not even a person, a clearly defined entity, imperfect, but at least perfectible? You're only a formless stream of water running down whatever slope one offers it, a fish without memory or reflection which, as long as it lives in its aquarium, continuing to mistake the glass for water, will bump against it a hundred times a day. Do you understand that your answer will have the effect—I won't say of making me stop loving you immediately, of course, but of making you less attractive in my eyes when I realize that you're not a person, that you're lower than all other things, that I can't place you above any of them? Obviously I would have preferred to ask you as a thing of no importance to give up *Une Nuit de Cléopatre* (since you oblige me to soil my lips with that despicable name) in hopes that you would go anyway. But since I've decided to tally such an account, to derive such consequences from your answer, I thought it would be more honest to let you know."

For some time, Odette had shown signs of agitation and uncertainty. Although she failed to grasp the meaning of this speech, she did understand that it might belong to the category of "scoldings" and scenes of reproach or supplication, and her familiarity with men enabled her, without paying attention to the details of what they said, to conclude that they would not make such scenes if they were not in love, that since they were in love it was pointless to obey them, that they would be only more in love afterward. And so she would have listened to Swann with the utmost calm if she had not seen that time was passing and that if he talked much longer, she would, as she told him with a smile that was tender, obstinate, and abashed, "end by missing the overture!"

On other occasions he told her that the one thing that was more likely than anything else to make him stop loving her was that she would not give up lying. "Even from the point of view of your desire to be attractive," he told her, "don't you understand how much of your charm you lose when you stoop to lying? With one confession, think how many faults you could redeem! Really you are much less intelligent than I thought!" But it was in vain that Swann expounded for her thus all the reasons she had for not lying; they might have undermined some general and systematic approach to lying; but Odette had none; she merely contented herself, whenever she wanted Swann not to know about something she had done, with not telling him about it. And so lying was for her an expedient of a particular order; and the only thing that could decide whether she ought to make use of it or confess the truth was a reason of a particular order too, the greater or lesser likelihood that Swann might discover she had not told the truth.

Physically, she was going through a bad phase: she was growing stout; and the expressive and doleful charm, the surprised and dreamy glances she had once had seemed to have disappeared with her first youth. So that she had become so dear to Swann at the moment, as it were, when he found her in fact much less pretty. He would look at her for a long time trying to recover the charm he had once seen in her, and he would not find it. But knowing that under the new chrysalis, what lived on was still Odette, still the same will, evanescent, elusive, and guileful, was enough to make Swann continue to put the same passion into trying to capture her. Then he would look at a photograph from two years before, he would remember how exquisite she had been. And that would console him a little for taking such pains over her.

When the Verdurins carried her off to Saint-Germain, Chatou, Meulan, often, if it was the warm season, they would propose, on the spot, staying there to sleep and not coming back until the next day. Mme. Verdurin would try to quiet the scruples of the pianist, whose aunt had remained in Paris.

"She'll be delighted to be rid of you for a day. And how could she worry, she knows you're with us; anyway, she can put the blame on me."

But if she was not successful, M. Verdurin would spring into action, find a telegraph office or a messenger, and inquire as to which of the faithful had someone they needed to inform. But Odette would thank him and say that she did not need to send anyone a telegram, because she had told Swann once and for all that by sending him one in front of everybody, she would be compromising herself. Sometimes she would be gone for several days, the Verdurins would take her to see the tombs at Dreux, or, on the advice of the painter, to Compiègne to admire sunsets as viewed from inside a forest, and then they would push on as far as the Château de Pierrefonds.[76]

"To think that she could visit real historic buildings with me. I've studied architecture for ten years and I'm forever being implored to take people of the highest standing to Beauvais or Saint-Loup-de-Naud[77] and would do it only for her, and instead she goes with the lowest of simpletons to wax ecstatic first over the dejecta of Louis-Philippe and then over those of Viollet-le-Duc! It seems to me you don't need to be an artist for that and even without a particularly delicate nose, you don't choose to go holiday making in latrines in order to be closer to the smell of excrement."

But when she had left for Dreux or Pierrefonds—without, alas, allowing him to go too, as though by chance, on his own account, because "that would make a deplorable impression," she said—he would plunge into that most intoxicating of romances, the railway timetable, which would present him with all the ways he might join her, in the afternoon, in the evening, that same morning! Not only the ways, but even more, almost: the authorization. Because after all, the timetable and the trains themselves were not meant for dogs. If one informed the public, via printed matter, that at eight o'clock in the morning a train left which arrived in Pierrefonds at ten o'clock, it was because going to Pierrefonds was a lawful act, for which permission from Odette was superfluous; and it was also an act that could have a motive completely different from the desire to meet Odette, since people who did not know her performed it each day, in large enough numbers for it to be worth the trouble of stoking the locomotives.

So she really couldn't stop him from going to Pierrefonds if he wanted to! Now, in fact, he felt that he did want to, and that, if he had not known Odette, he certainly would have gone. For a long time now he had wanted to form a clearer idea for himself of Viollet-le-Duc's restoration work. And in this weather, he was moved by an imperious desire for a walk in the forest of Compiègne.

It was truly hard luck that she was forbidding him the only spot that tempted him today. Today! If he went despite her prohibition, he might see her *today*! But whereas, if at Pierrefonds she had met someone who did not matter, she would have said joyfully: "Imagine finding you here!" and would have asked him to come see her at the hotel where she was staying with the Verdurins, if she met him, Swann, there, she would be offended, she would say to herself that she was being followed, she would love him less, perhaps she would turn away angrily when she saw him. "So, I no longer have the right to travel!" she would say to him when they returned, whereas really he was the one who no longer had the right to travel!

For a while he had had the idea, so as to be able to go to Compiègne and Pierrefonds without appearing to be doing it in order to meet Odette, of contriving to be taken there by one of his friends, the Marquis de Forestelle, who had a château in the vicinity. The Marquis, to whom he had communicated his plan without letting him know the reason for it, was beside himself with joy and marveled that Swann, for the first time in fifteen years, was at last consenting to come see his estate and, since he did not want to stay there, as he had told him, at least promised to take walks and go on excursions with him for a few days. Swann pictured himself already down there with M. de Forestelle. Even before seeing Odette there, even if he did not manage to see her, what happiness it would give him to step on that earth where, not knowing the exact location, at any given moment, of her presence, he would feel palpitating everywhere the possibility of her sudden appearance: in the courtyard of the château, now beautiful to him because it was for her sake that he had gone to see it; in every street of the town, which seemed to him romantic; on every road in the forest, rosy in the deep and tender sunset—numberless alternative asylums, where, in the uncertain ubiquity of his hopes, his multiplied heart simultaneously came to take refuge, happy and vagabond. "Whatever we do," he would say to M. de Forestelle, "let's take care we don't stumble on Odette and the Verdurins; I've just learned they're in Pierrefonds today, in fact. There's time enough for us to see one another in Paris, it wouldn't be worth the trouble of leaving Paris if they couldn't take a step without me or I without them." And his friend would not understand why, once he was there, Swann would change a plan twenty times, inspect the dining rooms of all the hotels in Compiègne without making up his mind to sit down in any of them even though no trace of the Verdurins had been seen, looking as though he were searching for the very thing he had said he wanted to avoid and then avoiding it as soon as he found it, because if he had encountered the little group, he would pointedly have gone off, glad he had seen Odette and that she had seen him, especially that she had seen him not bothering about her. But no, she would certainly guess that it was for her sake he was there. And when M. de Forestelle came to pick him up so that they could set off, he said to him: "Alas, no, I can't go to Pierrefonds today, Odette is there, as it turns out." And Swann was happy despite everything to feel that, if alone of all mortals that day he was not allowed to go to Pierrefonds, it was because for Odette he was someone different from the others, her lover, and that this restriction which was applied in his case alone to the universal right to freedom of movement was merely one of the forms of that slavery, of that love which was so dear to him. Decidedly it was better not to risk quarreling with her, to be patient, to wait for her to come back. He spent his days bent over a map of the Compiègne forest as if it were the Map of Love,[8] and surrounded himself with photographs of the château at Pierrefonds. As soon as the day arrived on which it was possible that she would be coming back, he opened the timetable again, calculated which train she must have taken and, if she had been delayed, those that were still available to her. He did not go out for fear of missing a telegram, did not go to bed in case, having returned on the last train, she wanted to surprise him by coming to see him in the middle of the night. In fact he heard the bell at the carriage gate, it seemed to him they were slow opening it, he wanted to wake up the concierge, went to the window to call out to Odette if it was she, for despite the instructions he had gone downstairs to give the servants himself more than ten times, they were still capable of telling her he was not there. It was a servant coming home. He noticed the incessant stream of passing carriages, to which he had never paid attention in the past. He listened to each one come from far off, draw near, pass his gate without stopping, and go on into the distance bearing a message that was not for him. He waited all night, quite uselessly, because the Verdurins had decided to return early, and Odette had been in Paris since noon; it had not occurred to her to tell him; not knowing what to do, she had gone and spent her evening alone at the theater and long ago, by now, had returned home to bed and gone to sleep.

The fact was that she had not even thought of him. And occasions such as this when she forgot Swann's very existence were more useful to Odette, did more to attach Swann to her, than all her coquetry. Because in this way Swann was kept in that state of painful agitation which had already been powerful enough to make his love blossom on the night when he had not found Odette at the Verdurins' and had searched for her all evening. And he did not have, as I had at Combray in my childhood, happy days during which to forget the sufferings that will return at night. Swann spent his days without Odette; and now and then he said to himself that to allow such a pretty woman to go out alone in Paris like that was as imprudent as to put a case full of jewels in the middle of the street. Then he would become indignant at all the people passing by as at so many thieves. But their faces, formless, collective, escaped the grasp of his imagination and did not feed his jealousy. Swann's mind would become exhausted, until, passing his hand over his eyes, he would exclaim: "We must trust in God," like those who, after having persisted in embracing the problem of the reality of the external world or the immortality of the soul, grant their tired brains the relief of an act of faith. But always the thought of the absent woman was indissolubly mingled with the simplest actions of Swann's life—having lunch, receiving his mail, leaving the house, going to bed— by the very sadness he felt over performing them without her, like the initials of Philibert le Beau, which, in the church at Brou,⁷⁹ because of the longing she felt for him, Margaret of Austria intertwined everywhere with her own. On certain days, instead of staying at home, he would go and have his lunch in a restaurant not far from his house whose good cooking he had appreciated once upon a time and to which he now went only for one of those reasons, at once mystical and preposterous, that we call romantic; in fact this restaurant (which still exists) bore the same name as the street in which Odette lived: *Lapérouse.*⁸⁰ Sometimes, when she had gone away briefly, it was only after several days that she thought of letting him know she had returned to Paris. And she would say to him quite simply, no longer taking the precaution as she once had of covering herself, just in case, with a little fragment borrowed from the truth, that she had just returned that moment by the morning train. These words were mendacious; at least for Odette they were mendacious, insubstantial, not having, as they would have had if they had been true, a basis in her memory of arriving at the station; in fact, she was even prevented from picturing them herself at the moment she uttered them, by the contradictory image of what she had been doing that was quite different at the moment she was claiming she had stepped off the train. But in Swann's mind it was just the opposite, these words, encountering no obstacle, encrusted themselves and assumed the immobility of a truth so indubitable that if a friend told him he had come by that train and had not seen Odette, Swann would be convinced it was the friend who was mistaken about the day or the hour, since his account did not agree with Odette's. Her words would have seemed to him false only if he had suspected beforehand that they were. For him to believe she was lying, a previous suspicion was a necessary condition. In fact it was also a sufficient condition. Then everything Odette said to him would appear suspect. If he heard her mention a name, it was certainly the name of one of her lovers; the supposition once forged, he would spend weeks grieving; he even contacted a private investigation agency once in order to find out the address and the daily routine of the stranger who would not let him breathe easy except when he went off on a trip, and who, he learned in the end, was an uncle of Odette's dead for the past twenty years.

Even though in general she did not permit him to meet her in public places, saying that people would talk, sometimes at an evening party to which he and she both had been invited—at Forcheville's, at the painter's, or at a charity ball in one of the ministries—he would find himself there at the same time as she. He would see her but did not dare stay for fear of irritating her by appearing to spy on the pleasures she was enjoying with other people, pleasures which—as he drove home alone, went to bed as anxious as I myself was to be some years later on the evenings when he would come to dine at the house, at Combray—seemed unlimited to him because he had not seen them come to an end. And once or twice on such evenings he experienced the sort of happiness which, had it not been so violently affected by the recoil from the abrupt cessation of anxiety, one would be tempted to call a tranquil happiness, because it consisted of a return to a peaceful state of mind: he had dropped in on a party at the painter's home and was preparing to go off again; behind him he was leaving Odette transformed into a brilliant stranger, surrounded by men to whom her glances and her gaiety, which were not for him, seemed to speak of some sensuous pleasure that would be enjoyed there or else-where (maybe at the "Bal des Incohérents,"[81] where he trembled at the idea that she would go afterward) and that caused Swann more jeal-ousy than the carnal act itself because he had more difficulty imagin-ing it; he was already on the point of passing through the studio door, when he heard himself being called back with these words (which, by cutting off from the party that end which had terrified him so, made the party seem in retrospect innocent, made Odette's return a thing no longer inconceivable and terrible, but sweet and familiar and abid-ing next to him, like a bit of his everyday life, in his carriage, and di-vested Odette herself of her too brilliant and too gay appearance, showed that it was only a disguise which she had put on for a mo-ment, for its own sake, not with a view to mysterious pleasures, and that she was already tired of it), with these words that Odette tossed at him, as he was already on the threshold: "Wouldn't you wait five min-utes for me? I'm leaving, we'll go back together, you can take me home."

True, one day Forcheville had asked to be taken back at the same time but, when they had arrived at Odette's door and he had asked per-mission to come in too, Odette had answered him, pointing to Swann: "Ah! That depends on this gentleman here, ask him. Well, all right, come in for a moment if you want, but not for long because I warn you he likes to talk quietly with me, and he doesn't much like having visi-tors when he comes. Oh, if you knew this fellow as well as I know him! Isn't that so, *my love*,[82] I'm the only one who really knows you?"

And Swann was perhaps even more touched to see her addressing him thus, in front of Forcheville, not only these tender words of predilection, but also certain criticisms such as: "I'm sure you haven't answered your friends yet about that dinner on Sunday. Don't go if you don't want to, but at least be polite," or: "Now, have you left your essay on Vermeer here so that you can do a little more on it tomor-row? How lazy you are! I'll make you work—you'll see!," which proved that Odette kept up with his social engagements and his literary work, that the two of them really had a life together. And as she said this she gave him a smile in whose depths he felt she was entirely his.

And so at these moments, while she was making orangeade for them, suddenly, as when a poorly adjusted reflector at first casts on the wall around an object large fantastic shadows which then fold and disappear into it, all the terrible shifting ideas he had formed for himself about Odette would vanish, would rejoin the charming body that stood there in front of him. He would have the sudden suspicion that this hour spent at Odette's house, in the lamplight, was perhaps not an artificial hour, invented for his own use (intended to mask that dismaying and delightful thing which he thought about endlessly without being able really to picture it, an hour in Odette's real life, in Odette's life when he himself was not there), with stage-set accessories and cardboard fruit, but was perhaps a real hour in Odette's life, that if he had not been there, she would have set out the same armchair for Forcheville and poured him not some unfamiliar drink, but that very same orangeade, that the world inhabited by Odette was not that other frightful and supernatural world where he spent his time locating her and which perhaps existed only in his imagination, but rather the real world, radiating no special sadness, comprising that table where he was going to be able to write and that drink which he would be permitted to taste, all those objects which he contemplated with as much curiosity and admiration as gratitude, for if by absorbing his dreams they had delivered him from them, they in return had been enriched by them, they showed him the palpable realization of his dreams, and they interested his mind, they assumed substance and shape before his eyes at the same time that they soothed his heart. Ah! If fate had permitted him to have but a single home with Odette so that in her house he would be in his own, if when he asked the servant what was planned for lunch, it was Odette's menu that he had learned in answer, if when Odette wanted to go out in the morning to walk down the avenue du Bois de Boulogne, his duty as a good husband had obliged him, even if he did not want to go out, to accompany her, carrying her coat when she was too warm, and at night after dinner if she wanted to stay at home informally dressed, if he had been forced to stay there with her, to do what she wanted; then how completely all those trifles in Swann's life which seemed to him so sad, would, on the contrary, because they were at the same time part of Odette's life, have taken on, even the most familiar of them—like that lamp, that orangeade, that armchair which contained so much of his dreams, which materialized so much desire—a sort of superabundant sweetness and mysterious density.

Yet he actually suspected that what he thus longed for was a calm, a peace that would not have been a favorable atmosphere for his love. When Odette ceased to be for him a creature always absent, longed for, imaginary, when the feeling he had for her was no longer the same mysterious disturbance caused in him by the phrase from the sonata, but affection, gratitude, when normal relations were established between them that would put an end to his madness and his gloom, then no doubt the actions of Odette's daily life would appear to him of little interest in themselves—as he had several times already suspected they were, for example on the day he had read through its envelope the letter addressed to Forcheville. Considering his disease with as much discernment as if he had inoculated himself with it in order to study it, he told himself that when he had recovered his health what Odette might be doing would leave him indifferent. But, from within his morbid state, in truth he feared death itself no more than such a recovery, which would in fact have been the death of all that he was at present.

After these peaceful evenings, Swann's suspicions would be calmed; he would bless Odette and the next day, first thing in the morning, he would send around to her house the most beautiful jewels, because those kind attentions the night before had excited either his gratitude, or the desire to see them repeated, or a paroxysm of love that needed to expend itself.

But at other times his pain would seize him again, he would imagine that Odette was Forcheville's mistress and that when the two of them had seen him, from the depths of the Verdurins' landau, at the Bois, the day before the Chatou party to which he had not been invited, entreat her vainly, with that look of despair which even his coachman had noticed, to go back with him, then return home on his own, alone and defeated, she must have had, as she pointed him out to Forcheville and said to him: "Look! How furious he is!" the same expression in her eyes, glittering, malicious, haughty, and sly, as on the day when Forcheville had driven Saniette from the Verdurins'.

Then Swann detested her. "But also, I'm too stupid," he would tell himself, "I'm paying with my own money for other people's pleasures. All the same, she ought to take care and not pull too hard on her bowstring, because I might very well not give anything more at all. In any case, let's forgo the supplementary favors for the time being! To think that only yesterday, when she said she wanted to attend the season at Bayreuth,[83] I was stupid enough to propose renting for the two of us one of the King of Bavaria's pretty castles in the vicinity. And anyway she did not seem all that delighted, she hasn't yet said either yes or no; let's hope she will decide against it. Good Lord! To spend two weeks listening to Wagner with her when she cares as much for it as a fish for an apple—what fun that would be!" And because his hatred, like his love, needed to manifest itself and to act, he took pleasure in pursuing his evil fantasies further and further, since, because of the perfidies he imputed to Odette, he detested her still more and could, if—something he tried to picture to himself—they were found to be true, have an occasion for punishing her and for satiating on her his increasing rage. Thus he went so far as to suppose that he was going to receive a letter from her in which she would ask him for money to rent that castle near Bayreuth, but warning him that he could not go there himself, because she had promised Forcheville and the Verdurins that she would invite them. Ah! How he would have liked her to be so bold! What joy he would feel as he refused, as he drafted the vengeful answer, the terms of which he took satisfaction in choosing, in uttering out loud, as if he had actually received the letter!

Yet this was in fact what happened the very next day. She wrote that the Verdurins and their friends had expressed a desire to attend these performances of Wagner and that, if he would be so good as to send her the money, she would at last, after having so often been entertained at their home, have the pleasure of inviting them in her turn. About him, she said not a word, it was implied that their presence would exclude his own.

And so that terrible answer, whose every word he had determined the day before without daring to hope that it would ever be used, he could now have the joy of sending off to her. Alas! He was quite aware that, all the same, with the money she had, or that she might easily find, she could rent something at Bayreuth since she wanted to, she who was incapable of telling the difference between Bach and Clapisson.[84] But still, she would live there more frugally. There would be no way, as there would have been had he sent her a few thousand-franc bills this time, of organizing every evening, in a castle, those exquisite suppers after which she would perhaps have indulged the whim—which it was possible she had never yet had—of falling into Forcheville's arms. And then at least he, Swann, was not the one who would be paying for this detested journey! Oh, if only he could have prevented it! If only she could have sprained her ankle before she left, if the coachman of the carriage that would take her to the station had agreed, whatever the price, to drive her to a place where for some time she would remain sequestered—this perfidious woman, her eyes glittering with a smile of complicity addressed to Forcheville, which Odette had become for Swann in the past forty-eight hours!

But she was never that for very long; after a few days the gleaming hypocritical gaze would lose some of its luster and duplicity, the image of a despised Odette saying to Forcheville: "How furious he is!" would begin to grow pale, fade away. Then, gradually the face of the other Odette would reappear and rise up, shining softly, the Odette who also offered a smile to Forcheville, but a smile in which there was nothing but affection for Swann, when she said: "Don't stay long, because this gentleman does not much like me to have visitors when he wants to be with me. Oh, if you knew this fellow as well as I know him!," the same smile she wore when thanking Swann for some instance of his courtesy, which she prized so highly, for some advice she had asked of him in one of those serious circumstances in which she had confidence only in him.

Then, thinking of this Odette, he would ask himself how he could have written her that outrageous letter of which no doubt until now she had not thought him capable, and which must have brought him down from the high, the unique rank which by his goodness, his honesty, he had won in her esteem. He would now become less dear to her, because it was for those particular qualities, which she did not find in either Forcheville or any other man, that she loved him. It was because of them that Odette so often showed a graciousness toward him that he counted for nothing when he was jealous, because it was not a sign of desire, and even gave proof of affection rather than love, but whose importance he began to feel again in proportion as the spontaneous relaxation of his suspicions, a relaxation often increased by the distraction he found in reading about art or talking to a friend, caused his passion to become less demanding of reciprocities.

Now that, after this oscillation, Odette had naturally returned to the place from which Swann's jealousy had for a time removed her, to the angle from which he found her charming, he pictured her as full of tenderness, with a look of consent, and so pretty thus that he could not help offering her his lips as if she had been there and he had been able to kiss her; and he felt as strong a gratitude toward her for this enchanting, kindly glance as if she had really given it to him, as if it were not merely his imagination that had just portrayed it in order to satisfy his desire.

How he must have hurt her! Of course he could find valid reasons for his resentment against her, but they would not have been enough to make him feel that resentment if he had not loved her so much. Had he not had grievances of equal gravity against other women, for whom he would nevertheless readily have done favors now, feeling no anger toward them because he no longer loved them? If someday he was ever to find himself in the same state of indifference toward Odette, he would understand that it was his jealousy alone that had made him find something atrocious, unpardonable, in this desire of hers, fundamentally so natural, arising from a touch of childishness and also a certain delicacy in her nature, to be able in her turn, since an occasion presented itself, to repay the civilities of the Verdurins, to play the mistress of the house.

He returned to this point of view—which was opposed to that of his love and his jealousy, and in which he placed himself sometimes through a sort of intellectual equity so as to allow for the various probabilities—from which he tried to judge Odette as if he had never loved her, as if to him she were a woman like any other, as if Odette's life had not been, as soon as he was no longer there, different, contrived in hiding from him, plotted against him.

Why should he believe that there, she would enjoy with Forcheville or with other men intoxicating pleasures which she had never experienced with him and which his jealousy alone had fabricated out of nothing? In Bayreuth as in Paris, if Forcheville happened to think of him at all, it might be merely as of someone who mattered a great deal in Odette's life, to whom he was obliged to yield his place, when they met at her house. If Forcheville and she gloated over being there despite him, it was he who would be to blame by trying in vain to keep her from going, whereas if he had approved of her plan, which was in fact defensible, she would have appeared to be there on his recommendation, she would feel she had been sent there, housed there by him, and for the pleasure she felt in entertaining those people who had entertained her so often, it was to Swann that she would have been grateful.

And—instead of letting her go off on bad terms with him, without having seen him again—if he sent her this money, if he encouraged her to take this trip and went out of his way to make it pleasant for her, she would come running to him, happy, grateful, and he would have the joy of seeing her, a joy which he had not experienced for almost a week and which nothing could replace. Because as soon as Swann could picture her without horror, as soon as he once again saw kindness in her smile, and as soon as the desire to take her out of reach of all other men was not added by jealousy to his love, that love again became above all a predilection for the sensations that Odette's person gave him, for the pleasure he took in admiring like a spectacle or questioning like a phenomenon the dawn of one of her glances, the evolution of one of her smiles, the emission of an intonation of her voice. And this pleasure, different from all the others, had ended by creating in him a need for her that she alone could satisfy by her presence or her letters, a need almost as disinterested, almost as artistic, as perverse, as another need that characterized this new period in Swann's life, in which the dryness, the depression of earlier years had been succeeded by a sort of spiritual superabundance, without his knowing to what he owed this unhoped-for enrichment of his inner life any more than a person in delicate health who from a certain moment grows stronger, stouter, and seems for a time to be on the road to a complete recovery: that other need which was also developing apart from the real world was the need to hear, and to understand, music.

And so, with the very chemistry of his disease, after he had created jealousy with his love, he began once more to manufacture affection, and pity, for Odette. She had turned back into the Odette who was charming and good. He felt remorse at having been severe toward her. He wanted her to come to him, and, before that, he wanted to procure for her some sort of pleasure, so as to see gratitude mold her face and shape her smile.

And Odette, sure of seeing him come back after a few days, as tender and submissive as before, to ask her for a reconciliation, acquired the habit of no longer being afraid to displease or even to provoke him, and she refused him, when it was convenient for her, the favors he valued most.

Perhaps she did not realize how sincere he had been with her during the quarrel, when he had told her he would not send her any money and would try to hurt her. Perhaps she also did not realize how sincere he was, if not with her, at least with himself, on other occasions when for the sake of the future of their relationship, so as to show Odette he was capable of doing without her, that a break was always possible, he decided to let some time pass without going to see her.

Sometimes this was after several days during which she had not given him any new reason to worry; and since, from the next few visits he would make to her, he knew he would not derive any very great joy but more probably some vexation that would put an end to his present state of calm, he would write to her that since he was very busy he would not be able to see her on any of the days on which he had said he would. Then a letter from her, crossing his, would ask him to change one of those very meetings. He would wonder why; his suspicions, his anguish would take hold of him again. He would no longer be able to abide, in the new state of agitation in which he found himself, by the commitment he had made in his earlier state of relative calm, he would hurry to her house and demand to see her on all the following days. And even if she had not written to him first, if she merely answered, with an acquiescence, his request for a brief separation, this would be enough to make him unable to go on without seeing her. For, contrary to Swann's calculations, Odette's consent had entirely changed his attitude. Like all those who enjoy the possession of a thing, in order to know what would happen if he ceased for a moment to possess it he had removed that thing from his mind, leaving everything else in the same state as when it was there. But the absence of a thing is not merely that, it is not simply a partial lack, it is a disruption of everything else, it is a new state which one cannot foresee in the old.

But there were other occasions—Odette was about to go off on a trip—when, after some little dispute for which he had chosen the pretext, he would resolve not to write to her and not to see her again before she returned, thus giving the appearance, and expecting the reward, of a more serious quarrel, which she would perhaps believe was final, to a separation the greater part of which was unavoidable because of the trip and which he was merely allowing to begin a little earlier. Already he imagined Odette uneasy, distressed at having received neither visit nor letter, and this image, by calming his jealousy, made it easy for him to break himself of the habit of seeing her. No doubt, at times, at the far end of his mind where his resolution had thrust her because of the entire interposed length of the three weeks of separation he had accepted, it was with pleasure that he contemplated the idea of seeing Odette again when she returned; but it was also with so little impatience that he began to ask himself if he would not readily double the duration of an abstinence that was so easy. It had lasted as yet only three days, a period of time much shorter than he had often spent without seeing Odette and without having as now planned it in advance. And yet at this point a slight irritation or physical discomfort—by making him consider the present moment an exceptional one, outside the rules, one in which even common wisdom would agree that he could accept the appeasement afforded by a pleasure and allow his will, until it might be useful to resume the effort, to rest—would suspend the action of the latter, which would cease to exert its pressure; or, less than that, the memory of something he had forgotten to ask Odette, whether she had decided which color she wanted to have her carriage repainted, or, with regard to a certain investment, whether it was common or preferred shares that she wanted to buy (it was all very well to show her that he could live without seeing her, but if, after that, the painting had to be done all over again or the shares paid no dividends, a lot of good it would have done him), and like a stretched piece of elastic that is let go or the air in a pneumatic machine that is opened, the idea of seeing her again, from the far distance where it had been kept, would come back in a single leap into the field of the present and of immediate possibilities.

It came back without encountering any further resistance, in fact so irresistible that Swann had had much less difficulty feeling the approach one by one of the fifteen days he was going to be separated from Odette than he had waiting the ten minutes which his coachman took to harness the carriage that was going to take him to her house and which he spent in transports of impatience and joy as he recaptured a thousand times in order to lavish his tenderness on it that idea of meeting her again which, by so abrupt a return, at a moment when he thought it was so far away, was once again with him in his most intimate consciousness. For this thought no longer encountered the obstacle of Swann's desire to attempt forthwith to resist it, a desire which had ceased to have any place in Swann's mind since, having proved to himself—at least this was what he believed—that he was so easily capable of it, he no longer saw any disadvantage in deferring an attempt at separation that he was now certain he could put into execution whenever he wished. And, too, this idea of seeing her again returned to him adorned with a novelty, a seductiveness, endowed with a virulence which habit had dulled, but which had been retempered in that privation not of three days but of fifteen (for a period of renunciation must be calculated, by anticipation, as having lasted already until the final date assigned to it), and had converted what had been until then an expected pleasure which could easily be sacrificed into an undreamed-of happiness which he was powerless to resist. Finally, the idea returned to Swann embellished by his ignorance of what Odette might have thought, perhaps done, seeing that he had given her no sign of life, so that what he was now going to find was the impassioning revelation of an Odette almost unknown to him.

But she, just as she had believed that his refusal to send her money was only a sham, saw nothing but a pretext in the information that Swann came to ask of her about the carriage to be repainted or the shares to be purchased. For she could not reconstruct the various phases of these crises through which he was passing and, in the idea she formed of them, she failed to understand the mechanism by which they worked, believing only in what she knew beforehand, in their necessary, infallible, and always identical outcome. An idea that was incomplete—all the more profound, perhaps—if one judged it from the point of view of Swann, who would no doubt have thought he was misunderstood by Odette, just as a morphine addict or a consumptive, persuaded that they have been prevented, one by an outside event just when he was about to free himself of his inveterate habit, the other by an accidental indisposition just when he was about to be restored to health at last, feel misunderstood by the doctor who does not attach the same importance they do to these alleged contingencies, mere disguises according to him, assumed, so as to make themselves perceptible again to his patients, by the vice and the morbid condition which, in reality, have not ceased to burden them incurably while they were feeding their dreams of reformation or recovery. And in fact, Swann's love had reached the stage where the doctor and, in certain affections, even the boldest surgeon, ask themselves if ridding a patient of his vice or relieving him of his disease is still reasonable or even possible.

Certainly, of the extent of this love Swann had no direct awareness. When he tried to measure it, it sometimes seemed to him diminished, reduced to almost nothing; for example, the lack of pleasure, the displeasure, almost, inspired in him, before he loved Odette, by her expressive features, her faded complexion, came back to him on certain days. "Really, I'm making some progress," he would say to himself the next day. "When I think about it carefully, I hardly enjoyed myself at all yesterday when I was in bed with her: it's odd, I actually found her ugly." And of course, he was sincere, but his love extended well beyond the realms of physical desire. Odette's body itself no longer had a large place in it. When his eyes fell upon Odette's photograph on the table, or when she came to see him, he had trouble identifying the figure of flesh or cardboard with the painful and constant disturbance that inhabited him. He would say to himself almost with surprise: "It's she!" as if suddenly someone were to show us in a separate, external form one of our own diseases and we found that it did not resemble what we were suffering. "She"—he tried to ask himself what that was; for one thing love and death have in common, more than those vague resemblances people are always talking about, is that they make us question more deeply, for fear that its reality will slip away from us, the mystery of personality. And this disease which was Swann's love had so proliferated, was so closely entangled with all his habits, with all his actions, with his thoughts, his health, his sleep, his life, even with what he wanted after his death, it was now so much a part of him, that it could not have been torn from him without destroying him almost entirely: as they say in surgery, his love was no longer operable.

By this love Swann had been so far detached from all other interests that, when by chance he reappeared in society telling himself that his connections, like an elegant setting that she would not in fact have been able to appreciate with much accuracy, could restore a little of his value in Odette's eyes (and this would perhaps indeed have been true had these connections not been lowered in value by that love itself, which for Odette depreciated all the things it touched by seeming to proclaim them less precious), what he experienced there, along with the distress of being in places and among people whom she did not know, was the disinterested pleasure he would have taken in a novel or a painting which depicted the amusements of a leisured class, just as, in his own house, he enjoyed contemplating the functioning of his domestic life, the elegance of his wardrobe and livery, the proper placement of his stocks, in the same way that he enjoyed reading in Saint-Simon, who was one of his favorite authors, about the "mechanics" of the daily life, the menus of the dinners of Mme. de Maintenon,[85] or the well-advised avarice and grand style of Lully.[86] And to the small extent that this detachment was not absolute, the reason for this new pleasure that Swann was enjoying was that he could emigrate for a while into the rare parts of himself that had remained almost foreign to his love and to his pain. In this respect the personality which my great-aunt attributed to him, of "young Swann," distinct from his more individual personality of Charles Swann, was the one in which he was now happiest. One day when, for the birthday of the Princess of Parma (and because she could often please Odette indirectly by making it possible for her to have seats at galas, jubilees, and other occasions), he had wanted to send her some fruit and was not sure how to order it, he had entrusted the task to a cousin of his mother's, a lady who, delighted to do an errand for him, had written to him, when sending him the account, that she had not got all the fruit at the same place, but the grapes at Crapote's, whose specialty they were, the strawberries at Jauret's, the pears at Chevet's, where they were the loveliest, etc., "each piece of fruit inspected and examined individually by me." And indeed, from the Princess's thanks, he had been able to judge the flavor of the strawberries and the mellowness of the pears. But more important, that "each piece of fruit inspected and examined individually by me" had soothed his pain, by taking his consciousness away into a region where he rarely went, even though it was his by right as the heir to a rich and solid bourgeois family in which there had been preserved by heredity, quite ready to be put at his service whenever he wished, a knowledge of the "best addresses" and the art of placing a proper order.

Certainly, he had forgotten for too long that he was "young Swann" not to feel, when he became that person again briefly, a keener pleasure than those he could have felt the rest of the time and to which he had grown indifferent; and if the friendliness of the bourgeoisie, for whom he had remained that person more than anything else, was less animated than that of the aristocracy (but in fact more flattering, for with them at least it is always inseparable from respect), a letter from a royal personage, whatever princely entertainment it offered, could never be as pleasant to him as a letter asking him to be a witness, or merely to be present, at a wedding in the family of old friends of his parents, some of whom had continued to see him—like my grandfather, who, the year before, had invited him to my mother's wedding—while certain others barely knew him personally but believed they were obligated to be polite to the son, to the worthy successor, of the late M. Swann.

But, because of the long-standing close ties he had among them, the nobility, to a certain extent, were also part of his house, his household, and his family. He felt he possessed, when contemplating his distinguished friendships, the same support from outside, the same comfort, as when looking at the fine lands, the fine silverware, the fine table linen, that had come to him from his own people. And the thought that if he were to collapse at home from the effects of a sudden illness it would quite naturally be the Duc de Chartres, the Prince de Reuss, the Duc de Luxembourg, and the Baron de Charlus whom his valet would run off to find, brought him the same consolation as to our old Françoise the knowledge that she would be wrapped in a shroud of her own fine sheets, marked, not mended (or so finely that it gave only a loftier idea of the care of the seamstress), a shroud from the frequent image of which in her mind's eye she derived a certain satisfying sense, if not of material well-being, at least of self-respect. But most important, since in every one of his actions and thoughts that referred to Odette, Swann was constantly governed and directed by the unavowed feeling that he was, perhaps not less dear, but less welcome to her than anyone else, than the most boring faithful of the Verdurins—when he returned to a world in which he was the highest example of excellence, whom one would do anything to attract, whom one was sorry not to see, he began to believe again in the existence of a happier life, almost to feel an appetite for it, as an invalid may feel who has been bedridden for months, on a strict diet, and who sees in a newspaper the menu for an official luncheon or an advertisement for a cruise to Sicily.

If he was obliged to give his excuses to the society people for not visiting them, it was precisely for his visits to her that he sought to excuse himself to Odette. He even paid for them (asking himself at the end of the month, supposing he had abused her patience somewhat and gone to see her many times, if it was enough to send her four thousand francs), and for each one found a pretext, a present to bring her, a piece of information she needed, M. de Charlus whom he had met going to her house and who had demanded that he accompany him. And, lacking one, he would ask M. de Charlus if he would please run over to her house, remark to her as though spontaneously, in the course of the conversation, that he remembered he had something to say to Swann, would she kindly send for him to come to her house right away; but most often Swann would wait in vain and M. de Charlus would tell him in the evening that his plan had not succeeded. So that if she was often away from Paris now, even when she stayed there she saw very little of him, and she who, when she was in love with him, used to say: "I'm always free" and "What do I care what others think?" would now, each time he wanted to see her, invoke social conventions or plead other engagements. When he mentioned that he might be going to some charity ball, opening, premiere where she would be, she would tell him that he was trying to flaunt their affair, that he was treating her like a prostitute. It reached such a point that, in order to try not to be debarred from meeting her anywhere, Swann, knowing that she was acquainted with and had considerable affection for my great-uncle Adolphe and having once been a friend of his himself, went to see him one day in his little apartment in the rue de Bellechasse to ask him to use his influence with Odette. Since she always adopted poetical airs when speaking to Swann of my uncle, saying: "Ah, yes, he's not like you, his friendship with me is a lovely thing, so grand, so handsome! He would never think so little of me as to want to show himself with me in every public place," Swann was perplexed and did not know quite how lofty his tone ought to be in talking about her to my uncle. He first posited Odette's a priori excellence, her axiomatic and seraphic superhumanity, the revealed truth of her virtues, which could be neither demonstrated nor derived from experience. "I must talk to you. You know that Odette is a woman superior to all other women, an adorable creature, an angel. But you know what life in Paris is like. Not everyone sees Odette in the same light as you and I. And so there are people who think the role I'm playing is rather ridiculous: she can't even allow me to meet her outside, at the theater. She has such confidence in you—couldn't you say a few words to her for me, assure her that she's exaggerating the harm I would do her by greeting her in public?"

My uncle advised Swann to let a little time go by without seeing Odette, who would only love him all the more for it, and Odette to allow Swann to meet her wherever he liked. A few days later, Odette told Swann she had just had the disappointment of discovering that my uncle was the same as every other man: he had just tried to take her by force. She quieted Swann when at first he wanted to go off and challenge my uncle, but he refused to shake his hand the next time he met him. He especially regretted this quarrel with my uncle Adolphe since he had hoped, had he seen him again from time to time and been able to chat with him in complete confidence, to try to shed some light on certain rumors relating to the life Odette had once led in Nice. For my uncle Adolphe spent his winters there. And Swann thought that perhaps it was even there that he had met Odette. The little that had been let slip by someone in his presence, relating to a man who was said to have been Odette's lover, had greatly disturbed Swann. But the things he would have regarded, before knowing them, as the most frightful to learn and the most impossible to believe, once he knew them were incorporated forever after into his sadness, he accepted them, he would no longer have been able to understand that they did not exist. Only each one indelibly revised the idea he was forming of his mistress. He was even given to understand, at one point, that this laxness in Odette's morals, which he would not have suspected, was fairly well known, and that in Baden and in Nice, when she used to spend a few months there, she had had a degree of amorous notoriety. He sought out certain philanderers in order to question them; but they were aware that he knew Odette; and besides, he was afraid of reminding them of her, of putting them on her track. But he to whom before then nothing could have appeared as tedious as anything relating to the cosmopolitan life of Baden or Nice, learning that Odette had perhaps led a rather riotous life in those pleasure towns, though he could never manage to find out if it had been only to satisfy a need for money which thanks to him she no longer had, or from some capricious desire which might return, now leaned with an impotent, blind, and dizzying anguish over the bottomless abyss that had swallowed up those early years of the Septennate[87] during which one spent winters on the Promenade des Anglais, summers under the lime trees of Baden, and in them he saw a painful but magnificent profundity such as a poet might have lent them; and he would have devoted to the reconstruction of the petty events of the chronicle of the Côte d'Azur of that time, if that chronicle could have helped him understand something of Odette's smile or the look in her eyes—honest and simple though they were—more passion than an aesthete examining the extant documents of fifteenth-century Florence in order to try to penetrate further into the soul of Botticelli's Primavera, bella Vanna, or Venus.[88] Often, without saying anything to her, he would gaze at her, he would daydream; she would say to him: "How sad you look!" It was not as yet very long since he had moved on from the idea that she was a good person, comparable to the best he had ever known, to the idea that she was a kept woman; inversely he had sometimes since then returned from Odette de Crécy, perhaps too well known among the fast crowd, among ladies' men, to this face whose expression was at times so gentle, to this nature so human. He would say to himself: "What does it matter that at Nice everyone knows Odette de Crécy? Reputations of this sort, even if true, are created out of other people's ideas"; he would reflect that this legend—even if it was authentic—lay outside Odette, was not inside her like an irreducible and baneful personality; that the creature who might have been led to do wrong was a woman with kind eyes, a heart full of pity for suffering, a submissive body which he had held, which he had clasped in his arms and handled, a woman whom one day he might come to possess entirely, if he succeeded in making himself indispensable to her. She was there, often tired, her face emptied for a moment of that feverish, joyful preoccupation with the unknown things that made Swann suffer; she would push back her hair with her hands; her forehead, her face would appear broader; then, suddenly, some ordinary human thought, some good feeling such as may be found in all individuals when in a moment of rest or reclusion they are left to themselves, would spring from her eyes like a beam of yellow sunlight. And immediately her whole face would brighten like a gray countryside covered with clouds which suddenly part, transfiguring it, at the moment the sun goes down. The life that was in Odette at that moment, even the future she seemed so dreamily to be watching, Swann could have shared with her; no evil disturbance seemed to have left its residue there. Rare though they became, these moments were not entirely useless. In memory Swann joined these fragments together, eliminated the intervals, cast, as though in gold, an Odette formed of goodness and calm for whom (as will be seen in the second part of this story) he later made sacrifices which the other Odette would never have won from him. But these moments were so rare, and he saw her so little now! Even in regard to their evening meeting, she would tell him only at the last minute if she could grant it to him, for, since she could count on his always being free, she first wanted to be certain that no one else would suggest coming around. She would maintain that she had to wait for an answer of the greatest importance, and if after she had sent for Swann friends asked her, when the evening had already begun, to meet them at the theater or at supper, she would give a joyful leap into the air and dress quickly. As she progressed in her preparations, each movement she made would bring Swann closer to the moment when he would have to leave her, when she would fly off with an irresistible force; and when ready at last, plunging into her mirror a final glance strained and brightened by attention, she put a little more red on her lips, settled a lock of hair on her forehead, and asked for her sky-blue evening cloak with gold tassels, Swann looked so sad that she could not suppress a gesture of impatience and said: "So that's how you thank me for letting you stay here till the last minute. And I thought I was being nice. I'll know better next time!" Now and then, at the risk of angering her, he would promise himself to try to find out where she had gone, he would dream of an alliance with Forcheville, who would perhaps have been able to enlighten him. In any case, when he knew who it was she had spent the evening with, it was very seldom that he could not discover among all his own acquaintance someone who knew, if only indirectly, the man with whom she had gone out and could easily obtain this or that piece of information about him. And while he was writing to one of his friends to ask him to try to clear up some point or other, he would feel how restful it was to stop asking himself his unanswerable questions and to transfer to someone else the fatigue of interrogation. True, Swann was scarcely better off when he had certain information. Knowing a thing does not always allow us to prevent it, but at least the things we know, we hold, if not in our hands, at any rate in our minds, where we can arrange them as we like, which gives us the illusion of a sort of power over them. He was happy each time M. de Charlus was with Odette. Between M. de Charlus and her, Swann knew that nothing could happen, that when M. de Charlus went out with her it was for the sake of his friendship with Swann and he would have no reluctance about telling him what she had done.

Sometimes she had declared so categorically to Swann that it was impossible for her to see him on a certain evening, she seemed so keen on going out, that Swann attached real importance to M. de Charlus's being free to go with her. The next day, though he did not dare ask many questions of M. de Charlus, he would compel him, by appearing not quite to understand his first answers, to give him further answers, after each of which he would feel more relieved, because he very soon learned that Odette had occupied her evening with the most innocent of pleasures. "But what do you mean, my dear Mémé? I don't quite understand . . . You didn't go straight from her house to the Musée Grévin? You had gone somewhere else first. No? Oh! How funny! You don't know how much you amuse me, my dear Mémé. But what a funny idea of hers to go on to the Chat Noir afterward, that's certainly her sort of idea . . . No? It was you? How strange. But in fact it's not such a bad idea; she must have known a good many people there? No? She spoke to no one? That's extraordinary. So you stayed there like that just the two of you all by yourselves? I can just picture it. You are kind, my dear Mémé, I'm very fond of you." Swann felt relieved. For him, to whom it had occasionally happened, when chatting casually with people to whom he was barely listening, that he sometimes heard certain remarks (as, for example: "I saw Mme. de Crécy yesterday; she was with a gentleman I don't know"), remarks which, as soon as they entered Swann's heart, solidified, hardened like an encrustation, cut into him, never moved from there again, how sweet by contrast were these words: "She knew no one, she spoke to no one," how they circulated comfortably in him, how fluid they were, easy, breathable! And yet after a moment he would say to himself that Odette must find him quite tiresome if these were the pleasures she preferred to his company. And their insignificance, though it reassured him, nevertheless pained him like a betrayal.

Even when he could not find out where she had gone, it would have been enough to soothe the anguish which he felt at these times, and for which Odette's presence, the sweetness of being close to her was the only specific (a specific that in the long run aggravated the disease, like many remedies, but at least momentarily soothed his pain), it would have been enough for him, if only Odette had permitted it, to remain in her house while she was out, to wait for her there until the hour of her return, into whose stillness and appeasement would have flowed and melted the hours which some magical illusion, some evil spell had made him believe were different from the rest. But she did not want this; he returned home; he forced himself, on the way, to make various plans, he stopped thinking about Odette; he even succeeded, while he was undressing, in turning over some fairly cheerful thoughts in his mind; and it was with a light heart, full of the hope of going to see some great painting the next day, that he got into bed and put out his light; but, no sooner, as he prepared to go to sleep, did he cease to exert upon himself a constraint of which he was not even aware because it was by now so habitual, than at that very instant an icy shiver would run through him and he would begin to sob. He did not even want to know why, dried his eyes, said to himself with a smile: "Delightful—I'm turning into a real neurotic." Then he could not think without a feeling of great weariness that the next day he would again have to begin trying to find out what Odette had been doing, use all his influence to attempt to see her. This compulsion to an activity without respite, without variety, without results was so cruel to him that one day, seeing a lump on his abdomen, he felt real joy at the thought that he might have a fatal tumor, that he was no longer going to have to take charge of anything, that it was the disease that would manage him, make him its plaything, until the impending end. And indeed if, during this period, he often desired death though without admitting it to himself, it was to escape not so much the acuteness of his sufferings as the monotony of his struggle.

And yet he would have liked to live on until the time came when he no longer loved her, when she would have no reason to lie to him and he could at last learn from her if, on the day when he had gone to see her in the afternoon, she was or was not in bed with Forcheville. Often for several days, the suspicion that she loved someone else would distract him from that question about Forcheville, would make

it a matter almost of indifference to him, like those new developments in a continuing state of ill health which seem momentarily to
have delivered us from the preceding ones. There were even days
when he was not tormented by any suspicion. He thought he was
cured. But the next morning, when he woke up, he felt in the same
place the same pain, the sensation of which, in the course of the preceding day, he had diluted in a flood of different impressions. But it
had not moved from its place. And in fact, it was the sharpness of this
pain that had woken Swann.

Since Odette never gave him any information about these very
important things which occupied her so fully each day (although he
had lived long enough to know that these things are never anything
else but pleasures), he could not try to imagine them for very long at
a time, his brain was working with nothing in it; then he would pass
his finger over his tired eyelids as he would have wiped the glass of his
lorgnon, and stop thinking altogether. Yet floating up from that great
unknown were certain occupations which reappeared from time to
time, vaguely connected by her with some obligation toward distant
relatives or friends from an earlier time, who, because they were the
only ones she regularly mentioned to him as preventing her from seeing him, seemed to Swann to form the stable, necessary framework of
Odette's life. Because of the tone in which she referred from time to
time to "the day I go to the Hippodrome with my friend," if, having
felt ill and thought: "Perhaps Odette would be kind enough to come
round to the house," he recalled abruptly that this was in fact that
very day, he would say to himself: "Oh no! It's not worth the trouble
of asking her to come, I should have thought of it earlier, this is the
day she goes to the Hippodrome with her friend. We must confine
ourselves to what's possible; it's pointless wearing oneself out propos-
ing things that are unacceptable and have already been refused in advance." And the duty incumbent upon Odette of going to the
Hippodrome, to which Swann thus yielded, did not appear to him
merely unavoidable; but the mark of necessity with which it was
stamped seemed to make plausible and legitimate everything that was
closely or distantly related to it. If, after a man passing in the street

had greeted Odette and aroused Swann's jealousy, she answered his questions by associating the stranger with one of the two or three paramount duties of which she had spoken to him, if, for example, she said: "That was a gentleman who was in the box of the friend with whom I go to the Hippodrome," this explanation would calm Swann's suspicions, since he did indeed find it inevitable that the friend would have other guests besides Odette in her box at the Hippodrome, but had never tried or managed to picture them. Ah! how he would have liked to know her, the friend who went to the Hippodrome, and how he would have liked her to take him there with Odette! How gladly he would have given up all his connections in exchange for any person Odette was in the habit of seeing, even a manicurist or a shop assistant! He would have gone to more trouble for that person than for a queen. Wouldn't she have given him, with what she contained of Odette's life, the only effective calmative for his pain? How happily he would have hurried to spend the days at the home of one of those humble people with whom Odette kept up friendly relations out of either self-interest or true simplicity! How willingly he would have taken up residence forever on the fifth floor of a certain sordid and coveted house to which Odette did not take him and in which, if he had lived there with the little retired dressmaker whose lover he would willingly have pretended to be, he would have had a visit from her almost every day! In these almost working-class neighborhoods, what a modest life, abject, but sweet, nourished with calm and happiness, he would have agreed to live indefinitely!

It also sometimes happened that when, after meeting Swann, she saw some man approaching her whom he did not know, he could observe on Odette's face the sadness she had shown the day he had come to see her while Forcheville was there. But this was rare; for on the days when, despite everything she had to do and her fear of what other people would think, she managed to see Swann, what now predominated in her attitude was self-assurance: a great contrast, perhaps an unconscious revenge or a natural reaction to the timorous emotion which, in the early days when she had known him, she had felt with him, and even far away from him, when she would begin a letter with these words: "My dear, my hand is shaking so hard I can scarcely write" (at least so she claimed, and a little of that emotion must have been sincere for her to want to feign more of it). She liked Swann then. We do not tremble except for ourselves, except for those we love. When our happiness is no longer in their hands, what calm, what ease, what boldness we enjoy in their company! When speaking to him, when writing to him, she no longer used any of those words with which she had sought to give herself the illusion that he belonged to her, creating occasions for saying "my," "mine," when she referred to him—"You are my property, this is the fragrance of our friendship, I'm keeping it"—and for talking to him about the future, about death even, as a single thing that would be shared by the two of them. In those days, to everything he said, she would answer admiringly: "You—you will never be like anyone else"; she would look at his long face, his slightly bald head, about which the people who knew of Swann's successes with women would think: "He's not conventionally handsome, granted, but he is smart: that quiff of hair, that monocle, that smile!" and, perhaps with more curiosity to know what he was than desire to become his mistress, she would say: "If only I could know what is in that head!"

Now, to all of Swann's remarks she would reply in a tone that was at times irritated, at times indulgent: "Oh, you really never will be like anyone else!" She would look at that head, which was only a little more aged by worry (but about which now everyone thought, with that same aptitude which enables you to discover the intentions of a symphonic piece when you have read the program, and the resemblances of a child when you know its parents: "He's not positively ugly, granted, but he is absurd; that monocle, that quiff of hair, that smile!" creating in their suggestible imaginations the immaterial demarcation that separates by several months' distance the head of an adored lover from that of a cuckold), she would say: "Oh, if only I could change what's in that head, if only I could make it reasonable."

Always prepared to believe what he hoped for, if Odette's behavior toward him left any room at all for doubt, he would fling himself avidly on her words:

"You can if you want to," he would say to her.

And he would try to show her that to soothe him, direct him, make him work, would be a noble task to which many other women might ask nothing better than to devote themselves, though it would only be fair to add that in their hands the noble task would have appeared to him merely an indiscreet and intolerable usurpation of his freedom. "If she did not love me a little," he would say to himself, "she would not want to transform me. In order to transform me, she will have to see more of me." Thus he regarded this reproach of hers as a sort of proof of interest, of love perhaps; and indeed, she now gave him so few that he was obliged to regard as such the various prohibitions she imposed on him. One day, she declared that she did not like his coachman, that he was perhaps turning Swann against her, that in any case he did not show the punctuality and the deference to Swann that she wanted. She felt that Swann wanted to hear her say: "Don't use him anymore when you come to see me," as he would have wanted a kiss. Since she was in a good mood, she said it; he was touched. That evening, chatting with M. de Charlus, with whom he had the comfort of being able to talk about her openly (for the least bit of conversation he had, even with people who did not know her, always somehow related to her), he said to him: "Yet I believe she loves me; she is so kind to me, what I do is certainly not a matter of indifference to her." And if, when he was setting off for her house, getting into his carriage with a friend whom he was to drop along the way, the friend said: "Why, that's not Lorédan on the box," with what melancholy joy Swann would answer him: "Oh Lord no! I tell you I can't use Lorédan when I go to the rue La Pérouse. Odette doesn't like me to use Lorédan, she doesn't think he suits me. Well, what do you expect! Women, you know, women! I tell you she wouldn't like it at all. Oh, Lord, yes; if I'd used Rémi, there'd be no end of trouble!"

This new manner, indifferent, distracted, irritable, which was now Odette's manner with him, certainly caused Swann to suffer; but he was not aware of his suffering; since it was only gradually, day by day, that Odette had cooled toward him, it was only by comparing what she was now to what she had been in the beginning that he would have been able to fathom the depth of the change that had taken place. Yet that change was his deep, his secret wound which hurt him day and night, and as soon as he felt that his thoughts were straying a little too close to it, he would quickly guide them in another direction for fear of suffering too much. He would certainly say to himself in an abstract way: "There was a time when Odette loved me more," but he would never look back at that time. Just as there was a bureau in his office which he took pains not to look at, which he made a detour to avoid as he came and went, because in one of its drawers he had locked away the chrysanthemum she had given him that first evening on which he had driven her home, and the letters in which she had said: "If you had forgotten your heart here too, I would not have let you take it back," and "At whatever hour of the day or night you need me, send word and my life will be yours to command," so too there was a place inside him which he never let his thoughts approach, forcing them if necessary to make the detour of a lengthy argument so that they would not have to pass in front of it: this was the place where his memory of the happy days resided.

But his meticulous prudence was foiled one evening when he had gone out into society, to a party.

It was at the home of the Marquise de Saint-Euverte, on the last, for that year, of the evenings on which she invited people to hear the musicians whom she would afterward use for her charity concerts. Swann, who had wanted to go to each of the preceding evenings in turn and had not been able to resolve to do so, had received, while he was dressing for this one, a visit from the Baron de Charlus, who was coming with an offer to return with him to the home of the Marquise, if his company would help him to be a little less bored there, a little less sad. But Swann had answered:

"You can't doubt how much pleasure I would take in being with you. But the greatest pleasure you could give me would be to go to see Odette instead. You know what an excellent influence you have on her. I believe she's not going out this evening before she goes to see her old dressmaker, and I'm sure she'd be delighted to have you accompany her there. In any case you'll find her at home before that. Try to amuse her and also to talk some sense to her. If you could arrange something for tomorrow that she enjoys and that we could all three do together . . . Also, try to begin planning for this summer, see if there's something she might want to do, a cruise we might all three take, I don't know. I'm not counting on seeing her tonight myself; still, if she wanted to see me or if you were to find a way, you would only need to send me word at Mme. de Saint-Euverte's up to midnight, and afterward at home. Thank you for all that you do for me—you know how fond I am of you."

The Baron promised to go and pay the visit that Swann wanted after he had driven him to the door of the Saint-Euverte house, where Swann arrived soothed by the thought that M. de Charlus would be spending the evening in the rue La Pérouse, but in a state of melancholy indifference to everything that did not concern Odette, and in particular to the accoutrements of fashionable life, which gave them the charm that is to be found in anything which, being no longer an object of our desire, appears to us in its own guise. As soon as he descended from the carriage, in the foreground of that fictitious summary of their domestic life which hostesses like to offer their guests on ceremonial occasions and in which they seek to respect accuracy of costume and setting, Swann enjoyed the sight of those descendants of Balzac's "tigers,"[89] the grooms, who normally followed along on the daily outing, now hatted and booted and posted outside in front of the house on the soil of the avenue, or in front of the stables, like gardeners lined up at the entrances to their flower beds. The particular tendency he had always had to look for analogies between living people and portraits in museums was still active but in a more constant and general way; it was society as a whole, now that he was detached from it, which presented itself to him as a series of pictures. In the hall which in the old days, when he went out regularly into society, he would walk into wrapped in his overcoat and leave in his tails, but without knowing what had happened there, his mind having been, during the few moments he had stayed there, either still at the party he had just left, or already at the party he was about to be shown into, for the first time he noticed, woken by the unexpected arrival of the late guest, the scattered pack of magnificent, tall, idle footmen sleeping here and there on benches and chests who, raising their sharp, noble, greyhound profiles, stood up and gathered in a circle around him.

One of them, of a particularly ferocious aspect and rather like the executioner in certain Renaissance paintings which depicts scenes of torture, advanced upon him with an implacable air to take his things. But the hardness of his steely gaze was compensated by the softness of his cotton gloves, so that as he approached Swann he seemed to be showing contempt for his person and consideration for his hat. He took it with a care to which the exactness of his balance gave something meticulous, and with a delicacy rendered almost touching by the evidence of his strength. He then passed it to one of his assistants, new and timid, who expressed the terror he felt by casting wild glances in all directions and displayed the agitation of a captive animal in the first hours of its domestication.

A few steps away, a sturdy fellow in livery mused motionless, statuesque, useless, like the purely decorative warrior one sees in the most tumultuous paintings by Mantegna,[90] lost in thought, leaning on his shield, while others beside him rush forward and slaughter one another; detached from his group of companions as they pressed around Swann, he seemed as resolved to take no part in this scene, which he followed vaguely with his cruel sea-green eyes, as if it were the Massacre of the Innocents or the Martyrdom of Saint John. He seemed in fact to belong to that race which has vanished—or which perhaps never existed except in the altarpiece of San Zeno and the frescoes of the Erimitani, where Swann had encountered it and where it dreams on still—and which issued from the impregnation of an ancient statue by one of the Master's Paduan models or some Albrecht Dürer Saxon.[91] And the locks of his red hair, crimped by nature but glued by brilliantine, were treated broadly as they are in the Greek sculpture which the painter from Mantua studied so constantly and which, if out of all creation it depicts only man, is at least able to derive from his simple forms richnesses so varied, as though borrowed from all of living nature, that a head of hair, in the smooth rolls and sharp beaks of its curls, or in the superimposition of the threefold flowering diadem of its tresses, looks at once like a bundle of seaweed, a nestful of doves, a band of hyacinths, and a coil of snakes.

Still others, also colossal, stood on the steps of a monumental staircase to which their decorative presence and marmoreal immobility might have induced one to give the same name as the one in the Ducal Palace—"Staircase of the Giants"—and which Swann began to climb with the sad thought that Odette had never ascended it. Oh, with what joy by contrast would he have gone up the dark, evil-smelling, and rickety flights to the little retired dressmaker's, in whose "fifth floor" he would have been so happy to pay more than the price of a weekly stage box at the Opéra for the right to spend the evening when Odette came there, and even on the other days, so as to be able to talk about her, to live among the people she was in the habit of seeing when he was not there and who because of that seemed to him to harbor something, of his mistress's life, that was more real, more inaccessible, and more mysterious. Whereas in the old dressmaker's pestilential and longed-for staircase, since there was no second, service stair, one saw in the evening in front of each door an empty, dirty milk can set out in readiness on the mat, on the magnificent and disdained staircase which Swann was mounting at that moment, on either side, at different levels, in front of each anfractuosity formed in the wall by the window of the lodge or the entrance to a set of rooms, representing the domestic service which they directed and paying homage to the guests on their behalf, a concierge, a majordomo, a steward (good people who lived the rest of the week somewhat independent in their domains, dined there at home like small shopkeepers, and by tomorrow would perhaps be in the bourgeois service of a doctor or manufacturer), heedful not to fail to carry out the instructions they had been given before being allowed to put on the dazzling livery which they wore only at rare intervals and in which they did not feel very much at ease, stood under the arcature of their portals with a stately glitter tempered by common good nature, like saints in their niches, and an enormous usher, dressed as though he were in church, struck the flagstones with his staff as each new arrival passed. Having reached the top of the staircase up the length of which he had been followed by a wan-faced servant with a little bunch of hair tied in a cadogan[92] at the back of his head, like a Goya[93] sexton or a scrivener in an old play, Swann passed in front of a desk where valets, seated like notaries in front of great registers, stood up and inscribed his name. He then crossed a little vestibule which—like certain rooms arranged by their owners to serve as the setting for a single work of art, from which they take their name and, deliberately bare, contain nothing else—displayed at its entrance, like some precious effigy by Benvenuto Cellini[94] representing a watchman, a young footman, his body bent slightly forward, lifting from his red gorget a face even redder from which burst forth torrents of fire, timidity, and zeal, and who, piercing with his impetuous, vigilant, distracted gaze the Aubusson tapestries hung before the drawing room where people were listening to music, appeared, with a military impassivity or a supernatural faith—an allegory of alarm, an incarnation of alertness, a commemoration of the call to arms—to be watching, angel or sentinel, from the tower of a castle or cathedral, for the appearance of the enemy or the hour of Judgment. Now Swann had only to enter the concert room, whose doors an usher loaded with chains was opening for him with a bow, as he would have handed over to him the keys to a city. But he thought of the house in which he might have been at this very moment, if Odette had permitted it, and the memory he glimpsed of an empty milk can on a doormat wrung his heart.

Swann rapidly recovered his sense of how ugly men could be, when, beyond the tapestry hangings, the spectacle of the servants was followed by that of the guests. But even the ugliness of these faces, though he knew it so well, seemed new to him since their features—instead of being signs usable in a practical way for the identification of a certain person who had until then represented a cluster of pleasures to pursue, worries to avoid, or courtesies to pay—now remained coordinated only by aesthetic relations, within the autonomy of their lines. And of these men in whose midst Swann found himself hemmed in, even the monocles which many wore (and which, formerly, would at the very most have allowed Swann to say that they wore a monocle), having now been released from signifying a habit, the same for everyone, appeared to him each with a sort of individuality. Maybe because he did not regard Général de Froberville and the Marquis de Bréauté, who were talking to each other just inside the door, as more than two figures in a painting, whereas for a long time they had been useful friends who had introduced him to the Jockey Club and supported him in duels, the general's monocle, stuck between his eyelids like a shell splinter in his vulgar, scarred, overbearing face, in the middle of a forehead which it blinded like the Cyclops' single eye, appeared to Swann like a monstrous wound that might have been glorious to receive, but was indecent to show off; whereas the one that M. de Bréauté added, as a badge of festivity, to the pearl-gray gloves, the opera hat, and the white tie, and substituted for the familiar lorgnette (as Swann himself did) for going out in society, bore, glued to its other side, like a natural history specimen under a microscope, an infinitesimal gaze teeming with friendliness that smiled constantly at the loftiness of the ceilings, the beauty of the preparations, the interest of the programs, and the excellence of the refreshments.

"Well now, here you are! Why, it's been an eternity since we last saw you," said the general to Swann and, noticing his drawn features and concluding from this that it was perhaps a grave illness that had kept him away from society, he added: "You look quite well, you know!" while M. de Bréauté asked: "My dear, what in the world are you doing here?" of a society novelist who had just positioned in the corner of his eye a monocle which was his only organ of psychological investigation and pitiless analysis and who answered with an air of mystery and self-importance, rolling the *r*:

"I am observing!"

The Marquis de Forestelle's monocle was minuscule, had no border, and, requiring a constant painful clenching of the eye, where it was encrusted like a superfluous cartilage whose presence was inexplicable and whose material was exquisite, gave the Marquis's face a melancholy delicacy, and made women think he was capable of great sorrows in love. But that of M. de Saint-Candé, surrounded by a gigantic ring, like Saturn, was the center of gravity of a face which regulated itself at each moment in relation to it, a face whose quivering red nose and thick-lipped sarcastic mouth attempted by their grimaces to equal the unceasing salvos of wit sparkling from the disk of glass, and saw itself preferred to the handsomest eyes in the world by snobbish and depraved young women in whom it inspired dreams of artificial charms and a refinement of voluptuousness; and meanwhile, behind his own, M. de Palancy, who, with his big, round-eyed carp's head, moved about slowly in the midst of the festivities unclenching his mandibles from moment to moment as though seeking to orient himself, merely seemed to be transporting with him an accidental and perhaps purely symbolic fragment of the glass of his aquarium, a part intended to represent the whole, reminding Swann, a great admirer of Giotto's *Vices* and *Virtues* at Padua, of Injustice, next to whom a leafy bough evokes the forests in which his lair is hidden.

Swann had walked on into the room, at the insistence of Mme. de Saint-Euverte, and, in order to hear a melody from *Orphée*[95] that was being performed by a flautist, had placed himself in a corner where unfortunately his only view was of two mature ladies seated next to each other, the Marquise de Cambremer and the Vicomtesse de Franquetot, who, because they were cousins, spent their time when attending a party, clutching their bags and followed by their daughters, looking for each other as though in a railway station, and did not rest easy until they had reserved, with a fan or a handkerchief, two seats side by side: Mme. de Cambremer, since she had very few acquaintances, being all the happier to have a companion, Mme. de Franquetot, who was in contrast extremely well connected, believing there was something elegant, something original, about showing all her fine friends that she preferred, to their company, an obscure lady with whom she shared memories of her youth. Full of a melancholy irony, Swann watched them listen to the piano intermezzo (*Saint Francis Speaking to the Birds* by Liszt)[96] which had come after the flute melody, and follow the vertiginous playing of the virtuoso, Mme. de Franquetot anxiously, her eyes wild as if the keys over which he ran with such agility were a series of trapezes from which he might fall from a height

of eighty yards, and at the same time casting at her neighbor looks of
astonishment, of denial which signified: "This is not to be believed, I
would never have thought a man could do this," while Mme. de
Cambremer, being a woman who had received a strong musical education, marked time with her head transformed into the arm of a
metronome whose amplitude and rapidity of oscillations from one
shoulder to the other had become such (with that sort of frenzy and
abandon in the eyes characteristic of a kind of suffering which is no
longer aware of itself nor tries to control itself and says "I can't help
it!") that she kept snagging her solitaires in the straps of her bodice
and was obliged to straighten the black grapes she had in her hair,
though without ceasing to accelerate her motion. On the other side of
Mme. de Franquetot, but a little in front, was the Marquise de Gallardon, occupied with her favorite thought, her alliance with the Guermantes, which in the eyes of the world and in her own was the source
of a good deal of glory along with some shame, the most brilliant of
them keeping her a bit at a distance, perhaps because she was tiresome, or because she was spiteful, or because she was from an inferior
branch, or perhaps for no reason. When she found herself next to
someone she did not know, as at this moment Mme. de Franquetot, it
would pain her that her own awareness of her kinship with the Guermantes could not be manifested outwardly in visible characters like
those which, in the mosaics of the Byzantine churches, placed one
below another, inscribe in a vertical column, next to a holy personage,
the words he is supposed to be uttering. At this moment she was pon-
dering the fact that she had never received an invitation or a visit
from her young cousin the Princesse des Laumes, in the six years the
Princesse had been married. This thought filled her with anger, but
also with pride; for, by dint of saying to people who were surprised
not to see her at the home of Mme. des Laumes, that it was because
she would have risked meeting Princesse Mathilde[97] there—for which
her ultra-Legitimist[98] family would never have forgiven her—she had
ended by believing this actually was the reason she did not go to her
young cousin's house. Yet she recalled having asked Mme. des

Laumes several times how she might contrive to meet her, but recalled it only confusedly and also more than neutralized this slightly humiliating memory by murmuring: "After all it's not up to me to make the first move, I'm twenty years older than she." Fortified by the efficacy of these unspoken words, she proudly threw back her shoulders, which seemed detached from her bust and on which her head was positioned almost horizontally so that one was reminded of the "restored" head of a haughty pheasant brought to the table in all its feathers. It was not so much that she was not stocky, mannish, and plump by nature; but the insults she had received had straightened her up like those trees which, born in a bad position at the brink of a precipice, are forced to grow backward to keep their balance. Obliged as she was, in order to console herself for not being altogether the equal of the other Guermantes, to keep telling herself that it was because of the intransigence of her principles and her pride that she did not see them very often, this thought had ended by shaping her body and by giving her an imposing sort of presence that passed in the eyes of bourgeois women for a sign of breeding and sometimes disturbed with a fleeting desire the clubmen's weary glances. If Mme. de Gallardon's conversation had been subjected to those analyses which, by recording the greater or lesser frequency of each word, permit one to discover the key to a language in code, one would have realized that no expression, even the most ordinary, recurred in it as often as "at the home of my cousins the Guermantes," "at the home of my aunt de Guermantes," "the health of Elzéar de Guermantes," "my cousin de Guermantes's baignoire."[99] When anyone spoke to her about a famous personage, she would answer that without knowing him personally she had met him a thousand times at the home of her aunt de Guermantes, but she would answer this in a tone so icy and in a voice so low that it was clear that, if she did not know him personally, it was by virtue of all the ineradicable and stubborn principles which her shoulders touched behind her, like those ladders on which gymnastics instructors make you stretch out in order to develop your chest.

Now as it happened, the Princesse des Laumes, whom one would not have expected to see at Mme. de Saint-Euverte's, had just arrived.

In order to show that she was not trying to advertise, in a drawing room to which she had come only out of condescension, the superiority of her rank, she had entered with her shoulders turned sideways even where there was no crowd to cleave through and no person attempting to get past her, staying deliberately at the back, with the air of being in her proper place, like a king who stands in line at the door of a theater so long as the management has not been informed that he is there; and, merely confining her gaze—so as not to seem to be signaling her presence and demanding attention—to a consideration of the design in the carpet or in her own skirt, she stood in the spot that had seemed to her the most modest (and from which she was well aware she would be drawn by a delighted exclamation from Mme. de Saint-Euverte as soon as the latter noticed her), next to Mme. de Cambremer, whom she did not know. She observed the pantomime of her music-loving neighbor, but did not imitate it. It was not that, the one time she came to spend five minutes at Mme. de Saint-Euverte's, the Princesse des Laumes would not have wished, so that the courtesy she was showing her might count double, to prove as friendly as possible. But by nature, she had a horror of what she called "exaggerations" and was anxious to show that she "did not have to" indulge in displays of emotion which were not in keeping with the "style" of the circle she moved in, but which still, on the other hand, could not help but impress her, by virtue of that spirit of imitation akin to timidity which is developed in the most confident persons by the atmosphere of a new environment, even if it is an inferior one. She began to wonder if this gesticulation was not perhaps a necessary response to the piece being played, which did not come quite within the scope of the music she had heard up to now, if to refrain was not to give proof of incomprehension with respect to the work and impropriety toward the lady of the house: so that, in order to express both of her contradictory inclinations by a compromise, she first merely straightened up her shoulder straps or put a hand to her blond hair to secure the little balls of diamond-flecked coral or pink enamel which formed her simple and charming coiffure, while at the same time examining her ardent neighbor with cold curiosity, then with her fan she beat time for a moment, but, so as not to forfeit her independence, on the offbeat. When the pianist ended the piece by Liszt and began a prelude by Chopin, Mme. de Cambremer gave Mme. de Franquetot a tender smile full of knowledgeable satisfaction and allusion to the past. When she was young she had learned to caress the phrases of Chopin with their sinuous and excessively long necks, so free, so flexible, so tactile, which begin by seeking out and exploring a place for themselves far outside and away from the direction in which they started, far beyond the point which one might have expected them to reach, and which frolic in this fantasy distance only to come back more deliberately—with a more premeditated return, with more precision, as though upon a crystal glass that resonates until you cry out—to strike you in the heart.

Living in a provincial family that had few friends, scarcely ever going out to a ball, she had intoxicated herself in the solitude of her manor house, with all those imaginary dancing couples, now slowing them, now speeding them, now scattering them like flowers, now leaving the ball for a moment to hear the wind blow in the pine trees, at the edge of the lake, and suddenly seeing, as he came toward her there, more unlike anything anyone had ever dreamed of than an earthly lover could be, a slender young man in white gloves whose voice had a strange, false lilt to it. But nowadays the old-fashioned beauty of that music seemed stale. Having fallen in the esteem of the discriminating public over the past several years, it had lost its position of distinction and its charm, and even those whose taste is bad no longer took more than an unacknowledged and moderate pleasure in it. Mme. de Cambremer cast a furtive glance behind her. She was aware that her young daughter-in-law (full of respect for her new family, except regarding the things of the mind about which, since she knew a little harmony and even some Greek, she was especially enlightened) despised Chopin and suffered when she heard it played. But far away from the surveillance of that Wagnerian who was off in the distance with a group of people her own age, Mme. de Cambremer abandoned herself to her delightful impressions. The Princesse des Laumes was enjoying them too. Though without a natural gift for music, she had had lessons fifteen years earlier from a piano teacher of the Faubourg Saint-Germain, a woman of genius who at the end of her life had been reduced to poverty and had returned, at the age of seventy, to giving piano lessons, to the daughters and granddaughters of her old pupils. She was dead now. But her method, her lovely sound, came back to life sometimes under the fingers of her pupils, even those who had become in other respects ordinary people, had abandoned music, and almost never opened a piano anymore. And so Mme. des Laumes could shake her head, with expert knowledge, with a just appreciation of the way the pianist was playing this prelude, which she knew by heart. The end of the phrase he had begun already sang on her lips. And she murmured, "It's always *ch*arming," with a double *ch* at the start of the word which was a mark of refinement and which, she felt, pursed her lips so romantically, like a beautiful flower, that she instinctively brought her eyes into harmony with them by giving them an expression just then of sentimentality and vague yearning. Meanwhile, Mme. de Gallardon was saying to herself how annoying it was that she only very rarely had the opportunity to meet the Princesse des Laumes, for she wanted to teach her a lesson by not responding to her greeting. She did not know her cousin was there. A movement of Mme. de Franquetot's head revealed the Princesse to her. Immediately she hurried toward her, disturbing everyone; but though she wanted to preserve a haughty and glacial manner which would remind everyone that she did not wish to be on friendly terms with a person in whose house one might find oneself coming face-to-face with Princesse Mathilde, and to whom it was not for her to make advances since she was not "of her generation," still she wanted to off-set this air of haughtiness and reserve by some remark that would jus-tify her overture and force the Princesse to engage in conversation; and so when she came near her cousin, Mme. de Gallardon, with a hard expression and a hand outthrust like a "forced" card, said to her: "How is your husband?" in the concerned tone she would have used if the Prince had been gravely ill. The Princesse, bursting into a laugh which was peculiar to her and which was intended at once to show others that she was making fun of someone and also to make herself look prettier by concentrating her features around her animated lips and sparkling eyes, answered:

"Why, he's never been better!"

And she laughed again. Whereupon Mme. de Gallardon, drawing herself up and contriving an even chillier expression, yet still concerned about the Prince's condition, said to her cousin:

"Oriane" (here Mme. des Laumes looked with an air of surprise and merriment at an invisible third party in whose presence she seemed anxious to attest that she had never authorized Mme. de Gallardon to call her by her first name), "I would be so pleased if you could stop in at my house for a moment tomorrow evening to hear a clarinet quintet by Mozart. I would like to have your opinion."

She seemed not to be offering an invitation, but to be asking a favor, and to need the Princesse's assessment of the Mozart quintet as if it were a dish composed by a new cook about whose talents it was valuable to her to obtain the opinion of a gourmet.

"But I know that quintet. I can tell you right now . . . I like it!"

"You know, my husband isn't well; it's his liver . . . It would give him great pleasure to see you," resumed Mme. de Gallardon, now placing the Princesse under a charitable obligation to appear at her soiree.

The Princesse never liked to tell people she did not want to go to their homes. Every day she would write notes expressing her regrets at having been prevented—by an unexpected visit from her mother-in-law, an invitation from her brother-in-law, the opera, an expedition to the country—from attending a soiree to which she would never have dreamed of going. In this way she gave many people the joy of believing that she was one of their friends, that she would readily have gone to visit them, that she had been kept from doing so only by princely inconveniences which they were flattered to see enter into competition with their soiree. Then, too, since she was part of that witty circle of the Guermantes in which something survived of the alert mentality unburdened by platitudes and conventional feelings which was handed down from Mérimée[100] and had found its latest expression in the theater of Meilhac and Halévy,[101] she adapted it even to social relations, transposed it even into her politeness, which endeavored to be positive and precise, and to approximate the plain truth. She would never develop at any length to a hostess the expression of her desire to be present at her party; she thought it friendlier to put to her a few little facts on which it would depend whether or not it was possible for her to come.

"The thing is," she said to Mme. de Gallardon, "tomorrow evening I have to go see a friend who has been asking me to make a date with her for ages. If she takes us to the theater, even with the best will in the world there won't be any chance of my coming to you; but if we stay in the house, since I know we'll be alone, I'll be able to leave her."

"Oh, by the way, did you see your friend M. Swann?"

"Why no! My beloved Charles, I didn't know he was here, I must try to attract his attention."

"It's funny that he should go to old Saint-Euverte's," said Mme. de Gallardon. "Oh, I know he's intelligent," she added, meaning he was a schemer, "but still and all, a Jew in the home of the sister and sister-in-law of two archbishops!"

"I confess to my shame that I'm not shocked," said the Princess des Laumes.

"I know he's a convert, and even his parents and grandparents before him. But they do say converts remain more attached to their religion than anyone else, that it's all just a pretense. Is that true?"

"I don't know a thing about that."

The pianist, who was to play two pieces by Chopin, after finishing the prelude had immediately attacked a polonaise. But now that Mme. de Gallardon had told her cousin that Swann was there, Chopin himself might have risen from the dead and played all his pieces in succession without Mme. des Laumes paying the slightest attention. She belonged to that half of the human race in whom the curiosity the other half feels about the people it does not know is replaced by an interest in the people it does. As with many women of the Faubourg Saint-Germain, the presence in a place where she happened to be of someone from her set, though she had nothing in particular to say to him, monopolized her attention at the expense of everything else. From that moment on, in the hopes that Swann would notice her, the Princesse, like a tame white mouse when a bit of sugar is offered to it and then taken away, kept turning her face, which was filled with a thousand signs of complicity unrelated to the feeling in Chopin's polonaise, in Swann's direction, and if he moved, she would shift in a corresponding direction her magnetic smile.

"Oriane, don't be angry," resumed Mme. de Gallardon, who could never stop herself from sacrificing her greatest social ambitions and highest hopes of someday dazzling the world to the immediate, obscure, and private pleasure of saying something disagreeable, "but people do claim that M. Swann is someone whom one can't have in one's house, is that true?"

"Why . . . you ought to know," answered the Princesse des Laumes, "since you've invited him fifty times and he hasn't come once."

And leaving her mortified cousin, she burst into laughter again, scandalizing the people who were listening to the music, but attracting the attention of Mme. de Saint-Euverte, who had stayed near the piano out of politeness and only now noticed the Princesse. Mme. de Saint-Euverte was especially delighted to see Mme. des Laumes because she had thought she was still at Guermantes looking after her sick father-in-law.

"Why, Princesse, I didn't know you were here!"

"Yes, I tucked myself away in a little corner, and I've been hearing such lovely things."

"What! Have you been here for a long time?"

"Why yes, a very long time which seemed very short to me—it was long only because I couldn't see you."

Mme. de Saint-Euverte tried to give her chair to the Princesse, who answered:

"Oh, please, no! Why should you? I'm comfortable wherever I sit!"

And, intentionally selecting, the better to display her simplicity, great lady though she was, a low seat without a back:

"Here, this hassock is all I need. It'll make me sit up straight. Oh, my Lord, I'm making too much noise again, if I'm not careful they'll turn on me and throw me out."

Meanwhile, the pianist having redoubled his speed, the musical emotion was at its height, a servant was passing refreshments on a tray and making the spoons clink, and, as happened every week, Mme. de Saint-Euverte signaled to him without his seeing her, to go away. A newlywed, who had been taught that a young woman must not appear bored, smiled with pleasure, and tried to catch the hostess's eye in order to send her a look of gratitude for having "thought of her" for such a treat. However, although she remained calmer than Mme. de Franquetot, it was not without some uneasiness that she followed the music; but the object of her uneasiness was, not the pianist, but the piano, on which a candle jumping with each fortissimo risked, if not setting its shade on fire, at least spotting the Brazilian rosewood. In the end she could not bear it any longer and, scaling the two steps of the dais on which the piano was placed, swooped down to remove the sconce. But her hands were just about to touch it when, with a final chord, the piece ended and the pianist stood up. Nevertheless the young woman's bold initiative, the resulting brief promiscuity between her and the instrumentalist, produced a generally favorable impression.

"Did you see what that young woman did, Princesse?" said Général de Froberville to the Princesse des Laumes, whom he had come up to greet and whom Mme. de Saint-Euverte had left for a moment. "Odd, wasn't it? Is she a performer?"

"No, she's just some young Mme. de Cambremer," answered the Princesse without thinking and then added hurriedly: "I'm only repeating what I heard, I haven't the slightest idea who she is; someone behind me was saying they were country neighbors of Mme. de Saint-Euverte, but I don't think anyone knows them, really. They must be 'country folk'! Anyway, I don't know if you're intimate with the brilliant society here, but I can't put a name to any of these astonishing people. What do you think they spend their time doing when they're not at Mme. de Saint-Euverte's evenings? She must have ordered them along with the musicians, the chairs, and the refreshments. You must admit these 'guests from Belloir's'[102] are magnificent. Does she really have the heart to rent the same 'extras' every week? It isn't possible!"

"Ah! But Cambremer is quite a good name, and an old one too," said the general.

"I see no harm in the fact that it's old," answered the Princesse dryly, "but still, it's not *euphonious*," she added, isolating the word *euphonious* as though between quotation marks, a little affectation in delivery that was peculiar to the Guermantes set.

"You think so? She's pretty enough to eat, though," said the general, who had not let Mme. de Cambremer out of his sight. "Don't you agree, Princesse?"

"She thrusts herself forward too much, I think; in so young a woman, that's not nice—because I don't believe she's of my generation," answered Mme. des Laumes (this expression being common to both the Gallardons and the Guermantes).

But then the Princesse, seeing that M. de Froberville was continuing to gaze at Mme. de Cambremer, added half out of spite against her, half out of friendliness toward the general: "Not nice . . . for her husband! I'm sorry I don't know her, since you've set your heart on her; I would have introduced you," she continued, although she probably would have done nothing of the kind had she known the young woman. "I will have to say goodnight to you, because it's the birthday of a friend of mine and I must go and pay my respects," she said in a tone of modesty and sincerity, reducing the fashionable party to which she was going to the simplicity of a ceremony which was tiresome but which it was obligatory and also rather touching to attend. "Besides, I'm supposed to meet Basin there; while I've been here, he has been seeing friends of his—people you know, I believe. They have the same name as a bridge: the Iénas."

"Before that it was the name of a victory, Princesse," said the general. "What do you expect—an old soldier like me," he went on, removing his monocle and wiping it, as he would have changed a bandage, while the Princesse instinctively looked away. "The nobility of the Empire, it's different of course, but really, for what it is, it's very fine of its kind. Those were men who fought, really, like heroes."

"But I have the deepest respect for heroes," said the Princesse, in a slightly ironic tone: "if I don't go with Basin to see this woman, the Princesse d'Iéna, it's not because of that, not at all, it's quite simply because I don't know them. Basin knows them, he loves them dearly. Oh no, it's not what you may think, they're not having an affair, I have no reason to object! Anyway, what use is it when I do try to object?" she added in a melancholy voice, because everyone knew that the very day after the Prince des Laumes married his ravishing cousin, he had deceived her, and he had not stopped deceiving her since. "But this is not the same, these are people he used to know, he's happy as a pig in clover, I think it's very nice. But I can tell you that even what he has told me about their house . . . Can you imagine, all their furniture is 'Empire'!"[103]

"Well, naturally, Princesse; it was their grandparents' furniture."

"Well, I'm not saying it wasn't, but it's no less ugly for all that. I understand perfectly well that one can't always have pretty things, but at least one's things should not be ridiculous. What do you expect? I can't think of anything more conventional, more bourgeois, than that horrible style—cabinets with swans' heads, like bathtubs."

"Actually I do believe they have some beautiful things, they must have that famous mosaic table that was used for the signing of the Treaty of . . ."

"Oh, I'm not saying they don't have things that are interesting from a historical point of view. But things like that can't ever be beautiful . . . because they're simply horrible! I've got things like that myself which Basin inherited from the Montesquious. Only they're in the attics of Guermantes where no one can see them. Anyway, really, that's not the point, I would rush around to their house with Basin, I would see them even in the midst of their sphinxes and their brass if I knew them, but . . . I don't know them! I was always told when I was little that it wasn't polite to go to the homes of people one didn't know," she said, assuming a childish tone. "So I'm just doing what I was taught. Can't you see those good people if someone they didn't know were to come bursting into the house? They might make me feel quite unwelcome!" said the Princesse.

And she coquettishly enhanced the smile which this supposition had brought to her lips by giving her blue eyes, which were fixed on the general, a dreamy, gentle expression.

"Ah, Princesse, you know very well they wouldn't be able to contain themselves for joy . . ."

"Not at all. Why?" she asked him with the utmost vivacity, either so as not to seem to know that it was because she was one of the foremost ladies in France, or so as to have the pleasure of hearing the general say it. "Why? What do you know about it? It might be the most disagreeable thing in the world for them. I don't know, but judging by myself, it already bores me so much to see people I know, I believe that if I had to see people I didn't know, even if they had 'fought like heroes,' I would go mad. Besides, you see, except when it's an old friend like you whom one knows quite apart from that, I don't know if heroism would take one very far in society. I often find it quite boring enough as it is to give a dinner party, but if I had to offer my arm to Spartacus going in to the table . . . No, really, Vercingétorix would never be the one I would send for, to make a fourteenth. I think I would save him for the large parties. And since I never give any . . ."

"Ah, Princesse, you're not a Guermantes for nothing. You have your share of it all right, the wit of the Guermantes family!"

"They always say 'the wit of the Guermantes *family*.' I've never been able to understand why. Do you know *other* Guermantes who have it?" she added in a bubbly, joyful burst of laughter, her features concentrated, interconnected in a web of animation, her eyes sparkling, blazing with a radiant sunshine of gaiety that could be kindled only by remarks, even if made by the Princesse herself, in praise of her wit or her beauty. "Wait, there's Swann. He seems to be speaking to your young Cambremer. There . . . he's next to old mother Saint-Euverte, don't you see him? Ask him to introduce you. But hurry up, he's trying to walk away!"

"How frightfully ill he's looking—did you notice?" said the general.

"My dear Charles! Ah! At last he's coming, I was beginning to think he didn't want to see me!"

Swann liked the Princesse des Laumes very much, and the sight of her also reminded him of Guermantes, the estate next to Combray, the whole countryside which he loved so much and had ceased to visit so as not to be away from Odette. Using the half-artistic, half-courtly formulae which he knew were pleasing to the Princesse and which he resumed quite naturally whenever he reimmersed himself for a moment in his old social milieu—and wanting anyway for his own sake to express the yearning he felt for the country:

"Ah," he said to some vague general audience, in order to be heard both by Mme. de Saint-Euverte, to whom he was speaking, and by Mme. des Laumes, for whom he was speaking, "here's the charming Princesse! See, she has come up from Guermantes expressly to hear Liszt's *Saint Francis of Assisi* and has only just had time, like a pretty titmouse, to go and pluck a little fruit from the wild plums and hawthorns and put them on her head; there is even a bit of dew on them still, a bit of the hoarfrost that must be making the duchess groan so. It's very pretty indeed, my dear Princesse."

"What, the Princesse has come up expressly from Guermantes? But that's too much! I didn't know, I'm embarrassed," exclaimed Mme. de Saint-Euverte naively, not being used to Swann's wit. Then, looking more closely at the Princesse's headgear: "Why you're quite right, it's meant to look like . . . what shall I say, not chestnuts, no—oh, what a ravishing idea! But how could the Princesse have known what was going to be on my program! The musicians didn't even tell me."

Swann, who was accustomed, when he was in the company of a woman whom he had kept up the habit of addressing in gallant language, to say things so delicately nuanced that many society people could not understand them, did not condescend to explain to Mme. de Saint-Euverte that he had merely been speaking metaphorically. As for the Princesse, she began laughing heartily, because Swann's wit was highly appreciated in her set and also because she could not hear a compliment addressed to her without finding it most exquisitely subtle and irresistibly droll.

"Well! I'm delighted, Charles, if you like my little hawthorn fruits.

Why did you speak to that Cambremer woman? Are you her neighbor in the country too?"

Mme. de Saint-Euverte, seeing that the Princesse appeared happy to chat with Swann, had moved off.

"But you are too, Princesse."

"I! But then those people have country places everywhere! How I would like to be in their place!"

"It's not the Cambremers, it's her own family; she's a Legrandin daughter and used to come to Combray. I don't know if you know you're the Comtesse de Combray and the chapter owes you a due?"

"I don't know what the chapter owes me, but I know that I'm dunned a hundred francs every year by the curé, which I could do without. Really those Cambremers have a most astonishing name.[104] It ends just in time, but it ends badly!" she said, laughing.

"It doesn't begin any better," Swann answered.

"Really, the two abbreviations together! . . ."

"Someone very angry and very proper didn't dare finish the first word."

"But since he couldn't stop himself from beginning the second, he should have finished the first—then he'd be done with it once and for all. Our jokes are in charming taste, my little Charles, but how tiresome it is not to see you anymore," she added in a caressing tone, "I so much like talking to you. Just think, I wouldn't even have been able to make that idiot Froberville understand that the name Cambremer is astonishing. Admit that life is a dreadful thing. It's only when I see you that I stop feeling bored."

This was probably not true. But Swann and the Princesse had the same way of looking at the small things of life, the effect of which—unless it was the cause—was a great similarity in their ways of expressing themselves and even in their pronunciation. No one noticed the resemblance because their two voices were so utterly unlike. But if in one's imagination one managed to divest Swann's remarks of the sonority in which they were enveloped, of the mustache from under which they issued, one realized that these were the same sentences, the same inflections, that these turns of phrase belonged to the Guermantes set. When it came to the important things, Swann and the Princesse did not have the same ideas about anything. But now that Swann had become so sad, always in the sort of tremulous condition that precedes the moment one is going to cry, he felt as compelled to talk about grief as a murderer is to talk about his crime. When he heard the Princesse say that life was a dreadful thing, he felt as comforted as if she had been talking about Odette.

"Oh, yes! Life is a dreadful thing. We must see each other soon, my dear friend. What's so nice about being with you is that you're not cheerful. We could spend an evening together."

"What a good idea! Why don't you come down to Guermantes? My mother-in-law would be wild with joy. It's supposed to be so ugly thereabouts, but I must say I don't dislike that countryside at all; I loathe 'picturesque' spots."

"I agree, it's wonderful," answered Swann, "it's almost too beautiful, too alive for me just now; it's a place to be happy in. Perhaps it's because I've lived there, but the things there speak to me so! As soon as a breath of wind comes up, when the wheat begins to move, it seems to me that someone is about to arrive, I'm going to hear some news; and those little houses by the edge of the water . . . I would be quite miserable!"

"Oh, my dear Charles, watch out, there's that dreadful Rampillon woman. She's seen me; please hide me. Remind me what it was that happened to her; I'm getting it all mixed up; she's just married off her daughter, or her lover, I can't remember which; maybe both of them . . . and to each other! . . . Oh no! I remember now, she's been dropped by her prince . . . Pretend to be talking to me, so that Bérénice woman won't come over and invite me to dinner. Anyway, I must fly. Listen, my dear Charles, now that I've seen you for once, won't you let me steal you away and take you to the Princess's? She'd be so pleased to see you, and Basin, too—he's meeting me there. If we didn't get news of you from Mémé . . . Just think, I never see you at all now!"

Swann declined; having told M. de Charlus that when he left Mme. de Saint-Euverte's he would go directly back home, he did not want to run the risk, by going on to the Princess of Parma's, of missing a note that he had been hoping all evening would be handed to him by a servant during the party, and that perhaps he would find in his concierge's keeping. "Poor Swann," said Mme. des Laumes that night to her husband, "he's always kind, but he appears quite unhappy. You'll see, because he has promised to come to dinner one of these days. I do find it absurd that a man of his intelligence should suffer over a person of that sort, who isn't even interesting—because they say she's an idiot," she added with the wisdom of people not in love who believe a man of sense should be unhappy only over a person who is worth it; which is rather like being surprised that anyone should condescend to suffer from cholera because of so small a creature as the comma bacillus.

Swann wanted to leave, but just when he was at last about to escape, Général de Froberville asked him for an introduction to Mme. de Cambremer and he was obliged to go back into the drawing room with him to look for her.

"Now, Swann, I'd rather be the husband of that woman than slaughtered by savages, what do you say?"

The words *slaughtered by savages* pierced Swann's heart painfully; and at once he felt the need to continue the conversation:

"Well, you know," he said to him, "some really fine men have lost their lives that way . . . For instance, if you remember . . . That navigator whose ashes were brought back by Dumont d'Urville, La Pérouse . . ." (And Swann was immediately happy, as if he had spoken Odette's name.) "He was a fine character, La Pérouse was, and one who interests me very much," he added with a melancholy air.

"Ah! Indeed yes. La Pérouse," said the general. "The name is well known. It's got its own street."

"You know someone in the rue La Pérouse?" asked Swann in some agitation.

"I know only Mme. de Chanlivault, the sister of that good fellow Chaussepierre. She gave us a nice theater party the other day. Her salon will be very elegant one of these days, you'll see!"

"Ah, so she lives in the rue La Pérouse. It's an appealing street, very pretty, and so melancholy."

"Why, not at all, in fact you haven't been there in some time; it's not melancholy these days, they're beginning to build there, they've got buildings going up in the whole neighborhood."

When at last Swann introduced M. de Froberville to young Mme. de Cambremer, since it was the first time she had heard the general's name she ventured the smile of joy and surprise she would have given him if no other name but that one had ever been uttered in her presence, for as she did not know the friends of her new family, each time a person was presented to her, she believed he was one of them, and thinking it would be tactful of her to look as though she had heard such a lot about him since she was married, she would put out her hand with a hesitant air meant as proof of the inculcated reserve she had to conquer and the spontaneous congeniality that succeeded in overcoming it. And so her parents-in-law, whom she still believed to be the most brilliant people in France, declared that she was an angel; especially since they preferred to appear, in marrying their son to her, to have responded to the attraction of her fine qualities rather than of her great wealth.

"One can see that you have the soul of a musician, madame," the general said to her, unconsciously alluding to the incident of the sconce.

But the concert was beginning again and Swann realized he would not be able to leave before the end of this new number. He was suffering at having to remain shut up among these people whose stupidity and absurd habits struck him all the more painfully since, being unaware of his love, incapable, had they known about it, of taking any interest in it or doing more than smile at it as at some childish nonsense or deplore it as utter madness, they made it appear to him as a subjective state which existed only for him, whose reality was confirmed for him by nothing outside himself; he suffered most of all, to the point where even the sound of the instruments made him want to cry out, from prolonging his exile in this place to which

Odette would never come, where no one, where nothing knew her, from which she was entirely absent.

But suddenly it was as though she had appeared in the room, and this apparition caused him such harrowing pain that he had to put his hand on his heart. What had happened was that the violin had risen to a series of high notes on which it lingered as though waiting for something, holding on to them in a prolonged expectancy, in the exaltation of already seeing the object of its expectation approaching, and with a desperate effort to try to endure until it arrived, to welcome it before expiring, to keep the way open for it another moment with a last bit of strength so that it could come through, as one holds up a trapdoor that would otherwise fall back. And before Swann had time to understand, and say to himself: "It's the little phrase from the sonata by Vinteuil; don't listen!" all his memories of the time when Odette was in love with him, which he had managed until now to keep out of sight in the deepest part of himself, deceived by this sudden beam of light from the time of love which they believed had returned, had awoken and flown swiftly back up to sing madly to him, with no pity for his present misfortune, the forgotten refrains of happiness.

In place of the abstract expressions *the time when I was happy, the time when I was loved,* which he had often used before now without suffering too much, for his mind had enclosed within them only spurious extracts of the past that preserved nothing of it, he now recovered everything which had fixed forever the specific, volatile essence of that lost happiness; he saw everything again, the snowy curled petals of the chrysanthemum that she had tossed to him in his carriage, that he had held against his lips—the embossed address of the "Maison Dorée" on the letter in which he had read: "My hand is shaking so badly as I write to you"—the way her eyebrows had come together when she said to him with a supplicating look: "It won't be too long before you send word to me?"; he smelled the fragrance of the hairdresser's iron by which he would have his "brush cut" straightened while Lorédan went to fetch the young working girl, the stormy rains that fell so often that spring, the icy drive home in his victoria, by moonlight, all the meshes formed from habits of thinking, impressions of the seasons, reactions on the surface of his skin, which had laid over a succession of weeks a uniform net in which his body was now recaptured. At that time, he was satisfying a sensual curiosity by experiencing the pleasures of people who live for love. He had believed he could stop there, that he would not be obliged to learn their sorrows; how small a thing Odette's charm was for him now compared with the astounding terror that extended out from it like a murky halo, the immense anguish of not knowing at every moment what she had been doing, of not possessing her everywhere and always! Alas, he recalled the accents in which she had exclaimed: "But I will always be able to see you, I am always free!"–she who was never free now!–the interest, the curiosity she had shown in his own life, the passionate desire that he should do her the favor–which he in fact dreaded in those days as a cause of tiresome inconveniences–of allowing her to enter it; how she had been obliged to beg him to let her take him to the Verdurins'; and when he had allowed her to come to him once a month, how she had had to tell him over and over again, before he would let himself give in to her, how delightful it would be to have the habit of seeing each other every day, a habit which she dreamed of whereas to him it seemed only a tedious bother, which she had then grown tired of and broken once and for all, while for him it had become such an irresistible and painful need. He did not know how truthfully he was speaking when, the third time he saw her, as she said to him yet again: "But why don't you let me come more often?" he had said to her with a laugh, gallantly: "for fear of being hurt." Now, alas, she still wrote to him occasionally from a restaurant or hotel on paper that bore its printed name; but now the letters of that name burned him like letters of fire. "It's written from the Hôtel Vouillemont?[105] What can she have gone there to do? And with whom? What has been going on there?" He remembered the gas jets being extinguished along the boulevard des Italiens when he had met her against all hope among the wandering shades on that night which had seemed to him almost supernatural and which indeed–since it belonged to a time when he did not even have to ask himself if he would vex her by looking for her, by finding her, so sure was he that her greatest joy was to see him and go home with him—was truly part of a mysterious world to which one can never return once its doors have closed. And Swann saw, motionless before that relived happiness, a miserable figure who filled him with pity because he did not recognize him right away, and he had to lower his eyes so that no one would see that they were full of tears. It was himself.

When he realized this, his pity vanished, but he was jealous of the other self she had loved, he was jealous of those of whom he had often said to himself without suffering too much "maybe she loves them," now that he had exchanged the vague idea of loving, in which there is no love, for the petals of the chrysanthemum and the letterhead of the Maison d'Or, which were full of it. Then his pain became too sharp, he passed his hand over his forehead, let his monocle drop, wiped its glass. And no doubt, if he had seen himself at that moment, he would have added to the collection of those which he had singled out for distinction the monocle he was removing like an importunate thought and from whose clouded face, with a handkerchief, he was trying to wipe off his worries.

There are tones in a violin—if we cannot see the instrument and therefore cannot relate what we hear to our image of it, which changes the sound of it—so similar to those of certain contralto voices that we have the illusion a singer has been added to the concert. We lift our eyes, we see only the bodies of the instruments, as precious as Chinese boxes, but at times we are still fooled by the deceptive call of the siren; at times too we think we hear a captive genie struggling deep inside the intelligent, bewitched, and tremulous box, like a devil in a holy-water basin; sometimes, again it is like a pure and supernatural being that passes through the air uncoiling its invisible message.

As if the instrumentalists were not so much playing the little phrase as performing the rituals it required in order to make its appearance, and proceeding to the incantations necessary for obtaining and prolonging a few moments the wonder of its evocation, Swann, who could no more see it than if it had belonged to an ultraviolet world, and who was experiencing something like the refreshing sense of a metamorphosis in the momentary blindness with which he was struck as he approached it, felt it to be present, like a protective goddess, a confidante of his love, who in order to be able to come to him in the midst of the crowd and take him aside to talk to him, had assumed the disguise of this body of sound. And while it passed, light, soothing, murmured like a perfume, telling him what it had to tell him, as he scrutinized every word, sorry to see them fly off so quickly, he involuntarily made the motion with his lips of kissing the harmonious fleeting body as it passed. He no longer felt exiled and alone since the little phrase was addressing him, was talking to him in a low voice about Odette. For he no longer felt, as he once had, that the little phrase did not know him and Odette. It had so often witnessed their moments of happiness! True, it had just as often warned him how fragile they were. And in fact, whereas in those days he read suffering in its smile, in its limpid and disenchanted intonation, he now found in it instead the grace of a resignation that was almost gay. Of those sorrows of which it used to speak to him and which, without being affected by them, he had seen it carry along with it, smiling, in its rapid and sinuous course, of those sorrows which had now become his own, without his having any hope of ever being free of them, it seemed to say to him as it had once said of his happiness: "What does it matter? It means nothing." And for the first time Swann's thoughts turned with a stab of pity and tenderness to Vinteuil, to that unknown, sublime brother who must also have suffered so; what must his life have been like? From the depths of what sorrows had he drawn that godlike strength, that unlimited power to create? When it was the little phrase that spoke to him about the vanity of his sufferings, Swann found solace in that very wisdom which, just recently, had seemed to him intolerable when he thought he could read it on the faces of the indifferent people who considered his love an insignificant aberration. For the little phrase, unlike them, whatever its opinion of the brief duration of the conditions of the soul, did not see in them, as these people did, something less serious than the events of everyday life, but on the contrary, something so superior that it alone was worth expressing. These charms of an intimate sadness—these were what it sought to imitate, to re-create, and their very essence, even though it is to be incommunicable and to seem frivolous to everyone but the one who is experiencing them, had been captured by the little phrase and made visible. So much so that it caused their value to be acknowledged, and their divine sweetness savored, by all those same people sitting in the audience—if they were at all musical—who would afterward fail to recognize these charms in real life, in every individual love that came into being before their eyes. Doubtless the form in which it had codified them could not be resolved into reasoned arguments. But ever since, more than a year ago now, the love of music had, for a time at least, been born in him, revealing to him many of the riches of his own soul, Swann had regarded musical motifs as actual ideas, of another world, of another order, ideas veiled in shadows, unknown, impenetrable to the intelligence, but not for all that less perfectly distinct from one another, unequal among themselves in value and significance. When, after the Verdurin evening, he had had the little phrase played over for him, and had sought to disentangle how it was that, like a perfume, like a caress, it encircled him, enveloped him, he had realized that it was to the closeness of the intervals between the five notes that composed it, and to the constant repetition of two of them, that was due this impression of a frigid and withdrawn sweetness; but in reality he knew that he was reasoning this way not about the phrase itself but about simple values substituted, for the convenience of his intelligence, for the mysterious entity he had perceived, before knowing the Verdurins, at that party where he had first heard the sonata played. He knew that even the memory of the piano falsified still further the perspective in which he saw the elements of the music, that the field open to the musician is not a miserable scale of seven notes, but an immeasurable keyboard still almost entirely unknown on which, here and there only, separated by shadows thick and unexplored, a few of the millions of keys of tenderness, of passion, of courage, of serenity which compose it, each as different from the others as one universe from another universe, have been found by a few great artists who do us the service, by awakening in us something corresponding to the theme they have discovered, of showing us what richness, what variety, is hidden unbeknownst to us within that great unpenetrated and disheartening darkness of our soul which we take for emptiness and nothingness. Vinteuil had been one of those musicians. In his little phrase, although it might present an obscure surface to one's intelligence, one sensed a content so solid, so explicit, to which it gave a force so new, so original, that those who had heard it preserved it within themselves on the same plane as the ideas of the intelligence. Swann referred back to it as to a conception of love and happiness whose distinctive character he recognized at once, as he would that of *La Princesse de Clèves* or of *René*,[106] when their titles returned to his memory. Even when he was not thinking of the little phrase, it existed latent in his mind in the same way as certain other notions without equivalents, like the notion of light, of sound, of perspective, of physical pleasure, which are the rich possessions that diversify and ornament the realms of our inner life. Perhaps we will lose them, perhaps they will fade away, if we return to nothingness. But as long as we are alive, we can no more eliminate our experience of them than we can our experience of some real object, than we can for example doubt the light of the lamp illuminating the metamorphosed objects in our room whence even the memory of darkness has vanished. In this way Vinteuil's phrase had, like some theme from *Tristan*, for example, which also represents to us a certain emotional acquisition, espoused our mortal condition, taken on a human quality that was rather touching. Its destiny was linked to the future, to the reality of our soul, of which it was one of the most distinctive, the best differentiated ornaments. Maybe it is the nothingness that is real and our entire dream is nonexistent, but in that case we feel that these phrases of music, and these notions that exist in relation to our dream, must also be nothing. We will perish, but we have for hostages these divine captives who will follow us and share our fate. And death in their company is less bitter, less inglorious, perhaps less probable.

Swann was therefore not wrong to believe that the phrase of the sonata really existed. Of course, although human from this point of view, it belonged to an order of supernatural creatures whom we have never seen, but whom despite this we recognize with delight when some explorer of the invisible manages to capture one, to bring it, from that divine world to which he has access, to shine for a few moments above ours. This was what Vinteuil had done for the little phrase. Swann sensed that the composer had merely unveiled it, made it visible, with his musical instruments, following and respecting its sketched form with a hand so tender, so prudent, so delicate, and so sure that the sound altered at every moment, fading away to indicate a shadow, revivified when it had to follow a bolder contour. And one proof that Swann was not mistaken when he believed in the real existence of that phrase was that any lover of music with the least discernment would at once have noticed the imposture if Vinteuil, having had less capacity to see and to render its forms, had sought to conceal, by adding lines of his own invention here and there, the lacunae in his vision or the failures of his hand.

It had disappeared. Swann knew that it would reappear at the end of the last movement, after a whole long passage that Mme. Verdurin's pianist always skipped. There were marvelous ideas in it which Swann had not distinguished at his first hearing and that he perceived now, as if they had divested themselves, in the cloakroom of his memory, of the uniform disguise of novelty. Swann listened to all the scattered themes which would enter into the composition of the phrase, like premises in the necessary conclusion; he was attending its birth. "O audacity as inspired, perhaps," he said to himself, "as that of a Lavoisier, of an Ampère[107]—the audacity of a Vinteuil experimenting, discovering the secret laws that govern an unknown force, guiding and urging on, across a region unexplored, toward the only possible goal, the invisible team in which he has placed his trust and which he may never discern!" The beautiful dialogue which Swann heard between the piano and the violin at the beginning of the last passage! The suppression of human speech, far from letting fantasy reign there, as one might have believed, had eliminated it; never had spoken language been such an inflexible necessity, never had it known such pertinent questions, such irrefutable answers. First the solitary piano lamented, like a bird abandoned by its mate; the violin heard it, answered it as from a neighboring tree. It was as at the beginning of the world, as if there were only the two of them still on the earth, or rather in this world closed to all the rest, constructed by the logic of a creator, this world in which there would never be more than the two of them: this sonata. Was it a bird, was it the soul of the little phrase, not yet fully formed, was it a fairy—this creature invisibly lamenting, whose plaint the piano afterward tenderly repeated? Its cries were so sudden that the violinist had to leap to his bow to collect them. Marvelous bird! The violinist seemed to want to charm it, tame it, capture it. Already it had passed into his soul, already the violinist's body, truly possessed, was shaking like a medium's with the summoned presence of the little phrase. Swann knew it was going to speak one more time. And he had so completely divided himself in two that the wait for the imminent moment when he would find himself confronting it again made him shudder with the kind of sob which a beautiful line of verse or a sad piece of news wrings from us, not when we are alone, but if we repeat it to friends in whom we can see ourselves as another person whose probable emotion moves them. It reappeared, but this time to hang in the air and play for a moment only, as though motionless, and afterward expire. And so Swann lost nothing of this very brief extension of its life. It was still there like an iridescent bubble floating by itself. Like a rainbow, whose brilliance weakens, fades, then rises again, and before dying away altogether, flares up a moment more brilliant than ever: to the two colors it had so far allowed to appear, it added others, variegated chords of every hue in the prism, and made them sing. Swann did not dare move and would have made all the other people be still too, as if the slightest motion might compromise the fragile, exquisite, and supernatural magic that was so close to vanishing. No one, in fact, dreamed of speaking. The ineffable word of one man who was absent, perhaps dead (Swann did not know if Vinteuil was still alive), breathing out above the rites of these officiants, was enough to hold the attention of three hundred people, and made of this dais, where a soul had thus been summoned, one of the noblest altars on which a supernatural ceremony could be performed. So that, when the phrase came unraveled at last, floating in shreds in the motifs which followed and had already taken its place, if at first Swann was irritated to see the Comtesse de Monteriender, famous for her naive remarks, lean toward him to confide her impressions even before the sonata had ended, he could not help smiling, and perhaps also found a deeper meaning that she did not see in the words she used. Awestruck by the virtuosity of the performers, the Comtesse exclaimed to Swann: "It's amazing, I've never seen anything so powerful . . ." But a scruple for accuracy causing her to correct her first assertion, she added this reservation: "anything so powerful . . . since the table turning!"

From that evening on, Swann understood that the feeling Odette had had for him would never revive, that his hopes of happiness would not be realized now. And on the days when she happened to be kind and affectionate toward him again, if she showed him some thoughtful attention, he would note these apparent and deceptive signs of a slight movement back toward him, with the loving, skeptical solicitude, the desperate joy of those who, caring for a friend in the last days of an incurable illness, relate as precious facts: "Yesterday, he did his accounts himself, and he was the one who spotted a mistake in addition that we had made; he ate an egg and enjoyed it— if he digests it easily we'll try a cutlet tomorrow," although they know these facts are meaningless on the eve of an unavoidable death. No doubt Swann was sure that if he had now been living far away from Odette, she would in the end have become unimportant to him, so that he would have been glad if she had left Paris forever; he would have had the courage to stay there; but he did not have the courage to leave.

He had often thought of it. Now that he had resumed his study of Vermeer, he needed to return at least for a few days to The Hague, Dresden, Brunswick. He was convinced that a *Diana with Her Companions* which had been bought by the Mauritshuis at the Goldschmidt sale as a Nicolas Maes, was in reality a Vermeer.[108] And he wished he could study the painting on the spot, in order to support his conviction. But to leave Paris while Odette was there, or even when she was absent—for in new places where our sensations are not dulled by habit, we retemper, we revive an old pain—was for him so cruel a plan that he was able to think about it constantly only because he knew he was resolved never to execute it. But sometimes, while he was asleep, the intention of taking the trip would revive in him—without his remembering that it was impossible—and in his sleep he would take the trip. One day he dreamed he was leaving for a year; leaning out the door of the railway car toward a young man on the platform who was saying good-bye to him, weeping, Swann tried to convince him to leave with him. The train began to move, his anxiety woke him, he remembered that he was not leaving, that he would see Odette that evening, the next day, and almost every day after. Then, still shaken by his dream, he blessed the particular circumstances that had made him independent, because of which he could remain near Odette, and also succeed in getting her to allow him to see her now and then; and, recapitulating all these advantages—his position; his fortune, from which she was too often in need of assistance not to shrink from contemplating a definite break with him (having even, people said, an ulterior plan of getting him to marry her); his friendship with M. de Charlus, which in truth had never helped him obtain much from Odette, but gave him the comfort of feeling that she heard flattering things about him from this mutual friend for whom she had such great esteem; and lastly even his intelligence, which he employed entirely in contriving a new intrigue every day that would make his presence, if not agreeable, at least necessary to Odette—he thought about what would have become of him if he had not had all this, he thought that if, like so many other men, he had been poor, humble, wretched, obliged to accept any sort of work, or tied to relatives, to a wife, he might have been forced to leave Odette, that that dream, the terror of which was still so close to him, might have been true, and he said to himself: "You don't know it when you're happy. You're never as unhappy as you think."[109] But he calculated that this existence had already lasted for several years, that all he could hope for now was that it would last forever, that he would sacrifice his work, his pleasures, his friends, finally his whole life to the daily expectation of a meeting that could bring him no happiness, and he wondered if he was not deceiving himself, if the circumstances that had favored his love affair and kept it from ending had not been bad for the course of his life, if the desirable outcome would not in fact have been the one which, to his delight, had taken place only in a dream: for him to have gone away; he told himself that you don't know it when you're unhappy, that you are never as happy as you think.

Sometimes he hoped she would die in an accident without suffering, she who was outside, in the streets, on the roads, from morning to night. And when she returned safe and sound, he marveled that the human body was so supple and so strong, that it continued to ward off, to outwit all the perils which surrounded it (and which Swann found innumerable now that his secret desire had computed them) and so allowed people to abandon themselves daily and almost with impunity to their work of mendacity, their pursuit of pleasure. And Swann felt very close in his heart to Mohammed II, whose portrait by Bellini he liked so much, who, realizing that he had fallen madly in love with one of his wives, stabbed her in order, as his Venetian biographer ingenuously says, to recover his independence of mind. Then he would be filled with indignation that he should be thinking thus only of himself, and the sufferings he had endured would seem to him to deserve no pity since he himself had placed so low a value on Odette's life.

Since he was unable to separate from her irrevocably, if he had at least been able to see her without any separations, his pain would in the end have abated and perhaps his love would have died. And if she did not want to leave Paris forever, he would have liked her never to leave Paris. At least since he knew that her only long absence was the yearly one in August and September, he had ample opportunity several months in advance to dissolve the bitter idea of it in all the Time to come which he carried within him in anticipation and which, composed of days identical with those of the present, flowed through his

mind transparent and cold, sustaining his sadness, but without causing him too sharp a pain. But that interior future, that colorless free-
flowing river, was suddenly assaulted by a single remark of Odette's
which entered Swann and, like a piece of ice, immobilized it, hardened its fluidity, made it freeze entirely; and Swann suddenly felt he
was filled with an enormous infrangible mass that pressed on the
inner walls of his being till it nearly burst: what Odette had said, observing him with a sly smiling glance, was: "Forcheville is going to be
taking a lovely trip, at Pentecost. He's going to Egypt," and Swann
had immediately understood that this meant: "I'm going to Egypt at
Pentecost with Forcheville." And in fact, if several days after, Swann
said to her: "Look, about this trip you told me you would be taking
with Forcheville," she would answer thoughtlessly: "Yes, my dear boy,
we're leaving the nineteenth, we'll send you a view of the Pyramids."
Then he would want to know if she was Forcheville's mistress, would
want to ask her directly. He knew that, superstitious as she was, there
were certain perjuries she would not commit, and, too, the dread,
which had restrained him up to this point, of irritating Odette by
questioning her, of causing her to hate him, had vanished now that he
had lost all hope of ever being loved by her.

One day he received an anonymous letter telling him that Odette
had been the mistress of countless men (several of whom it mentioned, among them Forcheville, M. de Bréauté, and the painter), and
of women too, and that she frequented houses of ill repute. He was
tormented by the thought that among his friends there was an individual capable of sending him this letter (because certain details revealed that the person who had written it had an intimate knowledge
of Swann's life). He wondered who it could be. But he had never had
any feelings of suspicion about the unknown actions of other people,
those which had no visible connection with what they said. And
when he tried to find out whether it was beneath the apparent character of M. de Charlus, or M. des Laumes, or M. d'Orsan, that he ought
to situate the unknown region in which this ignoble act must have
been conceived, since none of these men had ever spoken in praise of

anonymous letters in his presence and since everything they had said to him implied that they condemned them, he saw no reason for connecting this infamy with the character of one rather than another. That of M. de Charlus was a little deranged but basically good and affectionate; that of M. des Laumes, a little hard, but sound and straightforward. As for M. d'Orsan, Swann had never met anyone who in even the most dismal circumstances would approach him with a more heartfelt remark, a more discreet or appropriate gesture. So much so that he could not understand the rather indelicate role people ascribed to M. d'Orsan in the love affair he was having with a rich woman, and that each time Swann thought of him, he was obliged to thrust to one side that bad reputation which was so irreconcilable with the many clear proofs of his discretion. For a moment Swann felt his mind was darkening and he thought about something else in order to recover a little light. Then he had the courage to return to these reflections. But now, after being unable to suspect anyone, he had to suspect everyone. True, M. de Charlus was fond of him, had a good heart. But he was a neurotic, tomorrow he might weep at the news that Swann was ill, and today, out of jealousy, out of anger, acting under the influence of some sudden idea, he had wanted to hurt him. Really, that kind of man was the worst of all. Of course, the Prince des Laumes was not nearly as fond of Swann as M. de Charlus. But for that very reason he did not have the same susceptibilities with regard to him; and then although his was undoubtedly a cold nature, he was as incapable of base actions as of great ones. Swann regretted that in his life he had not formed attachments exclusively to such people. Then he mused that what prevents men from doing harm to their fellowmen is goodness of heart, that really he could answer only for men whose natures were analogous to his own, as was, so far as the heart was concerned, that of M. de Charlus. The mere thought of causing such pain to Swann would have revolted him. But with an insensitive man, of another order of humanity, as was the Prince des Laumes, how could one foresee the actions to which he might be led by motives that were so different in essence? To have a kind heart is everything, and M. de Charlus had one. M. d'Orsan was not lacking

in heart either and his cordial but not very close relationship with
Swann, arising from the pleasure which, since they thought the same
way about everything, they found in talking together, was more secure
than the excitable affection of M. de Charlus, capable of committing
acts of passion, good or bad. If there was anyone by whom Swann
had always felt himself understood and liked in a discriminating way,
it was by M. d'Orsan. Yes, but what about this dishonorable life he
was leading? Swann regretted never having taken it into account properly, having often confessed as a joke that he had never experienced
such keen feelings of sympathy and respect as in the company of a
scoundrel. It is not for nothing, he said to himself now, that when
men judge another man, it is by his actions. They alone mean something, and not what we say, or what we think. Charlus and des
Laumes may have their faults, but they are still honest men. Orsan
perhaps has none, but he is not an honest man. He may have acted
badly yet again. Then Swann suspected Rémi, who, it was true, could
merely have inspired the letter, but for a moment he felt he was on
the right track. In the first place Lorédan had reasons for resenting
Odette. And then how can we help but imagine that our servants, living in a situation inferior to ours, adding to our fortunes and our
faults imaginary wealth and vices for which they envy and despise us,
will find themselves inevitably led to act in a way different from people of our own class? He also suspected my grandfather. Each time
Swann had asked a favor of him, had he not always refused? And
then with his bourgeois ideas he might have thought he was acting for
Swann's own good. Swann also suspected Bergotte, the painter, the
Verdurins, admired once more in passing the wisdom of society people in not wanting to mix in those artistic circles in which such things
are possible, perhaps even openly admitted as good pranks; but he recalled certain honest traits in those bohemians, and contrasted them
with the life of expediency, almost of fraudulence, into which the lack
of money, the craving for luxury, the corrupting influence of their
pleasures so often drive members of the aristocracy. In short, this
anonymous letter proved that he knew an individual capable of villainy, but he could see no more reason why that villainy should be

hidden in the bedrock—unexplored by any other person—of the character of an affectionate man rather than a cold one, an artist rather
than a bourgeois, a great lord rather than a valet. What criterion
should one adopt for judging men? Really there was not a single person among those he knew who might not be capable of infamy. Was
it necessary to stop seeing all of them? His mind clouded over; he
passed his hands across his forehead two or three times, wiped the
lenses of his lorgnon with his handkerchief, and thinking that after all
men as good as himself associated with M. de Charlus, the Prince des
Laumes, and the others, he said to himself that this meant, if not that
they were incapable of infamy, at least that it is a necessity of life to
which each of us submits, to associate with people who are perhaps
not incapable of it. And he continued to shake hands with all of those
friends whom he had suspected, with the one purely formal reservation that they had perhaps tried to drive him to despair. As for the actual substance of the letter, he did not worry about it, because not one
of the accusations formulated against Odette had a shadow of likelihood. Swann, like many people, had a lazy mind and lacked the faculty of invention. He knew very well as a general truth that people's
lives are full of contrasts, but for each person in particular he imagined the whole part of his life that he did not know as being identical
to the part that he knew. He imagined what he was not told with the
help of what he was told. During the times when Odette was with
him, if they were talking about some indelicate act committed or
some indelicate feeling experienced by someone else, she would stig-
matize them by virtue of the same principles that Swann had always
heard professed by his parents and to which he had remained faithful;
and then she would arrange her flowers, she would drink a cup of tea,
she would worry about Swann's work. And so Swann extended these
habits to the rest of Odette's life, he repeated these gestures when he
wanted to picture to himself the times when she was away from him.
If anyone had portrayed her to him as she was, or rather as she had
been with him for so long, but in the company of another man, he
would have suffered, because that image would have appeared to him
quite likely. But to think that she went to procuresses, took part in

orgies with other women, that she led the dissolute life of the most abject of creatures—what an insane aberration, for the realization of which, God be thanked, the imagined chrysanthemums, the successive teas, the virtuous indignation left no room! Only from time to time, he would insinuate to Odette that, out of spite, someone had been reporting to him about everything she did; and, making use, in connection with this, of an insignificant but true detail, which he had learned by chance, as if it were the sole fragment among many others that he had allowed to slip out despite himself, of a complete reconstruction of Odette's life which he kept hidden inside himself, he would lead her to suppose that he was well informed about things that in reality he did not know or even suspect, for if quite often he adjured Odette not to alter the truth, it was only, whether he realized it or not, so that she would tell him everything she did. Undoubtedly, as he said to Odette, he loved sincerity, but he loved it as a procuress who could keep him in touch with his mistress's life. And so his love of sincerity, not being disinterested, had not made him a better person. The truth he cherished was the truth Odette would tell him; but he himself, in order to obtain that truth, was not afraid to resort to falsehood, that very same falsehood which he constantly portrayed to Odette as leading every human creature down to utter degradation. And so he lied as much as Odette because, while unhappier than she, he was no less selfish. And she, hearing Swann tell her the things she had done, would gaze at him with a look of mistrust, and, just to be on the safe side, of vexation, so as not to seem to be humiliating herself and blushing at her actions.

One day, during the longest period of calm he had yet been able to go through without suffering renewed attacks of jealousy, he had agreed to go to the theater that evening with the Princesse des Laumes. Having opened the newspaper, in order to find out what was being played, the sight of the title, *Les Filles de Marbre* by Théodore Barrière,[110] struck him such a painful blow that he recoiled and turned his head away. Illuminated as though by footlights, in the new spot where it had appeared, the word *marble*, which he had lost the ability to distinguish because he was so used to seeing it before his eyes, had suddenly become visible again and had immediately reminded him of the story Odette had told him once long ago, about a visit she had made to the Salon du Palais de l'Industrie with Mme. Verdurin, where the latter had said to her: "Watch yourself, now! I know how to make you melt. You're not made of marble, you know." Odette had sworn to him it was only a joke, and he had attached no importance to it. But he had had more confidence in her at that time than he did now. And in fact the anonymous letter mentioned love affairs of that kind. Without daring to lift his eyes to the newspaper again, he unfolded it, turned a page in order not to see the words *Les Filles de Marbre,* and mechanically began reading news from the provinces. There had been a storm on the Channel, damage was reported at Dieppe, Cabourg, Beuzeval. Immediately he recoiled again.

The name Beuzeval had reminded him of the name of another place in the same area, Beuzeville, whose name is joined by a hyphen to another, Bréauté, which he had often seen on maps, but without ever noticing before that it was the same as that of his friend M. de Bréauté, whom the anonymous letter mentioned as having been Odette's lover. In fact, in the case of M. de Bréauté, the accusation was not unlikely; but so far as Mme. Verdurin was concerned, it was a sheer impossibility. From the fact that Odette sometimes lied, one could not conclude that she never told the truth, and in the remarks she had exchanged with Mme. Verdurin and which she herself had described to Swann, he had recognized those pointless and dangerous jokes made, from inexperience of life and ignorance of vice, by women whose innocence they merely reveal and who—like Odette for example—are least prone to feel passionate love for another woman. Whereas on the contrary, the indignation with which she had denied the suspicions she had involuntarily aroused in him for a moment by her story squared with all he knew about his mistress's tastes and temperament. But at this moment, through one of those inspirations common to jealous men, analogous to that which reveals to a poet or scientist who has still only one rhyme or one observation the idea or law that will give them all their power, Swann recalled for the first time a remark Odette had made to him fully two years before: "Oh,

Mme. Verdurin! All she can think about these days is me. I'm her lit-tle pet. She kisses me, and she wants me to go shopping with her, and she wants me to call her *tu*."ᴵᴵᴵ Far from seeing, at the time, any sort of connection between this comment and the absurd remarks meant to simulate some sort of depravity which Odette had reported to him, he had welcomed it as proof of a warm friendship. Now the memory of Mme. Verdurin's affection had suddenly come to join the memory of her unseemly conversation. He could no longer separate them in his mind and saw them mingled in reality too, the affection lending something serious and important to the jokes which in return caused the affection to lose some of its innocence. He went to Odette's house. He sat down at a distance from her. He did not dare kiss her, not knowing whether it would be affection or anger that a kiss would provoke, either in her, or in himself. He said nothing, he watched their love die. Suddenly he made up his mind.

"Odette," he said to her, "my dear, I know I'm being hateful, but there are a few things I must ask you. Do you remember the idea I had about you and Mme. Verdurin? Tell me, was it true, with her or with anyone else?"

She shook her head while pursing her lips, a sign people often use to answer that they will not go, that it bores them, if someone asks: "Would you like to come watch the cavalcade go past, will you be at the review?" But a shake of the head thus usually assigned to an event in the future, for this reason colors with some uncertainty the denial of an event that is past. What is more, it suggests only reasons of per-sonal propriety rather than reprobation, a moral impossibility. When he saw Odette make this sign to him that it was untrue, Swann under-stood that it was perhaps true.

"I've already told you. You know perfectly well," she added, look-ing irritated and unhappy.

"Yes, I know, but are you sure? Don't say, 'You know perfectly well'; say, 'I have never done anything of that sort with any woman.'"

She repeated, as though it were a lesson, ironically, and as if she wanted to get rid of him:

"I have never done anything of that sort with any woman."

"Can you swear it on your medal of Our Lady of Laghet?"

Swann knew Odette would never swear a false oath on that medal.

"Oh, you make me so unhappy!" she exclaimed, abruptly dodging the grasp of his question. "Aren't you done? What's the matter with you today? Are you determined to make me hate you, to make me detest you? You see? I wanted to have a nice time with you again, the way we used to, and this is how you thank me!"

However, not letting her go, like a surgeon waiting for a spasm to subside that has interrupted his operation but will not make him abandon it:

"You're quite wrong to imagine I would hold it against you in the least, Odette," he said to her with a persuasive and deceptive gentleness. "I only talk to you about what I know, and I always know much more about it than I say. But you are the only one who can mitigate by your confession what makes me hate you as long as it has been reported to me only by other people. My anger toward you does not come from your actions, I forgive you everything because I love you, but from your duplicity, the absurd duplicity which makes you persist in denying things I know already. How can you expect me to go on loving you when I see you insisting upon something, swearing to something I know is untrue? Odette, don't prolong this moment, which is agony for both of us. If you want to, you can end it in a second, you'll be free of it forever. Tell me on your medal, yes or no, if you have ever done these things."

"But I have no idea," she exclaimed angrily, "maybe a very long time ago, without realizing what I was doing, maybe two or three times."

Swann had envisaged all the possibilities. Reality is therefore something that has no relation to possibilities, any more than the stab of a knife in our body has any relation to the gradual motions of the clouds overhead, since those words *two or three times* carved a kind of cross in the tissue of his heart. Strange that the words *two or three times*, no more than words, words spoken into the air, at a distance, can lacerate the heart this way as if they had really touched it, can make you as sick as if you had swallowed poison. Involuntarily Swann thought of the remark he had heard at Mme. de Saint-Euverte's: "That's the most powerful thing I've seen since the table turning." The pain he was now experiencing resembled nothing he had imagined. Not only because in the hours when he most entirely distrusted her he had rarely imagined such an extremity of evil, but because, even when he did imagine this thing, it remained vague, uncertain, not clothed in the particular horror that had issued from the words *maybe two or three times,* not armed with that specific cruelty as different from everything he had known as a disease with which one is stricken for the first time. And yet Odette, from whom all this harm came to him, was no less dear to him, quite the contrary, more precious, as if at the same rate that his suffering increased, the value of the sedative increased, of the antidote which only this woman possessed. He wanted to devote more care to her, as to a disease which one suddenly discovers is more serious. He wanted the frightful thing she had told him she had done "two or three times" not to be repeated. For this, he had to watch over Odette. People often say that when we inform a friend of his mistress's wrongdoings, we succeed only in attaching him to her more closely because he places no faith in them, but how much more so if he does place faith in them! But, said Swann to himself, how could he manage to protect her? He could perhaps keep her safe from a particular woman, but there were hundreds of others, and he realized what madness had come over him when he had begun, on the evening when he had not found Odette at the Verdurins', to want something that was always impossible—to possess another person. Happily for Swann, beneath the new sufferings that had just entered his soul like hordes of invaders, there lay a natural substratum, older, gentler, and silently industrious, like the cells of an injured organ that immediately set about preparing to restore the damaged tissues, like the muscles of a paralyzed limb that try to resume their former movements. These older, more autochthonous inhabitants of his soul employed, for a moment, all of Swann's strength in this dim recuperative work that gives the illusion of repose to a convalescent, to a surgical patient. This time it was not so much, as it usually was, in Swann's brain that this relaxation induced by exhaustion took effect, it was rather in his heart. But all the things in life that have once existed tend to recur, and like a dying animal shaken one last time by the throes of a convulsion which seemed to have ended, upon Swann's heart, spared for a moment, the same suffering returned of its own volition to carve the same cross again. He remembered those moonlit evenings when, lying back in the victoria that was taking him to the rue La Pérouse, he would voluptuously cultivate within himself the emotions of a man in love, without knowing the poisoned fruit they would necessarily bear. But all these thoughts did not last more than the space of a second, the time he took to bring his hand to his heart, catch his breath, and manage a smile to hide his agony. Already he was beginning to ask his questions again. For his jealousy, which had taken pains an enemy would not have taken to strike this blow, to introduce him to the most intense suffering he had yet known, did not believe he had suffered enough and sought to expose him to a wound that was deeper still. Thus, like a wicked deity, his jealousy inspired Swann and pushed him to his ruin. It was not his fault but only Odette's if at first his torment did not grow worse.

"My dear," he said to her, "it's in the past now. Was it with anyone I know?"

"No, of course not, I swear it wasn't. And anyway, I think I exaggerated, I don't think I went that far."

He smiled and went on:

"As you like. It doesn't really matter, but it's too bad you can't tell me the name. If I could picture the person it would keep me from ever thinking about her again. I say this for your own sake, because then I wouldn't be bothering you about it anymore. It's such a relief to be able to picture a thing! The truly horrifying things are the ones you can't imagine. But you've already been so kind, I don't want to tire you. I do thank you with all my heart for all the good you've done me. I'm quite finished now. Only this last question: How long ago was it?"

"Oh, Charles! Don't you see you're killing me? It's all so long ago. I never gave it another thought. And now it's as if you're positively trying to put those ideas in my head again. A lot of good it'll do you," she said, with unthinking foolishness and deliberate spite.

"Oh, I only wanted to know if it had happened since I've known you! It would be natural enough. Did it happen here? Could you tell me which particular evening, so that I could picture what I was doing at the time? I'm sure you realize it isn't possible that you don't remember who it was with, Odette, my love."

"Oh, I don't know, really I don't, I think it was in the Bois one evening when you came to meet us on the island. You had been to the Princesse des Laumes's for dinner," she said, happy to give him a specific detail that would attest to her truthfulness. "There was a woman at the next table; I hadn't seen her for ages. She said to me: 'Come around behind that little rock there and see the moonlight on the water.' At first I just yawned and said: 'No, I'm tired and I'm quite comfortable where I am.' She swore there had never been such moonlight. I said: 'What a joke!' I knew quite well what she was after."

Odette told this almost with a smile, either because it seemed to her quite natural, or because she thought she would thereby make it seem less important, or so as not to appear humiliated. At the sight of Swann's face, she changed her tone:

"You're a scoundrel, you like tormenting me, making me invent lies which I only tell you so you'll leave me in peace."

This second blow which Swann suffered was even more agonizing than the first. Never had he supposed the thing had been so recent, hidden from his eyes, which had not been able to discover it, not in a past which he had not known, but among evenings which he recalled so clearly, which he had experienced with Odette, which he had believed he knew so well, and which now assumed in retrospect an appearance that was false and atrocious; among them suddenly there opened up this wide gap, this moment on the island in the Bois. Odette, without being intelligent, had the charm of naturalness. She had described, she had mimed this scene with such simplicity that Swann, breathless, saw everything: Odette's yawn, the little rock. He heard her respond–gaily, alas: "What a joke!" He felt she would say nothing more this evening, there was no new revelation to expect just now; he said to her: "My poor dear, forgive me, I feel I'm hurting you, it's over and done with, I'm not thinking about it anymore."

But she saw that his eyes were still dwelling on the things he did not know and on that past era of their love, monotonous and sweet in his memory because it was vague, which was now being torn open like a wound by that minute on the island in the Bois, in the moonlight, after the dinner with the Princesse des Laumes. But he was so much in the habit by now of finding life interesting—of admiring the curious discoveries one can make—that even while suffering to the point of believing he could not endure such pain for long, he said to himself: "Life is really astonishing; it really has great surprises in store for us; immorality is actually more common than one would think. Here's a woman I trusted, who seemed so simple, so honest in any case, even if she was rather flighty, who seemed quite normal and healthy in her tastes; after an unlikely denunciation I question her, and the little she admits reveals much more than what one would have suspected." But he could not confine himself to these disinterested remarks. He tried to estimate the exact value of what she had told him, in order to know if he ought to conclude that she had done these things often, that they would happen again. He repeated to himself the words she had said: "I knew quite well what she was after," "Two or three times," "What a joke!" but they did not reappear in Swann's memory disarmed, each of them held a knife and with it struck him another blow. For a very long time, just as an invalid cannot stop himself from trying over and over again to make the motion that is painful to him, he repeated these words to himself: "I'm quite comfortable here," "What a joke!" but the pain was so intense he had to stop. He marveled that acts which he had always judged so lightly, so cheerfully, had now become as serious as a disease from which one may die. He certainly knew some women he could have asked to keep an eye on Odette. But how could he hope they would adopt the same point of view he now had and not hold on to the point of view he had had for so long, that had always guided him in love affairs, would not say to him, laughing: "You nasty jealous man—trying to rob others of a little pleasure"? By what trapdoor, suddenly opened, had he (who in the past had derived only refined pleasures from his love for Odette) been roughly dropped into this new circle of hell from which he could not see how he would ever get out? Poor Odette! He did not hold it against her. She was only half guilty. Didn't people say it was her own mother who had handed her over to a rich Englishman in Nice when she was hardly more than a child? But what painful truth was now contained for him in those lines from *Journal d'un Poète* by Alfred de Vigny[112] which he had read with indifference in the past: "When you feel you are falling in love with a woman, you ought to say to yourself: Who are her friends? What sort of life has she had? All one's future happiness depends upon it." Swann was surprised that simple statements spelled out by his mind, like "What a joke!," "I could see very well what she was after," could hurt him so. But he realized that what he believed to be simple statements were merely the pieces of the framework that still contained, and could give back to him, the pain he had felt during Odette's story. For it was indeed the same pain which he was feeling again. Though he now knew, though he had even, as time passed, forgotten a little, forgiven, the moment he said these words to himself again the old suffering made him once again what he had been before Odette spoke: ignorant, trustful; his cruel jealousy placed him once again, so that he might be wounded by Odette's confession, in the position of a man who does not yet know, and after several months this old story still upset him like a revelation. He admired the terrible re-creative power of his memory. It was only by the weakening of that generator, whose fecundity diminishes with age, that he could hope for an easing of his torment. But as soon as the power of any one of Odette's remarks to make him suffer seemed nearly exhausted, then one of those on which Swann's mind had dwelt less until then, a remark that was almost new, would come to relieve the others and strike at him with undiminished vigor. The memory of the evening he had dined with the Princesse des Laumes was painful to him, but it was only the center of his disease. The latter irradiated confusedly on all sides through the days before and after it.

And whatever point in it he tried to touch in his memories, it was the whole of that season, during which the Verdurins had dined so often on the island in the Bois, that hurt him. Hurt him so badly that gradually the curiosity which his jealousy kept provoking in him was neutralized by his fear of the new torments he would inflict on himself by satisfying it. He realized that the entire period of Odette's life that had elapsed before she met him, a period he had never tried to picture, was not the abstract expanse which he could vaguely see, but had consisted of specific years, each filled with concrete incidents. But if he came to know them, he was afraid that that past of hers, colorless, fluid, and tolerable, might assume a body that was tangible and loathsome, a face that was individual and diabolical. And he continued to refrain from trying to imagine it, no longer from laziness of mind, but from fear of suffering. He hoped that one day he might at last be able to hear the name of the island in the Bois, of the Princesse des Laumes, without feeling the old tearing at his heart, and thought it would be imprudent to provoke Odette into supplying him with new remarks, names of places, different circumstances which, when his illness was still scarcely abated, would reawaken it again in another form.

But often the things he did not know, that he now was afraid of knowing, were revealed spontaneously by Odette herself, and without her realizing it; in fact the distance that depravity put between Odette's real life and the relatively innocent life which Swann had believed, and quite often still believed, his mistress led, was a distance whose extent Odette did not realize: a depraved person, still affecting the same virtue in front of the people by whom he does not want his vices to be suspected, has no gauge by which to recognize how far the latter, whose continuous growth is imperceptible to himself, are drawing him little by little away from normal ways of living. As they cohabited, deep in Odette's mind, with the memory of the acts she was hiding from Swann, other actions were gradually colored by them, infected by them, without her being able to see anything strange about them, without their seeming out of place in the particular surroundings where she

kept them inside her; but if she described them to Swann, he was horrified by the revelation of the environment they betrayed. One day he
was trying, without hurting Odette, to ask her if she had ever had any
dealings with a procuress. Actually he was convinced she had not;
reading the anonymous letter had introduced the conjecture into his
mind, but in a mechanical way; it had met with no credence there, but
had in fact remained there, and Swann, in order to be rid of the purely
material but nonetheless awkward presence of the suspicion, wanted
Odette to remove it. "Oh, no! Not that they don't pester me," she
added, revealing by her smile a self-satisfied vanity which she no
longer noticed could not seem justified to Swann. "There was one here
yesterday who stayed more than two hours waiting for me, offered me
any amount I liked. It seems some ambassador had said to her: 'I'll kill
myself if you don't get her for me.' They told her I'd gone out. In the
end I went and talked to her myself so she would leave. I wish you
could have seen the way I spoke to her; my maid heard me from the
next room and told me I was shouting at the top of my voice. I said,
'Haven't I told you I don't want to? It's a poor idea, I don't like it. Really, I should hope I'm still free to do what I want! If I needed the
money, I could understand . . .' The concierge has orders not to let her
in again. He'll tell her I'm in the country. Oh, I wish you had been hiding somewhere. I think you would have been pleased, my dear. You
see, your little Odette has some good in her, all the same, even though
some people find her so detestable."

Moreover her very admissions, when she made them, of faults that
she supposed he had discovered, served Swann as points of departure
toward new doubts rather than put an end to the old. For her admissions were never of exactly the same proportions as his doubts. Though
Odette might subtract from her confession all the essential part, there
remained in the accessory part something Swann had never imagined,
that crushed him with its newness, and would permit him to change
the terms of the problem of his jealousy. And these admissions he
could no longer forget. His soul bore them along, cast them aside,
cradled them, like dead bodies. And it was poisoned by them.

One time she told him about a visit Forcheville had paid her on the day of the Paris-Murcia fete. "What? You already knew him back then? Yes, of course, that's right," he said, catching himself so as not to show that he had not known. And suddenly he began to tremble at the thought that on the day of the Paris-Murcia fete, on which he had received from her the letter he had kept so carefully, she had perhaps been having lunch with Forcheville at the Maison d'Or. She swore she had not. "Yet the Maison d'Or does remind me of something or other that I knew at the time wasn't true," he said in order to frighten her. "Yes, that I hadn't actually been there at all that evening when I told you I had just come from there and you had been looking for me at Prévost's," she answered (thinking from his expression that he knew this), with a decisiveness in which there was, not cynicism, but rather timidity, a fear of vexing Swann, which out of self-respect she wanted to hide, and also a desire to show him that she could be frank. Thus she struck with an executioner's neatness and energy though quite without cruelty, for Odette was not conscious of the harm she was doing Swann; and she even began to laugh, perhaps, it is true, chiefly so as not to seem humiliated, embarrassed. "It's quite true that I hadn't been to the Maison Dorée; I was coming away from Forcheville's house. I actually had been to Prévost's, I didn't make that up, and he ran into me there and asked me to come and look at his engravings. But someone else came to see him. I told you I was coming from the Maison d'Or because I was afraid you would be annoyed. See? That was rather kind of me, wasn't it? Even if I was wrong, at least I'm telling you all about it now quite frankly. What would I gain by not telling you I had lunch with him the day of the Paris-Murcia fete, if it was true? Especially since at the time we didn't know each other very well yet, you and I, dear." He smiled at her with sudden cowardice, changed by these crushing words into a creature without strength. So, even during the months which he had never dared to think about again because they had been too happy, during those months when she had loved him, she was already lying to him! Besides that time (the first evening they had "made cattleya") when she had told him she was coming from the Maison Dorée, how many others there must have been, each of them also harboring a lie which Swann had not suspected. He remembered that one day she had said to him: "I would simply tell Mme. Verdurin my dress wasn't ready, or my cab came late. There's always a way to manage it." From him too, probably, many times when she had murmured the sorts of words which explain a delay, justify a change in the hour of a meeting, they must have concealed, without his suspecting it then, something she was going to do with some other man, with some other man to whom she had said: "I'll simply tell Swann my dress wasn't ready, or my cab came late. There's always a way to manage it." And under all of Swann's sweetest memories, under the simplest words Odette had said to him in the old days, which he had believed like the words of the gospel, under the daily actions she had recounted to him, under the most ordinary places, her dressmaker's house, the avenue du Bois, the Hippodrome, he sensed, concealed within the surplus time which even in the most thoroughly itemized days still leaves some play, some room, and can serve as hiding places for certain actions, he sensed insinuating itself the possible subterranean presence of lies which made something ignoble out of all that had remained most dear to him (his best evenings, the rue La Pérouse itself, which Odette must always have left at other hours than those she had reported to him), propagating everywhere a little of the dark horror he had felt when he heard her admission about the Maison Dorée, and, like the loathsome beasts in the Desolation of Nineveh,[113] toppling stone by stone his entire past. If he now turned away each time his memory spoke the bitter name of the Maison Dorée, it was no longer, as still quite recently at Mme. de Saint-Euverte's party, because it recalled to him a happiness he had long since lost, but because it recalled to him an unhappiness he had only just discovered. Then the same thing happened to the name of the Maison Dorée as to that of the island in the Bois, it gradually ceased to hurt Swann. For what we believe to be our love, or our jealousy, is not one single passion, continuous and indivisible. They are composed of an infinity of successive loves, of different jealousies, which are ephemeral but by their uninterrupted multitude give the impression of continuity, the illusion of unity. The life of Swann's love, the faithfulness of his jealousy, were formed of the death, the faithlessness, of numberless desires, numberless doubts, all of which had Odette as their object. If he had remained for a long time without seeing her, those that died would not have been replaced by others. But the presence of Odette continued to sow Swann's heart with affection and suspicion by turns.

On certain evenings she would suddenly be full of kindness toward him again, and she would warn him severely that he ought to take advantage of it right away, under penalty of not seeing it repeated for years to come; they had to go back to her house immediately to "make cattleya," and this desire which she claimed to feel for him was so sudden, so inexplicable, so imperious, the caresses she lavished on him at these times so demonstrative and so unusual that this rough and improbable affection made Swann as unhappy as a lie or an unkindness. One evening when he had gone home with her thus after she commanded it, and she was kissing him and murmuring to him with a passion quite unlike her usual coldness, he suddenly thought he heard a noise; he stood up, looked everywhere, found no one, but did not have the courage to go back to his place next to her, whereupon she, in a paroxysm of rage, broke a vase and said to Swann: "One can never do anything right with you!" And he remained uncertain whether she had not hidden someone there with the desire of provoking the man's jealousy or inflaming his senses.

Sometimes he visited brothels hoping to learn something about her, though without daring to say her name. "I have a nice little one I know you'll like," the madam would say. And he would stay there for an hour chatting gloomily to some poor girl who was astonished that he did nothing more. One who was very young and beautiful said to him one day: "What I'd like would be to find a man who would be a real friend to me: then he could be quite certain I'd never go with another man again." "Really, do you believe it's possible for a woman to be touched that a man loves her, and never be unfaithful to him?" Swann asked her anxiously. "Well, of course! But it would depend on her character, wouldn't it now?" Swann could not help saying to these girls the same sorts of things that would have pleased the Princesse des Laumes. To the one who was looking for a friend, he said, smiling: "How nice—you've put on blue eyes to match the color of your belt." "And you too; you've got blue cuffs on." "What a lovely conversation we're having, for this sort of a place! I'm not boring you, am I? Perhaps you've got something else you have to do?" "No, I have plenty of time. If you were boring me, I would have told you. Actually, I like listening to you talk." "I'm very flattered. Aren't we having a nice chat?" he said to the madam, who had just come in. "Why yes, that's just what I was saying to myself. How well they're behaving! There! Now they come to my house to talk. The Prince said it himself, the other day, it's much nicer here than at his wife's house. It seems that in high society these days all the women put on such airs, it's a real scandal! But I'll leave you alone, I know when to be discreet." And she left Swann with the blue-eyed girl. But soon he stood up and said good-bye, she did not matter to him, she did not know Odette.

Because the painter had been ill, Dr. Cottard had advised him to go to sea for a while; several of the regulars talked about going along with him; the Verdurins could not reconcile themselves to being left alone, rented a yacht, then purchased it and so Odette went on frequent cruises. Each time she had been gone for a little while, Swann felt he was beginning to separate from her, but as if this mental distance were proportional to the physical distance, as soon as he knew Odette was back, he could not rest without seeing her. Once, having gone off for only a month, as they thought, either because they were tempted along the way, or because M. Verdurin had cunningly arranged things beforehand to please his wife and had informed the regulars only as they proceeded, from Algiers they went to Tunis, then to Italy, then to Greece, to Constantinople, to Asia Minor. The voyage had lasted close to a year. Swann felt absolutely calm, almost happy. Even though Mme. Verdurin had tried to persuade the pianist and Dr. Cottard that the aunt of the one and the patients of the other did not need them at all and that in any case it was imprudent to let Mme. Cottard return to Paris, which M. Verdurin assured them was in the midst of a revolution, she was obliged to give them back their freedom at Constantinople. And the painter left with them. One day, shortly after the three travelers[114] returned, Swann, seeing an omnibus go by headed for the Luxembourg, where he had business, had jumped inside and found himself sitting across from Mme. Cottard, who was making the rounds of the people whose "day" it was in full dress uniform, ostrich feather in hat, silk dress, muff, combination umbrella-sunshade, calling-card case, and freshly cleaned white gloves. Clothed in these insignia, when it was dry out she would go on foot from one house to the next in the same neighborhood, but for proceeding into a different neighborhood would use the omnibus with connection service. During the first few minutes, before the woman's native kindness perforated the starch of the petty bourgeoise, and also not very sure if she ought to talk about the Verdurins to Swann, she produced quite naturally, in her awkward, slow, soft voice which at times the omnibus drowned out completely with its rattling, remarks chosen from among those she heard and repeated in the twenty-five houses whose stories she climbed during one day:

"I don't need to ask you, monsieur, if a man in the swim such as yourself has gone to the Mirlitons,[115] to see the portrait by Machard[116] which the whole of Paris is rushing to see? Well, and what do you think of it? Whose camp are you in, those who approve or those who don't? It's the same in every house now, all they talk about is the portrait by Machard; you aren't fashionable, you aren't really cultured, you aren't up-to-date, unless you can give your opinion of Machard's portrait."

Swann answered that he had not see the portrait, and Mme. Cottard was afraid she had offended him by obliging him to confess it.

"Well, good, at least you admit it frankly, you don't think you're disgraced because you haven't seen Machard's portrait. I think that's admirable. Well now, I have seen it. Opinion is divided, you know, some people think there's too much polish in it, too much whipped cream, but I think it's just right. Of course she's not like the blue-and-yellow women by our friend Biche. But I must confess to you frankly, though you will not find me very fin-de-siècle, but I do say what I think—I don't understand his work. Good Lord, I can see the good points in his portrait of my husband, it's not as strange as what he usually does, but even so he had to go and put a blue mustache on him. Whereas Machard! Imagine, the husband of the friend I'm on my way to see at this moment (giving me the great pleasure of riding with you) has promised her that, if he's elected to the Academy (he's one of the doctor's colleagues), he'll have her portrait done by Machard. Obviously they're dreaming! I have another friend who claims she likes Leloir[117] better. I'm just a poor layman and perhaps Leloir is even superior technically. But I think the most important quality in a portrait, especially when it's going to cost ten thousand francs, is that it should be a good likeness, and pleasant to look at."

Having made these remarks, which were inspired by the loftiness of her plume, the monogram on her card case, the little number inked inside her gloves by the dry cleaner, and the difficulty of talking to Swann about the Verdurins, Mme. Cottard, seeing that they were still far away from the corner of the rue Bonaparte where the driver was to let her off, listened to her heart, which counseled other words.

"Your ears must have been burning, monsieur," she said, "during the voyage we made with Mme. Verdurin. We talked of nothing else but you."

Swann was very surprised; he had assumed that his name was never mentioned in the presence of the Verdurins.

"Anyway," added Mme. Cottard, "Mme. de Crécy was there, and that says it all. Wherever Odette is, she can never go for very long without mentioning you. And as you may expect she does not speak ill of you. What! You doubt it?" she said, seeing Swann make a gesture of skepticism.

And carried away by the sincerity of her conviction, and imputing no unfavorable meaning to the word, which she used only in the sense in which one employs it to speak of the affection between friends:

"Why, she adores you! Oh, I'm sure one couldn't say anything against you in front of her! One would be soundly scolded! Apropos of anything at all, if we saw a painting, for instance, she would say: 'Now, if he were here, he'd be able to tell us whether it was genuine or not. There's nobody like him for that.' And she was constantly asking:

'What can he be doing right now? If only he would do a little work! It's dreadful that a fellow with such gifts should be so lazy.' (You'll forgive me, won't you?) 'I can see him right now, he's thinking about us, he's wondering where we are.' She even made a remark that I found quite charming: M. Verdurin said to her: 'How in the world can you see what he's doing right now, since you're eight hundred leagues away?' And Odette answered: 'Nothing is impossible for the eye of a friend.' No, I swear, I'm not saying it just to flatter you, you have a true friend in her such as you don't often find. I can tell you besides, that if you don't know it, you're the only one who doesn't. Mme. Verdurin told me as much herself on our very last day (you know, when you're about to leave you always have the best talks): 'I'm not saying Odette doesn't care a great deal for us, but whatever we might say to her wouldn't have much weight compared to what M. Swann might say.' Oh, my Lord! The driver's stopping for me—here I've been chatting away with you and I nearly went right past the rue Bonaparte . . . Would you be so kind as to tell me if my plume is straight?"

And Mme. Cottard withdrew from her muff and held out to Swann a hand gloved in white from which escaped, along with a transfer ticket, a vision of upper-class life that filled the omnibus, mingling with the smell of the dry cleaner. And Swann felt himself overflowing with affection for her, as much as for Mme. Verdurin (and almost as much as for Odette, since the feeling he now had for the latter, being no longer mingled with pain, was hardly love anymore), while from the platform of the omnibus he followed her with his newly affectionate eyes as she courageously made her way up the rue Bonaparte, her plume high, lifting her skirt with one hand, holding in the other her sunshade and her card case with its monogram displayed, while her muff danced in front of her.

To compete with the morbid feelings that Swann had for Odette, Mme. Cottard, a better healer than her husband would have been, had grafted alongside them other feelings, normal ones, of gratitude, friendship, feelings which in Swann's mind would make Odette more human (more like other women, because other women too could inspire these feelings in him), would hasten her final transformation into the Odette who was loved with a peaceful affection, who had brought him back one evening after a party at the painter's home to drink a glass of orangeade with Forcheville and with whom Swann had glimpsed the possibility of living in happiness.

In the past having often thought with terror that one day he would cease to be in love with Odette, he had promised himself to be vigilant and, as soon as he felt his love was beginning to leave him, to cling to it, to hold it back. But now to the weakening of his love there corresponded a simultaneous weakening of his desire to remain in love. For one cannot change, that is to say become another person, while continuing to acquiesce to the feelings of the person one has ceased to be. Now and then the name, glimpsed in a newspaper, of one of the men he thought could have been Odette's lovers, restored his jealousy to him. But it was very mild and as it proved to him that he had not yet completely emerged from the time when he had suffered so much—but also when he had experienced such voluptuous feelings—and that the hazards of the road ahead might still permit him to catch a furtive, distant glimpse of its beauties, this jealousy actually gave him a pleasant thrill just as to the sad Parisian leaving Venice to return to France a last mosquito proves that Italy and the summer are not yet too remote. But most often, when he made the effort, if not to remain in this quite distinctive period of his life from which he was emerging, at least to have a clear view of it while he still could, he would notice that already he no longer could; he would have liked to observe, as though it were a landscape about to disappear, that love which he had just left behind; but it is so difficult to duplicate oneself and give oneself a truthful display of a feeling one no longer has that soon, darkness gathering in his brain, he could no longer see anything, gave up looking, took off his lorgnon, wiped its lenses; and he said to himself that it would be better to rest a little, that there would still be time later on, and would settle back with the incuriosity, the torpor of the drowsy traveler who pulls his hat down over his eyes in order to sleep in the railway carriage which he feels carrying him faster and faster away from the country where he has lived for so long and which he had promised himself not to let slip past without giving it a last farewell. Indeed, like the same traveler if he does not wake until he is back in France, when Swann happened upon proof close at hand that Forcheville had been Odette's lover, he observed that he felt no pain, that his love was far away by now, and he was sorry not to have been warned of the moment when he was about to leave it behind forever. And just as before kissing Odette for the first time he had tried to imprint on his memory the face which had been familiar to him for so long and which was about to be transformed by the memory of that kiss, so he would have wanted, in his thoughts at least, to have been able to make his farewells, while she still existed, to the Odette who had inspired him with love, jealousy, to the Odette who had made him suffer and whom he would now never see again. He was mistaken. He did see see her again, one more time, a few weeks later. It was while he was asleep, in the twilight of a dream. He was walking with Mme. Verdurin, Dr. Cottard, a young man in a fez whom he could not identify, the painter, Odette, Napoleon III, and my grandfather, along a path that followed the sea and overhung it steeply sometimes very high up, sometimes by a few yards only, so that one climbed and descended again constantly; those who were descending again were already no longer visible to those who were still climbing, what little daylight remained was failing, and it seemed then as though a profound darkness was going to spread over them at any moment. Now and again the waves leaped right up to the edge and Swann felt sprays of icy water on his cheek. Odette told him to wipe them off, he could not and was embarrassed by this in front of her, as he was embarrassed to be in his nightshirt. He hoped that in the darkness no one would realize, but Mme. Verdurin stared at him with a look of surprise for a long moment during which he saw her face change shape, her nose lengthen, and that she had a large mustache. He turned away to look at Odette, her cheeks were pale, with little red spots, her features drawn, ringed with shadows, but she was looking at him with eyes full of tenderness that were about to separate from her like teardrops and fall on him, and he felt he loved her so much that he wanted to take her away at once. Suddenly Odette turned her wrist, looked at a little watch, and said: "I

have to go," she said good-bye to everyone, in the same manner, without taking Swann aside, without telling him where she would see him
again that evening or another day. He did not dare ask her, he would
have liked to follow her and was obliged, without turning back toward
her, to answer with a smile some question of Mme. Verdurin's, but his
heart was pounding horribly, he felt he hated Odette, he would have
liked to cut out those eyes of hers that he had loved so much just a
moment ago, crush those pallid cheeks. He continued to climb with
Mme. Verdurin, which meant that with each step he moved farther
away from Odette, who was descending in the opposite direction.
After one second, it was many hours ago that she had left them. The
painter remarked to Swann that Napoleon III had vanished an instant
after she had. "They certainly must have arranged it together," he
added. "They must have met at the bottom of the hill, but they didn't
want to say good-bye at the same time for the sake of appearances.
She's obviously his mistress." The unknown young man began to cry.
Swann tried to comfort him. "Really, she's doing the right thing," he
told him, drying his eyes and taking off his fez so that he would be
more comfortable. "I told her a dozen times she should do it. Why be
sad about it? He above all would understand her." Thus did Swann
talk to himself, for the young man he had not been able to identify at
first was also himself; like certain novelists, he had divided his personality between two characters, the one having the dream, and another
he saw before him wearing a fez.

As for Napoleon III, it was to Forcheville that some vague association of ideas, then a certain modification in the Baron's usual phys-
iognomy, lastly the broad ribbon of the Legion of Honor on his chest,
had induced him to give this name; but in reality, and in everything
which the character in the dream represented to him and recalled to
him, it was indeed Forcheville. For, from incomplete and changing
images the sleeping Swann drew false deductions, having for the moment as well such creative power that he reproduced himself by simple division like certain lower organisms; with the warmth that he felt
in his own palm he modeled the hollow of a strange hand which he
thought he was clasping, and from feelings and impressions of which

he was not yet conscious, devised peripeteias of a sort which, through their logical linking, would produce at just the right moment in Swann's sleep the person required to receive his love or prompt his awakening. Utter darkness descended on him in an instant, an alarm sounded, inhabitants of the place ran past, escaping from houses in flames; Swann heard the sound of the waves leaping and his heart, with the same violence, pounding with anxiety in his chest. Suddenly the palpitations of his heart redoubled in speed, he felt an inexplicable pain and nausea; a countryman covered with burns flung at him as he passed: "Come ask Charlus where Odette ended up this evening with her friend, he used to go about with her in the old days and she tells him everything. It's them that started the fire." It was his valet who had come to wake him and who said:

"Monsieur, it's eight o'clock and the hairdresser is here, I've told him to come by again in an hour."

But these words, penetrating the swells of sleep in which Swann was plunged, had reached his consciousness only by suffering that deflection which causes a ray of light in the depths of water to appear to be a sun, just as a moment earlier the sound of the doorbell, assuming in the depths of those abysses the sonority of an alarm, had begotten the episode of the fire. Meanwhile the scene before his eyes turned to dust, he opened his eyes, heard one last time the sound of a wave of the sea as it receded. He touched his cheek. It was dry. And yet he could recall the sensation of the cold water and the taste of the salt. He got up, dressed. He had asked the hairdresser to come early because he had written to my grandfather the night before that he would be going to Combray in the afternoon, having learned that Mme. de Cambremer—Mlle. Legrandin—was spending a few days there. Associating in his memory the charm of that young face with the charm of a countryside he had not visited in such a long time, he found that together they offered him an attraction that had made him decide to leave Paris for a few days at last. Because the different chance events which bring us into contact with certain people do not coincide with the time during which we are in love with them, but, extending beyond it, may occur before it begins and repeat themselves after it has ended, the earliest appearances in our lives of a person destined later to captivate us assume retrospectively in our eyes the significance of a warning, a presage. This was how Swann had often looked back at the image of Odette when he met her at the theater, that first evening when he did not dream he would ever see her again—and how he now recalled the party at Mme. de Saint-Euverte's where he had introduced Général de Froberville to Mme. de Cambremer. We have such numerous interests in our lives that it is not uncommon, on a single occasion, for the foundations of a happiness that does not yet exist to be laid down alongside the intensification of a grief from which we are still suffering. And undoubtedly this could have happened to Swann elsewhere than at Mme. de Saint-Euverte's. Who knows, even, had he found himself elsewhere, that evening, if other happinesses, other griefs would not have come to him, which afterward should have appeared to him to have been inevitable? But what did seem to him to have been inevitable was what had taken place, and he was not far short of seeing something providential in the fact that he had decided to go to Mme. de Saint-Euverte's party, because his mind, wanting to admire life's richness of invention and incapable of posing itself a difficult question for very long, such as to determine what would have been most desirable, believed that in the sufferings he had experienced that evening and in the pleasures still unsuspected that were already germinating—between which the balance was too difficult to establish—there was a sort of necessary connection.

But while, an hour after he had woken, he was giving instructions to the hairdresser so that his brush cut would not become disordered on the train, he thought about his dream again, and saw once again, as he had felt them close beside him, Odette's pale complexion, her too thin cheeks, her drawn features, her tired eyes, everything which—in the course of the successive expression of tenderness which had made of his abiding love for Odette a long oblivion of the first image he had formed of her—he had ceased to notice since the earliest days of their acquaintance, days to which no doubt, while he slept, his memory had returned to search for their exact sensation. And with the intermittent coarseness that reappeared in him as soon as he was no longer unhappy and the level of his morality dropped accordingly, he exclaimed to himself: "To think that I wasted years of my life, that I wanted to die, that I felt my deepest love, for a woman who did not appeal to me, who was not my type!"

PART III

Place-Names: The Name

MONG THE BEDROOMS whose images I summoned up most often in my nights of insomnia, none resembled less the rooms at Combray, dusted with an atmosphere that was grainy, pollinated, edible, and devout, than the room at the Grand-Hôtel de la Plage, at Balbec, whose enamel-painted walls contained, like the polished sides of a swimming pool which tints the water blue, a pure azure salt sea air. The Bavarian decorator commissioned to furnish the hotel had varied the design schemes of the rooms and on three sides, along the walls, in the one I was occupying, had placed low bookcases, with glass panes, in which, depending on the spot they occupied, and by an effect he had not foreseen, one part or another of the changing picture of the sea was reflected, unfurling a frieze of bright seascapes, which was interrupted only by the solid pieces of mahogany. So much so that the whole room had the look of one of those model dormitories presented in "*modern style*"[1] furniture shows, where they are hung with works of art assumed to be likely to delight the eyes of the person who will be sleeping there, and representing subjects in keeping with the type of site where the room will be found.

But nothing resembled less this real Balbec, either, than the one I had often dreamed of, on stormy days, when the wind was so strong that Françoise as she took me to the Champs-Élysées warned me not to walk too close to the walls or the tiles might fall on my head and moaned to me about the great disasters and shipwrecks reported in the newspapers. I had no greater desire than to see a storm at sea, not so much because it would be a beautiful spectacle as because it would be a moment of nature's real life unveiled; or rather for me there were no beautiful spectacles except the ones which I knew were not artificially contrived for my pleasure, but were necessary, unchangeable— the beauties of landscapes or of great art. I was curious, I was avid to know only those things which I believed to be more real than myself, which had for me the value of showing me a little of the mind of a great genius, or of the force or grace of nature as it is manifested when left to itself, without the interference of men. Just as the lovely sound of her voice, reproduced in isolation by the phonograph, would not console us for having lost our mother, so too a storm mechanically imitated would have left me as indifferent as the illuminated fountains at the Exposition.[2] And so that the storm would be absolutely real, I also wanted the shore itself to be a natural shore, not a pier recently built by some municipality. In fact, because of all the feelings it awakened in me, nature seemed to me the thing most opposite to the mechanical productions of men. The less it bore their imprint the more room it offered in which my heart could expand. Now, I had remembered the name Balbec, which had been mentioned to us by Legrandin, as that of a seaside resort very close to "those funereal cliffs, famous for their many wrecks, wrapped six months of the year in a shroud of fog and the foam of the waves."

"In that place you can still feel beneath your feet," he said, "far more so than at Finistère itself[3] (and even though hotels are being superimposed upon it now without, however, the power to change the more ancient skeleton of the land), you can still feel the true end of the land of France, of Europe, of the Ancient World. And it's the last encampment of fishermen, precisely like all the fishermen who have ever lived since the beginning of the world, facing the eternal realm of the mists of the sea and the shadows of the night." One day when, at Combray, I had mentioned this seaside resort of Balbec in the presence of M. Swann in order to find out from him if it was the choicest spot for seeing the most powerful storms, he had answered me: "Yes indeed I certainly know Balbec! The church at Balbec, built in the twelfth and thirteenth centuries, still half Romanesque, is perhaps the most curious example of our Norman Gothic, and so singular! It's almost Persian in style." And that region, which until then had seemed to me similar in nature to the immemorial, still contemporaneous great phenomena of geology—and just as completely outside human history as the Ocean itself or the Great Bear,[4] with those wild fishermen for whom no more than for the whales had there been any Middle Ages—it had been a great delight for me to see it suddenly take its place in the sequence of the centuries, now that it had experienced the Romanesque period, and to know that the Gothic trefoil had come at the proper time to pattern those wild rocks too, like the frail but hardy plants which, when spring comes, spangle here and there the polar snow. And if the Gothic brought to those places and to those men a definition which they lacked, they too conferred one upon it in return. I tried to picture how those fishermen had lived, the timid and unsuspected attempt at social relations which they had made there, during the Middle Ages, clustered on a point along the shores of hell, at the foot of the cliffs of death; and the Gothic seemed to me more alive now that, having separated it from the towns in which until then I had always imagined it, I could see how, in one particular case, on those wild rocks, it had germinated and flowered into a delicate steeple. I was taken to see reproductions of the most famous of the statues at Balbec—the fleecy snub-nosed apostles, the Virgin in the porch—and my breathing stopped in my chest for joy when I thought that I could see them modeled in relief against the eternal briny mist. Then, on the sweet stormy evenings of February, the wind—blowing into my heart, which trembled under its gusts no less powerfully than my bedroom chimney, the plan of a trip to Balbec—mingled in me a desire for Gothic architecture with my desire for a tempest at sea.

I would have liked to leave the very next day on the handsome, generous 1:22 train whose hour of departure I could never read without a palpitating heart, in the railway company's advertisements or in announcements for circular tours: it seemed to me to incise at a precise point in the afternoon a delectable notch, a mysterious mark from which the diverted hours, though they still led to the evening, to the next morning, led to an evening and morning which one would see, not in Paris, but in one of those towns through which the train passes and among which it permitted us to choose; for it stopped at Bayeux, at Coutances, at Vitré, at Questambert, at Pontorson, at Balbec, at Lannion, at Lamballe, at Benodet, at Pont-Aven, at Quimperlé, and moved on magnificently overloaded with proffered names so that, among them all, I did not know which one I would have preferred, so impossible was it to sacrifice any of them. But without even waiting for it, I could have, by dressing quickly, left that very evening, if my parents had allowed me, and arrived at Balbec when the morning twilight was rising over the furious sea, from whose volleys of foam I would take refuge in the Persian-style church. But at the approach of the Easter holidays, when my parents promised to let me spend them for once in the north of Italy, now, in place of those dreams of tempests by which I had been so entirely occupied, wanting to see only waves running in from all sides, higher and higher, on the wildest coast, near churches as steep and rugged as cliffs, from whose towers the seabirds would shriek, now suddenly erasing them, taking away all their charm, excluding them because they were its opposite and could only have weakened it, the converse dream now occupied me, of the most dappled spring, not the spring of Combray which still pricked us tartly with all the needles of the frost, but the spring which was already covering the fields of Fiesole with lilies and anemones and dazzling Florence with golden grounds like those of Fra Angelico. From then on, only sunlight, perfumes, colors seemed to me of any value; for this alternation of images had brought about a change of direction in my desire, and—as abrupt as those that occur now and then in music—a complete change of tone in my sensibility. Thus it came about that a simple variation in the atmosphere was enough to provoke this modulation in me without any need to wait for the return of a season. For often, in one season, we find a day that has strayed from another and that immediately evokes its particular pleasures, lets us experience them, makes us desire them, and interrupts the dreams we were having by placing, earlier or later than was its turn, this leaf detached from another chapter, in the interpolated calendar of Happiness. But soon, like those natural phenomena from which our comfort or health can derive only an accidental and rather slender benefit until the day when science seizes hold of them, and producing them at will, puts into our hands the possibility of their appearance, withdrawn from the guardianship and exempted from the consent of chance, in the same way the production of those dreams of the Atlantic and of Italy ceased to be subjected solely to the changes of the seasons and of the weather. I needed only, to make them reappear, to pronounce those names—Balbec, Venice, Florence—in the interior of which had finally accumulated the desire inspired in me by the places they designated. Even in spring, finding the name of Balbec in a book was enough to awaken in me the desire for storms and Norman Gothic; even on a stormy day the name of Florence or Venice gave me a desire for the sun, for lilies, for the Palace of the Doges, and for Saint-Mary-of-the-Flowers.[5]

But if these names absorbed forever the image I had of these towns, it was only by transforming that image, by subjecting its reappearance in me to their own laws; in consequence of this they made it more beautiful, but also more different from what the towns of Normandy or Tuscany could be in reality, and, by increasing the arbitrary joys of my imagination, aggravated the future disappointment of my travels. They exalted the idea I was forming of certain places on the earth, by making them more particular, consequently more real. I did not at the time represent to myself cities, landscapes, monuments as more or less pleasant pictures, cut out here and there from the same material, but each of them as an unknown thing, different in essence from the others, a thing for which my soul thirsted and which it would profit from knowing. How much more individuality still did they assume from being designated by names, names that were theirs alone, proper names like the names people have. Words present us with little pictures of things, clear and familiar, like those that are hung on the walls of schools to give children an example of what a workbench is, a bird, an anthill, things conceived of as similar to all others of the same sort. But names present a confused image of people—and of towns, which they accustom us to believe are individual, unique like people—an image which derives from them, from the brightness or darkness of their tone, the color with which it is painted uniformly, like one of those posters, entirely blue or entirely red, in which, because of the limitations of the process used or by a whim of the designer, not only the sky and the sea are blue or red, but the boats, the church, the people in the streets. Because the name of Parma, one of the towns I had most wanted to visit ever since I had read *La Chartreuse,*[6] seemed to me compact, smooth, mauve, and soft, if anyone mentioned a certain house in Parma in which I would be staying, he gave me the pleasure of thinking I would be living in a house that was smooth, compact, mauve, and soft, that bore no relation to the houses of any real town in Italy, since I had composed it in my imagination with the help only of that heavy syllable, *Parme,* in which no air circulates, and of all that I had made it absorb of Stendhalian softness and the tint of violets. And when I thought of Florence, it was of a town miraculously fragrant and like the petals of a flower, because it was called the City of Lilies and its cathedral Saint-Mary-of-the-Flowers. As for Balbec, it was one of those names in which, as on a piece of old Norman pottery that retains the color of the earth from which it was taken, one can still see depicted the representation of some outmoded custom, of some feudal right, of some locality in an earlier condition, of an abandoned habit of pronunciation which had formed its heteroclite syllables and which I did not doubt I would rediscover spoken there even by the innkeeper who would serve me coffee with milk on my arrival, taking me down to watch the furious sea in front of the church, and to whom I would ascribe the disputatious, solemn, and medieval aspect of a character from a fabliau.[7]

If my health improved and my parents allowed me, if not to go stay in Balbec, at least to take just once, in order to acquaint myself with the architecture and landscapes of Normandy or Brittany, that one-twenty-two train which I had boarded so many times in my imagination, I would have wished by preference to stop in the most beautiful towns; but compare them as I might, how could I choose, any more than between individual people, who are not interchangeable, between Bayeux, so lofty in its noble red-tinged lace, its summit illuminated by the old gold of its last syllable; Vitré,[8] whose acute accent barred its ancient glass with black wood lozenges; gentle Lamballe, whose whiteness goes from eggshell yellow to pearl gray; Coutances, a Norman cathedral, which its final, fat, yellowing diphthong crowns with a tower of butter; Lannion with the sound, in its village silence, of the coach followed by the fly;[9] Questambert, Pontorson, naive and ridiculous, white feathers and yellow beaks scattered along the road to those poetic river spots; Benodet, a name scarcely moored, which the river seems to want to carry away among its algae; Pont-Aven, a pink-and-white flight of the wing of a lightly poised coif reflected trembling in the greeny waters of a canal; Quimperlé, more firmly attached, ever since the Middle Ages, among the streams about which it babbles as they bead it with a pearly grisaille like that which is sketched, through the spiderwebs of a stained-glass window, by rays of sunlight which have turned into blunted points of burnished silver?

These images were false for another reason also; namely that they were necessarily quite simplified; doubtless whatever it was that my imagination aspired to and that my senses took in only incompletely and without any immediate pleasure, I had enclosed in the sanctuary of a name; doubtless because I had accumulated there a store of dreams, these names now magnetized my desires; but names themselves are not very spacious; the most I could do was include in them two or three of the towns' principal curiosities, which would be juxtaposed there with nothing to connect them; in the name Balbec, as in the magnifying glass of the penholders you buy at a seaside resort, I saw waves rising around a Persian-style church. Perhaps indeed the simplification of these images was one of the reasons for the hold that they had over me. When my father decided, one year, that we would go spend the Easter holidays in Florence and Venice, not having enough room to insert into the name Florence the elements that usually make up a town, I was forced to produce a supernatural city from the fecundation, by certain springtime fragrances, of what I believed to be, in its essence, the spirit of Giotto. At the very most—and because one cannot attach to a name much more time than space—like certain of Giotto's paintings themselves which show us the same figure at two different moments in the action, here lying in his bed, there getting ready to mount his horse, the name Florence was divided into two compartments. In one, under an architectural canopy, I was contemplating a fresco on part of which was superimposed a curtain of morning sunlight, dusty, oblique, and gradually spreading; in the other (for, since I did not think of names as an inaccessible ideal but as a real atmosphere in which I was going to immerse myself, the life not yet lived, the pure and intact life that I enclosed in them gave to the most material pleasures, to the simplest scenes, the attraction they have in the works of the primitives), I was walking quickly—the sooner to reach the lunch that was waiting for me with fruits and wine from Chianti—across a Ponte Vecchio crowded with jonquils, narcissus, and anemones. That (even though I was in Paris) was what I saw, and not what was actually around me. Even from a simple realistic point of view, the countries we long for occupy a far larger place in our actual life, at any given moment, than the country in which we happen to be. Doubtless, had I myself paid more attention at the time to what was in my mind when I pronounced the words "go to Florence, to Parma, to Pisa, to Venice," I would have realized that what I saw was not a town at all, but something as different from anything I knew, something as delightful, as might be, for a human race whose whole life had been spent in the late afternoons of winter, that unknown marvel: a spring morning. These images, unreal, fixed, always alike, filling my nights and my days, differentiated this period of my life from those that had gone before it (and might have been confused with it in the eyes of an observer who sees things only from outside, that is to say who sees nothing), as in an opera a melodic motif introduces something new that one could not have suspected if one had only read the libretto, still less if one had remained outside the theater only counting the quarter hours as they passed. And besides, even from this point of view, of mere quantity, in our lives the days are not all equal. As they travel through the days, temperaments that are slightly nervous, as mine was, have available to them, like automobiles, different "speeds." There are arduous mountainous days which one spends an infinite time climbing, and downward-sloping days which one can descend at full tilt singing. During that month–in which I replayed over and over like a melody, without ever becoming sated, those images of Florence, Venice, and Pisa for which the desire they excited in me retained something as profoundly individual as if it had been love, love of a person–I did not cease to believe that they corresponded to a reality independent of me, and they introduced me to a hope as beautiful as that which a Christian of the earliest era might have nourished on the eve of entering Paradise. Thus without my worrying about the contradiction of wanting to look at and touch with the organs of my senses what I had created in a daydream and not perceived with my senses–though all the more tempting to them in consequence, more different from anything they knew–it was whatever reminded me of the reality of these images that most inflamed my desire, because it was a sort of promise that my desire would be gratified. And although the motive for my exhilaration was a desire for artistic delights, the guidebooks sustained it even more than the books on aesthetics and, more than the guidebooks, the railway timetable. What moved me was the thought that if this Florence which I could see near but inaccessible in my imagination was separated from me, in myself, by a tract which I could not cross, I could reach it indirectly, by a detour, by taking the land route. Certainly when I repeated to myself, thus giving such a high value to what I was going to see, that Venice was "the school of Giorgione, the home of Titian, the most complete museum of medieval domestic architecture,"[10] I felt happy. Yet I was even happier when, out on an errand and walking quickly because of the weather, which, after a few days of precocious spring, had turned back into winter (like the weather we usually found at Combray in Holy Week)–seeing on the boulevards that the chestnut trees, though plunged in an atmosphere as icy and as liquid as water, were nonetheless beginning, punctual guests, already in formal dress, and not allowing themselves to be

discouraged, to chisel out of their frozen masses the round shapes of
the irresistible greenery whose steady growth the abortive power of
the cold might hinder but could not succeed in restraining–I thought
that already the Ponte Vecchio was abundantly strewn with hyacinths
and anemones and the spring sunshine was already dyeing the waves
of the Grand Canal with so dark an azure and such noble emeralds
that when they came to break at the feet of Titian's paintings, they
might rival them in richness of color. I could no longer contain my
joy when my father, even as he consulted the barometer and deplored
the cold, began to seek out which would be the best trains, and when
I realized that by making one's way, after lunch, into the coal-
blackened laboratory, the magic chamber charged with working the
complete transmutation of everything around it, one could wake the
next morning in the city of marble and gold "bossed with jasper and
paved with emeralds."[11] So that it and the City of Lilies were not
merely fictive pictures which one could set up at will before one's
imagination, but existed at a certain distance from Paris that one absolutely had to cross if one wanted to see them, at a certain determined place on the earth, and at no other, in a word were quite real.
They became even more so for me, when my father, by saying: "So
you could stay in Venice from the twentieth of April until the twenty-
ninth and arrive in Florence on Easter morning" made them both
emerge no longer merely from abstract Space, but from that imaginary Time in which we situate, not one journey at a time but others simultaneously and without too much emotion since they are only
possibilities–that Time which re-creates itself so effectively that we
can spend it again in one town after we have spent it in another–and
devoted to them some of those particular days which are the certificate of authenticity of the objects on which one employs them, for
those unique days are consumed by use, they do not come back, one
cannot live them here when one has lived them there; I felt that it was
toward the week which began on the Monday when the washerwoman
was to bring back the white waistcoat I had covered with ink that the
two Queen Cities were heading, to absorb themselves in it as they

emerged from that ideal time in which they did not yet exist—those two Queen Cities the domes and towers of which I was soon going to be able, by the most moving kind of geometry, to inscribe on the map of my own life. But I was still merely on the way to the last degree of bliss; I reached it finally (for only then did the revelation come to me that on those wave-splashed streets, reddened by reflections from Giorgione's frescoes,[12] it was not, as I had, despite so many admonitions, continued to imagine, men "majestic and terrible as the sea, bearing armour that gleamed with bronze beneath the folds of their blood-red cloaks"[13] who would be walking through Venice next week, on the eve of Easter, but that I myself might be the minuscule figure, in a large photograph of St. Mark's that had been lent to me, whom the illustrator represented, in a bowler hat, in front of the porches), when I heard my father say: "It must be quite cold, still, on the Grand Canal; you would do well to put your winter overcoat and your heavy jacket in your trunk just in case." At these words I was lifted into a kind of ecstasy; I felt myself to be truly making my way, as I had until then thought impossible, between those "rocks of amethyst like a reef in the Indian Ocean";[14] by a supreme feat of gymnastics beyond my strength, divesting myself, as of a useless carapace, of the air of my bedroom that surrounded me, I replaced it by equal parts of Venetian air, that marine atmosphere as indescribable and particular as the atmosphere of dreams, which my imagination had enclosed in the name of Venice; I felt myself undergoing a miraculous disincarnation; it was immediately accompanied by that vague desire to vomit which one feels when one has come down with a severe sore throat, and they had to put me to bed with a fever so tenacious that the doctor declared they would not only have to give up the idea of allowing me to leave for Florence and Venice now but, even when I was entirely well again, spare me for at least a year any plans for traveling and any cause of excitement.

And also, alas, he forbade them absolutely to allow me to go to the theater to hear La Berma; the sublime artist whom Bergotte had regarded as a genius would have, by introducing me to something that was perhaps as important and as beautiful, consoled me for not having been to Florence and Venice, for not going to Balbec. They had to confine themselves to sending me to the Champs-Élysées every day under the supervision of someone who would keep me from tiring myself out, and that person was Françoise, who had entered our service after the death of my aunt Léonie. To go to the Champs-Élysées was unbearable to me. If only Bergotte had described it in one of his books, I probably would have wanted to get to know it, like all the things whose "double" someone had begun by putting into my imagination. It would warm them, bring them to life, give them a personality, and I would want to find them again in reality; but in this public garden nothing formed a part of my dreams.

One day, because I was bored in our usual spot, next to the merry-go-round, Françoise had taken me on an excursion—beyond the frontier guarded at equal intervals by the little bastions of the barley-sugar sellers—into those neighboring but foreign regions where the faces are unfamiliar, where the goat cart passes: then she had gone back to get her things from her chair, which stood with its back to a clump of laurels; as I waited for her I was pacing the broad lawn, sparse and shorn, yellowed by the sun, at the far end of which a statue stands above the pool, when, from the path, addressing a little girl with reddish hair playing with a shuttlecock in front of the basin, another girl, while putting on her cloak and stowing her racket, shouted to her in a sharp voice: "Good-bye, Gilberte, I'm going home, don't forget we're coming to your house tonight after dinner." The name Gilberte passed close by me, evoking all the more forcefully the existence of the girl it designated in that it did not merely name her, as one speaks of someone who is absent, but addressed her directly; thus it passed close by me, in action so to speak, with a force that increased with the curve of its trajectory and the approach of its target;—transporting along with it, I felt, the knowledge, the notions concerning her to whom it was addressed that belonged not to me, but to the friend who was calling her, everything that, as she uttered it, she saw again or at least possessed in her memory, of their daily companionship, of the visits they paid to each other, of the whole of that unknown existence which was all the more inaccessible and all the more painful to me for being conversely so familiar and so malleable for that happy girl who brushed me with it without my being able to penetrate it and hurled it up in the air in a shout;—letting float in the air the delicious emanation it had released, by touching them so precisely, from several invisible points in the life of Mlle. Swann, from the evening that was to come, such as it might be, after dinner, at her house;—forming, in its celestial passage among the children and the nursemaids, a little cloud of precious color, like that which, billowing over a lovely garden by Poussin,[15] reflects minutely like a cloud in an opera, full of horses and chariots, some manifestation of the life of the gods;—casting, finally, on that bald grass, at the spot where it was at once a patch of withered lawn and a moment in the afternoon of the blond shuttlecock player (who did not stop launching the shuttlecock and catching it again until a governess wearing a blue ostrich feather called her), a marvelous little band the color of heliotrope as impalpable as a reflection and laid down like a carpet over which I did not tire of walking back and forth with lingering, nostalgic, and desecrating steps, while Françoise cried out to me: "Come on now, button up your coat and let's make ourselves scarce," and I noticed for the first time with irritation that she had a vulgar way of speaking, and alas, no blue feather in her hat.

But would she come back to the Champs-Élysées? The next day she was not there; but I saw her there on the following days; I spent all my time circling around the spot where she played with her friends, so that once when they found they were short of players for their game of prisoners' base, she sent to ask if I wanted to make up the number on their side, and after that I played with her each time she was there. But this was not every day; there were days when she was kept from coming by her lessons, by the catechism, a tea, that whole life separate from mine which twice, condensed in the name of Gilberte, I had felt pass so painfully close to me, on the steep path at Combray and on the lawn at the Champs-Élysées. On those days, she would announce in advance that we would not be seeing her; if it was because of her studies, she would say: "It's an awful bore, I won't be able to come

tomorrow; you'll all be having fun without me," with a sorrowful air
that consoled me a little; but when she was invited to a party and I,
not knowing, asked her if she would be coming out to play, she would
answer: "I should certainly hope not! I certainly hope Mama will let
me go to my friend's." At least on those days, I knew I would not see
her, whereas other times, it was quite unexpectedly that her mother
would take her shopping, and the next day she would say: "Oh yes! I
went out with Mama," as though it were a natural thing and not, for
someone else, the greatest possible misfortune. There were also the
days of bad weather when her governess, who herself could not endure the rain, did not want to take her to the Champs-Élysées.

And so if the sky was dubious, from early in the morning I would
question it constantly, taking every omen into account. If I saw the
lady opposite, near the window, putting on her hat, I would say to
myself: "That lady is going to go out; so it's the sort of weather one
can go out in: why wouldn't Gilberte do the same as that lady?" But
the weather would darken, my mother would say it could lift again,
that a ray of sunlight would be enough, but that more probably it
would rain; and if it rained what was the good of going to the
Champs-Élysées? And so from lunch on my anxious eyes never left
the unsettled, cloudy sky. It remained dark. Before the window, the
balcony was gray. Suddenly, on its gloomy stone I did not see a color
that was less dull, but I felt a sort of effort toward a color less dull, the
pulsation of a hesitant ray that wished to discharge its light. A moment later, the balcony was as pale and reflective as a pool at dawn,
and a thousand reflections of its ironwork lattice had alighted on it. A
breath of wind dispersed them, the stone had darkened again, but, as
though tamed, they returned; it began imperceptibly to whiten again
and, in one of those continuous crescendos like those which, in
music, at the end of an overture, carry a single note to the highest fortissimo by making it pass rapidly through all the intermediary degrees, I saw it reach that fixed, unalterable gold of fine days, against
which the cutout shadow of the elaborate support of the balustrade
stood out in black like a whimsical vegetation, with a delicacy in the

delineation of its slightest details that seemed to betray a painstaking consciousness, an artistic satisfaction, and with such sharp relief, such velvet in the restfulness of its dark and happy masses that in truth those broad and leafy reflections resting on that lake of sun seemed to know they were pledges of calm and happiness.

Instantaneous ivy, fleeting wall flora! The least colorful, the saddest, in the opinion of many, of those that clamber over the wall or decorate the casement; for me, the dearest of them all since the day it appeared on our balcony, like the very shadow of the presence of Gilberte, who was perhaps already in the Champs-Élysées and, as soon as I arrived there, would say to me: "Let's start playing prisoners' base right away, you're on my side"; fragile, carried off by a breath, but also in harmony, not with the season, but with the hour; a promise of the immediate happiness which the day will deny or fulfill, and thereby of the highest sort of immediate happiness, the happiness of love; softer, warmer on the stone even than moss; hardy, for it needs only a ray of light to come into being and blossom into joy, even in the heart of winter.

And even on those days when all other vegetation has disappeared, when the handsome green leather that wraps the trunks of the old trees is hidden under snow, when the snow had stopped falling, but the weather was still too overcast to hope that Gilberte would go out, then suddenly, making my mother say: "Well now, it's actually nice out, perhaps you might try going to the Champs-Élysées after all," on the mantle of snow that covered the balcony the sun that had appeared was weaving gold threads together and embroidering black glimmers. That day we found no one, or one solitary girl about to leave, who assured me that Gilberte was not coming. The chairs, deserted by the imposing but chilly assembly of governesses, were empty. Alone, near the lawn, sat a lady of a certain age who came in all weathers, always dressed in the same clothing, magnificent and dark, to make whose acquaintance I would at that time have sacrificed, had the exchange been allowed me, all the greatest future advantages of my life. For Gilberte went up to greet her every day; she asked Gilberte for news of "her love of a mother"; and it seemed to me that, had I known her, I would have been someone quite different for Gilberte, someone who knew her parents' friends. While her grandchildren played farther off, she always read *Les Débats*,[16] which she called "my old *Débats*," and with an aristocratic affection would say, when speaking of the policeman or the woman who rented the chairs:[17] "my old friend the policeman," "the chair warden and I who are old friends."

Françoise was too cold to sit still; we walked to the pont de la Concorde to see the frozen Seine, which everyone including the children approached without fear as though it were a beached whale, immense, defenseless and about to be cut up. We returned to the Champs-Élysées; I was growing sick with misery between the motionless merry-go-round and the white lawn caught in the black web of paths from which the snow had been cleared and above which the statue had in its hand an added jet of ice which seemed to explain its gesture. Even the old lady, after folding her *Débats*, asked a passing nanny what time it was and thanked her by saying: "How kind of you!" then begged the man tending the paths to tell her grandchildren to come back, because she was cold, adding: "You are infinitely good. I am overwhelmed!" Suddenly the air was torn apart: between the puppet theater and the circus, on the clearing horizon, against the opening sky, I had just spied, as though it were a fabulous sign, Mademoiselle's blue feather. And already Gilberte was running as fast as possible in my direction, sparkling and red under a square fur hat, animated by the cold, the lateness, and her desire to play; a little before reaching me, she let herself slide along the ice, and either to help keep her balance, or because she thought it more graceful, or pretending to move like a skater, her arms opened wide as she came forward smiling, as if she wanted to take me into them. "Brava! Brava! That was very good. I would say, as you do, that it was champion, first-rate, if I were not from another age, if I did not belong to the Ancien Régime," cried the old lady, speaking on behalf of the silent Champs-Élysées to thank Gilberte for having come without letting herself be intimidated by the weather. "You're like me, faithful to our old Champs-Élysées despite everything; we're two brave souls, you and I. I tell you I love it, even this way. This snow—you'll laugh at me—reminds me of ermine!" And the old lady began to laugh.

The first of these days—to which the snow, image of the forces that could stop me from seeing Gilberte, imparted the sadness of a day of separation and even the aspect of a day of departure because it changed the appearance and almost prevented the use of the customary site of our only encounters, now changed, all wrapped in dustcovers—this day, however, caused my love to progress, for it was like a first sorrow that she had shared with me. There were only the two of us out of all our gang, and to be thus the only one there with her was not only like a beginning of intimacy, but also on her part—as though she had come out only for me, in such weather—it seemed to me as touching as if on one of those days when she was invited to a party she had given it up to come to find me in the Champs-Élysées; I gained more confidence in the vitality and the future of our friendship, which remained hardy in the midst of the numbness, loneliness, and ruin of the things around us; and while she put snowballs down my neck, I smiled with emotion at what seemed to me both a preference she was showing me by tolerating me as her traveling companion in this new and wintry land, and also a sort of loyalty she was cherishing for me in the midst of misfortune. Soon one after the other, like hesitant sparrows, her friends arrived all black against the snow. We began to play, and since this day so sadly begun was to end in joy, when I went up, before playing prisoners' base, to the friend with the sharp voice whom I had heard the first day shouting the name Gilberte, she said to me: "No, no, we know perfectly well you'd rather be on Gilberte's side, besides look, she's signaling to you." She was indeed calling me over to join her camp on the snowy lawn, which the sun, giving it glimmers of pink, the metallic worn surface of an old brocade, was turning into a Field of the Cloth of Gold.[18]

That day which I had so dreaded was, in fact, one of the only ones on which I was not too unhappy.

For, although I no longer thought, now, of anything else but of not allowing a single day to pass without seeing Gilberte (so much so that once when my grandmother had not returned by dinnertime, I could not help saying to myself immediately that if she had been run over by a carriage, I would not be able to go to the Champs-Élysées for a long time; we no longer love anyone else when we are in love), yet those moments when I was with her and which since the day before I had been awaiting so impatiently, for which I had trembled, for which I would have sacrificed everything else, were in no way happy moments; and I knew it very well for they were the only moments in my life on which I concentrated a meticulous, fierce attention, and that attention did not discover in them one atom of pleasure.

All the time I was away from Gilberte, I needed to see her because, constantly trying to form a picture of her for myself, in the end I could not do it, and no longer knew precisely to what my love corresponded. And then she had never yet told me she loved me. Quite the contrary, she had often claimed there were boys she liked better than me, that I was a good enough friend she was always willing to play with, though too distracted, not involved enough in the game; finally, she had often given me apparent signs of coldness that might have shaken my belief that for her I was someone different from the others, if the source of that belief had been the love Gilberte might feel for me, and not, as was the case, the love I felt for her, which rendered it far more resistant, since this made it depend entirely on the manner in which I was obliged, by an inner necessity, to think of Gilberte. But the feelings I had for her, I myself had not yet declared to her. Certainly, on every page of my notebooks I copied out her name and address endlessly, but at the sight of those indeterminate lines which I wrote without inducing her to think any more about me because of that, which made her take up so much apparent space around me without being any more involved in my life, I felt discouraged because they spoke to me not of Gilberte, who would not even see them, but of my own desire, which they seemed to show me as something purely personal, unreal, tedious, and impotent. The most urgent thing was that we should see each other, Gilberte and I, and that we should be able to make a reciprocal avowal of our love, which until then would not so to speak have begun. No doubt the various reasons that made me so impatient to see her would have been less imperious for a grown man. When we are older, more skilled in the cultivation of our pleasures, we are sometimes content with the enjoyment of thinking about a woman as I thought about Gilberte, without worrying about whether that image corresponds to the reality, and also with the pleasure of loving her without needing to be certain that she loves us; or we forgo the pleasure of confessing our warm feelings for her, in order to encourage the hardiness of hers for us, imitating those Japanese gardeners who, to obtain one lovelier flower, sacrifice several others. But during the period when I loved Gilberte, I still believed that Love really existed outside of us; that, allowing us at the very most to remove obstacles in our way, it offered its joys in an order which we were not free to alter; it seemed to me that if I had, on my own initiative, substituted for the sweetness of confession the simulation of indifference, I would not only have deprived myself of one of the joys of which I had dreamed most often but that I would have fabricated for myself in my own way a love that was artificial and without value, without any connection to the real one, whose mysterious and preexisting paths I would have had to forgo following.

But when I reached the Champs-Élysées–and when, before anything else, I would be able to confront my love, so as to subject it to the necessary corrections, with its living cause, independent of me–as soon as I was in the presence of that Gilberte Swann on the sight of whom I had counted to refresh the images that my tired memory could no longer recapture, of that Gilberte Swann with whom I had played yesterday, and whom I had just been moved to greet and recognize by a blind instinct like that which, when we are walking, sets one of our feet in front of the other before we have had time to think, immediately it was as if she and the little girl who was the object of my dreams had been two different creatures. For example if, since the day before, I had been carrying in my memory two blazing eyes in full and shining cheeks, Gilberte's face now presented me insistently with something that quite specifically I had not recalled, a certain sharp tapering of the nose, which, instantaneously associating itself

with certain other features, assumed the importance of those characteristics which in natural history define a whole species, and trans-
muted her into a little girl of the type that have pointed snouts. While
I was preparing to take advantage of this longed-for moment in order
to devote myself to submitting the image of Gilberte which I had prepared before coming, and which I could no longer find again in my
mind, to an amendment that would allow me, in the long hours when
I was alone, to be sure it was truly she whom I was recalling, that it
was truly my love for her that I was augmenting little by little like a
book as it is being written, she would pass me a ball; and, like the idealist philosopher whose body makes allowances for the external world
in the reality of which his intelligence does not believe, the same self
who had made me greet her before I identified her, hastened to make
me take the ball she was holding out to me (as if she were a friend
with whom I had come here to play, and not a sister soul with whom
I had come to be united), made me exchange with her, for the sake of
decorum, until the hour when she went off, a thousand friendly and
meaningless remarks and thus kept me both from preserving a silence
during which I could at last have laid hands once more on the urgent
truant image and from uttering the words that might have brought
about the decisive progress in our love, the hope of which I was
obliged each time to postpone until the following afternoon. It did,
however, make some progress. One day when we had gone off with
Gilberte to the booth of the vendor who was particularly nice to us—
for it was to her that M. Swann sent for his spice cake,[19] and for health
reasons, he consumed a great deal of it, suffering from ethnic eczema
and the Prophets' constipation—Gilberte showed me with a smile two
little boys who were like the little artist and the little naturalist in children's storybooks. For one of them did not want a stick of red barley
sugar because he preferred violet, and the other, tears in his eyes, was
refusing the plum his nanny wanted to buy for him because, he finally said with passion: "I like the other plum better, because it has a
worm!" I bought two one-sou marbles. I gazed with admiration at the
agates, luminous and captive in their separate wooden bowl, precious
in my eyes because they were as blond and beaming as young girls

and because they cost fifty centimes apiece. Gilberte, who was given a great deal more money than I was, asked me which I thought was the most beautiful. They had the molten transparency of life itself. I did not want to make her sacrifice a single one of them. I would have liked her to be able to buy them, liberate them, all. Yet I pointed to one which was the same color as her eyes. Gilberte took it, looked for its golden ray of light, stroked it, paid its ransom, but immediately handed her captive over to me saying: "Here, it's for you, I'm giving it to you, keep it as a souvenir."

Another time, still preoccupied by the desire to hear La Berma in a classical play, I had asked her if she happened to own a little book in which Bergotte talked about Racine, and which one could no longer find. She had asked me to remind her of its exact title and that evening I had addressed an express letter to her, writing on the envelope that name, Gilberte Swann, which I had so often copied out in my notebooks. The next day she brought me a packet tied up in mauve ribbons and sealed with white wax containing the little book, which she had asked someone to find for her. "You see? It really is the one you asked for," she said, taking from her muff the letter I had sent her. But on the address of this *pneumatique*[20]—which, only yesterday, was nothing, was merely a *petit bleu* which I had written, and which, now that a telegraph boy had delivered it to Gilberte's concierge and a servant had carried it to her room, had become this priceless thing, one of the *petits bleus* she had received that day—it was hard for me to recognize the insignificant, solitary lines of my handwriting under the printed circles apposed to it by the post office, under the inscriptions added in pencil by one of the telegraph messengers, signs of actual realization, stamps from the outside world, violet bands symbolizing life, which for the first time came to espouse, sustain, uplift, delight my dream.

And there was also one day when she said to me: "You know, you can call me Gilberte, I'm going to call you by your first name anyway. It's too tiresome otherwise." Yet for a while she went on simply calling me *vous*[21] and when I pointed this out to her, she smiled, and composing, constructing a sentence like the ones in grammar books of foreign languages whose only aim is to make us use a new word, she ended it with my given name. And remembering later what I had felt then, I could distinguish within it the impression that I had been held for a moment in her mouth, I myself, naked, without any of the social terms and conditions that also belonged, either to her other friends, or, when she said my family name, to my parents, and of which her lips—in the effort she made, rather like her father, to articulate the words she wanted to emphasize—seemed to strip me, undress me, as one removes the skin from a fruit of which only the pulp can be eaten, while her gaze, adopting the same new degree of intimacy as her words, reached me more directly also, while at the same time showing its awareness of this, its pleasure and even its gratitude, by accompanying itself with a smile.

But in the moment itself, I could not appreciate the value of these new pleasures. They were given, not by the little girl I loved, to me who loved her, but by the other, the one I played with, to my other self who possessed neither the memory of the true Gilberte, nor the inalienable heart which alone could have known the price of such a happiness, because it alone had desired it. Even after returning home I did not savor them, for, each day, the same need which made me hope that the next day I would be able to enjoy a clear, calm, happy contemplation of Gilberte, that she would at last confess her love for me, explaining why she had to hide it from me until now, also forced me to regard the past as nothing, to look ahead of me only, to consider the small attentions she had shown me not in themselves and as if they were enough, but as new rungs on which to set my foot, new rungs which would permit me to take another step up and at last attain the happiness I had not yet found.

If she gave me these signs of friendliness from time to time, she also hurt me by seeming not to be pleased to see me, and this often happened on the very days I had most counted on for the realization of my hopes. I was sure that Gilberte would come to the Champs-Élysées and I felt an elation that seemed to me only the vague anticipation of a great happiness when—entering the drawing room first thing in the morning to kiss Mama, who was already dressed to go out, the tower of her black hair fully constructed, and her lovely plump white hands still smelling of soap—I learned, seeing a column of dust standing by itself above the piano and hearing a barrel organ playing "En Revenant de la Revue"[22] under the window, that until nightfall winter would be receiving the unexpected and radiant visit of a day of spring. While we were eating lunch, the lady opposite, by opening her casement, had sent flying in the blink of an eye, from next to my chair—streaking the entire width of our dining room in a single bound—a beam of light that had settled there for its afternoon rest and returned to continue it a moment later. At school, during the one o'clock class,[23] the sun made me languish with impatience and boredom by trailing a glimmer of gold over my desk, like an invitation to a party I would not be able to attend before three o'clock, the hour when Françoise came to pick me up at the school gate and we made our way toward the Champs-Élysées through streets decorated with light, choked with crowds, where the balconies, unsealed by the sun and vaporous, floated before the houses like clouds of gold. Alas, in the Champs-Élysées I did not see Gilberte, she had not arrived yet. Motionless on the lawn fed by the invisible sun which here and there ignited the tip of a stalk of grass, while the pigeons that had landed on it looked like ancient sculptures which the gardener's pick had brought back up to the surface of the venerable soil, I stood with my eyes fixed on the horizon, expecting at any moment to see the image of Gilberte following her governess appear behind the statue, which seemed to hold out the child it was carrying, streaming with rays of light, to the benediction of the sun. The old lady who read *Les Débats* was sitting in her seat, still in the same spot; she hailed a park keeper, to whom she made a friendly gesture with her hand, calling out to him: "What fine weather!" And when the chair attendant approached to collect the price of the seat, she smirked and simpered as she put the ten-centime ticket away in the opening of her glove, as if it were a bouquet for which she was seeking, out of kindness toward the giver, the most flattering place possible. When she had found it, she performed a circular motion with her neck, straightened her boa, and fastened upon the attendant, showing her the bit of yellow paper sticking out over her wrist, the beautiful smile with which a woman, showing her bodice to a young man, says to him: "Recognize your roses?"

I led Françoise out as far as the Arc de Triomphe hoping to meet Gilberte, we did not find her, and I was returning to the lawn convinced that now she would not be coming, when, in front of the merry-go-round, the little girl with the sharp voice flung herself at me: "Quick, quick, Gilberte's already been here for a quarter of an hour. She's going soon. We were waiting for you to make up a game of prisoners' base." While I was going up the avenue des Champs-Élysées, Gilberte had come by way of the rue Boissy-d'Anglas, Mademoiselle having taken advantage of the fine weather to do some shopping for her; and M. Swann was coming to pick up his daughter. So it was my fault; I should not have left the lawn; for one never knew for certain which way Gilberte would come, if it would be later or earlier, and in the end this waiting caused me to be more deeply moved, not only by the whole of the Champs-Élysées and the entire extent of the afternoon, a sort of immense expanse of space and time at each point and at each moment of which it was possible that Gilberte's image would appear, but even by that image itself, because behind that image I felt there lay concealed the reason why it had been fired into my heart at four o'clock instead of two-thirty, topped by a hat for paying calls rather than a beret for playing, in front of the "Ambassadeurs"[24] and not between the two puppet theaters, I could divine one of those occupations in which I could not follow Gilberte and which forced her to go out or stay at home, I touched the mystery of her unknown life. It was this mystery, too, that disturbed me when, running on orders from the little girl with the sharp voice to begin our game of prisoners' base right away, I saw Gilberte, so brusque and lively with us, curtsying to the lady with *Les Débats* (who was saying to her: "What lovely sunshine, it's like a burning fire"), talking to her with a shy smile, with a formal air which called to my mind the different young girl that Gilberte must be at home with her parents, with the friends of her parents, when paying calls, in the whole of her other existence which eluded me. But of that existence no one gave me so strong an impression as did M. Swann, who came a little later to find his daughter. For he and Mme. Swann–because their daughter lived in their home, because her studies, her games, her friendships depended on them–contained for me, like Gilberte, perhaps even more than Gilberte, as was proper for gods all-powerful with respect to her, in whom it must have had its source, an inaccessible strangeness, a painful charm. Everything that concerned them was the object of a preoccupation so constant on my part that on the days when, as on these, M. Swann (whom I had seen so often in the past without his having aroused my curiosity, when he was on friendly terms with my parents) came to pick Gilberte up in the Champs-Élysées, once the pounding of my heart that had been excited by the appearance of his gray hat and traveling cape had subsided, his appearance still impressed me like that of a historical character about whom we have just been reading a series of books and whose least peculiarities impassion us. His relations with the Comte de Paris, which, when I heard them discussed at Combray, had left me indifferent, now assumed for me something wonderful, as if no one else had ever known the Orléans; they caused him to stand out vividly against the vulgar background of people of different classes out for a walk who were crowding that path of the Champs-Élysées, and in the midst of whom I admired his consenting to appear without demanding of them any special consideration, which none of them dreamed of giving him anyway, so profound was the incognito in which he was wrapped.

He responded politely to the greetings of Gilberte's friends, even to mine although he had quarreled with my family, but without appearing to know me. (This reminded me that he had, however, seen me quite often in the country; a memory I had retained, but somewhere in a dim place, because ever since I had seen Gilberte again, for me Swann was preeminently her father, and no longer Swann of Combray; as the ideas with which I now linked his name were different from the ideas which had once formed the network in which it was included and which I no longer ever used when I wanted to think about him, he had become a new person; I did attach him, however, by an artificial, secondary, and transversal line to our guest of earlier times; and since nothing had any value for me anymore except to the extent that my love could profit from it, it was with a burst of shame and regret at not being able to erase them that I returned to the years when, in the eyes of this same Swann who was at this moment before me in the Champs-Élysées and to whom, happily, Gilberte had perhaps not mentioned my name, I had so often in the evenings made myself ridiculous by sending word asking Mama to come up to my room and say goodnight to me, while she was having coffee with him, my father, and my grandparents at the table in the garden.) He told Gilberte he would let her play one game, that he could wait a quarter of an hour, and sitting down like anyone else on an iron chair, paid for his ticket with the same hand which Philippe VII[25] had so often held in his own, while we began playing on the lawn, putting to flight the pigeons whose beautiful heart-shaped iridescent bodies, like the lilacs of the bird kingdom, went to seek refuge as though in so many sanctuaries, one on the large stone vase to which its beak, by disappearing into it, imparted the gesture, and assigned the purpose, of offering in abundance the fruits or seeds which the bird seemed to be pecking from it, another on the forehead of the statue, which it seemed to crown with one of those enameled objects whose polychrome varies the monotony of the stone in certain ancient works of art, and with an attribute which, when the goddess carries it, earns her a particular epithet, and makes her, as does for a mortal woman a different first name, a new divinity.

On one of those sunny days that had not fulfilled my hopes, I did not have the courage to hide my disappointment from Gilberte.

"I had so many things to ask you," I said to her. "I thought that today was going to mean such a lot to our friendship. And as soon as you get here, you have to leave again! Try to come early tomorrow, so I can finally talk to you."

Her face shone and she was jumping with joy as she answered me:

"Tomorrow, you may depend upon it, my dear friend, I won't be coming at all! I've got a big tea party; nor the day after tomorrow, either, I'm going to a friend's house to watch the arrival of King Theodosius[26] from her windows, it will be splendid, and then the day after we're going to *Michel Strogoff*[27] and then after that, Christmas will be coming soon and the New Year's holidays. Maybe they'll take me to the Midi.[28] How nice that would be! Though it will mean I won't have a Christmas tree; anyway, if I stay in Paris, I won't be coming here because I'll be paying calls with Mama. Good-bye, there's Papa, he's calling me."

I returned home with Françoise through streets that were still bedecked with sunlight, as on the evening of a holiday that is over. I could scarcely drag my legs along.

"It's not a bit surprising," said Françoise. "This weather is not right for the time of the year, it's far too hot. Alas! My Lord, think of all the folk around and about that must be ill today. It makes one think that things are all awry in the heavens above, as well!"

I repeated to myself, stifling my sobs, the words in which Gilberte had exploded with joy at the prospect of not coming back to the Champs-Élysées for such a long time. But already the charm with which, by the mere act of thinking, my mind was filled as soon as I thought about her, and the special, unique position—painful though it was—in which I was inevitably placed in relation to Gilberte by the internal constraint of a mental habit had begun to add, even to this sign of indifference, something romantic, and in the midst of my tears a smile formed that was simply the timid adumbration of a kiss. And when it was time for the mail to come, I said to myself that evening as on every evening: "I'm going to get a letter from Gilberte, she's going to tell me at last that she has always loved me, and explain the mysterious reason why she has been forced to hide it from me until now, to pretend she could be happy without seeing me, the reason why she has disguised herself as the other Gilberte who is merely a playmate."

Every evening I liked to imagine this letter, I would believe I was reading it, I would recite each sentence of it to myself. All of a sudden I stopped in alarm. I realized that if I were to receive a letter from Gilberte, it could not be that one anyway since I was the one who had just written it. And from then on, I forced myself to turn my thoughts away from the words I would have liked her to write to me, for fear that by articulating them, I would exclude precisely those—the dearest, the most desired—from the field of all possible compositions. Even if through an improbable coincidence it had been precisely the letter that I had invented that Gilberte on her own account addressed to me, recognizing my work in it I would not have had the impression of receiving something that did not come from me, something real, new, a happiness external to my mind, independent of my will, truly given by love.

Meanwhile I reread a page which had not been written to me by Gilberte, but which at least came to me from her, that page by Bergotte on the beauty of the old myths that inspired Racine, and which, next to the agate marble, I kept near me always. I was moved by the goodness of my friend who had had someone find it for me; and because everyone needs to discover reasons for his passion, so much so that he is happy to recognize in the person he loves qualities which literature or conversation have taught him are among those worthy of inspiring love, so much so that he assimilates them by imitation and makes them new reasons for his love, even if these qualities were the most diametrically opposed to those his love would have sought so long as it remained spontaneous—as Swann had done once upon a time, with the aesthetic nature of Odette's beauty—I, who had at first loved Gilberte, back in Combray, because of all that was unknown about her life, into which I would have liked to hurl myself, become incarnated, abandoning my own life which was no longer anything to me, I now thought, as of an inestimable advantage, that of this life of mine, too well known, disdained, Gilberte might one day become the humble servant, the companionable and comfortable collaborator who in the evening, helping me in my work, would compare and collate pamphlets for me. As for Bergotte, that infinitely wise and almost divine old man because of whom I had first loved Gilberte, even before I saw her, now it was above all because of Gilberte that I loved him. With as much pleasure as the pages he had written on Racine, I looked at the paper closed with great seals of white wax and tied with a cascade of mauve ribbons in which she had brought them to me. I kissed the agate marble which was the best part of my friend's heart, the part that was not frivolous, but faithful, and which even though adorned with the mysterious charm of Gilberte's life remained close to me, lived in my bedroom, slept in my bed. But as for the beauty of that stone, and the beauty also of those pages by Bergotte, which I was so pleased to associate with the idea of my love for Gilberte, as if in the moments when that love appeared to me to be nothing at all they gave it a sort of substance, I saw that they were anterior to that love, that they did not resemble it, that their elements had been determined by talent or by the laws of mineralogy before Gilberte knew me, that nothing in the book or in the stone would have been different if Gilberte had not loved me and that consequently nothing entitled me to read in them a message of happiness. And while my love, ceaselessly expecting from the next day an avowal of Gilberte's love, annulled and undid each evening the badly done work of the day, in the darkness inside me an unknown seamstress did not leave the pulled threads in the scrap heap but arranged them, with no concern for pleasing me or working for my happiness, in the different order to which she gave all her work. Showing no particular interest in my love, nor beginning by deciding that I was indeed loved, she gathered up those of Gilberte's actions which had seemed inexplicable to me, along with her faults, which I had excused. Then the first and the second acquired a meaning. It seemed to say, this new order, that when I saw that Gilberte, instead of coming to the Champs-Élysées, attended a party, went shopping with her governess, and prepared to be away over the New Year's holidays, I was wrong to think: "It's because she's frivolous or submissive." For she would have ceased to be either if she had loved me, and if she had been forced to obey it would have been with the same despair that I felt on the days when I did not see her. It told me further, this new order, that I must after all know what it was to love since I loved Gilberte; it pointed out to me the perpetual concern I felt to show myself to advantage in her eyes, because of which I tried to persuade my mother to buy Françoise a waterproof coat and a hat with a blue ostrich feather, or better still not to continue sending me to the Champs-Élysées with that maid who made me blush (to which my mother answered that I was unfair to Françoise, that she was a good woman and devoted to us), and also that exclusive need to see Gilberte because of which months in advance I thought only of trying to learn at what time of the year she would be leaving Paris and where she would be going, finding even the most pleasant countryside a place of exile if she was not going to be there, and wanting only to stay in Paris all the time as long as I could see her at the Champs-Élysées; and it had no difficulty showing me that I would not find that concern, or that need, behind Gilberte's actions. She on the contrary appreciated her governess, without worrying about what I thought of her. She found it natural not to come to the Champs-Élysées, if she was going to make some purchases with Mademoiselle, pleasant if she was going out with her mother. And even supposing she would have allowed me to spend the holidays in the same place as she, at least in choosing that place she considered her parents' desires, the thousand amusements she had heard about, and not in the least that this was the place where my family was intending to send me. When she assured me from time to time that she liked me less than one of her other friends, less than she had liked me the day before because I had made her lose the game through my carelessness, I would ask her to forgive me, I would ask her what I should do so that she would begin to like me again as much as the others, so that she would like me more than them; I wanted her to tell me that it was already done, I begged her for it as if she could change her affection for me as she wished, as I wished, in order to please me, merely by the words that she would say, depending on my good or my bad behavior. Did I not know, then, that what I myself felt, for her, depended neither on her actions nor on my own will?

And, finally, this new order designed by the invisible seamstress showed me that if we may wish that the actions of a person who has hurt us up to now were not sincere, they are followed by a clarity against which our wishes are powerless and to which, rather than to them, we must address ourselves in asking what that person's actions will be tomorrow.

These new words were heard by my love; they persuaded it that the next day would not be different from what all the other days had been; that Gilberte's feeling for me, already too old to be able to change, was indifference; that in my friendship with Gilberte, I was the only one who loved. "It's true," my love answered, "there's nothing more to be done with this friendship, it won't change." And so, the very next day (or waiting for a public holiday if there was one coming up soon, or an anniversary, or the New Year perhaps, one of those days which are not like the others, when time makes a fresh start by rejecting the heritage of the past, by not accepting the legacy of its sorrows) I would ask Gilberte to give up our old friendship and lay the foundations of a new one.

I always had within reach of my hand a map of Paris which, because one could distinguish on it the street where M. and Mme. Swann lived, seemed to me to contain a treasure. And for pleasure, out of a sort of chivalrous loyalty also, apropos of anything at all, I would say the name of that street, until my father would ask, not being, as were my mother and grandmother, fully informed about my love:

"Now why do you talk about that street all the time, there's nothing extraordinary about it, it's a very pleasant street to live on because it's two steps from the Bois, but there are ten others quite like it."

I contrived at every turn to make my parents say the name Swann; of course I repeated it to myself in my own mind incessantly; but I also needed to hear the delicious sound of it and to have someone else play me this music the silent reading of which was not enough. The name Swann, which I had known for such a long time, was for me also, now, as happens for certain aphasics with the most everyday words, a new name. It was always present in my mind and yet my mind could not grow accustomed to it. I took it apart, I spelled it, its orthography was a surprise to me. And at the same time that it had ceased to be familiar, it had ceased to appear innocent. The joy I felt at hearing it I believed was so guilty that it seemed to me others guessed my thoughts and changed the conversation if I tried to lead it there. I resorted to subjects that still touched upon Gilberte, I recited the same words endlessly, and although I knew they were only words—words spoken far away from her, which she could not hear, words without potency that repeated what was, but could not modify it—yet it seemed to me that by dint of thus feeling, handling everything that touched Gilberte I would perhaps make something happy emerge from it. I told my parents again that Gilberte liked her governess very much, as if that proposition enunciated for the hundredth time were at last going to result in the sudden entrance of Gilberte, coming to live with us forever. I resumed my praise of the old lady who read *Les Débats* (I had hinted to my parents that she was an ambassadress or perhaps a royal highness) and I continued to celebrate her beauty, her magnificence, her nobility, until the day I said that from what I had heard Gilberte call her, her name must be Mme. Blatin.

"Oh, now I know who she is!" exclaimed my mother while I felt myself blushing from shame. "On guard! On guard! as your poor grandfather would have said. So she's the one you find so beautiful! Why, she's horrible and always has been. She's the widow of an usher. You don't remember when you were little the lengths I went to to avoid her at the gymnastics class where, though she didn't know me, she would come up to me and try to talk with the excuse of wanting to tell me you were 'too nice looking for a boy.' She always had a mania for getting to know people and she must indeed be rather mad as I always thought, if she really knows Mme. Swann. For though her background is quite common, at least there was never anything said against her so far as I know. But she always had to cultivate a new acquaintance. She's horrible, frightfully vulgar, and a troublemaker into the bargain."

As for Swann, in order to try to resemble him, I would spend all my time at the table pulling on my nose and rubbing my eyes. My father would say: "The child has no sense, he'll make himself quite hideous." I would especially have liked to be as bald as Swann. He seemed to me a person so extraordinary that I found it amazing that people I knew actually knew him too and that the chance events of an ordinary day might bring one face-to-face with him. And one time, my mother, in the course of telling us, as she did every evening at dinner, about the errands she had run that afternoon, merely by saying:

"Speaking of which, guess who I ran into in Trois Quartiers,[29] at the umbrella counter: Swann," caused the center of her story, so very dry for me, to blossom with a mysterious flower. What a delectable melancholy pleasure, to learn that that very afternoon, profiling his supernatural form against the crowd, Swann had gone to buy an umbrella! Among the great and tiny events, equally unimportant, this one alone awoke in me those peculiar vibrations by which my love for Gilberte was perpetually stirred. My father said I was not interested in anything because I did not listen when they talked about the political consequences that might follow from the visit of King Theodosius, at this moment the guest of France and, it was claimed, its ally. But how keenly, on the other hand, I wanted to know if Swann was wearing his traveling cape!

"Did you say hello to each other?" I asked.

"Why, naturally," answered my mother, who always seemed to be afraid that, were she to admit there was any coolness between them and Swann, people would have tried to bring about a reconciliation closer than she wished, because of Mme. Swann, whom she did not want to know. "It was he who came up and spoke to me, I didn't see him."

"Then you haven't quarreled?"

"Quarreled? Now what makes you think we might have quarreled?" she answered briskly, as if I had assaulted the fiction of her good relations with Swann and tried to effect a "rapprochement."

"He might be cross with you for not inviting him anymore."

"One isn't obliged to invite everyone; does he invite me? I don't know his wife."

"But at Combray he used to come."

"Well, yes! He came at Combray, and now in Paris he has other things to do and so have I. But I promise you we didn't look in the least like two people who had quarreled. We stood there together for a moment because they hadn't yet brought him his parcel. He asked after you, he told me you played with his daughter," added my mother, stunning me with the prodigious fact that I existed in Swann's mind, even more, that I existed there in so complete a manner that, when I trembled with love there before him in the Champs-Élysées, he knew my name, who my mother was, and could amalgamate around my qualifications as playmate of his daughter certain facts about my grandparents, their family, the place where we lived, certain details of our past life which were perhaps unknown even to me. But my mother did not seem to have found any particular charm in that counter at Trois Quartiers where she had represented for Swann, at the moment when he saw her, a definite person with whom he had memories in common that had inspired the impulse to approach her, the gesture of greeting her.

Nor did she or my father either seem to find, in talking about Swann's grandparents, about the title of honorary stockbroker, a pleasure that surpassed all others. My imagination had singled out and sanctified one particular family from within the social Paris just as it had from within the Paris of stone one particular house whose carriage entrance it had sculpted and whose windows it had made precious. But I was the only one who could see these ornaments. In the same way that my father and mother regarded the house that Swann lived in as similar to the other houses built at the same time in the neighborhood of the Bois, so Swann's family seemed to them of the same sort as many other families of stockbrokers. They judged it more favorably or less depending on the degree to which it shared in merits common to the rest of the universe and did not see in it anything unique. On the contrary, what they appreciated in it they encountered to an equal, or higher, degree elsewhere. And so, after having agreed that the house was well situated, they would talk about another that was better situated, but that had nothing to do with Gilberte, or about financiers a cut above her grandfather; and if they had seemed for a moment to be of the same opinion as me, it was because of a misunderstanding that would soon be dispelled. For, in order to perceive in everything that surrounded Gilberte an indefinable quality analogous in the world of emotions to what infrared may be in the world of colors, my parents would have needed that supplementary and ephemeral sense with which I had been endowed by love.

On the days when Gilberte had let me know she would not be coming to the Champs-Élysées, I would try to go for a walk that brought me a little closer to her. Sometimes I would lead Françoise on a pilgrimage before the house where the Swanns lived. I would make her repeat endlessly what, through the governess, she had learned relating to Mme. Swann. "It seems she puts a good deal of trust in her medals. You won't find her going off on a trip if she's heard an owl hooting, or something ticking like a clock inside the wall, or if she's seen a cat at midnight, or if the wood furniture creaks. Oh, yes! She's a person of great faith!" I was so in love with Gilberte that if, along the way, I saw their old butler walking a dog, my emotion would force me to stop, I would stare at his white whiskers with eyes full of passion. Françoise would say:

"What's wrong with you?"

Then we would continue on our way until we reached their carriage entrance, where a concierge different from any other concierge, and steeped even to the braid of his livery in the same painful charm I had felt in the name Gilberte, seemed to know that I was one of those people whom a primordial unworthiness would prohibit forever from penetrating into the mysterious life that he was charged with guarding and on which the windows of the entresol seemed conscious of being closed, resembling far less, between the stately fall of their muslin curtains, any other windows than they did Gilberte's own eyes. At other times, we would go down the boulevards and I would take up a position at the corner of the rue Duphot; I had been told that here one could often see Swann going past on his way to the dentist; and my imagination so differentiated Gilberte's father from the rest of humanity, his presence in the midst of the real world introduced into it such magic, that, even before I reached the Madeleine, I was moved at the thought of approaching a street where I might suddenly encounter that supernatural apparition.

But most often—when I was not going to see Gilberte—since I had learned that Mme. Swann went for a walk almost every day in the allée des Acacias, around the Grand Lac, and in the allée de la

Reine-Marguerite,[30] I would steer Françoise in the direction of the Bois de Boulogne. For me it was like those zoological gardens in which one sees diverse flora and contrasting landscapes brought together in one place; where, after a hill, one finds a grotto, a meadow, rocks, a stream, a ditch, a hill, a marsh, but knows they are there only to provide the frolicking of the hippopotamus, zebras, crocodiles, albino rabbits, bears, and heron with an appropriate environment or a picturesque setting; the Bois too, equally complex, bringing together as it does diverse enclosed little worlds—first a farm planted with red trees, American oaks, like an agricultural estate in Virginia, then a stand of firs at the edge of the lake, or a forest from which would rise suddenly in her supple fur, with the lovely eyes of an animal, some woman walking quickly—it was the Garden of Woman; and—like the Alley of the Myrtles in *The Aeneid*[31]—planted for their sake with trees of a single species, the allée des Acacias was a favorite spot of the most famous Beauties. Just as, from a long way off, the top of the rock from which it will dive into the water thrills the children who know they are about to see the sea lion, so, well before reaching the allée des Acacias, first their fragrance, which, radiating all around, allowed one to sense from a distance the approach and the singularity of a powerful, soft, vegetative entity, then, when I drew near, the glimpsed crest of their greenery, light and childishly graceful, with its easy elegance, its coquettish cut, its thin material, on which hundreds of flowers had swooped down like vibratile winged colonies of precious parasites, and, finally, even their name, feminine, indolent, and sweet—all of this made my heart pound, but with a worldly desire, like those waltzes which remind us only of the names of the beautiful guests whom the usher announces as they enter the ballroom. I had been told that in the avenue I would see certain fashionable women who, even though they were not all married, were habitually mentioned along with Mme. Swann, but most often by their professional name; their new name, when they had one, was only a sort of incognito which those who wanted to talk about them took care to remove in order to make themselves understood. Thinking that Beauty—in the order of feminine elegance—was governed by occult laws into the knowledge of which these women had been initiated, and that they had the power to bring it into being, I accepted in advance as a revelation the vision of their clothes, their carriages and horses, a thousand details deep within which I placed my belief as in an interior soul which gave the cohesiveness of a masterpiece to that ephemeral and shifting tableau. But it was Mme. Swann whom I wanted to see, and I waited for her to pass, as moved as if she were Gilberte, whose parents, steeped like all that surrounded her in her charm, excited in me as much love as she did, indeed a disturbance that was even more painful (because their point of contact with her was that domestic part of her life which was forbidden to me), and lastly (because I soon knew, as will be seen, that they did not like my playing with her) that feeling of veneration which we always have for those who wield unrestrained power to do us harm.

I assigned the first place to simplicity, in the order of aesthetic merits and social grandeur, when I saw Mme. Swann on foot, wearing a cloth polonaise, on her head a little toque trimmed with a pheasant wing, a bouquet of violets at her bodice, hurrying down the allée des Acacias as if it were merely the shortest way to return home and answering with a wink the gentlemen in carriages who, recognizing her figure from far away, bowed to her and said to themselves that no one was as smart. But in place of simplicity, it was ostentation that I put on the highest rank, if, after I had forced Françoise, who was exhausted and said her legs were "folding up," to walk back and forth for an hour, at last I would see, emerging from the avenue that comes from the Porte Dauphine–the picture for me of royal dignity, of a sovereign's arrival, an impression such as no real queen has since been able to give me, because my notion of their power was less vague and more founded upon experience–borne along by two flying fiery horses as slender and smoothly turned as in the drawings of Constantin Guys,[32] carrying an enormous coachman settled on his seat and wrapped in furs like a Cossack, next to a little groom who recalled the "tiger" of "the late Baudenord"[33] I would see–or rather I would feel it imprint its form on my heart with a neat and exhausting wound–a matchless victoria, in its design a little high and with allusions to the old forms showing through its "dernier cri" opulence, in the depths of which Mme. Swann lay back carelessly, her hair now blond with a single gray lock and girded with a thin band of flowers, most often violets, from which descended long veils, in her hand a mauve parasol, on her lips an ambiguous smile in which I saw only the beneficence of a monarch and in which there was, more than anything else, a cocotte's provocativeness, and which she inclined gently on the people who bowed to her. That smile in reality said to some of them: "I remember it very well—it was exquisite!"; to others: "How I would have loved to! What bad luck!"; to others: "Why yes, if you like! I'll stay in line for a moment longer and cut out as soon as I can." When strangers passed, she would still allow an idle smile to linger around her lips, as though it were turned toward the expectation or the memory of a friend, which made people say: "How beautiful she is!" And for certain men only she had a smile that was sour, stiff, reticent, and cold, and meant: "Yes, you beast, I know you have the tongue of a viper, that you can't keep from talking! But do I care about you? Do I?" Coquelin[34] went past holding forth among a group of attentive friends, and with his hand gave a broad theatrical hello to the people in the carriages. But I was thinking only about Mme. Swann and I pretended I had not seen her yet, for I knew that once she drew level with the Tir aux Pigeons[35] she would tell her coachman to cut out of the line and stop so that she could come back down the avenue on foot. And on the days when I felt I had the courage to pass close to her, I would drag Françoise in that direction. At a certain moment, in fact, in the footpath, walking toward us, I would see Mme. Swann letting the long train of her mauve dress spread out behind her, clothed, as the common people imagine queens, in fabrics and rich finery that other women did not wear, lowering her eyes now and then to the handle of her parasol, paying little attention to the people passing, as if her great business and her goal were to take some exercise, without thinking that she was being observed and that all heads were turned toward her. But now and then when she had looked back to call her greyhound, she would imperceptibly cast a circular gaze around her.

Even those who did not know her were alerted by something singular and excessive—or perhaps by a telepathic radiation like those that triggered bursts of applause from the ignorant crowd at moments when La Berma was sublime—that this must be some well-known person. They would ask one another: "Who is she?," or sometimes question a passing stranger, or promise themselves they would remember the way she was dressed as a reference for some better-informed friend who would immediately enlighten them. Others, half stopping in their walk, would say:

"Do you know who that is? Mme. Swann! That means nothing to you? Odette de Crécy?"

"Odette de Crécy? Why in fact I was just wondering . . . Those sad eyes . . . But you know she can't be as young as she once was! I remember I slept with her the day MacMahon resigned."

"You'd better not remind her of it. She's now Mme. Swann, wife of a gentleman in the Jockey Club who's a friend of the Prince of Wales. But she's still superb."

"Yes, but if only you'd known her then—how pretty she was! She lived in a very strange little house filled with Chinese bric-a-brac. I remember we were bothered by the newsboys shouting outside, in the end she made me get up."

Though I could not hear these comments, I did perceive all around her the indistinct murmur of celebrity. My heart raced with impatience at the thought that yet another instant was going to pass before the moment when all these people, among whom I was disconsolate not to find a certain mulatto banker by whom I felt I was despised, would see the young stranger to whom they had paid no attention bow (without knowing her, in fact, but I felt I was authorized to do so because my parents knew her husband and I was her daughter's playmate) to that woman whose reputation for beauty, improper behavior, and elegance was universal. But I was already very close to Mme. Swann, so I raised my hat to her with a motion so large, so extended, so prolonged, that she could not help smiling. People laughed. As for her, she had never seen me with Gilberte, she did not know my name, but for her I was—like one of the keepers of the Bois, or the boatman or the ducks on the lake to which she threw bread—one of those secondary, familiar, anonymous figures, as lacking in individual character as an "extra" onstage, of her outings in the Bois. On certain days when I had not seen her in the allée des Acacias, I would sometimes find her in the allée de la Reine-Marguerite, where women go who want to be alone, or to appear to want to be alone; she would not remain alone for long, soon joined by some friend, often wearing a gray "topper," whom I did not know and who would talk to her for a long time, while their two carriages followed.

That complexity of the Bois de Boulogne which makes it an artificial place and, in the zoological or mythological sense of the word, a Garden, I discovered again this year as I was crossing it to go to Trianon,[36] on one of the first mornings of this month of November when, in Paris, inside the houses, we are so close to the autumn spectacle, and yet denied it, as it rapidly comes to an end without our witnessing it, that we are filled with a yearning, a veritable fever for the dead leaves that may go so far as to stop us from sleeping. In my closed room, they had been coming for a month now, summoned by my desire to see them, between my thoughts and any object to which I applied myself, and they eddied like those yellow spots that sometimes, whatever we may be looking at, dance in front of our eyes. And that morning, no longer hearing the rain fall as on the days before, seeing the fine weather smile at the corners of the drawn curtains as at the corners of a closed mouth that betrays the secret of its happiness, I had felt that I might be able to look at those yellow leaves as the light passed through them, in their supreme beauty; and being no more able to keep myself from going to see the trees than in earlier days, when the wind blew too hard in my chimney, from departing for the seaside, I had left to go to Trianon, by way of the Bois de Boulogne. It was the hour and it was the season when the Bois seems perhaps most multiform, not only because it is more subdivided, but also because it is subdivided in a different way. Even in the open parts where one embraces a great space, here and there, in front of the dark distant masses of the trees that had no leaves or still had their summer leaves, a double row of orange chestnut trees seemed, as in a picture just begun, to be the only thing painted so far by the scene painter, who had not put any color on the rest, and it offered its avenue in full light for the episodic walk of figures that would be added later on.

Farther off, at a place where the trees were still covered in all their green leaves, one alone, small, squat, lopped, obstinate, shook in the wind a homely head of red hair. Elsewhere, again, there was a first awakening of this May of the leaves, and those of an ampelopsis as marvelous and smiling as a pink winter hawthorn had since that same morning been all in flower. And the Bois had the temporary and artificial look of a tree nursery or a park, where for botanical purposes or in preparation for a festival, they have just placed, among the trees of a common sort that have not yet been transplanted, two or three precious species with fantastic foliage which seem to be reserving an empty space around themselves, giving air, creating light. Thus it was the season when the Bois de Boulogne reveals the most numerous different varieties and juxtaposes the most numerous distinct parts in a composite aggregation. And it was the hour, as well. In the places where the trees still kept their leaves, they seemed to be undergoing a change in substance starting from the point where they were touched by the light of the sun, almost horizontal in the morning as it would be again a few hours later at the moment when in the early twilight it flames up like a lamp, projects over a distance onto the foliage a warm and artificial glow, and sets ablaze the topmost leaves of a tree that remains the dull and incombustible candelabrum of its burning tip. Here, it thickened the leaves of the chestnut trees like bricks and, like a piece of yellow Persian masonry patterned in blue, crudely cemented them against the sky, there on the contrary detached them from it as they clutched at it with their fingers of gold. Halfway up a tree clothed in Japanese ivy, it had grafted and brought into bloom, too dazzling to discern clearly, an immense bouquet as though of red flowers, perhaps a variety of carnation. The different parts of the Bois, merging more completely in summer in the thickness and monotony of their green, were now separated. Open spaces made visible the entrance to almost every one of them, or a sumptuous bit of foliage marked it like a banner. One could distinguish, as on a colored map, Armenonville, the Pré Catelan, Madrid, the Race Course, the shores of the lake. From time to time there would appear some useless construction, a fake grotto, a mill for which the trees parted to make room or which a lawn carried forward on its soft platform. One sensed that the Bois was not merely a wood, that it fulfilled a purpose foreign to the life of its trees, the exhilaration I was experiencing was not caused merely by an admiration for autumn, but by some desire. The great source of a joy which the soul feels at first without recognizing its cause, without understanding that it is motivated by nothing outside. And so I looked at the trees with an unsatisfied tenderness that passed beyond them and went on without my knowing it toward that masterpiece of lovely strolling women which they enclose each day for several hours. I went toward the allée des Acacias. I passed through old groves where the morning light imposed new divisions, pruning the trees, joining together the different stems, and composing bouquets. Deftly it drew toward itself a pair of trees; using the powerful scissors of a ray of light and a shadow, it cut off from each of them half its trunk and branches and, weaving together the two halves that remained, made of them either a single pillar of shadow, delimited by the sunshine around it, or a single phantom of brightness whose tremulous artificial contour was ringed by a net of black shadow. When a ray of sun gilded the highest branches, they seemed, steeped in a sparkling dampness, to emerge alone from the liquid emerald-colored atmosphere in which the entire forest was plunged as though under the sea. For the trees continued to live their own life and, when they had no more leaves, that life shone more brightly on the sheath of green velvet that wrapped their trunks or in the white enamel of the spheres of mistletoe that spangled the tops of the poplars, as round as the sun and the moon in Michelangelo's *Creation*. But forced as they have been for so many years by a sort of grafting to live a life shared with women, they conjured up for me the wood nymph, the lovely quick and colorful worldly beauty whom they cover with their branches as she passes beneath them, obliging her to feel as they do the power of the season; they recalled to me the happy time of my believing youth, when I would avidly come to the places where masterpieces of feminine elegance were created for a few moments among the unconscious and complicitous leaves. But the beauty which the pines and acacias of the Bois de Boulogne made me desire, trees more disturbing because of this than the chestnuts and lilacs of Trianon that I was going to see, was not fixed outside me in the mementos of some historic period, in works of art, in a little temple to the god of Love whose base is piled with golden palmate leaves. I reached the shores of the lake, I went on as far as the Tir aux Pigeons. The idea of perfection which I carried inside me I had conferred at that time upon the height of a victoria, upon the slenderness of those horses, as furious and light as wasps, their eyes bloodshot like the cruel steeds of Diomedes,[37] which now, filled as I was with a desire to see again what I had once loved, as ardent as the desire that had driven me down these same paths many years before, I wanted to see before my eyes again at the moment when Mme. Swann's enormous coachman, watched over by a little groom as fat as a fist and as childlike as Saint George, tried to control those wings of steel as they thrashed about quivering with fear. Alas, now there were only automobiles driven by mustached mechanics with tall footmen by their sides. I wanted to hold in front of my bodily eyes, so as to know if they were as charming as they appeared in the eyes of my memory, women's little hats so low they seemed to be simple crowns. All the hats were now immense, covered with fruits and flowers and varieties of birds. In place of the lovely dresses in which Mme. Swann looked like a queen, I now saw Greco-Saxon tunics with Tanagra[38] folds, and sometimes in the style of the Directoire, made of liberty-silk chiffons sprinkled with flowers like wallpaper. On the heads of the gentlemen who could have walked with Mme. Swann in the allée de la Reine-Marguerite, I did not find the gray hats of earlier times, nor any others. They went out bare-headed. And I no longer had any belief to infuse into all these newelements of the spectacle, to give them substance, unity, life; they went past scattered before me, randomly, without reality, containing in themselves no beauty that my eyes might have tried as they had in earlier times to form into a composition. These were ordinary women, in whose elegance I had no faith and whose dress seemed to me unimportant. But when a belief disappears, there survives it—more and more vigorous so as to mask the absence of the power we have lost to give reality to new things—a fetishistic attachment to the old things which our belief once animated, as if it were in them and not in us that the divine resided and as if our present lack of belief had a contingent cause, the death of the Gods.

How awful! I said to myself: can anyone think these automobiles are as elegant as the old carriages and pairs? I'm probably too old now—but I'm not meant for a world in which women hobble themselves in dresses that aren't even made of cloth. What's the use of walking among these trees, if nothing is left of what used to gather under the delicate reddening leaves, if vulgarity and idiocy have taken the place of the exquisite thing they once framed? How awful! My consolation is to think about the women I once knew, now that there is no more elegance. But how could anyone contemplating these horrible creatures under their hats topped with a birdcage or a vegetable patch even perceive what was so charming about the sight of Mme. Swann in a simple mauve hood or a little hat with a single stiff, straight iris poking up from it? Could I even have made them understand the emotion I felt on winter mornings when I met Mme. Swann on foot, in a sealskin coat, wearing a simple beret with two blades of partridge feathers sticking up from it, but enveloped also by the artificial warmth of her apartment, which was conjured by nothing more than the bouquet of violets crushed at her breast whose live blue flowering against the gray sky, the icy air, the bare-branched trees, had the same charming manner of accepting the season and the weather merely as a setting, and of living in a human atmosphere, in the atmosphere of this woman, as had, in the vases and flower stands of her drawing room, close to the lit fire, before the silk sofa, the flowers that looked out through the closed window at the falling snow? But it would not have been enough for me anyway for the clothes to be the same as in those earlier times. Because of the dependence which the different parts of a recollection have on one another, parts which our memory keeps balanced in an aggregate from which we are not permitted to abstract anything, or reject anything, I would have wanted to be able to go spend the last part of the day in the home of one of these women, over a cup of tea, in an apartment with walls painted in dark colors, as Mme. Swann's still was (in the year after the one in which the first part of this story ends) and in which the orange flares, the red combustion, the pink and white flame of the chrysanthemums would gleam in the November twilight, during moments like those in which (as we will see later) I was not able to discover the pleasures I desired. But now, even though they had led to nothing, those moments seemed to me to have had enough charm in themselves. I wanted to find them again as I remembered them. Alas, there was no longer anything but Louis XVI apartments all white and dotted with blue hydrangeas. Moreover, people no longer returned to Paris until very late. Mme. Swann would have answered me from a country house that she would not be back until February, well after the time of the chrysanthemums, had I asked her to reconstruct for me the elements of that memory which I felt belonged to a distant year, to a vintage to which I was not allowed to go back, the elements of that desire which had itself become as inaccessible as the pleasure it had once vainly pursued. And I would also have needed them to be the same women, those whose dress interested me because, at the time when I still believed, my imagination had individualized them and given them each a legend. Alas, in the avenue des Acacias—the Alley of the Myrtles—I did see a few of them again, old, now no more than terrible shadows of what they had been, wandering, desperately searching for who knows what in the Virgilian groves. They had fled long since as I still vainly questioned the deserted paths. The sun had hidden itself. Nature was resuming its rule over the Bois, from which the idea that it was the Elysian Garden of Woman had vanished; above the artificial mill the real sky was gray; the wind wrinkled the

Grand Lac with little wavelets, like a real lake; large birds swiftly crossed the Bois, like a real wood, and uttering sharp cries alighted one after another in the tall oaks which under their druidical crowns and with a Dodonean[39] majesty seemed to proclaim the inhuman emptiness of the disused forest, and helped me better understand what a contradiction it is to search in reality for memory's pictures, which would never have the charm that comes to them from memory itself and from not being perceived by the senses. The reality I had known no longer existed. That Mme. Swann did not arrive exactly the same at the same moment was enough to make the Avenue different. The places we have known do not belong solely to the world of space in which we situate them for our greater convenience. They were only a thin slice among contiguous impressions which formed our life at that time; the memory of a certain image is but regret for a certain moment; and houses, roads, avenues are as fleeting, alas, as the years.

Notes

Most of the information for the following notes was taken from the commentary in the Bibliothèque de la Pléiade edition of *À la recherche du temps perdu*, vol. 1 (Paris: Éditions Gallimard, 1987) and from Maxine Arnold Vogely's *A Proust Dictionary* (Troy, N.Y.: Whitston Publishing Co., 1981).

PART I: *Combray I*

1. **the *Débats roses*:** An evening edition of the *Journal des débats* begun in 1893.
2. **schoolroom:** Room in which children had their lessons or did their homework.
3. **Bressant-style:** Jean-Baptiste Prosper Bressant (1815–86) was a well-known actor who introduced a new hairstyle, which consisted of wearing the hair in a crew cut in front and longer in the back.
4. **Jockey Club:** One of the most exclusive and elegant of the Parisian clubs, founded in 1834.
5. **Comte de Paris:** Louis-Philippe-Albert d'Orléans (1838–94), grandson of King Louis-Philippe.
6. **Prince of Wales:** The future Edward VII, Prince of Wales from 1841 to 1901.
7. **marrons glacés:** Candied chestnuts traditionally presented on New Year's Day, especially in Paris.
8. **to Lyon:** The warehouse was situated near the Gare de Lyon, terminal station for the trains to Lyon.
9. **Twickenham:** Until 1871, the residence of the Comte de Paris, exiled in England.

10. **Sacré-Coeur:** A religious boarding school run by the nuns of Sacré-Coeur, a church in Paris.

11. **de Bouillon:** Branch of the de La Tour d'Auvergne family. Basin de Guermantes's mother, Oriane de Guermantes's mother, and Mme. de Villeparisis were sisters in the Bouillon family.

12. **Sévigné:** The Marquise de Sévigné (1626–96) is famous for her letters (over 1,500 have been published). Most of them written to her daughter, in a natural, racy, and picturesque style, they reveal her opinionated and spirited character and describe the life of the nobility at court and in the country, as well as historical and cultural events of her time. She was Proust's grandmother's favorite author.

13. **Maréchal de MacMahon:** Edmé Patrice, Comte de MacMahon, Duc de Magenta, Maréchal de France (1808–93). In 1873, he was elected President of the Republic by a monarchist coalition for a term of seven years. He resigned on January 30, 1879, before the end of his term.

14. **most prominent statesmen in the reign of Louis-Philippe:** The statesmen mentioned are probably the Duc d'Audiffret-Pasquier (1823–1905) and the Marquis d'Audiffret (1787–1878), who served respectively as president of the Chamber of Peers and as senator. Louis-Philippe, King of France, ascended the throne following the 1830 Revolution and abdicated following the 1848 Revolution.

15. **like Molé, the Duc Pasquier, the Duc de Broglie:** Louis Mathieu, Comte Molé (1781–1855), was prime minister under Louis-Philippe and a member of the Chamber of Peers. He was elected to the Académie Française after writing *Essais de morale et de politique*. Étienne-Denis Pasquier (1767–1862) was named president of the Chamber of Peers by Louis-Philippe, who made him a duke in 1841. Duc Achille de Broglie (1785–1870) was a member of the Chamber of Peers under the Restoration, then, under Louis-Philippe, president of the council and minister.

16. **Corot:** Jean-Baptiste Camille Corot (1796–1876), French painter especially known for his pastoral subjects and the serenity of his interpretations.

17. **Flora:** Proust inadvertently attributes both remarks to Flora.

18. **Maubant:** Henri-Polydore Maubant (1821–1902), a member of the Comédie-Française, specialized in the roles of noble father, king, and tyrant. He retired in 1888.

19. **Mme. Materna:** Amalie Materna (1844–1918), German opera star who created some of the great Wagnerian roles. She retired in 1897.

20. **Saint-Simon:** Louis de Rouvroy, Duc de Saint-Simon (1675–1755), French author of the *Mémoires*, which cover the period 1675–1723 and give a detailed picture of the life of the court at that time.

21. **Spain:** Saint-Simon was sent to Spain as *ambassadeur-extraordinaire* to negotiate the royal marriage of the Infanta of Spain to Louis XV.

22. **Maulévrier:** Jean-Baptiste-Louis Andrault, Marquis de Maulévrier-Langeron (1677–1754), Marshal of France. He is described in Saint-Simon's *Mémoires* of the year 1721.

23. **"'What virtues . . . abhor'":** The line is from Corneille's *La Mort de Pompée*, act III, scene 4, and actually reads, *"'Ô ciel, que de vertus vous me faites haïr."*

24. **"against my heart":** *À contrecœur,* "reluctantly."

25. **the miracle of Saint Théophile or the four sons of Aymon:** The *Miracle de Théophile,* composed by Rutebeuf, a thirteenth-century troubador, relates the adventures of Théophile d'Adana, who was not in fact a saint but a simple cleric, and who signed a pact with the devil, repented, and was saved through the intercession of the Virgin Mary. The story of the four sons of Aymon who offended Charlemagne, fled his wrath, and were finally reconciled with him is told in the late twelfth- or early thirteenth-century *chanson de geste, Renaud de Montauban.*

26. **mouth-rinsing bowls:** Bowls containing warm, flavored water presented at the end of the meal for rinsing the mouth and the fingers.

27. **"granité":** A grainy water ice or granita served as dinner course or dessert.

28. **Benozzo Gozzoli:** Florentine painter (1420–97), one of the creators of the frescoes of the Campo Santo at Pisa badly damaged during World War II. One scene depicts the sacrifice of Isaac, but there is no gesture of dismissal directed at Sarah.

29. **Indiana:** A novel by George Sand published in 1832.

30. **Hubert Robert:** Hubert Robert (1733–1808), French painter of landscapes and architecture, especially garden statues, porticos, ruins, and fountains; precursor of the Romantics.

31. **Turner:** Joseph Mallord William Turner (1775–1858), English painter, precursor of the Impressionists and of lyrical abstraction, much admired by Ruskin.

32. **Morghen:** Raphael Morghen (1758–1833), engraver commissioned by the Duke of Tuscany to make an engraving of Leonardo da Vinci's fresco of the Last Supper.

PART I: *Combray 2*

1. **ten leagues:** One league is equal to two to three miles. Proust refers to both leagues and kilometers.

2. **King Charles VI:** Charles VI *le Bien-Aimé* (1328–1422), King of France (1380–1422), experienced alternating periods of lucidity and madness. A tarot game was invented to entertain him.

3. **Saint Eloi:** (*c.* 588–660) Treasurer and goldsmith of Clotaire II and Dagobert I, King of the Franks in 632.

4. **Louis the Germanic:** King of the Franks (817–43). He had three sons who conspired constantly against him. The tomb of the sons of Louis in the church at Combray is a fiction.

5. **Sigebert's:** Sigebert was the name of three early kings of Austrasia—a part of the Merovingian kingdom of the Franks—in the sixth and seventh centuries.

6. **Second Empire:** The empire of Napoleon III, 1852–70, a period of financial and industrial expansion; its positivist and materialistic spirit was reflected in the pursuit of money and pleasure and its brilliant social life.

7. **Morris column:** The name given to columns on Paris streets on which plays and other entertainments are advertised. Named for the printer, Morris, who was the first concession holder.

8. *Le Testament de César Girodot . . . Le Domino Noir: Le Testament de César Girodot* was a comedy by A. Belot and E. Villetard. *Oedipe-Roi* was the French translation by Jules Lacroix of Sophocles' *Oedipus Rex. Les Diamants de la Couronne* and *Le Domino Noir* were comic operas with lyrics by Eugène Scribe and music by Daniel Auber.

9. *gentleman:* "Gentleman" is in English in the original, as is "a cup of tea."

10. **"'blue'":** *Bleu,* an express letter transmitted by pneumatic tube within Paris. (See note 20, p. 461.)

11. **Vaulabelle:** Achille de Vaulabelle (1799–1879), a French journalist and historian.

12. **Virtues and Vices of Padua:** Frescoes by Giotto in the Arena Chapel in Padua; seven virtues—Prudence, Fortitude, Temperance, Justice, Faith, Charity, Hope—face seven vices—Folly, Inconstancy, Anger, Injustice, Infidelity, Envy, Despair.

13. **"La Nuit d'Octobre":** *October* (1837), Poem by Alfred de Musset (1810–57), one of the series entitled *Les Nuits (Nights).*

14. **"'The white Oloossone' . . . 'The daughter of Minos and Pasiphaë'":** The first line is *La blanche Oloossone et la blanche Camyre.* The actual line, from

"La Nuit de Mai," is *La blanche Oloossone à la blanche Camyre*. The second line is *La fille de Minos et de Pasiphaë*. From Racine's *Phèdre*, act I, scene 1, line 36.

15. **"'Bhagavat' and 'Le Lévrier de Magnus'"**: Both poems by Leconte de Lisle. "Bhagavat" is from the collection *Poèmes antiques* (1852), and "Le Lévrier de Magnus" from *Poèmes tragiques* (1884).

16. *La Juive:* Opera by Fromental Halévy first performed in 1835 at the Paris Opéra.

17. **"Israel, break thy bond"**: A line from the opera *Samson et Dalila* by Saint-Saëns.

18. **Archers . . . without sound:** In the original, *Archers, faites bonne garde!/Veillez sans trêve et sans bruit.*

19. **Let you . . . Israelite:** In the original, *De ce timide Israelite/Quoi, vous guidez ici les pas!*

20. **Fields of our fathers . . . Hebron:** In the original, *Champs paternels, Hébron, douce vallée.*

21. **Yes, I am of the chosen race:** In the original, *Oui je suis de la race élue.*

22. **Malay kris:** A dagger with a ridged serpentine blade.

23. *Athalie* or *Phèdre:* Dramas by Jean Racine (1639–99). Their dates are respectively 1691 and 1677.

24. *dolce . . . lento:* Musical indications in Italian meaning "sweet and soft" and "slow."

25. **portrait of Mohammed II by Bellini:** Mohammed II, Sultan of the Ottoman empire from 1451 to 1481, was painted in Constantinople by the Venetian painter Gentile Bellini (*c.* 1429–1507).

26. *Le Cid:* 1636 tragedy by Pierre Corneille (1606–84), part of the classic repertory of the Comédie-Française.

27. **"the Queens of Chartres":** Statues on the western portal of Chartres Cathedral, for a long time assumed to be kings and queens of France but in fact representing characters from the Bible.

28. **The happiness . . . stream:** Racine, *Athalie*, act II, scene 7, line 688. The actual line is *Le bonheur des méchants comme un torrent s'écoule.*

29. **"theater in bed":** Allusion to Alfred de Musset's *Theater in an Armchair,* i.e., a play meant to be read to oneself from a book.

30. **proud as Artaban:** Expression derived from the novel *Cléopâtre* by Gauthier de la Calprenède (1614–63). The character Artaban has become proverbial for his pride.

31. **the "mechanics" of life at Versailles:** The phrase recurs several times in Saint-Simon's *Mémoires*.

32. **The woods are dark, the sky still blue:** *Les bois sont déjà noirs, le ciel est encor bleu.* A line by Paul Desjardins (1859–1940), French writer and thinker.

33. **Fall in love . . . plum:** In the original, *Qui du cul d'un chien s'amourose, Il lui parait une rose.* Literally, "He who falls in love with a dog's bottom / Will think it's a rose."

34. **Fabre:** Jean-Henri Fabre (1823–1915), French teacher and entomologist who retired in 1871 to devote himself to the study of insect life, one of his special interests being the Hymenoptera. He published ten volumes of studies, *Souvenirs entomologiques,* from 1879 to 1907.

35. **Balzac's flora:** The plant, sedum, appears in at least two of the novels in Balzac's *La Comédie humaine.*

36. **"for wounded hearts . . . shadow and silence":** *Aux coeurs blessés l'ombre et le silence.* Epigraph from a novel by Balzac, *Le Médecin de campagne* (The Country Doctor).

37. **Jacobin:** Member of a society of revolutionary democrats in France during the Revolution of 1789; hence, a political radical.

38. **Andromedas:** In Greek mythology, Andromeda was the daughter of Cassiopeia, who boasted that Andromeda was more beautiful than the daughter of Nereus, the Sea God. The daughter was punished for the mother's arrogance and, chained to a rocky cliff by the sea, was rescued by Perseus.

39. **Ar-mor, the Sea:** Ar-mor is the Celtic name for Brittany, meaning "on the sea."

40. **Anatole France:** French novelist, critic, and literary figure (1844–1924). He wrote about the Cimmerians in *Pierre Nozière* (1899).

41. **country of the Cimmerians in the *Odyssey*:** The Cimmerians were an ancient people from the north shore of the Black Sea who invaded Lydia in Asia Minor in the seventh century. In the *Odyssey,* Homer describes them as living in darkness.

42. **that erudite crook:** The crook in question is most likely Vrain-Lucas, who forged signatures which he attributed to Rabelais, Pascal, Joan of Arc, Julius Caesar, and Cleopatra. His story was told by Alphonse Daudet in *L'Immortel* (1888).

43. **burdened . . . across my brow:** Indirect quotation from Racine's *Phèdre,* act I, scene 3: *Que ces vains ornements, que ces voiles me pèsent! / Quelle importune main en formant tous ces noeuds / A pris soin sur mon front d'assembler mes cheveux?*

44. **some novel by Saintine:** Joseph Xavier Boniface, known as Saintine (1798–1865), French novelist best known for his novel *Picciola*.

45. **some landscape by Gleyre:** Charles-Gabriel Gleyre (1806–74), Swiss academic painter.

46. **the little hooded monk in the optician's window:** A figure in a box that predicted weather changes.

47. ***Chanson de Roland: Song of Roland,*** most famous of the *chansons de geste* of the Middle Ages.

48. **kith and kindred:** The humor of Françoise's mistake is more evident in the original. Instead of *parenté*, "family," "relations," she says *parentèse*, "parenthesis."

49. **Viollet-le-Duc:** Eugène Emmanuel Viollet-le-Duc (1814–79), French architect and writer who restored many monuments of the Middle Ages, including the Sainte-Chapelle, Notre-Dame, and the feudal château of Pierrefonds.

50. **that painting by Gentile Bellini . . . Saint Mark's:** The reference must be to Gentile Bellini's *Procession in St. Mark's Square*, valued especially for its quality as documentary evidence of the appearance of St. Mark's Cathedral in the fifteenth century.

51. **their pretty name:** *Boutons d'or*, or "gold buttons."

52. **"vacation house":** The irony is lost in translation, since the French *maison de plaisance*, though it means "country house," translates literally as "pleasure house" (as in "pleasure boat").

53. ***Lohengrin:*** Opera by Richard Wagner (1813–83), who was immensely popular in Europe in the late nineteenth century.

54. **Carpaccio:** Vittore Carpaccio (c. 1455–1525), Venetian painter.

55. **Baudelaire:** Charles Baudelaire (1821–67), French poet and critic.

56. **flowery Delos:** Greek island; in Greek mythology, the birthplace of Apollo and Artemis.

PART II: *Swann in Love*

1. **Planté:** Francis Planté (1839–1934), a French pianist and composer whose concerts were very successful beginning in 1872.

2. **Rubinstein:** Anton Grigorievtch Rubinstein (1829–94) was, along with Liszt, the most illustrious pianist of his time.

3. **Potain:** Pierre-Charles-Édouard Potain was elected to the Académie de Médecine in 1882, and to the Institute in 1893.

4. **the ride from** *The Valkyrie* **or the prelude from** *Tristan:* *The Valkyrie* (1854–56) and *Tristan and Isolde* (1865) are both operas by Richard Wagner.

5. *fishing for compliments:* In English in the original.

6. **conclave:** A meeting of Roman Catholic cardinals to choose a new pope. Proust is probably referring to the conclave of 1878.

7. **What is then . . . understand:** A quotation from the end of act 1 of *La Dame blanche,* an opera by François-Adrien Boieldieu. In the original, *Quel est donc ce mystère?/Je n'y puis rien comprendre.*

8. **Fleeting vision:** An allusion to Herod's aria in act II of *Hérodiade,* an opera by Jules Massenet. In the original, *Vision fugitive.*

9. **In these affairs . . . blind:** A quotation from the end of *Amphitryon,* a comic opera by André-Ernest-Modeste Grétry. In the original, *Dans ces affaires/Le mieux est de ne rien voir.*

10. **home:** In English in the original.

11. **Vermeer of Delft:** Jan Vermeer (1632–75), Dutch painter.

12. **Areopagus:** The ancient tribunal of Athens; used figuratively to indicate an assembly of virtuous, wise people. The reference seems to be to some fable, but its identity remains unclear.

13. *"Patronne's":* Feminine form of *patron,* "boss" or "manager."

14. **Reichstag:** German legislative assembly.

15. **Ninth . . .** *The Meistersingers:* The reference is to Beethoven's Ninth Symphony and Wagner's opera *The Meistersingers.*

16. *di primo cartello:* Italian term indicating singers of highest quality, who have "top billing."

17. **Academy:** Potain was elected to the Académie de Médecine in 1882. The Académie was founded (in 1880) primarily to advise the government on questions of public health.

18. **Gambetta's funeral:** Léon Gambetta, an important political leader and deputy to the National Assembly, was buried in January 1883.

19. *Les Danicheff:* Play by Pierre de Corvin-Koukowsky in collaboration with Dumas *fils* (see note 55 below).

20. **M. Grévy's:** Jules Grévy was president of the Republic from 1879 to 1887.

21. *gentleman:* In English in the original.

22. **Pieter de Hooch:** Dutch painter (1629–83?) known for his handling of light and perspective.

23. **cattleyas:** Orchids with large, richly colored flowers developed by the English horticulturist W. Cattley.

24. **Our Lady of Laghet:** Notre-Dame de Laghet is a place of pilgrimage situated in the Alpes-Maritimes, to the north of Turbie and close to Nice.

25. **Zipporah . . . Sistine Chapel:** The figure of Zipporah appears in the Sistine Chapel in a series of frescoes by Botticelli depicting the life of Moses, her husband.

26. **Antonio Rizzo:** The Correr Museum in Venice possesses a bronze bust of Andrea Loredan (who, unlike Pietro Loredan, was never a doge) attributed to the Paduan sculptor Andrea Briosse (1471–1532), known as Riccio or Rizzo.

27. **Ghirlandaio:** Ghirlandaio (1449–94), Florentine painter, one of the best of the Italian primitives. The reference here is to his *Portrait of an Old Man and His Grandson,* which hung in the Louvre in Proust's day. The old man in the picture, a nobleman, has a large prominent nose covered with warts.

28. **Tintoretto:** Jacopo Robusti Tintoretto (1518–94), Venetian painter whose self-portrait hung in the Louvre in Proust's day.

29. **La Maison Dorée:** An elegant restaurant opened in 1840 and situated at 1, rue Lafitte, at the corner of the boulevard des Italiens.

30. **the Paris-Murcia fete . . . Murcia:** A fete given on December 18, 1879, in aid of the victims of the flooding that occurred in the Murcia province of Spain on October 14 and 15, 1879.

31. **Prévost's:** Tearoom at 39, boulevard Bonne-Nouvelle, which opened in 1825 and owed its reputation to its chocolate.

32. **Tortoni's:** A café at 22, boulevard des Italiens.

33. **Café Anglais:** A café at 13, boulevard des Italiens.

34. **the "Valse des Roses" or "Pauvre Fou" by Tagliafico:** Both pieces in "bad taste." The "Valse des Roses" was the best-known composition of Olivier Métra, conductor at the Châtelet and the Folies Bergères; Joseph Dieudonné Tagliafico was a French opera singer who made his debut in 1844 at the Théâtre Des Italiens. He wrote a ballad whose correct title is "Pauvres Fous" (Poor Lunatics).

35. **Watteau:** Antoine Watteau (1684–1721), French painter said to have spent hours in the Luxembourg Gardens sketching the faces and figures of the passersby.

36. **the rue Abbatucci:** Former name, from 1868 to 1879, of part of the rue de La Boétie, in the eighth arrondissement.

37. **the Vicomte de Borelli:** Raymond de Borelli (1827–1906) was a society poet.

38. **the avenue de l'Impératrice:** In the sixteenth arrondissement, it runs from the place de l'Étoile to the Porte Dauphine. It was created in 1854 and called by this name until the 1870s, when, with the fall of the Empire, it was renamed avenue du Bois de Boulogne, finally becoming avenue Foch in 1929.

39. **the Tour du Lac:** The *lac* in question is the lake (in fact two lakes) in the Bois de Boulogne. In Proust's day, the favorite promenade routes led from the avenues to the lake. *Tour du Lac* must refer to a road around the lakes.

40. **Éden Théâtre:** Theater erected in 1882 for the performance mainly of ballets; it was located on the rue Boudreau near the Opéra.

41. **Hippodrome:** A stadium located, from 1875 to 1892, between the avenue de l'Alma and the avenue Marceau. It held ten thousand spectators and presented races, ballets, horse shows, and other performances.

42. **darling:** In English in the original.

43. **Château de Blois:** Historic castle on the Loire River, and a favorite residence of the French kings during the sixteenth century. It combines styles from the thirteenth to the seventeenth centuries and is in fact remarkable for its elaborate Renaissance chimney pieces, which rise to the ceiling.

44. *La Reine Topaz:* The *Topaz Queen,* a comic opera with music by Victor Massé first performed in 1856.

45. *muffins* **and** *toasts:* In English in the original, including the eccentric plural of "toasts."

46. **"Thé de la rue Royale":** Ancient establishment which at the turn of the century was located at 3 and 12, rue Royale and served afternoon tea in the English style.

47. *Serge Panine:* 1881 novel by Georges Ohnet first produced as a play in 1882. Ohnet (1848–1918) was a dramatist and the author of sentimental novels immensely popular with the public and disparaged by the critics. His *Le Maître de Forges,* mentioned elsewhere, was a novel and play produced with great success during the 1884 season.

48. **Olivier Métra:** Métra (1830–89) was a French composer and conductor best known for his waltzes.

49. **the Righi:** Mountain in Switzerland, with villages at its foot and hotels at intervals on the way to the summit, from which there is a wonderful panorama. The Riviera and Switzerland, along with the English things one could find there, were very much in vogue at the time.

50. *"Blanche?* **Blanche de Castille":** "White"; Blanche de Castille (1188–1252) was the wife of Louis VIII and mother of Louis IX.

51. **Suger and other Saint Bernards:** *The Chronicle of Saint-Denis,* a history of the kings of France, was begun by Abbot Suger in the twelfth century and continued at the Abbey of Saint-Denis until 1286.

52. **Henry Plantagenet:** Henry II of England (1133–89) married Eleanor of Aquitaine in 1152. The latter was not the mother of Blanche de Castille, but her grandmother.

53. **Rembrandt or Hals:** *The Night Watch* by Rembrandt (1606–69) is an open-air scene depicting militia and a variety of other types of faces; *The Regents* by Franz Hals (1580–1666) is a group portrait of lady governors of the Almshouse of Haarlem. It hangs in the museum of Haarlem.

54. **the Ninth and the *Winged Victory:*** The reference is to Beethoven's Ninth Symphony and *The Winged Victory of Samothrace,* a Greek statue of a draped and winged woman found on the island of Samothrace in 1863 and now standing at the top of the Daru Staircase in the Louvre.

55. **play by Dumas:** Alexandre Dumas, known as Dumas *fils* (1824–95), French dramatist and novelist. The Japanese salad appears in his play *Francillon.*

56. **"*speech*":** In English in the original.

57. **the La Trémoïlles:** A celebrated family whose duchy was one of the oldest in France.

58. **lost wax:** The wax model from which a metal sculpture is cast.

59. **the Palais de l'Industrie:** The Palais de l'Industrie (Hall of Industry) was built for the Exposition of 1855 on the site of the present Grand Palais and Petit Palais beside the Seine. It housed the annual salons of painting and sculpture.

60. **Fénelon:** François de Salgnac de la Mothe-Fénelon (1651–1715), French theologian who was in charge of the education of the grandsons of Louis XIV. In his *Treatise on the Existence and Attributes of God,* he defines God as "universal intelligence" and "infinitely intelligible." He posits that nothing is intelligent except through God, but intelligence is "real in His creatures"; our ideas "are a perpetual mingling of God's infinite being which is our object, and of the limits He gives always and essentially to each creature."

61. **Trémouailles:** Brichot is pronouncing the name incorrectly; it should be "Trémoïlles."

62. ***Se non è vero:*** First words of the adage *Se non è vero, è ben trovato:* "If it isn't true, it's still a happy thought."

63. **the Duc d'Aumale:** A pun on the name of the fourth son of King Louis-Philippe and the word *mâle,* "male."

64. **Baronne Putbus:** According to *Gotha's Almanac,* the Putbus family

dated back to the twelfth century, at which time it owned a château and fifteen villages in Pomerania.

65. "'sonata-snake'": The Marquise Diane de Saint-Paul, a brilliant pianist and a scandalmonger, was known in Proust's circle as the *"serpent à sonates,"* or "sonata-snake." The nickname is a play on the word for rattlesnake, *serpent à sonnettes.*

66. **Gustave Moreau:** French painter (1826–98), whose subjects were products of imagination and fantasy and whose refined and sensual aestheticism interested Proust.

67. **the Île des Cygnes:** "Island of the Swans," an island in the larger of the two lakes in the Bois de Boulogne.

68. **the Primavera:** Painting by Botticelli which hangs in the Uffizi Gallery in Florence.

69. **Moses pour water into a trough:** Botticelli depicted the child Jesus playing with a pomegranate in his *Madonna della Melagrana;* in the Sistine Chapel, one of the scenes from Botticelli's *Trials of Moses* shows the prophet drawing water for the flocks of the daughters of Jethro.

70. **Chatou:** A village on the banks of the Seine ten miles from Paris, a popular spot, in the latter part of the nineteenth century, with fishermen, boaters, and Impressionist painters.

71. **Labiche comedy:** Eugène Labiche (1815–88) was a French dramatist and author of comedies of manners and vaudevilles.

72. **Bossuet:** Jacques Bénigne Bossuet (1627–1704), theologian, moralist, and one of the great orators of French history.

73. **Dante's last circle:** The last book of *The Divine Comedy* places the greatest sinners in the ninth circle of Hell.

74. *Noli me tangere:* "Do not touch me"–words attributed by John to Jesus Christ addressing Mary Magdalen.

75. *Une Nuit de Cléopatre:* "A Night with Cleopatra," a work by Victor Massé (1822–84), composer of *La Reine Topaze* and *Paul et Virginie. Une Nuit de Cléopatre* was first performed in 1885.

76. **the tombs at Dreux . . . the Château de Pierrefonds:** The royal chapel of Dreux contains the tombs of the princes of Orléans. The château of Pierrefonds, at the edge of the forest of Compiègne, was originally built by Louis d'Orléans in the fifteenth century, fell into ruins, was bought by Napoleon I, and was eventually entrusted to the care of Viollet-le-Duc by Napoleon III in 1857. Restoration work was completed in 1884.

77. **Beauvais or Saint-Loup-de-Naud:** The Cathedral of Saint-Pierre de

Beauvais, built in the thirteenth and fourteenth centuries, is famous for its Gothic choir. The Roman church of Saint-Loup-de-Naud, in the *département* of Seine-et-Marne, is one of the oldest in France.

78. **the Map of Love:** An allegorical map devised by the novelist Madeleine de Scudéry (1607–1701) and introduced in her novel *Clélie* (1654–60). The Map of Love shows three different roads leading to true love.

79. **the church at Brou:** The church at Brou, near Bourg-en-Bresse, was built by the order of Margaret of Austria in memory of her husband, Philibert le Beau (1480–1504), Duke of Savoie.

80. *Lapérouse:* This restaurant lies outside Odette's "smart" territory, on the quai des Grands-Augustins quite close to the quai d'Orléans, where Swann lives.

81. **"Bal des Incohérents":** "Ball of the Incoherents." The Incoherents were artists who mocked the official salons and organized highly successful exhibitions of their own starting in 1882. They celebrated the opening day with a costume ball.

82. *my love:* In English in the original.

83. **the season at Bayreuth:** Inaugurated in 1876, the Festspielhaus, Wagner's model theater at Bayreuth, became the international center of the cult of Wagner beginning in 1882. The five castles of Louis II of Bavaria (1845–86) were inspired by Versailles or by the German legends that Wagner used in his operas.

84. **Clapisson:** Antonin-Louis Clapisson (1808–66), whose music had already gone out of fashion in 1880, was a French composer of comic operas.

85. **Mme. de Maintenon:** Françoise d'Aubigné de Maintenon (1635–1719) secretly married Louis XIV in 1684. Saint-Simon entitled one section of his *Mémoires* "Mechanics, private life and conduct of Mme. de Maintenon," and detailed the items of her table.

86. **Lully:** Jean Baptiste Lully (1632–87), Italian-born French composer.

87. **Septennate:** Seven-year term of a French president. The term Proust is most probably referring to is that of Edmé Patrice, Comte de MacMahon, which began in 1873 and ended with his resignation in 1879.

88. **Botticelli's Primavera, bella Vanna, or Venus:** Primavera, the goddess of spring, is depicted in Botticelli's *Spring;* the "bella Vanna" in *Giovanna Tomabuoni and the Three Graces;* and Venus in *The Birth of Venus.*

89. **Balzac's "tigers":** In both French and English a "tiger" was a gentleman's groom, either a boy or a small man. In his pastiche of Balzac (in *Pastiches et mélanges*), Proust refers to "Paddy, the famous tiger of the late Baudenord."

90. **paintings by Mantegna:** Mantegna, an Italian painter and engraver (*c.* 1430–1506), was part of a team that decorated the Church of the Erimitani at Padua between 1449 and 1456. In the Ovetari Chapel of that church are the *Scenes from the Life of Saint John and Saint Christopher*. In *The Martyrdom of Saint John* a warrior meditates, leaning on his shield. Mantegna painted the *Altarpiece of San Zeno*, at Verona, between 1456 and 1459.

91. **some Albrecht Dürer Saxon:** Dürer (1471–1528) was influenced by Mantegna, whose engravings he copied.

92. **cadogan:** Hairstyle in which a bunch of hair is folded twice at the back of the head and tied with a ribbon.

93. **Goya:** Francisco de Goya (1746–1828), Spanish painter several of whose paintings hung in the Louvre in Proust's day, though it is unclear which painting Proust is referring to.

94. **Benvenuto Cellini:** Florentine goldsmith, sculptor, and writer (1500–1571). It is not clear which work by Cellini Proust has in mind here.

95. *Orphée: Orphée et Eurydice* (1762) by Christoph Willibald Gluck (1714–87), a German-born composer whose music is considered French. The flute solo occurs in act 2, as Orpheus is searching the Elysian Fields in the Underworld for his lost beloved, Eurydice.

96. **Liszt:** Franz Liszt (1811–86), Hungarian pianist and composer who lived in Paris for some years (*c.* 1840). One of the two *légendes* he wrote for piano solo is titled *St. François prédicant aux oiseaux*.

97. **Princesse Mathilde:** Daughter of Jérôme Bonaparte. Princesse Mathilde (1820–1904) entertained the most brilliant members of the artistic and literary world. Among her guests were Taine, Renan, the Goncourts, and Flaubert.

98. **Legitimist:** In French history, a supporter of claims to the monarchy based on the rights of heredity.

99. **baignoire:** Literally, "bathtub"—a ground-floor theater box, projecting and rounded like a bathtub.

100. **Mérimée:** Prosper Mérimée (1803–70), widely traveled French writer noted for his exoticism.

101. **Meilhac and Halévy:** Henri Meilhac (1831–97) was a French author of drawing-room comedies and opera libretti; Ludovic Halévy (1834–1908), French librettist, was his collaborator.

102. **"'guests from Belloir's'":** Belloir's, in the rue de la Victoire in Paris, rented supplies for dances and parties.

103. **"'Empire'":** The style of furniture which became popular during the Empire (1804–15) favored mahogany and was cubic and massive, with gilded

or antique green and bronze trim and dark marble tops. Common decorative devices were sphinxes, laurel wreaths, Winged Victories, sheaves, and cornucopias. Napoleon's symbol, the bee, replaced the royal fleur-de-lis.

104. **most astonishing name:** The joke here, on the name Cambremer, sees it as being made up of abbreviations of *Cambronne* and *merde* (shit). *Le mot de Cambronne*, "Cambronne's word," said to have been uttered by Cambronne, a general at Waterloo, is the traditional euphemism for *merde*.

105. **the Hôtel Vouillemont:** The Hôtel Vouillemont was in the rue Boissy d'Anglas. In an 1863 guide to Paris it was described as a quiet first-class hotel.

106. *La Princesse de Clèves* **or of** *René*: *La Princesse de Clèves* (1678), a novel by Mme. de La Fayette, tells the tragic story of the frustrated love of a young married noblewoman for a gallant young duke; *René* (1805) is a tale by Chateaubriand recounting the passion between a brother and sister.

107. **of a Lavoisier, of an Ampère:** Antoine-Laurent de Lavoisier (1743–94), a French chemist, one of the fathers of modern chemistry, to which he contributed the law of conservation of matter; André Marie Ampère (1775–1836), French mathematician and physicist who propounded the theory of electromagnetism.

108. **Nicolas Maes . . . Vermeer:** Nicolas Maes (*c.* 1634–93), Dutch painter. It is unclear who painted *Diana with Her Companions* and Maes was once considered as a possible candidate.

109. **You're never as unhappy as you think:** The allusion here is to the forty-ninth maxim of François, Duc de La Rochefoucauld (1613–80), French moralist and author of *Maximes* (1665): "One is never either as happy or as unhappy as one imagines."

110. *Les Filles de Marbre* **by Théodore Barrière:** The play (literally, "Girls of Marble") (1853) is about courtesans who are cold and unfeeling.

111. **to call her** *tu:* In French, the distinction is still made between the formal "you," *vous*, and the informal *tu*; and in the period in which this novel is set, the formal "you" was far more prevalent even among children and within families.

112. *Journal d'un Poète* **by Alfred de Vigny:** A journal written by Alfred de Vigny (1797–1863), French poet, novelist, and dramatist. The passage quoted is dated April 22, 1833, and is an exact quotation.

113. **the Desolation of Nineveh:** An allusion to Ruskin's *The Bible of Amiens,* which appeared in Proust's translation in 1904. Ruskin points out the beasts of Nineveh on the facade of the cathedral of Amiens crawling "among the tottering walls and peeping out of their rents and crannies."

114. **the three travelers:** Four, actually.

115. **the Mirlitons:** An annual art show held each February by the Cercle de l'Union Artistique, a club created by the merger of the Cercle des Champs-Élysées and Les Mirlitons.

116. **Machard:** Jules-Louis Machard (1839–1900) first showed in the Salon of 1863. He was a fashionable portrait painter for many years.

117. **Leloir:** Probably Jean-Baptiste-Auguste Leloir (1809–92), a French academic historical and religious painter who also did occasional portraits.

PART III: *Place-Names: The Name*

1. *"modern style":* In English in the original.

2. **Exposition:** These illuminated fountains were installed on the Champs-de-Mars for the Exposition of 1889.

3. **at Finistère itself:** *Département* at the western extreme of Brittany; the name derives from the Latin, *finis terrae*, "land's end."

4. **the Great Bear:** Name of the constellation also called the Plow or the Big Dipper.

5. **Saint-Mary-of-the-Flowers:** Santa Maria del Fiore, the cathedral of Florence which Proust refers to by its French name, Sainte-Marie-des-Fleurs.

6. *La Chartreuse:* "The Charterhouse," referring to *La Chartreuse de Parme* (The Charterhouse of Parma, 1839), a novel by Stendhal (Henri Beyle; 1783–1842).

7. **fabliau:** A short, usually comic, frankly coarse, and often cynical tale in verse popular in the twelfth and thirteenth centuries.

8. **Vitré:** *Vitré* is also an adjective meaning "glazed," "having window-panes."

9. **the coach followed by the fly:** A play on the expression *faire la mouche du coche,* literally be the fly in the coach, i.e., buzz around, be a busybody.

10. **the school of Giorgione . . . medieval domestic architecture:** Here and elsewhere in this passage Proust is quoting or adapting John Ruskin's *Modern Painters* and *Stones of Venice.* Giorgio de Castelfranco, known as Giorgione (*c.* 1478–1510), was an Italian painter who spent his life in the vicinity of Venice. He and Titian frescoed the outside walls of certain buildings during the period when they worked as housepainters.

11. **"bossed with jasper and paved with emeralds":** Variation of quotation from Ruskin's *Stones of Venice.*

12. **reddened by reflections from Giorgione's frescoes:** Modified quota-

tion from Ruskin. In his *Modern Painters,* he says, "I saw the last traces of the greatest works of Giorgione yet glowing like a scarlet cloud on the Fondaco de' Tedeschi."

13. **"majestic ... blood-red cloaks":** Modified quotation from Ruskin's *Stones of Venice.*

14. **"rocks of amethyst like a reef in the Indian Ocean":** Modified quotation from Ruskin's *Stones of Venice.*

15. **Poussin:** Nicolas Poussin (1594–1665), French classic painter. The reference is probably to *L'Empire de Flore,* which shows the chariot of the sun driven over the clouds behind four horses. The scene below is a garden.

16. **Les Débats:** *Le Journal des débats politiques et littéraires* (Journal of Political and Literary Debates), founded in 1789 and published until August 1944. It styled itself "republican conservative" in 1890, then "republican and liberal" in 1895. There were two editions each day, the evening edition being called the *édition rose* or "pink edition."

17. **who rented the chairs:** In French public gardens, folding chairs of wood and iron were set up and available for use by the public for a price; old women would come around from time to time collecting the "rent," the equivalent of about one penny. The chairs are still there, but rent is no longer charged.

18. **Field of the Cloth of Gold:** An allusion to the ostentatious camp (including a tent of gold cloth) that François I set up in 1520, between Guines and Ardres (in the *département* of Pas-de-Calais), to receive Henry VIII of England, whom he hoped to turn into an ally against Charles V. Proust, here, is making a pun that is lost in translation: in the French, the same word, *camp,* means both "side" or "team" in a game, and also a military "camp" or, in this case, "field" in the phrase *camp du drap d'or,* Field of the Cloth of Gold. In addition, the name Champs-Élysées means, literally, Elysian Fields.

19. **spice cake:** The French *pain d'épices* is defined in dictionaries as "gingerbread." But unlike our gingerbread and our spice cake, it is a rather heavy and not very sweet breadlike cake made of rye flour, honey, sugar, and spices, including anise, and is mildly laxative.

20. *pneumatique:* Express letter sent by pneumatic tube. This delivery system existed in Paris as late as the 1970s or 1980s; as the telephone system was very slow to develop, casual appointments were made and messages transmitted by *pneumatique,* also know as a *petit bleu,* literally "little blue."

21. **vous:** The formal "you"; the informal is *tu.*

22. **"En Revenant de la Revue"**: A popular song with political significance sung for the first time by Paulus at the Alcazar in 1886.

23. **At school, during the one o'clock class**: During the period in which the novel takes place, it was usual—and not only in France—for children and working parents to come home for lunch and then return to school and work.

24. **"Ambassadeurs"**: A restaurant with a fine terrace which in Proust's day was on the Champs-Élysées near the place de la Concorde.

25. **Philippe VII**: Title assumed by the Comte de Paris, who became head of the royal house and claimant to the throne in 1883.

26. **King Theodosius**: Probably an allusion to the visit of Czar Nicholas II in 1896.

27. *Michel Strogoff:* The very successful theater adaptation by Jules Verne and A. Dennery of Verne's novel (1876), performed for the first time at the Châtelet in 1880.

28. **Midi**: The south of France (from *midi,* "noon").

29. **Trois Quartiers**: One of the great stores of Paris at the time, located in the first arrondissement at the corner of the boulevard de la Madeleine and the rue Duphot.

30. **allée des Acacias . . . allée de la Reine-Marguerite**: The allée des Acacias, also called the allée de Longchamp, was one of the most important streets in the Bois de Boulogne, and the scene of elegant promenades until the 1920s. The allée de la Reine-Marguerite was another large avenue in the Bois and was probably named for Marguerite de Valois, sister of François I.

31. **the Alley of the Myrtles in *The Aeneid:*** In book 6, lines 440–44 of Virgil's *Aeneid,* Aeneas, having descended into the Underworld, encounters in a forest of myrtles the mythological heroines who have died of love: "Those consumed by the wasting torments of merciless love / Haunt the sequestered alleys and myrtle groves that give them / Cover; death itself cannot cure them of love's disease" (*Aeneid of Virgil,* trans. C. Day Lewis, Oxford University Press, 1952).

32. **Constantin Guys**: French black-and-white and watercolor artist and draftsman (1805–82), famous for his sketches of the Parisian life of pleasure under the Second Empire.

33. **the "tiger" of "the late Baudenord"**: Baudenord and his groom, or "tiger," are characters in two volumes of Balzac's *La Comédie humaine.*

34. **Coquelin**: Actor (1841–1909) who for twenty-six years was highly successful as *premier comique* at the Comédie-Française.

35. **Tir aux Pigeons:** Literally "pigeon shoot," a shooting club in the Bois whose buildings were visible from the allée des Acacias.

36. **Trianon:** Name of two châteaux in the park of Versailles.

37. **the cruel steeds of Diomedes:** The allusion is a mythological one to Diomedes, the King of Thrace, who fed his horses on human flesh.

38. **Tanagra:** Simple terra-cotta statuettes and figurines dating from about 300 B.C. found in the Greek village of Tanagra, mostly of young women and children in costumes with graceful draperies. They were much in vogue at the turn of the century, and the fashion inspired by them reached its height in about 1908.

39. **Dodonean:** In Dodona, in Epirus, the priests of Zeus' sanctuary gave oracles by interpreting the sound of the wind in the sacred oaks.

Synopsis

and mental attitudes (100). Prestige of Mlle. Swann as a friend of Bergotte's (101, cf. 419). The curé's visits to Aunt Léonie (104). Eulalie and Françoise (109). The kitchen maid gives birth (111). Aunt Léonie's nightmare (111). Saturday lunches (112). The hawthorns on the altar in Combray church (114). M. Vinteuil (115). His "boyish" daughter (116). Walks around Combray by moonlight (116). Aunt Léonie's intrigues (119). Aunt Léonie and Louis XIV (121). Strange behavior of M. Legrandin (122–35). Plan for a holiday at Balbec (132). The way by Swann's (or the Méséglise way) and the Guermantes way (137).

The way by Swann's. View over the plain (137). The lilacs of Tansonville (138). The hawthorn lane (140). Apparition of Gilberte (143). The lady in white and the man with her (Mme. Swann and M. de Charlus) (144). Dawn of love for Gilberte: glamour of the name Swann (145, cf. 429). Farewell to the hawthorns (148). Mlle. Vinteuil's friend comes to Montjouvain (150). M. Vinteuil's sorrow (151). The rain (153). The porch of Saint-André-des-Champs, Françoise and Théodore (154). Death of Aunt Léonie; Françoise's wild grief (156). Exultation in the solitude of autumn (158). Discord between our feelings and their habitual expression (158). "The same emotions do not arise simultaneously in all men" (159). Stirrings of desire (159). The little room smelling of orris root (161, cf. 12). Scene of sadism at Montjouvain (161).

The Guermantes way. River landscape: the Vivonne (170); the water lilies (172). The Guermantes; Geneviève de Brabant, "the ancestress of the Guermantes family" (175). Daydreams and discouragement of a future writer (176). The Duchesse de Guermantes in the chapel of Gilbert the Bad (178). The secrets hidden behind shapes, scents, and colors (182). The steeples of Martinville; first joyful experience of literary creation (183). Transition from joy to sadness (186). Does reality take shape only in memory? (188).

Awakenings (190, cf. 14).

PART II: *Swann in Love*

The Verdurins and their "little clan." The "faithful" (195). Odette mentions Swann to the Verdurins (198). Swann and women (198). Swann's first meeting with Odette: she is "not his type" (203). How he comes to fall in love with her (204). Dr. Cottard (207). The sonata in F-sharp (213). The Beauvais couch (215). The little phrase (216). The Vinteuil of the sonata and the Vinteuil of Combray (222). Mme. Verdurin finds Swann charming at first (223). But his "powerful friendships" make a bad impression on her (225). The little working girl; Swann agrees to meet Odette only after dinner (226). Vinteuil's little phrase, "the national anthem of their love" (226). Tea with Odette; her chrysanthemums (228). Faces of today and portraits of the past: Odette and Botticelli's Zipporah (231). Odette, a Florentine painting (232). Love letter from Odette written from the Maison Dorée (234). Swann's arrival at the Verdurins' one evening after Odette's departure (235); anguished search in the night (237). The cattleyas (240); she becomes his mistress (242). Odette's vulgarity (249); her idea of "smart" (251). Swann begins to adopt her tastes (255) and considers the Vendurins "magnanimous people" (258). Why, nevertheless, he is not a true member of the "faithful," unlike Forcheville (259). A dinner at the Verdurins': Brichot (260), Cottard (260), the painter (263), Saniette (270). The little phrase (273). Swann's jealousy: one night, dismissed by Odette at midnight, he returns to her house and knocks at the wrong window (282). Forcheville's cowardly attack on Saniette, and Odette's smile of complicity (286). Odette's door remains closed to Swann one afternoon; her lying explanation (287). Signs of distress that accompany Odette's lying (290). Swann deciphers a letter from her to Forcheville through the envelope (292). The Verdurins organize an excursion to Chatou without Swann (294). His indignation with them (296). Swann's exclusion (300). Should he go to Dreux or Pierrefonds to find Odette? (303). Waiting through the night (306). Peaceful evenings at Odette's with Forcheville (309). His pain returns (311). The Bayreuth plan (312). Love and death and the mystery of personality (320). Charles Swann and "young Swann" (321). Swann, Odette, Charlus, and Uncle Adolphe (323). Longing for death (329).

An evening at the Marquise de Saint-Euverte's. Detached from social life by his love and his jealousy, Swann can observe it as it is in itself (335): the footmen (336); the monocles (338); the Marquise de Cambremer and the Vicomtesse de Franquetot listening to Liszt's "Saint Francis" (340); Mme. de Gallardon, a despised cousin of the Guermantes (341). Arrival of the Princess des Laumes (342); her conversation with Swann (353). Swann introduces the young Mme. de Cambremer (Mlle. Legrandin) to Général de Froberville (357). Vinteuil's little phrase poignantly reminds Swann of the days when Odette loved him (358). The language of music (364). Swann realizes that Odette's love for him will never return (366).

The whole past toppled stone by stone (385). Bellini's *Mohammed II* (368). An anonymous letter (369). *Les Filles de Marbre* (373). Beuzeville-Bréauté (374). Odette and women (374). Impossibility of possessing another person (377). On the island in the Bois, by moonlight (379). A new circle of hell (381). The terrible re-creative power of memory (381). Odette and the procuresses (383). Had she been lunching with Forcheville at the Maison Dorée on the day of the Paris-Murcia fete? (384, cf. 234). She was with Forcheville, and not at the Maison Dorée, on the night when Swann had searched for her in Prévost's (384, cf. 237). Odette's suspect effusions (386). "Lovely conversation" in a brothel (386). Odette goes on a cruise with the "faithful" (387). Mme. Cottard assures Swann that Odette adores him (389). Swann's love fades; he no longer suffers on learning that Forcheville has been Odette's lover (392). Return of his jealousy in a nightmare (392). Departure for Combray, where he will see the young Mme. de Cambremer, whose charm had struck him at Mme. de Saint-Euverte's (394). The first image of Odette seen again in his dream: he had wanted to die for a woman "who was not his type" (396).

PART III: *Place-Names: The Name*

Dreams of Place-names. Rooms at Combray (399). Room in the Grand-Hôtel at Balbec (399, cf. 8). Dreams of spring in Florence (402, cf. 405). Words and names (403). Names of Norman towns (405). Abortive plan to visit Florence and Venice (405). The doctor forbids me to travel or to go to the theater to see La Berma (409); he advises walks in the Champs-Élysées under Françoise's surveillance (410).

In the Champs-Élysées. A little girl with red hair; the name Gilberte (410). Games of prisoners' base (411). What will the weather be like? (412). Snow in the Champs-Élysées (413). The reader of *Les Débats* (Mme. Blatin) (413, cf. 430). Signs of friendship: the agate marble, the Bergotte book, "You may call me Gilberte" (418); why they fail to bring me the expected happiness (420). A spring day in winter: joy and disappointment (421). The Swann of Combray has become a different person: Gilberte's father (423). Gilberte tells me with cruel delight that she will not be returning to the Champs-Élysées before the New Year (424). "In my friendship with Gilberte, I was the only one who loved" (429). The name Swann (429, cf. 145). Swann meets my mother in Trois Quartiers (431). Pilgrimage with Françoise to the Swanns' house near the Bois (433).

The Bois, Garden of Woman. Mme. Swann in the Bois (433). A walk through the Bois one late autumn morning "this year" (438). Memory and reality (441).

For the best in Classics Literature, look for the Penguin

The Master and Margarita
Mikhail Bulgakov
Translated by Richard Pevear and Larissa Volokhonsky
Introduction by Richard Pevear
An artful collage of grotesqueries, dark comedy, and timeless ethical questions, Bulgakov's devastating satire of Soviet life was written during the darkest period of Stalin's regime and remained unpublished for more than twenty-five years after its completion. This brilliant translation was made from the complete and unabridged Russian text.   *ISBN 0-14-118014-5*

Heart of Darkness
Joseph Conrad
Edited with an Introduction and Notes by Robert Hampson
Marlow, a seaman and wanderer, travels to the heart of the African continent in search of a corrupt man named Kurtz. Instead he discovers a horrible secret in this exploration of the subconscious and the grim reality of imperialism. This edition includes more than seventy pages of critical commentary, together with Conrad's "The Congo Diary," the record of his 1890 journey upon which the novel is based.   *ISBN 0-14-018652-2*

The Portable Faulkner
William Faulkner
Edited by Malcolm Cowley
In prose of biblical grandeur and feverish intensity, William Faulkner reconstructed the history of the American South as a tragic legend of courage and cruelty, gallantry and greed, futile nobility and obscene crimes. This essential collection offers a panorama of life in Yoknapatawpha County by means of stories and episode from ten of Faulkner's books, including the "The Bear," "Spotted Horses," and "Old Man"; as well as the Nobel Prize Address, a chronology of the Compsons, and a unique map surveyed by Faulkner himself.   *ISBN 0-14-243728-X*

The Immoralist
André Gide
Translated by David Watson
Introduction by Alan Sheridan
This new translation of Nobel Laureate André Gide's masterpiece presents the confessional account of a man seeking the truth of his own nature as he awakens sexually and morally.   *ISBN 0-14-218002-5*

The Power and the Glory
Graham Greene
Introduction by John Updike
Set in a terror-ridden Mexican state, Greene's masterpiece is a compelling depiction of a "whiskey priest" struggling to overcome physical and moral cowardice and find redemption. *ISBN 0-14-243730-1*

Hunger
Knut Hamsun
Translated with an Introduction and Notes by Sverre Lyngstad
First published in Norway in 1890, *Hunger* probes into the depths of consciousness with frightening and gripping power. Like the works of Dostoyevsky, it marks an extraordinary break with Western literary and humanistic traditions. *ISBN 0-14-118064-1*

The Good Soldier Švejk
Jaroslav Hašek
Translated with an Introduction by Cecil Parrott and
Illustrations by Josef Lada
This novel portrays the "little man" fighting officialdom and bureaucracy with the only weapons available to him—passive resistance, subterfuge, native wit, and dumb insolence. *ISBN 0-14-018274-8*

A Portrait of the Artist as a Young Man
James Joyce
Introduction and Notes by Seamus Deane
Joyce's rich and complex coming-of-age story of the artist Stephen Dedalus—one of the great portraits of modern "Irishness"—is a tour de force of style and technique. *ISBN 0-14-243724-4*

Death in Venice and Other Tales
Thomas Mann
Translated with a Preface by Joachim Neugroschel
In an acclaimed new translation that restores the controversial passages censored from the original English version, "Death in Venice" recounts a ruinous quest for love and beauty. Also included are eleven other stories, among them "Tonio Kröger" and "The Blood of the Walsungs."
ISBN 0-14-118173-7

For the best in Classics Literature, look for the Penguin 🐧

The Confusions of Young Törless
Robert Musil
Translated by Shaun Whiteside
Introduction by J. M. Coetzee
Musil's devastating parable about the abuse of power that lies beneath the calm surface of bourgeois life takes a dark journey through the irrational undercurrents of humanity and its often depraved psychology.

ISBN 0-14-218000-9

Anna Karenina
Leo Tolstoy
Translated by Richard Pevear and Larissa Volokhonsky
Introduction by Richard Pevear
WINNER OF THE PEN/BOOK-OF-THE-MONTH CLUB TRANSLATION PRIZE
One of the world's greatest novels, *Anna Karenina* is both an immortal drama of personal conflict and social scandal and a vivid, richly textured panorama of nineteenth-century Russia. While previous versions have softened the robust, and sometimes shocking, quality of Tolstoy's writing, Pevear and Volokhonsky have produced a magnificent translation that is true to his powerful voice.

ISBN 0-14-200027-2

Kristin Lavransdatter I: The Wreath
Sigrid Undset
Translated with an Introduction and Notes by Tiina Nunnally
Originally published in 1920 and set in fourteenth-century Norway, the first volume of *Kristin Lavransdatter* chronicles the courtship of a strong-willed and passionate young woman and a dangerously charming man. This new translation—a finalist for the PEN Center USA West Translation Prize—brings Undset's magnificent epic to life with clarity and lyrical beauty.

ISBN 0-14-118041-2

CLICK ON A CLASSIC
www.penguinclassics.com

The world's greatest literature at your fingertips

Constantly updated information on more than a thousand titles,
from Icelandic sagas to ancient Indian epics, Russian drama to
Italian romance, American greats to African masterpieces

•

The latest news on recent additions to the list, updated
editions, and specially commissioned translations

•

Original essays by leading writers

•

A wealth of background material, including biographies
of every classic author from Aristotle to Zamyatin, plot
synopses, readers' and teachers' guides, useful web links

•

Online desk and examination copy assistance for academics

•

Trivia quizzes, competitions, giveaways, news on
forthcoming screen adaptations